TERMINAL WORLD

Ace Books by Alastair Reynolds

TERMINAL WORLD
Alastair Reynolds

ACE BOOKS, NEW YORK

THE BERKLEY PUBLISHING GROUP
Published by the Penguin Group
Penguin Group (USA) Inc.
375 Hudson Street, New York, New York 10014, USA
Penguin Group (Canada), 90 Eglinton Avenue East, Suite 700, Toronto, Ontario M4P 2Y3, Canada
(a division of Pearson Penguin Canada Inc.)
Penguin Books Ltd., 80 Strand, London WC2R 0RL, England
Penguin Group Ireland, 25 St. Stephen's Green, Dublin 2, Ireland (a division of Penguin Books Ltd.)
Penguin Group (Australia), 250 Camberwell Road, Camberwell, Victoria 3124, Australia
(a division of Pearson Australia Group Pty. Ltd.)
Penguin Books India Pvt. Ltd., 11 Community Centre, Panchsheel Park, New Delhi—110 017, India
Penguin Group (NZ), 67 Apollo Drive, Rosedale, North Shore 0632, New Zealand
(a division of Pearson New Zealand Ltd.)
Penguin Books (South Africa) (Pty.) Ltd., 24 Sturdee Avenue, Rosebank, Johannesburg 2196,
South Africa

Penguin Books Ltd., Registered Offices: 80 Strand, London WC2R 0RL, England

This is a work of fiction. Names, characters, places, and incidents either are the product of the author's imagination or are used fictitiously, and any resemblance to actual persons, living or dead, business establishments, events, or locales is entirely coincidental. The publisher does not have any control over and does not assume any responsibility for author or third-party websites or their content.

Published by arrangement with the Orion Publishing Group.

PRINTING HISTORY
Gollancz edition / March 2010
Ace hardcover edition / June 2010

Library of Congress Cataloging-in-Publication Data

Reynolds, Alastair, 1966–
    Terminal world / Alastair Reynolds. — Ace hardcover ed.
        p.   cm.
    ISBN 978-0-441-01866-6
    I. Title.

    PR6068.E95T47 2010
    823'.92—dc22   2010010550

PRINTED IN THE UNITED STATES OF AMERICA

10   9   8   7   6   5   4   3   2   1

'And Earth is but a star, that once had shone.'
The Golden Journey to Samarkand, James Elroy Flecker

PART ONE

CHAPTER ONE

The call came in to the Department of Hygiene and Public Works just before five in the afternoon. Something messy down on the ledge, maybe a faller from one of the overhanging buildings up in Fourth, maybe all the way from Circuit City. The dispatcher turned to the wall map, surveyed the pin lights and found a clean-up van close enough to take the call. It was one of the older crews, men he knew. He lifted the black handset of his telephone and spun the dial, taking a drag on his cigarette while the switchboard clunked and whirred.

'Three oh seven.'

'Got a smear for you, Cultel. Something out on the ledge, just west of the waterworks. Not much else out there so you should spot it easy enough. Take the service duct on Seventh and Electric and walk the rest of the way. Keys on the blue hook should get you through any municipal locks.'

'We're loaded here. And we're about a minute from coming off shift. Can't you pull in someone else?'

'Not at rush hour I can't. We wait for another van, smear's going to start attracting a crowd and smelling bad. Seagulls are already taking an interest. Sorry, Cultel, but you're going to have to suck it up and earn some overtime.'

'Fine. But I was serious about being loaded. You'd better get another van to meet us, case we have to move some stiffs around.'

'I'll see what I can do. Call in when you've peeled it off the concrete; we'll start the paperwork at this end.'

'Copy,' Cultel said.

'And watch your step out there, boys. It's a long way down, and I don't want to have to call Steamville and tell them they need to deal with a couple of smears of their own.'

In the clean-up van, Cultel clicked off his handset and hung it back under the dashboard. He turned to his partner, Gerber, who was digging through a paper bag for the last doughnut. 'You get all that?'

3

'Enough.'

'Another fucking ledge job. They know how much I love ledge jobs.'

'Like the man said, suck it up and earn some overtime.' Gerber bit into the doughnut and wiped the grease off his lip. 'Sounds good to me.'

'That's because you've got a sweet tooth and expensive girlfriends.'

'It's called having a life outside of scraping pancakes off pavement, Cultel. You should try it sometime.'

Cultel, who always did the driving, grunted something derogatory, engaged the flywheel and powered the van back onto the pick-up slot. Traffic was indeed already thickening into rush hour, cars, taxis, buses and trucks moving sluggishly in one direction, almost nose to tail in the other. Being municipal, they could go off-slot when they needed to, but it still required expert knowledge of the streets and traffic flow not to get snarled up. Cultel always reckoned he could make more money driving taxis than a clean-up wagon, but the advantage of ferrying corpses around was that he mostly didn't need to make conversation. Gerber, who generally had his nose into a bag of doughnuts, didn't really count.

It took them twenty minutes to make it to Seventh and Electric. The service duct was accessed by a sloping ramp between two buildings, the ramp facing out from Spearpoint, an arched grillwork door at the bottom of it. Cultel disengaged the pick-up shoe and flywheeled down the slope, hoping he'd still have enough spin to get back up it when they had the smear loaded. No sign of the other van yet. He snatched the keyset from the blue tag, grabbed the equipment from behind his seat and left the corrugated-sided van, Gerber carrying a camera and a heavy police-style torch.

When Cultel was new in Hygiene and Works, the cops were always first on the scene at a faller, with the clean-up crew just there to go through the menial business of peel-off and hose-down. But the cops couldn't keep up lately, and so they were perfectly willing for Hygiene and Works to handle the smears, provided everything was documented and signed off properly. Anything that looked like foul play, the cops could always get involved down the line. Mostly, though, the fallers were just accident victims. Cultel had no reason to expect anything different this time.

They passed through the municipal gate and walked down the concrete-lined service duct, which was dark and dank, with bits of cladding peeling off every few spans. Rainwater run-off seeped through the cracks and formed into a slow-moving stream deep enough to soak through Cultel's shoes. It smelled a little bit of sewer. Beyond, at the far end of the service duct, was a half-circle of indigo sky. Cultel could already feel the cool evening wind picking up. Back from the ledge, with buildings all around, you didn't feel it much. But it was always colder towards the edges. Quieter, too: it didn't take much to absorb the hum of traffic, the rattle of commuter trains, the moaning of cop car sirens as they wound their way up and down the city's lazy spiral.

Beyond the duct, the concrete flooring gave way to Spearpoint's under-lying fabric. No one had ever bothered giving the black stuff a name because it was as ubiquitous as air. The ledge began level and then took on a gradually steepening slope. Cultel watched his footing. The stuff was treacherous, everyone knew that. Felt firm as rock one second, slippery as ice the next.

Gerber waved the torch downslope. 'There's our baby.'

'I see it.'

They edged closer, walking sideways as the angle of slope increased, taking increasingly cautious footsteps. The faller had come down about thirty spans from the very edge. In the evening gloom Cultel made out a head, two arms, two legs, all where they ought to have been. And something crumpled beneath the pale form, like a flimsy, translucent gown. You could never be too sure with fallers but it didn't look as though this one had come down very far. Dismemberment was com-monplace: limbs, heads tended to pop off easily, either with the impact or from glancing collisions on the way down, as the faller bumped against the sides of buildings or the rising wall to the next ledge. But this jigsaw came with all the pieces.

Cultel looked up, over his shoulder, and lifted the rim of his hat to get a better view. No buildings or overhangs near enough for the faller to have come off. And even if they'd stepped off the next highest ledge, with the way the winds were working they'd have ended up at the base, back behind the rising tide of buildings. Should have been a lot more damage, too.

'Something's screwed up here,' Cultel said.

'Just starting to feel that way myself.' Gerber raised the camera to his eye singlehandedly and flashed off two exposures. They crept forwards some more, planting each footstep gently, hardly daring to breathe. Gerber directed the torch a bit more steadily. It was then that Cultel knew what they were dealing with.

Crushed beneath the form: that wasn't any gown. It was wings.

'It's—' Gerber started saying.

'Yeah.'

What they had was an angel. Cultel looked up again, higher this time.

5

Not just to the nearest line of buildings, but all the way up. Up past the pastel flicker of Neon Heights, up past the hologram shimmer of Circuit City. Up past the pink plasma aura of the cybertowns. He could just see them circling around up there, leagues overhead, wheeling and gyring around Spearpoint's tapering needle like flies around an insect zapper.

And he thought to himself: *How the fuck did one of them get down here? And why did it have to happen on my watch?*

'Let's bag and tag,' Gerber said. 'Thing's creeping me out already.'

'You ever dealt with one of these?'

'First time. You?'

'Once when I was new on the job. Fell onto the third rail of the Green Line elevated. Fucking thing was toast by the time we pulled it off. Then again three, maybe four years back. That one was a lot more mashed up than this. Not a whole lot you could recognise at first glance.'

Gerber fired off another shot with the camera. In the after-flash Cultel had the weird feeling that the corpse had twitched, shifting almost subliminally from one position to another. He crept up beside the fallen creature and knelt down with his equipment next to him. Overhead the seagulls really were taking an interest, mewling and squabbling in the evening air. Cultel examined the creature, taking in its nearly naked form, the wings the only visibly broken part of it. It had come to rest with its head lolling to one side, looking at him with huge midnight-blue eyes. It could have been alive, except there was nothing happening behind those eyes.

'Damn thing must have been alive almost all the way down,' he said. 'This was a controlled landing, not a crash.'

'What a way to go,' Gerber said. 'You think it was suicide, or did it just, you know, lose its way?'

'Maybe there was a fault with its pack,' Cultel said, fingering the hard, alien alloy of the angel's propulsion harness. 'Hell, who knows? Cover all the angles, then we'll get it zipped up and into the van. Sooner this is off our hands the better.'

They got the angel bagged and tagged, taking care not to worsen the damage to the wings or break any of the creature's stick-thin limbs. Lifting the bag, Cultel could easily manage it on his own. It was like carrying a sack of bones and not much else. They didn't even need to hose down the ground. The angel hadn't shed a drop of whatever passed for blood in its veins.

The other van hadn't arrived when they called back to the dispatcher.

'Sorry, Cultel. Had to send them over to the boundary with Steam – had a report that the zone was shifting around again.'

'Well, you might want to rethink that. We got the smear.' He glanced at Gerber, grinning in the moment. 'You ready for this? It's an angel.'

'No reports of anything falling down from the Levels, three oh seven.'

'This one didn't fall. It must have flown almost all the way. Then died.'

'As they do.' He could hear the practised scepticism in the dispatcher's voice. Didn't much blame him, either. It wouldn't be the first time an angel corpse had been faked up for someone's twisted amusement. Might even be the kind of sick joke someone in Hygiene and Works would play on another clean-up crew, to see how gullible they were.

But Cultel knew this was a real one.

'You want us to squeeze the angel in, we will. Might get a little crumpled in there, but we'll manage. Just so you understand, I'm not taking responsibility for any breakages. I take it you'd like us to ship this thing over to Third?'

'If you think it's the real deal.'

'I'll take the fall if it isn't.'

'Fine; stop by at Third. But remove anything technical. Bag them separately, and we'll box them over to Imports.'

Cultel hung up.

'Why Third? We never deal with Third,' Gerber said.

They secured the angel, closed up the van and flywheeled back up the access ramp. It was another twenty-minute drive to the Third District Morgue, dodging through short cuts and back alleys, winding their way a little further up the spiralling ledge. The building was an ash-grey slab with a flat roof and a frontage of small square windows, lower than any of the office and apartment blocks crowding in around it. They drove to the rear and backed the van up to the dock, where a white-coated receiving clerk was waiting for them.

'Dispatch phoned through,' the clerk said as Cultel unlocked the van's rear doors. 'Said you had something juicy for Quillon.' He scratched a pen against his nose. 'Been a while, you know. I think he was starting to wonder if you'd forgotten about the arrangement.'

'Like we'd forget,' Cultel said, countersigning the delivery form.

'What's this all about?' Gerber asked.

'Quillon likes to get first dibs on anything freaky,' the clerk explained. 'Kind of a hobby of his, I guess.'

Gerber shrugged. 'Each to their own.'

'Suits everyone,' the clerk said. 'Quillon gets his kicks. The other morgues don't have to wade through a ton of paperwork – and there's always a lot of triplicate when one of these things comes in.' He peered at the bagged form as Cultel and Gerber eased it onto a wheeled stretcher. 'Mind if I take a look?'

'Hey, be my guest,' Cultel said.

The clerk zipped the bag down half a span. Wrinkled his nose at the dead, pale, broken thing inside.

'They look so beautiful flying around up there, wings all lit up and glowing.'

'Cut him some slack.' Cultel zipped the bag tight. 'He's not been having the best of days.'

'You sure it's a he?'

'Now that you mention it—'

'Wheel it through to Quillon if you want,' the clerk said. 'Take the freight elevator to the third. He'll be up there someplace. Gotta wait down here to see in another delivery.'

'Busy night?'

'Busy week. They say the boundary's getting itchy feet again.'

'What I heard,' Cultel said. 'Guess we'd better batten down the hatches and get our watches wound.'

They pushed the wheeled stretcher into the building. It was all green walls, stark white tiles and the chlorine reek of industrial cleaning solution. The lights in the ceiling were turned down almost to brown. Most of the staff had gone home for the day, leaving the morgue to the night shift and the ghosts of former clients. Cultel hated the place, as he hated all morgues. How could anyone work in a building where all they did was cut open bodies? At least being on the clean-up crew got him out into fresh air.

They took the freight elevator to the third floor, heaved open the heavy trelliswork door and rolled the stretcher out into the corridor. Quillon was waiting at the far end, flicking the butt of a cigarette into a wall-mounted ashtray. It had been three or four years but Cultel recognised him straight away. Which wasn't to say that Quillon hadn't changed in all that time.

'When I heard there was a delivery coming in, I was hoping it was the new medicines,' Quillon said, in his slow, measured, slightly too-deep voice. 'Cupboards were any barer, we'd have to start turning away dead people.'

'We brought you a present,' Cultel said. 'Be nice.'

'How's work?'

'Ups and downs, Quillon, ups and downs. But while there's a city and corpses, I guess you and I don't have to worry about gainful employment.'

Quillon had always been thin, always been gaunt, but now he looked as if he'd just opened his eyes and climbed off one of the dissection tables. A white surgical coat draped off his thin-ridged shoulders as if it was still on the hanger and a white cap covered his hairless skull. He wore glasses, tinted slightly even though the lights in the morgue were hardly on the bright side. Green surgical gloves that still made his fingers look too long and skeletal for comfort. There were deep shadows under his cheekbones and his skin looked colourless and waxy and not quite alive.

No getting away from it, Cultel thought. The guy had picked the ideal place of employment.

'So what have you got for me?'

'Got you an angel, my friend. Came down on the ledge.'

Quillon's reaction was hard to judge behind the glasses. The rest of his face didn't move much, even when he spoke. 'All the way down from the Celestial Levels?'

'What we figured. Funny thing is, though, there's not much sign that this one was going fast when it hit.'

'That's interesting.' Quillon said this in the uninflected tones of someone who'd be hard pushed to think of anything less interesting. But Cultel wasn't sure.

'Had some gadgetry on it, we removed all that. What you've got is essentially just a naked corpse with wings.'

'That's what we deal with.'

'You ... um ... cut many of these things open, Quillon?' Gerber asked.

'The odd one or two. Can't say they drop in with great regularity. Have we met?'

'I don't think so. What is it about them you like so much?'

'I wouldn't say "like" comes into it. It's just a speciality, that's all. We're set up for it here. Got the positive-pressure room, in case anything toxic boils out of them. Got the blast-proof doors. And once you've done one, the paperwork's fairly routine.'

'Takes the pressure off the other morgues,' Cultel said.

Quillon flexed his scrawny neck in a nod. 'Everyone's a winner.'

There was an awkward moment. The two of them by the trolley, Quillon still standing there with his green-gloved hands at his sides.

'Well, I guess we're done here,' Cultel said. 'Docket tells you everything you need to know. Usual deal: when you're through with the bag, send it back to Hygiene and Works. Preferably hosed down.'

'I'll see to it.'

9

'Well, until next time,' Cultel said, backing into the still-open freight elevator.

'Until next time,' Quillon said, raising a forearm by way of farewell.

'It's been great meeting you,' Gerber said.

Cultel closed the elevator doors. The elevator descended, the motor whining at the head of the shaft.

Quillon stood still at the end of the corridor until the panel over the door told him that the elevator had reached the ground floor. Then he walked slowly up to the stretcher, examined the docket and placed one gloved hand on the black zip-up bag containing the angel.

Then he wheeled it into the examination room, donned a surgical mask, transferred the bag onto the dissection plinth and carefully removed the angel from the bag.

It seemed to Quillon to be beautiful even in death. He had placed the angel on its back, its eyes closed, the ruined wings hanging down on either side so that their tips brushed the tiled floor, the floor's sloping runnels designed to channel away bodily fluids. Under the hard lights of the dissection plinth, it was as ghost-pale, naked and hairless as a rat foetus.

Not expecting to be disturbed, he took off his glasses.

He pushed a squeaking-wheeled trolley next to the table, pulling aside the green sheet to expose an assortment of medical tools. There were scalpels, forceps, bone-cutting devices, gleaming sterile scoops and spatulas, and an array of glass and stainless-steel receptacles to receive the dissected tissue samples. These tools had once struck him as laughably crude, but now they fell to hand with an easy, reassuring familiarity. A microphone dangled from the ceiling; Quillon tugged it closer to his face and threw a heavy rocker switch in its side. Somewhere beyond the room, tape reels started whirring through recording heads. He cleared his throat and enunciated clearly, to make himself heard through the distorting mask.

'Doctor Quillon speaking. Continuation of previous record.' He glanced up at the row of clocks on the far wall. 'Time is now ... six-fifteen p.m. Beginning autopsy of a corpse, docket number five-eight-three-three-four, recently delivered to the Third District Morgue by the Department of Hygiene and Public Works.' He paused and cast his eyes over the corpse, the appropriate observations springing to mind with a minimum of conscious effort. 'Initial indications are that the corpse is an angel, probably an adult male. Angel appears uninjured, save for impact damage to the wings. There are some longitudinal bruises and scars on the limbs, together with marked subepidermal swelling – recent

10

enough to suggest they might be contributory factors in the angel's death – but the limbs appear otherwise uninjured, with no sign of major breaks or dislocations. Indications are that the angel's descent was controlled until the last moment, at which point it fell with enough force to damage the wings but not to inflict any other visible injuries. Reason for the descent is unknown, but the likely cause of death would appear to be massive maladaptive trauma due to sudden exposure to our zone, rather than impact onto the ledge.' He paused again, letting the tape continue recording while he reached for a syringe. He punched the needle into a small rubber-capped bottle – one of the last dozen such bottles in the morgue's inventory – and loaded the tube, taking care not to draw more than was strictly necessary.

'In accordance with protocol,' he continued, 'I am now administering a lethal dose of Morphax-55, to ensure final morbidity.' He tapped the glass until there were no more bubbles, then leaned over to push the needle into the bare skin of the angel's chest.

In the six years that he had been working as a pathologist, Quillon had cut open many hundreds of human bodies – victims of accident, homicide, medical negligence – but only eleven angels. That was still more than most pathologists saw in their careers.

He pressed the tip of the syringe against skin.

'Commencing injection of—' he started.

The angel's left arm whipped over to seize his hand.

'Stop,' it said.

Quillon halted, but it was more out of reflex than a considered response to the angel's actions. He was so startled that he almost dropped the syringe.

'The angel is still alive,' he said into the microphone. 'It has exhibited comprehension, visual awareness and fine motor control. I will now attempt to alleviate the subject's suffering by . . .' He hesitated and looked into the dying creature's eyes, which were now fully alert, fully and terrifyingly focused on his own. The angel still had his hand on Quillon's wrist, the syringe hovering dagger-like above the angel's sternum.

'Let me do this,' he said. 'It'll take away the pain.'

'You mean kill me,' the angel said, speaking slowly and with effort, as if barely enough air remained in his lungs to make the sounds. His eyes were large and blue, characteristically lacking visible structures. His head rolled slightly on the dissection table, as the angel took in his surroundings.

'You're going to die anyway,' Quillon said.

'Break it to me nicely, why don't you.'

'There's nothing nice to break. You've fallen out of the Celestial Levels into Neon Heights. You don't belong down here and your cells can't take it. Even if we could get you back home, too much damage has already been done.'

'You think I don't know that?' The angel's piping, childlike voice was just deep enough to confirm him as male. 'I'm fully aware of what's going to happen. But I don't want your medicine. Not just yet.' The angel let go of his hand, allowing Quillon to place the syringe back on the trolley. 'I need to ask you something.'

'Of course.'

The angel was looking at him, the blue eyes windows into an alien soul. His head was only a little smaller than an adult human's, but almost entirely hairless, beautiful and unworldly, as if it were made of porcelain and stained glass rather than living matter and machines. 'You must answer me truthfully.'

'I will.'

'Are you Quillon?'

He was silent for a few seconds. He had often wondered how it would happen, when his pursuers finally caught up with him. Strangely, he had never envisaged the encounter taking place in the morgue. He had always assumed that the time would come in some dark alley, a packed commuter train, or even his own apartment as he clicked on the light after returning home. A shadow moving into view, a glint of metal. There would be no reason to ask his adopted name. If they had managed to track him down that efficiently, his real identity would have been beyond question.

The only reason for asking, in other words, would be to taunt him with the sure and certain knowledge that he had failed.

'Of course,' he said, with as much dignity and calm as he could muster.

'That's good. They said I'd be brought to you.'

The unease had begun deep in his belly and was now climbing slowly up his spine.

'Who said that?'

'The people who sent me here, of course. You don't think any of this happened by accident, do you?'

Quillon thought about killing the angel there and then. He still had the Morphax-55 to hand, ready to inject. But the angel knew he was capable of doing that and was still talking. His mind raced. Perhaps trying to kill the angel would be the very trigger that caused him to kill Quillon.

He kept his composure. 'Then why did you fall?'

12

'Because I chose to. This was the quickest – if not the least risky – way.' The angel swallowed hard, his whole body flexing from the table. 'I was under no illusions. I knew this was a suicide mission; that I would not be returning to the Celestial Levels. But still I did it. I fell, and stayed alive long enough to be brought to you. They said when an angel falls into Neon Heights, it almost always gets taken to Quillon to be cut open. Is that true?'

'Most of the time.'

'I can see why that would work for you.'

The tape reels were still running, recording every detail of the conversation. Quillon reached up and clicked off the microphone, for all the good that would do.

'Can you?'

'You were once one of us. Then something happened and . . . now you live here, down amongst the prehumans, with their stinking factories, buzzing cars and dull electric lights.'

'Do I look like an angel?'

'I know what happened to you. You were remade to look prehuman, your wings removed, your body reshaped, your blood cleansed of machines. You were sent to live among the prehumans, to learn their ways, to prove that it could be done. There were others.' The angel drew an exhausted, rasping breath. 'Then something went wrong and now there's just you, and you can't ever go back. You work here because you need to be on guard, in case the Celestial Levels send agents down to find you. Ordinary angels can't reach you, so you know that whatever they send will have to be unusual, or prepared to die very soon after finding you.'

'There's just you and me in this room,' Quillon said slowly. 'Why haven't you killed me yet?'

'Because that's not what I was sent to do.' The angel inhaled again, the breath ragged and wet-sounding. 'I came to warn you. Things are moving in the Levels. You're back on the agenda.'

'What do you mean, things are moving?'

'Signs and portents. Indications of unusual instability in the Mire. Or the Eye of God, if you're religious. You're not religious, are you, Quillon?'

'Not really.'

'If you were, you'd say God was getting restless again. You've probably noticed the pre-shocks down here. Boundary tremors, warnings of zone slippage. There's something inside Spearpoint that no one really understands, not even the angels, and it's got a lot of us rattled. The people who sent you down here, the ones you're hiding from? They want you back.'

'I'm useless to them now.'

'Not what they believe, unfortunately. There's information in your head that they'd very much like to suck out. And if they can't, they'll kill you anyway to make sure no one else gets their hands on it.'

'Who else cares?'

'The people who sent me. We want that information as well. Difference is we'd rather you stayed alive.'

'Are the others here?'

'Yes. They're like you, to some extent: modified to work down here. But without the expertise you brought to the first infiltration programme, the modifications aren't as effective. They can't stay as long and they don't blend in as well.' The angel studied him. 'Inasmuch as you blend in, Quillon.'

'How near are they?'

'Chances are they already have you under observation. They may already be covering likely exit points, in case you try to leave Neon Heights.'

'Then I'll hide.'

'You're already hiding and it hasn't worked. They'll have a chemical trace on you by now, sniffing you out by your forensic trail. Running's your only option. Being here is already pushing them to the limit. They won't be able to track you if you cross zones.'

'Leave Neon Heights?'

The angel licked his lips with a fine blue tongue. 'Spearpoint. All the way down, all the way out. Into the great wide open.'

The thought made Quillon shiver. 'There's nothing out there.'

'There's enough for survival. If you've adapted to life down here, you'll cope. What matters above all else is that the information in your head never reaches your enemies.'

'Why do they care now?'

'The work you were involved with was only ever the tip of a project, a covert programme designed to create an occupying force. An army of angels with sufficient built-in tolerance to take over the rest of Spearpoint.'

'I know.'

'Without you, the work stalled. But now the prospect of a zone shift has heightened the urgency. They want that occupying force, which means they want your knowledge.'

'And what do your people want?'

'The same knowledge, but to use for different purposes. Not to take over the rest of Spearpoint, but to provide for emergency assistance if the worst does happen.'

'Seems to me the safest thing would still be to have me killed.'

'That was ... considered. I won't lie to you.' The angel gave him a weak, pitying smile. 'But in the end it was agreed that you were too valuable for that. We can't see your knowledge wasted.'

'Then help me get back home.'

'Not an option. Best we can do for you is warn you to get out. After that, you're on your own.' The blue eyes regarded him with deep, penetrating intelligence. 'Can you leave Spearpoint without being followed, Quillon?'

'I don't know.'

'Because if you can't be certain, there's very little point in trying. There's no one you can turn to?'

After a moment Quillon said, 'There is someone.'

'A prehuman?'

'A man who's helped me from time to time.'

'Can he be trusted?'

'He knows what I am. He's never betrayed me.'

'And now?'

'I've no reason to assume otherwise.'

'If this man can help you, then go to him. But only if your trust in him is absolute. If you're not sure of that, you have to get out on your own.'

'How long am I supposed to be away?'

'You'll know when it's safe to return. Soon there's going to be a change in the power balance in the Celestial Levels.'

'I can't just drop everything and leave. I've got a life down here.'

'Our intelligence says you have no one, Quillon. No wife. No family. Hardly any friends. Just your work. You cut open corpses and lately you're starting to look like one. If you want to call that a life, fine by me.'

Quillon stared down at the angel. 'Did you really sacrifice yourself for this?'

'To reach you, Quillon? Yes. I did. Knowing that I would die, and that my death would not be an easy one. But I also knew that if I could reach you, and persuade you to take your own survival seriously, something good might come of it. Something that would make my own death seem a very small price to pay.'

'I don't even know your name.'

'Do you remember yours?'

'No. They scrubbed that from me when they layered in the new memories.'

'Then we'll part as strangers. It's better that way.'

'I understand,' Quillon said softly.

'I'll take that injection now, if you have no objections.'

Quillon's hand closed around the syringe of Morphax-55. 'If I could do more for you, I would.'

'You don't have to feel bad about this. It was my choice to come here, not yours. Just don't waste this chance.'

'I won't.' Quillon made sure the syringe was still free of air. He touched his other hand to the angel's bare sternum, applying gentle pressure. 'Hold still. This won't hurt.'

He pushed the syringe in and squeezed the plunger.

The angel sighed. His breathing became slower and more relaxed.

'How long?'

'Couple of minutes. Maybe less.'

'Good. Because there's something I forgot to tell you.'

CHAPTER TWO

The whirr of gears, the clunk and chatter of an electromechanical telephone exchange, relays tapping in and out, the purr of a dialling tone, Fray picking up after ten or eleven rings.

'Who the fuck?'

'Quillon.'

'My favourite monster.' Fray paused. Bar sounds in the background: rowdy laughter, the chinking of glass, a television or wireless turned up loud, the time-bell of a boxing match. 'Kind of early, aren't we? I don't have the sewing kit with me right now.'

'I'm in trouble. We need to talk in person.'

'Where are you calling from?'

'A delicatessen, on my way home.' Quillon cupped one hand around his mouth, conscious of the shopkeeper eyeing him from the front of the store. The man had wanted Quillon to use the public booth down the road, rather than the private one tucked away at the back of the store. 'They're on to me,' he said.

'You think, or you know?'

'Something happened today. That's all I can tell you right now.'

'All right,' Fray said after long seconds. 'One thing I know: you're not the kind to jump at shadows unless there's good reason. Forget about going home. You think you can make it up here without being followed?'

'I'll do my best.'

'Stay vigilant, stay alert, but try to act perfectly normal and relaxed at the same time.'

'That's a good trick, Fray.'

'You could do this once. Start getting back into the groove.'

Fray hung up. Quillon stood with the telephone still pressed against his ear, struck by the feeling that he had set something in motion that could not be stopped. Fray was an avalanche waiting to happen. It only took a tiny nudge to set him off, but from that point on the only option open to him was to gather momentum, rumbling and roaring towards some cataclysmic, landscape-altering event.

Quillon replaced the handset, walked to the front of the store and threw a handful of coins onto the counter.

'Thanks,' he said.

'Cheer up,' the shopkeeper said, scratching at the roll of fat under his chin. 'Might never happen.'

He took the car off the slot, parked it at the kerb and reached over to the passenger seat for his bag. It had travelled with him all the way from the morgue. The bag was finished in black leather, scuffed to a fleshy brown at the edges. It had a black leather handle, a label marked *Doctor M. Quillon*. It was secured by a gold clasp and opened like a concertina, disclosing an assortment of padded pockets and receptacles. He locked the car and adjusted his hat. Fifth was a bad neighbourhood and it was getting late. He wondered if he'd see the car again.

The Pink Peacock was easily missed. It lay at the end of a blind alley that terminated in the rising black wall of Spearpoint's underlying fabric, a cliff that soared into the heavens, rising ever higher until it jogged back to form the next shelf. Bracketed on one side by a fleapit hotel and on the other by the derelict offices of a failed taxi business, there was little to identify the nature of the premises. A metal fixture marked where the peppermint-green neon illumination used to hang, until Malkin gave up having it repaired. Metal bars fenced the outside windows, the glass so grimed by dirt and cigarette smoke that it was difficult to tell if the lights were on inside. Posters and graffiti covered the walls in layers of archaeological thickness.

Quillon walked to the end of the alley and knocked on the door. It opened a crack, a fan of pink-red light spilling across the asphalt.

'Here to see Fray.'

'You're the cutter?'

Quillon nodded, though the dismissive term repulsed him. The doorman – it wasn't the usual one – grunted and let him in. Inside, the sudden humidity fogged over Quillon's small, round, blue-tinted spectacles. He took them off and rubbed the flat lenses on his sleeve before slipping the glasses back onto the narrow ridge of his nose. The lights were turned down, but that was the way Malkin and most of his customers preferred it.

Malkin himself was behind the bar, polishing glasses while he kept one eye on the fight that was still playing out on the television. He was rake-thin and mean-looking, with cryptic tattoos on his forearms, all smudged purples and liver-reds. They looked like they'd been done with a piece of scrap metal and a bottle of low-grade transmission oil. Malkin wore a yellowing vest and a towel draped around his shoulders, the vest showing off his scrawny, leathery-skinned neck with the thin circumferential scar where – Quillon could only assume – Malkin had survived being garrotted. Certainly there had been some damage to his larynx, because when he opened his mouth all he could produce was a croaking noise, a sustained guttural rasp that forced his clients to lean in close when they wanted to understand.

'That time of year again?' Malkin asked. 'Must be getting punchy, because I could have sworn it wasn't long since your last visit. When was it, June, June Prime?'

'August. And that's not why I've come.'

'Always welcome to drop by, you know that.' Malkin reached for a bottle behind the bar. 'Your usual?'

'No ice.'

Malkin poured out a measure of Red Eye. 'How's life down in the morgue, anyway? Cut open anything interesting lately?'

'This and that.'

Malkin put the bottle back on the shelf. 'You know, we could always use a man with a steady hand on the blade. A man who knows his way around anatomy, so to speak. What to cut and what not to cut, if you get my drift. What you can live with for a few hours and what you can't.'

'I'm sure you and Fray know more than enough on that score already.'

'Well, maybe. But Fray's not the man he used to be, and my problem is I like to make them squeal. Sometimes I go too far too fast, you know?' Malkin looked as if he was expecting sympathy, for being too enthusiastic with his interrogation and torture methods. 'You, though, you've got the necessary restraint. All I'm saying – and I know I speak for Fray in this matter – there's always potential employment here, if work dries up in the morgue.'

'Thanks for the offer. Work's not very likely to dry up in a hurry, though.'

'I take your point. It being a morgue and all.'

'Anyway, I'm not looking for a new line of work.' Quillon took a sip of the Red Eye. It was sharp and he felt it trickle down his throat in fiery rivulets. Alcohol had no significant effect on the angel nervous system, even given his modified physiology. But the taste wasn't unpleasant, and it helped him fit in with the bar's other customers, insofar as any were bothering to pay attention to the thin man in a coat talking to the thin man behind the bar.

'You in trouble?' Malkin asked.

'I've never been out of it.'

'I mean, something other than whatever shit it was brought you into Fray's sphere of influence.' Malkin fixed him with his small, pale yellow eyes. They were the exact colour of urine drops on the rim of a toilet. 'Which, incidentally, I have never seen fit to pry about.'

'That's good.'

'Just like it's never occurred to me to pry about what exactly happens each time you come up here and go into that back room.'

'That's also good.'

Malkin was part of Fray's organisation, but to the best of Quillon's knowledge he did not know the truth of Quillon's identity. Fray, Quillon believed, had never told a living soul what he knew.

'Well, he's in the back. Usual haunt.'

Quillon reached for change, but Malkin shook his head. 'On the house tonight. The least we can do, you choose to pay us a visit.'

Fray could normally be found in a small room set back from the rest of the bar, entered by a narrow stoop-under archway. The windowless nook was only just big enough to accommodate the table and chairs around it. With its narrow entrance, there was a claustrophobic sense of entrapment about the place. Today Fray nursed a cigarette and a half-empty shot glass, and according to his usual custom was sitting alone. There was something in his demeanour, some subtle, hard-to-articulate quality of expression and posture that caused people to orbit away from him. He was a big man, black-skinned, almost too big for the chair he was sitting in. His hair had been black when they first met, but in nine years it had turned first to grey and then to a brilliant pure white.

'Starting to think I'd imagined that phone call,' Fray said, his voice a low, threatening rumble. He blinked and twitched. 'Uptown traffic's a bitch, right?'

'I made it, didn't I?'

'So take a seat. Look like you plan on spending more than five seconds in my presence.'

Quillon eased into a chair opposite the bottled force that was Fray. 'Thanks for agreeing to see me.' He took off his hat and placed it on a wall hook. Fray sucked on the cigarette, the orange tip the only bright thing in the gloom of his favoured nook. His hand shook terribly, as if there was a hook in it and someone was jerking an invisible string.

'I took the liberty of calling Meroka. She's on her way.'

'Who's Meroka?'

'One of my extraction specialists. You'll like her.'

'Who said anything about "extraction"?'

'I did. And we're doing it. Pieces are already falling into place.'

'Aren't we jumping the gun a little here?'

'You told me enough on the telephone.' Fray sipped from his own drink. 'Joining the dots, that's one of my specialities. I joined the dots where you were concerned, didn't I?'

'That was your job back then,' Quillon said. 'Before you hung up your badge.'

'Worst mistake I ever made. Other than not turning you in.'

'Do you want to know what happened or not?' Without waiting for an answer, Quillon told him about the angel and their conversation during the examination and autopsy. 'Then I called you. I drove by my apartment – I know you told me not to go home, but I didn't stop or slow down – and then I came here.'

'Told you not to do that, Cutter.'

'No one saw me.'

'You hope. Did you notice anyone there who shouldn't have been?'

'Only a van from the Boundary Commission, badly disguised as a vehicle from Hygiene and Works. I assume that didn't have anything to do with the mess I'm in.'

'Right now I wouldn't assume anything. It isn't just the local administration getting twitchy. They're stockpiling pharms all over the city. You probably heard about that.'

'There've been some shortages in drug deliveries,' Quillon said, thinking back to the morgue's dwindling inventory. 'I just assumed there was a problem in the supply chain.'

'There isn't. This is coordinated and deliberate, and it smells of someone being very scared indeed. Word is it goes all the way up and all the way down. That includes the Celestial Levels, in case you weren't paying attention. A big shift, a major realignment, would hurt the angels just as badly as it hurts us. So yes, it could all be tied in.' Fray gave him a grin that was somewhere between pitying and sympathetic. 'Hate to break it to you, but you're a loose end. Could be someone's decided to tidy you up before the big one hits.'

'Judging by what the angel said, they had more in mind than just tidying me up.'

'Getting at those buried memories, in the hope that you know something vital about the infiltration process? Doesn't that strike you as a long shot?'

'Maybe I do know something. It isn't beyond the bounds of possibility.'

'The angel give you any idea about how long you need to lie low?'

'Not really. He said something about a change in Celestial Levels, some kind of coup. If it works, I can return. If it doesn't, it's always going to be dangerous for me here – and dangerous for anyone who tries to shelter me.'

'This coup – are we talking about something imminent?'

'Could be months away for all I know. But however long it takes, that's how long I'll have to keep out of Spearpoint. It isn't just about protecting my own neck, either. If I'm valuable, then I'm valuable to the people who sent the angel down as well.'

'Whose motives we don't know for sure.'

'They gave me the weapon, Fray. That suggests they have my best interests in mind.'

'This weapon you still haven't shown me.'

'I've got it with me.' Quillon took another sip of the Red Eye. 'You mentioned your extraction specialist. That was news to me. Whenever we talked about this, it was always you who was going to get me out of Spearpoint.'

Fray leaned back in his chair. 'Maybe it's escaped your attention, but I'm getting a little ragged around the edges lately. The drugs aren't doing it for me any more, not unless I dial up the dosage.'

'Looks to me as if you've dialled it up about as far as it'll go,' Quillon said. The decline since their last meeting was worse than he had expected.

Fray accepted this diagnosis with a powerful, twitch-like shrug. He scratched a finger under his right eye. 'There's no way I can go deeper than Steamville, much less survive beyond Spearpoint. I'll see you to the station, but from then on you'll be in Meroka's hands. You don't have to worry about her. She has her quirks, but she gets the job done. Already more than a dozen successful extractions under her belt.'

'Out of how many attempts?'

'Oh, please. What matters is that she can do this, and she's ready and waiting. You'll take the train. Now – you going to show me what the angel gave you?'

'Is it safe here?'

'Provided you don't think it'll blow up on us.'

Quillon lifted the medical bag onto the table and sprung open the gold clasp. 'I suppose if the angel meant to hurt me, he had ample opportunity in the morgue. But that's only my theory.'

'We'll roll with it for now.'

The bag yawned open. Quillon reached into it and dug to the bottom. He pulled out a heavy bandaged object, like a severed hand wrapped in linen. Quillon let the linen unroll across the table, revealing that it contained eight smaller packages, each individually wrapped. 'This is how it came out of him, in pieces.'

'What do you mean, "out of him"?'

'The pieces were surgically implanted. I noticed bruising and swelling as soon as I saw him on the table. That was the only way to do it. If the angel had come down bearing some obvious item of advanced technology, it would have been separated by the clean-up crew and sent up to the Bureau boys before I ever got a look at it.'

'Proves they were serious about getting it to you, at least. It wasn't just an afterthought.'

'No, I don't think so.'

'There's a problem, though. Why send down something that isn't going to work? Nothing from the Celestial Levels functions down here. You know that as well as anyone.'

'I don't think the angels would have gone to so much trouble if they knew it would be a futile gesture.'

Quillon unwrapped the pieces one by one, placing them on the bare table with the wrapping beneath them. The linen had been white before, but now it was soaked through with pink and yellow discoloration. None of the components was any larger than the palm of Quillon's hand, and each was still covered in a thin slime of blood and tissue.

Fray tapped a finger in the air, pointing at the objects and mouthing silently. 'Sure you didn't miss anything?'

'He told me precisely where to cut and how many parts I'd find. This is all we have.'

Fray took one of the larger parts, smeared off most of the residue onto the edge of the linen and held it up to his eyes with a trembling hand. Like the other pieces, it was made of a hard, matte-silver metal.

'Expecting it to be heavier.'

'Everything they make is light,' Quillon said. 'They're light. They've got very good at it.'

'How long did it take before you stopped saying "we", Cutter?'

'Protective camouflage. It doesn't mean I've forgotten who or what I am.'

Quillon retrieved a fresh sheet of linen from the medical bag and set about cleaning up the other seven parts. Fray watched with an expression of quiet fascination, as if he was studying the opening moves of a high-stakes card game. One by one, Quillon put the cleaned parts back down on the table.

'Anything leaping out at you?' Fray asked.

'I don't know where to start.' Quillon sifted through the parts, fingering each in turn. The angel hadn't given him any detailed instructions on what to do with the pieces. It wasn't even clear that the angel had known the exact nature of the weapon it had been carrying. Eight pieces, which will fit together. That was all he had been told.

Fray jabbed a finger. 'That piece looks like it might go with that one.'

Quillon picked up a kind of elongated pipe, ribbed with lateral flanges, and decided – provisionally – that it might be a barrel or focusing device. There was another piece, a thicker cylinder with an open end, which appeared to slot into place on one end of the barrel. He slid the pieces together and felt a tiny, microscopic click – too precise to be accidental.

'Good call.'

'Anything started ticking yet?' Fray asked.

Quillon said nothing. He tried pulling the pieces back apart, but they were fixed solidly together. He couldn't even see a visible join where one piece fitted over the other. It was as if the parts had fused seamlessly.

He picked up the other pieces in turn, searching for something that would mate in a clear fashion with the component he had already assembled. There was nothing obvious, but during his examination he spotted two other pieces that appeared to fit together. As carefully as he dared he pushed them together, and felt the same tiny click as the parts engaged. He had made something like a pistol grip, but scaled for a small, delicate hand.

'Wild stab in the dark here, Cutter, but I think it might possibly be a gun.'

'I'm not fond of guns.'

'I am,' said a new voice. 'Especially when they're shiny. Guess this is the new package, right?'

Quillon turned around from the table as the woman entered the nook. She was short enough not to need to duck under the low arch. Her clothes were utilitarian and drab: shapeless trousers, heavy toe-capped boots that might have belonged to a welder, a dark olive coat that was several sizes too big. She had a nondescript, melt-into-the-crowd face and very short hair, mostly dark but flecked with grey at the temples. He guessed her age at somewhere between fifteen and twenty.

'Meroka, meet Doctor Quillon,' Fray said. 'He is, as you correctly surmised, the new package. I've just been telling him how you're going to do such an excellent job of getting him out of Spearpoint.'

'Hope you told him it isn't going to be no joyride.'

'I'm under no illusions,' Quillon said.

'Looking at three hard days to get you out, if all goes to plan, which mostly it won't. Three days of dirt and worry and less sleep than you've ever had in your life. Then we have to find the people Fray's lined up to take you to Fortune's Landing, and hope they haven't changed their minds.'

'You can throw in danger as well,' Fray said. 'Cutter's ticked off some angels. They've got deep-penetration agents in Neon Heights, and they'll be aiming to stop him leaving town.'

'You didn't mention angels on the phone, Fray. You said there was local heat. In my book that ain't the same thing.'

'Must've slipped my mind.' He contorted his face into a mask of fake contrition. 'Not that a little thing like that would be enough to scare you off, would it?'

'I've dealt with angels. They don't worry me.'

'What I figured. Bonus is, Cutter's come into a little inheritance. It's what we're trying to put together now.'

Meroka looked at the gore-stained puzzle on the table.

'That's the weapon you were talking about?'

'It's angel technology. Supposed to give him an edge, so he can get out with his skin intact.'

'Looks like something a dog sicked-up.'

'You don't want to know where it came from, trust me.' Fray brushed fingers through the white thatch of his hair. 'Well, any new insights, Cutter?'

Quillon stared at the still-unassembled gun. For a moment the parts seemed impossible to reconcile. Then, with a shudder of intuitive understanding, it all made sense to him. One element fitted under the other and formed an aperture into which the barrel could be slid and locked. The grip assembly slotted into the rear of the whole, entering at a slight angle to the line of the barrel. He pushed it home, anticipating the click that would signify correct assembly. The click arrived, but at the same moment the weapon also came alive in his hand. A tracery of luminous blue lines appeared over it, flickering and branching as if the weapon were validating its own operational integrity. The change was so sudden that he nearly dropped it.

'Guess you got that right,' Fray said.

'So it would seem.'

'What I said before still stands, though. That's angel technology. It shouldn't work down here.'

'If it does, then we're all—' Meroka started saying.

The gun spoke.

'Thank you for reassembling me. Be advised that I am programmed to blood-lock to the individual now holding me.' Its voice was hard and metallic, with a slight feminine edge. 'If you wish blood-lock to be assigned to another individual, they must handle me within the next thirty seconds. Blood-lock may only be assigned once, to one individual. I am now initiating the thirty-second countdown. You will be alerted when blood-lock is established.'

'I guess that's you,' Fray said to Quillon, with a sly smile on his face, as if he was enjoying every moment of this.

'Or maybe it should be me,' Meroka said. 'After all, I'm the one doing the protecting around here.'

Quillon held on to the weapon, although part of his mind was screaming at him to release it. 'There's intelligence in this thing,' he said. 'That shouldn't be possible. Machines can't *think* down here.'

Fray shrugged. 'Things keep working for a while.'

'Not when they've been taken apart and put back together again,' Quillon said.

'Give me the gun,' Meroka said.

'It's Cutter's toy now.' Fray looked up at her, daring Meroka to contradict him. 'The angel meant it for him.'

The gun said, 'Blood-lock has now been established. Please be advised that ambient conditions are such that my operational effectiveness in energy-discharge mode is now eighty-one per cent and falling.'

'What?' Fray said.

'Assuming that present conditions remain stable, I will become inoperable in energy-discharge mode in five hours, twenty-two minutes, with an estimated error margin of plus or minus eight minutes. Functionality will be severely compromised within three hours, forty-five minutes.'

'It's already failing,' Quillon said, turning the barrel to face the wall, making sure his finger was nowhere near the trigger.

'Five hours and change,' Fray said. 'What time is it?'

'I got nine,' Meroka said, lifting up her sleeve to examine her watches. 'Last downbound train's ten-fifteen.'

'Still doable, wouldn't you say?' asked Fray.

'If we move now,' Meroka said.

'Slow down,' Quillon said, feeling like a man on a moving sidewalk that was accelerating ever faster. 'I came here to discuss the *possibility* of leaving, that's all. I thought we might make arrangements for tomorrow, or the day after ... not start the journey right now, with no preparation.'

'Things have moved up a notch,' Fray said. 'Besides, the angel told you not to stick around. Tomorrow might already be too late.'

'Meroka and I don't know each other. How can I be sure she's any good?' Quickly he added: 'No disrespect.'

'None taken,' Meroka said.

'Meroka works for me. That's all the recommendation you need.' Fray looked expectantly at Meroka. 'May be a silly question, but I take it you came equipped?'

She screwed up her face. 'Shit, I forgot.'

'Meroka,' Fray said warningly.

She allowed her coat to hang open. Stitched to the inside seam was an array of armaments and equipment, each item in a little pouch or hoop of its own. There was a sub-machine gun, a revolver, an automatic, some kind of blunderbuss, something like a pistol-sized crossbow and a vicious assortment of edged weapons, some of which were evidently for throwing and some for close combat.

There were also bullets, magazines, powder boxes and an apothecary's wet-dream of colour-coded vials and stoppered bottles.

'I didn't forget.'

'Told you she was good,' Fray said, pushing back his chair so that he could stand up. 'And now it's time to let you in on a little operational secret, Cutter. I guess it never occurred to you that it wouldn't be very smart for a man in my position to allow himself to be cornered in a room like this?'

'Now that you mention it . . .'

Fray produced a bunch of heavy iron keys from his pocket, then pushed a shoe against a section of the wall behind him. What had appeared to be a part of the panelling hinged inwards, into darkness.

'What's that?' Quillon asked.

'What it looks like. A secret tunnel.' He passed the keys to Meroka. 'Go ahead. I'll bring up the rear.'

'You don't need to come with us, Fray. I can do this on my own.'

'I don't doubt it, Meroka, but I told Cutter I'd see him to the station. Least I can do.'

Meroka stooped through the door, then straightened up once she was inside. Quillon followed her into a short, narrow tunnel, bending almost double to squeeze through. Ahead was another door blocking their passage. This one was made of plated metal and looked like it could stop a train, or at the very least a determined safe-cracker. Meroka poked a key into the dark eye of a lock and twisted it with a grunt. There was a *thunk* as the mechanism worked. She pushed at the door, which must have been very nearly airtight. As it swung wide, warm, humid air gusted against Quillon's face. The tunnel stretched on much further.

'Where does it lead?'

'Out,' Meroka said.

Fray pushed the outer door almost closed, leaving only a pencil-thin shaft of light leaking through from the interior of the Pink Peacock. Fray must have had a spare set of keys, since he was able to lock the secondary door on his own. The bar sounds, which had been muffled but present a moment earlier, were now entirely absent. It was just the three of them and the sound of their own breathing. They advanced into darkness, the gloom relieved only by the wavering light from Meroka's pen-sized electric torch.

When Quillon touched the dark, marble-like surface of the wall it gave off an ancient, reptilian cold. He had heard rumours of tunnels such as this, cutting back into Spearpoint's fabric from within the oldest buildings, but this was the first time he had seen the evidence with his own eyes. He had taken his tinted spectacles off to see better in the darkness. The tunnels had been bored, it could only be presumed, during an earlier phase, centuries or millennia ago, when local conditions allowed the use of high-energy cutting equipment such as plasma lances. Nothing that now worked in Neon Heights could inflict more than a scratch on the dense black fabric. It would have taken lifetimes to manually dig this far.

'You never told me about these tunnels,' Quillon said to Fray.

'That's sort of the idea with a secret, Cutter.'

'I didn't think you and I had any. Now I'm wondering what else I didn't need to know.'

'Fray's a businessman,' Meroka said, butting in on their conversation. 'He may have made you think you had some special relationship going, but the bottom line is you're just one of his clients. Ain't that right, Fray?'

'Cutter's more than a client,' Fray said. Despite his size he was keeping up with the pace.

'What's the deal with the name?' Meroka asked.

Quillon took off his hat so he didn't have to stoop as much, clutching it against the dark prize of his medical bag. 'Fray's idea of wit. I'm a pathologist. I cut things open. It means he doesn't have to use my real name when it might be overheard. But for what it's worth, I'd much rather you called me Quillon.'

'Good enough for Fray, good enough for me. Cutter it is.'

'Thanks. Is it going to be like this all the way to . . . what was the place you mentioned?'

'Fortune's Landing,' Fray said.

'I've heard of it. That's about all.'

'You'll do fine there,' Fray said. 'It's on one of the semaphore lines, so you won't feel out of touch.'

'I trust Meroka will make introductions for me when we arrive.'

'I don't go that far,' she said. 'I drop you off with some nomads we've had dealings with. Bunch of traders who loop between the main towns, selling and bartering what they can, generally trying to stay out of the way of the Skulls and the vorgs.'

'People I can trust?'

'They'll see you right,' Fray said. 'But once you get to Fortune's Landing you're on your own. Which is no problem, you being a medicine man and all that. Those ladylike hands of yours, I'm sure you won't have too much trouble finding employment.'

'I hope it's not the same kind Malkin had in mind.'

'He gets carried away with the torturing thing,' Fray admitted. 'But you've got to admire a man who enjoys his work.'

'You said you cut things open,' Meroka said. 'How's that going to help you if they've already got the pathologist's job covered?'

'I was trained as a doctor. I can diagnose ailments, prescribe drugs and perform simple surgical procedures.'

'That's good,' Meroka said. 'Plenty of diseases out there to treat, that's for sure. Provided they don't get you first.'

'You're a ray of sunshine. I can see the next three days are just going to fly by.'

'Give her time,' Fray said. 'She's an acquired taste. Besides, none of it's personal with Meroka. She likes you really; she just doesn't want to get too close to the commodity.'

'Might have something to do with how few of them ever show up again,' Meroka added.

'Fray seems to think I'll make it back. Don't you, Fray?'

'Absolutely,' he called from the rear. 'Not a doubt in my mind.'

'Fray's an optimist,' Meroka said scathingly. 'Always did tell him it was his biggest flaw.' But there must have been some tiny flicker of curiosity in Meroka, some realisation that Quillon was not just another client, because a short while later she said, 'So how'd you two hook up, anyway? Fray got you into one of his business insurance schemes?'

'It isn't a protection racket,' Fray said. 'I don't do protection rackets.'

'But you're not above setting your enemies on fire,' Meroka said.

'That's different.'

Quillon stooped even more, having the impression that the tunnel was becoming tighter the further they went into it. 'How far are we going?'

'Far as we have to. Need to pick up the pace or we'll miss the train. You all right back there, Fray?'

'I'm fine.'

But Fray was clearly beginning to flag. Quillon could hear it in his increasingly laboured breathing, the gradual weakening of his voice. The tunnel began to bend around to the left. Although neither Meroka nor Fray made any mention of it, Quillon was conscious of passing a separate shaft running off to the right. Warm, foetid air gusted out of the dark mouth. They were surely an awesome distance into the fabric of Spearpoint now: Quillon sensed the crushing press of all this ancient matter, resentful at the tunnels cut through it, nothing on its mind except the need to close them up for all eternity. For all the hazards that awaited him in the inhabited part of Neon Heights, he was very keen to leave this place.

'I'd heard about these tunnels,' he said, 'but I didn't know whether they were real or not. Part of me just assumed they were another urban myth, like the giant rats in the sewer drains.'

'They're real enough,' Fray said.

'Then is the rest of it real as well? The stories about the things inside them?'

'Been using these tunnels for half my life,' Meroka said. 'Been deep, too. In all that time, I ain't never seen anything I couldn't explain. Been spooked a few times, but ...' She paused, as if she had given away too much by admitting to having been frightened.

'We've all been spooked,' Fray said. 'There's no shame in it. Thing is, though, these tunnels aren't any kind of secret. Cops know about them: I did, before I left the force. We'd use them to intimidate suspects. Threaten to leave them alone in here. Didn't exactly go out of our way to spike the scare stories.'

'Scare stories?' Quillon said.

'Bad shit happens down here,' Meroka said. 'Get lost down here quicker than you can blink. Or bump into people you don't want to bump into – which would be me, on a bad day. But the rest of it? So much steaming horseshit, metaphorically speaking.'

'I couldn't have put it more eloquently,' Fray said.

'And the Mad Machines?' Quillon asked.

'Man's been reading too many bedtime stories,' Meroka said, just as her torch flickered out, plunging them into absolute darkness. 'No machines, big or small, Cutter. Just because the tunnels exist don't mean all the other made-up crap turns out to be real as well.' She shook the torch until it faltered back to life.

'So neither of you has ever seen anything strange, in all the times you've been coming through these tunnels?'

'Seen some dead bodies,' Meroka said. 'Seen some things I'd rather not know what they used to be. But big scary machines, wandering around in here? 'Fraid not. Spearpoint's just a big old spike jammed into the ground. Nothing's changed in here for thousands of years.'

'Have you ever been lost?'

'Happened once or twice. Especially when the package was doing too much talking.'

'Hint taken.'

Meroka wasn't done, though. 'Being lost isn't the worst thing that can happen. At least if you get lost, you might wander out again. Cross a zone, that's a different story.'

'You'd hardly fail to notice if you crossed a zone,' Quillon said.

'Yeah, you'd notice. But that doesn't mean you'd feel it coming, or be able to cross back over. You think you know Spearpoint pretty well, Cutter, but all you really know is life on the skin, out on the ledges. The zones are big out there. Someone like Fray, he hardly ever needs to leave Neon Heights.' Her voice took on an admonitory tone. 'Different story once you get inside. Now they get smaller and smaller, crowding in around the Eye of God, or the Mire, or whatever you want to call it. Shit gets blurred together, hard to map. Reason my light isn't working so well: it can feel us getting closer to the transition.'

'Do we have to cross over?'

'Not until we leave the tunnel and get to Steamville. Unless things have shifted around in here since last time. Which is a possibility. Clock boys are already worked up about it, and not just in Neon Heights. Rest of us saw this coming way back. Last two, three years, easily. Serious movement. Something heavy heading down the pike.' Without waiting for his opinion she added, 'Blame the angels myself. Anything unexplained, they're top of my shit list.'

'I see.' Quillon swallowed hard. 'And this assumption is based on . . . what, exactly?'

'I'd just take it as a given, I were you,' Fray said.

'Angels piss me off,' Meroka said. 'That's all you need to know.'

They walked on in silence, Quillon unwilling to press her on the matter for fear that she would start wondering exactly why he was so interested. At least it told him one thing: Fray must have kept their mutual secret. Unless she was lying for reasons of her own, Meroka knew nothing of his origins, and that meant Fray had never broken his word.

'How close are you taking us to the boundary?' Quillon asked.

'Within half a league. Can't be more accurate than that.'

Presently he had the sense of the tunnel widening, and when he tried to reach out he could only touch the nearest wall. 'Keep right,' Meroka said again, and though he could see almost nothing except the wavering spot cast by Meroka's torch, he knew they were edging past a huge duct or shaft leading much deeper into Spearpoint.

In the darkness he heard a quick rustle of fabric. There was a flash of yellow light and a bang that echoed and echoed into a diminishing infinity. In the after-image of the yellow flash he saw Meroka's fist holding one of her guns, the revolver, firing it into the warm draught. He steeled himself, wondering what she had seen or sensed. Then her torch beam alighted on a scampering black form, a soot-black rat. Part of its tail was missing. The rat looked up at them with ochre eyes and rubbed its snout with its forepaws.

He heard the click as Meroka put the safety catch back on and slipped the gun into her coat.

'Nothing to see. Let's move.'

'We're only a few hundred spans from the exit,' Fray said, wheezing heavily now. 'Reckon I'd better turn around here, or I'll be slowing you down too much. Meroka'll take care of you the rest of the way. Send me a postcard from Fortune's Landing. Anonymous, of course – don't want everyone knowing you've skipped town.'

In the gloom of the tunnel, Quillon shook the bigger man's hand. 'I'll be sure to. And thanks for coming this far. You didn't need to.' He paused and remembered something he had meant to give to Fray earlier. 'Would you shine the torch over here?' he asked Meroka. He waited until the beam fell on his medical bag, then opened the fasteners. He took out a small package from near the top. 'It's not as much as usual, but our supplies haven't been restocked for weeks. I'm afraid you'll just have to make do until I can find another source.'

Fray took the package of Morphax-55, crumpling the white paper in his fist. 'You saved any for yourself, Cutter?'

'Enough.'

Fray passed the package back. 'I'm pretty sure you'll need this more than I do. I'm not going anywhere; you are. If you don't make it back from the outside, I don't know where I'd find another supplier.'

'I'm sure you'd find someone,' Quillon said. But he knew better than

32

to press the point. He returned the antizonals to his bag, secretly grateful that Fray had turned them down.

'When you two are done,' Meroka said, 'we got a train to make.'

'Go,' Fray said, squeezing Quillon's hand once before releasing his grip. 'And enjoy the scenery.'

CHAPTER THREE

They emerged from the tunnel through a low door that led into the back room of an all-night launderette. Quillon replaced his hat and pushed his spectacles back onto his nose, even though the steam fogged them almost instantly. With its pale green walls, sacks of soiled linen and churning coin-operated machines, the launderette was a bright, steam-filled oasis. Despite the lateness of the hour two people were sitting apart on the hard benches waiting for their washing cycles to end, staring into the hypnotic vortices of their whirling clothes. In that moment he would gladly have joined them, choosing life in the launderette over the uncertainties that lay ahead beyond Spearpoint.

Then they were outside, in the night and the rain. Quillon caught himself looking around, eyeing the surrounding streets, buildings and vehicles for a potential spy or assailant.

'Try not to look like you've got a target on your head,' Meroka said.

They took the funicular down to the next ledge, then rode the elevated. Slot-cars and slot-cabs buzzed by in racing blue flashes. Blade, the female pop singer, winked at them from an animated neon advertisement covering the whole side of a tenement building, while she took sultry puffs from a Mariner cigarette. The few pedestrians about were stooped under umbrellas, or had their hats jammed low against the weather. Quillon felt conspicuous, wondering what explanation he would offer if anyone questioned him about his association with the scowling, illegally armed Meroka. But none of the vehicles slowed, no one in the passing slot-buses or overhead trains gave them more than a second glance, and the other pedestrians seemed much more concerned with avoiding puddles and potholes than noticing Quillon and his new accomplice.

It was nearly ten by the time they got to the station. Quillon looked up at the cluster of golden clocks set into the stonework above the arched entranceway.

'Can we still make it?'

Meroka nodded at one of several all-night diners across the other side of the road from the station 'Wait in there. I'll buy the tickets.'

'Shouldn't I stay with you?'

'Don't want you hanging around in the station. Angels want you this badly, they'll have every station scoped. We get in, get out, fast. On the train and out.'

'Understood.'

He watched Meroka vanish into the station, then walked into the yellow glow of the all-night diner. There was a long zinc-topped bar, a trio of morose-looking customers perched at one end of it, none of whom acknowledged his arrival. The bartender gave him a noncommittal look. Quillon pulled up a red-cushioned stool at the far end and ordered a coffee and a doughnut. He lit a cigarette and smoked it hard. Like alcohol, the plant extract in the cigarette had no detectable effect on his nervous system, but smoking eased the tightness in his lungs. They were changing, just like the rest of him.

When the coffee arrived he forced half the cup down immediately. He ate the doughnut in a few dutiful mouthfuls, wiped sticky residue from his lips and studied the station entrance, waiting for Meroka to emerge. Perhaps they had cut things too fine after all.

Five minutes later she came out and walked over to the all-night diner. There was nothing on her face to say how the transaction had gone. She pushed open the door and took the stool next to Quillon's.

'We're ready?'

'Finish your drink.'

They sat in brooding silence, like a pair of lovers after a public tiff. Every now and then Meroka glanced at the clocks behind the counter, checked her own watches or the times shown above the station entrance. It was already ten minutes past the hour, with the train due to leave in less than five minutes. It must already be in the station, waiting to depart.

'Shouldn't we be on our way?'

'You want to do this on your own, be my guest.'

'Did you see anyone inside?'

'One or two.'

'I mean anyone who looked suspicious.' He caught the bartender's eye and slipped a bill onto the counter, waving aside any change. 'Like they might be the ones after me.'

She gave him a sidelong look. 'You think they'd be that obvious?'

'No,' he said. 'But I'm assuming you're good enough at your job to spot the signs most people would miss.'

Meroka simmered, clearly distressed at not being able to come back with a suitably cutting response. 'Didn't see anyone,' she said eventually. 'But that don't mean no one's there. They're good, they're going to be hard to spot. Even for me.'

Quillon checked his own watches. 'Then there's nothing for it but to hope for the best. Isn't it time?'

'Train ain't leaving for another three minutes.'

'It'll take us at least two minutes to get to the platform.'

'Ninety seconds,' she said, with fierce certainty.

They sat in silence for another half-minute, at which point Meroka nodded and they were moving. He was aware of the bartender watching them, of the expert disinterest of the other three patrons. They crossed the street and entered the station. Above the arch, all the mechanical clocks paused their minute hands at the top of the hour, as if the hidden mechanisms behind their faces were drawing breath. Then the hands resumed their progress and it was less than a minute until the train departed.

They walked quickly through the vaulted gloom of the station, never quite breaking into a run. Down blue-tiled staircases, onto wooden flooring, the smell of steam, oil and ozone heavy in the air. Meroka had cut their departure to the second, but at least it meant there were no crowds pressing around the boarding gates, where the station clerks checked tickets. They were waved through and instructed not to dawdle. The platform alongside the waiting train was nearly empty, all other passengers and luggage already aboard. The only people now standing on the platform were station staff, pillbox-hatted guards with crisp white gloves and silver whistles at the ready, porters waiting by empty trolleys. At the head of the train was an internal-combustion-powered loco-motive, the fiery red of a transistor radio. On the opposite side of the platform, waiting to be relieved after it had climbed all the way up from the next zone down, was a black steam engine at the end of a long line of freight cars. The black engine was veiled in its own steam, hissing from pipes and valves as if the machine was on the point of exploding from its own pressure.

They boarded the red-engined train, climbing into the vestibule at the end of a carriage. Meroka lingered nervously at the threshold, looking up and down the steam-cloaked platform. Most of the doors were already closed. One of the guards blew his whistle. The locomotive answered with a blast of its air horn. The train began to inch forwards. Meroka closed the door.

Quillon saw the figure at the same moment she did. A man, little more than a walking silhouette, emerged from the white fog around the steam engine on the other side of the platform. He wasn't wearing a railway uniform, rather a wide-brimmed hat and a knee-length coat cinched at the waist. He could have been an evening commuter waiting for the last train home. Something in his left hand caught the scarlet gleam of a signal light.

'That's one of them,' Meroka said, as the same paralysing realisation formed in Quillon's own mind.

What was the man going to do? Get on the train, or wait as it rolled out of the station, picking up speed as it hit the descending grade, the start of the long spiral all the way down to Steamville? The moment stretched agonisingly.

Quillon wanted to act for himself, wanted to take the initiative, but it had been too long since he had faced a similar crisis and the certainty of action he had once relied upon was not there. He watched in a state of numb indecision as the man grabbed the handrail of a passing carriage and swung himself aboard, opening the door and letting himself in, the difficult sequence of movements completed with a weirdly inhuman elegance, as if Quillon had just seen a movie run through the projector backwards. The man had stepped onto the train only four or five carriages from where they were standing.

'We're leaving,' Meroka said, opening the door again.

Quillon looked down at the platform, the wooden boards moving by more quickly with each instant that he delayed. It was already fast enough that if he did not judge his landing well he would be seriously injured.

'It's going too fast.'

'Do it, Cutter.'

He couldn't. He was paralysed with fear and indecision, part of him wanting to place his complete trust in Meroka, another part unable to surrender. She grabbed his wrist and for a moment he thought she was going to launch herself into space and take him with her. The train was rocketing now, picking up speed quickly as the front portion reached the descending grade beyond the platform. His only instinct was to hold on tighter to the handrail, refusing to be dragged free.

'It's too fast,' he said again, this time on a falling note, because he knew that any possibility of jumping was now behind them. 'I'm sorry.'

'You blew the extraction,' Meroka said. 'Less than a minute into the journey ... and you fucking *blew* it.'

Something snapped inside him. He shoved Meroka against the wall of the carriage, surprising himself with his own violence and the suddenness with which it had emerged.

'Listen to me,' he said, still pinning her in place. 'I may seem meek and mild to you, and maybe I am compared to you, but there's something you need to understand.' He pushed harder, with a savagery he had not expected in himself. 'I am not your damned package. I'm a man who's spent nine years surviving alone, nine years after I killed two of my colleagues because they murdered someone I loved. And when I say "killed" I mean that I tortured them with drugs, slowly and painfully, until they died, because that's what happens when you get on the wrong side of me. And I've been down here for nine years, minding my own business, never so much as treading on a fly. Until today, when my world turned upside down again. I've had to go from that, to this, in less time than it takes most people to pick somewhere nice to eat. I left work and now – only a few hours later – I'm leaving the city. So I apologise if my adjustment isn't as quick as you'd like, but you're just going to have to deal with it.'

He released the pressure on Meroka. She moved her chin back and forth, licked her lips.

'You finished, Cutter?'

'For now.'

She reached up to readjust the collar of her coat, where he had held her. 'For something that looks like it crawled out of the ground, you have some strength, I'll give you that. Felt good to get that off your chest, didn't it?'

'I'm just saying, it would be a mistake to underestimate me.'

'You serious about the torturing and killing part?'

He closed his eyes against the memory of what he had been forced to do. 'Yes.'

She slammed the door shut, the rushing air of their progress doing most of the work for her. Outside, the train rattled and swayed over a silvery labyrinth of criss-crossing rails. 'Well, guess we're on the train now, whether we like it or not.'

'We don't know how many of them were hiding in that station, apart from the one who got aboard. For all you know we'd be dead if we'd jumped off.'

Meroka looked down the long corridor that ran the length of the carriage on the left-hand side. 'Whereas it's a stone-cold certainty that there's one of them on the train now.'

'I don't know that he saw us. He may just have got on this train on the off chance that we were on it.'

'He saw us. Saw you, anyway.'

'We should move along the train, closer to the front. Maybe he won't have time to reach us.'

'Next stop's twenty minutes away, when they switch the engine. He'll have time.'

'That doesn't mean we should just wait here for him, does it?' Quillon breathed in and out, trying to find some calm, however transitory it might prove. 'We're not defenceless. We're both armed. There's two of us, just one of him.'

'Just the one we saw. Doesn't mean he don't have friends already inside.'

Meroka looked along the corridor again. They could only see as far as the opposite end of this carriage, where the corridor jogged inwards to pass through the connecting bellows between one coach and the next. Four or five carriages down, Quillon thought, trying to hold the image in his mind like a photograph, scanning it for details he might have missed at the time. If the agent was working his way towards them now, the first warning they would have would be when he came around that corner.

'You ready with that angel gun?' Meroka asked.

Quillon squeezed his palm around the waiting weapon, still safe in his coat pocket. He drew it out slowly. 'Do you still work?'

'Operational effectiveness is now sixty-three per cent and falling,' the gun answered, quietly enough that its voice would not have been heard in the adjoining compartments. 'I will become inoperable in energy-discharge mode in four hours, three minutes. Functionality will be severely compromised within two hours, twenty-five minutes. Error margins are available for these estimates.'

'I'll skip the error margins.' He returned the gun to his pocket, before someone happened along the corridor. 'Four hours is still good, isn't it? Once we've lost this tail, we'll be fine. Won't we?'

'Yeah. We'll be fine.' Meroka opened her coat and selected one of her own weapons, a bulky machine-pistol with squared-off, utilitarian lines. It had a stamped-metal barrel and a straight grip enclosing a long magazine. Meroka thumbed a lever on the side of the black-painted housing, clicking it to its third setting. 'Anything else you need reassuring about?'

'I thought you didn't do reassurance.'

'Got two choices. Wait at the front of the train for him to find us. Which he will, sooner or later – and he'll know he's got us cornered. Or take the fight to him.'

'I'm guessing you like the second one best.'

Meroka concealed the gun back inside her coat, the flap covering her hand and sleeve.

'Stay behind me. Don't shoot at anyone until I do.'

They started walking down the corridor, passing compartments on the right. The first two were empty, and the third contained only one passenger, a young woman looking out of the window. Neon Heights slid by in a rain-smeared blur of mingled colours, the succession of advertisements and slogans tending to a rushing electric white as the train gathered speed. The next compartment was empty, and the one after that contained two men who were smoking and laughing. The next and last compartment in that coach was also empty, with only a couple of discarded newspapers on the seats. Quillon could feel the descending grade now, the train winding its anticlockwise way down the long, gentle spiral cut into Spearpoint's side, losing a league in altitude for every thirty leagues it travelled along the tracks. There was still a long way to go before he reached the ground. He didn't want to think about exactly how far it was.

Meroka paused at the bend in the corridor, whipping out her gun and swinging around the blind corner. Quillon waited until she gave him the nod and followed behind, through the swaying connecting bellows between the two carriages. Then she held him back while she swung around into the next corridor.

'Clear,' she said quietly.

They moved along the next series of compartments. Again some were empty and some were partially occupied. Only one was anywhere near full, the second along, with five rowdy businessmen trading stories, their shirt collars and ties loosened, the smell of an evening's hard drinking hanging in the air. In the next compartment sat a mother and daughter, bolt upright in their seats, the girl wearing a bonnet, the mother a veil that covered the upper half of her face, both of them dressed in the elaborate and formal clothes that marked them as respectable citizens of Steamville, returning from what must have been an arduous and costly excursion to Neon Heights. On the mother's lap, clutched as if it were the most precious artefact in the universe, lay a large brown envelope. The girl was pale of complexion, thinner than she should have been and in the grip of a constant shivering tremor. The mother probably couldn't have afforded the expense of a full operation in Neon Heights, but she might have had the means to pay for a set of X-rays, the images intended to guide the hand of an affordable surgeon back in Steamville.

He wanted to talk to them. He had the tools in his bag to perform basic tests of neurological function. Even if he couldn't do anything for the girl, he could at least settle the mother's doubts, reassure her that she had done all that she could.

He must have hesitated. The girl turned to look at him through the partition glass. The mother met his gaze, eyes dark and unreadable behind her veil, but there was inexpressible sadness and resignation in the lines around her mouth. The tendons stood out on the backs of her hands, clutching the envelope with its fearful cargo of medical truth.

Then Meroka was looking back at him, urging him to follow.

'I'm sorry,' Quillon mouthed, as if that made a difference.

Then a man came around the bend of the corridor, beyond Meroka. He saw her twitch, ready to bring out the pistol. The man wore the cap and waistcoated uniform of a railway worker. He was shorter and bulkier than the figure they had seen on the platform, his frame filling the width of the corridor. In his hand was a ticket clipper; in the other a pocket timetable.

'Be with you in a minute,' the man called, before sliding open the first compartment door and vanishing inside.

Meroka kept moving. There was only one person in the fourth compartment, deeply asleep, and no one in the fifth. The guard spoke to whoever was in the sixth compartment; there was the sound of his ticket punch, and then he emerged back into the corridor, to be met by Meroka, standing there with one hand still tucked into her coat and Quillon behind her, the angel gun held out of view.

'If I could just see your tickets,' the guard said, 'then you can get right on back to your compartment.'

Meroka reached into her coat with the other hand and produced the tickets. The guard took them from her and squinted down the length of his nose, eyes narrowing behind glasses. 'I think you need to turn around,' he said, not unhelpfully. 'Looks like you overshot your compartment back in the third coach. Guess you were coming back from the dining car?'

'Guess so,' Meroka said.

The guard jabbed a finger over his shoulder. 'It's all first class behind me, right to the end of the train.' He held his clipper up to the tickets and punched them together, then handed them back to Meroka, beaming with the satisfaction of a job well done.

'We need to get past you,' she said.

The pleasant demeanour began to crack. 'Maybe you didn't quite understand me, miss. These tickets of yours are second class only. You really don't have any business going into the first-class section.'

'How would you know about our business?' Meroka asked.

'Let's not make more of this than we need to. You miscounted the number of coaches, that's all. Easy mistake, anyone could do it. You just need to turn around and—'

It was all too quick for Quillon. One instant the guard was looking down at Meroka, the next she had the machine-pistol pushed right up into his face, the barrel digging into the fleshy mound of his cheek. The guard dropped the ticket punch and timetable, falling back against the partition between the corridor and the compartments.

'You could have made this so much easier,' Meroka said. She spun him around, then nodded at Quillon to open the sliding door into the empty compartment next to the one the guard had just been checking. She propelled the guard through, then gave him a hard kick in the testicles, sending him sprawling onto one of the cigarette-stained couches.

'Don't shoot me,' the guard said, recovering his glasses just as they slipped from his nose.

'You think I can trust you to sit here and be awfully nice about not stopping this train as soon as we're out of your sight?'

'Of . . . of course.'

'Yeah, right.' Still holding the machine-pistol in her left hand, Meroka dug back into her coat and produced a small silver-plated device resembling a cross between a tiny pistol and a needle-less hypodermic. She tossed it over to the stunned guard. 'Pick it up,' she said, as the device tumbled down between his buckled legs. There was, Quillon noticed, a growing dark spot on his groin.

'What do you want—'

'Got two choices here, fat man. Either you press that against your neck and squeeze, or I have to shoot you. What's it going to be?'

'What's in it?' the man asked, picking up the device with nervous, fumbling fingers. 'How do I know it isn't going to kill me?'

'You don't.'

'I'd do it if I were you,' Quillon said, hoping and praying that the device was loaded with some kind of tranquilliser.

'Trigger finger's getting itchy here,' Meroka said.

The guard must have realised that he had very little option, for he pressed the tip of the device against the skin of his neck, just above the starched collar of his uniform, jammed his eyes shut and pulled the spring-loaded trigger. The device clicked and hissed, firing its chemical payload through his skin. The effect was rapid. The guard's fingers loosened, the anaesthetic device dropping to the floor. His eyes opened, rolled senselessly, and then the guard slumped against the back of the seat, only his uniform distinguishing him from another drunk commuter dozing off the booze.

'Please tell me I was right to convince him to use it,' Quillon said.

Meroka ducked in and retrieved the device, slipping it back into her coat. 'He's tranked. It'll wear off in half an hour or so.'

'So now we just ... leave him? Shouldn't we remove his uniform or something, make him look less like a guard?'

'Yeah. You do that, while I go on and kill the man who's on his way down the train to kill you.' Meroka came back out of the compartment and slid the partition door closed.

As she spoke the adjoining door slid open. A man poked his head out of the gap, appraising Meroka and Quillon. 'Something the matter here?' he asked, in a low, threatening rasp of a voice. He had the thickset face of a born troublemaker, the beady, questioning eyes of someone who wouldn't consider the evening complete if he didn't get into at least one good brawl.

'No, we're fine,' Meroka said, the machine-pistol once more secreted within her coat.

'Where's the guard? He was here a moment ago.'

'We didn't see any guard,' Quillon said. 'He must have turned back and gone the other way.'

'How'd you know which way he was going if you didn't see him?' The man emerged into the corridor, suspicion deepening in his face. He tried to see past Meroka, through the compartment door she had just slid shut. 'Who's in there? No one inside just now.'

'Not your problem,' Meroka said. 'Trust me on this.'

'Let me past.' The man grabbed Meroka's shoulder and made to shove her against the corridor's outside wall. Meroka didn't give him a chance. She pulled the machine-pistol out and rammed it under the man's chin.

'I did tell you it wasn't your problem, didn't I?'

The big man made a choking sound.

'It would probably be a good idea to get back in your compartment,' Quillon said, wondering if Meroka had enough tranquilliser to knock out everyone on the train. The big man, for all that he might have been spoiling for a confrontation, evidently knew better than to argue with the gun pressed under his jaw. He started shuffling backwards, his eyes straining to look down as Meroka forced his head up at an unnatural angle.

That was when a figure appeared around the corner at the end of the corridor. Quillon, looking past both Meroka and the man she was holding at gunpoint, had only an instant to recognise the newcomer as the same man they had seen on the platform. In the half-light of the platform he had passed for normal. Here in the brightness of the railway carriage there was nothing about the hatted man that could ever be right. Quillon didn't even have the sense that he was looking at another angel. The figure was a grey-skinned ghoul, a corpse going through the parodic motions of life.

Meroka acted swiftly. She jerked back the machine-pistol and used her right boot to kick the big man off kilter, sending him careering back into the newcomer. The newcomer looked stick-thin even in his coat, but he had unexpected resources of strength and balance. In what seemed like slow motion, the ghoul began to draw the glinting weapon they had seen him carrying on the platform. With the same slowness Meroka lowered the barrel of the machine-pistol, aiming it squarely at the ghoul. Most of him was still hidden behind the big man, who – Quillon realised – the ghoul was supporting with his free hand, improvising a shield. Quillon began to bring the angel gun up.

The ghoul was the first to fire. He shot through the big man, punching a red-rimmed hole from his back to his chest, neat and central through the sternum. Quillon flinched away, gore spattering the left side of his face like a drizzle of warm rain, bone and blood, muscle and lung tissue erupting from the wound in a widening fan. The ghoul had missed Quillon, but only by a tiny margin. An eyeblink later, Meroka returned fire, releasing a deafening burst of bullets from the machine-pistol, the barrel spitting blue flame, shell casings ratcheting from the side, the torso of the big man – he had died instantly the moment the ghoul fired – turning into a pulverised red chaos. Meroka kept on firing until she had exhausted the magazine. The ghoul staggered back, his coat plastered with blood and tissue, at last relinquishing the human shield. He came to rest with his spine against the rear wall and produced a hideously exaggerated smile, as if invisible hooks were pulling up the extremities of his mouth.

Behind the blue-grey lips was a compacted horror of black teeth and tongue, as if there was too much squeezed into too little space.

'I am but one of many,' the ghoul said, his voice like wind through trees, dry and spectral. 'You are but one, Quillon.'

The ghoul let go of his weapon.

'Did you come alone?' Meroka asked, dropping the magazine and reaching into her coat for a spare.

'Of course I didn't.'

'Where are the others?'

'All around you. There's no point in running.' The ghoul coughed black treacle out of his mouth. 'There are too many of us, and now we know exactly where you are and exactly where you think you are going.'

'But you probably don't know about this,' Quillon said, aiming the angel gun. He waited an instant for the ghoul's eyes to alight on it, another instant for a flicker of recognition to show in his face.

'That won't work down—'

Quillon fired. The gun twitched in his hand – it wasn't so much recoil as a kind of quickening, the weapon stirring from sleep. Crimson light, bright enough to etch an after-image in his vision, lanced from the barrel. The beam boiled into the ghoul and turned half of him to black char in no more than a second. The smell hit Quillon an instant later.

Along with the realisation that he had just killed for the third time.

CHAPTER FOUR

The angel left a slick of black blood as they dragged it to the nearest outer door. Bits of it kept flaking off like charred newspaper. If there was anything useful on the corpse, some weapon or gadget that might help them, it was going to have to remain undiscovered.

Meroka pulled open the window, then reached down to the door handle. She had to push it open against the force of the wind. The train was passing over a latticework bridge, spanning one of the points where some impossibly ancient cataclysm had chipped a crevasse in the black fabric of Spearpoint, ripping a tapering cleft all the way down to the next ledge. She shoved the dead ghoul and the body tumbled to the tracks, the train's forward motion snatching it away. Quillon only just had time to see the angel slip through a gap in the rails and plummet into the dark void under the bridge. There would be precious little to recognise after it had hit the ground again, leagues below. He imagined the corpse providing some puzzle for a counterpart to himself, a striving young pathologist in Horsetown's equivalent of the Third District Morgue.

They were struggling with the other body when a partition door slid open further down the carriage and two of the rowdy businessmen peered cautiously out. So did the mother who had been sitting in the next compartment along. None of them said anything. They merely looked at Meroka and Quillon, at the remaining body and the tableau of carnage surrounding them.

'As you were,' Meroka said.

All three moved quietly back into their compartments.

'Perhaps we shouldn't throw him overboard after all,' Quillon said.

'What do you care?'

'He was an innocent man. If he falls all the way down to the next ledge, no one will ever know what happened to him. At least if we leave him on the train he'll be found by someone.'

'With your fingerprints all over him.'

'The least of my worries, Meroka.' There was no need to add that his fingerprints were purposefully nonspecific, making a unique match very hard to prove.

They moved the dead man into the empty compartment and slid the door closed on him. Propped up in the seat, a hole blown through his chest, there was no way he could be mistaken for anything other than a corpse. But at least he wasn't lying in the corridor any more.

'Still another ten minutes from the stop,' Meroka said, checking her watches. 'Better find us an empty compartment somewhere else.'

'Do you think there's another angel on the train?'

'If that thing was an angel, it wasn't like any I've ever seen. Fucker didn't even have wings. You sure you know who's really after you?'

As they walked towards the rear of the train, Quillon said, 'It was an angel, just not like the ones we see flying overhead. The angels have been trying to find a way to survive beyond the Celestial Levels for years. That thing – the ghoul – was one of their deep-penetration agents, surgically and genetically adapted to function down here.'

'Looked half-past dead to me.'

'He was dying from the moment he crossed into our zone. But just being able to operate down here at all is a significant step forwards for them.'

'You know a lot about angels.'

'When they're trying to kill you, you make a point of studying your enemy.' He paused as they passed a washroom. 'I need to get this mess off my face, Meroka. Do you mind?'

'Don't take all week.'

He went inside and locked the door. The light came on automatically, bathing everything in a liverish yellow. He took off his hat and glasses and looked at himself in the mirror, trying to match his face against the ghoul's, trying to convince himself that there was a world of difference. He'd been able to pass as human in daylight, when he had first come to Neon Heights. But forced into exile, cut off from home, he was reverting to type. He had shaved his head when the hair started falling out. He had taken to wearing spectacles when the blue tint of his eyes began to deepen unnaturally. As he dabbed away at the spatter and gore with soap, water and a handful of scratchy paper towels, his skin seemed little more than a translucent membrane stretched perilously tight over alien bone-structure. He had been amongst humans long enough to know how weird he was starting to look.

Half-past dead.

He reached behind his back and felt through the fabric of his coat and clothes for what should have been the hard ridge of his shoulder blade. It wasn't there. Instead he felt a soft, cancerous bud. There was one on the other side as well, precisely symmetrical.

For years he had practised a kind of chemotherapy on himself, dosing himself with a cocktail of drugs, holding the process of reversion at bay. When that began to fail, he had gone back to Fray. Black-market surgery, performed in a squalid annexe of the Pink Peacock, kept the wing-buds from growing back. Every twelve months, the buds had been meticulously cut away, the wounds stitched and bandaged. Then every six, as the growth rate began to accelerate. Then every three.

And now he was overdue.

By the time Meroka and Quillon had disembarked, a snorting black dragon of a steam engine was already being backed into place where the internal-combustion locomotive had been, ready to take the train on the next leg of its journey. Everything happened with stopwatch precision, fixed to a routine that hadn't changed in centuries.

'Maybe we should have stayed on it,' he said, as they followed the handful of other disembarking passengers away from the platform to the station hall.

'Either way it's a risk,' Meroka said. 'Least now we aren't stuck on that thing with nowhere else to go.'

From somewhere behind them came a scream, followed by shouting and a growing commotion.

'Sounds as if they just found the body,' Quillon said, making a conscious effort not to alter his stride.

'You can look back,' Meroka said in a low voice. 'Everyone else is.'

He risked a wary glance over his shoulder. Passengers and station staff were gathering around the coach where the confrontation had taken place, including some of the rowdy businessmen. There was a great deal of enthusiastic shouting and finger-pointing. A white-whiskered man in a railway uniform began blowing a code on his whistle, the whistle-blasts echoing off the station's high metal roof. Two men emerged from the end of the coach, supporting the barely conscious form of the guard.

'That's them!' called one of the businessmen, singling out Meroka and Quillon. 'They were there! I saw them! They killed that man!'

Quillon turned around slowly, trying to look agreeably perplexed, as if he had no possible idea what he was being accused of. 'Is something the matter ...' he started to say, not even sounding convincing to himself.

'Stop there,' another man called, a black-bearded, uniformed figure who might have been a senior guard, stationmaster or perhaps an agent of the railway police. He began to unbuckle something from his belt, advancing steadily on Meroka and Quillon. The item turned out to be a long-nosed service revolver, which the man gripped two-handed and began to level at his targets. 'Stop,' he declaimed, his voice booming out in actorly fashion. 'Stop or I will shoot!'

'This isn't going to end well,' Meroka said. She began to reach into her coat again.

'No more deaths,' Quillon said. 'Please.'

The bearded man fired a warning shot, ringing high into the vaulted roof – disturbing the night's audience of roosting bats and birds, a vast eruption of sooty wings. 'This is your last warning!' he called again. 'Stop now!'

Meroka flung something at the man. For an instant Quillon had the absurd impression that she had thrown him a candy or a glass marble. It landed near his feet and exploded, a bright concussive flash louder even than the discharge of his revolver. The grenade threw up a screen of choking blue-white smoke. Meroka tossed another into the melee for good luck, then spun around and started running. Quillon followed her, his medical bag swinging ridiculously from his left hand, drawing his right hand and the angel gun from his pocket so that he could run more freely. They exited the platform area and passed through a wide doorway into the black-and-white-tiled booking hall and waiting room, where late-night travellers were only now beginning to register the commotion outside. A station official, more alert than most, was just putting down the handset of a wall-mounted telephone. He spotted the two fugitives and dashed across to the outer door, bravely set on blocking their escape. Meroka pulled out the machine-pistol and fired off a burst from the fresh magazine she had loaded on the train, aiming not at the station official but at the tilework mosaic above the open door. Shards and chips exploded away, the official shielding his eyes as the pieces rained down on him. Quillon risked another glance over his shoulder. The bearded man with the service revolver wasn't far behind them, stumbling slightly as if he was still dealing with the effects of the smoke grenade. He stopped for a moment, leaning over with one hand on his knee, the other still holding the gun, and then resumed his pursuit. Other officials – not to mention several passers-by – were hard on his heels.

Just then Quillon registered one of the passengers in the waiting room. With elegant, unhurried calm, the man began folding his newspaper. He placed it down on the vacant chair next to him – no one else was sitting anywhere near him – and rose slowly to his feet. He wore a long grey coat, cinched at the waist, a low-brimmed hat and patent leather shoes. The ghoul reached a black-gloved hand into his coat pocket, as if he was searching for a cigarette lighter.

Quillon was holding the angel gun, but he didn't dare risk a shot now. As sparsely occupied as the waiting room was, there were still people between him and the ghoul, who was now walking slowly out of the seating area, the black slash of his mouth beginning to curve up at the ends.

Meroka grabbed Quillon's arm and dragged him out into the night, just as the service revolver roared again. Rain hit his face, dirty and cold where it had sluiced down from the higher levels. For a moment the world was a moving confusion of cabs, trams, slot-cars and slot-buses. He stood transfixed. Then Meroka picked a cab and ran straight at it, making the driver slam on his brakes to avoid hitting her. She flung open the passenger door and stood by it until Quillon was inside, sitting behind the driver on the left. Then she climbed in after him, slammed the door and told the cabman to start driving.

'Where we going?' he asked, turning back to talk through the glass panel.

'Just drive,' Meroka said.

Quillon looked behind. He saw the ghoul emerge from the station entrance, then walk slowly towards one of the other cabs. Then they pulled away, and a slot-bus swerved in to block his view. When it had cleared all he could see was a rain-washed confusion of moving headlights. The cabman kept asking where he was meant to drive, and Meroka kept giving him the same non-answer. 'Just get us away from the station,' she said.

Quillon tore his attention from the rear view and fished out a ten bill. He tapped his wrist against the glass screen. 'We can pay you. Take this up front.'

The driver snatched the bill out of his fingers. 'Still be good to know where we're going.'

'Hit a right here,' Meroka said.

The driver yanked at the wheel, guiding his pick-up shoe into the diverging slot, the vehicle jerking sharply as it followed the shoe. The cab sped down a side road lined by cheap hotels and low-rent tenements. This was not a prosperous part of Neon Heights, lying as close as it did to the edge of the zone. No one lived here if they could afford to live further away from the boundary, where the likelihood of being caught in a zone shift was much reduced.

'Hit a left,' Meroka said.

The cab veered sharply, rejoining thicker traffic. Just as they cleared the bend Quillon saw headlights swing onto the side road. 'I think we're being followed,' he said.

'You *think*?' Meroka asked.

'I saw the ghoul going for another cab. Someone's behind us.'

'Hit another right,' Meroka said.

The cabman shook his head. 'Can't do that. Takes us too close to the boundary.'

She tapped the gun barrel against the glass. 'Do it anyway.'

He glanced around, saw the weapon and gave an unimpressed shrug, as if this was the kind of thing he expected to happen at least once a shift. 'It won't get you far. We'll be off-grid in a couple of blocks.'

'This cab got flywheels and batteries?'

'Of course.'

'Then do what I said.'

He made a right at the next intersection, diving down a dark street walled on either side by abandoned tenements, with the occasional vacant lot between them. The ride became rougher, and not just because of the bad condition of the asphalt under the tyres: years of dirt and garbage had compacted into the slot and not enough traffic came this way to keep the electrical path clear. The cab kept surging as the pick-up shoe lost traction current, the flywheel kicking in jerkily. Quillon glanced back. They had come quite some way down the dark street and nothing had turned off the main thoroughfare to pursue them. Perhaps he had been wrong about the other cab after all. He exhaled.

Headlights swung onto the street.

'It's them.'

'Which way is the boundary?' Meroka asked the cabman.

'Straight ahead.'

'Then keep going. Cutter – see if you can take them out, prove to me what a badass you really are.'

Quillon started to wind the window down and then halted, his hand trembling. 'I can't shoot at the cab. I'll risk hitting the driver.'

'Then fucking *improvise*.' Meroka glared at him, her eyes wild and angry. 'The slot. See if you can burn it out.'

Quillon drew the angel gun from his pocket. He twisted around and leaned cautiously out of the left-hand window. The other cab was gaining on them slowly, headlamps flickering as it hit the power breaks in the slot, blue sparks lighting under it as the current jumped the gap. With the unsteady motion of their own cab, it was difficult to keep the gun aimed at the slot. Holding his nerve, he squeezed gently on the trigger, flinching in expectation of the crimson beam. Nothing happened. He squeezed again and this time the beam lanced out, but with what seemed to Quillon to be less brilliance than before. It missed the slot and blew a manhole-sized crater in the asphalt. He re-centred his aim and tried another shot. Again the weapon was unresponsive. He pumped the trigger a couple of times. This time the beam sputtered out almost as soon as it had appeared. He twisted back into the cab. He thought he had hit the slot, but as the pursuing car reached the damaged spot it continued moving, flywheel and its own momentum carrying it over the dead stretch.

'Something's not right,' he said, shaking the gun as if that might make a difference. 'It's dying on me, but there should still be several hours of good function left.'

'Ask it,' Meroka said, winding down the window on her own side. She fired a burst from the machine-pistol, not appearing to care whether she hit the slot or the cab. She exhausted the magazine in a single burst then slumped down low to slip in a replacement. A shot rang against the small aperture of the cab's rear window, punching a neat little hole surrounded by white fracture lines.

'This isn't my problem!' the cabman called. 'I let you out now, you don't have to pay! You even get your ten back!'

'If you stop,' Meroka said, 'I'll shoot you.' She twisted around and resumed firing, only the fact that she was holding the weapon outside of the cab preventing Quillon from being deafened.

'You're not working properly,' he told the gun. 'What's wrong?'

'Earlier estimates based on stable zone conditions,' the gun responded, its voice slower and more machinelike than before. 'Transition to lower-state zone detected. Operational effectiveness in energy-discharge mode is now ... twenty-two per cent and ... falling. I will become inoperable in ... thirty-five ... minutes. Functionality will be ... severely compromised within ... eight. In order to preserve optimum functionality ... I am now sacrificing ... all ... nonessential ... all nonessential functions ... all nonessential *funk funk funk* ...'

The gun fell silent.

Two more shots rang against the cab. Meroka delivered another burst of bullets. Quillon leaned out of his own side and squeezed the trigger repeatedly until the gun emitted a single pulse of the crimson beam. This time even Quillon didn't care whether he hit the road or the cab. Someone in the cab was trying to kill him. That eclipsed all other considerations.

Suddenly the cab swerved hard to the left. Meroka yanked herself back in, swapping out the machine-pistol magazine again.

'Did I tell you to turn?'

'Slot was about to end,' the cabman said.

'Turn right again.' She leaned out and resumed firing.

The cabman spun his wheel to the right, the pick-up shoe disengaging from the slot, the cab surging forwards on the stored energy of its flywheel. Shots clanged against the right-side door, and then they had the shelter of another dark side street. At first, the flywheel gave them an edge, but the wheel's slowly dying scream attested to the fact that it was losing speed all the time. Quillon risked looking back, unsurprised when the other cab came off-slot at the same point, headlamps dimming as it lost current. He leaned out and tried firing the angel gun; nothing happened until the sixth or seventh squeeze of the trigger, and then all he got was a flash of crimson, the beam appearing to exhaust itself of energy long before it washed against the pursuing car. The cab slowed as the driver swerved it around the wrecks of abandoned cars still parked on the deserted street, fender kissing metal with a series of agonised squeals. Each time they lost momentum, the flywheel unable to push the cab back up to its previous speed. The only consolation was that the other cab had to negotiate the same set of obstacles.

'Can't go any further,' the driver said, desperation in his voice. 'Shoot me if you want, but we're about to hit the no-man's-land. From now we'll start to feel it.'

'Keep driving,' Meroka said.

'I'll black out. I'm not good with zone shifts.'

Quillon placed down the angel gun – he wasn't certain it was going to be much more use to him anyway – and dived into his medical bag. He produced a stoppered vial of small white pills. He tipped six into his hand and passed two through the hole in the glass screen. 'Take these,' he said, with as much commanding authority as he could muster.

'You trying to poison me?'

'These are antizonals. You're going to cross the zone anyway. You may as well take them.'

Meroka snatched two of the pills for herself. 'Do what the nice man says,' she told the cabman.

With one hand on the wheel he held the pills up to his lips, hesitated for an instant, then popped them down.

'We just need to get to the other side,' Quillon said. 'After that, you can make your way back to Neon Heights. The pills will stave off the worst effects of the zone transition.'

'I already feel weird.'

'That's the transition coming up, not the pills. They'll take a few minutes to have any effect.'

As he spoke one of the electric watches on Quillon's sleeve began to buzz, alerting him to an imminent transition. He could already feel the physiological effects gaining in strength. He felt light-headed, he was sweating and his heart was beginning to race. The transition from Neon Heights to Steamville was mild in comparison to the hell that the angel had gone through when it plummeted from the Celestial Levels. All Quillon could hope for was that it would prove too much for the ghoul, already stressed by the time it had spent in Neon Heights. But if the ghoul had once been an angel, then so too had Quillon. He had no idea how he was going to take the transition. All he could do was place maximum faith in his physical resilience, his medical judgement and the arsenal of potions in his bag.

It would have to suffice.

The high whine of the flywheel had become a low, complaining moan. The car was bouncing along at half the speed it had been maintaining before coming off the slot. At the end of the road, the remaining buildings thinned out to the desolate urban no-man's-land. Almost nothing stood intact; any buildings that had been here before the last zone shift had long since succumbed to weather and rot and fire – not to mention the occasional intrepid pillager – with only the barest shells remaining. On the other side of the wasteland – a strip running away in either direction, more or less concentric with the gentle curvature of the shelf – was the outskirts of Steamville, a tentative margin of low, dark buildings lit predominantly by gaslight.

Quillon looked back again, hoping to see some sign that the other car was abandoning the chase. But it was still behind them, and if anything it was gaining ground. The rutted, barely serviceable road had now reduced their speed to little more than a brisk running pace. Vehicular traffic between zones was rare, most people preferring to use the trains, elevators and other public transit systems, all of which had been carefully engineered to tolerate many crossings.

Quillon tensed. The feelings of transition intensified, sharp nausea rising in his throat. There was a moment of absolute cosmic cold, as if a billion tiny doors had opened in every cell of his body, letting in the draught of creation. The cab lurched and stalled and then resumed its ailing progress. The sensations of transition gradually eased, but even as they abated there remained an impression that something profound had changed. It was the first time he had left Neon Heights in nine years.

'I don't feel good,' the cabman said.

'It'll pass,' said Quillon. 'Keep driving.'

From somewhere under the floor came a sudden metallic crunching sound, followed by a violent shuddering. The cab slowed to below walking pace.

'Flywheel's just seized,' Meroka said. 'Couldn't cope with the shift. Switch to batteries.'

The driver threw a toggle on his dashboard. 'I'm switching. But they won't get us far.'

The cab resumed its hesitant progress, the electric transmission making a shrill whining sound. Another shot clanged into the back, ricocheting off into darkness. Meroka leaned out and fired off another burst from the machine-pistol. This time the burst ended abruptly. She leaned back in, gritting her teeth as she worked the safety lever back and forth, then tried firing again. The gun gave a short burst then jammed again. 'Everything's quitting on us,' Meroka said, flinging the machine-pistol aside. She reached into her coat and pulled out a heavy black revolver.

'They're slowing,' Quillon said. 'I think.'

'Try the angel gun again.'

He leaned out and squeezed the trigger, but even though he kept trying, the weapon now appeared totally inert. He was about to throw it away, but some impulse made him place it back in his pocket. Most technologies were damaged beyond repair when they passed from a high zone into a low zone, but for all he knew the angel gun had the ability to heal itself, or at least effect some kind of temporary recovery.

'Car's stopping,' Quillon said. 'Maybe he's decided to give—' But he had not completed his sentence before one of the other cab's front doors was flung open and the ghoul came out, articulating his grey-coated frame like a spider emerging from a burrow. There was no sign of the other cabman.

'You were saying?'

The ghoul paused to reach back into the cab for his hat, pressing it down on the hairless grey-green dome of his head. He started walking, taking determined paces away from the abandoned cab, long legs rising and falling in exaggerated, puppet-like strides. Every few steps he raised his gun and shot at the cab.

'He's gaining,' Quillon said.

'Stop,' Meroka told the driver.

He looked back at her, incredulous. 'Stop?'

'Stop.' To emphasise her point she brought the revolver around and shot through the glass screen, boring a smoking hole in the dashboard.

The cabman snatched his hands away from the wheel as the cab crunched to a halt.

Meroka opened the passenger door on her side. She levered herself out, using the door handle for support while she kept her feet in the passenger compartment, and emptied the revolver at the ghoul. The figure stumbled back, the hat blowing off, but the ghoul kept his footing. He resumed his advance, limping on one side, his right foot dragging across the ground, the ankle bent horribly, his shadowed face all but unreadable. Shots chimed into the door, one shattering the window. Meroka was oblivious, calmly swinging open the revolver's cylinder to reload it. Halfway through the task she paused, dug into her coat and passed a much smaller, more ladylike revolver to Quillon.

'Is it loaded?'

'Pull the trigger once, then you're good. You know where to find the trigger?'

'I'll manage.'

Through the remains of the screen the cabman said, 'You got anything for me?'

'Yeah,' Meroka said. 'Advice. Keep your fucking head down.' She began to empty the revolver again, popping up to shoot through the door's ruined window, the long barrel jerking up with each shot. Her bullets ripped ragged holes through the ghoul's clothes and flesh, yet he absorbed the impacts as if they were pebbles being tossed into a deep lake. Even when Quillon leaned out of the other side and fired the smaller revolver – the little gun whipping back into his hand with fierce recoil, for all that it looked like a toy – he had the impression that he was shooting into a mirage, an insubstantial figment that wasn't really there.

Then – just when he had begun to think nothing they had was going to do more than slow him – the ghoul staggered again, one of Meroka's shots blasting half his hand away, along with the revolver he had been carrying. The ghoul knelt down and retrieved the gun with his good hand. He staggered up and forwards, continued shooting. He had now crossed half the distance from the abandoned cab.

'What's that sound?' Meroka asked as she paused to slip bullets into the revolver.

'What sound?'

'The one coming from the angel gun.'

Quillon had had too much on his mind to notice it until she spoke, but now that she had drawn his attention to the gun he couldn't ignore it. It was on the back seat of the cab, where it must have fallen out of his pocket. It was buzzing, and the buzzing was growing steadily louder, as if an increasingly angry wasp was loose inside it. He reached for the gun, closing his fingers around it, and it was hot, so hot that he flinched back and yelped involuntarily. The buzzing grew stronger. A pink glow leaked from the previously invisible seals where the weapon had fused together.

'I think you'd better do something with that,' Meroka said.

He put down the revolver and dug into his coat pocket for a handkerchief. He bundled it around his hand and grabbed the buzzing gun. The heat penetrated the cloth almost instantly. The gun was rattling in his hand, as if it was on the point of shaking itself to pieces. He leaned out and was about to lob the gun in the direction of the ghoul when the rattling ceased abruptly, the gun still hot, but no longer buzzing.

'Cutter!' Meroka snarled. 'Throw the damn thing, before it blows us all up!'

But Quillon brought the gun back towards him. He still had the handkerchief wrapped around it, but even through the fabric sensed that the weapon's form had altered slightly. Although the gun remained hot to the touch, he had the conviction that it had completed some profound, larval transformation to a more primitive state of being.

He aimed at the ghoul and squeezed the trigger again. There was no energy discharge this time, but there was a result. His aim had been approximate, but as he fired he thought he felt the gun twist in his hand. Now there was recoil, and the thunder of a bullet being released from the chamber.

Then there was silence, and the ghoul wasn't coming any nearer.

Meroka waited a minute, then got out of the cab and walked carefully over to the last point where the ghoul had been. She still had the heavy revolver aimed in front of her. Quillon climbed out of his own side, leaving the medical bag in the cab, and followed slowly behind her.

'Do you think he's dead?'

Meroka found something pink-grey with the tip of her boot, an offcut of soiled meat, and kicked it into the dirt.

'Say that's a fair bet, Cutter.'

'I didn't expect him to get as far as he did.' Quillon looked down at the scattered remains, mentally reassembling the parts that had not been blown out of all recognition. He could see how the ghoul worked. He had been an angel once, and then knives and genetic intervention had remodelled him for life under the Celestial Levels. It was the same kind of forced adaptation that had been worked on him, but less elegant, less refined. If Quillon had been remade with watchmaker precision, the ghoul was a disposable cigarette lighter.

'You think this was a suicide mission?' Meroka asked.

Quillon still had the angel gun in his hand. His hand was shaking. 'Almost certainly.'

'What made them come down here, they knew they were going to die?'

'Belief, I suppose. The burning conviction that they were acting correctly, serving the true cause. Aided and abetted by some form of psychosurgical brainwashing, I don't doubt.' He paused, studying her expression for the slightest clue that she knew his true nature. 'It's all entirely feasible.'

'You know a lot about how they operate.'

'As I said, it helps when they're after you.'

Meroka found another piece of meat and stubbed her boot against it. 'Good call with the gun, by the way. You were right not to listen to me.'

'Can I get that in writing?'

'Quit while you're ahead, Cutter.'

Then she bent double and ejected a thin stream of vomit over the ghoul's remains.

CHAPTER FIVE

Quillon clutched his medical bag as if it were his final link to his life of the last nine years. They were on the upper deck of a rumbling, rattling steam-coach with hard wooden seats. They had walked for an hour before finding it, leaving the hapless cabman to make his own way back to Neon Heights. The coach was gas-lit, the few other passengers on the upper deck huddled in coats and scarves. Above the windows were monochrome advertisements for brands of soap and bleach, distemper and cold remedies. Quillon recognised none of them. He had travelled only a few leagues from Neon Heights and already it felt as if he had sailed off the edge of the world.

'Slight change of plan coming up,' Meroka said. 'Can't risk the trains any more, so we've got to find ourselves another way down.'

'What will that entail?' Quillon asked, clutching his medical bag to his lap.

'A trip to the bathhouse. There's a man there can help us, name of Tulwar. He's a friend, associate, of Fray's. Looks after Fray's interests in Steamville, now that Fray can't get down here so much these days.'

'Is this someone we can trust?'

'Why shouldn't we be able to trust him?'

'In all the conversations Fray and I had, I don't think the name Tulwar ever came up once.'

'Tulwar's reliable. He won't fuck us over.'

Quillon looked out of the window, abject tiredness and zone sickness dulling his will to continue the conversation. If he had to trust this Tulwar, so be it. It was only one remove from trusting Meroka, or Fray, for that matter. He had never felt so hopeless.

Buildings slid by outside at little more than a brisk walking pace, the architecture not unlike that of Neon Heights. But the lights were brown, quivering and quavering with the random flickering of gas filaments, and nowhere was there the cold, steady radiance of televisions, the pink auroral glow of neon tubes, the actinic flash of slot-cars and electric trains. Electricity existed in Steamville – the continued functioning of his own nervous system attested to that – but the machinery needed to generate and distribute it on a useful scale could not be made to work reliably. Steam and gas power, on the other hand, were still readily applicable technologies. There had been efforts, Quillon knew, to pump electricity in from outside the zone, and to make machines that were rugged enough to continue functioning once inside it. But all these efforts, along with similar endeavours elsewhere in Spearpoint, had come to naught. There was an old adage amongst Spearpointers: what works, works.

As the steam-coach trundled from block to block, so the signs of inhabitation and civilisation grew steadily more apparent. The seedier tenements gave way to long rows of well-maintained facades, each frontage bathed in its own lemony pool of gaslight from the tall black lanterns lining the avenues. They passed pedestrians and horseback riders, abroad even at this late hour. Meroka had chosen well with her own clothes: they had looked unremarkable in Neon Heights, and unremarkable here. Quillon presumed that he had achieved a similar effect with his own garments, although that was undoubtedly more by luck than judgement. With his long black coat, black-brimmed hat and anonymous black bag, he fancied that he cut a vaguely clerical figure, a minister or priest conveying some fallen child to sanctuary.

'Show me the angel gun,' Meroka said.

Quillon withdrew it from his pocket. It was still warm to the touch, but not as hot as before. Furtively, he unwrapped the handkerchief and let Meroka look at the weapon, keeping it low down in his lap where the other passengers wouldn't see it.

'It shot something,' Quillon said. 'Not a beam this time. Some kind of bullet.'

'Whatever it was made a serious mess of that thing chasing you. Must've been high-explosive, I reckon.'

'I don't think it has any intelligence left in it now. It's just inert metal. Probably can't change again, either. And I've no idea how many shots are left in it, if any.'

'Got to hand it to them angels – they're clever. But why can't they do something useful with that cleverness, like making life easier for the rest of us?'

'They're not as clever as you think,' Quillon said, choosing his words carefully. He had already slipped a couple of times, mentioning to Meroka that he had been living 'down here' for nine years. She seemed not to have picked up on it, but he was wary of making any more similar errors. 'They're good with gadgets, with making little toys like this gun. Sometimes, it seems as if they've made something genuinely new, something that didn't exist in the world before. But it's almost never the case. All they do is dig back into the past, hundreds or thousands of years if necessary, and find a solution someone already came up with. There's nothing new under the sun, and if you asked an angel to explain how this gun really worked, how it locked on to my blood, how it changed itself, I don't think you'd be very satisfied with the answers you got.'

'So angels are as dumb as the rest of us, then. They've just got shinier toys.'

'Something like that.'

'You ever been up there, Cutter?'

'To the Celestial Levels?' The directness of her question unsettled him. 'No. I've had no cause.'

'Never been sick enough to need their medicine, then?'

'I'm healthier than I look.' He bundled the gun back into the handkerchief and returned it to his pocket. 'What about you?'

'Ain't ever needed their medicine. If I did, I'd spit it back in their faces. Rather die than let one of those fuckers touch me.'

'And does Fray feel the same way you do?'

'You know him that well, why not ask him yourself?'

'Not exactly an option now,' Quillon said.

'I guess it isn't. Still, you knowing him as long as you have . . . exactly how far back do you go, anyway?'

'Don't tell me you're interested in me all of a sudden.'

'I'm interested in Fray's past. You're a piece of the jigsaw, that's all. You're his drug supplier, or one of them – I figured that much out. But when did you get mixed up with him? And what's he got on you to keep you bringing the goods?'

Quillon grimaced. Exactly how much did Meroka know of his past? How much was she deliberately testing him on? He had no idea what information Fray had given her, only that to have told her almost anything beyond the bare essentials would have constituted a grievous betrayal of trust.

'You know of Fray's old line of work, I take it?'

'Him being a detective and all? Not exactly the biggest secret around here. 'Specially as he still hangs his badge behind the bar in the Pink Peacock. You meet him on one of his cases?'

'Something like that.' He sighed, knowing that this would not be sufficient to end her probing. 'Fray was working on a murder investigation, one that had been dropped by the rest of the department. A body had been discovered at the bottom of a lift shaft in a pharmaceuticals warehouse in the Second District. I happened to feature in that investigation.'

'Suspect, or a witness?'

'Both. I didn't kill the woman in the lift shaft, but he was right to have his doubts about me. I had killed two people.' When Meroka said nothing – he'd been expecting some kind of reaction, either dismissive or admiring – he coughed and went on: 'But I only did so because they killed the woman, someone who mattered to me.'

'And Fray found all this out?'

'Fray worked out what had happened. I stated my case. At that point there were just the two of us. No one else knew about how far he'd carried the investigation.'

'You think about killing him?'

'There'd been enough murder. I'm a doctor, a healer. I'm meant to put lives back together, not end them.'

'Which is why you were so keen to keep your hands on that shiny little gun, I guess.'

'There wasn't a lot of time to think things through,' Quillon said. 'If I made the wrong decision, I apologise.' He waited, in vain, for Meroka to offer him a crumb of acknowledgement, then said, 'Fray left the force soon after. When he started expanding his activities, so to speak, he found that he had to cross over into the other zones more often than he had before. I was able to supply him with clinical-grade Morphax-55, stronger and purer than anything he could have obtained elsewhere.'

'So that's all it was. Simple protection racket, like I said. You fenced him the drugs or he turned you in.'

'No,' Quillon said carefully. 'There was more to it than that. Fray helped me. Fray kept helping me. I owe more to him than just my freedom. That's why I came to him this time.'

'Helped you how?'

He couldn't tell her about the wings, of course. Couldn't explain how they had to be cut away, the wounds stitched closed, while the pain of the cutting – it could only be done under a weak local anaesthetic – caused Quillon to thrash and writhe on the makeshift operating table where Fray did his sterile knifework. All the while knowing that the wings would start regrowing almost immediately, and that this pain would have to be revisited upon him at increasingly short intervals.

He couldn't tell her any of that.

'He helped me to keep ahead of the people looking for me. That's all.'

'Sounds like he got the good side of the bargain.'

'He didn't,' Quillon said.

They exited the steam-coach a few blocks further on. Meroka led him through the bustle of late-night revellers spilling out of bars and bordellos and gambling houses, barging through anyone who didn't have the wisdom to get out of her way, Quillon following in the wake she opened up. Jugglers, fire-breathers and hustlers provided rowdy entertainment, while a big-busted woman with too much make-up was standing on a pile of crates, bellowing along to the music from a steam organ. The calliope had been wheeled into the middle of the street and was piping its way through a score punched onto cards, while its operator kept it stoked with wood and monitored the steam pressure. Quillon recognised the tune as belonging to the singer Blade.

'I didn't know they had her music down here,' he said.

'Got it arse over tit, Cutter. That tune's been doing the rounds here for years. It's Blade who's picked up on it.'

He smiled at his ignorance. 'I didn't realise.'

'City's more complicated than people figure. Ain't just shit and bricks crossing between the zones. Spend some time moving around and you realise that Spearpoint's more like a living thing, with stuff flowing in all directions. Shouldn't need to tell you how tangled up bodies get inside.'

'No, you shouldn't.' Quillon let Meroka pick a path through the hurly-burly. 'You like it here, don't you? In Spearpoint, I mean.'

'Damn right I do. Left the place enough times. Got to be something dragging me back to it.'

The calliope stood in front of a pale green, wooden-boarded building with an elaborate portico and many red-painted balconies. Chains of pastel-coloured paper lanterns illuminated the frontage. A carved ser-pentine lizard lorded it over the entrance, entwined around a sign identifying the premises as the Red Dragon Bathhouse. Evidenced by the lights, and the amount of steam issuing from its windows and chimneys, the bathhouse was still open for business.

'This is the place,' Meroka said.

'How do you know Tulwar's going to be in?'

'Tulwar's always in. Being in is what Tulwar does. It's sort of his party trick.' She paused. 'You got a strong stomach, Cutter?'

'I'm a pathologist.'

'Enough said.'

Meroka walked up the steps to the entrance and spoke quietly to the burly, long-whiskered doorman waiting under the portico. He gave

Quillon an appraising glance, then nodded once, admitting them into the bathhouse. Meroka clearly knew her way. She led Quillon along a winding corridor from which branched various steaming chambers, bathing pools and changing rooms. The air was oppressively humid, reeking with scented oils and perfumes. Quillon already felt stifled under his coat, sweat beading around his collar and forehead. He removed his glasses quickly, wiping and replacing them before Meroka had a chance to look at his eyes. Now and then a towelled patron passed them by – it was always a glistening, overweight man, ambling from one room to another. The bathhouse girls wore long silk dresses, their hair elevated off their necks by jewelled pins. They could have been made from wax.

At the end of the corridor was an office. Meroka knocked on the glass-panelled door and entered. There were two women in the office. An older woman sat behind a lavish leather-topped desk, dipping a pen into an inkwell as they arrived. Her grey hair was tied back with a floral-painted papier-mâché clasp. A much younger woman – one of the bathhouse girls – was in the process of being reprimanded, judging by the severe expression on the older woman's face, and the way the younger one kept her head down, her chin trembling slightly as if she was trying hard not to cry.

'Let this be a lesson, Iztle,' the older woman said. 'Go now, and we'll speak no more of the matter. But I won't give you the benefit of a second warning.'

The girl gathered her skirt and sidled out, moving as if she travelled on hidden castor wheels.

'Ah, Meroka,' the older woman said. 'How unexpected of you to grace us again. Your charming presence has been much missed here in the bathhouse.'

'Sorry I didn't give you more notice, Madame Bistoury.'

'It would have made precious little difference if you had.' She pinched reading glasses from her nose. 'Who, might I ask, is your companion?'

'Name's Quillon,' Meroka said.

'On his way up or down?' Madame Bistoury scrutinised him carefully. 'Down, I think; he doesn't have the look of someone who's been outside. You may remove your hat, sir. And it must be very difficult to see anything behind those heavily tinted spectacles.'

'I'm fine, thank you,' Quillon said, touching a finger to the rim of his hat.

'As you will.'

'We came to see—' Meroka began.

'Tulwar, of course. Who else?'

'I figured you'd be glad we didn't come as clients, lowering the tone of the place and all.'

'One must clutch at such crumbs of consolation, of course. How are you finding your guide, Mister Quillon – if that's your surname? I trust you have a robust tolerance for profanity? All I will say in her defence is that Meroka was not always this way. Once, she could almost be allowed to circulate in polite society. I did warn her, of course. I've seen it so many times before. But she wouldn't listen.' She put the reading glasses back on and scratched something into one of the ledgers spread open on the desk. 'Well, I won't keep you. You know exactly where to find Tulwar. Do pass on my regards, won't you?'

'Count on it,' Meroka answered.

'Mister Quillon: good luck with the rest of your journey, wherever it takes you.'

'Thank you,' Quillon said.

They left Madame Bistoury to her accounting. Quillon said nothing, letting Meroka show him the way. She led him to a plain door in one of the corridors, marked for employees only. Two flights of stairs took them down into what could only be the basement, or part of it. It was oppressively warm, with only faint gaslight filtering down from windows at the top of the basement walls. Meroka walked across stone tiles to a heavy door with a circular, metal-barred window in its upper half. A dim orange light wavered through the glass. She hammered on the door.

'Tulwar!'

The orange light was suddenly eclipsed. Now all was darkness beyond the door. There came a laboured shuffling sound, accompanied by a heavy, bellows-like wheezing. A man-shaped form, carrying a hand-lantern, loomed beyond the door. A metal cover slid aside beneath the barred window and a gruff voice spoke through it.

'Wasn't expecting you tonight, Meroka.'

Quillon recognised the accent as belonging to Steamville. It was softer, slower, more drawling than the way people spoke in Neon Heights.

'We hit a few snags,' Meroka said. 'Are you going to let us in?'

'Do I have a choice?'

'I guess that depends on whether you want to keep on Fray's good side or not, Tulwar.'

'It's always an idea.'

The speaker opened the door and hinged it wide enough to survey his visitors. A face, sinisterly underlit by the handheld lantern, hovered in the darkness. Quillon caught a wild white eye set into a deeply wrinkled socket. The other eye was lost in shadow. The rhythmic bellows sound that he had taken for breathing was, he now realised, nothing of the sort. It was definitely coming from the man but it continued uninterrupted even as he spoke.

Tulwar stood aside to let them pass through the door. It was even hotter in the main boiler room. Quillon made out the boiler's vague presence, a squatting black kettle as large as a small house, an ever-devouring monster that would never be sated, no matter how much wood was stuffed into its belly. A labyrinth of ironwork pipes and return tubes threaded into the ceiling, distributing steam to all quarters of the Red Dragon Bathhouse.

Tulwar closed the door behind him. Quillon still couldn't make out much of their new host.

'You've been busy tonight,' Tulwar said.

'What gives you that idea?' Meroka asked.

'It's all over town. Someone found a body on the train, and there's talk of something going down in the railway station on the other side of the boundary.'

'Fancy.'

'You telling me you had nothing to do with any of that?'

'All right. Maybe a bit. Let's just say we've run into a few unforeseen complications with an extraction.'

The eye settled on Quillon. 'This gentleman?'

'Guy's got half of the Celestial fucking Levels on his case.'

'Special customer.' The head nodded approvingly. 'What's he done to get on the wrong side of the angels?'

'Better ask him. These aren't your ordinary angels we were dealing with.'

'I dealt with a few of the stranger variants in my time.' Tulwar led them past the boiler, heat bleeding off it even though the stoking hole was currently shut. He paused and tapped the back of his hand against a pressure valve until the phosphorescent dial quivered back to its proper setting. The hand made a dull ringing tone, as of wood on metal. 'But it was a long time ago.'

'They're infiltration units,' Quillon said, feeling a prickle of uneasiness down in his belly. 'That's my understanding, anyway. Modified to be able to survive down in Neon Heights. No machines in their blood. They don't have wings, either. Unless you see one up close, they're normal enough to blend in.' He paused and swallowed. 'You've had much experience with angels?'

'Fought and killed several hundred of them,' Tulwar said offhandedly.

'You were some kind of soldier?'

'Some kind of soldier,' Tulwar echoed. 'I'm guessing Meroka didn't fill you in about me?'

'Not exactly.'

'You'll get the full picture soon enough. Mind you don't trip on the cable.'

'What cable?'

'The one coming out of me.'

Tulwar escorted them out of the main boiler room into a separate annexe that appeared to serve as his quarters. He swung the door to behind him, but not completely shut. He placed the handheld lantern on a table in the middle of the room, then lit a slightly brighter version suspended from the ceiling. The filament flared in intensity, gradually dispelling some of the darkness. The table was circular and set with cards – arranged into the depleted regiments of some half-finished game – accompanied by a glass and a tall bottle of liquor with a sepia-coloured label Quillon didn't recognise. The room was fractionally cooler than the adjacent boiler room, aided by a slowly rotating ceiling fan, which must have been driven by steam pressure. There was a serving hatch in one corner – presumably it led to the bathhouse kitchens – and a neatly made bed in the other.

'My little abode,' Tulwar said. 'Sit yourselves down.'

'We don't have a lot of time to talk,' Meroka said. 'If we're going to make the next connection for Horsetown—'

'Have a seat anyway.' The eye turned to fix itself on Quillon. 'You too, whoever you are.'

'Quillon.' He took a chair, his mind reeling, but trying to let none of his consternation show on his face. Tulwar shuffled to one end of the room and slid open a cupboard under the serving hatch. There was a chink of glasses, then Tulwar came shuffling back. He put two new glasses down on the table and began pouring slugs from the bottle into them.

'Line of work?'

'I'm a doctor, a pathologist, from the Third District Morgue in Neon Heights.'

'How did a doctor get mixed up in something that meant he had to get out of Spearpoint?'

'It's a long story.'

'No one's going anywhere for a moment.' Tulwar pushed one of the glasses at Quillon and the other towards Meroka. 'Drink up. I'm sure you could both use some.'

'We're taking antizonals,' Quillon said, even as Meroka downed half her glass in a single gulp.

'So am I. The liquor won't be the thing that kills you.' With something close to menace Tulwar added, 'Bottoms up.'

Tulwar pulled up his own seat and sat opposite them, giving Quillon the first chance to get a good look at him. He controlled his reaction as best he could, but Tulwar was not for the faint-hearted. He was a big man, largely hairless, clearly older than Quillon or Fray, but his age was otherwise hard to judge. He only had one visible eye. The right one was lost behind an eyepatch seemingly made of cast iron, leather and wood, the patch extending around the side of his face, down to his cheek and up to his temples. There were two rectangular metal plates on either side of his skull, secured with screws. Only his right arm – the one that had been holding the lantern – was living; his other arm was a mechanical prosthesis connected by a heavy shoulder harness of leather and metal. The arm was human in shape, ending in a wooden hand with elegantly jointed fingers, tensioned wire tendons running in grooves in the wood.

Tulwar wore a white blouse shirt, unbuttoned halfway down his chest. Covering most of his torso was some kind of buckled-on apparatus, a green-painted chest-plate mottled with rust and condensation, with steam-pressure dials twitching under thick glass. The bellows sound, Quillon now realised, was coming from inside that machinery. A segmented copper hose emerged from one side of it and trailed off across the floor and through the gap where Tulwar had left the door ajar.

'Might I ask what happened to you?' Quillon enquired.

'Take a guess.'

'If I knew nothing about you, I'd say that you were the victim of an industrial accident. But that wouldn't account for the symmetry of the metal plates on either side of your head. Nor the fact that you mentioned killing angels. Were you a soldier, Tulwar?'

'What do *you* think, *Doctor*?'

'It's been generations since anyone went to war against the angels. Even then it was only one or two cyborg polities, and that was a long time ago. But they say cyborgs live nearly as long as angels. Is that what you used to be, Tulwar?'

'Judge for yourself.'

Quillon took a careful sip from his own glass. 'You would have been neurally integrated into your battle armour, much of your nervous system bonded directly to the armour's sensory interface. Those plates in your head were probably where the primary input trunks fed through your skull. The missing eye might be an old injury that was never repaired, or it might have been where the organic eye was replaced by some kind of targeting device. I don't know how you lost the arm, whether that was deliberate or not. I do know that your internal organs would have been extensively modified, your heart and lungs replaced with an oxygen-exchange pump, the rest of your insides plumbed directly into the battle-armour's recycling system. Inside it, you could live indefinitely. Without the armour, you'd be dead in seconds. Even in the polities.'

'I seem to be clinging on.'

'Only because someone was very ingenious. Someone found a way to keep you alive, in a world where even the simplest electrical device cannot function. You run on steam, from a wood-burning boiler.'

Tulwar started to unbutton the rest of his shirt. 'You want a closer look, see what really makes me tick?'

Meroka took another gulp from her glass and looked away. 'No offence, Tulwar, but you're hard enough on the eyes before you start the guided tour.'

Quillon raised a hand. 'It's not necessary.'

'Come on, *Doctor*. And you a man of medicine. How could you possibly turn down an offer like that?' Tulwar tugged the shirt wide around his navel area, exposing a hinged inspection panel curving across the base of the chest-plate. He began to undo the catch at the other end. 'I'm not ashamed of what I am. I was proud to be a soldier; proud to be given the honour of defending the polity against angels. So what if the war took half of me away? I still earned these scars.'

'I don't need to see inside you,' Quillon said.

'Not even a little bit curious?'

'Of course I am. If I could help you I would. But I'd have to examine you properly, and there wouldn't be any point in doing that until I've returned to Spearpoint. At the moment, this little bag is all I'm travelling with.' Quillon paused delicately. 'I take it you've been like this for a while?'

'Longer than you'd credit.'

'Then you're probably not going to catch anything before I have a chance to come back.'

Tulwar locked the catch and began to button his shirt again. 'You'd do that?'

'You're a friend of Fray's. That's all the recommendation I need.'

Amusement glittered in Tulwar's eye. 'Friend. That what he said?'

'That's what I said,' Meroka cut in. 'Quillon's only repeating what I told him.'

'"Underling" might have been a more apposite term to describe my relationship to Fray, don't you think?'

'That's between you and the man upstairs.'

'You shouldn't speak of Fray as if he's God,' Tulwar said disapprovingly. 'Especially you, Meroka, being so religiously inclined. She's never without her Testament, Doctor. Goes everywhere with her, it does. You'd never think it, would you, with that tongue of hers?'

Quillon started to say something, then thought better of it.

'Fray's been good to you,' Meroka said. 'He set you up down here, didn't he, when you became an embarrassment to your own side? Gave you a place to hide, a nice, steady supply of steam?'

'He gets his cut from Madame Bistoury, so let's not pretend there's anything philanthropic about it. Do you see him paying me many visits, enquiring about my welfare, asking if there's something I'd rather be doing than shovelling coal into a boiler for the rest of my time on Earth?'

'You know he doesn't get out much more than you do, Tulwar.'

'At least Fray gets to leave the basement occasionally.'

Quillon put down his glass and looked at Meroka. 'We shouldn't take too long before moving on, should we?'

'Oh, don't mind us,' Tulwar said, breaking into a lopsided smile. 'Meroka and I fight like cats, and bicker incessantly over Fray, but we go back a long way. It's just our act.'

'Although sometimes it starts wearing thin,' Meroka said.

'Go easy, I'm having a bad day. We're down a consignment of wood, which means steam pressure might have to be dropped. That hurts me as much as it hurts the bathhouse. Ordinarily I'd put out the feelers for some more fuel, but it's not like anyone else is rolling in wood either. Been the same all winter. Supplies running low, having to be dragged in from further and further away, and what you get isn't the best quality. Firesap's in just as short supply. It's going to be a cold one, too. You wouldn't think I feel it down here, but you'd be wrong.' He gave a philosophic shrug. 'Good for business, though. You think this is cold, wait until you've left Spearpoint.' Tulwar gave Quillon a lingering look. 'Hope you've got the constitution for it, Doctor. It can take its toll.'

'Speaking of leaving,' Meroka said, 'I don't think it would be a good idea to go on the train.'

'Forget it,' Tulwar agreed. 'After that trouble you caused, there'll be more than just angels trying to track you down. Police in Neon Heights will already have tubed descriptions down to the Steamville constabulary. They'll have every station scoped by now.'

'We'll need to use one of the alternatives, then. Is that an option?'

'We'll sort something out. In the meantime, given the amount of ammunition you appear to have discarded on the way down, you're welcome to replenish your supplies.' He jerked his head in a kind of stiff-necked nod, over his shoulder. 'Through the back door, remember? Take what you need, and leave anything you don't.'

'Thanks,' Meroka said.

'Pick up some new watches as well. Good for antizonals?'

'We have all we require,' Quillon said, patting the bag.

'Fine.' Tulwar refilled his drink and offered the bottle to Quillon, who declined with a polite elevation of his hand. 'While you're in there, there are some medical issues I'd like to go over with Doctor Quillon.'

Meroka nodded and went into the back room, seemingly glad to have the chore to herself. Tulwar waited silently until she was out of earshot, then made the lopsided smile at Quillon.

'You're good, I'll give you that,' he said.

'Good at what?'

'Good at hiding what you really are. Unless I'm mistaken, Meroka hasn't got a clue what she's escorting out of Spearpoint. Probably all the better for you. She's about as keen on angels as I am, *Doctor Quillon*.'

'You seem to be under some misapprehension.'

'No, I don't think so. It's all about smell, you see.' Tulwar tapped a wooden finger against the side of his nose. 'I could smell an angel halfway across the street. Doesn't matter what they look like. Sure, you've been made to look human – pretty damn well, I have to say. But they still didn't get it quite right.' Tulwar frowned, drawing the skin tight at the corners of the metal plates in his head. 'Did Fray know, when he set up this extraction? Of course he knew. How could Fray *not* know?'

Quillon looked down at his hands. Part of him wanted to persist with his denials, but a shrewder part knew that there was no point in doing so.

'Fray knew,' he answered quietly.

'What I figured. And Meroka?'

'Not as far as I'm aware.' Quillon stiffened in his seat. 'I'm sorry that we've ended up in this position. No deception was intended, I assure you.'

'You're a walking deception.'

'What good would it do for the truth to be revealed? I'm running from angels. My cover is the only protection I have. Do you think I'm going to advertise what I am?'

'Let me tell you about Meroka,' Tulwar said. 'She wasn't always like this. She likes women. That's her bag. I'm not making any judgements here, just telling you how it is. Once upon a time there was someone special, someone she really loved. But that woman got ill with something they can't treat down here. The angels, though? Maybe. They can do wonders up there, in the Celestial Levels. So they were petitioned, there are channels for that, and asked if they'd consent to fix the woman, make her better. They do this, take a certain number of deserving cases each year, just the same way it works on Ascension Day. But the woman – her name was Ida – couldn't afford to go all the way up there on her own, and no one around her could afford it either. The angels said they couldn't help: they weren't really interested, I think. They suck your soul out up there, read your mind, but that's only of use to them if your mind hasn't been half eaten away to begin with. So Ida got worse, and Ida's friends tried to find the means to send her up there, but by the time they scraped enough together it was too late. They dosed her with antizonals but she still didn't get further up than Circuit City. Meroka was with her. Died in her arms. That's why she doesn't go a bundle on angels. That's why she won't go a bundle on you, she finds out.' Tulwar studied Quillon for several silent moments. 'So what do you think's going to happen now?'

'I've no idea.'

'Take a stab.'

'Perhaps you're going to kill me, or reveal my nature to Meroka, or turn me in to the authorities, or keep me hostage until you're able to hand me over to the angels.'

'And get on Fray's bad side? He could end me, if I betrayed him. He's been good to me, I can't deny that. Even if he is a stupid, unimaginative fuck who wouldn't recognise an opportunity to better himself if it landed on his skull.'

'He's been good to me,' Quillon said.

'Then we're in the same boat. Both hiding from something, both owing Fray. There are few things I'd rather do right now than reach across this table and strangle you. But as the old saying goes, the enemy of my enemy—'

'Is my friend. But there's something you need to understand. We're not all monsters. I made enemies precisely because I refused to countenance an evil deed.'

Tulwar looked towards the back room, where Meroka was still busy sorting through the munitions stockpile. 'What kind of deed?'

'There was an experimental programme. The stated intention was to modify angels so that we could live under conditions similar to those in

Neon Heights. The theory was that we could engineer in resilience to a future zone shift, so that we wouldn't all have to die if the boundary moved catastrophically.'

'So the angels are nervous as well.'

'About what?'

'The big one. I'm sure you've noticed the signs – everyone getting more jittery by the day.'

'It might not happen for a hundred years, or a thousand.'

'Some folks think otherwise. Your angel programme suggests that at least a few in the Celestial Levels have grounds for concern.'

Quillon leaned forwards, lowering his voice even as he spoke more urgently. 'That's the point, though: the programme's stated objectives were a sham. We were sent to Neon Heights to test our ability to survive inside a different zone, with only the simplest of medicines to assist us. Obviously, those conditions couldn't be simulated in the Levels: it had to be done covertly. I understood that, just as I understood that we had to maintain maximum secrecy at all times. But there was more to it than just a proof of concept. The ultimate purpose of the programme was to prepare an occupying force, a division of zone-tolerant angels able to storm and conquer large tracts of Spearpoint. There were four members of the infiltration party. Two of us didn't know anything about that ultimate purpose. When one of us found out … the other two had no choice but to silence her. But she'd already shared her fears with me. They'd have silenced me eventually. I chose not to give them the chance. I killed them, using medicine. That's why I'm hiding now.'

'At least you were built for the terrain,' Tulwar said.

'It's been easier for me than it has for you. But there's one thing you need to understand. When they sent me down to Neon Heights they equipped me to live there undetected. They suppressed my real memories and gave me the ghost memories of someone who had been born and raised in the Heights. I've been wearing that mask for nine years, long enough that it feels like a part of me. I still care about the Celestial Levels. But I also care about Neon Heights, and for that matter the rest of Spearpoint. If something big is coming, then the last thing we should be doing is fostering more divisions between our different enclaves.'

'And if I kill you, or turn you in, that's what I'll be doing?'

'All I know is that the knowledge I carry – the knowledge I'm *told* I carry – could be a force for good, as well as evil. I really don't care about my own life. But I do care about Spearpoint, and if my continued survival benefits it, then I have a moral obligation to keep myself alive.'

'This woman they killed – the one who got too close to the truth. She wasn't just a colleague, was she?'

'No,' Quillon said. 'She wasn't.'

'She have a name?'

'Aruval. That was her cover. I don't remember her real name.'

'I lost someone special once. To angels, as well. I don't know if that means I ought to empathise with you or hate you even more.'

'I can't help you there,' Quillon said.

Tulwar leaned back, only the wheezing *chuff* of his life-support system filling the silence. He bent over to inspect one of the dials in his belly. 'Need to put some more fuel in shortly. Needle's starting to drop.'

'Does that mean you've made a decision?'

Meroka came back in through the door, her coat hanging visibly heavier about her frame. Quillon imagined every pocket crammed with instruments of bloody death and dismemberment. Somehow he didn't think she had lingered overly long on the watches.

'What decision?' she asked.

'About when to leave,' Tulwar said breezily. 'I was just telling the good doctor how we get the wood for the furnace, and what we send back down in the empty hoppers.'

'Right,' Meroka said. She dropped five or six clockwork watches on the table. 'So we're taking the meat wagon again. I can't tell you how fucking delighted I am about *that*.'

The funicular had little in common with the swift electric commuter services that connected Neon Heights' different levels. At the top end, in Steamville, stood a wood-fired stationary steam engine. This in turn drove a giant horizontal winding wheel, connected to a haulage rope long enough to reach all the way down to the Horsetown terminus, half a league beneath the Steamville end of the operation and as far out again in horizontal terms. Even though the cars never went down the slope empty – there was always something to send down to Horsetown – it was never quite enough to balance the weight of the ascending cars. The enterprise, one of a dozen or so similar funiculars dotted around Spearpoint's base, was slow, unreliable and prone to appalling, limb-shattering accidents. But it was still the most efficient means of moving goods – and occasionally people – between Steamville and Horsetown.

Once Tulwar's contact had delivered them to the upper terminus, there was bribery to be done before Meroka and Quillon found themselves shivering in one of the dozen cars of a downbound corpse consignment. It was an insulated wooden cabin mounted on the steeply angled chassis of a funicular carriage, with hatched compartments in the roof where ice was shovelled in to keep the corpses from warming up. The dead were bunked on horizontal racks, covered with thin white sheets.

Tulwar had found them extra coats and scarves – the Red Dragon Bathhouse had a well-stocked supply of lost clothing – but it did not take long for the cold to penetrate. The actual descent would only last a few minutes, but there was at least half an hour's wait at either end, while the procession of cars was slowly drawn forwards to be loaded and unloaded. Quillon struggled with his gloves, trying to sort through his medical bag to find the right type of antizonals for the crossing ahead of them, a dose that could be safely taken on top of the pills they had already ingested. He was off the chart now, in prescribing terms. The best he could do was navigate a course between his own instincts and Meroka's previous experiences in making this journey. 'Just dose me up,' she kept saying.

He doled out the extra pills with icy fingertips, having removed his gloves to open the vial.

'Take these for now,' he said, palming two pills.

'That all?'

'Too much would be as dangerous as too little. I don't even know what kind of cumulative damage your nervous system has already sustained.'

'Damage is already done, Cutter.'

'Nonetheless, we don't want to do any more harm on top of that. You know what Fray's like. For all I know, you're only one miscalculated dose from ending up exactly like him.'

Meroka took the pills with sullen bad grace, but at least resisted the urge to augment them with her own drugs. The cabin lurched into motion, descending in near silence save for the occasional creak and squeal of strained rope or metal on metal. They sat opposite each other, on the lowest level of the planked racks where the bodies were stored. Quillon and Meroka were sharing the carriage with corpses making their final downward journey after Ascension Day. Those who didn't adhere to the custom tended to refer to practitioners as ghost-riders, pre-corpses or, less charitably, angel-meat.

While advanced medical services were unavailable to most citizens of Spearpoint by dint of the fact that they lived in the wrong zone, there was one exception. Those who were sufficiently close to death that they had little to lose could submit to being scanned, and perhaps even healed, in the Celestial Levels. To do so they would have to leave their own zone and travel as rapidly as possible through Spearpoint's intervening enclaves, until they reached the domain of the angels. Most citizens could only hope to undertake such a journey alone, having saved for it over many years. If the sudden onset of massive maladaptive trauma hadn't killed them by the time they arrived, then they stood a chance of having their minds preserved after death, in the imperishable, massively redundant data-stores of the Celestial Levels. In most instances something could be recovered, and in a few cases the accumulated damage – perhaps even the underlying illness that had necessitated the journey in the first place – could be made good. Nonetheless, less than one in a hundred souls who travelled to the Celestial Levels ever came back down alive. For the majority, Ascension Day was a one-way trip – unless coming back down as a corpse counted.

Quillon put the gloves back on and tucked his hands under his armpits. His breath was a jet of white vapour. Ice crystals had already started to form on Meroka's eyebrows. He had made no allowance for how the cold would affect their metabolisms, impeding or accelerating the uptake of the antizonals. Nothing could be done now; it would have been sheer guesswork even if it had occurred to him to take the cold into consideration. He checked his clockwork watches and found that they were beginning to read different times. How much of that was due to the imminent transition, and how much to the watches being of cheap manufacture, he couldn't guess.

'Might I ask something?' he said, as much to keep his teeth from chattering as from a desire for information. 'Back in the bathhouse, Madame Bistoury – that was her name, I think – mentioned something about you not always being the way you are now. And then what Tulwar said about the Good Book, and that tongue of yours—'

'Two different things, Cutter.'

'Would you care to enlighten me? We're going to be together a little longer, and yet I barely know the first thing about you.'

'Seems to be working out fine for us.'

'I'm still entitled to my curiosity. I've read about certain kinds of long-term neurological trauma: brain damage associated with repeated zone crossings and the use of high-strength antizonals. In certain cases this damage can manifest as impairments or idiosyncrasies of the speech centre. There are instances of people becoming . . . profane after suffering brain injuries. Often distressingly so. Is that what happened to you?'

'Congratulations,' she said sourly. 'You've hit the nail on the fucking head.'

'You needn't feel any shame about it.'

'Who said anything about shame?'

'I'm sorry. I just presumed that it must occasionally lead to situations of social awkwardness. But what you have is a medical problem, no more or less. It may even be treatable, with the right therapies.'

'Thanks. I'll be sure to look them up.'

'And the other matter – the Testament?'

'Never mind the other fucking matter.'

The transition came, arriving more quickly than it had when they crossed the no-man's-land between Neon Heights and Steamville. The carriage kept descending at a steady rate, carrying them smoothly through the boundary. Meroka's eyes met his own, acknowledging the moment when it came. He was cold already, but when the transition passed through his body, the cosmic chill of it made the carriage seem cosily warm by comparison. That fierce, sucking cold lingered in his bones for minutes. Then he began to feel, if not better, then at least no worse than he had any right to expect. His heart was racing a little, he was perspiring excessively (despite the temperature in the carriage) and his surroundings were wheeling around him. But all such unpleasantnesses were nothing more than the anticipated residual effects of zone sickness. Had the pills not cushioned the brunt of the transition, he would be bent double and vomiting. He had, he knew, judged the dose more or less correctly.

'Is it always this bad?' he asked Meroka, when at last the wheeling sensation had begun to abate, and it seemed safe to open his eyes.

'Only the first hundred times. Then it gets easier.'

Quillon's first thought, when they had bribed the relevant parties into allowing them to leave the transhipment dock unmolested, was that there was nothing about Horsetown that he had not already seen in Steamville, half a league up Spearpoint's rising thread. The warehouses and clerical offices bordering the funicular terminus were, at least to Quillon's eyes, architecturally and functionally similar to those at the upper terminus. The lamps burned wood resin rather than gas, the illumination more sparsely distributed and more subdued in its effects, but he was still surprised by how fundamentally civilised and well ordered the community seemed. Looking down from Neon Heights at night, Horsetown had been little more than a black margin bordering Spearpoint's footslopes, a place that appeared to have no nocturnal existence at all. He saw now how inaccurate that impression had been, and felt a small, visceral tingle of shifting preconceptions.

But when his eyes had begun to adjust to the oil lamps, the darkness between the buildings beginning to yield its secrets, he only had to glance up and have the wild, shimmering glare of Neon Heights brand colours onto his retina. It was, he realised, why the citizens of Horsetown favoured wide-brimmed hats, even at night. They didn't want to keep looking up, didn't want to be permanently reminded of a place of swift machines and electric marvels; a place only a few would ever know, and even then only when they passed through it on Ascension Day.

Beyond the transhipment dock, Quillon slowly revised his initial impressions. Only a handful of buildings were made of anything other than wood, with brick reserved for civic and corporate structures of obvious importance. Nearly everything else had the ramshackle look of having been rebuilt many times, with new structures perched on the sagging, tumbledown remnants of the old. Streets and thoroughfares were ludicrously narrow, even allowing for the fact that the only form of motive power lay in horses. Nowhere were the buildings taller than four or five storeys high, but the manner in which they sagged in over the streets, with opposing buildings almost meeting overhead, occasioned more vertigo in Quillon than he had ever felt when staring up at one of Neon Heights' fifty-storey blocks. Like lovers pushing out their tongues to kiss, the buildings were linked by covered walkways of unsettling flimsiness. Walls were criss-crossed with black-painted timbers, buff-white rendering smeared between them. Every horizontal surface was white with pigeon droppings. Between the gaps in the buildings lay the utter emptiness of the great plains stretching away from Spearpoint's base, a blackness only relieved – or in some way intensified – by the dim lights of tiny, huddled communities scattered across the land all the way to the horizon. Meroka and Quillon were near Spearpoint's base now; the winding spiral of the ledge met the ground less than half a turn from their present position.

The smell was the worst. It hit him almost as soon as he cleared the ordered precincts of the transhipment area. It came in stately, fugal waves, like a symphony. Beneath everything was a permanent sewer stink, impossible to separate into its human and animal components. Above that, and only fractionally more tolerable, was the heavy chemical reek of the various industries associated with the production of animal by-products, the abattoirs, the smoking plants, the glue factories and tanneries. And with every frigid breath he sucked into his lungs, Quillon tasted woodsmoke. He was still wearing two layers of coats, and grateful for them.

'You thought it was going to get warmer, closer to the ground,' Meroka said as he drew the collar higher around his face. 'Maybe that's how it used to be.'

'And now?'

'Been getting colder beyond Spearpoint for years. Only reason you don't feel it in Neon Heights is you've got the heat coming off all those levels below you, warming up the air, giving the angels some thermals to play with. Down here, though? Ain't no more levels to go. This is what it's going to be like from now on. And we're the lucky ones, sitting on the equator like we do. Further north, further south? Gets cold enough to freeze a witch's tits.'

What if the Earth really was turning colder? Quillon wondered. And what if no one in the warm, lit levels of Spearpoint had been bothering to pay attention?

There would be no possibility of renting horses until morning. Besides, Meroka had said they would need all their energy for the day's ride, and that this would be their last chance for a decent night's sleep before they left Spearpoint. She found them a room above a gaming house, not too far from the rental stables she normally used. There were two metal-framed beds with thin sheets, a draughty window and something scuttling around in the overhead floorboards, rushing back and forth as if it had a long list of errands to do. None of that mattered. Meroka washed her hands and face at the rusty old basin in one corner of the room, removed her coat, then lay down on the bed and fell into immediate sleep. Quillon extinguished the oil lamp and removed his own coat, spectacles and hat. Exhaustion closed on him like a velvet vice.

He woke to colourless, wintery daylight pushing through the curtains. Meroka was gone. He could still see the imprint of her head on the pillow she had been using. The room key was still on the nightstand, along with his medical bag. He rose from the bed, stretching the stiffness out of his bones. He stripped to the waist, tolerating the cold long enough to wash. He turned until he could see his back in the tarnished mirror over the basin, spinal column showing through his skin with anatomical clarity, his wing-buds soft and obscene, like a pair of tiny clenched fists growing out of his back. He dressed again and was settling his hat on his head when he saw the little black book by Meroka's bedside.

Something compelled him to pick it up. The Testament was bound in black leather, creased and worn like his medical bag. He opened it gently, half-expecting some kind of trap to spring out into his face. The pages were translucently thin, the ink on one side showing through the other. Dense columns of scripture, with numbers at the start of every paragraph, some parts in plain font, others italicised or printed in boldface. The book looked older than Meroka, though he could not say precisely why he was certain of this. He turned the pages, something furtive in the sound the sheets made as they whisked against each other.

And in that time, before the gates of paradise were closed to them, men and women were as children. And so plentiful were the fruits and bounties of paradise that they lived for four-score years, and some lived longer than that. And in that time the Earth was warm and blue and green and many were its provinces.

He closed the book, hearing footsteps coming up the creaking staircase from below, then along the landing. There was a knock at the door.

He put the Testament down on the table as Meroka entered, subtly conscious that it was not quite as he had found it, and that she could not fail to notice this.

'Time to ship,' she said. 'Got us some horses.'

Meroka reached for the Testament and slipped it into a deep pocket of her coat, without giving it a second glance.

CHAPTER SIX

Quillon had never been close to a horse before. The ghost-white creatures, with their preposterously slender legs, blade-sharp faces, nervous
dark eyes and scarlet flaring nostrils, seemed not quite of a part with the
rest of the world. He tucked his bag into a vacant pocket in one of the
panniers, jammed a boot into one of the stirrups and – inelegantly, he
was sure – managed to lever himself astride. Although there was a saddle
between his posterior and the horse's back, he could nonetheless feel
the sinuous undulation of its spine as it hoofed the ground, willing and
eager to get going. There was a tiny mind in that skull, he knew, but it
was attached to a large, strong animal, and it was capable of entertaining
at least one idea. The stable owner showed him how to take the reins,
giving him just enough tuition to be able to stop the horse if needed.
Meroka would ride ahead, and his horse, he was assured, would follow
hers over a cliff.

They had taken antizonals and were symptom-free for the time being.
Soon they were ambling through Horsetown, following the descending
curve of the ledge all the way to the ground. The cobbled streets were
treacherous with ice, so there was never any prospect of breaking into a
trot. Occasionally his horse stumbled, Quillon seizing the reins in panic.
The horse seemed to resent this intrusion of human authority into its
business, so he soon learned to leave well alone.

They had been riding for two hours when it occurred to Quillon that
the road was no longer sloping to any visible degree, that there was little
sense of the ground level beyond the surrounding buildings being lower
than their present elevation. He supposed, with a shiver of realisation,
that they were now riding on the face of the Earth itself, having completed the descent of Spearpoint. There had been no obvious point of
transition to mark this passage. Even if there had been a clearly defined
foundation, some point where the spiral shelf reached a definite ter-
mination, thousands of years of weathering and human habitation had
smothered it under rubble and windblown dirt. They were still very

clearly in Horsetown, and therefore still potentially in reach of his enemies. The Godscraper's effective domain extended much further than the geometric limit of its base.

But as they rode on, even Horsetown became more attenuated. The streets widened, increasingly large gaps appearing between the buildings. Trees began to assert the presence of forest beyond the city's margins. The landscape was rocky and undulating, broken here and there by the pale sentry of a semaphore tower, the cranked arms moving constantly, sending information to the next tower in the chain, relaying news and intelligence far beyond Spearpoint.

The horses now travelled on roads of compacted dirt rather than cobbles. Now that their footing was surer, Meroka even broke them into the occasional trot. Quillon bounced around in the saddle until, more by accident than intention, he settled into a rhythm, putting weight through his legs into the stirrups to absorb the rise and fall of the horse's back. He wasn't cold now; there was enough heat boiling off the animal to keep him nicely warmed, and his own exertions helped. They were following the line of an aerial ropeway, suspended from wooden pylons. An endless succession of buckets, laden with freshly cut wood, was being hauled to Spearpoint. There were hundreds of ropeways like this, feeding the structure's unquenchable appetite for fuel. They came in from all directions, stretching away to the great woods and forests beyond the horizon. Some of the wood would be burned in stoves in Horsetown, some would end up in Tulwar's boiler, more still would feed the electricity-generating power stations of Neon Heights. As the buckets creaked overhead it was easy to imagine that the supply was limitless.

They had been riding for nearly three hours when he felt the first suggestion that the antizonals were wearing off. He took another pill and called ahead for Meroka to do likewise, but even after he had swallowed and digested his, the effects of zone sickness lingered. Belatedly he checked his watches, the clockwork ones Tulwar had given him, and saw the hands beginning to diverge. There was no question but that they were approaching the end of the zone.

It was nearing midday, the sun a cold yellow coin that had climbed as high as it was going to get. Ahead lay a rustic trading post, with a dozen or so horses hitched around it. Beyond, the road deteriorated even more severely. Quillon saw weed-choked cracks and cavernous potholes that looked a hundred years old.

This was as far as the horses could go, it transpired. Animals were even worse at tolerating zone shifts than humans, and there remained comparatively little scholarship on the arcane matter of veterinarian antizonals. Quillon was certain that nothing in his bag would do more good than harm, and besides, Meroka had only paid to ride the horses this far. They dismounted, hitched the horses to vacant posts, removed their gear from the panniers and went inside to eat. They washed the meal down with strong coffee and collected their belongings.

They crossed the boundary via the ropeway, riding one of the empty buckets returning to the forests. It was quicker than walking, even if it did mean climbing a rickety platform and timing their entry into the moving receptacle. There was a door in the side, which made it easier. From on high, clutching his hat to his head against the wind, Quillon saw that the staging post was also helping the buckets move. Behind the compound, teams of horses were driving a huge wheel, which was in turn coupled to the ropeway.

'I should at least examine you for zone sickness before we attempt the crossing,' Quillon said, as the bucket bobbed on its way.

'We'll be fine. Gets easier on the other side. If you could take Steamville, you'll cope.'

'Do machines work there?'

'Mostly. But there aren't that many of them, and them that exist tend to end up in the wrong hands. You aren't in the clear just yet.'

It was his third crossing since leaving Neon Heights, and perhaps the easiest. For the first time, the shift was in the opposite direction, taking him closer to the conditions he had grown accustomed to. Although there would still be a need to monitor the two of them for zone sickness, he could feel his body breathing a colossal sigh of sub-cellular relief. It was as if they had scaled a high mountain, breathed perilously thin air and were now descending again. The blood sang gladly in his veins.

'I don't even know where we are now,' he said, smiling at the depth of his own ignorance. 'What this place is called, how far it extends, who runs it.'

'Ain't much to say, Cutter. Out here there are just zones. They go on for hundreds of leagues, most of 'em. Some go on further than that. The one with the Bane in ... Well, never mind that for now. Ain't no government or Boundary Commission, neither. Ain't much resembling law and order, come to think of it. You got a few townships, places like Fortune's Landing, that make a living cutting and exporting wood and firesap to the 'scraper, and you got a few caravans that live off trading. That's about as far as civilisation goes, though. We sure as fuck aren't including the Skullboys.'

'Who are the Skullboys?'

'With luck on our side, you won't get to find out.'

The bucket bobbed its way to the trading post on the other side of the boundary. It was similar to the one they had left behind, if a little more rustic and run-down. Meroka threw open the door as the bucket approached the platform, and they stepped off – Meroka catching Quillon's sleeve as he nearly lost his balance and keeled over the low-railinged side.

'You're all skin and bones under that suit,' she said, letting go slowly.

They rented new horses and rode for the rest of the day, travelling west from Spearpoint. The lowering sun bestowed a pale honeyed light but offered nothing that Quillon would have dignified by calling warmth. He nestled into his coats and tugged his hat down further on his head. His hands were numb on the reins.

He had drifted into something like sleep, lulled by the horse's motion, when Meroka drew her ride to a halt. Quillon's horse stopped before he had a chance to tug on the reins. It snuffled the dry, cold ground and snorted disappointedly, as if until that moment it had been expecting a verdant green meadow. A breeze stirred dirt around the animals' hooves.

They must have come a long way. At some point the track had pulled away from the line of the ropeway, forging its own meandering path across the plain. They had passed the occasional hamlet, the occasional copse or small wood, but the forests were still far away. The ground had risen slightly in the last couple of leagues and was now descending, littered with rocks and boulders. A few hundred spans further on their trail met a wider path, one that showed evidence of heavy and frequent traffic. Wagon ruts etched its chalky yellow surface. But no one was moving on it now.

'This is the place,' Meroka said with sudden decisiveness. 'Come morning, they'll be along for you. Next stop, Fortune's Landing.'

'Assuming Fray got word through.'

'He won't let us down. Regardless, we'll figure something out.' She dismounted, swinging off the saddle and thudding to the ground. 'We'll camp here. Ain't gonna be the height of luxury, but you'll cope.' She set about unpacking the saddlebags. 'Anyone or anything comes along, keep out of sight.'

Quillon nodded and – less elegantly – got off his own horse, and began to empty the bags of what they needed for the night. The horse snorted and started to walk away but he grabbed the bridle and gave it a sharp yank, as he had seen Meroka do. She was already scouting a sheltered spot in the shadow of a house-sized boulder, tucked away from easy visibility of anyone on either the pass or the wider road.

They spread groundsheets, made pillows out of the saddlebags, preparing to sleep under the stars. It would be cold, even with thermal blankets, but Quillon told himself that he would only have to put up with it for one night.

'You can sleep now if you want,' Meroka said, sounding as if that was the last thing she had in mind. 'Or you can tuck in to the rations. Long as you don't mind eating cold. Can't risk a fire.'

Quillon understood. The darkening air was perfectly clear. Venus was already bright in the western sky, and the cold eye of Mars shone balefully in the east. Soon one of the Moon's two halves would rise, but until then the Milky Way was quite visible, numberless stars describing a spine of pearly luminescence across the vault of the heavens. It was a glorious evening for stargazing, but not one for subterfuge. Even if they concealed the flames, the column of smoke would be visible from afar, and it would stand every chance of drawing unwanted attention.

'How do you feel?'

'Fine, Cutter. You worry about yourself.' Meroka was by her horse, taking off its bridle and slipping on a leather halter that would allow it to graze on what meagre pickings it could find. She let the rope trail on the ground, not tied to anything. The horse would take it as a signal not to stray too far.

Meroka didn't seem to have an appetite, so Quillon tucked into the rations by himself, not caring that the food was neither warm nor particularly fresh. As he ate, the day's light diminished still further. Occasionally a bat or nocturnal bird flitted overhead, and now and then he heard the inquisitive snuffling of some small mammal, foraging in the darkness. There were undoubtedly wild things out there that could do them real harm, but Meroka seemed unconcerned and so he took that as an indication that he need not be too troubled himself. In any case the horses would give them fair warning of any predators.

Sleep still out of the question, he walked around the perimeter of their little camp until he came to a rise that took him half a dozen spans higher.

'Don't go far,' Meroka said, raising her voice only as much as was necessary.

'I just want to see how far we've come,' Quillon replied.

He had barely given Spearpoint a glance since leaving, preferring to concentrate on the rigours of the journey ahead and not be reminded of the pitifully small progress they had made. Now, though, sensing that the first phase of his exodus was nearing its end, he felt ready to face the truth. In the morning he would be with friends, or at least people who would give him shelter and value his talents.

They had come no more than fifteen leagues from the base of Spear-point, which was itself fifteen leagues across at its widest point. From its base it soared into the sky, gently tapering as it rose, until, fifty leagues above the ground, it was no more than a third of a league wide. But it kept on rising beyond that point, never narrowing beyond a thickness of one-third of a league, a quill-thin black column pushing beyond the veil of the atmosphere itself, into the impassable vacuum of space. Had the whole thing been dark it would still have stood out against the deepening purple of the eastern sky. Most of it, however, was gloriously aglow with evidence of inhabitation.

The city lights twinkled. Quillon tracked up from the base, striving to identify the zones and their interior districts against the mental map he carried, mindful that it would be easy to misjudge familiar scales and heights from this new perspective. He thought he could see the band of Spearpoint that was Neon Heights, beginning five or six leagues from the base and rising until the neon glow met the brighter but colder lights of Circuit City. Beneath Neon Heights was the much fainter, ember-like glow of Steamville, and beneath that, Horsetown was almost lost in darkness, its fires and torches scarcely visible at this distance. The spiral structure of Spearpoint's outer skin – the ever-winding shelf that rose in a continuous, clockwise gradient from the base to the very summit, beyond the air itself – was only intermittently discernible, where it was traced by a line of buildings or delineated by the faint, ascending thread of an electric train. Very few buildings were tall enough to reach from one level of the shelf to the next.

The shelf was widest at the base, and narrowed in width in harmony with Spearpoint's own tapering form. Even seen from this modest dis-tance, the city-districts appeared to be little more than a coating of light, a phosphorescent daub on the rising, screwlike structure. It seemed impossible that people could live and work in those perched com-munities and not be constantly assailed by the thought that they were a dizzying number of leagues from the ground, teetering on the edge of oblivion. But that was simply not how it felt when one was up there, in Neon Heights or Steamville or even within the glittering plasma-light precincts of Circuit City. For even as it diminished in width, the ledge remained more than wide enough to support a teeming grid of streets, and with the edge usually screened from view by at least one row of buildings, it required no great effort of will to put it out of mind. True, there was always the wall that supported the shelf on its next coil around Spearpoint, but for the most part that was either a dark cliff leaning over the streets and houses, or simply hidden behind a barricade of taller structures, traversed by elevators and funiculars. It too could be ignored most of the time, as could the levels of Spearpoint soaring far above.

The Mire, that node of confusion where the zones tended towards a state of unimaginable, unmappable compactedness, was somewhere level with Quillon's viewpoint, inside Spearpoint's awesome base. He imagined it as a boiling, seething knot. The zones radiated out from that focus, becoming larger and more tectomorphically stable with increasing distance, but their essential nature – whether they supported high or low degrees of technological sophistication – was, insofar as anyone had been able to ascertain, determined according to entirely random factors. And yet, had randomness been the sole factor, high and low societies should have been mingled together, with no regard for their vertical placement. There was no reason why the angels should claim the high reaches of the Celestial Levels, or why horses should be the primary form of motive power near the base. But there was more to the present order of things than fortuitous happenstance. This was clear from the profoundly dark blotches in Spearpoint's illumination, the places where nothing lived and nothing moved. There were blotches at all levels, right up to the Celestial.

The zones determined basic technological limits, but the mere possibility of a particular technology working in a given zone did not necessarily imply that people could live there. A zone like Horsetown, where almost nothing of any complexity could be made to work, could only exist near the base, where there was a ready supply of the basic amenities. Air, water and heat were all to hand, with nothing needing to be pumped or transported in by anything other than the simplest of machines, and there was also the possibility of trade in goods and resources with outlying communities, such as the small hamlets they had already passed.

By the same token, while it was feasible for angels and other post-human entities to survive in zones further down Spearpoint from the Celestial Levels, they gained little advantage in doing so, and rather more pertinently preferred not to breathe the same air as lesser 'pre-human' mortals. They lived high up because no one else could, enjoying the possibility of flight in those silent currents where the sky was a deep blue at the zenith and the warm airs rising from Spearpoint's lower levels made for ideal gliding conditions. Quillon could see them now: tiny specks orbiting the narrowing column, glowing like embers around a fire.

He thought again of the angel that had fallen down from those far reaches to crash onto one of Neon Heights' ledges, and how the angel's dying message had brought him to this desolate place.

Quillon did not know how long he had been staring at Spearpoint when Meroka sidled up alongside. He had not heard her approach; had in fact been completely unaware of any sounds or movements in his vicinity. He started slightly, gathering his composure.

'Homesickness's a bitch,' Meroka observed.

'You think I'm feeling homesick already?'

'Don't have to think, Cutter. See it in your face. You're telling yourself, maybe it wasn't as bad as I thought. Maybe I should've stayed.'

Her tone niggled him. 'Staying was never an option. I knew exactly what I was letting myself in for.'

'All the same, you got a lump in your throat and a tear in your eye.'

'If you say so.' He turned away, irritated with himself for allowing her to get to him. 'You're such an expert on homesickness, Meroka. But you'd never admit to feeling it, would you?'

'Shut up,' she said.

'Gladly. But I suggest you don't begin a conversation unless you have some vague intention of continuing it.'

'I said *shut up*. Something's coming.'

He lowered his voice. 'Something?'

'Along the main trail.' She nodded into darkness. 'Go fetch your horse. Bring it back to the camp. Don't make any noise doing it.'

The horse had not wandered far, encumbered by its rope. It walked back uncomplainingly. Meroka trudged out of the gloom with her own horse, its pale hide ghostly in the evening light. Only then did Quillon hear something that might have been the rumble of hooves and wheels, an engine's howl, whooping and hollering carried on the night's air.

With the horses tethered out of sight of the road, they crouched low by their bedding.

'Who do you think it might be?' Quillon asked in a whisper. 'The people we're supposed to be meeting?'

'Too soon for that.'

'Maybe the message got confused.'

'It's not them.' By way of explanation, she added, 'Too many horses, too many wheels.'

The rumble grew quieter and then louder, and sometimes fell away completely, but was always coming closer. The fragments of conversation almost resolved into something he could understand. The dialect had a guttural, harsh quality – words stripped down to single vowels and emotive grunts.

'The horses spook, this turns nasty, you hide,' Meroka said. 'It's safe, I fire three times.'

'And if I don't hear three shots?'

'Been nice knowing you.'

He caught movement then: a glimmer of torchlight in the distance. Meroka crept slowly away from the camp, eventually pausing and crouching low, overlooking the main road where it was joined by the narrower trail of the pass. The trails were paths of shimmering mercury against the shadowed darkness of the surrounding terrain. He heard the click as she released the safety catch on one of her weapons. She would be visible against the purple skyline, but if she remained perfectly still she would be hard to distinguish from a rock or boulder.

Cautiously, before the horses and wagons were too close, he crept over to Meroka's side and flattened himself against the ground. He had drawn out the angel gun again.

'Not a good idea,' she hissed.

'I'm sticking with you. If you get shot, how long do you think I'll last out here anyway?'

Meroka said nothing, leaving Quillon to draw his own conclusions about her likely answer. He lay very still, trying to ignore the hard stones digging into his chest. The rumble and clatter of the approaching procession grew louder, and with it came the lights of torches, casting a sullen, moving glow on the roadside. With the rumble and clatter came also the sharper overtone of buzzing, revving motors. He heard raucous, drunken laughter.

Gradually his eyes picked out the salient details. There were riders at the front, white- and grey-armoured men astride massive, burly horses that were also armoured, their muscular forms almost hidden behind a cunning arrangement of jointed and quilted plates, with animal bones nailed and tied on to the armour for effect. The riders wore metal masks covering the upper parts of their faces, the masks' empty eye sockets and exposed teeth either resembling skulls, or actually fashioned from them. Behind the riders, flanked on either side both by horsemen and men driving powered vehicles, came a trundling array of huge wagons, each of which was pulled by at least two horses, sometimes as many as six. Most of the wagons consisted of a wide platform, railed on four sides, with a tent or wooden hut in the middle. Thuggish-looking guards stood on the balconies, carrying various forms of weaponry. There were guards with pikes and swords, others with pistols, rifles and small machine guns, while some of the larger wagons sported artillery pieces at their corners, swivel-mounted cannon or brutish weapons with multiple barrel clusters, shields and double-handed grips for their operators. Some of the riders held pennanted staffs, while flags and banners trailed from the tents and huts on the backs of the wagons. The torches – some of them carried by the horsemen, some attached to the wagons – cast a wavering orange light over the entire spectacle. The tricycles and quadcycles accompanying the procession were ramshackle in appearance, seemingly welded together from the salvaged parts of older wrecks. They had skeletal chassis with machine guns, spikes and ramming devices bolted onto the frames. They bounced along quickly, apparently incapable of slowing down to keep pace with the horses and wagons. They were constantly having to swerve off the main track, making S-bends and loops, suspension jinking the vehicles high into the air, their riders only just managing to stay in their seats. As the procession neared it seemed inconceivable to Quillon that Meroka and he would avoid detection.

'Skullboys,' she said.

'The Skullboys I wasn't supposed to meet.'

'Kind of hoped we wouldn't cross paths.' She had the gun before her, held low to the ground just in front of her face. 'Lie still and shut up, we'll be all right. Seems they're in a hurry to get somewhere. Skullboys only look for trouble when they're in a fighting mood.'

'What kind of mood is this?'

'Shut up.'

The head of the procession gradually drew level with their position. With all the noise and spectacle, Quillon wondered how long it would be before one or both of their horses made a sound. The Skullboys were making a decent enough racket of their own, perhaps enough to drown out the horses, but the guards standing at the corners of the heavy wagons looked sober, vigilant and alert. Quillon thought it unlikely that night-vision technology would work here, but he still felt luminously bright, a warm human smudge against the cooling ground.

Yet the procession kept passing, and the horses remained quiet enough not to be heard. Dozens of wagons rumbled past, each seemingly larger than the last, until even the combined muscle of multiple horses proved insufficient and the wagons had to be hitched to traction engines: black behemoths of whirling metal flywheels and gushing ghost-white steam. Behind the traction engines came wagons holding metal cages as large as small houses. There were people in the cages, glimpsed in dismal huddles between the bars. Men and women, tied together and shackled, wearing little more than rags.

'Prisoners,' Meroka whispered, as if they could have been anything else. 'Skullboys buy 'em from villages and towns along the way, or sometimes just take 'em without asking.'

'Have they done anything wrong?'

'Some of 'em. Not all.' She paused. 'Some just didn't get out the way fast enough.'

'What will happen to them now?'

'Nothing good.'

'You can tell me, Meroka. I'd rather know the risks.'

She drew an audible breath as the procession continued to pass, almost blanketed in dust and steam. 'Some of 'em, the women mostly, they'll be sold on as slaves, or used by the Skullboys themselves.'

'Why are they like this?'

'Mostly they're pissed off and surly for the sake of it. Anyone who gets kicked out of the respectable communities around here – your murderers, rapists, thieves – there's a good chance they'll end up being recruited into the Skulls. They might only be borderline psychotic to start with, but by the time they've been force-fed the same drugs that the rest of 'em are on, they start drooling and snarling like they were born to it.'

'What drugs are we talking about here?'

'Not your common or garden antizonals, Cutter. Skulls need to cross between zones to do their dirty business, but they can't get hold of the good stuff. So they improvise. Brew up their own replacements, or take what the vorgs will give them in return for victims. Over time, it all messes with their heads. Turns them a little cranky. And that's before you factor in all the other shit they put into themselves.'

'You mentioned the vorgs back at Fray's place. Who are they?'

'*What* are they, you mean. Carnivorgs. Fucked-up, biomechanical machines. But you don't have to worry about them.'

'Just like I didn't need to worry about the Skullboys?'

'Skullboys make a point of being mobile. Vorgs don't. They can't get this deep into the zone.'

The line of caged wagons was almost past now. Smaller vehicles brought up the rear, pulled by more teams of horses. Quillon started to relax, daring to believe that they would remain undetected. The maximum noise and fury had moved on, and their own horses had retained enough dim cunning to keep quiet. Then he noticed the last and smallest of the cages – half the size of any that had passed so far, and containing what he first took to be only one prisoner, a young woman standing up at the bars, wearing a tattered dress or gown with the sleeves torn away. Her arms were very thin, yet knotted with hard muscle. She was either bald or her hair had been shaved almost to the scalp. She was not alone, for at the woman's side was a child of indeterminate sex, a boy or girl clothed in rags, face hidden behind a wild thicket of dirty black hair. No more than four or five years old at the most, Quillon judged, and he doubted that the mother – if she was indeed the child's parent – was more than fifteen.

'What will happen to them?' he asked, meaning the woman.

'Most likely end up as slaves.'

'This is barbaric.'

'Welcome to the real world, Cutter. You want to stand up and make a point, you're more'n welcome. Just give me time to get away first.'

'You mean, what's done is done, we just stand by and accept it?'

'Skullboys are everywhere, Cutter. They own the Outzone. You piss off one lot of 'em, word soon gets around. Fine if you don't plan on coming back too often. Me, I've got a living to make.'

The procession was ending, the last few wagons and riders roaring and rattling into the night, the whooping cries gradually fading. But he could still see the woman and child in the cage. She seemed to be looking almost directly at him, as if she had seen something in the darkness. He flinched, telling himself it was no more than coincidence, and then the woman turned slowly away to face the direction of travel, drawing the child closer to her side. As the woman presented her back to him, he made out a large scar or birthmark on the back of her skull, reaching almost all the way from the crown to the nape.

He wanted desperately to act, but he knew it was senseless; that Meroka was right. How ludicrous he must seem to her now, he thought: fresh from the city, stung with bruising indignation at the inhumanity he had only now begun to take notice of. But it had been out there all along, not just for years or decades but for millennia. A grinding toll of cruelty and injustice, going on, ceaselessly, for every waking moment of his life.

'I know it's hard,' Meroka said eventually, when the clamour of the Skullboy caravan had all but faded, 'but you get used to it. It's get used to it or go insane. I already made my choice.'

'I can't blame you for that.' They had stood up from the ground and put their guns away.

'It's not that I don't care. But there are lots of them and not many of us.' Long silences stretched between each sentence, Meroka assembling the words with obvious effort. 'If everyone in Spearpoint got together, made an army . . . came down here, maybe that would make a difference. And that's likely, right? Swarm'll forgive us before that happens.'

'What's Swarm?'

'Just one more thing you don't need to worry about, Cutter.'

CHAPTER SEVEN

It was the horses, not the lightening sky, that eventually roused him to alertness. They were whinnying, and in the still-present darkness he could hear Meroka cursing and muttering as she tried to quieten the animals. He divested himself of the blanket and stood up, shivering slightly, for the air had cooled and he had been tolerably warm under the covering. He felt light-headed, as if he had rushed to his feet too quickly. The horses were still upset about something. He looked in the direction of the road, but there was no sign of anyone else coming along it, and certainly no audible indication of another Skullboy caravan.

Still unsteady on his feet, the light-headedness persisting, he made his way to the commotion. Meroka was a shape in the dark, one hand on the muzzle of each horse, trying to settle them. Their eyes and teeth flashed white and wild and terrified. Their ears were flattened back.

'Something's got 'em riled, Cutter.' She was out of breath with the effort of restraining the animals, which were still thrashing and kicking against her grip.

'That much I surmised.' He took hold of his own horse and laid a hand on the sweat-sheened column of its neck. He could feel its pulse, like an overwound clock. 'Did you see or hear anything?'

'Been as quiet as a crypt all night. Then they start this shit.'

At the back of his mind the truth was already forming, although he was reluctant to give it room. 'How do you feel, Meroka?'

'Like I've been up all night, and the day before.'

'I mean, apart from that.'

She turned to look at him, her face little more than a featureless oval. 'Why you asking?'

'Because I'm not feeling well myself. Either that food I ate was bad, or else ...' He halted, still holding the horse, and used his other hand to tug up his sleeve, exposing enough of his forearm to read his watches. The dials and hands glowed feeble blue-green. It was hard to read them, with the agitated horse jerking its head up and down. He concentrated until he could be certain. The watches were beginning to show different times, the minute hands no longer winding around in perfect lockstep. The cumulative difference between the fastest and slowest watch was already a quarter of an hour.

'Something wrong?'

'I checked the synchronisation before I slept. The watches were all keeping good time. Now they're drifting.'

'So what're you saying?'

It was hard to come out with the words. He almost felt that by voicing his suspicion he was in danger of concretising it into reality. 'My symptoms match those of zone sickness. My watches are telling me something's happening. And our horses aren't happy. Animals sense these things sooner than people or machines.'

'Could just be a squall.'

'Yes. It could just be a squall.' But he thought about Fray's suspicion that there was something big coming down the line.

More than a squall, for certain.

'I think we're in trouble,' he said. 'I need to gauge the change-vector and issue us both a dose of antizonals.'

But even as he spoke, some fight seemed to go out of the horses. They stopped kicking the ground and yanking their heads, their eyes narrowing and their ears pricking forwards. They snorted and snuffled, letting the humans know that while they were in no way placated, whatever had stirred them up appeared to have passed, for now.

Quillon still felt light-headed and unsteady, but even that was beginning to ease. He released his horse, letting it wander off, then adjusted his watches back into synchronisation, as near as he could judge it. He would monitor them carefully from now on.

'You were saying?'

'Maybe it was a squall after all.'

'Squalls happen. I feel all right. What about you?'

'Whatever it was seems to be passing.'

'The boundary must have wandered over us for a few moments, before snapping back.'

Again Quillon listened into the night, but still there was nothing to be heard. 'I don't think I'm going to be able to get much more sleep, though. I feel wide awake.'

'Got a long wait until your ride arrives.'

'I'll be fine. Perhaps you're the one who ought to be getting some rest. I can look after the horses.'

'You insist,' she said, after several moments' reflection. 'But don't go dozing off on me.'

'No plans to doze off, I assure you.'

Satisfied that the horses were as settled as they were going to get, Meroka lay down under a blanket. Quillon watched her dark form, observing the regularity of her breathing until he was certain she was asleep. Meroka also had a taxing day ahead of her. She had to take both horses back alone, riding one and guiding the other, through the pass and back to the base of Spearpoint.

He found a hummock in the ground that made a passable seat and lowered himself onto it, the wheels of his mind spinning with dizzy alertness. The horses snuffled and snorted, but were otherwise docile. They had enviably short memories, animals. He examined his watches, the luminous dots on the dials and hands forming a series of circular constellations. The hands were all moving in lockstep again now. Watches were carefully engineered (and later selected by the purchaser) so that they would respond to zone changes in subtly different ways, rather than all of them slowing or speeding up in unison. But it still took attention to read the signs accurately, and care to ensure that the watches were wound and functioning properly. In Neon Heights, the majority of citizens had become lax in the business of watch-reading, secure in the knowledge that the ever-present Boundary Commission would alert them to a zone shift as soon as it happened. Most of them only wore watches as fashion accessories, barely remembering how to interpret the signs. The same applied to the other districts, in varying measure. But out here watches were all one had. There was no Boundary Commission, and Quillon would be entirely reliant on his own judgement as to when to administer antizonal medicine, and of what type and dosage.

But when the shift came again, the watches barely had time to respond. What had been light-headedness before was now a vicious, vicelike pressure mounting behind his eyeballs. The suddenness of the pain, the intensity of it, made him gasp. He stood up, more out of a flight reflex than any conscious volition, clutching the sides of his head. The pain increased, until it felt as if a sharp wedge were being driven down through his skull, splitting his brain between the hemispheres. Vomit rose in his throat. He staggered directionlessly, the landscape seeming to tilt madly into the sky. He pivoted around, fighting the urge to vomit, and saw the horses lying still on the ground like piles of black sacks, as if they had been shot. They were either dead or unconscious; he couldn't tell and he sensed it wouldn't make much difference either way if he didn't keep himself from slipping under. Already there was a dreamlike quality to his actions, a feeling that his mind was isolating itself from the real world, slamming down protective barriers.

He found Meroka. Something was very wrong with her. She was palsying under the blanket, her body convulsing. Her zone tolerance was not as robust as his own. He was disorientated and in pain, but if Meroka did not receive the right medication quickly, she would not survive very long. Yet to administer the wrong kind of antizonal would be worse than not treating her at all. He knelt down and touched her, hoping the pressure of his hand would calm her or at least bring her to consciousness, but she kept shaking. He found her mouth and his hand came away wet with blood and spittle.

This was not a squall. The squall had just been a wave breaking on a shoreline. This was an inundation: another zone completely swamping the one they had been inside. And so far it wasn't passing; it wasn't snapping back to its earlier configuration.

He bent over and retched. The pain was still inside his head, the dizziness and sense of detachment, but the nausea eased slightly. He forced himself to look down, to survey his watches. It could only have been a minute or so since the episode had begun – not enough time for the hands to have diverged to any useful extent. But the second hands were still ticking around. None of the watches had stopped. If one or more of them had, then it might – *might* – be an indication that the shift was to a lower-state zone, where even the simple clockwork of a watch was too complex and finicky to function. Since the watches were all still ticking, he could only draw the opposite conclusion. The shift was in the other direction, to a higher-state zone, where the clockwork operated too well, too freely. Tolerances had slackened; gears and cams were now whirring faster than they were supposed to.

He reached for his medical bag, snapped it open with trembling fingers. His vision was beginning to tunnel, his hand-to-eye coordination degrading. Like a drunk trying to untie shoelaces he fumbled open the rack that contained the direction-specific antizonals, the rubber-topped vials and the waiting hypodermics. They swam in and out of focus. He checked his watches again; all still running. The minute hands beginning to pull apart, the second hands ticking at visibly different rates. He took one of the syringes and plunged it into a vial. Drew out a measure of thick, resinous fluid.

Every instinct told him to treat himself first. He was the physician, Meroka the patient. Still he went to Meroka, leaning down on her to quell her movements, drawing back the blanket to expose an arm, finding bare skin under her sleeve, locating a vein, pushing the thick needle in, depressing the plunger. All the while seeing the hypodermic in his hand, like a glittering glass toy held at an absurd distance, Meroka's body stretching halfway to the horizon.

The drug worked quickly. Her convulsions became less violent, less frequent. He knelt back and staggered to his feet, hoping he had done the right thing. Too soon to tell: even the wrong antizonal could have an initially calming effect, lulling the physician into thinking he had made the right decision. He looked at the watches again, relieved to see that they were still telling him the same story.

He injected himself with the other syringe, and then returned both to their slots in the medical mag. If they could not be sterilised, he would at least make sure that Meroka was only injected using one syringe, and he the other.

He began to feel an improvement almost immediately. His vision started to clear, the headache fading. There would still be grogginess for some while, a sluggish quality to his thoughts and actions, but if he had made the right choice, the antizonal would gradually free him from the immediately obvious symptoms of zone sickness. Until either the ambient conditions changed again – for better or worse – or the drug had time to wear off, which it would.

The horses were still lying on the ground, inert as shadows. Perhaps they were dead after all – he could see no sign that they were still breathing. But the prognosis was better for Meroka. She had stopped convulsing and was now lying on her side, almost as if she had been watching him inject his own dose.

As he walked over, she moved a hand across her face. The sky had begun to lighten in the east and now he could make out her open eyes, the blood daubed around her mouth.

'I'm a mess,' Meroka said, slurring almost to the point of incomprehension.

'You bit your tongue.'

'What happened?'

'The squall came back.' He knelt beside her. 'Worse this time. It got you so fast you didn't even have time to wake up before you went into palsy. I think the horses might not have made it. I took a risk and decided the shift was in the upward direction. Fortunately, it appears I was right. I injected both of us with what I hoped was the right form of antizonal.'

'I feel like shit.'

'You may not believe it, but that's probably a good sign. Can you sit up?'

Meroka did as he suggested, letting out only a single groan of discomfort. 'Something hurts in my chest.'

'You might have done some damage when you were convulsing – fractured a rib, perhaps, or torn a muscle. I didn't get to you fast enough.'

'Guess you had problems of your own.' She pinched her fingers into the corners of her eyes, digging out grit. 'You did good, Cutter. Made the right judgement.'

'I hope so. In daylight, I'll give you a proper examination, see if I can work out what you've done. In the meantime, it's best if we stay here and monitor our progress. If I've overshot, I'll need to administer a corrective dose.' He tapped at the row of watches on his still-exposed wrist. 'We'll know soon enough.'

Meroka got to her feet. 'That's not going to work.'

'We weren't planning on going anywhere until your friends arrive to take me. I don't see that anything has changed, barring the zone shift. Are you worried that they won't be able to get here now?'

'They've got drugs. Maybe not as good as your city stuff, but it won't stop 'em getting through.'

'What, then?'

'You say we've shifted up?'

'Most likely, yes. If we hadn't, you and I would probably be starting to feel even worse now.'

'How far up?'

'I don't know – I couldn't make that kind of measurement, not in the time I had. That's why I may have overshot. Or undershot, for that matter. But the severity of the symptoms ... that would suggest to me that this isn't a small shift.'

'Not the same as just going from Neon Heights to Circuit City, then?'

'More severe than that, I suspect.'

'Severe enough that vorgs might be able to survive here, when they couldn't before?'

'I can't say. I haven't had a wealth of experience with vorgs.' He paused, the remark hanging in the air like a neon-lit challenge. 'Should we be moving on?'

'Need to look at the horses.'

Quillon placed a restraining hand on his patient. 'You need to stay where you are, until we know I got that dosage right.'

Meroka brushed him aside and stood up, more steadily than he would have imagined possible. He watched her stalk off in the direction of the fallen animals, taking the occasional lurch or stumble, but somehow managing not to fall down. Either she had gained a sudden, medically unlikely tolerance for the zone transition, or she was as tough as saddle leather. Quillon couldn't draw any measure of superiority from the fact that he felt clear-headed and in full control of his faculties. Tolerance was a genetic gift, not something you acquired through diligence and determination.

She stopped at the fallen horses, knelt down and touched the neck of Quillon's animal, under the hard, round swell of its cheek. She waited silently and then moved to the other one.

'Both dead.'

'I'm sorry. I can't say I'm surprised, though.'

Meroka stood up. 'None of that medicine of yours would've made a difference?'

'Human-specific antizonals don't even work on monkeys, Meroka. Do you think you can make it back on foot?'

'Who said anything about going back?'

'That was the arrangement. You hand me over to these people who are supposed to show up. You return to Spearpoint.'

'Things're different now.' She left the horses and started up the slope towards the higher ground, talking back to Quillon all the while. 'Can't stay here, not now. Not if the vorgs are on their way.'

'What about the people? They'll be expecting to find us here now.'

'They'll figure we had to shift things around. If they're coming from that way,' she gesticulated in the vague direction of the main path, 'then they're going to be in one motherfucking hurry to get away from the old boundary. There are other routes they can take, avoiding this place.'

'Then we'll never meet them.'

'Didn't say that. Just that we gotta be flexible now. There's another meeting point, ten, twelve leagues further on. Done some business there already. That's where they'll head, 'less the zone shifts again.'

'And if they're not there?'

'Then we need to find some new friends, someone else who can give you a ride to Fortune's Landing.' Meroka paused – he'd had the sense that she was going to say something else. 'Hey, Cutter. Maybe you ought to see this.'

'See what?'

'Just get up here.'

He followed the rise to where Meroka was standing, exactly where he had stood earlier that night, looking back at Spearpoint. It was still there, still illuminated against the purple- and orange-streaked dawn sky, a light-studded dagger pushed up through the skin of the world, twinkling in the cold distance, too near to make him feel as if they had travelled any significant distance, too far away to offer the promise of sanctuary.

'At least the shift doesn't seem to have affected it,' Quillon said.

'Keep watching.'

He did, and then he saw what she meant. Because even in the few seconds that had passed since his arrival at her side, he had seen a patch of illumination go out, a swathe of lights – a whole precinct or district – turn suddenly dark. The lights did not return; there was a ribbon of blackness cutting across Spearpoint that had previously been illuminated. And as he kept watching, another ribbon appeared below that one – the lights flickering on and off this time, as if some ancient, overstrained generator had just cut out and then restarted, before losing the battle against the darkness. It didn't end there, either. In seemingly disconnected parts of Spearpoint, squares and rectangles of darkness appeared – not just in Neon Heights but in the upper levels, taking out parts of Circuit City and even the angel spaces. The squares and rectangles pushed out fingers and filaments of blackness, joining disconnected areas, squeezing the visible light into narrow, harried motes and margins, as if the visible lights were people being herded into stifling pens by armies of dark enforcers. The motes and margins dwindled to nothing, and the pace of the shutdown appeared to be quickening, across all of Spearpoint. No part of the city was spared, irrespective of the prevalent technology. Only those low-lying gas- and fire-lit quarters did not seem to be strongly affected, but their contribution to Spearpoint's brilliance was so limited and feeble that it was as if the darkness had already taken them. As the brighter lights died, electric, neon and plasma-banks guttering out, so the faint, ruddy glow of the lanterns and fires of Steamville and Horsetown shone unchallenged for the first time, a sombre orange-tinged radiance that only reached a small distance up Spearpoint's rising flanks. The rest of the vast structure, save for a few motes and margins that had not yet been entirely eclipsed, was pitifully dark.

Then he saw the angels. They had been in flight before, circling the high elevations, tiny moving dots reflecting pastel light from their glowing wings. Now they were falling, tumbling down on the buffeting thermals, wings flickering and fading into darkness.

'Looks like you got out at the right time,' Meroka said.

For a moment he couldn't answer her, stunned into silence by the callous offhandedness of her remark. In Quillon's lifetime there had been squalls and shifts that had occasionally interfered with part of the city, but nothing remotely on the scale of the blackout he was now witnessing. This was a storm to rival anything that had happened in recent generations, perhaps even centuries. Nor was it some vicious but temporary spasm, the Mire lashing out with petulant fury before returning to normality. The lights would have begun to come on again by now if that were the case, but the darkness only grew more sullen with each minute that passed. A few spots of illumination remained, dotted here and there at different altitudes, but they looked likely to be choked out and swallowed at any moment.

'You think I care about myself now?' he asked. He stilled his tongue, waiting for her to say something, something he could spit back in her face. 'That's a city, Meroka. Thirty million people. Right now most of them are either going to be dealing with the onset of crippling zone sickness – what we just went through, only without drugs – or they're coming to the realisation that they've just lost every life-support system they've ever known. Or both.' He paused. 'Air. Water. Medicine. It's all over, until the zones snap back. *If* they snap back.' He spoke with a fierce resolution, barely recognising his own voice. 'They're either hurting or they're going to hurt, really badly. All of them, except for the very few that anyone's going to be able to help. The Boundary Commission was right: something big was coming. But they couldn't have imagined anything on this scale. This is the end of everything.'

'They'll fix things, Cutter. The lights'll come back on.'

'Meroka, listen to me. I spoke to Fray about this. The authorities knew something awful was going to happen. They were waiting, getting ready for it to hit. Not some local reorganisation of boundary lines, but something big, something catastrophic. That's why there was a drug shortage. They've been stockpiling antizonals, knowing this was coming at us.'

'So it'll be all right. They're in control.'

'Look,' he said, forcing her to stare back at the darkening spire. 'It's getting worse. There are fewer lights than even a minute ago. The parts that held out until now are failing. Does it look to you as if there's anyone in control? Does it look to you as if that's a city about to pick itself up and carry on?'

'It's only been a few minutes.'

She was right and he knew it – it was too soon to make rash assumptions – but in his heart he felt an icy conviction that things were not going to improve quickly.

'Even if they stockpiled drugs, there won't be enough to go around.

They'll be lucky if they can get enough medicine to the people supposed to be in charge, let alone to the citizens.'

'It's not our problem right now,' Meroka said. 'Doesn't mean I don't care, all right? Doesn't mean I haven't got a heart. But the zone change has happened here as well, only we don't have a city around us to hide in.'

'We've got the drugs,' Quillon said.

She inhaled deeply. 'Ain't nothing we can do for the city now. Take us two, three days to get back without the horses anyway, and what use are we going to be then? That dinky little bag of medicines won't stretch far, will it?'

'If I could do something, I would.' But Quillon knew he would need to tap deeply into his supply of antizonals just to keep the two of them alive from now on.

'We keep moving,' Meroka said. 'Just like I was telling you. Find the other meeting place, and hope someone shows up. What we don't do is spend any longer here. Place is already starting to creep me out. I can *smell* those fucking vorgs.'

'We just leave the horses?'

'What did you have in mind?'

'I don't know. Bury them or something.' He shrugged helplessly. 'So it's not so obvious we were here.'

Meroka seemed to give the idea at least a moment's consideration before answering. 'Done much horse burying?'

'What do you think?'

'Take you a day with a little shovel like that, open a grave big enough, assuming the ground doesn't turn to rock as soon as you get under the topsoil. Then you've still got the other horse to get rid of. Two days, and that's assuming you've got the strength to move a ton of dead meat when you're done shovelling.'

'So we just leave? Just leave and start walking?'

'Couldn't put it simpler if I tried.'

'This is easy for you, isn't it? Change plans, change gear, keep moving. It's what you do. But I'm not you, Meroka. I'm frightened and I'm not sure you really know what you're doing.'

She looked around theatrically. 'You see anyone else around offering you advice?'

'No.'

'Then it doesn't look like you've got a fuck of a lot of choice, does it?'

Meroka went back down to the camp and began to sort through their belongings, throwing aside what they could not carry on foot. Quillon lingered for a while before walking down the slope to join her. Behind him, Spearpoint's darkness had only intensified, even as the sky paled towards daylight and the steel-cold promise of a new day.

CHAPTER EIGHT

They walked into dawn and then sunrise, following the wide, wheel-rutted path that the Skullboys had already traversed, Meroka never once looking back, as if she had seen all that she needed to.

Quillon envied her that pragmatic acceptance – taking it to be that, rather than some fundamental lack of curiosity – but he could not stop turning around to view Spearpoint, always with the hope that something might have changed, that there might be a glimmer of light where before there had been darkness. But as the day brightened, it became increasingly difficult to tell in any case. Spearpoint was no longer a black sliver against night skies, but a distant blue-grey mass, a mountain of impossible steepness, its intrinsic blackness muted by leagues of intervening atmosphere, making it virtually impossible to tell whether there were lights burning or not. Certainly he saw no evidence of movement, no trains or flying things, but that didn't mean that there wasn't some kind of civil recovery in progress. The complex, energy-hungry infrastructure of transit systems would be the last thing to return, in any district.

Across the land, the semaphore towers stood deathly still.

Meroka's pace was unforgiving, but he still insisted that they stop every couple of hours, either to re-administer the antizonals or to perform enough tests to satisfy himself that he had estimated the dose well. He had been monitoring his watches carefully. While they were no longer keeping synchronous time, the cumulative differences were no more than he would have expected if the zone had remained fixed after the convulsive change of the previous night. They would need to keep taking the drugs, but at least the situation did not seem to be worsening. Based on the dosages he was giving out now, there was sufficient vector-specific medicine in the box to last the two of them somewhere between a week and ten days. When that was exhausted, there were other drugs, less effective, less finely tuned, but which would still keep them alive for a few days more. But not weeks, and definitely not months. The medicines had been calculated to serve him under entirely more benign conditions, where it would only have been necessary to administer a tiny fraction of the daily dosage he was now measuring out.

During their second stop, when the day had brightened even further, he found Meroka kneeling on the ground with a map spread before her. The map was tattered, brown at the edges as if it had been rescued from a fire. Meroka was making corrections to it with the stub of a pencil, crossing out one zone boundary and adding another.

'You think that's accurate?' he asked.

'Unless you got a better guess, I'm going with it. We hit another boundary, I can make some refinements. For now, this is as good as we've got.'

The map had two sides. One face showed the terrain within a few hundred leagues of Spearpoint, the dashed line of the equator cutting almost perfectly through the city's base. Quillon saw the road or trail they had followed since Horsetown, the point where it met the track where the Skullboys had passed, and along which they were now moving. They had been going due west; now they appeared to be moving in a south-westerly direction, although without a gyroscope or an accurate fix based on celestial navigation, there was no means of verifying this. Aside from the roads and semaphore tracks, a number of landmarks and surface communities had been marked on the map, but few of them meant anything to him. Fortune's Landing – one of the names he did recognise – lay to the south, at least a hundred leagues from their present position. He knew it to be the nearest large community to Spearpoint, but it might as well have been halfway around the world for all the hope he had of getting there without Meroka's assistance. Even with the map, he would be all but lost.

The other side of the map was not much of an improvement, but at least he recognised more of the landmarks. Soul's Rest was the largest community anywhere on Earth, with the exception of Spearpoint, and that really was halfway around the world. It lay far to the west, beyond the Daughters, the three mountains punched in a sloping line with the regularity of bullet holes, beyond even the Mother Goddess, the tallest of all mountains, so tall and wide that from its footslopes it no longer seemed a mountain, but merely a gentle steepening of the ground. It lay west of the shrunken waters of the Long Gash and the Old Sea – marked in black on the map, although he had a suspicion that the waters had retreated even further since the map was drawn. Here, as on the other face, were the sinuous margins of zone boundaries. In Spearpoint, zones were large enough to encompass the precincts and districts of a city.

Where Quillon and Meroka now stood the zones were larger still, but the zones on the other side of the map were expansive enough to swallow entire geographies, whole mountain ranges, plains and former seas. Despite the vastly different scales between one side of the map and the other, Meroka was even attempting to redraw the zone boundaries on this side as well, as if it mattered.

Quillon's eye fell on a patch of the map that was completely blank, a featureless absence to the east of the northernmost Daughter. It was as if all the details and inked shadings had been bleached away.

'What's that?'

'The Bane. But you don't need to worry about that. It's a long way from wherever we'll find ourselves.' She looked up, the pencil in her mouth. 'Trust me.'

'Why isn't there anything marked on that part? Hasn't anyone been into it?' The emptiness, the Bane, was hundreds of leagues across – big enough to swallow everything on the other side of the map.

'No one goes in. No one comes out. It's just a big old dustbowl; makes the rest of this cold, dry shit-bucket of a planet look like the Garden of fucking Eden on a good day.'

'It's a good job you're not religious,' Quillon said sarcastically.

'Can't help what comes out of my mouth, Cutter. Don't mean it correlates with what's in my head.' Satisfied with her corrections, she put the pencil away and folded up the map, doing so very carefully, so as not to tear the fragile document. 'Break over,' she announced. 'Got to keep moving.'

Meroka was right about that. They couldn't stay in this zone indefinitely, even if they had a limitless supply of drugs. They hadn't been born to it, and it was still killing them – just somewhat more slowly than if there had been no medicines. But in the long run, they needed to cross into another zone, one to which they were better adapted. Quillon had only the vaguest idea of the old configuration of boundaries, let alone the new one, so he wasn't sure how much faith to put in Meroka's hand-corrected map.

They would just have to travel, and hope that sooner or later the watches registered the shift to conditions they could live in.

Of course, there were no guarantees that would happen. There was no law of nature that said zones retained their characteristics when they shifted size and shape. They were not like countries moving around on a map, retaining political and cultural identities even as their margins shrank or enlarged, even as they oozed and squirmed halfway across the world like roving amoebas. When a zone shifted, almost anything could change – including the very character of the zone itself. Even if there had been a way out of this zone before, a passage into a more habitable volume, there was no guarantee that one existed now. They might be hemmed in on all sides by zones that were even less hospitable than this one.

But they couldn't think about that. Not now. All they could do was keep moving, and hope that something better lay ahead.

'Fires,' Meroka said an hour after noon, pointing to a series of smoke lines rising from the horizon. 'Bad news for someone. Could be Skullboys burning some villages, or villages burning a few Skullboys. Lot of scores being settled today.'

'How far do you think we've come?'

'Four leagues. Maybe five.'

Whenever Quillon looked back, Spearpoint did not seem any more distant than the last time. It was as if the whole edifice was crunching slowly along in their wake, following them like a sick animal. He fancied he could make out thin lines of smoke rising from different levels, braided and tugged by the crosswinds and thermals as they rose.

'And this meeting point? How much further is it?' Without an obvious scale on the map, he hadn't been able to work out how far they had to go.

'Ten, twelve leagues.'

'That's what you said last time.'

'Figured the pill needed sugaring. But rest easy – I'm telling the truth now. We'll be there by this time tomorrow.'

'If we make it through the night, with all these machines and vorgs you keep going on about.'

'You think I made them up, just to gee you along?'

'I'm just saying. There isn't any sign of anything behind us. No fires that way, and no sign of anything coming along the same road.'

Meroka slowed and for the first time since leaving the camp, turned to face the way they had come.

'Your call, Cutter. You can mosey on home now if you think your luck's in. Maybe you won't meet anything coming the other way, either. But I'm going on, with or without you.'

'I'm with you,' he said, readjusting the strap on his backpack where it had begun to dig into his shoulder. 'All the way. All I ask is that you tell me the truth. No sugaring, all right? No matter how bad things look, I can take it.'

Meroka began walking again. 'You think so?'

'There's really only one way to find out.'

After a few paces she said, 'It's a bit more than twelve leagues.'

'Thanks.'

'More like fifteen. And that's God's honest truth. But we can make it. We keep walking until we drop. You can rest all you like when we get there.'

'Pity the horses died,' Quillon said, gritting his teeth against the ordeal that lay ahead.

They came upon the wreckage and the bodies three hours later, when the sun was a good way towards the western horizon. A yellow-and-black-liveried steam-coach had come off the road and tipped over onto its side, smokestack buckled like a smashed limb, steam still hissing from its ruptured joints. One spoked wheel had broken from its axle and come to rest in the rut. The one that was still tilted to the sky was turning backwards and forwards as the breeze caressed it, squeaking gently. Luggage lay in piles where it had toppled from the roof. Two bodies lay on the ground, flung violently as the coach crashed. From their postures – one head-down, as if they had been rammed into the earth by a giant hand, the other lying on their side with one leg bent under them – it was quite clear that they had not survived the accident or ambush. Perhaps they had even been dead before they hit the ground.

Meroka kept walking so unconcernedly that Quillon began to wonder if she was just going to keep on past the wreck without giving it a glance. He even began to wonder if he was hallucinating it, or that Meroka was somehow hallucinating the absence of a wreck where one existed. Figments and mirages were to be expected when the antizonal dosage began to wear off, or was not quite correct to begin with. A steam-coach, however, seemed entirely too specific to be the product of Quillon's imagination.

Meroka was fully aware of it, however. Quite casually, she dug into her coat and drew a gun, a long-barrelled, brass-ornamented thing of vague provenance. She had better weapons, Quillon knew, but they would be useless now, their functionality ruined by the passage through the low-state zone of Horsetown. It didn't matter that they were in a high-state zone again; the iron rule was that what had been damaged remained damaged, for evermore. The only reason she hadn't thrown anything away, he presumed, was that the guns still had some residual value, either as scrap metal, bludgeoning instruments or as broken goods a skilled gunsmith might be able to repair.

He took out the angel gun. Meroka stepped off the road and crept around the ruined steam-coach, paying little heed to the bodies on the ground. The wagon wheel kept squeaking, an eerie melancholy rhythm that only emphasised the silent desolation of the road. Quillon followed her and knelt by the figure that had landed head-down. It was a youngish man, wearing a dark, long-hemmed coat of tanned animal hide. The impact had broken his neck. Quillon doubted that had killed him, though. There was a bullet hole in his forehead, the wound circular and neat as if it had been made by a piece of industrial punching machinery. Quillon tilted the head slightly in search of an exit wound, but there was none.

'I was hoping this might have been an accident,' he said aloud, 'that they were travelling when the zone storm happened, fell unconscious and lost control. But this man's been shot.'

'Shot?' Meroka called back.

'Clean through the forehead.'

'Someone was a damned fine marksman, to hit a steam-coach driver.'

'It would have been fast. I don't think he felt anything.'

'Problem is,' Meroka said, 'this wagon wouldn't have been travelling empty.'

Quillon moved to the second body, the one with the broken leg, and found another dead man. This one was older, with a sharp, red-veined nose, straggly grey moustache, long grey hair down to his collar and small round glasses similar to his own, one coin-sized lens now a star of shattered glass. He also had a bullet wound through the centre of his forehead. The two men must have been sitting high up at the front of the coach, steering it as if it was still being drawn by a team of horses.

'This man's been shot as well,' Quillon said.

'You don't say.' Meroka peered into the now-horizontal windows of the steam-coach, steadying herself on the door handle and the rails either side of it.

'You sound sceptical. But if someone was a good enough shot to hit one of these men, I suppose they could also have hit the other man. They wouldn't have had to reload.'

'Oh no,' she said, on a falling note. 'Why did it have to be a family?'

Quillon stood up and made his way over to her. 'How many?'

'Four. Mum and Dad and two girls.'

'Have they been shot?'

'No. Looks like they just died in here. Zone sickness, I figure. Want to take a look?'

'Not that I can help them, but ...' He watched as she scrambled up onto the side of the steam-coach and opened the door, then dropped elegantly into the compartment. 'What are you doing?'

'Looting. What does it look like?'

'I'm not sure this is right.'

'Don't go growing a conscience on me now, Cutter. These people are dead and gone. Anything they can give us that helps us, we take. Pretty soon someone else'll be along anyway.' She tossed something out of the compartment, a brown bottle. Quillon caught it – more by luck than judgement – and surveyed the sepia-coloured label and the pale pills the cork-stoppered bottle contained. 'Something we can use?'

'I don't know.' The label was written in a fussy, antique script with lots of capitals and exclamation marks.

'Tell me later.' Meroka grunted. Then: 'Hey.'

'Hey what?'

'Pa's got himself quite a firearm here. Still has a good grip on it.'

'Rigor mortis,' Quillon said, 'suggesting that these people have been dead at least three hours.'

Meroka's hand emerged clutching a heavy black weapon with a wooden stock and multiple barrels. 'Volley-gun. Always wanted to get my hands on one of these. Friend of mine had one once, but—'

'Is it something special?'

'Impractical, but pretty good for scaring the living crap out of people. Kicks like a mule, too, 'specially if you fire all the barrels at once. You don't so much aim as choose a hemisphere.' She worked a catch and folded down part of the weapon. 'Breech loader, with separate hammers on each barrel, able to be fired individually or all at once. Good to go, as well. Got off a couple of shots, but the rest of the rounds are still chambered. Now why would anyone walk around with one of these half-loaded?'

'I'm presuming that's a rhetorical question?'

'You either keep the thing loaded, all barrels, or you keep it empty, 'cause you don't trust it not to go off.'

'Meaning they used it,' Quillon said. 'Presumably against the people who shot those men in the forehead. But where did they go?' A worm of anxiety was beginning to uncoil in his stomach. 'Three hours isn't that long.'

'I don't think it happened the way you're thinking,' Meroka said.

'It wasn't an accident.'

'Could have been an accident made the carriage crash over – the drivers blacked out or something – then someone found them afterwards and decided to do some shooting and looting. These people stuck in here, they probably survived the crash. Don't see no broken bones or

110

nothing. But they'd have been suffering from the zone shift just the same as us.'

'They'd have taken some kind of antizonals.' Quillon looked dubiously at the bottle he was still holding. 'But whatever it was it only bought them time, not the ability to function in this zone as if nothing had happened. Even if they managed to stave off unconsciousness, and somehow avoided going into seizure the way you did, they'd have been in a very poor way. No hope of getting very far from the carriage, which is probably why they stayed inside, hoping someone was going to come along and help them. Eventually zone sickness would have overwhelmed them.'

Meroka climbed out, carrying a haul of looted goods. A part of Quillon still felt what they were doing was wrong, but he didn't doubt that Meroka had their best interests at heart. Even the watches she had taken – he could see them glittering in her hand, the straps around her fingers – were for strictly utilitarian purposes. There was an old Spearpoint saying: you can never have too many watches. She had taken some clothes – gloves, a scarf, some kind of fur hat – and a small linen bag. 'Some more pills and potions for you,' she said, slinging the bag in his direction.

'If they were coming this way,' Quillon said, the bag landing at his feet like a shot carcass, 'they'd have been bound to meet the Skullboys. Maybe they were the ones who killed the drivers.'

'Skullboys aren't that good a shot. Anyway, they didn't have to meet 'em.' She lowered herself down from the coach. 'That meeting place, it's not far if you're in one of these steam-coaches. The Skullboys could have passed right through on the main track before these people joined it from the other road. Never had to set eyes on each other.'

Quillon gathered up the bag, glass and porcelain receptacles chinking around inside it. 'Maybe we ought to be moving on?'

'No argument from me. Just wanted to see what we could salvage.'

'We can't bury these poor people, can we.' A statement this time, not a question.

Meroka shook her head. 'Same deal as for the horses. You check those other two?'

'Give me a moment.'

'See if one of them has some bullets.'

He returned to the bodies and explored their coat pockets and wrists, taking a pair of heavy company watches from each man, as well as a cased timepiece from each man's coat pocket. The watches and timepieces were all wound and ticking, with their multiple dials showing different times.

'You want me to take their coats as well?' he asked, fearing the answer she was likely to give.

'Just the clockwork, and anything that shoots or cuts.'

The men were carrying no guns or knives, but one of them did have a heavy holster strapped to his leg. The holster was empty now, and Quillon fancied that it would have been about the right size to take the volley-gun Meroka was now sporting. Perhaps the traveller had crawled out of the overturned carriage, retrieved the company-issued weapon and returned to the rest of his family, hoping to hold out long enough for help to arrive, or for the zone to snap back to its former state. He opened the man's coat and found a single bandolier reaching from shoulder to hip, with several rounds still in it. He unbuckled the bandolier, reckoning that the man in the coach must not have had time to look for it.

'I found some bullets,' he called.

'Good,' Meroka replied. 'I just found something I hoped I wouldn't.'

She reached down and scooped up an object from the ground, something that must have been there all along, unnoticed until now. At first glance Quillon thought it was a weirdly knotted stick or an animal bone, still with ropes and wires of sinew attached.

But when he caught the evil glint of metal, he knew it was neither of those things.

'Vorgs were here,' Meroka said. 'One of 'em, anyway. Left us a little present.'

It was a limb, a silver-grey mechanical arm, but more like the forelimb of a wolf or dog than a human arm. It had been wrenched away from the main body at the shoulder. It was jointed halfway along and at the wrist, and beyond the wrist end was a small, simplified hand or paw – three clawed fingers and an opposed thumb, with curved nails or claws gleaming cobalt blue, as if they were made from some harder, sharper metal than the rest of it. The skeletal bones and articulation points were elegantly slender and ingeniously compact, as if they had evolved under viciously stringent selection pressures. But there was more to it than just sleek machinery. There was a nervous system attached to the arm, or the remains of one: the sinews Quillon had already noticed. There was something like musculature. These organic parts were slimy and haphazardly organised, coloured a liverish purple. It looked as if a robot had dipped its arm into the waste vat at an abattoir, ruining its steely perfection with a coating of random gobbets of meat and gristle.

But metal and meat and gristle, Quillon now knew, was what the carnivorgs were.

'Maybe there was just one,' Meroka said, holding the arm at the shoulder joint, turning it this way and that with open revulsion. 'Broke away from the other vorgs, maybe. Some of 'em are outcasts, but they still trail the main packs, looking for scraps and easy pickings.'

'What happened to it?'

'Maybe the guy in the carriage got a good shot. Maybe the vorg was already injured, or it knew it had to skedaddle before the others got here.'

'You said they might be behind us,' Quillon said. 'That's why we've been walking this way. You never said anything about running into them ahead of us.'

'We haven't. We've only found a part of one.'

'Meaning they were here.'

'One of 'em. But it could be leagues away by now, or lying dead in a ditch somewhere.' She cast away the severed arm. 'Not our problem now. But we shouldn't hang around here.'

'I still don't understand. We know there was a carnivorg here, but we still don't know who shot the drivers.'

'Nobody did.'

'You haven't even looked at the wounds.'

'Don't have to. Soon as I found that a vorg had been sniffing around here, it all made sense. There *was* an accident. The steam-coach crashed and the men hit the ground. They were probably already dead by then, and definitely dead by the time the vorg got to them.'

'What do you mean, "got to them"?'

'Those holes you saw, they weren't made by bullets. That was where the vorg drilled into their skulls. That was where it got to their brains and took what it wanted.' Meroka tapped a finger against her own forehead. 'Good prefrontal lobe tissue, the kind they like best. Rich in synaptic structure, all ready to be sucked out and wired into the vorg's own nervous system.'

'Are you telling me it ate their brains?'

'What they do. How they survive, on the border where smart machines stop working. They could culture their own tissue, I guess ... but vorgs aren't that smart any more, and anyway, this is quicker, easier. Meat machines.' She stopped and looked at him with narrowed, judgemental eyes. 'You know, for a pathologist, or whatever it was they used to call your line of work, you're kind of squeamish around dead things.'

Quillon gave her a tight smile, trying to fight the bile climbing up his throat. 'That was the part of the job I never liked.'

*

It was nearly dark when they made out another fire – not just smoke, now, but actual flames, flickering orange and crimson amongst a complication of solid dark shapes directly ahead of them, on the road itself. Black smoke pushed into the oppressively low ceiling of the sky.

'This isn't good,' Meroka said.

'Has anything been good since we left Spearpoint?'

'Don't get clever with me, dickhead. I mean someone's been ambushed. For real this time.' Meroka was just as rattled as he was, even if she wouldn't admit it to his face. She had the volley-gun in her hands at all times, preferring it to any of her own weapons. Now and then, even as she kept on walking, she would flinch and aim the sheath of clustered black barrels at some crouching spectre only she could see. 'This is how Skullboys operate, when they don't get what they want. Slash and burn.'

'So perhaps we should consider giving this disaster a wide berth,' Quillon said.

But Meroka wanted to get closer. She wouldn't say why, but Quillon guessed for himself. She was thinking that whoever had been ambushed, whoever had been caught and set alight, might well be the same people who were meant to take Quillon away. She had to know, because if that was the case they were going to need to change plans.

They came closer to the fire. They could hear it now – the occasional dull thump as something exploded, the splinter and crash of something collapsing. Human voices occasionally pushing through the crackle and roar of the flames.

Frightened voices. Cries and screams of anguish and fear.

An icy terror, a premonition of something unspeakably wrong, settled over Quillon like a lowering shroud. 'Maybe this is as far as we should go.'

'We have to know what happened. You want to stay here, take your chances with whatever's waiting out there, it's your funeral.' Meroka pushed the volley-gun ahead of her like a battering ram. 'Me, I'd stick with the one who has the most barrels.'

'Whatever's happening here, it isn't our problem.'

'Everything's our problem now, Cutter.' She shot him a challenging look, as if everything rested on this one decision. 'You coming or staying?'

He followed her, even made an effort to walk by her side, but the fear was still there. He gripped the angel gun, comforted by it even though he had no idea whether it was still capable of firing.

'Try not to shoot at the first thing that moves,' she cautioned. 'Might turn out to be a friend of mine.'

Gradually his eyes began to resolve the dark, burning forms into individual shapes. It wasn't just one thing on fire, it was a whole collection of things, strewn across the road and on either side of it, stretching far into the distance. They approached a black hump in the road, like a half-buried boulder, which turned out to be a dead horse, still armoured. Meroka kicked at the dead animal's intricately fashioned carapace.

'Skullboy,' she said.

'They did this?'

'This used to be them. Weren't you paying attention back there?'

He realised now that the dead horse was wearing the same armour they had seen when the Skullboy caravan passed them by, half a lifetime ago, before the storm.

'Someone got them.'

'Give the man a gold star for observation.'

They came upon a dismounted rider a little further on, perhaps the same one who had been on the dead horse. The man was dead, his half-skull helmet lying by his side, but there was no sign that a carnivorg had tried sucking his brains out. He had, however, been gashed across the throat with something sharp.

'Can't say they didn't have it coming,' Meroka said, kicking the man with her boot before walking on.

'Have we seen enough? It's the Skullboys. What more do we need to know?'

'I'm hoping we might find something we can use. One of those machines, or a horse that hasn't died.'

The flames were warm on Quillon's face now. Ahead was another fallen rider – this one trapped under his horse. This man was still alive, whimpering as they approached, his legs buckled and crushed beneath the massive bulk of his charge. Meroka went straight up to him and put a heel on his chest-plate, pushing down as if she meant to squeeze the last gasp of breath from his lungs.

'Not looking so fucking fierce now, are you?' he heard her say, addressing the man in a low, confidential tone, as if the two of them were friends at a dinner party. 'You're dying, you piece of shit. Shrivelling up like a day-old turd. Hope it's hurting good. Bet you always wondered how being crushed under a dead horse would feel.'

'Meroka,' Quillon said, coming to her side. 'This isn't necessary.'

'It's very fucking necessary. Trust me on this, Cutter: I've seen what these bastards do to people.'

'Two wrongs ...' he started saying, then shook his head, knowing exactly how Meroka would respond to that sentiment. 'At least let me examine him. He's still alive, despite the zone shift. Must have a fair degree of inherited tolerance.' The man's mouth, where it was visible through a matted thicket of beard, was lathered with blood, spittle and foam. He had stopped whimpering, looking at them with fiercely defiant eyes.

'I told you they have drugs,' Meroka said, refusing to budge her foot.

'Let me look at him. He's going to die anyway. You don't need to help him on his way.'

She grunted something, but removed her heel. Quillon put down the angel gun so that he could use both hands to open his medical kit.

'Do you understand me?' he asked.

'He understands you. Just won't admit to it.'

Quillon shrugged – he had no reason to doubt her. 'I don't know if you have any idea what's happened. There's been a zone storm. Worse than anything in recent experience. Spearpoint ... well, you can't have missed that.'

'Spearpointer,' the trapped rider said, and then, despite his evident discomfort, managed to spit in Quillon's face. Quillon wiped away the pink-tinged foam. 'Fuck you, Spearpointer. Die like rest of us. Soon.'

The man spat again, but this time it was weaker and his aim less effective. The spit splashed back onto his beard, lying there like a slug trail. The man groaned, unable to hide his pain.

'How long do you think he's been lying here?' Quillon asked.

'Long enough,' she said, touching the fallen horse. 'It's cold. Couple hours at least, with him under it.'

'You're going to die,' Quillon told the man. 'Even if you didn't have zone sickness, that horse has almost certainly been on you for too long. It's cut off your circulation. Toxins have accumulated in your blood, trapped in your legs. If I were to release the pressure on you, those toxins would be released, and you'd die.'

The man wheezed and made a kind of death-mask smile. 'You too.'

'Yes, you were saying. The thing is, I can take some of your pain away.' Quillon could barely drag his eyes off the dying Skullboy, so his hands had to dig through the medical kit unassisted.

'Don't you go giving him no precious medicines,' Meroka said.

'I'll give him what I see fit.' He found a vial of granulated Morphax-55, recognising it by its shape. 'Open your mouth,' he told the man.

The Skullboy widened his lips, revealing a cave entrance of sharpened and metal-capped teeth, through which emerged a hellish, kitchen-waste stench of rotting meat and vegetables. His tongue had been split into two, the double-pronged end probing between his teeth.

'I'm going to put this under your tongue,' he said. 'There'll be no pain. Will you let me do that?'

'Making a big mistake,' Meroka said.

The Skullboy lifted his tongue, inviting Quillon to administer the Morphax-55. He thought of just tipping the bottle in and hoping for the best, but that was wasteful and would risk contaminating the bottle itself. Instead he cupped his left hand and poured out what he judged to be a sufficient number of pills. He would take away the Skullboy's pain, both from the horse and the zone sickness, and ease his passing, and feel that he had done some small measure of good, however insig-nificant the act was when set against the unthinkable misery playing out around him. Using the fingers of his right hand, he pinched at the pills with his thumb and forefinger until he had about half of them, as many as he could carry in one go, and transferred that quantity to the Skullboy's mouth. The tongue was still elevated, flexing and questing in a vile way, but permitting him to deposit the pills. Then he went back for the rest, and was placing them when the Skullboy clamped down his teeth hard on Quillon's fingers, the agony instant and exquisite, sharpened teeth and edged metal cutting flesh to the bone, crunching into the bone itself, threatening to sever his thumb and forefinger. Quillon let out a yelp of surprise and pain. With his right hand still trapped in the Skullboy's mouth, he snatched at the angel gun with his left. He jammed the barrel against the Skullboy's forehead and jerked the trigger. Nothing happened, so he tried again, with the Skullboy still biting down on his fingers. But the gun was dead. In a berserk fury he grabbed hold of the barrel instead and started hammering the grip against the Skullboy's head, grunting with pain and exertion, knowing nothing but fury and the need to murder another human being. The gun cracked against bone, and on the fifth or sixth swing he felt some-thing give way under the skin, the skull beginning to fracture, and at that same moment there was a bang, concussive and vast as if the world itself had just cracked open, and the Skullboy's mouth turned slack. Quillon staggered away, blood already welling up from the wounds in his fingers, dropping the angel gun, barely able to look at what Meroka had to done to the Skullboy's head.

He saw enough. Meroka had emptied several barrels of the volley-gun in one go, at practically point-black range. Little remained of the

117

Skullboy's head except for his jaw. Brain and bone sprayed away on either side, plastered onto the road in the shape of an obscene, pinkish-grey butterfly.

'Could've told you that was going to end in tears,' Meroka said.

CHAPTER NINE

Quillon dug into his medical kit with his good hand until he found a bottle of disinfectant. He passed it to Meroka. 'Open this for me.'

'Please.'

'Just open the damned ... thing.'

'Hey,' she said, sounding impressed. 'The doctor has his limits after all.' She unscrewed the cap, extracted the wadding from the top and passed the bottle back to Quillon. Without preamble he splashed it over his fingers, the blood still gushing from the wounds, the sting of the disinfectant like liquid fire where it touched.

'Damn,' Quillon said, but this time in response to the pain, not his irritation with Meroka. He poured more, and this time almost passed out as the antiseptic fluid penetrated the wounds, sinking its own chemical teeth into his flesh.

'You need someone to stitch those cuts?' Meroka asked.

'No.' He forced authority into his voice, even though he was almost weeping. 'Cut a length off those bandages. At the bottom of the case. *Please.*'

To her credit she was fast and efficient, shouldering the volley-gun while she worked, scissoring off a strip of bandage, cutting the strip into two and helping him wrap one strip around his thumb and the other around the index and forefinger, so that he could still retain some use of his hand.

'Pins in the upper compartment,' Quillon said.

Meroka secured the bandages, and then did something Quillon hadn't been expecting, which was to pat him on the shoulder, almost maternally. 'Sorry for the lecture. Guess it was surplus to requirements.'

'Somewhat.'

'You going to be all right?'

'Given our circumstances, I suspect I'll be doing very well if it's this wound that kills me.'

'Still need to keep an eye on it – fuckers've been known to keep dead meat lodged 'twixt their teeth, turning rotten, just so's they can poison people when they bite.'

'Information that, strangely enough, you neglected to mention earlier.'

'You're the doctor. Guess I just assumed you knew what you were doing.' She dug into her coat and produced a small pistol. 'Take this. I think you've about exhausted the possibilities with the angel gun, unless you're planning to shove it down someone's throat and choke them with it.'

Quillon took the pistol awkwardly with his bandaged hand.

'Thanks,' he said.

They walked on.

Meroka reloaded the volley-gun as she strolled, one of the burning wagons looming ahead, its wooden and fabric skin all but consumed, leaving only a sagging metal frame that was itself beginning to succumb to the fire. The frame, Quillon realised, was one of the cages they had seen when the caravan passed. The blazing heat from the other wagons was now almost unbearable, but he held his bandaged hand up to shield his face, gun pocketed so that he could carry his bag, and advanced as close as he dared. Meroka was only a little way ahead, shielding her own face with one hand and holding the volley-gun in the other.

'They got out,' she called, above the roar and hiss of the fire. 'Door's open.'

'You think someone let them leave?'

'Could be, if there was anyone around who wasn't already blacking out.'

'Someone other than the Skullboys, you mean?'

'Yeah. Or they all just broke out. Amazing what you'll do when burning to death is a real possibility.'

Quillon nodded, although – having seen how secure the cages looked – he doubted that any amount of adrenalin-fuelled strength would have made enough of a difference to the captives. It was much more likely they had been freed by bystanders, locals with a grudge against the Skullboys.

'I hope all of them got out.'

Meroka walked on a little further, pushing the volley-gun's barrel ahead of her, then said, 'These two certainly didn't.'

The wagon in question had come to rest in the ditch at the roadside, sufficiently far from the other vehicles that the flames had, at least until recently, managed to avoid it. Its rear wheels were now ablaze, the spokes columned in fire, tongues of flame beginning to lick along its chassis. Before very long the whole thing would be alight, the fire engulfing the cage resting on its back. For now, though, the flames had yet to reach the cage and the two people inside it were still alive.

It was the woman and child. Quillon remembered the birthmark on the back of the woman's head, and then she turned to face him. She was exactly as he remembered her from the night before: the same tattered, sleeveless dress, the same combination of thinness and hard-earned strength, the same hairless head. She was staring right at him, and the child – could have been a girl or a boy – was still at her side. He expected the woman to say something, to call out to them and ask to be freed, but instead she just kept on staring, her deep-set eyes emotionless and her strong jaw clenched in resignation, as if she had long ago reconciled herself to never leaving the cage. Even the child – a girl, Quillon decided – had a look of defiant acceptance, as if she had been studying her mother intently, learning to stare at the world with the same blazing refusal to show weakness.

'Why didn't anyone let them out?' Quillon asked, as Meroka slowed, aiming the volley-gun directly at the cage.

'I know,' Meroka said, before stopping and turning back to look at him.

'Are you going to tell me?'

Meroka raised the gun until it was pointed right at the woman. 'Turn around.'

The woman did nothing. Her expression registered only the tiniest shift, to a kind of imperious disdain.

'I said, turn the fuck around.' Meroka altered her aim slightly. 'Do it, or I put a hole through the sprat.'

The child gave no sign of being in any way alarmed by having the volley-gun pointed right at her head. Either she was too backwards or uneducated to understand the significance of the gesture, or she was heroically brave.

'Finger's getting twitchy,' Meroka said.

The woman seemed to consider, then turned slowly around so that she had her back to Quillon and his companion. He could see the birthmark much more clearly now, the woman's hairless skull bathed in flickering orange from the nearby fires.

Except it wasn't a birthmark. Or at least no birthmark Quillon had ever seen with his own eyes. It was far too regular, far too precise and geometric to be the work of nature: more like a tattoo or a brand, a mark of ownership or fealty. It was a five-pointed star, with circular dots at the tip of each point.

'She's a witch,' Meroka said. 'That's what it means.'

'There are no such things as witches,' Quillon said, but with rather less certainty than he might have wished.

'Maybe not. But there are such things as tectomancers. That's what we're looking at here.'

'Are you certain?'

'I know the score, Cutter. She's got the mark. Makes her one of them.'

Quillon didn't know what to think. Until leaving Spearpoint, he had never been required to have an opinion on the existence or otherwise of tectomancers. He knew that they were poised somewhere on the brink between myth and reality; dismissed as superstition by some, accepted as a real phenomenon – albeit frightening, rarely encountered and misunderstood – by others. On consideration he would probably have admitted to accepting their reality, while balancing that acceptance with a grave scepticism as to the actual scope and efficacy of their powers. There was simply too much scholarship to dismiss tectomancers as a fiction, something made up to frighten children and the superstitious, and yet within that scholarship their gifts had almost certainly been exaggerated, blown out of all proportion by fearful witnesses and avid retellers of second-hand experience. At no point, though, had Quillon expected to actually encounter one. Even if one accepted their reality, and that some of the powers credited to them were real, it was still a given that tectomancers were exotically rare. It was said that they were born to normal mothers, mothers who did not carry the mark of the baubled star. Just as some diseases only manifested when ill-fated parents met and produced a child – the causative factor carried silently by mother and father – so a tectomancer could be presumed to be the result of inherited influences that had lurked undetected in previous generations. But tectomancy was something other than a disease. Tectomancers might not have long life expectancies, but that wasn't because of their condition bestowing any systematic infirmity. It was because they tended to be hounded to early deaths, often involving stones or pyres. They were, in other words, regarded exactly like witches.

And he appeared to be staring at one.

'Do you believe?' he asked Meroka.

'It don't matter whether I do or don't, Cutter. What matters is what the Skullboys and the halfwit fucking inbreeds who live out here believe. And to them there's no doubt at all. She's a walking bad omen. Something you lock up in a cage and set fire to. That's why no one let her out. Too chickenshit to face the consequences of freeing her.'

The woman turned slowly back to face them. Something in the regal bearing of her posture disarmed all Quillon's assumptions – it was like watching a fashion model turn around after displaying some fabulously expensive item of high couture. She was inside the cage, but the thin woman in the ragged dress still seemed to have a subtle power beyond her confinement.

'But we're not chickenshit,' Quillon said, noticing that the fire had advanced since their arrival, now beginning to lick at the bottom of the cage. 'We can let them out. Someone has to.'

'Or we can walk on, because this isn't our problem.'

'I think it's just become our problem.'

'Like that Skullboy, the one who nearly bit your hand off back there?'

'This is different. I was wrong then, but I'm right now.'

The woman kept staring. She had said nothing yet. Perhaps she was incapable of speech, but Quillon had the feeling she was observing them, witnessing their exchange without a shred of doubt in her mind as to how events were going to run. She would speak only when it suited her, and perhaps not at all.

'Cutter, listen to me. There's a lot of superstitious horseshit surrounding tectomancers. Like how they can part waves, walk on water and heal the sick. But if only one-tenth of it's true, this is not something to be messed with lightly.'

'So it's superstitious horseshit, apart from the bit that happens to be true?'

'Don't mock me, Cutter. I've seen enough weird shit out here to know that you don't get to pick and choose what you believe in.' Meroka paused and looked to her right. A figure came stumbling out of the screen of smoke between two burning wagons, his arms reaching before him, moaning softly. It was a Skullboy, his helmet gone and his eyes gouged out, leaving only blood-clotted sockets. Snot and drool spilled from his nose and mouth. Meroka aimed the volley-gun and fired a single shot, blowing the Skullboy's right leg away below the knee. 'Maybe they can alter zones,' she went on as the figure crashed to the ground, 'maybe they can't. Way I figure it is, it don't really matter what they can and can't do. It's what people believe, what they project onto them. Just because of what people think they are, tectomancers are a magnet for all kinds of trouble we'd be better off avoiding. And that's before we deal with the powers they do have.'

She jerked the gun at something else in the smoke, squinted at whatever figment she had seen, then eased the barrel back towards the cage.

'From what little I know of the matter,' Quillon said, over the whimpering and groaning of the fallen Skullboy, 'it's not going to make much difference to the power of a tectomancer whether they're in a cage or not.'

'Meaning what?'

'Meaning that woman is no more dangerous to us freed than she is caged. Meaning we should have the courage of our convictions. We're not going to walk away from here and leave a woman and child to burn to death.'

'There are at least two other options.' Meroka hefted the volley-gun. 'This is one of them. I'm sure you can find another in that box of yours, you look hard enough.'

'Kill them?'

'Way I see it, we'd be doing them a favour.'

Quillon thrust the medical bag in Meroka's direction, not bothering to wait until she had her hand on it, the bag dropping to the ground as soon as he let go. 'I'm going to release them. If you have a problem with that, shoot me now and be done with it.'

'Can't say it isn't tempting.' Meroka watched him with slitted, venomous eyes, as if she really was only a twitch away from killing him. 'What you planning on using to bust that cage open, anyway? Sarcasm and fingernails?'

Quillon picked his spot and climbed into the wagon as far from the burning end as possible, avoiding the worst of the flames, but still singeing the palms of his hands against the fabric. He coughed and righted himself, placing a steadying hand against the side of the cage. The metal was itself beginning to warm.

'I am what she says,' the woman said, her voice commanding and calm, as if it would have been remiss of her not to confirm Meroka's fears. 'I am a witch. I have the gift of tectomancy.'

There was a hinged latch securing the door of the cage, which would have presented no difficulties were the latch not also padlocked. Meroka, Quillon realised, must already have seen the lock.

'Can you pick a lock?' he called down. 'Honest answer, Meroka.'

She grimaced, as if the answer itself caused her anguish. 'Not in the time you've got.'

'You should heed her warnings,' the woman said. 'There is a power in me beyond your understanding. Let me out, and everything changes.'

'You may believe that,' Quillon said.

'And you don't?' the woman asked, her voice almost masculine in its deepness, her searing calm beginning to unsettle him.

'If you are a tectomancer, your being caged shouldn't make any difference to your abilities.'

'Then you know something of our ways.'

'Enough to know that if I *was* a tectomancer, I'm not sure I'd be in such a hurry to convince people of that fact.' He took Meroka's pistol from his pocket, forcing his bandaged fingers around the grip and into the trigger guard, not trusting his left to aim accurately enough. 'Stand back, please – I'm going to try to shoot away this lock.'

The woman stood her ground for a moment, and then she stepped a couple of paces back – but it was more as if the child had made the decision for her, tugging on her mother's dress. In the strong outline of the girl's face he thought he could see something of the mother, the same prominent chin and broad cheekbones, although the girl did not look anywhere near as starved. He nodded and aimed the barrel at the lock, holding it only a few fingers' widths away. Was that too close, or not close enough? He had no idea. Nor had he any idea whether shooting away the padlock was even remotely feasible. He raised his free hand to shield his eyes and squeezed the trigger. When nothing happened he realised that the safety catch must still be set. He released it and aimed the pistol again.

The gun discharged and in the same instant – as near as he could judge – there was the ricocheting sound of bullet on metal. He stared down, hoping to see a shattered padlock, but instead he'd done little more than gouge the casing. He squeezed the trigger again but the gun didn't fire.

'Stand aside,' Meroka said.

He hadn't been aware of her climbing onto the wagon, but there she was, the volley-gun at the ready.

'For what it's worth,' she said, directing the barrel cluster at the padlock, 'I still think it's a bad idea.'

'She's no witch,' Quillon said. 'Delusional, maybe. But not a witch.'

The volley-gun went off. The padlock did not so much break as cease to exist, along with a good portion of the latch. Meroka flung the rusty, blackened remains aside. The cage door creaked open.

She aimed the volley-gun at the woman and child. 'That's our good deed for the day. Now get out of here.'

The woman advanced, drawing the child with her. 'You fear me,' she said, directing the statement at Meroka.

'Yeah. Kind of. But seeing as I'm the one with the big bastard gun with lots of barrels, I wouldn't push the point.'

Meroka hopped back onto the ground, still aiming the weapon at the

125

cage and its former prisoners. The woman had reached the door now. She was standing on the threshold, almost as if she was uncertain whether she really wanted to leave. Her feet were bare and dirty, as were the girl's.

The girl looked up with apprehensive eyes. 'They're here,' she said.

'What's that sound?' Quillon asked.

It was a droning noise he had not been aware of until that moment. It was coming from above, or within, the bellying canopy of fire-lit clouds.

'Skullboys,' Meroka said.

'They're in the air now?'

'They have some blimps. Don't usually operate this close to Spear-point, but I guess everything's changed now. We really don't want to be hanging around here much longer.'

'The storm came,' the mother said, looking into Quillon's eyes now.

'Yes.' His mouth was suddenly quite dry, more than could be explained by the heat of the fires. 'It was a bad one. A major tectomorphic shift. The people who took you prisoner fell ill because of it. Do you feel unwell yourself?'

'Do I seem ill to you?'

'I'm a doctor. I have drugs – medicines – that can help you and your ... I presume she's your daughter?'

'We have no need of your medicine.' She spoke clearly enough, but Spearpointish was evidently not her native language.

'Your zone tolerance must be unusually strong,' Quillon said.

'Your city wisdom means nothing to me. I am strong because of what I am.'

'Yes. A witch. Well, we'll let that pass for now. All I'm saying is, if there's anything you need ...' He paused awkwardly, conscious of Meroka chewing on something impatiently, waiting for the least excuse to fire the remaining barrels of the volley-gun.

'Need to be on our way, Cutter.'

'You have done what had to be done,' the woman said. She stepped down from the wagon, then lifted her daughter down after her, the muscles in her arms turning firm as steel cables as she took the girl's weight. 'You showed courage. You have our gratitude. Now put us from your thoughts.'

'We can't just leave you, not with everything that's been happening.'

'We can give it a shot,' Meroka said.

'Your friend spoke the truth,' the woman said, eyeing Meroka with haughty derision. 'I bring ill-fortune. That is why we travel alone. That is why you will never see us again.'

'Ignore Meroka. You say you feel no ill-effects of the storm, but there could still be hidden dangers working their way to the surface. No one alive has lived through a storm like this, and please don't tell me you're any different. At the very least let me examine your daughter.'

'We haven't got time for this,' Meroka said.

'Then we'll move. The four of us can travel together.'

'No,' the woman said. 'We travel alone. But your friend is right. You must leave now.'

She had turned her head away from him, allowing him a better look at the pattern on the back of her skull. The skin was reddened where it formed the bauble-tipped star.

'Let me see that,' Quillon said. Something in his tone of voice must have worked, because the woman did not pull away as he reached up and touched the back of her head, gently tracing the border of the pattern.

'You know the sign of a tectomancer,' the woman said.

'Yes,' he said, for the sake of argument. 'But this isn't it. It's . . . I don't know. Some kind of badly done tattoo, or a superficial burn or chemical injury. Probably a tattoo. I can see puncture scars where she's been pricked with a needle, to get the ink into her skin. It's not due to pigmentation.'

'What are you saying?' Meroka asked.

'I'm saying this is faked,' he said. 'Someone's made this woman look like a witch. Someone shaved her hair and made this mark on her skin, so she looks like a tectomancer.'

'You know nothing,' the woman said. 'The mark of a tectomancer waxes and wanes with the seasons.'

Quillon took hold of the woman's wrist. It was like holding a hawser, something taut and dangerous when under tension. 'Someone did this to you,' he said urgently. 'Maybe it was the Skullboys, trying to make you into something you weren't, so they could sell you on to the next bunch of superstitious fools they chanced upon. But it isn't real. No matter what you've been told, no matter what you've been made to believe, you *aren't* a witch. You're a woman, a mother. A woman with unusual zone tolerance, yes. But no witch. And we don't fear you, do we, Meroka? We only want to help.'

'If she isn't one, why is she working so damned hard to make us think she is?' Meroka said.

'I don't know,' Quillon said, letting go of the woman's wrist.

'Maybe she's just bugfuck.'

'How sane do you think you'd be if you'd been captured by Skullboys, branded to look like a witch, locked in a cage, all the while knowing that you were probably going to be burned alive? Throw in a few psychoactive drugs, some suggestion, and I think that could easily push someone over the edge.'

'You say so, Cutter. Me, I think we'd be doing well if we all said goodbye now and went our separate ways.'

'Your friend is wise,' the woman said, nodding gravely. 'You should do as she says.'

'If I did as she said, you'd still be in that cage.'

'Can't argue with that,' Meroka said darkly, looking around anxiously.

'At least let me examine the girl,' Quillon said again. 'But not here. If we walk a while and find somewhere to stop, I can perform some simple tests.'

'In the dark?' Meroka asked.

'Then we wait until daylight.' He turned back to the woman. 'Neither of you have shoes. Can you walk? I'm afraid we lost our horses last night.'

He sensed the woman reviewing the possibilities open to her, her mind swarming with calculations. As deluded as she might be – and he had not quite made up his mind about that – there was an undeniable intelligence about her, an electric emanation that made his skin prickle. Her eyes were shockingly alert and sharp, her focus disarmingly penetrating.

He wondered if she saw him for what he truly was.

'We will walk with you,' she said. 'You may make your examination, if it pleases you. Then we will leave.'

'My name is Quillon. I'm a doctor from the city. Meroka is ...' He paused, searching for the words. 'My guide. She knows her way around the Outzone. We were heading along this road, hoping to meet some friends of hers who might be able to help me reach Fortune's Landing.'

The woman looked at Quillon with dwindling interest. 'You have travelled from the Godscraper?'

'Yes.'

'I hope you said your farewells. Your city is dead.' Then she paused and added: 'I am Kalis. My daughter is Nimcha. That's all you need to know.'

Then she started walking, the girl at her side, picking a path through the rutted verge, away from the burning procession.

'Charming conversationalist,' Meroka said, walking alongside Quillon, far enough behind the woman and girl that it was unlikely they would be overheard. 'Real easy-going manner.'

'You can talk.'

'With me it's neurological.'

'For all we know it's neurological with her. Perhaps she just needs time to decide if she can trust us or not.'

'You just rescued her, Cutter. What more does she want?'

'I would think it self-evident. She's placed her trust in people before, and it's cost her dearly. Shouldn't we give her the benefit of the doubt, until she's had time to recognise that we don't mean her any harm?'

'We talking weeks or months here?'

'In the morning, if she's still with us, I'll examine the child. And the mother too, if she'll let me. If they need drugs, I'll do what I can. Then they can go their own way.'

Meroka shook her head. 'This is another one of those things that isn't going to end well.'

It was all very good being doctorly, insisting on looking after the woman and her child, but if he didn't rest he would be exhausted beyond measure by dawn. Certainly, he would be in no fit state to conduct an examination for the subtle indicators of latent zone sickness. There were preparations in his bag that could give him a few hours of chemically stimulated alertness, but even under normal circumstances he would pay for it afterwards. Given that he was also taking antizonals, the combination of drugs could easily prove fatal. He would just have to manage on his own reserves of endurance.

Meroka, by contrast, did not seem tired at all. She was in her element now, doing the thing she did best of all, which was survival. And, perhaps, a little retribution on the side. He watched as she spotted a Skullboy lying on the ground near one of the powered vehicles, now furiously alight. She left the verge and started walking towards him. The Skullboy had been still until her approach, but as she neared he began to claw at the road, attempting to haul himself away even though his legs trailed uselessly behind him, crushed or paralysed. From the rear, Quillon saw Meroka's coat flap open as she dug into her personal armoury. Something glinted in her hand. He heard a short, sharp crack and the Skullboy jerked once and then lay perfectly still. Meroka walked back, returning whatever weapon she had just used to the sanctuary of her coat.

'You still think she's a fake?' she asked nonchalantly, as if she had just stepped aside to dispose of a cigarette. 'There's still something screwed-up about her, that's for sure. Makes me nervous having her around.'

'You should see the effect you have on people.'

'Don't tell me you haven't felt it.'

'All right – there's something unnerving about her. I'm not saying she's normal, or that there isn't something a little strange going on in her head. But I've yet to see any objective evidence that she has superhuman powers.'

'The girl creeps me out as well. You seen the way she stares?'

'Like her mother, she's been through a lot.'

'She's fucked up,' Meroka said.

Quillon shrugged. 'Then we'll all get along famously.'

They reached the head of the burning procession. Ahead lay darkness and the open road, arrowing onwards into the coming night. Kalis and Nimcha walked confidently ahead, seeming to feel neither the coldness of the air nor the hardness of the worn and rutted ground under their feet. They were walking in the middle of the road, two ragged figures the colour of ash, the baubled star vivid on the back of the woman's head, the girl's filth-matted hair blowing sideways as the wind picked up. Overhead, the clouds began to curdle and race, vaults of star-dappled sky opening up between their harried edges. The droning sound hadn't gone away. Now it was harsher, like a bone saw.

Kalis halted. Nimcha stood perfectly still by her side, the two of them waiting like stone sentinels in the road. Instinctively Quillon slowed his own pace, wondering what was ahead.

'They've seen something,' Meroka said. 'Hand me that pistol again, Cutter.'

'Why?'

'Might be an idea to reload it.'

He reached into his pocket and passed her the weapon. 'Why don't you keep it? I can't shoot very well with my left hand anyway.'

'You'll do your best. We run into vorgs, I don't want to be the one doing all the work. Hold this.' Meroka passed him the volley-gun while she attended to the pistol, loading it as quickly and effortlessly as if she had been doing it since birth. While she was reloading they walked on slowly, the crunch of each footstep painfully loud, until they had almost caught up with the woman and girl. They were both still staring further down the road.

Meroka was about to pass the pistol back to Quillon when a hoarse voice bellowed out from the darkness on the left side of the road.

'Hello! Hello, hello, hello! Got us some fellow travellers!' The voice paused to laugh at itself. 'Nice night for it, too! Why don't you folks stop there for a moment, so we can all get acquainted?'

It was a Skullboy. He stepped out of the gloom, pointing a long rifle or musket at Quillon and Meroka. He was heavily armoured, the covering made from plates of metal and scavenged composites, with bones nailed on the outside to form ribs and spikes. His helmet was metal, covering most of his face and with sides that flared down to his shoulders, the effect enhanced by various bits of skull and bone fixed onto the metal, forming grotesquely enlarged eye sockets through which his own eyes were only dimly visible. He wore a plated skirt that extended down to his knees, with spike-augmented boots on his feet.

Meroka raised the pistol, and for an instant Quillon thought she was going to fire. Then she lowered it: not because she had decided the Skullboy posed no threat, but because he had not come alone. Emerging from the same gloom were at least five others, all carrying weapons of similar fierceness.

'We're screwed,' she said quietly, with all the sense of occasion as if she had just drawn a bad hand in a low-stakes card game. Quillon was still holding the volley-gun, the only thing that might have saved them, and he didn't have the faintest idea what he should do with it. Meroka was stuck with the pistol, unable to draw anything more substantial.

'We mean you no harm,' Quillon said, trying to keep the quaver out of his voice.

That made the Skullboy laugh, which was not the effect he had intended. The Skullboy turned around to address his companions. 'Man means us no harm, boys! Ain't that a relief! And there we were, shitting ourselves with consternation!'

The other Skullboys – none of them dressed quite alike, yet all obviously belonging to the same faction – found this uproarious. They were not all men, either. He heard the mad cackle of a woman, sounding as if her mind was already broken beyond repair.

'We're just passing through,' Quillon said. 'That's all. Let us go, and you'll hear no more of us.'

'Just passing through?' the Skullboy asked, as if the question was reasonable and sincerely meant.

'We were caught by the storm. We lost our horses and now we're just trying to get to safety.'

'Lost your poor little horses? All four of you? Including the two of you in rags?'

Meroka said nothing. Quillon couldn't tell if she was simply shocked

into silence, or had decided there was nothing to be gained by nego-
tiating with these thugs.

'They're friends of ours,' Quillon said.

'Friends you decided to let out of their cage, by any chance? We heard
about them, see. Was on our way to collect them from these other
friends of ours when the storm changed things around.' The Skullboy
touched a hand to the jaw-piece of his helmet, the carved yellow spikes
of his teeth moving behind the mouth-slit. 'Unless, of course, that wasn't
your doing?'

'She isn't a witch,' Quillon said, his heart beginning to race.

'That's an area of expertise for you, is it?'

'She's a fake. That mark on her head wouldn't fool a child, let alone
an adult.'

'So we got ourselves an authority,' the Skullboy said. He was up in
Quillon's face now, seemingly unconcerned by the volley-gun. His breath
was an open sewer. He jabbed the barrel of his weapon against Quillon's
medical bag. 'Figuring there must be something awful precious in there,
you clutching it so tightly.'

'Medicines,' Quillon said, resignedly. 'That's all. I'm a doctor. I carry
medicines.'

'Medicines.' The man said the word mockingly, as if it implied a world
of lily-livered scholarship he wanted no part of. 'Now ain't that a wonder,
boys? Especially as we might know some people who could use some
medicines.'

'You don't seem to be doing too badly,' Quillon said.

'Well, we've found ourselves a temporary supply. But it's not something we can count on for ever.'

'What's in that bag won't last for ever either.'

'No, but it'll tide us over.'

'You're making a mistake, dickhead,' Meroka said, speaking at last. 'A
bad one.'

One of the other Skullboys – Quillon fancied it was the woman he
had already heard laugh, though it was difficult to tell under all that
armour – strode over to Meroka. 'Maybe you should shut your trap,
before it gets you into trouble.'

'I'd say trouble's already here and taking off its boots, wouldn't
you?'

The Skullboy slapped her hard across the face, then tore the still-
loaded pistol from her hand, flipped it around and pushed the barrel
against her forehead, pressing it into the skin like a leather punch.

Meroka didn't flinch back. If anything she leaned in to the pressure.

'Don't shoot her,' the leader said. 'You'll only stir up her brains. You know they don't like that.'

The other one made a clicking sound and withdrew the pistol. The barrel left a circular indentation in Meroka's forehead.

'They?' Quillon asked, although he suspected he already knew the answer.

The leader ripped the volley-gun out of Quillon's grip, then stared down at his prize. 'You could have shot us,' he said, with something close to wonder. 'Nasty thing like that, we'd have stood no chance.'

'I didn't want us to get off on the wrong footing,' Quillon said.

That earned him a stab in the stomach from the man's rifle, but it was intended to hurt, not wound. The four of them – Quillon, Meroka, Kalis and Nimcha – were escorted off the road, their hands tied behind their backs with rope. No one had bothered checking Meroka's coat. It was as if they didn't care.

After a few hundred paces across rough ground, they came to a flatbed steam-truck with high slatted sides. It had the tall, spoked wheels of a traction engine. The vehicle's huge iron flywheel was turning slowly, steam hissing from valves. Two Skullboys were waiting on the high platform between the back of the squat black boiler and the front of the flatbed. It was lit up with lanterns and ready to roll.

'Load her up, boys,' said the leader. 'Time to go see our friends with the long teeth!'

One of the Skullboys hopped off the steam-truck and dropped the tailgate, forming a ramp up into the slatted, open-air compartment built onto the flatbed. The four prisoners were marshalled aboard. The first Skullboy closed the tailgate, then climbed aboard the control platform. The others split into pairs and clambered onto the running boards stretching the length of the flatbed. They grasped handholds and aimed their guns into the holding pen. The steam-truck – which seemed to lack any form of suspension – wheezed and snorted into motion, bumping and yawing across the cold, broken ground until it reached the comparatively level and smooth surface of the road. It started heading in the same direction Quillon and the others had been walking before their capture. Though they were now imprisoned, there was a dreamy sense of continuation.

'I'm sorry,' he said to Meroka. 'I should have asked you to show me how to use the volley-gun. Perhaps I might have made a difference.'

'Don't kill yourself, Cutter. Would have been touch and go even if I'd been holding it.'

He wondered if she was just being uncharacteristically kind, or merely stating the unembellished facts of their predicament.

'I still feel I should have done something.'

'Maybe it isn't me you should be talking to.'

He nodded and turned to Kalis, expecting her to be staring out into the black distance, detached from reality. He started under the pressure of her gaze.

'It will be all right,' she said.

The girl – Nimcha – was listening, of course. She had said nothing, but that didn't mean she was incapable of understanding. Kalis was just doing what any mother would have done under the same circumstances, which was to buffer her child from the full, lacerating bore of the truth. It was not going to be all right, by any measure. But what good would it do Nimcha to know this now?

'Perhaps I should have left you in the cage,' he said. 'Not to die, but for someone else to rescue you. Then you wouldn't be in this mess.'

'You did what you had to do. It was for the best.'

'This is for the best?'

'It will be all right,' she said, with savage self-assurance. 'Do not think to fight these men. You cannot beat them.'

'Do you know where they're taking us?' he asked.

'Yes,' Kalis said. 'I know. And it will still be all right.'

So she is insane after all, he thought. Even now, with the threat of death closing in on them, she still clung to her delusion. He began to wonder if the mark on Kalis's head was of her own doing, part of the web of self-deceit she had spun around herself. She was truly, tragically deranged, in that case. Under better circumstances he would have been sorry for her, and even sorrier for her daughter, who had to labour under her mother's warped view of the world.

The steam-truck swerved off the road, the ride becoming bumpier again. Its lanterns swept ahead, glancing off featureless, frost-mottled terrain, only the occasional rock or boulder serving to give a sense of scale. The driver might have been steering a random course, were it not for the visible marks in the ground, wheel ruts criss-crossing each other, showing that the steam-truck had come this way more than once.

They had gone perhaps a league at little more than walking pace when the driver brought the snorting machine to a halt. Nothing about the location suggested anything significant, but here the confusion of earlier wheel marks curved around, turning back on themselves.

The leader stepped down from the platform and walked to the rear of the flatbed. He kept glancing over his shoulder at something in the distance. For all the ferocity of his mask and armour, there was something nervous about him now. Quickly he flipped down the ramp and thrust his rifle up at the prisoners.

'Surprised you didn't try shooting your way out and making a run for it, back when we cornered you.'

'Futile gestures aren't really my style,' Quillon said. 'And it would have been futile, wouldn't it?'

'Pretty much.'

'There you go then. We've saved ourselves a lot of fuss and bother for nothing.'

'You know, you being a medical man and everything – maybe you're worth more to us alive than dead.'

'Hurt my friends and you'll get nothing from me.' With Nimcha in earshot he had been careful not to talk of killing. He hoped that when death came for the girl it would be fast and painless. He didn't want her knowing what was going to happen ahead of time.

'Oh, I don't know,' the leader said. 'We can be persuasive.'

'You'd be surprised how little good that would do you.'

'Think you're strong-willed?'

'No stronger than the next man. But how much trust would you place in a doctor if you'd given him reason to hate you? The drugs in my bag all look remarkably similar, to the uneducated. Would you trust me not to reach for something that might kill you, when you think I'm going to help you?'

'Saying we're uneducated?'

'Not to put too fine a point on it, I think you're as dumb as rocks.'

'Far be it for me to agree with Cutter,' Meroka said, 'but the man's got a point there.'

'Well, it was just a thought.' The Skullboy fell silent for a moment, and then in one easy movement swung the stock of his rifle into Quillon's face. He felt it mash against his nose, breaking something. He felt his spectacles crunch as the glass in one of the lenses shattered. He fell back, staggering into the flatbed's slatted side, Meroka making an effort to arrest his fall, but uselessly so with her hands tied, Quillon slumped to the ground, the pain arriving belatedly in his skull, all lit up and electric like a late-running commuter train.

'They're here,' one of the other Skullboys said.

Meroka, Kalis and Nimcha were herded out of the steam-truck. Quillon watched them through a gauze of pain. Their hands were untied, then Quillon's. At gunpoint, Meroka was made to remove her backpack and coat. The leader spread the coat open on the ground, beaming at the vicious delights it held. Someone grabbed Quillon's coat by the collar and hauled him roughly to his feet. The ruined glasses slid from his ruined nose. He wanted to grab for them but his hands were still tied. He watched as a booted foot pulverised them to mangled metal and brilliant blue shards.

'You too, city boy.'

Quillon was too stunned to speak, even if he'd had something to say. Blood drooled from his nose into his mouth. All he could do was submit to the men with guns and allow them to poke and prod him down the ramp, until he stood on the ground next to the other three prisoners.

'Walk,' the leader said.

There was something in the distance, picked out in furtive glimpses by the wavering lanterns. At first he thought it was a copse of silvery trees, standing alone in the emptiness. Then he realised that it was a huddle of steely figures, perhaps a dozen in all, some of them standing, some of them on the ground. For a lulling moment Quillon thought he was looking at armoured men, another party come to take them away from the young thugs with guns. Not that that would necessarily improve their situation, but at least it would delay the ultimate outcome. Yet as they covered the ground and the lantern light fell more strongly on the assembled group, he saw what he had been dreading.

They were not people. They were not human. They were not even, properly speaking, living things.

'Vorgs,' Meroka said.

CHAPTER TEN

The machines were man-sized, more or less man-shaped, with legs and arms and heads. Some of them stood erect, some of them crouched on all fours, while others sat on their haunches like trained dogs. There was indeed something canine or vulpine about them, something of the night and the wolf. Their bodies and limbs were little more than skeletal chassis, with their internal workings disgustingly visible. He recalled the severed limb Meroka had found by the crashed steam-coach, the vile melding of metal and meat: chrome-coloured joints and pistons, the liverish contamination of muscle and sinew and living nervous system, the one entwined with the other. Now he saw the creatures in their entirety and it was no better.

Organs and machines glistened under their chrome ribcages. Lunglike things, veined and wired, bellowed slowly in and out. Steel hearts pumped and whirred. There was even some kind of hideous digestive system, a tight-packed biomechanical nightmare of scarlet tubes, purple kidneys and silvery valves. The only thing protecting these delicate assemblies from damage was a thin, perforated meshwork.

It was their heads that he liked least of all. They were elongated, tapering frames, more like the skull of a horse than a man. They ended not in mouths but in a complex mechanism of drills, cutting tools and probes. They didn't seem to have living eyes, rather goggling masses of camera lenses. He could see something grey and doughy inside the framework. The carnivorgs' head-mechanisms were constantly clicking and swivelling, devices extending and retracting, as if the machines were going through some nervous autonomic anticipation, dogs drooling at the bell.

Most of them, anyway. One of the carnivorgs was already engaged in its business. It was crouched on the ground, neck stretched forwards like a dog drinking from a bowl. It was eating someone's brain, one of its head-probes sunk into the victim's skull. It was a middle-aged woman, her greying hair fanned on the ground under her head. Her body twitched as the carnivorg extracted the neural material it needed for its own functioning. Quillon hoped the woman was dead, and that the movements her body made were merely a side effect of the extraction process. But he wondered. At one time, the treatment for a certain kind of psychosis had been to push an ice pick up through the orbit of the eye, into the frontal lobe; the ice pick was then stirred around until it reduced the problematic brain tissue to non-functioning porridge. If a person could live through that, then Quillon thought it entirely likely that someone could live through the far more precise and directed extraction of tissue by a carnivorg.

Abruptly the machine withdrew its probe, rising on its rear legs, its forelimbs reaching up in an oddly endearing fashion as it cleaned the human contamination from its snout.

'Keep walking,' the Skullboy leader said, jabbing his rifle into the small of Quillon's back.

'Don't give them the girl,' Quillon said, finding the strength to speak at last. His tongue was thick, each utterance costing him pain. 'They won't miss her, will they? At least let her go, even if you give the rest of us to the machines.'

'Sorry,' the man said. 'Got ourselves an arrangement here. It's all meat to them.'

Two of the machines – including the one that had just stood up – moved to the body and hoisted it aloft, carrying her between them as if she were no more substantial than smoke. The party halted. The two machines walked to meet the waiting humans, while the other vorgs clicked and whirred their snout-mechanisms. They moved like puppets, gliding across the ground with feather-light footfalls as if they were being worked by hidden strings. Up close, they had the rank odour of a butcher's shop on a hot day, mingled with something acrid and mechanical, like an overheating axle-box.

'Vorgs/give/this/one/back,' said the vorg that had just finished dining. Its voice was crudely synthesised and atonal, no better an approximation of human speech than the buzzing drone of an artificial larynx. Together with its silent partner, the vorg knelt to place the woman on the ground. 'Vorgs/take/what/vorgs/need/now. This/one/still/good. Humans/bring/back/later. Vorgs/need/more/brain.'

Quillon's hopes crashed. She was still breathing.

'Take her, boys,' the leader said to his companions. 'But go easy; it's just a loan.'

'I see,' Quillon said, watching as two of the thugs took the woman back towards the steam-truck. 'Easier to rape her after she's been lobotomised, I suppose. Puts up less of a fight.'

'You'd be happier if the boys had their fun first?' the man asked.

No answer seemed adequate, but Quillon couldn't remain silent now. 'Why do you do this? Are you so scared of the vorgs that you have to do their work for them?'

'Nothing about being scared. It's all about *reciprocity*.' He said the last word slowly, as if he had been practising it. 'We're not friends. Just ... business partners.' He turned to face the vorg that had spoken. 'We got four subjects for you here.' Held up a hand with his fingers outstretched. 'Four. With the woman we got you last time, that brings us up to five again. Does that mean we have us a deal?'

'Vorgs/happy. Bring/first/donor. Vorgs/want/brain.'

'You can see they're alive and healthy. How about you give us a little sample of what you promised first, so we can see if it's as good as before?'

At first the vorg did not seem to understand the Skullboy. Quillon had the sense that something had stalled, some decision–action impulse blocked in the butcher-shop horror of its half-cybernetic, half-organic mind. If the vorg was in any sense intelligent, it was the opportunistic slyness of an organism that had learned to live on scraps, without ever thinking to improve its station.

Then the vorg said, 'Vorgs/make/good/drug. Vorgs/give/gift. This/one/time/only. Bring/human/for/gift.'

The leader began to undo the clasp of his helmet. 'That'll be me, boys, if none of you has any objections.'

'Vorgs/make/drug. Human/accept/gift.'

The leader tugged his helmet off. He was thick-necked, his thuggish head bald, the cranium scarred and pocked like one of the Moon's two halves. His ears were tiny and piggy. He knelt and the skeletal machine towered over him. Its snout-mechanisms swapped around, different devices clicking into position before being swivelled or retracted, as if the vorg could not quite remember what it was meant to do. At last a syringe-like needle emerged, long and gleaming. With the swiftness of a striking snake the vorg plunged the needle into the leader's neck. A pump whirred. The leader grunted and stumbled back, the needle popping free. He cuffed his hand over the puncture wound in his neck.

'Still hurts like a bitch, boys!' he declared, with a kind of wild glee at his own discomfort. 'But the fog's lifting already! Looks like we've got us a deal, vorg.'

'Give/vorgs/brain.' The machine's buzzing inflection was unchanged from before.

What was the least cruel? Quillon wondered. Let Nimcha go first and be spared the sight of the others becoming food for the carnivorgs, especially her mother? Or should he put himself forward, offering himself as a sacrifice before the machines worked their way to the girl? She would die either way, but there seemed a special evil in the adults watching the child be taken first of all.

'Get out of my way,' Meroka said, barging free of the men with guns.

'Give/vorgs/brain.' The machine-creature tracked her with its eyeless head.

'You think I'm going to give you the satisfaction of pleading or running?' Meroka said, kneeling down on the ground.

The other vorg – the one that had not been feasting when they arrived – stalked over to her. They had tails, Quillon realised for the first time – segmented counterweights, spined with the same kind of blue-metal material as their claws. The tails swished and swayed with a life of their own. It was as if the vorgs were hungry and excited, prey animals at the kill.

'Meroka,' Quillon said. 'I'm sorry it came to this.'

She looked up at him, cupping her hands around the back of her head. 'Me too, Cutter. But you don't have to apologise. It's me who fucked things up, not you.'

'It's no one's fault.' He turned to look at Kalis. 'Forgive us. It wasn't meant to end like this.'

He had expected Nimcha to be screaming in terror by this point, but the girl looked through him as if he were made of glass. Perhaps, after all, there was just as much wrong with the daughter as the mother.

Never mind, he told himself. It was hardly a problem now.

'Now, Nimcha,' Kalis said. 'Now.'

Nothing happened.

The vorg knelt down facing Meroka, still leaning over her. It reached out with its clawed forelimbs, bracing her into position like a lover about to plant a kiss. Meroka lifted her chin, a last act of defiance before the vorg did its work. Its mouthparts swivelled and clicked, the thick chromed tube of its skull-opening apparatus locking into position. The tip consisted of three intermeshing circular drills. They began to rotate as the apparatus telescoped slowly out from the head. If the other vorg had moved quickly to inject the antizonal drug into the Skullboy, this machine felt no need to hasten its work.

'Now!' Kalis said, with increasing shrillness. 'Do it, Nimcha!'

Quillon's attention flicked back to the girl. She looked confused, her eyes wide and uncomprehending.

He felt the faintest ghost of something skirl through his mind, the flutter of a moth's wing across his cerebellum.

There was a shot, then another.

The vorg keeled over, a hole punched right through its abdomen, a gory tapestry of organs and machine parts splattered on the ground behind it. The drill kept whirring, the telescoping apparatus moving in and out with neurotic repetition.

The other vorg, and the party of machines waiting in the distance, became agitated. They all sank onto their forelimbs, taut as springs, tails lashing back and forth. Their heads gyred from side to side and their mouthparts moved furiously.

The Skullboys pointed their rifles into the darkness. There was another shot and one of them dropped to the ground, screaming at the fist-sized hole that had just appeared in his shin.

Six people came out of the night. They were not Skullboys. They were uniformed, with black body armour over dark uniforms, five of them with helmets on their heads, carrying heavy machine guns slung from shoulder straps and gripped two-handed, with curving magazines and thick, perforated barrels.

The sixth member of the party was a woman, her helmet in one hand, a small service revolver in the other. She had very dark skin and was taller than most men Quillon had met. 'Take out the vorgs,' she said, her voice calm with the confidence of authority. 'Leave that one alive for Ricasso. It'll make his day.'

One of her party swung his machine gun and discharged it, blue-pink muzzle exhaust flaring out like a flamethrower. He doused the vorgs, the machines exploding apart under the impact of the bullets. Two of them sprang away, jaguaring into the darkness. The others writhed and thrashed, even as they were reduced to bloody scrap. Then the shooter selected semi-automatic fire and delivered a volley of shots into the one remaining vorg, the one that had spoken, blasting away one leg and one forearm. The vorg keeled over and pawed at the ground ineffectually, unable to achieve locomotion.

'The rest of you can surrender,' the tall woman said, before turning to examine Meroka. She had elegant, birdlike features, the whites of her eyes flashing bright in the gloom. 'You, kneeling on the ground: get up. This isn't the day you die.'

Without raising herself Meroka said, 'And who the fuck are you?'

'You imagine I owe you an introduction, after rescuing you?'

Meroka stood to her full height, fixing the woman with insolent disregard. 'If I'm being rescued, why am I being told what to do?'

The woman holstered her service revolver, evidently satisfied that her men had the situation within control. 'Because you are now under our jurisdiction. I am Captain Curtana of the rapid scout *Painted Lady*. You are now clients of Swarm.'

'What if we'd rather not be clients?'

'You are now clients of Swarm,' Curtana repeated. 'And that's a Spearpoint accent if I'm not mistaken, which puts you considerably out of your depth.' She nodded curtly at her men. 'Take them to the ship. There's no fuel to be had here.'

'And the prisoners, Captain?' one of the men asked.

'Which ones? Theirs or ours?'

'The Skulls, Captain. Do you want them executed, or brought aboard as prisoners?'

'We don't need any more ballast than we already have.'

'I'll have them shot, then.'

Curtana appeared to weigh the decision before answering. 'No, we can spare the bullets tonight. Take their weapons and anything else useful they have on them, then let them go. They'll be dead by morning anyway; we don't need to help them on their way.'

Quillon wondered what it meant to be 'clients' of Swarm, and suspected the answer was not going to be one he much cared for. The four of them were now being shepherded away from the Skullboys and the smoking, meat-spattered carnivorgs. Their hands were still bound. Two of Curtana's men lingered behind at the scene of the shooting, with Curtana and the other three escorting Quillon's party. Guns were present and visible. If they weren't exactly being marched at gunpoint, there was a definite sense that they had no option but to comply with their new hosts. They were no longer about to be fed to machines, so Quillon could not deny that their immediate prospects had improved. As to how temporary that improvement might be, he dared not venture an opinion. He knew precisely nothing of Swarm, and had no idea what it meant to be under its jurisdiction.

'Who are these people?' he whispered to Meroka, blood still seeping from his mashed nose. 'What is Swarm? I've never heard of it.'

'That's because it doesn't usually come this close to Spearpoint.'

'Until now.'

He was avoiding eye contact with her, not wanting her to see what was normally hidden behind his spectacles.

'Lot of things changed last night.'

'So it would seem. I'll ask again: what is Swarm?'

'Swarm is . . . Swarm. History ain't your strong point, is it?'

'Medicine was enough for me. What did I miss?'

'Long time back – we're talking centuries here, lot of centuries – Swarm was the military arm of Spearpoint. Kind of its eyes and hands, letting it see and reach much further than it does now. Swarm could get halfway around the world and back, bringing supplies and news. Then some shit happened – something about an expedition gone wrong – and there was a split. Bad blood ever since. We don't talk about them and they hate our fucking guts.'

'How do they treat their prisoners, exactly?'

'We don't take prisoners,' Curtana said loftily, for she must have overheard. 'We take ballast instead. It's a subtly different concept. I'm sure your companion will be happy to explain.'

'I don't think that'll be necessary.'

'Do any of you need medical attention?' Curtana said, glancing at his nose. 'We have a surgeon aboard *Painted Lady*.'

'I'll mend.'

'Your companion seems able enough, judging by her tongue. What about the mother and daughter?'

'I don't know. We haven't been travelling together for very long.'

'That wasn't my question.'

'I don't know. They were being held prisoner by Skullboys. The Skullboys were ambushed and we did what we could to rescue the two of them.'

'Do they speak?'

'Why don't you ask them?'

'Please don't try my patience, Mister . . .' She ended the sentence on a rising lilt, inviting him to continue.

'Quillon.'

'Also a citizen of Spearpoint,' Curtana observed. 'Although there's something odd about you. And you'd be?'

'Meroka.'

'What are you doing outside Spearpoint?'

'Counting my fucking blessings. What do you think?'

'Then you're not unaware of recent developments.'

'It would be hard for anyone not to have noticed,' Quillon replied. 'Not if they've an ounce of humanity. There are thirty million people suffering in Spearpoint now, dying a slow and painful death through zone sickness.'

'And it hasn't occurred to you that there might be even more people dying a slow and painful death beyond Spearpoint? Sorry, I forgot: they don't actually count, do they? They're not real people at all, since they have the misfortune not to live in your precious city.'

'Please don't put words in my mouth,' Quillon said. 'I'm against needless suffering wherever it happens. But let's not pretend this hasn't happened before. People out here are tough and adaptable: they've had to be, to get by all this time. The zone shift, as bad as it is, is just one more thing they'll eventually get used to.'

'Plus or minus a few million graves, I suppose.'

'All I'm saying is, you can't expect Spearpoint to adapt as readily. It's a delicate mechanism, like an expensive watch.'

'In other words, something that was just waiting to fall apart and stop working. Something too complicated, too fussy, too interdependent for its own good.' Curtana strode on, eating up the ground with her long legs. She wore riding pants and brown leather boots laced to the knee. She was tall and elegant and fiercely composed, the polar opposite of Meroka. 'Face it, Mister Quillon – it was a catastrophe waiting to happen. The wonder is that it didn't happen much sooner.'

'And I suppose Swarm's utterly unaffected by the zone shift?'

'Mobility and flexibility have always served us well. It's nothing we need be ashamed of.'

At that moment there was a short burst of shooting, a single concentrated volley with no return fire. Quillon slowed his pace involuntarily. The shooting had come from behind them, from the place where they had left the Skullboys in the hands of Curtana's other two officers.

It had sounded very much like an execution.

'What will happen to us?' Quillon asked. 'I'm still short on specifics when it comes to what it means to fall under Swarm jurisdiction.'

'You'll be taken back to Swarm at the earliest convenience. There, your usefulness will be assessed. We're an inclusive society – despite what you may have heard – and we believe in giving newcomers a chance to prove their worth.' Curtana's tone became stern, almost as if she was addressing children. 'But we're not gifted with limitless patience. We're well off by Outzone standards, but that doesn't mean we can afford to go throwing our resources around.' She gave Quillon a long, appraising glance, as if that was the first time she had paid real attention to him. 'You're obviously an educated man, so I've little doubt that we'll find something for you to do. Of course, you'll be accorded all the usual rights of a Spearpoint citizen, which is to say you'll be assumed to be a spy, saboteur or seditionist until proven otherwise.'

'No holding on to old grudges, then,' he said.

They walked on into the roar of the engines, until the grey shape of Curtana's ship began to emerge from the night, hovering just above the ground. Her engines were angled up, propeller blades directed to provide downward thrust to counteract the static lift from her rigid envelope. Quillon was not at all surprised to see an airship, for he had spotted enough of them during the day, even if they had never been more than distant dots foraging just above the horizon.

'Nice blimp,' Meroka said. 'You steal it from the Skullboys?'

Curtana said nothing, but Quillon sensed that she was only ever one provocation away from doing something they might all regret. He willed Meroka to keep her mouth shut.

That *Painted Lady* was a military craft would have been obvious to even a casual observer, for the airship's form was both purposeful and vicious. Her envelope was a slender cigar, spined with anti-fouling devices, barbed and bayoneted with jagged slicing edges, ramming spikes and retractile cutters. Her stiff fabric – reinforced here and there with aluminium sheeting – had been patched and repaired so many times that the vessel's scars suggested to Quillon not so much vulnerability as the stubborn resilience of a very hardy organism, something that had evolved the ability to shrug off wounds that would have ended lesser creatures.

Beneath the envelope, her single gondola was plated with angled metal sheets, lending her a chiselled, formidable look, as if she was expected to serve double-duty as an icebreaker. Her few full-sized windows were protected by armoured shutters. Elsewhere, visibility was provided by cowled slits and swivelling periscope stations. Ball turrets were stationed beneath the front of the gondola, under the belly, at either side and at the rear, each sprouting the twin pipe-entwined barrels of air-cooled rotary machine guns. Another turret poked through the envelope to afford protection from above. She had *wings*, braced out from the side of her envelope on adjustable-tension cables, the wings able to flex to provide both positive and negative lift, in much the same way that angels modified their own flying surfaces.

Her propulsion outriggers – jutting from the gondola fore and aft, with two piston engines on each side – were edged to function as blades in the event of close action, ready perhaps to slice through another vessel's envelope, wing-struts, control rigging or even crew. She was grey and blue-green metal-shades, save for a pink stencilled butterfly sprayed onto the envelope, the butterfly's faded, bullet-riddled shape already eaten into by rectangular patch repairs. She had no number or other means of identification; nothing to mark her higher allegiance to Swarm.

Two armoured and uniformed airmen were waiting on the ground, guarding the lowered ramp leading into the gondola's belly, the ramp flexing and scuffing against the ground as *Painted Lady* struggled to hold position. Curtana raised a hand and the airmen saluted back in the same fashion. 'Keep right behind me,' she told Quillon, ignoring the other three captives. 'The updraught from those engines is enough to suck you right into the blades if you step anywhere under them. Trust me, I've seen it happen. Took all week to scrape the mess off the envelope.'

The inside of the gondola, the limited part that he was allowed to see, was all unpainted utilitarian metal, engineered for maximum lightness. The interior struts were perforated; the floor a metal grid over a service trough containing various pipes and amenities. There were storage lockers, rifle, crossbow and sword racks, shelves of battle-hardened instruments, stencilled instruction panels with terse, admonitory warnings in old-fashioned, angular stencilled script about such and such a procedure and how vital it was that Action A be performed before Action B, with dire consequences for deviation. There were curtained alcoves and doored-off compartments. There were speaking tubes and periscopes and complex, optical-looking devices whose function Quillon couldn't even begin to guess at. All of this he was ushered past with maximum haste, until they reached a small, empty room at the back of the gondola, where it began to taper down to a fishtail steering vane. There was nothing in the room except two long benches, converging together at the room's narrow end, and only the narrowest slits of windows along either tapering wall. Some kind of gaslight burned in an armoured lamp, recessed into the ceiling. Their hands were untied. Meroka and Quillon took the bench on one side, Kalis and Nimcha the other.

'Your coats, please,' Curtana said. 'And that bag of yours, Mister Quillon.'

'We'll freeze,' Quillon said. The metal skin of the airship was icy to the touch.

'I'll send down warm clothes and blankets. The bag, please. Now.'

'I'll be wanting my coat back,' Meroka said, as Quillon handed over the medical bag.

'Everything you owned is now the property of Swarm, so get used to the idea. In return you'll be protected and well looked after.'

'Until you decide we're spies after all,' Quillon said, passing her the medical bag.

'We're not savages,' Curtana said. 'Many of our clients go on to become useful, productive citizens of Swarm.'

'Unlike those men you had shot back there.'

Curtana opened her mouth to speak, and for a moment he thought she was going to defend herself, pointing out that she had not ordered an execution. 'They resisted disarmament,' she said, voicing what could only have been a supposition, since she had not spoken to the other officer since ordering him to disarm and release the Skullboys. 'What you need to understand – and understand fast – is that you're not in Spearpoint now. We've always made our own law out here, and that isn't going to change any time soon.'

Curtana left, closing the door on them. It was heavy, with a small grilled window in the top half. Quillon had no doubt that this compartment was routinely used for prisoner storage. The walls might be thin enough to let in the cold, but they were likely strong enough to contain unarmed men. Not that he had the least intention of trying to escape anyway.

The airship loitered long enough for the other members of the landing party to return, and then they were aloft, the engines no longer fighting against the envelope, but providing forward momentum instead. The metal walls vibrated, the angle of the floor tilting as the craft nosed steeply into the sky.

'At least you knew about Swarm,' he said to Meroka.

'I wasn't planning on coming into range of it. Fray likes to keep track of its movements, as far as he's able. Normally it stays much further west. He'd have known if it was this close to Spearpoint before we left.' Quillon noticed that she was holding the Testament, the small black book he had leafed through in Horsetown, while Meroka was out of the room.

'What is Swarm, exactly?'

'You'll see soon enough, if that's where they're taking us.'

'At least it's a form of civilisation.'

'They aren't going to open their arms to us, Cutter. Maybe to the woman and the girl, seeing as they obviously aren't from Spearpoint. But you and me?' She paused, staring at him intently. 'You've got weird fucking eyes, anyone ever tell you that?'

Quillon turned to look at Kalis and Nimcha again. They were huddling into each other, the shaven-headed mother with her arms around the straggle-haired daughter, still barefoot, still clothed in little more than rags.

'Might I examine your daughter?' he asked Kalis.

The woman tugged the girl closer to her, flashing warning eyes at Quillon.

He raised a hand gently. 'We all know what happened back there, Kalis.'

'Do we?' Meroka asked.

'When the vorg was about to kill Meroka, you said something to Nimcha. It sounded very much like "do it" to me. I've been thinking about it ever since. What could you have been asking her to do? After all, she's just a girl. She had nothing on her she could have used. But even when you said it, I felt something.' He glanced at the grilled window, making sure they were not being observed. He doubted that eavesdropping was a possibility; the noise of the airship was much too loud for that. 'It wasn't a zone shift, or even a tremor,' Quillon continued, 'but it felt as if something was trying to happen.'

'What are you talking about?' Meroka asked, her tone insistent.

Quillon rose from his bench. He steadied himself with one hand against the perforated strut spanning the ceiling. Before she could flinch away, he stroked the other hand across Kalis's mark.

'I was right about this, wasn't I?' he asked her. 'It's self-inflicted. You made this mark yourself, or got someone to do it for you, to make people think you were the tectomancer. It's a good effort, I'll give you that, and it was obviously enough to convince the Skullboys. But it's not a true birthmark. It's a tattoo, and it wasn't done long ago.'

'You don't know anything,' Kalis said.

'And all that business since we met, that way you have of talking – the stilted, mad-woman things you keep coming out with? You're not mad at all. Or at least no madder than anyone would be if they'd been locked up, with a high likelihood of either being fed to the vorgs or burned alive. That would push anyone over the edge, if they were already insane to begin with. But you weren't. You were wise and resourceful enough to know that there was only one way to protect your daughter. You had to divert attention from her. You had to become the tectomancer, so no one would think it was Nimcha.'

'You feeling all right?' Meroka asked. 'Maybe you should have taken some of those meds, before they took that bag away.'

'I'm fine, thank you.' He smiled tightly. 'A little bruised around the edges, but otherwise in adequate command of my faculties. Might I look at Nimcha, Kalis? I promise no one else will learn of this. You've nothing to lose, since I'm already certain of the truth.'

'The truth of what?' Meroka asked.

Kalis offered no resistance when he stroked his hand through the filthy mass of Nimcha's hair, parting it just enough to see the scarlet mark showing through the skin. Meroka had left the bench and was looking over his shoulder.

'It's quite real,' he said, glancing again at the grilled window. 'This is pure pigmentation. I don't think it's tattoo, a scar or brand-mark. It could be a stain of some kind, but then it would have had to have been done when she was shaved, and yet it hasn't faded in all the time it's taken her hair to grow this long.'

'We talked about this,' Meroka said. 'Whether or not tectomancers are real, she isn't one.'

'We're talking about the daughter now.'

'It's still fake.'

'It isn't. Is it?' Quillon asked Kalis. 'You know perfectly well that it isn't. She's had this since she was born, hasn't she? And you've always known how dangerous it was, how that mark alone could get her killed, regardless of any actual power that came with it. If the rumour got around that one of you had the mark, then at least you could deflect attention onto yourself. And if Nimcha's powers really did manifest themselves, and drew attention to her, you'd be able to claim they originated with you.'

'If you speak of this,' Kalis said, 'I will kill you.'

'I'm not going to speak of it to anyone. But so far you haven't managed to keep the secret very well, have you?' Feeling he had spoken too harshly, he added, 'Look, Kalis, I can't imagine what you've gone through to protect your daughter this far. Even when you were in that cage, you didn't let anyone know that she was the one they really wanted. That must have taken all the love a mother could give.' Quillon shook his head. 'No, I won't speak of it. None of us will. Right, Meroka?'

'Nothing to speak of,' she said.

'Good,' Quillon said. 'That makes everything a lot simpler. But I'm serious, Meroka – it has to stay our little secret. They can't find out about her.'

'They?' Meroka asked.

'Curtana and the rest of her crew,' Quillon said. 'The rest of Swarm, for that matter.'

Meroka looked sceptical. 'It took you a couple of hours to figure out what she is. You think you're going to be able to keep that from them for ever?'

'We'll just have to do our best, won't we? When the surgeon comes he can't be allowed to examine the girl too closely.'

'I still don't get it,' Meroka said, looking at Kalis. 'Why couldn't you just act like a normal mother, instead of shaving your hair, marking your skin, putting on the witch act?'

'She had no choice,' Quillon said. 'Someone out there must have had a shrewd idea one of them had the power. If Nimcha caused a local zone shift, that might have been enough to draw suspicion her way. What Kalis did may seem drastic to us, but she knew it was the best thing, the only thing, she could do for her daughter. It bought Nimcha time.'

'Wake-up call, Quillon. They were captured by Skullboys. They were on their way to a burning.'

'Nimcha might have been released, or at least spared execution.'

'Happy endings all around.'

'I'm not saying that. Just that from Kalis's perspective, this was the lesser evil.' Quillon picked dried blood from his upper lip. 'I don't think we should be judging her. We weren't in her shoes.' He paused, sifting through the jumbled memories of recent events. 'And we know she's real now, don't we? Kalis – when you implored Nimcha to act, I felt something. The zone responded. It didn't shift, but it certainly noticed. It was listening, and it tried to obey. It was as if she called out to it, but lacked the strength or focus to make it follow her will. Is that what happened?'

After a great silence Kalis said, 'I hoped that you would not feel it, or remember what I said.'

'You're amongst friends. But we've got to know the truth, and all of it.' Deciding the direct approach was best he added, 'How long have you known about her?'

Kalis's eyes darted between Quillon and Meroka, both of whom were still standing up. 'Please,' she said, nodding to indicate that they should return to their own bench.

'Taking their sweet time with those blankets and clothes,' Meroka growled.

'She was one when the mark appeared,' Kalis said. 'It wasn't long after she'd learned to speak. She had hair by then, but one day she fell and hurt her head. I had to clean the blood away, and that was when I saw the mark.' She looked hard into his eyes, forcing him to imagine the shock of discovering her daughter's nature. 'It was then that I knew.'

'And you knew – just like that?' Quillon asked.

'Of course. There have always been children with the gift, for as long as the world is old.'

'Some combination of inheritance factors,' Quillon mused. 'Out there, in the general population. But it's only when they come together in the right combination that a child like Nimcha is born. How old was she when the power showed itself?'

Kalis thought for a moment. 'Nearly three. She could read and write, like any child of that age. That was when it came through.'

'As if it was waiting for certain brain structures to become sufficiently mature,' Quillon said. 'That's what this is: not magic, not possession by demons. It's just something buried deep in the blood, waiting for the right set of circumstances to emerge. Much like an inherited disease, although obviously more complicated – and much rarer – since it can't depend on just a single inheritance factor.'

'It is not a disease,' Kalis said.

'But it may still be something medicine can understand, and help her with if need be.'

'She has no need of help.'

'If the power threatened her life, would you still say that?' Quillon asked.

'It does not.'

'The power brought hatred down on you, caused the two of you to end up in a cage.'

'It saved us as well.'

'Perhaps it might have, had she been able to command it more effectively. I felt something, certainly – I'm sure all of us did. But it wasn't enough to stop the vorgs, or hurt the Skullboys. It's an undeveloped talent, something that needs to be nurtured and shaped.'

'You misunderstand,' Kalis said darkly.

'Evidently.'

'She was weak and frightened when the vorgs came. The power is not always strong in her. Today it was weak, because of what she had already done.'

'She'd used the power already tonight?'

'Not tonight, city man. Yesterday. When the change came. When your city died. When you watched the angels fall.' Kalis ran a hand through her daughter's hair, dirty fingernails parting filthy, grease-knotted strands, exposing the vivid crimson emblem of the baubled star. 'Nimcha brought the storm. Nimcha brought the end of your world.'

He opened his mouth to answer, but the best he could do was smile and shake his head.

'Told you she was crazier than a bag of snakes,' Meroka said.

CHAPTER ELEVEN

A face appeared in the grilled window of the door. It was a man none of them had seen so far: grey-bearded, pale, with an aquiline nose and narrowed, hawkish eyes under heavy brows. He surveyed the four then worked the lock. He entered clutching a medical bag that was only a little less scuffed and careworn than Quillon's. Behind him loomed another airman, burdened with blankets and clothes, and behind that man was a third, gripping a machine gun in shiny black gloves.

'Apologies for my tardiness,' said the bearded man. 'My name is Gambeson; I have the honour ... the pleasure ... of being the surgeon on this mission.' He wore a long leather coat, emblazoned across the chest and shoulders with what Quillon presumed to be various symbols of rank and distinguished service. The coat had been donned hastily, one of the buttons tucked through the wrong hole. Beneath it Quillon could see a white surgical smock, not unlike the one he wore during his normal duties at the Third District Morgue. 'I've been instructed ... commanded ... to give each of you a thorough medical examination,' Gambeson went on, 'partly for your own sakes and partly for the security of Swarm.'

'Because we might be carrying something?' Quillon asked. His eyes kept being drawn to the white tunic, stained here and there with the ochre of dried blood.

'Swarm, by its very nature, has to be cautious ... vigilant ... against infection. I'm given to understand that two of you are from Spearpoint?'

'That would be Meroka and me,' Quillon said. 'We're from Neon Heights.'

'I'm afraid the internal details of Spearpoint mean very little to me.' Gambeson's hawk-like features were turned fully towards Quillon, the surgeon's coppery eyes alert with observation. 'I was told you'd been hurt, hit in the face?'

'My nose may have been broken. Other than that there's no lasting damage.'

'And you know this for a fact?' Gambeson asked.

'Being a doctor as well, yes.'

'I had my doubts . . . suspicions. Rather an intriguing collection in that bag of yours, to start with. A veritable cornucopia of drugs and surgical instruments.' The surgeon's breath was warm and smelled faintly of leather. 'I'm sure we'd have a great deal to talk about, Doctor . . .'

'Quillon.' He looked at Nimcha and Kalis, knowing that he must do everything in his power to protect the girl. His heart raced in his chest. He knew he was on the edge of something irrevocable, a point from beyond which there was no return. 'There *is* something, actually.'

'Something?'

'I've been having a little trouble focusing, since I was hit in the face. I'm wondering if something didn't get . . . dislodged.'

'Let me see. Stand up, will you?'

Gambeson looked over his shoulder, perhaps making sure the other men were still behind him, and then produced a silver instrument from his medical bag. It had a delicate, precision-tooled look, with an elegant knurled handle.

'You've been dealing with injured men,' Quillon said, in not much more than a whisper. 'Where are they? Perhaps there's something I can do to help.'

Gambeson peered into his eyes one at a time, squinting into the eyepiece of his instrument. 'Be very still, Doctor Quillon.'

'I can show you how to use my medicines to best advantage. I can also operate, if it comes to that.'

Gambeson lowered the instrument, frowning slightly, and rubbed one of its hinged lenses against his coat sleeve before raising it again. 'I must insist that you be still. And silent.' He looked at Quillon's eyes again, but this time with a deepening frown, a recognition of wrongness. He pulled back sharply, as if he had seen his own death in those deep, dark pools of midnight blue.

'What are you, Doctor Quillon? What the *hell* are you?'

'Perhaps it would be best if you continued your examination in private,' Quillon suggested.

He was taken to another room, through a part of the gondola he had not seen before. As they passed through one section, a gloved and masked airman came down a spiral ladder descending from the ceiling, the open hatch offering a glimpse of the sepulchral vault of the airship's envelope. He heard the resonant, organ-like throb of the air rushing by her skin, the droning skirl of her engines. The craft was larger than he had grasped on the ground. He could not guess at the size of its crew, even allowing for injuries. It seemed entirely possible that there might be many dozens of airmen aboard *Painted Lady*.

'You know what I am,' he told Gambeson, when the doctor faced him alone in the tiny chamber, which appeared to be little more than a walk-in medicine cabinet. 'Or at the very least you have an inkling.'

Gambeson closed the door behind them.

'What you are is an impossibility, Doctor Quillon. Nonetheless, you are standing before me, so I must confront ... accept ... your true nature.'

'Have you ever seen anything like me?'

'I've had the pleasure of dissecting angels once or twice. They were dead long before they came to me. How could they not be, when they can't survive beyond Spearpoint for more than a few hours? Nonetheless, their bodies may be collected and ... pickled ... and conveyed to those, such as I, who find amusement ... interest ... in them.' He had prepared a basin of hot water and was dabbing the dried blood from Quillon's face with a tenderness that bordered on the maternal. 'They were very old corpses, Doctor Quillon. They'd been dead for centuries, according to the provenance, which I have no reason to doubt. But angels don't change very much, if at all. And I remember the structure of their eyes very well. Would you mind removing your garments?'

'Of course not.'

Quillon shrugged off his replacement coat, donned hastily from the pile before Gambeson led him away from the others. He unbuttoned his shirt and removed his vest. He stood before Gambeson, his own wraith-like image reflected back at him from the bottles on the shelving, a pale, hairless, attenuated thing with ribs like radiator bars.

Gambeson studied him expressionlessly. 'Turn around please, Doctor. I would like to see your ...' He swallowed as Quillon presented his back to his examiner. 'Wings. Might I touch ... examine ... them?'

'Be my guest.'

Quillon felt Gambeson's cold fingertips touch first his left and then his right wing-buds. He kneaded them gently, exploring the underlying structure, the tiny bones and muscles that were struggling to assume functionality.

'What are you?' he said again, softly this time.

'You would have discovered my nature soon enough, Doctor. I saw no point in prolonging the matter. I am what you imagine me to be, but both more and less than that. I was an angel, once. I was born in the

154

Celestial Levels, and I would have looked very like those pickled bodies you cut open. Then I was changed.'

'Why?'

'For the purposes of infiltration,' Quillon answered blandly. 'There were four of us. We were altered, surgically and genetically, to make us look human. Or prehuman, as angels would say. We were sent down to Neon Heights, to live amongst normal men and women, to prove that it could be done. What would have killed unmodified angels was merely troublesome to us. With the right antizonals, we could still function.'

'Why didn't they remove your wings, alter your eyes?'

'They did. Nine years ago you'd have needed detailed blood and urine chemistry to tell I was anything other than human. Unfortunately, the infiltration exercise went wrong.'

'In what way?'

'There was a . . . disagreement.' He smiled thinly as he glossed over Aruval's death, his own role in murdering the other two infiltrators. 'I was left behind, stranded in Neon Heights. Eventually our specialised drugs ran out. I made do with what I could find, but while I was able to stave off zone sickness, I couldn't stop my underlying physiology from beginning to reassert itself. The circumstances I found myself in hadn't been anticipated. The best I could do was suppress the changes with chemistry and surgery.'

'There are scars under your wings.'

'They were cut back whenever they grew too obviously. It had to be done over and over again. There was nothing I could do about my eyes, so I concealed them as best I could. I had help from human friends in Spearpoint.'

'They trusted you?'

'We trusted each other. I'm hoping you and I can come to the same accommodation.'

'You lied to me about being a doctor, then.'

Quillon turned around slowly. 'No, that's the truth. Most of it, anyway. I am, or was, a pathologist. I worked in the Third District Morgue. And before I was sent down to Neon Heights I was a kind of physician. There's very little I don't know about bodies, be they angel or human. My offer to help you still stands.' He paused. 'Would you mind if I dress again? I'm fully aware that I don't conform to the usual standards of aesthetic normality.'

'You're a master of understatement, Doctor.' Gambeson passed him his vest. 'Why would you help us? And please don't give me any specious half-truths about moral imperatives.'

155

'It wouldn't be a half-truth. Besides, I want to convince you of my good intentions. And I hope if I do so it will reflect well on my comrades. They don't have much else to offer.'

'They know what you are, of course.'

'No,' Quillon said, buttoning his shirt. 'They don't. Not at all. And for now you would be doing me a very great favour if things stayed that way.'

'Why haven't you told them?'

'The woman and the child, we're barely acquainted. The other one, Meroka, has excellent reason to hate the likes of me.'

'She'll learn the truth eventually.'

'I know. I'm just hoping I can earn enough respect for her not to throw me out of the nearest window when it happens. I'm sure she's capable of it.'

'A firebrand.'

'She has her reasons.'

Gambeson pursed his lips. 'For now, I would indeed like to keep you apart. There's a small holding cell, which I'm afraid is even less salubrious than the place where we're holding your friends. But you'll be ... comfortable ... warm, and I'll make sure you're served a decent ration, such as we can spare.'

'That would be kind, Doctor.'

'I may wish to examine you some more in the morning. In the meantime, though, I'm afraid other patients call on my time.'

'I can help,' Quillon said.

'Your offer is noted. It will, of course, need to be reviewed by Captain Curtana. I can't promise that she'll see eye to eye with you. Many of us have a well-earned dislike of angels, over and above anything we might feel for Spearpoint.'

'I understand.'

Gambeson hesitated. 'Your companions: now that we're speaking candidly, as it were, as two medical men – is there anything about them I need to know? Any matters that have come to your attention?'

He shook his head as casually as he was able. 'Nothing that I'm aware of. They could all use food, water and a good wash. Beyond that, there doesn't seem to be much wrong with them.'

'Even the mother and daughter?'

'They've survived on their own for long enough. They're stronger than they look.'

Quillon attempted to sleep during the remainder of the night, but his efforts were fruitless. The pain from his smashed nose was all but gone;

what disturbed him was the profound unfamiliarity of his surroundings, the discomfort of the bench he was expected to use as a bed, the bucking and swaying motion of the airship and the habit of the engines, just when his brain was beginning to adjust to their endless monk-like droning, to subtly change tone and volume. That and the many worries circling his mind, chasing each other like the Moon's two halves.

It had been an impetuous decision to reveal his identity to Gambeson, one that he had barely had time to evaluate, but it had served its intended function. He had given the doctor – and by extension the rest of the crew – something other than the girl to puzzle over. He would be the object of their fascination now; Nimcha just a semi-mute child of only subsidiary interest. He was not so naive as to think he could protect her secret for ever, but under the present circumstances a delaying action was the best he could offer. As to what would happen when Nimcha's true nature was eventually revealed, he dared not speculate.

It scarcely mattered whether or not he believed Kalis when she said that Nimcha had caused the storm. That was not the way the world worked, or at least not the one he lived in. It was not that he refused to believe in tectomancers. And granted, she might have some mild, demonstrable power over the zones ... but it could only be a local influence. Surely. To believe otherwise was to surrender every rational instinct he had ever cherished. No child could have brought about what he had witnessed happening to Spearpoint.

What mattered – the only thing that mattered – was what everyone else would think when they discovered that mark on her head. How were the Swarmers liable to take it? Not well, he suspected. They might have their airships and machine guns, but superstition wasn't something that went away just because you had engines and bullets.

In his mind's eye he kept seeing a child's body tumbling though leagues of air, falling like a rag doll.

One less piece of ballast.

When at last he gave up on sleep he went to the holding cell's narrow slit of a window and watched the sky lighten to orange. From his present vantage point he could not see Spearpoint, so he had no idea how far they had come or in which direction they were now moving. Beneath *Painted Lady* the unlit landscape offered no clues. Fires burned here and there, semaphore towers stood motionless, but for all the sense these portents made to him they could have been constellations in an alien sky.

Once, when the sky had nearly brightened to dawn, he fancied he saw another ship shadowing them at a distance. He had begun to dismiss it as a phantom when, a little later, *Painted Lady* changed course and the other ship came nearer. Manoeuvres ensued, the engine drone rising and falling, and for one instant he heard a short, sharp discharge, a guttural rip of sound that could have been some ship-borne gun-battery being deployed. Afterwards the airship resumed steady flight, and when he swept the sky he saw nothing but wisps and quills of morning cloud.

Gambeson came to see him again shortly after sunrise. He was given another examination, more thorough than the last. Gambeson was cordial, but rebuffed almost all of Quillon's questions. In daylight Quillon was struck by how much older the man looked compared to the night before. His beard seemed whiter, his eyes more wrinkled, his face more lined and drawn. Quillon wondered if he had slept at all since their conversation.

'My offer still stands,' Quillon said, when Gambeson was packing his instruments away.

'It could never be that easy, Doctor. That you are a Spearpointer would be reason enough for most of our crew to distrust you. But an angel trying to pass himself off as human?' Gambeson shook his head in mock exasperation.

'You seem the exception to this rule, Doctor.'

Afterwards, he was taken not back to the others but to another room in the airship. It had small, shuttered windows, the shutters hinged open to admit stripes of wintry daylight. It must have been somewhere near the front, since the walls tapered slightly along their length. The room contained a large table, the kind that could be spread with charts, and the concave walls were lined with books and map rolls, secured in place with leather clasps. The cumulative weight of the books and maps must have been considerable. Quillon could only conclude that each and every one had been deemed essential to the airship's operation. Once or twice, strangely, he heard birdsong coming from somewhere nearby, as if a small aviary was located next door.

There were three other people in the room, Gambeson amongst them. Seated next to the surgeon behind the chart table was Captain Curtana. She also had the look of someone who had not seen much sleep lately. Her hair had been tied back, but a few lank strands hung down against her cheek. Her skin, which had appeared nearly black at night, was merely a rich brown, shading to yellow under her eyes, where she looked puffy and exhausted. Once again Quillon was struck by the elegant structure of her face, the birdlike delicacy of her features. She wore the same kind of side-buttoned tunic as the other airmen, although hers had been tailored for a woman. The tunic was unbuttoned to the breast, revealing a white shirt underneath, stained around the collar. Quillon couldn't tell if she was still wearing her service revolver, but nothing about her mood – impatient, ready to dispense summary justice and move on to the next item of business – seemed in any way intended to put him at ease.

'Remove your shirt and vest,' Gambeson said, before Quillon had been shown where to sit. 'Show us what you are.'

Quillon did as he was told. He turned around slowly, bringing his wing-buds into view. He could feel his audience staring, horrified and fascinated at the same time.

'He says they'll keep growing if he doesn't cut them back,' Gambeson said. 'Eventually, if he's to be believed, he'll have a full set of wings, and the nervous system and musculoskeletal structure to use them. He could fly away from us without any great difficulty.'

'We could catch him, though?' Curtana asked, as if his escape were not merely possible, but a distinct and looming probability. 'He couldn't actually outfly us?'

'He'd have the edge in agility,' Gambeson said. 'Just like Skullboy raiders. But that wouldn't keep him out of our gun sights for ever, and even with thermals and gliding I doubt he'd have a range of much more than fifty leagues.'

'I was just thinking – we could always use some target practice,' Curtana said.

'I think you'll have a wait on your hands before those wings are flight-capable. Quite a specimen, isn't he?'

'That's one word for it, Doctor. Revolting's another.' Curtana snapped her fingers at Quillon. 'Put your clothes on, before I lose my breakfast. And take a seat.'

He was ushered, none too gently, into the waiting chair on the other side of the table.

'Have you decided what you're going to do with me?'

'There are a number of avenues open to us,' Curtana said. 'First, it might help if I explained that we're at war. Actually, we've always been at war. War is sort of what we do, when we're not grubbing around looking for the next firesap supply. The Skullboys don't go away, and there's only room for one dominant force in this airspace. Lately, though, things have been getting more intense. The storm's given the Skulls a chance to recombine, to aggregate together in serious numbers. They've no real chance of taking down Swarm – we're still too strong, too organised for that. But they can make life harder for us, interfering with our scouting and reconnaissance activities, forcing us to commit more ships to a given task than we'd ordinarily need, leaving Swarm less well defended. It's not just our problem, either. Ground intelligence has it that they're also planning a move against Spearpoint and the other surface cities, now that the storm's made them so vulnerable.' Quillon started to speak, but Curtana raised a silencing hand. 'I merely state these things to clarify the difficulty of our position. Under other circumstances we might be inclined to extend the hand of trust and forgiveness. But these are not such circumstances. The possibility of a saboteur on one of our ships, or a destabilising element, cannot be tolerated.'

'I'm neither of those things,' Quillon said.

'Doctor Gambeson: your findings?' she asked.

Gambeson coughed before speaking. 'Nothing's changed since my earlier report. He's a human–angel hybrid. We've never seen anything like him before, and neither have the textbooks. His story is that he was surgically modified to look human, and that the concealment ... camouflage ... is beginning to wear off.'

'Do you find this plausible?'

'Confronted with a human–angel hybrid, a man with atrophied wings growing out of his back, I'd have to say that there are very few things I *wouldn't* find plausible.' Gambeson scratched at the corner of his eye, finding something small and gritty lodged there. 'I have no particular reason to disbelieve him. Short of an autopsy, though, there's really no way to verify his story. All we can do is keep him under observation and see how he changes. If his angel morphology becomes more dominant, that will bolster his story.'

'Is that your recommendation?' asked the other man present. 'Just let him stay aboard, observing him like a laboratory specimen?'

'I see no immediate harm in it.'

'You have no idea of his capabilities.'

Gambeson shrugged at the other man. 'Nor do you, Commander Spatha. On the other hand, I've had the luxury of examining him. He's actually quite frail; one of your men could easily overpower him and probably break his limbs without too much difficulty. He doesn't weigh much more than a child. Angels need very delicate bone structure. They couldn't fly otherwise.'

'He could be dangerous in other ways,' Commander Spatha said.

Quillon thought he recognised him as the man who had been sent back to deal with the Skullboys who had taken the four of them prisoner. He had a lean face with uncommonly pale, practically colourless eyes, his hair scrupulously parted and oiled. He was still wearing his tunic, but unlike Curtana he had it buttoned to the collar, and somehow managed to make it look as if the uniform was as stiff and fresh as the day it had been issued.

'Yes, he might retain the ability to walk through walls, or exert a hypnotic influence over us, despite being held captive,' Gambeson said, not bothering to hide his sarcasm. 'But that could just as well apply to our other clients.'

'I haven't eliminated them from suspicion either,' Spatha said.

'Commander Spatha has a point, though,' Curtana said, with a hint of grudging concurrence in her voice. 'Do we know that Quillon isn't carrying something contagious?'

'If he is, we're already exposed. That's a risk we entertain whenever we bring a prisoner ... client ... aboard. To settle your fears, I've seen nothing in his blood samples that indicates any kind of elevated immune response. Setting aside the residual effects of zone sickness, he appears quite well, considering what he is.'

'If I knew I was infectious, I'd have told you,' Quillon said.

'Your companions don't know what you are,' Curtana answered. She had her hands clasped on the table. 'Does that mean you lied to them?'

'I've told them the truth, that I am Doctor Quillon, a pathologist from Neon Heights.'

'That was your cover, according to Doctor Gambeson's report,' said Spatha.

'It's also what I've become. I've lived amongst humans for nine years, and I was sent down to them with an overlay of ghost memories to help me blend in more easily.'

'Where did those memories come from?' Curtana asked.

'The terminally ill,' Quillon replied. 'When people are close to death, they sometimes travel to the Celestial Levels. Ascension Day, they call it. They're scanned, their neural patterns recovered against the day when they can be put back into a living body. As a by-product, memories are also extracted and stored.'

Curtana narrowed her already fatigue-slitted eyes. 'Is it common knowledge that this goes on?'

'No.'

'Another untruth, then,' Spatha said, making a note in whatever logbook or journal he had open on the table before him.

'I'm telling you now.'

'But you've disclosed none of this to your companions?' asked Curtana.

'While my identity could be concealed, it seemed prudent to do so. They have reason to dislike angels.'

'Doctor Gambeson tells us you've volunteered your medical services,' Curtana said.

Quillon nodded. 'That's correct.'

'You've examined his belongings, Doctor Gambeson?'

The surgeon produced Quillon's medical bag and set it on the chart table. 'I've tested his samples – those I can identify – and the quality is at least as good as anything we have in our normal arsenal.'

'He could have stolen the bag,' Spatha said.

'I think he knows how to use them, Commander. Meroka – the city woman – had been given expert treatment for zone sickness. I've examined her. The residual effects were almost immeasurably small. The dosage must have been calculated with a degree of skill.'

Curtana examined the bag as she spoke. 'Can we be sure Quillon did it?'

'No, but it would have to have been administered relatively recently. Who else could have done it?'

'What do you mean by "normal arsenal"?' Quillon asked. 'What other kind is there?'

Commander Spatha stood from the table. He sauntered around to the back of Quillon's chair, polished boots creaking as he walked, and leaned down until Quillon could feel the cold rasp of his breath on the back of his neck.

'Let me make my formal introduction,' he said quietly, as if he were sharing a confidence with Quillon, an amusing bon mot or dry aside. 'I am the security officer aboard this vessel. I have been tasked to safeguard Swarm from the activities of foreign elements. As such it is my duty to attend to matters of counter-espionage, including the detection and interrogation of spies.' Without warning he grasped Quillon's bare scalp and tugged down hard, snapping his head back so violently that Quillon almost fell out of the chair.

'Whatever you think,' he said, choking under the strain, 'I am not a spy.'

'Then you should be careful how you frame your questions.'

'If I was a real spy, don't you think I'd have been better prepared?'

Spatha yanked Quillon's head back again and he felt something crick in his neck. He struggled for breath, feeling as if he was being strangled. He thought of Malkin, Fray's barman, the scar around his throat. Was this how it had felt?

'That's enough for now,' Curtana said warningly. 'You're not going to get much out of him dead. Besides, I'm sure Ricasso will find him fascinating.'

When Quillon was able to speak he said, 'Who's Ricasso?'

'Enough questions,' Spatha said, emphasising his point with another vicious tug on Quillon's scalp. 'I say we dump him now,' he told Curtana. 'Throw him overboard, before he has a chance to sabotage anything.'

'And the other three, while we're at it?' Curtana asked, with the mildest note of scepticism.

'The woman and the child aren't even from Spearpoint,' Quillon said, speaking through clenched teeth as Spatha yanked his head back again. 'You've no quarrel with them.'

'And the other Spearpointer?' Spatha asked.

'Meroka's nothing to do with me. We only met a few days ago. She was just my escort out of the city.'

'Maybe he's the diversion,' Spatha said. 'A decoy to keep us amused while one of the others does the real work.'

'We were going to die,' Quillon said insistently. 'If I had serious intentions to infiltrate Swarm, do you think I'd have put myself in such a dangerous position that I had to be rescued from certain death?'

'He has a point,' Curtana said. 'If we hadn't intervened, Quillon and his friends would have been vorg meat within the hour.'

'A ruse,' Spatha said dismissively. 'For all we know, they were in collusion with the Skullboys.'

Curtana glanced at her surgeon, some unspoken communication passing between them, before continuing, 'I think that will be all for now, Commander Spatha. Your concerns are noted.'

Spatha released Quillon with a snap of his wrist, enough to draw a final grunt of pain from his captive.

'Ballast,' he said. 'That's all you are. Useful until we need lift. Then you become useful in an entirely different way.'

'At least there's that,' Quillon replied.

CHAPTER TWELVE

They took him back to the others. He was only wearing the shirt and vest on his top half now, his coat still in the examination room. The door was opened and he was flung into the rear compartment, landing on his knees, his back to the ceiling. He could still feel Spatha's fingernails digging into his scalp, clenching into him as if his skin were soft wet clay.

'What the fuck happened to you?' Meroka said, stirring from half-sleep, with the Testament still in her hands.

He struggled awkwardly to his feet. Kalis and Nimcha were sitting where he had left them, partly wrapped in blankets. He wondered if they had slept any better than he had.

'They questioned me,' he said, placing one hand on the ceiling strut to steady himself. 'Interrogated, more accurately. They're worried that I'm a spy. I tried to convince them otherwise, but ... I don't know.' He wiped spittle from his chin. 'I'm not sure they believe me.'

'You don't look good,' Meroka said, wonderingly. 'First time I've seen you properly in daylight, Cutter, without that hat and those glasses you always wear. You look like ... some baby bird, dropped out of its nest. Not the cute kind. The hairless, shrivelled-up, ugly-as-fuck kind.' She kept staring at him, Quillon trying to avert his eyes without making it obvious that that was what he was doing.

'Has anything happened while I was away?' he asked, hoping to strike the right note of easy-going nonchalance.

'Something not right about you, Cutter. Something *definitely* not right.'

'How is Nimcha?'

Kalis stared at him with lingering disquiet before answering, 'She did not sleep well. Her dreams were troubled.'

'I'm sorry. They've taken my things. If I had them, I might be able to do something. Might I examine her, all the same?'

'No,' Nimcha said, recoiling into the blankets. 'I don't want him to touch me.'

'I won't hurt you,' Quillon said.

'You look like a dead man. I've seen dead men.'

He looked around to make sure the door was closed and that no one was listening at the grille.

'I hoped to draw attention away from your daughter, Kalis. To some extent, I think I succeeded, but the distraction's not going to keep working indefinitely. We have to think seriously about how we protect Nimcha's secret.'

'I did not think you believed,' Kalis said.

'I'm not sure I do.' Quillon phrased his words with all the care he could muster. 'I accept that Nimcha may have abilities that aren't easily explained. I've told you I felt something, and I won't deny that now. But what happened the night before last, the zone shift? That definitely wasn't her doing.'

'You know this?' Kalis asked.

He nodded, glad to be on firm ground again. 'Yes. I do. No one could be sure when it was going to happen, and it's either our good or bad luck that it happened when it did, but the storm's been expected for a long time. Even before I left Spearpoint, the men and women who are paid to worry about that kind of thing were getting nervous. They were making more checks than usual, scurrying around trying to make sure the city was ready for the change when it hit. Their instruments were picking up the precursor signals, the indications that the zone instabilities were growing larger, in anticipation of a major readjustment.' He sighed, not wanting to humiliate Kalis, but at the same time keen that she should understand that her daughter's powers could not be as vast as she imagined. 'This has been going on for a while,' he added. 'It's only recently that the rest of us have realised the authorities were getting nervous.'

'How long?' Kalis asked.

What did it matter? he wondered. But nonetheless he tried to give her an honest answer, thinking back to what Fray and Meroka had told him. 'Two years, give or take.'

'Nimcha is five years old now. I told you that she was nearly three when her powers first showed.'

'No,' Quillon said, aiming to correct her gently. 'That isn't possible. Nimcha is just one girl. I can accept that she has some influence over the local conditions of the zone, here and now, in the place where she stands. That's not to say I understand it, but I know what I felt and I must trust the evidence of my own senses. But to go beyond that, to start believing that this one girl caused *everything* that's happened in the last couple of days ... that she's been building up to it for years ... I'm sorry, but that's simply more than I can credit.'

'She had to bring the storm,' Kalis said, with surprising calm, as if she had not really expected anyone to believe her. 'She knew that the Skullboys would suffer, and that we might be able to escape. You cannot deny that it worked. You found us. If she had not brought the storm, you would never have done that.'

'Crazy as a bag of snakes the woman may be,' said Meroka, 'but she does have a point.'

'I cannot accept that all this was the work of one little girl,' Quillon said. 'It would mean that, just to escape from that cage, she had to plunge Spearpoint in darkness, eclipsing the one beacon of civilisation left on this planet.'

'Got the job done,' Meroka said.

'She did not mean to cause what happened,' Kalis said suddenly. 'She only did what she had to do. Her power is strong, but her control over it is still ... not what it should be.' She looked down at the rumpled folds of the blanket still covering her legs. 'But what had to be done was done. I encouraged her in this. She was the instrument; I was the one who guided her. You cannot blame her for what happened.'

'There's no blame to be attached to anyone,' Quillon said forcefully. 'This was merely a coincidence of factors – you encouraged Nimcha to act, and at the same time the zone shift arrived. From your point of view, it was natural to believe that her influence had something to do with that. But that's not what happened. It *cannot* be what happened.'

'Why not?' Kalis asked.

'Because if Nimcha is what you think she is, then ...' He trailed off, struggling to articulate his thoughts. 'She wouldn't just be a child with unusual abilities. She'd be the single most important human being now alive; someone with the power to change everything.'

'And you do not think that this is possible?'

'I'll believe in anything when I see evidence for it. But evidence isn't the problem here.'

'What is, then?'

'This isn't the way it's meant to happen.' It was not so much rage as a kind of wild indignation, a sense that he had been displaced from his proper position in the order of things, like a planet demoted to a lesser orbit. From the moment the angel arrived on his mortuary table, he had been under the illusion that he was the master of his own destiny, the main actor in a story of his own shaping. But if Nimcha was all that her mother claimed, then she had been the one shaping the story all along. It was Nimcha who had caused the instabilities that had led the Boundary Commission to suspect that the storm was imminent ... the very instabilities that, it seemed increasingly likely, were behind the angels' renewed interest in retrieving him from Neon Heights. It was Nimcha, in other words, who had been indirectly responsible for his fleeing the city. He felt now as if she had been pulling him towards her like a magnet.

'I know what you're feeling,' Meroka said. 'You're thinking, this was my little adventure, it was all revolving around *me*. And now it's not. You're just a detail, swept up in the stuff she's making happen. Welcome to the way most of us spend our lives feeling, Cutter. We're just turds swirling our way down the pipe.'

'She did not ask for this,' Kalis said. 'She did not choose this path.'

'I don't envy her.'

'Neither should you pity her. Just ... understand. That is all I ask.'

'I'll do my best.'

'Turn around,' Meroka said.

He looked at her, trying to feign honest bemusement. 'I'm sorry?'

'Turn around, Cutter. So we can see your back.'

'I don't see—'

'Turn the fuck around. Now.' She rose from the bench and he saw, mesmerised by the chrome glint of it, that she carried a blade. For a moment the only thought in his head was the wonder of how she had kept it about her.

'What are you, Cutter? I'd like to know. Because you sure as hell aren't normal.'

Quillon stepped back, raising his hands defensively, not willing to give in to her demands quite so easily. 'I don't understand.'

'The others may not have seen anything like you before,' Meroka said, 'but I have. Those eyes aren't something you forget in a hurry. No fucking wonder you kept them hidden so long. You knew exactly what I'd make of them.'

'This is not what you think.'

'Turn around. Ain't repeating myself.'

Something in her voice commanded him to obey. He presented his back to her, facing the door, holding his hands above his shoulders. He felt the clean whisk as the knife cleaved through the fabric of his shirt and the vest under it. The cold line of it arrowed down his spine. Meroka grabbed the torn fabric and ripped it wide.

Kalis let out a small, startled gasp. Nimcha's scream was pure dire incomprehension. Meroka spat. He felt the gobbet impact between his shoulder blades.

'Always had my doubts, Cutter.'

'This is not what you think,' he said again, less pleadingly this time, for the damage was already done. He could still feel the cold line traced by the knife, and he guessed that for all her skill she had drawn blood. He imagined the droplets racing down his back like a procession of scarlet beetles.

She stepped closer. He felt an edge touch his throat.

'Tell me what the fuck this means. In words of two syllables or less.'

Nimcha was still screaming. Her screams were becoming continuous and hysterical, as if she were in the throes of an unspeakably vivid night terror. It could not just be the sight of his wing buds. Meroka saw them for what they were, the mark of his true and secret nature, but to Nimcha they could only have been two slightly pendulous, symmetrical lumps on either side of his spine. He was peculiar enough without them, but surely his emaciation wasn't enough to pitch the child into nightmares. Unless it was just one strangeness too many ...

'Speak,' Meroka said, increasing the pressure on the blade.

'Fray knew what I am,' he said, hardly daring to move his lips. 'Fray trusted me. You trusted Fray. Isn't that good enough for you?'

'Fuck Fray. Tell me what you are.'

'An angel made to look like a man. That's all. Not your enemy. Angels hate me as well. They want me dead. All of that was true.'

'What the fuck were you doing in Neon Heights?'

'Trying not to die.'

'Don't get smart with me, Cutter.'

'It's the truth. I was sent down to blend in with humans, to prove that it could be done. To prove that we could be modified both to blend in and survive the different zone conditions. I thought that was all there was to it. I was wrong. There was an agenda I knew nothing about.' He tried to swallow, conscious of the blade pushing against his skin, eager to part it. 'I ... rebelled. From that point on I became a fugitive. Fray helped me build a new life. He always knew what I was and he always knew that I meant no harm. That's the truth, Meroka. Fray knew how you felt about angels. Is it any wonder he didn't want you finding out about me? You were supposed to get me out of Spearpoint. That was all.'

Nimcha was still screaming. But the scream had a different quality to it now. It was beginning to break up into choked grunts and gurgling, as if she was starting to go into convulsions.

'Tell her to shut up,' Meroka said.

'She cannot,' Kalis answered.

'Let me look at her,' Quillon said. 'Whatever you have against me, we can deal with it later. But for now let me examine Nimcha.'

Meroka released the pressure on the blade by the smallest increment. 'You want this blue-eyed freak anywhere near the girl, Kalis?'

Quillon spoke as calmly as he was able. 'I won't hurt her. If I had anything against her, do you think I'd have insisted we rescue them? At least let me look.'

Meroka pulled the blade from his throat. 'We're not finished, Cutter. Not by a long fucking margin.'

He went over to Nimcha, Kalis supporting her daughter as best she could. Nimcha had stopped screaming now, but she was still convulsing. Her limbs thrashed constantly and her eyes had rolled back into their sockets. Drool was spooling out of her mouth in a continuous stream. Her skin was beginning to darken.

'She's choking,' Quillon said. 'She's swallowed her tongue. Support her head, Kalis. I'm going to try and reach in. Meroka: bang on the door and get them to bring either Gambeson or my medical bag.'

'You couldn't sound any colder if you tried, Cutter.'

'That's because I'm doing my job.' The fingers on his right hand were still bandaged from where the Skullboy had bitten him. He used that hand to force her mouth open, and the left to reach in and try to retrieve her tongue. Nimcha thrashed under him, making a difficult task harder. She was trying to bite him. He pushed his fingers deeper, until he found the tongue. Not for the first time, he was paradoxically grateful for his slender fingers. As his bones elongated and thinned, so he became a better surgeon.

'I have it,' he said. 'She should be able to breathe more easily now.'

Nimcha began to calm almost immediately, her convulsions easing, her normal complexion starting to return. Her breathing was deep, her eyes now closed.

'It has never been that bad before,' Kalis said.

'This happens often?'

'Lately. Along with the bad dreams. I fear for her. She has had the mark since she was young. But it has never made her sick.'

'The two might not be connected.' But that was as much consolation as he could offer her. If the convulsions were not linked to the mark of tectomancy, then the alternatives – epilepsy, a brain tumour – were no more reassuring. He was just about to ask her more about the bad dreams when the door opened. It was Gambeson, equipped with his own medical bag. An airman stood behind him.

'I was told there was screaming. Is something the matter?'

'We were just getting better acquainted,' Quillon said, turning around so that Gambeson could see his slashed shirt and vest. 'Meroka took it about as well as I'd been expecting.'

'Did she hurt you?'

'No, I'm fine.' He flashed a glance at Meroka, who was still regarding him with poisonous distrust. 'I can't blame her for disliking what I am.'

'And I won't have our clients at each other's throats,' Gambeson said. 'Touch him again, Meroka, and I'll personally sign your death warrant. Is that understood?'

'Whatever you say,' she answered sullenly.

'Take that knife from her,' Gambeson told the airman. 'And search her properly this time.' Slowly his attention shifted to the child. 'Was she the one screaming?'

'She was disturbed by my wings,' Quillon said. 'It's understandable. She won't have seen anything like me before. It must have been quite upsetting for her.'

'Has this sort of thing happened before?' Gambeson asked Kalis.

Quillon wondered if Gambeson detected the momentary hesitation in her answer. 'No, this has not happened before. But she is resting now. I do not think it will happen again.'

'I'll do my best to reassure her,' Quillon said.

'I can examine her privately,' Gambeson said. 'There's no reason why she has to be treated like a prisoner.'

'I think we'd all rather stay together for now,' Quillon said.

Gambeson looked sceptical. 'Even you, Doctor? Given that your fellow clients ... companions ... now know everything about you?'

'I think we can resolve our differences amicably.' Quillon directed a querying glance at Meroka. 'Can't we?'

'Very well,' Gambeson said, not bothering to wait for her answer. 'It's probably just as well that you don't need my immediate attention. The captain's anticipating close action, I'm afraid. It could come at any time in the next day, but we must all be at maximum readiness.' He paused and studied Quillon again. 'I expect you'd appreciate a new shirt, Doctor. I'll have one sent down. And perhaps a pair of tinted goggles, so you don't have to go around explaining those eyes at every turn.'

'That would help,' Quillon said.

They were flying over water. To the south lay the same sparsely wooded, barely inhabited plains they had been traversing for many hours. The occasional hyphenated scratch of a long-abandoned road or railway line, the spindly remains of a disused semaphore tower, were the only tangible signs that civilisation had ever reached this region. Yet just when the monotony of it was becoming unbearable, the plains had given way to precipitous cliffs, plunging away beneath *Painted Lady* to drop at least a league below the former ground level. It was impossible to tell how deep the water was. It was a cold and sullen sea, slug-black, flecked by ice, running in what Quillon judged was an approximately east-west direction. He could see the far, northern side of it, where equally impressive cliffs staggered out of the waters, the dismal plains resuming beyond them. It must have been fifty or a hundred leagues to those cliffs; at least an hour's flight. As the sun lowered after noon, vast shadows bit into the cliffs, deepening from purple to black.

He thought back to Meroka's map, remembering the black ink of the Long Gash and the Old Sea. Could they have come so far that they were already crossing those waters?

'There are many names for that sea,' Kalis told him. 'We are on the eastern edge of it now. They say it is so deep and long you could hide your Spearpoint in it, if you laid it on its side. They also say it was once much larger, extending all the way to the Night Maze and the Three Daughters. That was before the world became colder and the seas started to shrink.' She shrugged, as if she placed no great faith in these titbits of planetary lore. 'I have seen none of these places, nor have I ever met anyone who has. I do not even know for sure that they exist, or that the world was once warmer.'

'I don't know what to believe,' Quillon said dispiritedly. 'It all seems irrelevant now, doesn't it? If the world can change the way it just has, then anything's possible. The world could return to the way it was, the trees could come back and the waters rise again.'

'If you think so,' Kalis said doubtfully.

'You don't?'

'If I were you, I would have stayed in my city. It will always be safer and warmer there.'

'You've seen what happened to my city. I was lucky to get out when I did.' He glanced at his surroundings. 'If this can be considered lucky.'

'Why did you leave?' Kalis asked.

'I had no choice. People wanted to kill me for something I did.'

'Where were you going?'

'To Fortune's Landing. That was the idea, anyway.'

'I have seen Fortune's Landing. It is not so great.'

'I was told I could make a living there.'

'Perhaps.' But he could see in her eyes how unlikely she regarded this proposition. 'You would have been better off in Soul's Rest, city man.'

'It looked a lot further away on the map.'

'Closer now, if this is the Long Gash. Perhaps they are taking us there.'

'Have you seen it?'

She shook her head. 'I have heard people speak of it. That it is much bigger than Fortune's Landing; that the city wall is twice as tall, decked in gold, and that the narrowest street in Soul's Rest would be a promenade in Fortune's Landing. That there are enough people inside the wall that you need never see the same face twice. That they have machines, electricity and television, as in Spearpoint.'

'Do you believe this?'

'I do not know. In some parts of the world, so I have heard, they say the same about Fortune's Landing.'

'Ah.'

'Perhaps Soul's Rest is bigger now. It is said that the two cities were once the same size, and that both are older than Spearpoint. Did you know this?'

'I confess it had escaped me.'

'It is said that they were founded at the same time, by two brothers who were also twins and also princes. They came from another land, a palace in another kingdom. This was before the Moon became two.'

'I see.'

Kalis inhaled a measured breath. Her tone of voice told him that this was something she had recited many times before. 'The palace was made of purest silver, with two great towers, taller than any other in the kingdom. The king had built it as a tribute to his wife, who had died giving birth to his sons. When the king's enemies destroyed the palace, he was heartbroken, for it was as if they had torn the memory of his wife from his heart. Fearing for his sons, he sent them out into the desert to found two new cities. Thus was his heart broken twice, for he knew he must say goodbye to his beloved princes for all time. Yet before they left, he made for them two suits of silver armour, and that armour would bring them luck because it was made from the same metal as the fallen towers, metal that the king had dug out of the palace ruins with his own fingers. And so the princes travelled, crossing land and sea, and when after many months they had grown weary of journeying, they set down their armour, gathered it into mounds and on top of the mounds founded two new cities. The sons built new towers, taller even than the old palace, and at last climbed to the top of them, and then – using the last pieces of their armour – they held mirrors to the sun, and flashed messages all the way back to the kingdom, so that the king would know

172

that his sons were safe. And so the king, who was still heartbroken, was at last able to sleep peacefully, for he had lost everything except that which mattered the most. He died that night, but his heart was full of contentment and before he slipped into death he dreamed of his wife again, the two of them young and in love in the gardens of the palace. And so the cities were founded, and because one brother was named Spirit, or Soul, so his city became Soul's Rest. The other brother was named Opportunity, or Fortune, and so his city became Fortune's Landing. And that is why those cities have those names, and why they are also twins.' She paused and studied Quillon intently. 'It is just a story,' she added, as if there had been any doubt in his mind. 'For bedtime. But because you had not heard it, I thought you would like to.'

'Thank you,' Quillon said. 'After all that you've said, I'd like to see Soul's Rest now, if only to find out if there's still a tower that might be older than Spearpoint. But I'm not sure that's where we're being taken. They've mentioned returning us to Swarm, but nothing about a ground city.'

'They do not like cities, or those who live on the ground,' Kalis said.

'They don't much like Spearpointers either, from what I can gather.'

'We are all dirt-rats to them. Even you.'

None of the crew had given any guidance in the matter, but it seemed probable to him that *Painted Lady* was travelling directly westwards, following more or less the same trajectory that Meroka and he had been pursuing when the storm hit. The shadows were lengthening in the opposite direction from the airship's motion; Spearpoint was falling steadily away behind them, falling further and further out of reach.

'How fast do you think we're moving?' Quillon wondered. 'Fifty leagues an hour, I'd guess. We flew all through the night and we haven't slowed down once since this morning. If that's the case, then we could easily be more than five hundred leagues from home by now. In four days we could circumnavigate the world. I never really grasped how small our planet is until now.' He paused before continuing, 'Have you ever been this far west, Meroka?'

She did not answer him. He was not expecting her to. Meroka was still disgusted at Quillon, both for what he was and the way she had been deceived about it. She was also bitter about the loss of her Testament, and blamed Quillon for that as well. Curtana's men had found a recess in the book's spine where the blade had been hidden.

What was clear, though he was careful not to speak of it in front of Nimcha, was that *Painted Lady* did not have the sky to herself. He had seen another ship at dawn, and during the day he had made several other sightings of distant, stalking craft. They were too far away for him to discern more than the skimpiest details, but from the efforts *Painted Lady* made to put space between herself and these other airships, Quillon thought it doubtful that they were other elements of Swarm. The close action that Gambeson had spoken of was still a possibility. There must, he was certain, have been an earlier skirmish: an engagement that had resulted in the injuries Gambeson was now tending to. The ship had appeared intact when he had seen her from the ground, but he knew very little about dirigibles.

With the approach of twilight came a change in the weather. The cloudless day had given way first to a high layer of rib-like clouds, and then to a gathering cloud-bank that was all but indistinguishable from fog. It thickened by degrees, white mist curling around *Painted Lady* like a glove, obscuring even those useless glimpses of the Long Gash. Quillon marvelled at the iron nerve of the navigators, still driving the ship forwards. But it was only by the drone of the engines that he could tell they were moving at all. He could hardly make out the whirling pro-pellers at the ends of the outriggers, and it was only by concentrating all his senses on the task that he was able to judge that the ship was changing course with some regularity, swerving, veering and shifting altitude. None of this could be accidental, so he was forced to assume that the ship was engaged in deliberate manoeuvres, either in pursuance or evasion of some stealthy, cloud-garbed enemy. The guns fired occa-sionally, the recoil of heavy airborne artillery felt through the gondola almost before their ears had registered their sound. The bursts seldom lasted more than a second or so, suggesting to Quillon that the crew were opening fire on phantoms of light and shadow, loosing a few rounds before realising their error. Curtana must have authorised them to use discretionary fire, which could only mean that the danger was sufficiently grave to justify the expenditure of ammunition.

He had been in the care of Curtana and her crew since the moment of his capture, but it was only now that the significance of this was striking home. The fact that he was a prisoner would be immaterial if the airship ran into an enemy it couldn't outgun. Everyone sensed the same helplessness, or so it seemed from the mood of his fellow captives. Nimcha was silent, and most of the time her mother simply stared through the walls, fixated on something only she could see. Even Meroka had little to say, and nothing at all to him.

The intermittent shooting continued, single cannon rounds and tooth-grating bursts of rapid fire, and then there came a volley that didn't end as quickly as the others had. The airship swerved violently, the engines roaring louder than he had ever heard them, and through the window he saw *something* loom out of the mist, a fleeting grey shape like a bloated whale, snatched away by cloud before his eyes had registered more than the vaguest of impressions. All he was sure of was that he had seen another airship, that it had been very close and that it had most definitely not been a phantom.

The firing resumed. This time he had the sense that it was directed and disciplined, with Curtana's crew trying to estimate the course of the invisible enemy through their intimate, hard-won knowledge of airmanship and aerial combat. Even above the roar of the engines he heard shouted orders, the snap and crackle of small-arms fire, and felt the drumming of booted feet on metal plates. Then he heard something different, a rapid series of metallic twangs, as if someone outside the gondola was hammering along its length.

They were being shot at.

Painted Lady steered hard once more, her guns and cannon roared, and again something large and grey bellied out of the mist. This time Quillon had enough time to recognise weapons and armour and engines. The other ship was at least as large as *Painted Lady*; at least as fearsomely armoured and equipped. But it hadn't been some mirage-like reflection. The other ship made even *Painted Lady*'s spikes and ramming devices look like serene accoutrements. The gondola was covered in barbs and crenulations of what was either actual bone – the remains of some vast and terrible animal – or wood that had been carved and sharpened to the same effect. The bonework extended onto the envelope, garlands of skulls and femurs and pelvises wrapping the toughened, metal-plated skin. There was a grisly figurehead at the front of the gondola – a carved or mummified corpse in mortal torment, arms flung wide, ribcage pulled apart to expose glistening innards, gouged holes for eye sockets, mouth wrenched open in an eternal scream.

'Skullboys,' Kalis said.

Quillon nodded. 'I was hoping we'd seen the last of them. But Curtana's made it this far. She must be used to dealing with them, if they're in the air as well.'

The shooting continued. There was more shouting; a scream from somewhere; much too nearby to have been one of the Skullboys.

'That sound like someone in command of things to you?' Meroka asked, the first words she had said to him in hours.

Another round clanged against the gondola. This one punctured the metal, letting in a finger of grey daylight. Nimcha jerked back from the hole into her mother's arms, eyes wild and wide with fright.

'You'd better get on this side,' Quillon said.

'You think it's going to make any difference what side they sit on?' Meroka asked.

Guns roared fire into the mist. Quillon squinted into the swirling white haze but he couldn't see any trace of the enemy now. He did not doubt for a moment that they were still out there.

'Nimcha can bring the change again,' Kalis said. 'Would that silence your doubts, if she did it again?'

'She'd better not,' Meroka said.

'If it helped us—' Quillon began.

'It won't, trust me.'

'A little while ago you wouldn't even credit her with those powers.'

'Right now I'm not prepared to take the chance that I'm wrong. Kalis, listen to me. If you control that daughter of yours, you tell her *not* to do anything, understood?'

'She has her own will,' Kalis said.

'And I've got a pair of hands that are pretty good at strangling. The only things keeping us from those Skullboys are engines and guns, and we need 'em both.'

'You're assuming it has to be a shift to a lower state,' Quillon said. 'What if she changes the zone so that more advanced technologies are available?'

'One way we lose, the other way we gain nothing.'

Quillon turned to Kalis. 'She might be right. The risk's much too great.'

An airman opened the door, carrying a service revolver which he was in the process of reloading.

'Quillon,' he said. 'You're to come with me. Doctor Gambeson's orders. He thinks it's worth taking a risk on you.'

Quillon made to move from the bench. 'What's prompted that change of heart?'

'Ask him, not me. You'll only ever be one mistake away from a bullet, so try not to slip up.'

Quillon took the tinted goggles from his shirt pocket, ready to don them as soon as he had left the room. 'I'll do my best.'

'What about the rest of us?' Meroka asked. 'We're supposed to just sit here and lap this shit up, right? We're sitting targets. If you're under attack, wouldn't it make sense to let us join in the fight?'

'Including the girl?'

'I can use a gun. You might want to mention that to your boss.'

'Captain Curtana's got a few things on her plate at the moment.'

'Judging from all the shouting and screaming, she's not the only one.

Wouldn't it make sense to use every skilled hand you can get?'

The man fumbled the last bullet into his revolver, snapping shut the cylinder and spinning it. 'I'll speak to her. In the meantime Quillon comes with me.'

He was taken out of the room and led through the narrow companionways of the gondola. They walked past the small medicine locker where Gambeson had performed his first, tentative examination. The door was open and most of the shelves were now bare of bottles and preparations.

'How many wounded?' Quillon asked.

'Seven at the last count. We were already carrying four seriously injured men.'

'I presume there was an earlier engagement?'

'This is the first close action we've seen on this mission, actually. The injured men came from a semaphore station. Swarm's always maintained good relations with the signal guilds – it's the only way we can communicate when our fleet is separated. We were supposed to be delivering antizonals when the storm hit. The station was overrun with Skullboys; most of the signalmen were killed before we could get to them. We extracted eight survivors, of which six needed medical attention. Two died shortly afterwards, despite Gambeson's best efforts.'

'He's a very good doctor, but he's still just one man.'

'So are you, Quillon. Do you really think you'll make that much of a difference?'

'I'll do what I can. You rescued us; that places me in your debt.'

'Half the crew still think you should be thrown overboard, along with the mother and daughter. People are beginning to wonder what you are. You think wearing those goggles is going to put an end to the scuttlebutt?'

'If you know why I wear them, what's to stop you telling everyone else?'

'Doctor Gambeson asked me not to.'

'It's that simple?'

'When a man's saved your leg, you do as he asks. But I can't speak for everyone else.'

'We'll just have to win them round, won't we?' Quillon said. 'Speaking personally, surviving to the end of the day would be a good start.'

The airman pushed doors open and led him through into the sickbay. Quillon reeled, momentarily unable to process the sight that greeted him. The shuttered room was much too small for the number of injured men that had been squeezed into it, their beds and bunks locked together like the pieces of a child's puzzle, with scarcely any room for Gambeson to pass between them. The air reeked with chemical disinfectant, barely disguising an underlying stench of disease and decay. Yellow bandages, blood- and pus-stained, littered the floor. Quillon's feet crunched on the broken glass of a bottle, a sticky brown residue of spilled medicine oozing from it. Bullet holes riddled the wall. Death was loitering in the room, Quillon thought, awaiting an opportunity to pounce.

'Ah, Doctor Quillon,' Gambeson said, looking over his shoulder as he bent down over one of the men, inspecting a chest dressing. 'Good of you to come.' He gestured in the vague direction of a shelf. 'I've had your bag brought down. I trust everything's still in it, and you of course have my authority to use any of our supplies as you see, um, fit. Might I rely on you to proceed without my direct supervision?'

'Of course,' Quillon said.

'The gentleman in the furthest bed may be the one most urgently in need of your attention.'

Quillon collected his bag and went to the man. He had been shot in the arm, and judging by the amount of blood on his bandages he appeared to have received only the most basic attention.

'Mister Cudgel,' Gambeson said, directing his remark to the airman who had accompanied Quillon. 'You may leave us now. I'm sure you have more pressing business to attend to.'

'I was told to keep Quillon under guard.'

'And I'm countermanding that order, even if it came from Captain Curtana herself.' Gently he added, 'I need hardly remind you that I have that authority, at least in the sickbay.'

'Ask the captain to let Meroka fight,' Quillon said urgently. 'I promise none of us will do anything to endanger the ship.'

'The doctor speaks good sense,' Gambeson said. 'I believe we would do well to take him at his word.'

Quillon opened his bag and reached bony fingers into its black heart. Very quickly he was lost in the business of healing, all sense of time and his own needs eclipsed by the exigencies of the task. It was not the first time he had dug bullets out of people. Fray had occasionally called on that skill, when his own men had need of back-room surgery. Then, as now, the work had called for a steady hand, scrupulous detachment and a willingness to improvise with less than ideal instruments and supplies. Gambeson's sickbay was at least as well equipped as Fray's back-room clinic in the Pink Peacock (the same room where Fray had cut Quillon's wings away) but it could never have been intended to serve this many sick and wounded.

The fighting continued, although he was only distantly aware of it. The ship swerved, dived and lurched. The engines roared and quelled. Gunfire sounded from just outside the gondola, from the defensive positions along the railinged balcony. Once, a pair of little silver-edged holes appeared in the metal walls on either side of the sickbay, neat as full stops.

'It's not always like this,' Gambeson said, looking up from his patient.

'You don't have to apologise, Doctor. I'm just grateful for the chance to be doing something.'

'Your being from Spearpoint hasn't helped your cause, I'm afraid. Rightly or wrongly, there's still a good measure of animosity within Swarm. I wish it were otherwise, but people will be ... people. Grudge-bearing is part of our nature.'

Gambeson had been careful not to mention Quillon's angel nature in the sickbay.

'Spearpointers don't see Swarm in quite the same light,' Quillon said ruefully. 'Most of them haven't even heard of it.'

'Out of sight, out of mind. We've never had that luxury, Doctor. Even when we're halfway around the world, Spearpoint's influence is still present. Even in the way we talk.'

'Your accent is unfamiliar, but we don't seem to have much difficulty understanding each other.'

'We shouldn't. What you call Spearpointish we call Swarmish, but in truth it's the same language. Spearpoint split from Swarm less than a thousand years ago. That's really not that long, compared to how long some of the ground communities have been out there, going about their own business. The woman – Kalis? Swarmish isn't her first tongue. She can speak it, but it's awkward for her. The girl has a little more fluency – she's probably been in contact with the dirt-rats ... the surface communities ... that speak Swarmish, or a variant of it. Most of the signalling guilds use it, and their influence tends to spread out from the semaphore stations.'

'You seem well informed,' Quillon observed.

'Too many late-night discussions with Ricasso, I suppose.'

Quillon raised a nearly hairless eyebrow. 'A name I've heard twice already.'

'He and I share similarly unfashionable interests. With Ricasso it's the deep history of our world, its origins and ontological underpinnings. For reasons that I need hardly elaborate on, I've long been fascinated by the history of medicine, as practised throughout the zones. There's no shortage of common ground.'

Quillon thought back to what had happened at the Skullboy ambush. 'Which still doesn't tell me anything about Ricasso, or why he would be interested in a live carnivorg.'

'Ricasso's the leader of Swarm,' Gambeson said. 'The closest thing we have to a king, I suppose. He's also Curtana's godfather. Whatever she says Ricasso takes as gospel. You couldn't drive a hair between those two.'

'And if she doesn't think I'm trustworthy?'

'You'll be lucky to see Swarm, I'm afraid.' He glanced back down at the work his hands were doing. 'There's no one I'd rather serve under than Captain Curtana. She's the bravest woman I've ever known, and the best airship commander in Swarm. There's nothing she doesn't know about dirigible flight. But she'll do whatever she deems necessary to protect this ship and bring her crew back alive.'

'Up to and including disposing of her clients?'

'I've known her take far colder decisions than that, and not lose a minute's sleep afterwards. And she's right, as well. Too much depends on us. There's no law out here except Swarm. We're all that's holding back the darkness.'

'There's always Spearpoint.'

'Just a city, Doctor. That's all. It may be the *last* city, but it's not the world. And the world is what's at stake now.'

'You make us sound like parasites, leeching away at a dying patient while Swarm struggles to keep it alive.'

'That's how most of us see it.'

'And you?'

'I'm prepared to see things in a different light.' Gambeson looked at Quillon with a thin smile. 'I'll need persuasion, of course ... rigorous proof. One doesn't take such things lightly.'

The doors opened and two airmen brought in another patient, cradling the slumped and bloodied form between them. The injured airman wore a heavy coat, a helmet and goggles covering most of the face. 'Took a shot in the shoulder!' one of the men said, lifting the lifeless form onto the only vacant bunk in the room, laying it on sheets that were still sodden and stained from the last patient. 'Fell back against the gondola and knocked herself out.'

'It's Meroka,' Quillon said numbly, as the helmet was removed from the unconscious form. Even from the other side of the room he could see that her eyes were closed and her breathing shallow.

'Captain gave her permission to use one of the fixed-mount spinguns,' the airman explained. 'She was giving it hell, too. Took out at least two Skullboy gunners, from what we could see.'

'I knew she'd prove her worth,' Quillon said.

'Do you want to attend to her?' Gambeson said, tying off the bandage he was applying. 'I can take over your patient now.'

'It might be for the best if you look after her. She certainly won't thank me for touching her.'

'She won't know, either.' Something shifted in Gambeson's expression. 'In fact I insist on it. You're my colleague now, Doctor Quillon. I authorise you to treat this patient.'

CHAPTER THIRTEEN

He could not have said precisely when the engagement ended, but there came a point when he realised that the airship had been flying smoothly for some time, and that it had also been some while since he had heard a discharge from any of her weapons. The cloying fog had dispersed, although it was now far too dark to see any surface features.

'We're in the Night Maze now,' Gambeson said, when he queried the other physician as to their position. 'The captain knows this landscape better than the back of her hand, and she likes nothing better than the challenge of dead reckoning, nosing her way through canyons with only a map, gyroscope and starlight for guidance. She's very good at this sort of thing. Mark my word: by morning she'll have shaken the Skullboys off our tail.'

'Is that the last we'll see of them?'

'For now. They don't usually come east of the Three Daughters, or west of the Long Gash. It's all too close to the Bane, which is about the only thing that frightens them.' He was using the dregs of a bottle of sterilising solution to clean his fingers. 'You did well, Doctor Quillon. I'll personally vouch for the fact that you saved lives in this room.'

'I hope someone vouches for Meroka as well.'

'No need, I suspect. The crew will respect anyone who shoots down a Skullboy, no matter where they're from. Taking a bullet won't have hurt her cause either.'

Meroka was still unconscious. The bullet had gone clean through her shoulder without damaging any major structures, but the wound had still been deep and required thorough cleansing. They would need to be on guard against sepsis now. He did not think she had suffered any serious head trauma after falling – it was just shock and exhaustion taking their toll now – but he was also quietly relieved that she had not yet woken.

The engagement heralded a change in the status of the new clients. Quillon was allocated a bunk in one of the small storage rooms near the chart room. He was still not at liberty to wander the airship freely, but it was a definite improvement on the earlier arrangements. With Meroka still in sickbay – barring any other complications, she would remain there for the remainder of the journey – Kalis and Nimcha had the tail-end compartment to themselves. The battle damage had been repaired in a makeshift fashion, and when he visited them he found that they had been given extra clothes and bedding to fend off the cold.

'I think we'll be all right now,' he said, when he was certain no one was listening. 'Meroka was hurt, but I'm certain she'll make a good recovery. As for the rest of the crew, they seem to be willing to accept that we mean them no harm.'

'They will not accept Nimcha if they learn what she is,' Kalis said quietly, her daughter sleeping on the bunk, her form barely discernible under blankets.

'Then we'll just have to make sure they don't,' he said. 'I've done my best to convince Gambeson that neither of you requires any medical attention. Given everything else on his hands, I doubt he'll trouble you now.'

'And later?'

He could only offer the truth, as disheartening as it was. 'I have no idea what will happen to us when we reach Swarm. I don't even know exactly what Swarm *is*, or how they'll welcome us. But I can guarantee something. I'm always going to be the one who will draw their attention, if it comes to that. Nimcha looks like an innocent girl. I look like a freak.'

She nodded slowly, perhaps wary of agreeing. 'Will you be all right?'

It was, as far as he was able to recall, the first time Kalis had shown any concern for his welfare.

'I'm adaptable.'

'You have been kind to us, Cutter.'

He realised that she thought that was his name, after hearing Meroka use it so many times. 'Quillon,' he said. 'And no, I haven't been kind. I've just done what any decent human being would do. Even one with wings.'

He saw that part of Nimcha's blanket had slipped off and bent down to gather it up. She murmured something in her sleep, then turned slightly on the bench. She seemed restful, not at all in the grip of night terrors. He felt a gush of intense protectiveness towards her, but at the same time he sensed that he was close to a ticking bomb. She was just a girl. But if he had harboured any doubts before, he now believed with the utmost conviction that there was a power in her head that could remake the world, and just as easily shatter it again.

Somewhere near midnight he was summoned to Captain Curtana's private quarters. They were alone. She dismissed the attending airman as soon as he had delivered Quillon to her door.

'Have a seat, Doctor. You can take those goggles off now. How you see through them I don't know, but Gambeson tells me you did sterling work.'

'I'm glad he was satisfied.'

'I suppose I can't rule out some ulterior motive for saving lives, but I confess at the moment it's escaping me what it might be. You have my personal gratitude.' There was a bottle of amber-coloured liquid on her desk, accompanied by a pair of small, wide-bottomed glasses. 'Do you drink? It may seem a silly question, but I have no idea what kind of tolerance is the norm amongst angels, or whether such a tolerance would apply to one such as you.'

'I drink.' He corrected himself. 'Or rather, I may drink, for now at least. Alcohol doesn't affect me, but I still have taste buds.'

She poured a measure of the liquid into each of the glasses, finishing the bottle. 'To your health, then, Doctor Quillon.'

He took the glass and sipped at it. It tasted the way he imagined firesap tasted, the aviation fuel that was distilled from some kind of wood secretion or resin: viscous and fiery, with a metallic finish.

The room was very small. The desk was designed to fold back into the wall when not in use. He presumed there was a folding bed somewhere in the room as well, although for now it was well disguised. There were a few shelves, and a number of technical-looking books, their spines printed with the angular, old-fashioned script that he now recognised as the written form of Swarmish. Almost no other signs of per-sonalisation, save for a couple of framed black and white photographs. Both of them showed the same man, though he was younger in one than in the other, his hair and moustache dark where the older man's were white. He wore an airman's uniform in both pictures, with many medals or signifiers of rank on the chest: almost as many when he was young as when he was older. In the earlier picture he was standing on the ground with an airship looming behind him, most of it out of shot. In the other he was caught in a stiff, overly formal posture at the wheel, looking distinctly uncomfortable at being the centre of attention.

Quillon ventured, 'I think I recognise that ship. Was that man one of *Painted Lady*'s former captains?'

'You're very observant, Doctor. That's a useful trait amongst spies.'

'And amongst doctors.'

184

'Touché.' She drank from her own glass, finishing it in one gulp. 'Actually, I don't think you're a spy. A spy would do everything possible not to draw attention to himself, and he certainly wouldn't have gone to such involved lengths to get aboard my ship.'

'That's something of a relief.'

'Nor is it very likely that you're a saboteur. You've had opportunity, and you haven't acted. Perhaps you're saving yourself for some devilish masterstroke, but I'm inclined to think otherwise.'

'I'm not a saboteur. Or a spy. You can eliminate my friends from similar suspicions while you're at it.'

'I don't need to. The fact that Meroka was last seen trying to kill *you* rather rules her out of suspicion, I think. Unless it's all some incredibly cunning ruse to get us off our guard, but ... I don't think so.' Curtana smiled guardedly. 'Now all I have to do is persuade Commander Spatha, and we'll be home and dry.'

'You're in charge of this ship, aren't you?'

'Technically.'

'Then why do you need to persuade him of anything? Doesn't he have to listen to you, not the other way around?'

'It's not as simple as that. Spatha isn't part of my regular crew. He's been foisted on me to keep me and my crew in line.' Curtana looked regretfully at the bottle she had poured from. 'I probably shouldn't be telling you any of this, but you're going to find out sooner or later anyway so you may as well hear it now. Swarm's undergoing one of its periodic spasms. For years there's been little or no challenge to Ricasso's rule, but that's all changing. Look, we're not a democracy, all right? Democracies are fine and noble things when you've got all the time in the world to make your decisions. In the air ... not how it works. You need one hand on the wheel, someone you can trust absolutely. That's Ricasso. He was a captain once, and the other captains decided they wanted him to take all the big decisions. Just the captains, not the citizenry. When Ricasso says something, there's this thing we do called the show-of-flags, but it's not really a vote. It's a show of confidence. Actually it's not even that, because it's more ceremonial. And it never, ever goes against Ricasso. Until recently.'

'What happened?'

'Some captains started getting ideas above their station, is what. There are about twenty of them, all told. *Ghost Moth* is the figurehead, although Spatha – who isn't even a captain – is the one really pulling the strings. Together with the dissenting captains, it looks like they're trying to engineer Ricasso's fall from power.'

'What have they got against him?'

'Ricasso plays the long game. He's repeatedly shied away from direct confrontation with the Skullboys, saying we'd be better off consolidating our power, improving our flexibility, developing improved forms of zone tolerance, before tackling them. They think he's too soft.'

'Is he?'

'They forget what an iron-spined bastard he can be when the cause is right. Truth to tell, so do I sometimes. Ricasso's content to hold the Skulls at bay, picking off the odd one here and there instead of declaring all-out war.'

'Whereas Spatha and the others don't agree.'

'They've managed to draw concessions from Ricasso. He's still in charge, and he still has majority support. But the minority – the *Ghost Moth* dissenters – have chipped away at some of his power. Show-of-flags is now binding on all decisions – it's not just some ceremonial rubber-stamping like it used to be. Ricasso's been allowed to pursue his interests, and not take Swarm into direct and deliberate confrontation with the enemy. In return, the dissenters have pushed through rearmament of dozens of ships, sticking guns and armour on anything with a gasbag and an engine. Everything's become more disciplinarian than it used to be. We used to be very lax about rank and uniforms. I mean, we took airmanship seriously – you have to, out in one of these ships – but that's not the same thing. Now it's all rigid command hierarchies, saluting your superiors, war-readiness exercises, courts martial . . .' She shook her head in abject disgust. 'I don't know where it's all going. What I do know is that anyone even suspected of having sympathies with Ricasso is now under special observation by Spatha and his dissenters. They've put security officers on our ships, spying turd-sucking scabs like Spatha himself.' Curtana looked momentarily rueful. 'I've said too much, haven't I?'

'Merely clarified your feelings. I find it helps.'

'Helps if you know which side I'm on, that's for sure. Here's the thing, though, Doctor. I very much want to believe everything you've told me. I want to be able to accept you for what you say you are. But I've got a tiny, nagging problem.'

'Which is?'

'Doctor Gambeson. He's been with me for years. Knows Ricasso like a brother. Isn't a man on this ship whose counsel I'd trust over his. And Gambeson tells me he's fairly certain that you're still lying about something.'

'Is he?'

'It was much too pat, the way you presented yourself to him. You could have kept your secret much longer, but you seemed in almost indecent haste to reveal it to us. It was almost as if you wished to provide a distraction, to deflect Gambeson's professional interest. You gave him a puzzle that you knew – or at least suspected – that he'd find impossible to ignore.'

'I can't help what I am,' Quillon said.

'No, and no one's saying you aren't an object of genuine fascination. But when Gambeson comes to me with a hunch like that, I am compelled to listen. And he tells me that he thinks you're protecting one of the others.' She raised a finger, rebuffing any attempt he might have made to interject. 'His instincts may or may not be correct. He's also told me that he doesn't think you present an immediate threat to the security of either this ship or Swarm. In truth, I think he likes you, or at least would like the chance to spend more time talking to you. But understand one thing, Doctor: if deception is being practised here, I will learn of it sooner or later. I need hardly add that I would act in any way that I saw fit, with the full authority of command behind me. I would also not be responsible for any interest that Commander Spatha might choose to take in you from that point on.'

'He's already showing interest.'

'Believe me, you haven't seen the half of it.'

Quillon reflected on what he was being told. There was, he supposed, an outside chance that this was all some psychological gambit cooked up between the captain and her security officer, designed to lull him into sharing everything with Curtana. His instincts, however, told him that she was being entirely frank.

'I am hiding nothing,' he assured her.

'I hope that's the case, Doctor. For both our sakes.'

There was a lull. He wondered if this warning was the sole purpose of the conversation. 'What will happen to us when we reach Swarm?' he asked cautiously.

'You'll be evaluated. I've already told you that we believe in giving newcomers a chance to prove their worth. Doctor Gambeson's doubts aside, you could have done worse than you have. The same can be said for Meroka. She took a bullet for us, and I won't let that go unmentioned.'

'I'm sure she'll be delighted.'

'You're not defending her, by any chance? The impression I got from Gambeson was that she was on the point of slicing you open.'

'Meroka was just making a point, that's all.'

Curtana nodded as if she had just had some lingering prejudice confirmed. 'In other words, you Spearpointers will stick by each other to the bitter end.'

'Tell me the same isn't true in Swarm, Captain.'

'No, you're probably right.' She conceded his point wearily, as if her appetite for argument had just run out. 'You realise you'll probably never see it again, don't you? The Godscraper? Do you still call it that?'

'Some of us. But I confess I haven't thought much further ahead than tomorrow morning.'

'Not unwise, under the circumstances. The fact is, though, that we very rarely come within three hundred leagues of Spearpoint, and we usually don't even venture into the same hemisphere. It has nothing to offer us, and we have nothing to offer it in return.'

'Things might be different now,' Quillon said.

'Because of a little storm? I don't think so. It's changed their world more than it's changed ours. When the zones shift, we shift with them. Spearpoint's fatal weakness is that it's never had that flexibility. It's an evolutionary dead end; a form that can't adapt.'

'It's done well enough to last this long. Anyway, if Spearpoint moved, the Mire would move with it. Doesn't that rather exempt it from criticism?'

'So what?' she asked, disinterestedly. 'The Mire has to be somewhere. All I care about is that it isn't here, getting in my way when I have a ship to fly.'

'I'm given to understand that you're very good at it.' He looked at the photographs again, then back at Curtana, gauging the similarity of the face he saw in the images against the one opposite him. Like Curtana he was dark-skinned, but the resemblance went deeper than that. He could see the same eyes, the same delicate features. 'That man ... is he by any chance your father?'

'Was,' she corrected. 'He died ten years ago. Got into an encounter with Skullboys over Sunburn Flats.'

'And he flew this ship?'

'And his father before him, and his grandfather, and his great-grandfather all the way back to when they laid her keel. Been in the family for more than ten generations. She's a hundred and fifty years old. Not the oldest ship in Swarm by any measure, but one of the oldest. That's why I won't see her endangered. She'll go down in flames one day, but it won't be under my command.'

'I would have thought being on some long-range scouting mission qualified as hazardous in anyone's book.'

'That's what she was built for,' Curtana said. 'I'm talking about the danger from internal elements, such as people I can't be sure aren't lying to me.'

'I don't know what I can do to convince you of my good intentions.'

'I'm sure you'll think of something.' Curtana seemed on the verge of dismissing him when a thought occurred to her. She reached into a drawer under the fold-down desk and produced a small black volume that Quillon recognised. 'We confiscated this from your friend, on the assumption she might have another weapon concealed somewhere inside it.'

'And?'

'We found nothing. She may as well have it back.' Curtana riffled the translucent pages before handing the book over. 'Are you a religious man?'

Quillon shifted awkwardly on the seat. His wing-buds were catching on the high fretted back.

'Not especially.'

'That's one thing we have in common, at least. Frankly, I wouldn't have expected it of Meroka, either. That tongue of hers—'

'She can't help it, I assure you.'

Something in his words or expression drew a smile on Curtana's serious face. 'Defending her again, Doctor?'

He fingered the Testament. 'Merely stating the facts.'

'Ricasso thinks there's hidden wisdom in that book. Truths smeared almost out of all recognition. He's not a believer himself – he doesn't hold with all that fire and brimstone, Mire as God's Eye burning through the world stuff – but he doesn't dismiss the practical value of close study of the Testament. But then Ricasso believes a lot of strange things. That's another thing Spatha and the dissenters don't like about him.'

'I presume you know him quite well?'

'I don't have a lot of choice,' Curtana said. 'I'm his god-daughter.'

In the early morning he returned to sickbay. It was not as crowded as it had been the evening before and some screens had been set up between the makeshift beds. Quillon had already been informed that one of the crewmen had died from unavoidable complications, while two others had been deemed well enough to be discharged as walking wounded. Gambeson was half-awake, riffling through notes and the depleted remains of his medical rations. He had the caved-in, shop-soiled look of a man who had not slept in weeks.

'I'm told we should be back in Swarm by mid-morning,' Gambeson said, pausing to scratch at his beard, which had grown progressively more unruly since their first encounter. 'Not a day too soon, in all honesty. We won't lose any more men, but it's been a close-run thing. You can take some credit for that, Doctor.' He held a bottle up to the light, inspecting the thimbleful of medicine still inside, perhaps deciding that it was too precious to discard.

'I wondered how Meroka was faring.'

'Much improved. I spoke to her earlier. She may be sleeping now, but if you wish to talk to her yourself, I won't object.'

'You'd better clear another bed,' Quillon said, steeling himself. 'You may have a new patient coming in.'

Gambeson made an effort to smile, but he was clearly much too exhausted for that. He nodded in the direction of one of the screened-off beds. Meroka had been moved since the night before, and was now next to one of the shuttered windows. Quillon parted the screens, certain that if Meroka was awake, she would have heard their conversation.

She was. She had.

'We haven't got anything to talk about, Cutter.' She sounded drowsy, the words slurred. He could see that the dressing on her shoulder had been changed recently.

'You hate me that much?'

'I hate what you are, and the fact that you lied.'

'That would mean hating Fray as well.'

'My problem, not yours.'

'I envy you, Meroka. It must be refreshingly simple to live in your world. Everything's so clear-cut, isn't it? Angels bad. Humans good. No matter that the angels aren't all the same, and some of the humans have done far worse things to each other than angels ever have.'

'You finished sermonising?'

'For now.'

'Then get the fuck away from me.'

'I hope you'll forgive me in time,' Quillon said. 'For what it's worth, I enjoyed your company, when you weren't convinced I was the devil incarnate.' He paused and drew out the Testament. 'I brought you this. Based on what Tulwar said, I'm assuming it means something to you, other than as a means of safekeeping weapons.' He placed the Testament down on her chest, where she could reach it with her good arm.

Then he left, before she could say a word.

Later that morning they approached a high crater wall, castellated with notches, rimmed in amber fire by the ascending sun. Quillon was allowed onto the command bridge, and then onto the balcony that ran around the gondola, affording the best view. The airship was still maintaining a ground speed of fifty leagues per hour, according to the instruments he had glimpsed on his way through the bridge. That was faster than most trains, even the electric express service between Neon Heights and Circuit City, but there was little more than a breeze on the outside. He kept having to resist the urge to check that his hat was still jammed on his head.

'You were expecting it to be gustier,' Spatha said, joining him on the balcony.

Quillon prickled at the security officer's unheralded arrival. 'Are we moving with the wind?'

'We'd have a much faster ground speed if that was the case. The air's fairly still today. But an airship's not like an aeroplane. Yes, we know about aeroplanes, Doctor Quillon – we don't use airships simply because we haven't grasped the possibilities of heavier-than-air flight. In this zone, and most of the airspace we operate in, you simply cannot build an internal-combustion engine with a sufficiently high power-to-weight ratio to make it effective. Dirigibles, on the other hand, can still be made to work.'

'I never thought otherwise,' Quillon said, though in truth he had given the matter no thought whatsoever.

'An aeroplane cuts through air like a knife. An airship drags air with it, like a glove. We're close enough to the envelope to feel the benefit of that here.'

'Thank you for answering that question for me.'

'We'll be at Swarm shortly. Once there, you'll cease to be under the specific jurisdiction of *Painted Lady*. I expect you think that's the last you'll see of me.'

'I imagine that's not really in my hands.'

'Come with me, Doctor, I'd like to show you something – I think you'll find it invigorating. You do have a head for heights, don't you? Of course. How could you not?'

'What would happen if I stayed here?'

'You might meet with an unfortunate accident. We're not overlooked by any part of the gondola here. If you were to slip over that railing, no one would notice.'

'I might.'

Spatha winked. 'You could always try flapping those little wings.'

Knowing he had no choice, he followed Spatha around the curve of the gondola to a gate in the railing. They were intermittently in view of the gondola's bridge and windows, but everyone aboard seemed far too preoccupied with the approach to the crater wall to care about what was happening outside. They were in safe airspace now, the sky empty of Skullboy marauders. Spatha opened the gate's latch. It led to one of the starboard engine spars, a narrow plank with a waist-high wire hand-guide on the trailing side, the engine a distant snarling mass at the far end of it. The spar was supported by tensioned cables rising up to meet the top of the gondola and the brooding undercurve of the envelope.

'Walk it, Doctor,' Spatha invited.

'If you're going to kill me, why don't we just get it over with now?'

'I'm not going to kill you.' Spatha sounded affronted and startled. 'I'm just satisfying myself that you can meet one of the standard requirements for operational crew. We must all be prepared to go out on those engine spars, when needs must. Things malfunction and need repairing. Propeller pitch can't be adjusted from within the gondola, only by someone out there. In the heat of battle, or when we hit an uncharted zone boundary, there isn't time to wait until a technician arrives. All crew have to be able to do it.'

'I thought I was a client, last I heard.'

'Let's just say that you've entered a transitional state.'

Quillon knew there was no point resisting. He stepped out onto the spar, feeling the vibration of the engine through the soles of his shoes. There was nothing to prevent him from falling forwards, and only the thin guide-wire to arrest him should he fall back. The wire provided more of a psychological than an actual benefit. He clutched it nonetheless. Spatha, who was not holding on to anything, nodded for him to walk further out. 'You can't reach the engine from here.'

The gangway was only wide enough for one man to pass at a time. Quillon had not felt any vertigo when he had been inside the airship, not even when he had looked down at the ground sliding beneath her from the balcony. Now it arrived in full, paralysing force. The terrain was beginning to rise up to meet the crater wall, but it was still an upsettingly long way to the ground. It was a fallacy that angels didn't suffer from fear of heights. Fear of heights was a very sensible phobia to cultivate, even if you had wings. But Quillon didn't even have wings. He just had the useless stumps of wings, confined under the fabric of his shirt.

'Further, Doctor. All the way out. Show us what you're made of.'

Quillon could barely raise his eyes to the engine, let alone work out how far he had already come. The wind began to increase as soon as he left the airship's cocoon of still air. The plank trembled and thrummed, like a horse shivering to dislodge a mosquito. He kept inching along sideways, his back to the direction of motion, hands on the wire, sliding along it rather than letting go completely.

'Have you proved your point?' he asked, raising his voice above the engine and the wind.

'Not yet. Carry on.'

He risked a sideways glance. Spatha was right there, his arms folded, leaning into the wind, a grin of quiet amusement on his face, no less at ease than if he had been standing on solid ground. Quillon redoubled his grip on the wire and continued his shaking, fear-drenched advance. The wind dug its talons into him, trying to rip his coat from his frame. Now his hat really was beginning to loosen, but he could not bring himself to let go of the wire, not even with one hand. The hat popped off, and he felt cold air skim his scalp.

'Just a little further, Doctor. You're doing fine, for a Spearpointer. We'll have you on engine duty in no time.'

'I had you down as a xenophobic zealot,' Quillon said. 'I didn't realise you were also a sadist.'

'We all have our hidden depths.'

He must have been two-thirds of the way to the end of the strut. All he was conscious of was being suspended in space between two fixed landmarks: the engine, and the much larger bulk of the airship. Now the terror of reaching the engine was beginning to ebb, to be replaced by the equally potent terror of returning to the airship. He continued his sideways progress, his heart beating too fast, his hands dead and cold on the wire. The engine was nearly in reach. He could feel the heat belching from its exhaust nozzles. The noise was savage, feral, like the world being torn in two.

'Reach out, Doctor. Place a hand on the cowling. That's all I ask for today.'

He dared to let go of the wire with his left hand, leaning to his left to touch the engine. He gripped the wire as well as he could with his right hand, the one the Skullboy had sunk its teeth into, and his feet were still firmly planted on the plank, with its anti-slip coating. But even so he slipped, or had his feet kicked out from under him. It was so sudden that he could not say which had happened. All he knew was that he went from reaching to hanging, holding on to the wire with his right hand, his wrist twisting violent as his body was sucked back under the wire into open air. Still the wind tried to rip him free. He gasped something, gulped in terror and shock, seeing Spatha standing over him,

Spatha's boots still on the plank, Spatha's arms still folded. Quillon's feet were dangling into space. His left hand grasped at nothing. His right hand began to lose its grip on the wire.

Spatha moved with startling speed. Anchoring himself with one hand, he grasped Quillon's sleeve with the other and hauled him back onto the plank.

'There you are, Doctor. I've got you now.'

Quillon wanted to spit something back at him, but all he could feel was pathetic, shaming gratitude that he had not been allowed to die. His calm still unruffled, Spatha helped him to his feet. Wordlessly they began to work their way back towards the gondola. 'I think we'll call it a day for now,' Spatha said eventually, when he had reached the gate.

'You've made your point,' Quillon said, forcing the words out between gasps for breath.

'I've not even begun,' Spatha said.

But then Quillon saw something that rendered any possible reply superfluous. They were cresting the crater wall, slipping through one of the deeper notches, plunging cliffs of weathered rock sliding by on either side, seemingly close enough to scrape the propellers.

Beyond, sheltered inside the crater, lay what could only be Swarm.

He could not begin to count the ships. There must have been a hundred, a hundred and fifty of them, at the very least. They were packed together densely at the core, more dispersed around the edges of the perimeter, and although the entire formation was holding position within the crater wall, the individual craft were in constant nervous motion. They were all imaginable shapes and sizes and colours, the sole constancy being that they were all airships, and that each craft had at least one propeller. Some had many more than that, and some – like *Painted Lady* – were augmented with wings and fins, scalloped and elegant and painted with dazzling designs in glorious heraldic colours. She was, now that he had something to measure her against, by no means the largest airship. Patrolling the edge of the formation, quartering back and forth, were ships of similar size and armament to Curtana's. Quillon guessed that these must be Swarm's scouts and protectors, fast, agile airships tasked with guarding the weaker, slower ships. There were some with huge, multi-decked gondolas, large as skyscrapers turned sideways, pinned under enormous, sagging, sluglike envelopes, propelled by an absurd number of tiny whirring engines. Some of these huge craft were even joined together, connected by bridges and ladders of swaying rope. Much tinier ships – little more than teardrop-shaped balloons with a single cabin tucked under them – buzzed though the gaps between the behemoths as if they were nothing more substantial than cloudbanks. There were too many of the tiny ships to begin numbering them in the main count; they were, Quillon supposed, merely the ferries and taxis serving the aerial city that Swarm constituted.

He couldn't see all the way through it. The ships were packed too densely for that, darkening into purple gloom as they robbed each other of sunlight. He was aware only that the very largest ships – fat, juicy maggots that were anything up to a quarter of a league from nose to tail – were cloistered deep within the formation. He could see parts of them as the formation shifted, but never the whole thing.

And then there was the sound, which he was only now becoming properly aware of. Even above the noise of *Painted Lady*'s own engines, he could hear the cumulative drone of Swarm. Not just four engines but – he could easily believe – four thousand: four thousand variable-pitch airscrews whisking the air, either to hold station or to maintain darting patrol patterns. Four thousand subtly different engine notes, not one tuned to exactly the same tone as any other, but combining, merging, threading, echoing off the crater walls to form one endless, throbbing, harmonically rich chorus that was utterly, shockingly familiar.

The hum of the city.

PART TWO

CHAPTER FOURTEEN

Painted Lady docked under the belly of a much larger dirigible, a dark green juggernaut that Quillon presumed was a dedicated repair and refurbishment facility for servicing long-range airships. She had a long, narrow central gondola, flanked by half a dozen berthing positions where entire ships could be locked into place, constrained by ropes, cables and an arrangement of massive grapples. Two other craft were already docked, one running her engines on a test cycle, the other with her envelope flayed open like a skinned carcass, exposing a lacy internal skeleton of metal stiffening hoops and lateral struts, the gasbags deflated so that she generated no lift of her own. Airmen of both sexes crawled over the autopsied form, industrious as beetles. Some of them were roped up for safety, but others were entirely dependent on hand- and footholds, blithely dismissive of the possibility of falling.

'*Iron Prominent*,' Curtana said, nodding at the flayed-open ship. She was still standing at the control pedestal, having guided *Painted Lady* all the way in.

'You can tell all of these ships apart?' Quillon asked.

'I can tell that one.' She was smiling for once; he could only assume that for one reason or another it pleased her to see the other ship. 'Are you all right? You seem to be trembling.'

He decided not to speak of the business with Spatha for now, having yet to work out where Curtana's sympathies lay. 'I missed my footing outside, almost slipped between the rails.'

'Happens to us all sooner or later.' She paused to make some inscrutable adjustment to one of the brass-handled controls. 'I flashed Ricasso about our arrival. He's aware that we're carrying new arrivals.'

'How much did you tell him?'

'I told him he'd find one of them very interesting indeed and left it at that. Frankly, he'll be at least as interested in his new toy.'

'Can I trust him?'

'If you can trust me, you can trust Ricasso. He'll know all about you as soon as I hand in my journal, anyway. What happened to your hat?'

'The wind took it.'

'Take one of the airmen's caps from stores. You're starting to look like something sent to scare children.'

'Thank you. What will happen to the others?'

'Meroka will be transferred to the hospital aboard *Purple Emperor*, until she's well enough to be assessed. Kalis and Nimcha will remain in quarantine, also in *Purple Emperor*. We're fairly well acquainted with the diseases in Spearpoint, but dirt-rats are a different story.'

'I examined them both myself. I didn't find anything.'

'On the other hand, you probably weren't looking for anything specific. It's just a precaution, that's all.'

'Who will be the examining surgeon?'

She gave him an odd glance. 'I don't know; it'll depend on too many factors. Why are you interested?'

'Natural curiosity. I also thought it might be less traumatic for the mother and child if they dealt with someone they already knew.'

'Such as you?'

'If it came to that. I've proven my adaptability, I hope.'

'I still haven't forgotten our little conversation last night, Doctor. I meant every word.'

'I never doubted it.'

After a moment, she said, 'Did you find time to visit Meroka and return the item I gave you?'

'I did.'

'And how did she take it?'

'We still have some fences to mend.'

Once the process of securing *Painted Lady* was complete, then began the business of unloading her. A rickety metal platform, a kind of aerial quay, was now in position along one side of the gondola. It was already beginning to fill up with boxes, crates and canisters, as airmen and stevedores worked in chains to liberate whatever hard-won cargo Curtana had brought back. The sick were unloaded on stretchers; engines were already being fussed over by armies of oil-stained technicians, clambering around the struts and wires with wild, death-defying abandon, as if the embattled ship was a prize for the looting. Meanwhile, the small airships – the ferries and taxis Quillon had noticed before – were jostling for parking slots on the other side of the quay, their envelopes bulging against each like overripe fruit. Some of them, he now realised, served as ambulances, the sick being stretchered aboard with particular urgency. Curtana, who was standing next to Quillon, watched all this activity with visible apprehension, breaking her silence to scold some hapless worker for being too careless with a spanner, or stepping where he was not meant to.

'How long will it be before you go out again?' he asked, keeping a firm hold on the rail as the quay swayed worryingly under his feet, the metal plates parting to reveal the crater floor, half a league below.

'A week,' she said. 'Maybe two. Depends on how long they take to patch up all that damage.'

'I imagine you can't wait. This must be claustrophobic, after being away so long.'

'Shore time has its advantages as well. But if I didn't like having a lot of sky to myself, I wouldn't be captain of a long-range scout.' She cupped her hands around her mouth and bellowed, 'Be careful with that! Ricasso'll have your hide if there's a scratch on his pet!'

The stevedores were using a crane to winch something out of *Painted Lady*'s gondola. It was a nailed-up wooden crate, as big as the cage he had rescued Kalis and Nimcha from. The quay tilted alarmingly as the weight was transferred to it, buckling like a rope bridge on the point of snapping. No one around him seemed in the least bothered.

'I don't suppose anyone's ever going to tell me what Ricasso wants with the vorg,' Quillon said, reaching up to secure his airman's cap, which did not quite fit him.

'He likes tormenting them. You can't really blame him for that.'

'I'm not sure I entirely approve of tormenting.'

'You can argue the point with Ricasso. That's him arriving now.'

One of the small airships was moving in to dock at the far end of the quay. It was markedly different from the others, its black sedan-sized gondola painted to a high gloss and ornamented with gold reliefwork. In contrast to all the other ships, whose envelopes showed evidence of make-and-do repair work, this one was a seamless crimson. It completed its docking efficiently, and a stair-equipped door folded down. Two airmen stepped out, both wearing ostentatiously impractical uniforms with white gloves and gold epaulettes, and assumed flanking positions either side of the door. A figure emerged: a huge, jocular-looking man with an enormous belly, a head of abundant white curls and a tiny white goatee beard. His uniform, such as it was, was somewhat less lavish than those of his guards. He wore black trousers and a black tunic, a red sash the only sartorial hint of his evident status. The quay shifted under his weight, despite already being burdened with several tons' worth of crates and boxes and fuel cans. The work of unloading continued, but the airmen and stevedores were now all too conscious of Ricasso's arrival. It was obvious to Quillon that their every move was being conducted under his exacting scrutiny.

Ricasso said something, but with engines still droning all around them, it was impossible to pick up his words. One of the stevedores pointed to the large crate, and Ricasso – outpacing his guards, and with cavalier disregard for the swaying of the quay – strode eagerly over to inspect it. He called out something else, and one of the stevedores presented him with a crowbar. Ricasso levered off one of the planks from the side of the crate, wafted dust from his face and peered into the dark gap he had just created.

'Very good, Curtana!' he called, his voice audible for the first time. 'You've made a fat old man very happy! It's a fine specimen!'

'We had to shoot it,' Curtana said.

'You did well to bring it to me alive at all.' He handed the plank and the crowbar back to the worker, rubbed his palms on his knees and strode over to the part of the quay where Curtana and Quillon were standing, ducking nimbly as an entire engine, its propeller still attached, was craned through the air. 'It's good to have you back!'

'Good to be back.'

He embraced Curtana, all decorum cast aside. Up close, he was even larger than Quillon's initial assessment. He tried to estimate the man's age, but the clues were conflicting. His hands and wrists were age-spotted, but they were corded with muscle. His cheeks were plump and unlined, his hair thick but nearly white; deep wrinkles surrounded his eyes, but they were eyes that sparkled with effervescent enthusiasm. In his thirties, certainly – perhaps even his forties, but with the vigour of a man a third his age. 'I feared we'd lost you, when you were so late flashing in,' Ricasso said. His voice was deep, almost impossibly resonant: designed for oration.

'You must have known the semaphore networks were down, that we wouldn't be able to contact you until we were within heliograph range.'

'That's the thing: we knew almost nothing. Yes, that the storm had been worse than anything in living memory – that was obvious. Beyond that, it was all guesswork. We had no idea how extensive the loss of the semaphore networks was, whether it was a local collapse or a planetwide failure. All we knew was that, one by one, we were losing contact with our long-range scouts. We thought the worst, quite frankly. Then *Iron Prominent* flashed in, and late last night we heard from *Cinnabar*. I hardly dared believe that *Painted Lady* might make it back as well, but here you are.'

'Bearing gifts.'

His tone turned gently reproving. 'It wouldn't make a jot of difference if you hadn't brought me anything, Curtana. As you well know.'

'Is Agraffe all right?'

'He's fine; don't you worry. I've had him aboard *Purple Emperor* since he got back, debriefing Intelligence on the extent of the storm. What about your own crew?'

'We've taken losses, but it could have been worse. You were flashed about our new guests, I take it?'

'The survivors of the signalling station, yes, and the refugees.' It was only then, it seemed to Quillon, that Ricasso became even peripherally aware of him. 'This gentleman's one of the latter, isn't he?'

'Doctor Quillon, from Spearpoint,' Curtana said. 'We picked him up along with three travelling companions.'

'They fled Spearpoint after the storm hit?' Ricasso asked, directing his query at Curtana.

'No, they were already outside. In fact two of them aren't even Spearpointers, so far as we can tell.'

Quillon decided that if he didn't say something, he might never be asked. 'I'm grateful to Curtana for rescuing us. We were about to be killed by carnivorgs.'

Ricasso's gaze shifted onto him. 'How did you come to be mixed up with vorgs?'

'We had the great misfortune to run into Skullboys.'

'Mm. It's a dangerous world, beyond Spearpoint.'

'I noticed. Might I enquire about your interest in vorgs?'

'Is he normally this forward?' Ricasso asked Curtana.

'Actually, we were lucky to run into him. He's a surgeon. Well, some kind of doctor, anyway. Gambeson was stretched thin – he could barely cope before we ran into the marauders on our way back.'

'You volunteered your services, Doctor?'

'It was the least I could do. I'm sorry that one of the men still died.'

'Gambeson says there'd have been more deaths if it hadn't been for Doctor Quillon,' Curtana said.

'Trying to buy our confidence, Doctor?'

'If I imagined it might be bought, I'd give you everything I have. I've nothing to offer but my skills.'

'I normally like to see a man's eyes when he's talking to me.'

Quillon reached up to touch the goggles. 'It's medical. My eyes have an unusually strong sensitivity to daylight. We can talk about it privately, if it interests you.'

'It might,' Ricasso said slowly.

'This is the man I said you'd be keen to meet,' Curtana said. 'I thought we might continue this conversation aboard *Purple Emperor*.'

'Discretion being the order of the day?'

'Something like that. Meroka, the other Spearpointer, was injured, but Gambeson says she should make a full recovery. He has the other two under precautionary quarantine.'

'You can't take any chances with dirt-rats. But there's no reason why they can't all be moved to *Emperor*, is there?'

'None that I'm aware of,' Curtana said.

'I want the vorg shipped there immediately. Tell them to put it with the others, but keep it in the cage for now.' Ricasso turned to Quillon. 'And you, Doctor, can come with me.'

They were aloft, bobbing more than flying, the little gold-encrusted craft having more in common with a balloon than a dirigible. With three passengers inside there was only enough room for the pilot and one guard. The swaying motion, and the sumptuous plush seats, conspired to lull Quillon into a pleasant drowsiness. Curtana had already succumbed. She was asleep almost before they had undocked from the service airship, her forehead leaning against the window, snoring gently.

'I'm not sure she's slept since we were rescued,' Quillon said.

'It wouldn't surprise me. It's a rare mission when she doesn't come back pushed to the brink of exhaustion. I feel a duty of protection, of course.' Ricasso sat opposite Quillon with his legs spread wide, his belly sagging between like a partially deflated gasbag. 'I knew her father very well; he was a superb man. Died defending us, of course. Skullboy incursion of 5273. In my darker moments I worry that she won't feel she's served Swarm unless she meets a similar end.'

'She told me you're her godfather.' Quillon hesitated. 'What should I call you, by the way?'

'Ricasso, like everyone else. I'm not a great stickler for formality, as you'll discover.'

'Do you ... run Swarm?'

'Technically speaking, yes.' He lowered his voice conspiratorially. 'On a day-to-day level, not at all. I've delegated that kind of thing to my very capable administrative staff. Frankly, I've got better things to do with my time than *govern*. It's all rather tiresome.'

'I heard you're interested in scholarship.'

'Indeed. And yourself, Doctor?' His face lit up with inquisitiveness. 'Are you perchance a man of letters?'

'I've studied medicine.'

'There's a hint in the title. I mean more generally. Do you have an interest in history?'

'No more or less than anyone else, I imagine.'

'Well, I hope that isn't the case, because most people – in my admittedly very limited experience – aren't interested at all. And you can't really blame them for that, I suppose.'

'You feel differently.'

'For my sins. Most would consider it no more than a harmless, slightly eccentric diversion, something to keep a bored old man out of mischief. I'm perfectly content for them to keep believing that, but I know they're wrong.'

'There's a saying in Spearpoint – history is just the same card game, reshuffled. Nothing ever really changes; nothing ever happens that hasn't happened already, probably a thousand times. So what's the point in studying the past? All it will tell you is that the future's going to be more of the same, like the weather.'

'You use the same calendar as us, Doctor. I mentioned the Skullboy incursion of 5273 just now.'

Quillon grasped his seat's armrests as the little ferry performed a sharp swerve – far sharper than seemed possible for a dirigible – and plunged between two looming ships, skimming the envelope of one and just passing beneath the gondola of another.

'I fail to see the relevance.'

'If history's always been the same, if nothing's ever changed, why do we bother with a calendar in the first place? Granted, it makes the bookkeeping a little simpler. Gives dirt-rats something to scribe on their gravestones. But there's got to be more to it than that, don't you think? The mere existence of a dating system implies that something happened, something that was deemed sufficiently noteworthy to mark the commencement of things. Something suitably epochal.'

Curtana, who had woken from her drowse, said, 'Here we go.'

'Humour an old fool, my dear.'

They were in the thick of Swarm now, surrounded on all sides by airships and the ropes and bridges linking them. The sky and the ground were only intermittently visible. It was deceptively easy to imagine that these huge structures were fixed landmarks, like a city of toppled skyscrapers.

'From what little I know of the matter,' Quillon said, 'our calendar derives from the Testament. It says that the Eye of God shone through the skin of the world, five thousand, two hundred and eighty-odd years ago. Before that there was just formless chaos, darkness without light.'

'The Eye of God being more or less synonymous with what, in more enlightened times, we would now refer to as the Mire, the chaotic origin point for the zones. Is that not correct?'

'No one really takes that seriously,' Quillon said.

'Other than the many millions of people who still read the Testament, or one of the other major religious texts.'

'Even the most ardent of them don't take all of it literally,' Quillon said. 'They read it for moral guidance, comfort during hardship. Not as a veiled history lesson about the origin of the world.'

'And if they did?'

'They'd be deluding themselves.'

'You sound rather sure of that, Doctor. Not even a glimmer of doubt? Come now – you can't be that close-minded. Not after everything that's happened recently.'

'It's just a bad storm, that's all.'

'And yet the Testament says – and I'm quoting from memory here, so forgive me if I don't get it exactly right – "*and in that time it is written that the powerful shall come, those who move the mountains and the skies, and the mark of the keepers of the gates of paradise shall be upon them, and they shall be feared*".' He smiled, pleased with himself, for it was undoubtedly an accurate recollection. 'The tectomancers, in other words.'

'No one's moved any mountains or skies that I'm aware of.'

'We'll allow a little latitude for poetic interpretation. Keep in mind that the Testament's been passed down through more than three hundred generations. Is it any wonder certain concepts have been muddied?'

'More than muddied, if you ask me.'

'So you don't believe in tectomancers, despite all the scholarship to the contrary?'

Quillon answered as truthfully as he was able. 'I believe some individuals have certain, very limited control over the zones. If that makes me close-minded, so be it.'

'I'm not asking you to open your mind to all manner of nonsense, Doctor, merely to allow for the possibility of things you might previously have dismissed, or failed to give any consideration to whatsoever. Such as the fact that the world was not always this way, and by implication doesn't have to be this way in the future.'

'If the world was very different,' Quillon said, 'there wouldn't necessarily be room in it for Swarm.'

'Something that you no doubt think must have escaped my attention.

206

Well, it hasn't. Truth to tell, Doctor, there's actually a purpose to my scholarship. I have a duty to evaluate any threat, any change in circumstances, that might affect Swarm and its citizenry. Call it strategic thinking, if you must. It seems to me axiomatic that you can't predict the future state of our world, much less plan how you're going to adapt to it, unless you understand how the world became the way it is.'

'And the fact that you enjoy nosing through dusty old maps and legends is entirely coincidental,' Curtana said, with the long-suffering air of someone who had been through similar discussions more times than she cared to remember.

'A happy marriage of desire and necessity, that's all,' Ricasso said. He looked at Quillon sadly. 'I'm sorry, Doctor. My hopes were raised. It's not your fault, of course.'

'About what?'

'I hoped you might prove a suitable foil, a sympathetic ear for my more outlandish ideas. You're set in your ways, though, and I can hardly fault you for that. Medicine is a fixed discipline; it requires diligence, not imagination.'

Quillon did not allow the barb to rankle him. 'Doctor Gambeson told me you enjoy your conversations with him.'

'Gambeson's the exception to the rule. Besides, as often as not he's away from Swarm. I used to enjoy discussions with Curtana's father, but now that he's no longer with us—'

'I wouldn't want to give the impression that I'm completely closed to new ideas,' Quillon said.

'Of course not,' Ricasso said, reassuringly. 'I'm sure, in your own way—'

'It would still be good to talk privately.'

Ricasso leaned over and patted Quillon on the knee, the way an uncle might reassure a small boy. 'I insist on it, dear fellow. I'm sure we'll find a lot of common ground.'

The pilot lowered a grilled hatch to speak to her passengers. 'Coming up on *Purple Emperor*, sir. I'll bring us into the main docking port, unless you've any objections.'

'That'll be fine,' Ricasso answered. 'Take a good look, Doctor. Not many people get this close to her. Quite something, isn't she? Even for a Spearpointer?'

'She's enormous.'

'There's no larger machine on the planet. Nearly two hundred and fifty years old, as well. That's almost prehistoric where airships are concerned.'

They had punched through to Swarm's secret core. *Purple Emperor* nestled there like a jewel, ornamented with the lesser finery of smaller ships maintaining close, swaddling formation. She was, by any measure, a truly preposterous machine: vast and dark as a thundercloud, threatening in her very size, but at the same time conveying a sense of ludicrous ponderousness and vulnerability. Her envelope must have been more than half a league from end to end, twice the size of any ship Quillon had glimpsed so far. The main gondola, running nearly the whole length of the envelope, was a dozen decks tall, lit up with chains of golden windows, festooned with balconies and promenades. There were a dozen smaller gondolas linked to the main one by covered walkways. She had numerous outriggers, mounted in triple and quadruple layers, each supporting a dozen or more engines, the airscrews ranging in size from mere propellers, no larger than those on *Painted Lady*, to slowly gyring blades as long again as a single airship. Ships at least as large as *Painted Lady* were docked at various stations, and they resembled nothing more than opportunist parasites nibbling the crusted underbelly of some tremendous, oblivious sea monster.

'I've never seen anything quite like her,' Quillon said.

'They should have cut her up years ago,' Curtana said. 'She's too big, too old. Slows down the entire formation, and keeps our best ships tied up feeding and protecting her, like a big fat mewling baby.'

'Never one for sentiment, our Curtana,' Ricasso reflected.

'If Swarm didn't have to spend half its resources protecting worn-out, bloated relics like *Purple Emperor*, we could really do something. Take on the Skullboys at their own game for once, instead of skulking around them. Become more mobile, more assertive.'

'More like the Skullboys, in other words,' Ricasso said.

'I didn't say that.'

'One thing I'm still not entirely clear about,' Quillon said. 'What is it that Swarm does, exactly?'

'Everything that Spearpoint does, and more,' Ricasso said grandly. 'Which is to say, Swarm endures; it provides shelter and comfort for its citizens, it clothes, feeds and educates them and gives them work to do when they are old enough. If that was all, it would still be enough: nobody requires Spearpoint to be anything other than a city, do they? It is a thing unto itself, sufficient in that regard. So with Swarm. But we are much more than just a city in the air, and that is where we differ from the Godscraper. Spearpoint's civilising influence, if you can call it that, extends no more than a handful of leagues from its base. We are not like that. Swarm's influence covers the entire planet – there's nowhere we can't go, nowhere we can't extend our reach. Our shadow has touched every square span of the Earth's surface.'

'Even the Bane?' Quillon asked, recalling the blank spot on Meroka's map.

'No one goes there, no one even lives there, so it doesn't count,' Ricasso answered. 'Elsewhere is what matters. Half the communities on this planet think Spearpoint's a myth. But they've all heard of Swarm, and most of them know what we stand for.'

'Which is?'

'Self-preservation,' Curtana answered, before Ricasso had a chance to speak. 'That's all. We grub around looking for the last drop of firesap, or bully some hapless dirt-rats into forging new engines or bullets for our ships. Funny how persuasive four hundred loaded spinguns aimed down at you from the sky can be.'

'We stand for more than just staying alive,' Ricasso said. 'We're the last beacon of enlightenment in a world where the lights are going out one by one.'

Curtana looked like she'd heard this one before. 'Oh, please. We're just another semi-organised rabble. The difference is we have ranks and airships and the delusion that we're doing something noble and uplifting.'

'If your father heard you speak—'

'He'd agree with me. And so would the Ricasso he used to know. We had a purpose once, I'm not arguing with that.'

'Before Spearpoint turned its back on us.'

'I'm not talking about that. I mean afterwards, long afterwards. Until recently, in fact. We were trying to make something better of the world, acting as – yes, I'll admit it – a civilising force, where none existed. Helping the surface communities to better themselves. Establishing lines of communication and commerce, offering guidance and support to towns and communities that dared stand up to the Skullboys. Proving that it didn't have to be Spearpoint or nothing, that there was an alternative.'

Ricasso said, 'We probably shouldn't bicker in front of our guest.'

'He's got eyes and ears and a brain,' Curtana replied. 'He'll have worked out most of it for himself. He did ask the question, didn't he?'

Quillon smiled awkwardly. 'I didn't mean to reopen old wounds.'

'You didn't,' Ricasso said, leaning forwards to pat Quillon on the knee reassuringly. 'Curtana and I may have our differences, but fundamentally ... Look, you know what they say about your fiercest critics, how you should keep them close at hand? Well, there's none fiercer than Curtana.

Her only saving grace is that she thinks I'm still open to reasoned persuasion, rather than being jettisoned overboard.'

'Yes,' Curtana said. 'I'm foolish enough to think he may not be a completely lost cause.'

'And as foolish as it makes me, I'm proud to have her as my god-daughter,' Ricasso answered.

They docked without ceremony, Quillon experiencing a disorientating sense of landing on solid ground as the little craft engaged with the rock-steady fixture of *Purple Emperor*. The landing door was lowered again, and almost immediately a uniformed man leaned in through the open hatchway. He had a youthful, handsome face, pale and freckled, a light, downy growth of beard, flashing green eyes and a head of reddish hair, worn raffishly long. He nodded at Ricasso, but that was clearly just a formality for the benefit of the other observers. Curtana rose from her seat and embraced the man without speaking. They kissed and descended the steps, still holding each other. The guard motioned for Quillon to follow them down onto the platform. They'd berthed next to one of the smaller gondolas, on the starboard side of the ship. Immediately Quillon was struck by how very much more palatial the surroundings were, compared to the businesslike austerity of *Painted Lady*. Although there were other ships docked, there was none of the boisterous activity of the servicing facility. The deck was carpeted, and the attending airmen behaved more like hotel concierges, their uniforms as discreetly understated as their manner. Even the engine drone sounded muted and deferential.

He was led indoors, and then through a long connecting bridge that brought them to the central gondola. The interior of the gondola was galleried and surprisingly airy, for all that the vast envelope loomed over it. It hummed with civic purpose. Staff – civil servants of various kinds, he supposed – seemed to be rushing everywhere on errands, clutching satchels and papers, conducting urgent, hushed conversations with each other as they strode the long hallways. Quillon heard the chatter of typewriters through open doors. He heard the pneumatic *whoosh* of message tubes gliding along overhead service pipes. Aside from the absence of electricity, it was not so different from a busy administrative department in Neon Heights. It was just that he was up in the air, leagues above the ground . . .

After descending to one of the gondola's lower levels they came at last to a lavish stateroom, hemmed by many smaller offices and parlours. The stateroom was half lounge and half place of business, with a long table at one end and an arrangement of settees, armchairs, coffee tables and drinks cabinets at the other. Along one side was a ceiling-high sloping window, affording a spectacular view of the surrounding ships, with only shifting, furtive glimpses of sky and ground between them. The remaining walls were lined with bookcases and framed maps and charts, some of obvious antiquity. The engine drone was no more audible than the noise of city traffic in an air-conditioned office.

Ricasso fixed drinks for his guests, then dismissed the guard. He ushered the party to the lounge chairs and bade them sit down in front of a low table. Something like a game of chequers appeared to be in progress, judging by the gridded board spread out on the table, and the many black markers placed in various formations on the grid.

'I won't keep you long, Curtana,' Ricasso said. 'I know you and Agraffe have far more pressing matters to attend to now.'

The red-headed man blushed. 'I think I've told you everything useful.'

'You were out on a scouting mission?' Quillon asked.

'North of the Bane,' Agraffe said, leaning against Curtana in one of the settees. 'Trying to re-establish contact with an old fuel supply station we haven't used for years.' He paused and looked momentarily worried. 'Um, this isn't a state secret, is it?'

'You can speak freely in front of Doctor Quillon,' Ricasso said. 'If he learns anything we'd rather he didn't, we always have the option of throwing him overboard.'

'Fuel's a constant problem,' Curtana said. 'Firesap grows on trees, as the saying goes, but there aren't as many trees as there used to be. You probably noticed this in Spearpoint. Great swathes of forest are dying back. It's the climate change, we think. The world's cooling. No one knows why.'

'Our atmosphere isn't stable,' Ricasso said, sounding like a man about to veer off on one of his pet theories. 'I've done the calculations. It's like a bucket with a leak in it. Someone filled it to the brim a long time ago, and now it's draining out. Earth's gravity simply isn't strong enough to retain a warm, breathable atmosphere over thousands of years. The atmosphere's thinning, and as a consequence it can't trap heat so efficiently.'

'I don't think anyone in Spearpoint believes that the cold spell is going to continue,' Quillon said.

'Even as their wood supply chains extend further and further from the city? Even as the lights go out? Yes, we have our intelligence, Doctor. We may not like Spearpoint, but we know what it's up to.'

'We rely on ground stations for our fuel,' Agraffe said. 'Not just the fuel, either. Also the sungas we use in our lifting cells, and the explosives we use in our weapons, and the food we eat. There's a limit to what you can manufacture and recycle up in the air, so we've always had to maintain good relations with surface facilities.'

'Dirt-rats,' Quillon said.

'Even dirt-rats have their uses,' Curtana replied.

'Things have been getting worse during the last few years,' Agraffe went on. 'Stations that we used to rely on aren't there any more. Partly it's due to the dying back of the forests, meaning that the raw materials just aren't as easy to come by. But that's not the only reason. The cold's hitting the Skullboys as well, so they've been forced to become more aggressive. It used to be that we kept to our territories and they kept to theirs. But now we're coming into conflict almost every time we send out a ship. A number of our old ground facilities have fallen under Skullboy control. They've started to take the fight to the air now. They don't have our expertise, but what they do have is strength in numbers, and the willingness to die.'

'Desperate times,' Ricasso said. 'And that was before the storm came to stir things around even more, as if we didn't have enough to deal with. It's all verging on the auspicious, wouldn't you say?'

'If I were superstitious,' Curtana replied.

'We've endured crises before,' Agraffe said. 'There's no reason why we can't get through this one.'

'The boundless optimism of the young,' Ricasso said, smiling fondly. 'I envy you that, I really do. But this isn't just some temporary bottleneck we'll pass on through and emerge the other side leaner and stronger. The world is changing. It's never done that before, at least not within Swarm's history.'

'What will you do?' Quillon asked.

'While the semaphore lines are down, we have to rely on scouts for long-range intelligence. There's a resupply facility to the north of the Bane – that's what Agraffe was verifying for us. It was mothballed, but according to Agraffe is still serviceable. More importantly, there's a stockpile of useful fuel, so we can land and replenish very quickly. Two, three days, if the pumps work and the firesap's still good. Equally importantly, the Skullboys don't know about it.'

'It's not a long-term solution,' Agraffe said, 'but it should stave off our worries for another twelve months to a year, depending on the volume and quality of the fuel in the storage silos. We didn't have time to do more than a few simple tests.'

'We're waiting for one more scout to come in,' Ricasso said. '*Brimstone* is late, but we'll give her one more day. Then we move, heading for

Agraffe's fuel concentration depot. We'll take a different route so we don't run into the same marauding parties that caused Agraffe so much difficulty on his return. If *Brimstone* is still operable, she'll have to maintain independent action until the semaphore lines are working again. Then she can re-establish contact with the main fleet. We don't do this lightly – Swarm never abandons one of its own unless there's no alternative. In this case there is none. Our tanks are running perilously low. We must have that fuel.'

'I don't doubt the severity of the situation,' Quillon said.

'I suppose it will be a matter of concern to you, to be taken even further from Spearpoint?' Ricasso asked.

'My relationship with Spearpoint isn't as straightforward as you might think.' Quillon reached up and touched the goggles, glancing at Curtana for confirmation. 'May I?'

'Go ahead,' she said. 'He's going to find out sooner or later, no matter what you do.'

He removed the goggles, waited for his eyes to adjust to the brightness of the stateroom, and looked at Ricasso and Agraffe in turn. 'It's quite a long story,' he said. 'And the eyes aren't the end of it. I am ... anatomically distinct.'

'Some kind of hybrid,' Ricasso said, pausing only to refill his glass, as if he needed extra sustenance to deal with the apparition sitting before him.

'Yes. But I'm slowly reverting to full angel physiology. Very soon these simple disguises won't suffice. I already look ... odd. I'm only going to look odder.'

Agraffe said, 'I can understand why you'd feel a little ambivalent about returning to Spearpoint.'

'It's my home. But they were also trying to kill me. You'll appreciate me being slightly ... conflicted.'

'People? Ordinary human beings?' Ricasso asked.

'Angels. Not that ordinary human beings wouldn't have a go if they knew what I was.'

Curtana bristled. 'Not all of us.'

'No, you've been most hospitable, given the alternatives. I'm grateful.'

'We managed to keep him a secret from most of the crew,' Curtana told Ricasso. 'They're good airmen, for the most part – they wouldn't be working under me if they weren't – but that doesn't mean they'd be ready to accept Quillon. They're superstitious, and ... well.' She looked into her lap. 'No one much likes the angels.'

'I can understand angels being disliked in Neon Heights, or anywhere in Spearpoint that isn't part of the Celestial Levels,' Quillon said. 'But why should Swarm's citizens care either way? Aren't angels just another kind of Spearpointer?'

'It goes deeper than that,' Curtana said. 'There's bad blood between us and Spearpoint. But there's extra-strong bad blood between us and the angels.'

'Meroka said Swarm used to be Spearpoint's military arm,' Quillon said.

Ricasso looked equivocal. 'More than that. Back then Swarm *was* Spearpoint. You couldn't tell where one ended and the other began. What you call Spearpoint was just Swarm's fixed focus. But administratively, politically, culturally, the city was diffuse. Its influence was much more widespread than it is now. It had true satellite communities, daughter-cities, spread halfway across the world, bound by the same laws and statutes, the same civil rights.'

'And then all that changed,' Agraffe said, sounding like a man warming to the topic. 'There was a zone storm, a big one. Maybe not as big as the one we've just experienced, but big enough. The map shifted. Once things had settled down, we surveyed the changed boundaries and reported back to Spearpoint.'

'There are places we can't go,' Ricasso said. 'Zones where nothing works. Not just machinery, but basic biological processes. The Bane's the largest of them, but there are others. After the storm, it appeared that a navigable path had opened up into part of the Bane. We called it the Salient: it was a projection of the existing zone into what had once been dead space. We could live in it, and more importantly, our ships and instruments could function there. It was possible for a ship to travel into the Salient and report back.'

'But Spearpoint wanted more than that,' Curtana said. 'They had intelligence – very shaky, dubious intelligence – that there was something important inside the Bane. It had been hidden until now, but with the Salient pushing as deep into the Bane as it did, there was a possibility of reaching it.'

'There were tensions between Spearpoint and some of its satellite communities,' Ricasso said. 'They wanted more autonomy. Spearpoint – under the influence of the Celestial Levels – wanted to strengthen its authority. After the zone shift, there were fears that one of these dissident states might try to stake its own claim on whatever was in the Bane, thereby altering the power balance across much of the planet. That, needless to say, couldn't be tolerated. And so Spearpoint – or rather the angels – decided that it was going to commit much more than just a small survey mission to the Salient. Fully half of Swarm was organised into a taskforce. We weren't just going to stake a claim; we were going to occupy, and hold, for as long as it took.'

'What happened?' Quillon asked.

'Swarm's captains had serious qualms,' Curtana said. 'They were worried that the storm might not have played out completely. If the zones underwent another adjustment, there'd be a chance that the Salient might collapse, or disconnect from its mother-zone.'

'Marooning the fleet,' Quillon said.

'It would have been a death sentence,' Ricasso replied. 'A slow one, but a death sentence all the same. It's no wonder the captains wanted reassurance.'

'They got it, too,' Agraffe said. 'They were assured that the best analysts in the Celestial Levels had run computer simulations which showed that the Salient was stable. On that understanding, they agreed to the expedition. But they'd been lied to. The angels had decided that the Salient had to be explored at all costs, even if that meant placing Swarm in jeopardy.'

Quillon could see where things were heading. 'It collapsed, didn't it.'

'Swarm was deep inside when the zones resettled,' Curtana answered. 'They were cut off; didn't have a hope. Even then, we were so naive that we didn't immediately assume there'd been any deception. What was left of Swarm regrouped. We couldn't do anything for the ships lost in the Salient. They were beyond help; beyond heliograph signalling range. The only thing left to them was death from zone sickness. But then, slowly, the truth began to emerge. The simulations that had been suppressed because they didn't show the results Spearpoint wanted. The voices that had been silenced or discredited. Our betrayal.'

'As far as we were concerned, it was tantamount to a declaration of war,' Ricasso said. 'So we took it as such. Spearpoint had abandoned us, so we abandoned it in return. We withdrew from protection duties. One by one its satellite communities broke away from control. Over time, they all withered. Now they're not even remembered. And we claimed the skies for our own.'

'I can't speak for Spearpoint,' Quillon said, 'but I'm sorry this happened.'

'Justice has been served,' Agraffe replied loftily. 'It's just a shame that we had to wait so long.'

'That's a pretty harsh judgement, considering no one alive in Spearpoint was responsible for the crime.'

'Collective responsibility doesn't end with death of any single citizen,'

Curtana said. 'It goes on. The city betrayed us. The city still remembers, even as it tried to forget.' She shrugged. 'Now ... it's getting a taste of its own medicine.'

'Surely you can't wish death by zone sickness on anyone.'

'Why shouldn't I? They brought it on us. And they wanted you dead, Doctor. Don't tell me your sympathies lie with Spearpoint now, after it forced you into exile.'

'They're good people,' he told her. 'Most of them.'

'Sometimes bad things happen to good people,' Ricasso said. 'That's just the way things are. You can't lose sleep over it, Doctor. I'd have thought a medical man would appreciate that more than anyone.'

CHAPTER FIFTEEN

Swarm was moving north, uncoiling out of the temporary sanctuary of its crater like some black mass of hornets, belligerent and purposeful. Thousands of engines were revved to military power. The snarling, braying noise drummed off the landscape for leagues around. It was the sound of a city carving a path through the sky.

Out on the balconies, the sound was nearly unbearable, especially aboard *Purple Emperor,* which was never very far from its flanking escort of sleek, weapons-barbed protector vehicles. A small army of airmen had to work outside all the while, tending to the engines, the demented cat's cradle of rigging and struts and torsion spars, the rip-prone envelopes, the finicky, temperamental windspeed and barometric pressure gauges, the guns and cannon that needed continual testing, calibration and adjustment. The airmen wore goggles, helmets and earmuffs, rendering them all but indistinguishable from each other. If there had been something casual about Swarm while it loitered in the crater, the impression was now one of the unbending application of strict procedure. Swarm had owned the skies for centuries; finally Quillon understood something of the authoritarian discipline that had made that possible. It had saved his life, and given his companions shelter. But it was still a thing to be feared, even as it went through the paradoxical business of burning fuel in the hope of finding further reserves of the same dwindling commodity. It was a creature that had to keep moving or die, and that made it both awesome and ever so slightly tragic.

They had waited a day for *Brimstone* to come in. When no word of the ship had arrived – no distant flash of a heliograph send at the limit of visibility – Ricasso had reluctantly given the order to move north, towards the fuel facility that Agraffe had surveyed. Collectively, Swarm could only travel at half the speed of its fastest ships, maintaining little more than twenty-five leagues per hour; less if there was headwind. Swarm's strength at this point lay in numbers rather than agility, but it was also amorphous and adaptable, and (so Quillon was reassured) capable of rebuffing almost any conceivable attack.

His status remained difficult to assess. Ricasso had allocated him generous quarters near his own stateroom, replete with every luxury one could reasonably expect aboard an airship. He shared his meals with Ricasso, Curtana, Agraffe and – when his own duties permitted it – Doctor Gambeson. No topic of discussion was out of bounds, not even matters that Quillon would have supposed were sensitive operational secrets, such as the severity of the fuel shortage. He could only conclude that Ricasso and the others either trusted him completely, or had absolutely no intention of ever letting him leave Swarm. The truth probably lay somewhere between those poles.

But in other senses he was not at liberty to do as he pleased. He was confined to *Purple Emperor*, and only allowed to move around a very small part of her, effectively a self-contained section encompassing the stateroom and the infirmary, plus a short stretch of private balcony. Partly this was for his own protection, to keep his true nature secret from as many personnel as possible. But it also reinforced his impression that regardless of Ricasso's fascination with him, he was still a prisoner.

Meroka had continued to improve. She was out of the infirmary now, although still bandaged and sore. She was not yet well enough to be allowed near the guns again, even for training exercises – they were simply too heavy and cumbersome for someone in her condition. Instead, she was being schooled in navigation and Swarm communications, skills that – for the airmen – were at least as vital as being able to load and aim a spingun. He found her at one of the heliograph stations, practising the transmission of test signals between *Purple Emperor* and other nearby ships, working the shutter with increasing speed and confidence. She not only had to learn the apparatus, but also the code system for ship-to-ship messaging. A female signals officer remained with her at all times, but it was clear that Meroka was anything but a slow pupil.

He watched her for several minutes before she became aware of his presence. She was sending and receiving in bursts, alternately working the shutter and noting incoming flashes in a practice log. Through the windows he saw the stuttering mirror-flash of the other sender, the shutter flicking open and shut only slightly faster than Meroka was able to work hers.

'She's good, isn't she?' Quillon said, addressing the signals officer.

'Better than your average dirt-rat,' the woman said, which he supposed was meant as praise. 'All right, you can take a break now. It's hard on the wrist to begin with, isn't it?'

'I'll cope,' Meroka said.

'Gambeson tells me you're doing well,' Quillon said.

'Good for Gambeson.'

'He's not the only one concerned for your welfare.'

'You wouldn't know concern if it bit you, Cutter.' Meroka eyed the signals officer. She was not one of *Painted Lady*'s crew and so was unlikely to know Quillon's secret. Quillon imagined Meroka having to bite down hard against the temptation to refer to his angel nature. 'It's not in you. Not in any of you. You're colder than snakes. I learned that the hard way.'

'I know what happened,' he said softly. 'Tulwar told me. All I can say is, I'm sorry. You deserved better treatment. Both of you.'

'"Sorry"? That's the best you've got?'

'If I could undo what happened, I would. But it would never have been in my power.'

'Guess that gives you a clear conscience, then.'

'I didn't say that.'

'This isn't about making me feel better, Cutter. It's about atoning for your own sins. *Sorry*, but I can't lift that particular burden. Got enough of my own.' She paused and looked at the signals officer. 'Break over. Can we get back to the lesson?'

'You're wrong about me,' Quillon said.

'And you're wrong about me, if you think there's some forgiveness deep down inside, if only you can find it. Truth to tell, Cutter, there's only more hate. That's what I am. Clinical-grade hate, all the way through. Keep digging, you'll only come out the other side.'

'I don't believe you.'

'Then you're in for more misery and frustration than you realise.' Without another word, Meroka returned to the heliograph, grabbing the shutter lever and initiating another send, all the anger and fury of her life working its way into her wrist as she wrenched the mechanism back and forth.

Quillon took his leave.

'The girl was convulsing again,' Gambeson told him, when they were alone in a side-room off the infirmary. 'Her mother says it's normal, but I'm not sure she isn't hiding something.' He looked at Quillon enquiringly. 'Are you certain they haven't been taking antizonals? It could be a side effect.'

Where Kalis and Nimcha were concerned, he had to tread even more carefully than with Meroka. Curtana still suspected he was hiding something, but he hoped that the gyro-needle of her suspicion wasn't zeroing in on the mother and daughter yet. Perhaps she still thought Meroka was the one he was most likely to be protecting. Kalis and Nimcha, after all, were both dirt-rats, not Spearpointers. Dirt-rats, as far as he could judge, were not considered to be capable of much more than nuisance-action. They brought disease, parasites and moral laxity. Sabotage and espionage were deemed to be beyond their remit. But still: Curtana's suspicion wouldn't fixate on Meroka indefinitely, and then it would have nowhere else to go but the mother and daughter. Quillon craved the chance to speak to them in private. But he could not risk displaying an undue attachment, and was therefore obliged to show no more than the plausible concern of one traveller for his companions.

'They refused the drugs I offered, so I can't see any reason for them to have taken any illicitly,' Quillon said. 'They just have unusually robust tolerance, that's all.'

'It's not uncommon amongst surface-dwellers,' Gambeson mused. 'And, at least out here, the zone shift hasn't been too severe. We've been flying through stable conditions ever since the storm, keeping well away from boundaries. But that only makes the convulsions even more of a mystery. I suppose you think us terribly primitive, lacking X-rays and brain-imaging devices?'

'You can hardly be blamed for living somewhere where machines like that won't work.'

'It's not for want of trying, believe me. There are some basic electrical systems in Swarm, but the crew spend more time repairing them than using them. Building complicated medical equipment is quite beyond the bounds of possibility. The zone simply won't tolerate it. The cellular grid doesn't have the necessary resolution, as Ricasso would say.'

'We all have to make the best of what we have,' Quillon said. 'I've seen the medical care you offer on this ship, and I've been impressed. Granted, you don't have much in the way of clever machines to help you, but you've compensated by being superb physicians.'

'But it would need more than a superb physician to look inside that girl's skull and see what's making her ill. Perhaps we were right to quarantine her after all. It could be viral meningitis, or something similar.'

'I don't think it's anything like that. I believe Kalis when she says the convulsions aren't a cause for concern. She's the girl's mother, after all. If anyone's going to know, it's her.'

'And you're satisfied that the mother isn't a cause for concern herself?'

Quillon tried to look puzzled by Gambeson's line of questioning. 'The mother? She's as strong as a horse.'

'I was thinking more along mental lines. You've seen that mark on her head.'

'It's just a tattoo.' Skirting dangerously close to the truth, he added, 'Someone did it for a cruel joke, or so they could pass her off as a tectomancer. It's not as if she did it to herself.'

'I just wonder what persuaded someone to persecute her in that fashion. She's hardly the most *normal* person I've ever met. The way she stares . . . her entire manner . . . it's discomfiting. I wouldn't be surprised if she drew some of that persecution down on herself.'

'She's been through a lot.'

'Enough, perhaps, to destabilise her, to push her over the edge?'

'She seems rational enough to me,' Quillon said. 'Uneducated, certainly, Swarmish isn't her native tongue, and she's unfamiliar with your culture and technology. She's probably illiterate. But she isn't stupid – she has an excellent command of oral history, and she's managed to keep herself and her daughter alive out there. In my book that makes her neither deranged nor irresponsible.'

'She cares for the girl; that's not in doubt. I just hope there isn't anything seriously wrong with either of them.'

'I suppose if I spoke to them I might be able to tease something out,' Quillon said.

'You don't sound very keen.'

Good, Quillon thought. *That was the idea.*

'They've already asked for you, actually,' Gambeson continued. 'Provided you respect the terms of the quarantine, I've no objections.'

'Shouldn't I be quarantined as well? I was in contact with both of them.'

'The quarantine's mainly a sop . . . a concession . . . to the captain and her officers. But since it causes no harm, and may even do some small good, I am willing to indulge them in that.'

'I'll be brief.'

He went to see Kalis and Nimcha, closing the quarantine door behind him. The room was spartan, but warm and clean and infinitely preferable to the conditions they had been forced to endure aboard *Painted Lady*. There were separate beds with clean sheets and pillows. Mother and daughter were wearing Swarm clothes, utilitarian and slightly too large for both of them, but a considerable improvement on the rags he had found them in. A wind-up gramophone player had been provided, together with an assortment of cylinders, but there was no sign that Kalis had played them; the cover was still on the box. Nor was Nimcha showing interest in the pile of child's picture books she had been given to read. Quillon leafed through them and understood why. The illustrations and texts were predominantly concerned with romanticised airship-based adventures, the ground little more than a smudgy abstraction. Clearly nothing of interest ever happened on the ground.

Mother and daughter, in any case, seemed much more interested in the view through the room's single large window. They were standing at it when he came in, their backs to the door. As the escort ships jockeyed around *Purple Emperor*, the view shifted constantly, the sky and the land showing through the packed mass in furtive glimpses.

'Where are we?' Kalis asked.

'North,' he said.

It was as accurate an answer as he could give. They were a day out from the crater now. The air was chillier than it had been at the equatorial latitudes of Spearpoint and the Long Gash, so much so that even with coat and gloves he could only tolerate brief, bracing spells on the balcony. The airmen never stopped their work, which only became more taxing as the cold took its toll on fabric and machines. Once, with a sense of dreamlike unreality, he had watched a lone airman stumble from a spar and drop into the rushing air, the sound of the engines stealing any exclamation that the man might have made. Snatched away by Swarm's motion, the airman tumbled off the envelope of one of the escort ships moving behind and below *Purple Emperor*.

Then he was gone, and it was as if nothing had happened.

'Where are we going?' Kalis persisted.

He had been given no guidance as to what he was and was not allowed to discuss with them. 'There's a refuelling point somewhere ahead of us. That's where they're taking Swarm.'

'Will we return to Spearpoint?' Kalis asked directly.

It was an odd question because Swarm itself had never been near Spearpoint, not since the Sundering, and even *Painted Lady* had not come closer than a day's ride from the base of the structure.

'If anything, Swarm will take us even further away. I don't think they've got any plans to go anywhere near Spearpoint. They don't like it very much.'

'The further we go, the more ill she will become,' Kalis said. 'She dreams of it now. The dreams make her sick.'

'You told me of bad dreams. Are these the same ones?'

'She dreams of a dark tower and the Eye of God burning inside it. It

222

draws her nearer. Only she can close the Eye. When she cannot do this, she becomes sick.'

'The tower wants me to make it better,' Nimcha said.

Quillon took a deep breath. 'You're saying Spearpoint is the thing causing your bad dreams and convulsions?'

'She has told you,' Kalis said. 'Why would you doubt her?'

'I don't know.' He lowered himself into a high-backed white chair. 'I don't know anything any more. I accept that Nimcha has power over the zones – at least, I think I do. Does that mean I should automatically accept that the Mire – the Eye of God – has power over Nimcha? Perhaps you're right, and I should just take this as the natural order of things. Or perhaps I'm going quietly insane.'

'The zones begin and end in the Eye of God. Nimcha speaks to the zones. Therefore the Eye speaks back to Nimcha. Is this so hard to accept?'

'Let's deal with the practicalities for now. I've told Gambeson that the convulsions aren't a cause for concern. But if what you tell me is correct, then my reassurance was premature. But on the other hand, I can't exactly tell him the truth.'

Kalis said sternly, 'No one must know.'

'You realise this puts me in a bind. Gambeson only wants to do the best for Nimcha. But he can't be allowed to examine her too closely.'

'You must keep him away,' Kalis insisted.

'There's a limit to how long I can deflect him. If he was a poorer doctor he wouldn't care so much.'

'You must make them go back to Spearpoint,' Nimcha said. 'Then the dreams will end, and I won't have the pain in my head any more.'

'They won't go back,' Quillon said. 'They just won't. I'm sorry. I wish it was some other way. But you can't grasp the amount of hatred they have for that place.'

'She will get more and more ill,' Kalis said. She left the rest unspoken, but he knew what she was implying. Nimcha could easily die if the convulsions worsened.

'I don't know what I can do. I can't tell them why we have to return to Spearpoint, because that would mean telling them about Nimcha. And I won't be able to talk them into it unless there's a reason.'

'What if you gave them a reason?' Kalis asked.

'Just like that? Against the grain of everything they believe in? I'm barely more than a prisoner, Kalis. They have no reason to listen to anything I say, much less to accept that we should return to Spearpoint.'

'Then we must leave Swarm,' the mother decided.

'And survive out there somehow, on our own? Even if they agree to let us go? We're thousands of leagues away from where we were picked up. It would take a year to cross all that land on foot, assuming we somehow managed not to get ourselves killed on the way. Our record's not too good in that regard. We barely made it out of Spearpoint's shadow!'

'You will find a way,' Kalis said, as if the mere act of commanding him was enough to make the thing possible.

'I don't think you understand the difficulties.'

'You will find a way,' she repeated. 'And it must be soon.'

'I can close the Eye of God,' Nimcha said. 'I can put things back the way they used to be.'

'Before the storm?' Quillon asked, half-humouring her, half-believing every word the girl said.

'Not before the storm,' Nimcha answered. 'Before everything.'

Ricasso, as was his usual habit at the start of their evening meetings, stood at the stateroom window, one hand behind his back and a slender-stemmed glass in the other, charged with whatever pale spirit had taken his fancy, his attention on the visible portion of the fleet. With the lowering of the sun, the envelopes, engines and gaily painted empennages of the airships turned dark, save for the illuminated parts of their gondolas. Collisions, always a liability when Swarm moved in tight formation, were now even more of a hazard. Ricasso obviously had supreme faith in his airmen. But he seemed to feel that his own vigilance was a necessary component to the enterprise, as if by watching the bobbing, shifting gondolas, he too helped to keep them from straying too close.

'Night's always been a double-edged sword,' he said quietly, as Quillon was let into the stateroom. 'It gives us cover from the Skullboys and other enemies. But there isn't an airman alive who wouldn't rather navigate by day.'

'Have we far to go?'

'We'll reach the fuel tomorrow, by noon if all goes well. We'll spend a day or two replenishing the tanks. Depending on the stocks, we'll either suck the wells dry or leave a ship or two behind to safeguard them until we're next in the area.'

'And then what?'

'We think about where we're going to get our next fuel from. We can't ever rely on one facility. That's how it is, Doctor. It never ends.' Ricasso turned from the window and worked the slats, closing them on the darkening view. 'Don't pity us; it's what we're used to. We wouldn't have it any other way.'

Quillon still knew very little about Ricasso, beyond what Curtana had told him. He didn't seem to have a wife or partner or any immediate family. He had been a captain, like Curtana, like her father and grandfather before her. His ship, Quillon had learned, had been *Cinnabar*, and he was said to have flown her over the snow-cap of the Mother Goddess, higher than almost any captain had ever taken a ship before. He had gained the respect of a majority of his serving colleagues, and by dint of that had been ... 'elected' was probably the wrong word – put forward as Swarm's de facto leader. It wasn't democracy, as Curtana had already pointed out, but it was as close to it as Swarm was likely to get. Quillon had seen the show-of-flags when the decision was taken to move north, each airship dropping a string of brightly coloured banners from its gondola. The imprimatur had been near-unanimous, but that was only because there was, this time, no practical alternative. When the decision was less clear-cut, unanimity could not be counted on.

Ricasso had been close to Curtana's father and he clearly looked on Curtana as something more than just another captain. All the same, Quillon doubted that favouritism had played much of a role in her ascendancy. Her father's genes might have had some bearing, but she was clearly a superb and much-admired captain in her own right, and woe betide anyone who thought otherwise. She had her differences with Ricasso – Curtana hadn't quite concealed her exasperation at the amount of time he spent on his scholarly interests – but at the same time she left Quillon in no doubt that she considered Swarm under Ricasso to be vastly preferable to the alternative. She was a captain of a fighting ship, but she saw her duty as the protection of an essentially pacific entity, rather than being one cog in an ever-more-belligerent war machine.

'All this travelling from one fuel supply to the next, though,' Quillon said. 'It could be considered something of a futile existence.'

'You've distanced yourself from that remark, so I'll take no particular umbrage with it. But is living in a city any different? Spearpoint exists only to keep existing. A city's only ever three hot meals away from anarchy. We're just the same. The difference is, we get to see a bit of the world while we're waiting.'

'I suppose.'

'You sound sceptical, Doctor.' Ricasso touched a finger to his forehead, as if some revelatory insight had just struck him. 'Doubtless you're thinking of all the great art and music Spearpoint gives to the world, its endless cultural achievements. Things that transcend mere survival.

Well, we have our own art. It might not be to your taste, but it's still art.'

'Do airships feature in much of it?'

'I see you're already acquainted. That doesn't make it any less worthwhile, though. I'm willing to bet streets and buildings feature in quite a lot of yours.'

'You're probably right.'

'We make music as well. You might like some of it. Granted, living with the background noise of several thousand constantly functioning piston engines does tend to colour one's appreciation of harmony ... I'm informed that, to the unschooled ear, our music sounds very mechanical and droning, almost like lots of engines being run at the same time.'

Quillon smiled. He couldn't tell if Ricasso was teasing him. 'And our music?'

'The music of Spearpoint, or the part of it you come from? I'm not sure. All I know is that the piece I once had the misfortune to hear sounded like many vehicles trying to squeeze into the same place at the same time. All frantic and cacophonic, with horns and squeals and elements that sounded like metal being scraped with sharp fingernails.'

'I think I know the very piece.'

'Do you care for music, Doctor?' Ricasso had perambulated to a drinks cabinet and was in the process of preparing something for Quillon, chinking coloured bottles together like a boy with his first chemistry set.

'Not really. Or rather, I was brought up with the music of the Celestial Levels, and anything else can't help but sound rather flat and uninspired by comparison.' He paused. 'It was ... lovely. But I think I needed a head full of machines to get the full effect. When they took them away, they also took away a large part of my ability to appreciate music. All I really have left now is the memory of having appreciated it. Like waking from a dream filled with a sense of exultation, but being completely unable to recall exactly what it was about the dream that was so delightful.'

Ricasso directed Quillon to take one of the lounge chairs. He passed him the drink he had just fixed, which was a chemical green colour. 'When you're not listening to music of unspeakable beauty, do angels ever give much thought to why they exist in the first place?'

'Only angels could survive in the Celestial Levels.'

'Undoubtedly the case, but not what I was asking.' Ricasso paused to move one of the black markers on the chequerboard game that was still in progress on the table. 'Consider this, Doctor. Could angels have come into existence in any other zone, and then colonised the Celestial Levels?'

'I don't think so,' Quillon answered carefully. 'The machines inside us couldn't function anywhere else. That's why they had to be removed before I could descend to Neon Heights. My body is reverting to angel physiology, but without the machines I'll never become exactly the way I used to be.'

'These machines, then. How are they made? Who designs them?'

'No one. The machines make themselves. They copy and self-repair, endlessly. Angels are born exactly the same way that pre— I mean, ordinary humans are – their blood just contains machines inherited from the mother.'

'So you understand the basic nature of these machines – enough to make use of them, enough to remove them without killing the host – but you couldn't make them again if you had to?'

Quillon had the sense that he was being steered into a trap. 'I suppose not.'

'But then why would you need to? You've had the machines inside you for thousands of years. They haven't let you down yet, and they probably won't let you down in the future. But someone must have made them once.'

'And I suppose there's a passage about it in the Testament?'

Ricasso's smile was one of self-recognition. 'Actually, this time there isn't – or if there is, it's so camouflaged with metaphor that even I haven't teased it out. But the point still stands: angels are merely people with some highly technical modifications. They appear uniquely suited to life in the Celestial Levels, but maybe that's just the way it looks to us now, after thousands of years. There'll have been a degree of adaptation, to be sure, but not enough to produce creatures such as you out of wholecloth. There must have been something *like* angels from the very beginning, before the zones formed. Before, as the Testament informs us, the gates of paradise were closed, and the angels were effectively locked into the Celestial Levels.'

'The Testament also tells us that people were once like children, and lived to be twice as old as we do now.'

'I don't claim to have fathomed all the mysteries. But I do have a theory about the angels. Once, they were very common. They may even have been the dominant form. There were two kinds of people: those who lived on the ground, who looked much like myself, and who were biologically much the way we Swarmers are now. And there were those who had augmented themselves to fly, and to make use of machines;

machines that allowed them to tap into a realm of the senses mere humans will never comprehend. Perhaps it was a matter of personal choice, whether you became an angel or stayed with the old anatomy. Or perhaps choice had nothing to do with it. Perhaps it was even a punishment or penance, to be remade as ordinary men, and cast down to the ground. But one thing is clear to me. Even if the angels owned the skies, even if they dared to traverse the airless spaces above the atmosphere, most of them would not have been able to survive when the zones formed. Just as an angel could not exist here, in the zone we now inhabit, so most angels would have perished when the zones came into being. Only a few would have been fortunate enough to find themselves in a zone that could still support the kind of being they had become. And so they thrived – or at least did not die – while all the others dropped from the sky like stones. And that is why there are angels in the Celestial Levels now. Not because of some unique convergence of function and form, but because they were lucky.'

'It's a theory,' Quillon allowed.

'It's more than that. In our travels we occasionally come into contact with surface traders who specialise in artefacts of an antiquarian nature. I have a particular fondness for old bones, as it happens. In fact I've made it a minor hobby of mine to collect the skeletons of fallen angels. There is no part of the Earth where they cannot be found. It's as if they were everywhere, until the zones killed most of them.' He paused and took a gulp from his drink. 'I apologise if this is distasteful to you. I mean no offence. All that really interests me is the nature of our world. The angels are a part of that mystery, so I've naturally applied myself to the question of their origin with some considerable vigour. But I'm just as interested in the origins of Spearpoint, or Soul's Rest, or the carnivorgs—'

'I know about your interest in vorgs,' Quillon said.

'Do you, Doctor?'

'I saw one of them being captured and put in a crate for you. I saw it being unloaded from *Painted Lady*.'

'Then you know all my innermost secrets.' Ricasso hesitated and looked at his watches. For all their animosity, Quillon reflected, the wearing of watches was at least one thing that Spearpointers and Swarmers had in common. 'It's not too late. Would you like to see my monsters?'

'As long as they don't try to suck my brains out.'

'Very little chance of that, I assure you. They pose no danger now. I'm even hoping some small good can come of them.'

They finished their drinks and left the stateroom. Ricasso whispered something to the guards and they were escorted away from the part of *Purple Emperor* Quillon had begun to become at least moderately familiar with. Ricasso bustled ahead, flushed with enthusiasm at the chance to show off. They descended to another level – they were surely near the bottom of the gondola now – and through a series of dark, echoey storage rooms lined with stacked towers of lashed-down crates holding – so Quillon was informed by the yellowing labels – various consumable supplies and replacement parts. Some of the crates near the back walls looked dusty and neglected, as if they hadn't been opened in years. It was a measure of *Purple Emperor's* vast size that all this dead tonnage could be tolerated, even forgotten about.

At length they came to a room near what Quillon estimated must be somewhere near the rear of the gondola. Ricasso opened the impressively armoured door with a hefty key, and then repeated the procedure with another door just beyond the first. 'Can't be too careful,' he said. 'They couldn't do much damage even if they did get out, but it wouldn't reflect well on me.'

'I thought you were in charge.'

'I am, but there's no shortage of dissenters who'd snatch at every chance to dethrone me.' He affected a high, whining tone of voice. '"Neglecting his responsibilities." "Wasting his time with pet dis-tractions." "Tinkering when he should be running Swarm" – you get the idea.' He grunted and shifted back to his normal register. 'The fact that I'm doing all this *because of* Swarm escapes them entirely.'

He led Quillon into what at first glance appeared to be a kind of airborne dungeon or torture chamber. Cages ran along one side, benches along the other, littered with all manner of tools ranging from delicate and precise to brutal and frightening. In the absence of windows the room was lit by a series of pink-tinged lanterns, suspended on chains, which were already illuminated when they entered. From somewhere came the thudding pulse of an internal-combustion engine. Above the benches, wheels and cables and shafts spun endlessly. Rubber belts transmitted this power to the waiting tools and devices.

'This is my laboratory,' Ricasso said proudly, doing a little about-turn on his heels. 'It's where I attempt to do my ... what I like to call *"science"*.' He paused meaningfully, studying Quillon's reaction. 'Are you familiar with the word?'

'I don't think so.'

'Frankly, I'd be surprised if you were. There's not a lot of it about these days.'

Quillon smiled tightly. He had snatched a sidelong glance at the contents of the cages and was unnerved by what he had seen.

'You'll have to enlighten me.'

'We conduct applied science, Doctor, all of us. We live in a world surrounded by technologies, and we know how these technologies work and equally importantly we know when they won't. We train people to make the best of use of them. We put them in guilds and military organisations. Some of them we put in hospitals and morgues. We place absolute, unflinching faith in their abilities. We – generally speaking – can repair or rebuild or duplicate almost anything, from a flintlock pistol to a piston-engine to an electric train or television set, a neural-imaging device or energy-discharge weapon. It allows us a lustre of competence. But that's all it is. Scratch beneath our superficial understanding, and all you'll find is a yawning void of ignorance. We don't truly understand any of it. It's all just toys we've been handed down to play with.'

'It doesn't seem to be doing us any harm.'

'Yes, or we wouldn't be here. But that's only because the world has been stable for thousands of years, so we haven't been tested. We've been let off the hook. But now the world is changing, and we haven't got a clue as to how it works or what we can do about it, and what worries me most of all is that there isn't going to be much time to get back up to speed. Hence,' he said with a small gestural flourish at his surroundings, '*science*, or at least the pathetically small area of it to which I am able to make some tiny, trifling contributions.'

'I'm still not quite sure I understand.'

'I want to make sense of the world, Doctor. I want to undo the screws, take off its elegant face, glimpse the glittering movement, poke around in the gears and then decide if it's broken or not. Then I want to know if there is anything we can do to put it back together again. There may not be, but at least we'd have the satisfaction of knowing.'

'We'd be satisfied by our own impotence?'

'We won't know unless we try.' Ricasso stroked his hands against an assemblage of glassware, a thing of spiral tubes, cone-shaped retorts and slowly dripping filters. Something thick and clear and resinous was building up in a catchment flask, drop by laboured drop. 'Look, it's not as if I blame us for not taking much interest in science. Intellectual curiosity will only get you so far. The zones, by their nature, place bedevilling restrictions on what we can hope to do. Every workable device has already been incorporated into our arsenal of useful gadgets. We've worked through the permutations over and over again. There's no point speculating about what you'd do if you didn't have to work under the constraints of the zones, because we do, and that's God-given. Or so it appears.'

One of the caged things stirred predatorily. 'You think otherwise.'

'The zones aren't stable. We know that. But what if the zones are radically, *catastrophically* unstable? The storm's already plunged Spearpoint into squalor and darkness. It's already shaken up the Skullboys and made our existence more precarious than it was before. Everything we've seen to date, though, may be nothing compared to what could be on its way. For now, people are able to survive almost everywhere on the planet, but there's no reason that has to be the case for ever. What if the Bane swelled to encompass the territories that are now habitable?'

'We'd move,' Quillon said.

'Until we couldn't move any more. And then what? Just give up and die, like the angels did?'

'There's no reason to expect anything like that's going to happen soon.'

'I hope you're right, Doctor, with every atom of my existence. Whatever atoms are. But that's not the only danger we face. The zones might stay the way they are now, and we'd still be in trouble. The world is cooling, the atmosphere thinning, the forests dying. That's got nothing to do with zones or storms. But it narrows our options just as effectively.'

'And your solution?'

'I don't have one. Yet.' Ricasso started towards the leftmost cage. 'But I'm directing my efforts in that direction. It seems to me that however you look at it, it's a problem of zone tolerance. If the zones change, we need to be able to withstand whatever fate throws at us. And if the world becomes progressively less habitable, we have to find a way to survive without it.' He read something in Quillon's face. 'You think I'm joking.'

'Where do we go, if we don't have the world?'

'Somewhere else. We've done it before; we can do it again. The Testament tells us that we were once allowed through the gates of paradise. Beyond the gates, it also tells us, lay numberless gardens, each with its own sun and moon. Other worlds, Doctor! Other planets, like our own, but elsewhere in space.'

'That's one interpretation.'

'Some of the older ground-based cultures maintain that Spearpoint was once a bridge, or ladder, to the stars, before it was decreed that the stars were not for us. It's easy to laugh at such beliefs. But what is Spearpoint, if not a very tall structure that pierces the atmosphere? It's situated almost on the equator – you know that, don't you?'

'I suppose,' Quillon said. 'What bearing does that have?'

'It might be telling us something, something very useful indeed. To construct a cosmic funicular you must first—'

Quillon almost laughed. 'A what?'

'You've been up there, Doctor. You know that even the Celestial Levels are only the start of it. It goes on and on, rising into the airless void. No one can live up there, so there must be another reason for its existence. What is to say that men did not climb up the tower – or ride up it by means of a winch, and launch themselves into the gulf between the worlds?'

'Common sense?'

Ricasso shook his head in gentle disappointment. 'You're too much a prisoner of your times, Doctor. You can't see through the prism of the present. I don't blame you for that; I was much the same, once upon a time. But you have to train yourself to see further.' Ricasso paused and smiled. 'Enough speculation; I've undoubtedly said too much. Let us instead deal with something inarguably concrete and practical.' He touched the side of the cage, and the thing inside stirred languidly, metal grating on metal like a steel chain being gradually unwound. The vorg had been relieved of its rear limbs, but it still maintained a degree of ambulatory prowess by virtue of its blue-clawed forelimbs. The elongated, tapering head had locked on to Quillon. It was tracking his movements. The segmented metal tail scraped the ground, swishing from side to side. It smelled of burning oil and rotten meat.

'Give/brain/tissue/vorg. Vorg/want/feed. Vorg/make/good/drug. Vorg/help.'

'Wouldn't it be safer just to kill it?'

'It would. But they're useful to me, and potentially vital to all of us. They used to be robots, I think. Perhaps they were our slaves, before the zones came. Mechanical workers, serving human and angel masters. They were obviously given a degree of cleverness, so that they didn't have to be told how to do *everything*. And, perhaps, a measure of adaptability and self-repair, so they weren't always breaking down. After the change, some of the robots were able to keep on as they were. Others stopped working more or less immediately, because they ended up in zones where complex machines simply couldn't function. And some were on the border. They didn't die out immediately, but their circuits didn't work as well as they used to. So they adapted. They found that they could incorporate organic matter into their mechanisms, using living tissue to bypass systems that no longer functioned. It was probably only a small substitution to begin with, but it allowed the vorgs to operate where other machines couldn't, and where humans found it uncomfortable. So they kept altering themselves, until they ended up the way we see them now. Half-machine, half-flesh. Flesh that's almost always dying and decaying, so they have to keep replenishing it. So they became carnivorous cyborgs, or carnivorgs.'

'You can't tell me there's some good in these horrors.'

'Only in the sense that they're rather adept at chemical synthesis,' Ricasso said. 'Feed them what they need, and they'll make almost anything for you in return. It's how they trade.'

'They were making something for the Skullboys.'

'A kind of antizonal medicine,' Ricasso said. 'They can do that, certainly. But that's not what we need now. We need something better, something more potent and long-lasting. An antizonal's only effective until it wears off, and even then it has to be tailored carefully to the patient, the change-vector and the zone conditions. Is that not so, Doctor?'

'It's true enough.'

'And we accept it, because it's what we've learned to accept. Most of us keep to our zones. We cross over occasionally, but very seldom with the intention of staying. Antizonals suffice. They let you leave Spearpoint. They allow us to take Swarm through zone changes, when we're forced into it, which I assure you is not very often. Your city, your Spearpoint, is structured into districts by virtue of the zones. There's an entire economy dependent on what can and can't be moved from zone to zone. Sure, the zone boundaries shift around sometimes, but can you imagine the wonderful, unholy chaos if people didn't have to obey them any more? If people could live where they wanted to, instead of where they've ended up as an accident of birth?'

'I'd like to see it happen,' Quillon said. 'I wouldn't necessarily want to be there when it did.'

'Chaos, undoubtedly. But that doesn't change my larger point. A drug that allows us to ignore the zones would be of enormous benefit in the future. Even if the zones don't alter, the world is still changing, and the zones prevent us from leaving. We need that drug whatever happens.'

'I don't disagree. But I'm afraid there's no such thing.'

'There soon will be. That's what I've been working on down here. I'm very close, Doctor. Quite spectacularly close.'

Quillon noticed now that there was a fine transparent line reaching into the cage. It plunged through the vorg's metal ribcage, into the glistening mass of organs that enabled the semi-living entity to function. Something pale and watery oozed along the line into one of the glass retorts, drip-drip-dripping through a filtration device.

'You milk them.'

'Something like that. They produce secretions. I refine and analyse the secretions. We're on the sixteenth batch now – I call it Serum-16. It's a slow, painstaking process, getting anywhere near a useful drug. The vorgs aren't clever enough to work out the molecular formula of the compound they need to synthesise, so it's a question of trial and error, working through the permutations.' Ricasso scratched the white hair on the back of his neck. 'It takes patience, and a ready supply of vorgs.'

'And they just ... do this?'

'They don't have much choice. If they refuse, I kill them. Then I dismantle them and feed their remains to the other vorgs. They're not fussy about a little biomechanical cannibalism.'

'Even so.'

'They have a highly developed survival instinct, so they don't particularly want to die. I keep them alive, and they give me the drugs. It's a very equitable arrangement. Secretly they harbour fantasies of taking over the ship, of course. They imagine they can assemble a fully operative vorg from the partially dismembered versions I have captive. Needless to say, it isn't going to happen.'

Quillon was glad to move away from the cages. 'How do you test the drug?'

'On rats and zebra finches, mainly, although anything with a reasonably developed nervous system will do. I mean actual rats, Doctor – not people from the ground. They have to come from outside our own zone, of course, or else they're already too well adapted to be useful subjects. I place one control group on normal antizonals, another on no drugs at all, and I test the third group with the serum.'

'And?'

'The results are ... encouraging. There's still work to be done, but there's no doubt in my mind that the project will succeed. Within twelve months I hope to test it on my first human subjects. Within a year I hope to begin widespread production and dispensing of the end-stage serum. I'll need many more vorgs, of course, but that's not an insurmountable problem. Freed of dependence on antizonals, there'll be almost nowhere Swarm can't reach.'

'I could help you with this,' Quillon said. 'The testing of the batches must be laborious – wouldn't you appreciate a second pair of hands down here?'

'We barely know each other, Doctor.'

'You know me well enough to show me all this. All I'm talking about

234

is lifting some of the work from your shoulders. It's not as if you'd need to teach me any medicine.'

'You seem very keen.'

'Of course I'm keen. Something like this could help the whole planet, not just Swarm.'

'I don't disagree. Equally, I see the need for caution and strict control. It's both a cure and a weapon. We can't go racing into this. If the Skullboys got their hands on it, there'd be nothing to contain them.'

'But maybe they wouldn't be Skullboys any more, if they had access to drugs that didn't turn them into murderous, drooling lunatics.'

'An experiment you'd be willing to sanction, Doctor?' Ricasso's tone showed that he had no great inclination to wait for an answer. 'No; it'll need to be dispensed with care. It's chemical wildfire. Or it will be, when I reach the production batch.'

'What happened to the previous runs?'

'They just didn't work out,' Ricasso said. 'You don't need to worry about them.'

CHAPTER SIXTEEN

From a distance the fuel concentration depot was a dismal, rusting thicket of skeletal docking towers. It looked like a huddle of skyscrapers that had been flayed of glass and chrome and masonry, leaving only an armature of iron bones. They pushed up from a forlorn, mouse-grey landscape, a rugged, boulder-strewn steppe almost entirely denuded of vegetation. Only a few low-lying hills sheltered the towers from distant observation. Some had fallen, toppling onto the buildings and storage tanks below; others were leaning so precariously that it would have been brazen madness to bring an airship anywhere near them. That didn't stop some of Swarm's captains from doing just that. One by one the heavy tankers were brought in, engines droning against the prevailing wind, until they mated with the towers. Guylines were usually sufficient to stabilise the ships in favourable conditions. Here the towers flexed and swayed unnervingly under the varying loads, rivets popping free and girders springing away like flicked playing cards. Airmen scrambled down ladders to reach the pumps and valves on the ground. Some of the machines had been tested when Agraffe visited the site, but many had not been activated in years. They were iced over and seized tight with a thick caking of rust. Hammers clanged and flame-guns roared as the airmen tried to coax the petrified mechanisms back into something resembling serviceability. Even when it began to flow the fuel came desperately slowly, the ageing pumps barely able to lift it to the airships. The smaller craft could get in lower, nosing between the towers, but the tankers were much too big for that. Even now no one was exactly sure how much fuel remained in the tanks, or how much of that was not contaminated beyond the point of recovery. What was certain was that Swarm was not going anywhere for two or three days. All the while, the airworthy escort ships maintained a perimeter patrol, surveying the horizon for signs of enemy craft. This was a watering hole, and watering holes drew the hungry as well as the parched.

It was a predictably nervous time. *Painted Lady* was still undergoing repairs, so she was not one of the ships tasked with protection duties. This chafed at Curtana almost as much as the fact that she had not been given permission to command another vessel in the interim. Quillon sensed her bristling impatience whenever they were together. She was glad to be with Agraffe, who was also 'grounded' aboard *Purple Emperor* while his ship was patched back together. But she was also itching to get away from Swarm's hustle and bustle, back to the gin-clear skies where her hand was on the wheel and her authority total. When she wasn't talking or listening, Curtana stole appraising glances through the nearest window, as if judging the meteorological conditions.

He liked both of them. Agraffe was opinionated, hopelessly wedded to Swarm's rightness in all things, but at no point had Quillon sensed even a speck of animosity in the man concerning his own nature. Agraffe didn't like Spearpointers, that was clear, but it was a general prejudice and he was perfectly willing to make exceptions in individual cases. When Curtana or Ricasso or Gambeson were not around, Agraffe gave Quillon long and enthusiastic lectures on everything from the properties of high-altitude noctilucent clouds to the functioning of navigational gyroscopes and the business of aerial cartography. 'I'm a good captain,' he confessed to Quillon once, 'but she's better than me. Always will be. That's no condemnation of my own abilities, though. It's just that she's Curtana and the rest of us aren't. There's only one Mother Goddess, and there's only one Curtana. The rest of us are foothills.' He smiled quickly. 'Not that I'm putting her on a pedestal or anything.'

'How much of that is natural talent, and how much did she learn from her father?'

'Anyone's guess. All I know is that ship listens to her hand on the helm like it wants her to command it. I've taken her out once – *Painted Lady*, I mean. She fought me all the way. Oh, I got her under control eventually – but it was more brute force than airmanship. Then Curtana takes over and it's like she's soothing an animal. That was when I knew I'd never have what she has.' He said this in the relieved tones of a man who had not only abandoned an impossible goal, but realised that there was no humiliation in doing so.

By way of consolation Quillon offered, 'I'm sure it would be the same if she tried to fly your ship.'

'That's the point, though. I've seen her take command of *Iron Prominent* – that's my ship. She's got her own quirks, her own temper. And Curtana just shrugged and took the reins, and she was flying almost as well as if I'd been at the helm. Not *as* well, but damned close. She's born to it, Doctor. She's a creature of the air, like yourself.' He shook his head in marvel and wonderment. 'We're lucky to have her. We're lucky we even live in the same century she does.'

'You don't mind the time apart?'

'We make up for it.' Agraffe hesitated. They were on one of the balconies, watching the refuelling operations from what was either a generously safe distance or a perilously close vantage point, depending on Quillon's vacillating state of mind. The air smelled charged and flammable, waiting for a spark, a mistake, a moment's inattention. 'What about you, Doctor? Was there anyone in Spearpoint?'

'There was, once.'

'I don't even know if angels have lovers, or whether the sexes come into it.'

'It's rather complicated.'

'As I suspected.'

'We have sexes. There are male angels and female angels. We have other sexes. We have reproductive organs and we look different from each other, at least in our own eyes. But those differences are subtle enough that a human physician wouldn't necessarily see them. We're . . . aerodynamic. I'll leave the rest to your imagination.'

Agraffe gave an uncertain smile. 'But when you came down to Neon Heights—'

'I was human enough to pass close physical examination, yes. Now I'm in a state of transition. I'm not sure if I'll ever look exactly like an angel again. But I will certainly look . . . unusual.'

'And this other angel . . . was she . . . was the angel . . . a woman?'

'Her name was Aruval. I loved her when she was an angel, and I loved her when we had both been changed to look human. We were sent down together, part of the same infiltration party.' He swallowed, conscious of a sudden dryness in his throat. Below, one of the airships was undocking from its refuelling point, pushing back like a pollen-laden bee departing a flower. 'Aruval didn't know the whole truth about the infiltration programme. Nor did I. We thought the purpose was merely to prove that it could be done, and then leave it at that. But our masters wanted to go much further. They wanted to engineer an army of infiltrators, an invading force that could sweep through Neon Heights and the rest of Spearpoint. The cosmetic modifications were almost an irrelevance. What really mattered was our enhanced zone tolerance.'

'Aruval found this out?'

'Almost by accident. The other two were in on the secret. Aruval grew suspicious when she caught them concealing extra drugs and weapons that we knew nothing about. She revealed her fears to me, but neither of us was ready to act until we knew more about what was going on. Then they killed Aruval. They tried to make it look like an accident, of course, and perhaps I'd have believed them if she hadn't already confided in me. But by then I knew.'

·'How did they kill her?'

'The three of them were off on a mission. One of our drug supplies had become tainted so we needed to obtain more stocks. Fortunately it was one of the less complicated drugs and there was a close commercial analogue in Neon Heights. They went to break into a pharmaceutical warehouse in the Second District. I stayed behind in the safe house, as I usually did. I was the medical specialist, you see. I'd been closely involved in the infiltration programme all along, working with the surgeons, the machine-programmers and the drug developers. I knew what had been done to us, and I knew what we all needed to stay alive. I monitored the others – and myself, of course – and made tiny adjustments to our therapeutic regime.' Quillon took a heavy breath of cold, faintly toxic air. 'Anyway: Aruval was pushed down a lift shaft in the warehouse. They said they'd run into security guards, had to make a quick exit, become separated, and Aruval had mistaken a service door for the open lift shaft. They were supposed to go back the next day and recover the body, or at least burn the warehouse down – anything to prevent Aruval from ending up on an autopsy table. But I knew the truth. I also knew that, once I'd helped with the disposal of her body, I'd be next. They were preparing to go deep, and I was a very conspicuous loose end. So that night I informed them that I needed to correct a slight imbalance in their medication. They submitted, as they always did. They had no reason to presume I suspected a thing. That may seem strange to you, but you must bear one thing in mind. Our faces were not our own. We had complete muscular control of them, but they were not the faces we had been born with. Nor did we have a lifetime's experience reading nuances of expression, or hearing deception in each other's voices. It was easier than you'd think to lie to each other.' Quillon looked down at his gloved hands, tight on the railing. 'I murdered my colleagues. I mixed fatal doses. I administered them. It was not a good way to die.'

'You had no other choice.'

'That made precious little difference, when they started dying.'

'And afterwards?'

'I attempted to hide the evidence of their crime, and mine. I was only partially successful. A man – a good man – came after me. He was a policeman, and he knew only that at least one murder had taken place.

He had no way of knowing that this was an internal matter amongst the angels, so he pursued his case with a certain dogged relentlessness. And it led him to me. His name was Fray.'

'I guess he didn't turn you in.'

'We came to an arrangement. I always wondered if he might betray me, but he never did. It was not his fault that I had to leave Spearpoint. In fact, I'd have been dead if he hadn't helped me escape. So I don't hate all humans. I don't even hate most of them.'

'I guess you're wondering what's happened to Fray, and anyone else you left behind.'

'It's crossed my mind.'

'There'll have been emergency provisions, Doctor. Spearpoint isn't Swarm, but it still has governments and committees and civil contingency plans. I'm sure of it.'

'I didn't see much evidence of civil contingency plans taking hold after I left. I saw what looked like a city taking its terminal breath.'

'Then you were lucky to get out when you did. So was Meroka.'

'Strangely enough, that's not quite how it feels.' Quillon reached up to steady his airman's cap, which a freak gust had threatened to dislodge. Day by day, even the cap seemed to fit him less tightly, the bones of his skull contracting. 'But I don't suppose I should be surprised. I can't be the only exile who's ever felt like a traitor, and I doubt I'll be the last.'

'Incoming,' Agraffe said quietly, as if it was a response to Quillon's statement.

'I'm sorry?'

'Incoming,' he repeated, and directed Quillon's attention to an almost invisibly small dot on the horizon.

'Is it one of ours?'

'Of course,' Agraffe said, mildly affronted. 'It's not on fire.'

The new ship was *Brimstone*, and *Brimstone* brought news. She had caught up with Swarm, having returned to the earlier rendezvous point a day after the other ships had departed. A tethered balloon had been left in the crater, loaded with a coded message informing *Brimstone* of Swarm's intentions.

Like the other returning scouts, she had seen close action. Her envelope, gondola and control surfaces were peppered with bullet and shell holes. Half her empennage had been torn bloodily away. She was down one engine, and had been forced to thrash the others to stand a chance of making this rendezvous. Injury and sickness had depleted her crew, taking her captain and senior officer, as well as many hands. Months of work would be required to return *Brimstone* to operable condition, assuming she was not retired and recycled and her name attached to some newer, if not markedly superior, craft.

None of that was of any particular consequence, however, compared to the information she conveyed.

The intelligence was twofold. Partly it concerned improved data on the new zone patterns. *Brimstone* had surveyed change boundaries across several thousand leagues and had detected that the habitable zones now pushed some way – possibly all the way – into what had once been the Bane. Much was still unknown, the global charts largely useless, but it was a start on remapping the world. Across Swarm, cartographers were busy inking in the new boundaries: solid where they were certain, dashed where they were questionable, a series of dots where they were little more than conjecture. Hatched lines and inked shades indicated the probable conditions within each zone, annotated with symbolic summaries of what would and wouldn't work.

More crucially, *Brimstone* had intercepted a semaphore transmission. Far to the east of Swarm's present position, at least one signalling chain had resumed – or perhaps never entirely ceased – transmission. The guilds on Radial Nine were keeping the Skullboys at bay, at least for now. A number of repeating stations had been lost, but when atmospheric conditions were favourable, messages could be leapfrogged across twice the usual distance. The towers were therefore not sending at anything like their usual rate, but they were working, and something like news – albeit scrappy and disjointed – was flowing along the chain. The direction of transmission was almost entirely away from Spearpoint, to an even greater extent than before the storm. Even if that news had been indecipherable, it would have confirmed that someone was still alive, someone very desirous of communicating with the outside world.

But the news was decipherable, and the news was not good. Spearpoint was in agony, just as Quillon had suspected. The only saving grace was that it hadn't died yet.

Across the structure, the old zones had shifted convulsively, making a mockery of the old districts, the old certainties. It was pointless now to speak of any difference between Neon Heights and Steamtown. Steamtown's zone had swelled and now encompassed a much greater volume of Spearpoint, both up and down. The former zones of Neon Heights and Circuit City had shrunk, and what had been the Celestial Levels was now distended, stretched to the point of rupture, its frayed extremities reaching much further down. Horsetown had fractured, meaning that there was no longer a low-technology moat surrounding Spearpoint; no longer any effective barrier to mechanised incursion. Already there were reports of Skullboys massing around the base, and beginning to launch raids onto the low-lying ledges, one or two turns up the spiral. By the same token, angels – or creatures very like angels – had been reported descending beneath the old limit of the Celestial Levels. They were pushing into zones that, ordinarily, would have proven lethal. They weren't dying, yet.

But the city was dark and almost without power, amenities and transportation. Systems that had been highly tuned to one zone no longer functioned. For all that the angels were descending, the Celestial Levels were devoid of light and the flickering indicators of ceaseless, soul-catching computation. Electrical generators lay silent and smoking in the former Neon Heights, the trains and slot-cars and funiculars deathly inert. The steam stations lower down were still theoretically viable, but there was no ready supply of wood to feed them, and their workforces had been decimated by crippling zone sickness. Against this background, the civil contingency schemes stood little chance of being implemented according to plan. Even if there were stockpiles of antizonals secreted around Spearpoint, it was all but impossible to organise their efficient distribution and dispensation. The very people who were supposed to coordinate the effort were themselves victims of the storm, and the hospitals and clinics where the drugs were meant to be doled out in orderly fashion were now little more than dank, terror-filled asylums, crammed with panicked, dying or hallucinating citizens, the staff and patients all but indistinguishable from each other. Unsurprisingly, those precious stockpiles of drugs were being pilfered enthusiastically. There was no central authority operating in any of the former zones, no effective police force or martial law. In this power void, criminal elements were seizing what they could, and leveraging themselves into positions of local influence, however tenuous and short-lived it might prove. They were intercepting antizonals and fuel. No one dared guess how long Spearpoint had before the drugs ran out, and zone sickness took its inevitable toll. Spearpoint might endure for weeks, maybe – depending on certain barely known variables – months. It was almost certainly not going to see out the winter.

Sooner or later Radial Nine would succumb. Sooner or later there would be no one capable of transmitting from any of the sender stations in Spearpoint. Until such a time arrived, there was only one rational thing left to do. It might be pointless, it might be in vain, it might be a shout into uncaring silence, it might be an abnegation of centuries of proud independence. Still it had to be done.

Spearpoint was doing the one thing it had never done in its existence. It was asking for help.

Later that day, while the refuelling operation was still underway, Quillon was called to Ricasso's stateroom. He had been asking after Meroka, gladdened to hear that her progress was continuing, disappointed that she still did not wish to speak to him. It was earlier than they usually met and he wondered exactly what Ricasso wanted to discuss. Even as he ruminated over the possibilities, sifting through the many questions he meant to ask Ricasso, he felt a stirring tingle of disquiet. Nothing about the atmosphere in the stateroom seemed calculated to dispel his unease. Ricasso stood at his usual window, but there was a tension emanating from his portly figure that Quillon had not detected before. He conjectured that *Brimstone* must have brought some other news, something so utterly, viciously demoralising that it could only be shared at this level, between people already bound by one secret. Then he saw that the room also contained Curtana, Agraffe, Doctor Gambeson and Commander Spatha, and also a seated Meroka – who did not look at all happy about having to be within ten spans of him – and he began to suspect that *Brimstone* had very little to do with his problems.

'Sit down, Doctor,' Ricasso said, failing to turn from the window. It was nearing dusk and the ships were still gathering around their feeding points, the operation even more fraught than it had been during the hours of clear daylight. Worse, a milk-white fog was curling in from the north-west, pushing exploratory fingertips over the surrounding hills. It would be on them soon. That probably accounted for some of Ricasso's mood, but not all of it.

'Is something the matter?' Quillon asked, sinking into his customary seat. The furnishings had not been altered, but the chair felt noticeably less accommodating than before.

'Tell him,' Curtana said.

'We know about the girl,' Doctor Gambeson said. 'We know about the mark on her head, and we know what it means.'

'A tectomancer,' Ricasso said, drawling the word out syllable by syllable.

'Can we take it as a given,' Gambeson went on, 'that this was the matter you were so keen for us not to discover, Doctor? So much so that you placed your own life at risk, by revealing your own nature, in the hope that it would distract us?'

'I don't know anything about the girl,' Quillon said.

Spatha walked around to where he was seated and leaned in until his breath was warm in Quillon's face. 'Let's skip this part, shall we? The bit where you feign ignorance, until you realise how futile it's going to be? You examined the mother and the girl, Quillon. You can't have missed that mark, or failed to realise its significance.'

'He saw the mark,' Meroka said, speaking for the first time since Quillon had entered. 'He just didn't take it as seriously as you stupid dumb fucks are taking it.'

Something like a smile twitched across Spatha's face. 'Then why did he hide it from us?'

'Because he knew how you'd react.' Despite her bandages, Meroka sat with her arms folded across her chest, looking as if she was ready to pick a fight – and continue it, and probably win it – with anyone in the room foolish enough to make eye contact with her. 'I took a bullet for you idiots, all right? I helped defend your piece-of-shit blimp. But that doesn't mean I don't think you're all a bunch of superstitious, hypo-critical fuckheads. You've got your guns and your clever gyroscopes, but you're still only one scary little birthmark away from wetting yourselves. Me and Cutter, we don't have much to say to each other right now. But I'll give the lying, treacherous bastard this much: he knows you better than you know yourselves. Reason he protected that girl wasn't because he believes in all that witchery hokum. He did it because he knew you wouldn't be able to stop yourselves, and he didn't like to think what you'd do to her.'

'Oh, we're a bit more educated than that.' Curtana said. 'And inci-dentally, they're dirigibles, not blimps.'

'Whatever you say, little Miss Sky-Princess. But I'll tell you one thing. Where I'm sitting, I'm seeing a lot of scared, fidgety Swarmers.'

At last, and with imperial slowness, Ricasso turned from the window. 'I take it you're not a believer, Meroka?'

'Are you?'

'I don't believe.' He paused theatrically. 'In anything. I question. I *doubt*. I doubt and I doubt consistently and systematically. It's called thinking scientifically.'

'I hope you understand what the fuck that means,' Meroka said, 'because I sure don't.'

'I wouldn't expect you to, my dear. The world isn't exactly conducive to scientific thinking. Not in its present condition. But it's changing, and so must we. Those of us who can, anyway.'

'Still doesn't answer my question about tectomancers,' Meroka said.

'Whether the girl is a tectomancer or not,' Spatha said, 'she cannot remain in Swarm. She'll be a destabilising element.'

'I thought I was the destabilising element,' Quillon said. 'Or are you planning to throw all three of us overboard now?'

'Tell them, Cutter.' Meroka said. 'Tell them she's harmless, that they don't have anything to fear.'

'It's not about whether she's harmless or not,' Spatha said.

Quillon glanced at Ricasso, his mind spinning as he tried to correlate everything he had learned about the man so far. Fragments of conversations, impressions of the personality beneath the bluster and political effrontery, swirled in and out of focus. Ricasso was worried about Nimcha's effects on Swarm, but he was also a man driven by curiosity, a man who would not easily let a puzzle slip through his fingers. Quillon hoped so, anyway. He was putting more than just his own fate in Ricasso's hands.

'She's not harmless,' he said. 'She's anything but.'

'Cutter,' Meroka hissed. 'Think very carefully about where you're going with this.'

'I'm telling the truth. I'm sorry, Meroka, but there's no other way. They have to know what they're dealing with here. They have to know that she's an instrument of change. That doesn't mean she's evil, or even a force for destruction. But she isn't the girl she looks like. She's something bigger than any of us, bigger than Swarm or Spearpoint. I don't think there's anything more important in the world right now than Nimcha. And they have to know that now.'

Ricasso took a deep breath. 'For once, Doctor, I don't think you're holding anything back.'

'I'm not.'

'The question is, why didn't you tell us all this when you came aboard?'

Quillon looked around at his other hosts. Curtana was studying him with something between loathing and fascinated admiration. Agraffe appeared to be finding the whole thing slightly comical; he looked like a man trying hard not to laugh. Spatha was stony-faced and implacable. Meroka was still turning the full bore of her hate onto him. If they had been alone in the room, he suspected she would have made a concerted effort to rip his windpipe out.

'The best thing would have been if you never discovered Nimcha's nature. That's how I was hoping it was going to work out. Kalis, Meroka and I did our best to make sure you didn't find out, but it was a losing battle. Kalis's courage ... we couldn't betray that. Not unless there was no possible alternative. Unfortunately, I think we've just reached that stage. If I let you believe she's just a girl with an interesting birthmark, someone who looks like a tectomancer but isn't, you'll have every reason to get rid of her.'

'There's no reason she couldn't have remained aboard,' Curtana said. 'No one outside this room knows about her now. They wouldn't have to know in the future.'

'But it's like me,' Quillon said. 'I know my own nature isn't the best-kept secret in Swarm. Despite your best efforts, the scuttlebutt was all over *Painted Lady* when we docked. Now there must be thousands who know something of what I am. If you can't keep me secret, what hope is there for Nimcha?'

Curtana shook her head. 'We'd have found a way. Besides, aren't you still trying to argue us into holding her inside Swarm?'

'Under different terms. As a protected asset, not a prisoner. Prisoners you can always throw to the wolves when the rations run dry, or offer to the lynch mobs for appeasement.'

'That's not exactly how we operate,' Curtana sneered.

'Everyone has their limits. But if I can convince you that Nimcha is worth more than that, maybe there's a chance of protecting her.' Quillon looked at Ricasso, still uncertain that his judgement had been correct. 'Isn't there?'

'You've intrigued me, Doctor, I'll give you that. But we're still missing one tiny detail.'

'Which is?' Quillon asked.

'Objective evidence. Some hint that that thing on her head really isn't just a birthmark. Show me that the girl can move zones, and I might begin to take an interest in her.' He gave a shrug of enormous world-weariness, as if potential tectomancers were a phenomenon he encountered at least half a dozen times in a year. 'Until then, I'm afraid she's just another passenger – no matter what you, personally, happen to think.'

Quillon turned in his seat to face Meroka. 'You were there. You know what happened.'

She stared at him biliously. He could feel the lacerating force of her fury. Not necessarily because of what he had done, he believed, but because of what he stood for.

'Quillon's right,' she said slowly and quietly, but with an underlying venom. 'The girl's got something.'

'They were accomplices when we found them,' Spatha said. 'The fact that she agrees with him now proves nothing.'

'I'll get you your proof,' Quillon told Ricasso. 'Let me speak to Kalis and Nimcha. I don't know if she has the strength or control to initiate a full change, but if Nimcha can perturb the zones like she did when we were about to be killed by the vorgs, you'll feel it. We'll all feel it.'

Ricasso turned back to the window. Already the fog was beginning to enshroud the outermost elements of Swarm, paling the ships into diffuse grey smudges that would soon be indistinguishable both from the sky and each other.

'Might be an idea to hold fire on that,' he said.

CHAPTER SEVENTEEN

Quillon's liberty, such as it was, had not been rescinded. He was surprised by that; grateful and suspicious in equal measure. Spatha seemed to have something to do with his not being returned to confinement and he found that difficult to fathom. He was still allowed access to a limited number of rooms aboard *Purple Emperor*, he was still allowed to assist Gambeson in his surgical work, and he was still permitted to see and speak to Kalis and Nimcha. They knew something of what had happened, of course. Gambeson had examined Nimcha and he had not concealed his surprise at the discovery of the birthmark. Kalis had given away as little as she could, but in her heart she had known that her silence would count for nothing now. Quillon did his best to reassure her that neither she nor Nimcha was in danger, but even as he spoke he could taste the callow, ringing hollowness of his own promises. He really didn't know how safe they were, or how wise it had been for him to confess the truth to Ricasso.

'You did what you thought was right,' Kalis said, trying to console him even as he tried to do the same for her, which only made his guilt more intense. 'You must not blame yourself. They would have learned the truth sooner or later. They always do. It is why we have always kept moving.'

'You expected better of me.'

Kalis took his hand, somehow thinner and more feminine than her own. He felt as if she could crush his bones just by twitching. 'The blame is not with you.'

'We have a friend in Ricasso, I think. And Curtana, Agraffe and Gambeson too, although they don't have Ricasso's influence.'

'I have not met Ricasso.'

'You will, I'm sure of it. He's curious about the way things work, and I'm hoping that will count in our favour. He's already interested in Nimcha. I just have to tip the balance a little further, by convincing him that she really is what we say. Then, I think, he'll protect her from anything and everyone.'

'You trust this man?'

'I don't know him well enough. But I already know there's a man I absolutely don't trust, and it's not Ricasso. I have to give him the benefit of the doubt. I think he means well, and that he won't hurt Nimcha.' Quillon realised that Nimcha was staring at him, expectant and fearful at the same time, as if he were a parcel that might contain a present or a bomb. 'He knows what I am, and he hasn't hurt me. That's not much to stake our future on, but it's all I have.'

'And this other one, the man you do not trust?'

'I don't know about him either. If I can keep him interested in me, rather than you, I'll consider that a success. But he wants something, and I don't know what it is.'

'Be careful, Quillon,' Kalis said.

He was leaving the room when Meroka appeared at the end of the narrow, wood-panelled corridor leading to it. Both halted in their tracks. Quillon raised his hands defensively.

'I was just seeing how they are.'

'Don't have to explain yourself to me, Cutter.' She wore one of the heavy coats the airmen used for outside work, slung over both shoulders like a cape.

He closed the door behind him. 'You don't approve of what I said in the stateroom.'

'What makes you think you can read my mind?'

'You gave every impression of wanting to get your hands around my throat. I don't much blame you; it must have come as quite a shock to hear me speak so openly to Ricasso. But I had no choice. I just hope you can see that.'

She shifted a bundle of books from one arm to the other. They were brightly coloured, like the picture books Quillon had already leafed through.

'You took one hell of a fucking gamble in there.'

'I had to give Ricasso a reason to protect Nimcha. He's about the only thing standing between her and mob justice. You saw how Spatha was acting. Would you rather I let him decide her fate?'

'It was still a gamble.'

'I'd have been more than willing to discuss it with you beforehand.' He flashed a quick sarcastic smile. 'Still, at least we're talking now. That has to be an improvement, doesn't it?'

'Never going to be the same between you and me. Just in case you had other ideas.'

She approached until they were close enough to touch. Quillon stood his ground. 'It must cost a lot of energy to keep hating my guts. Wouldn't it be more productively channelled into some other activity?'

'Works for me.'

'It would make sense if I hated you in return, Meroka, but I don't. I'm still grateful for what you did to help me escape. Doesn't that make our relationship somewhat lopsided?'

'I hate lots of things. Don't much care if they hate me back or not.' She moved to push past him. The bundle of books slid apart, some of them hitting the floor. 'Shit, Cutter!' she said.

He knelt down to pick up the books. Some had fallen shut, others had landed splayed open. They were similar to the ones he had already examined. Colourful, airship-fixated pictures and little rectangles of simple text. Stories for children, about adventure and magic in kingdoms of the air.

'What are you doing with these?'

Meroka snatched the books back off him and returned them to the pile she had been carrying.

'Taking them to the mother and girl.'

'There's no point. Kalis is probably illiterate and Nimcha can't read yet. It's not even their mother tongue.'

'I know.'

'Then why—'

'Because someone has to, Cutter. And I don't see you doing it.'

She pushed past, opening and closing the door, vanishing into the room and leaving him alone.

The fog had closed in completely overnight, and now it surrounded Swarm like a packing of soft white cotton. The wind had died down, which made station-holding fractionally easier, but the risk in every action was now compounded by the possibility of collision, either between ships or between ships and the refuelling towers. Already there had been one small fire, caused by a friction spark as an outrigger glanced against one of the towers' support struts. The fire had been doused quickly enough, but it had done nothing to alleviate the tension among the captains and officers, all of whom were beginning to show strain. Anxious to protect its secret cache, and not be caught in a vulnerable condition by any enemy raiders that chanced by, Swarm wanted to finish the refuelling as quickly as possible. The only saving grace, so far as Quillon could ascertain, was that the fuel tanks were both largely uncontaminated and still yet to be tapped out.

Protector ships were on constant vigil. It was harder for them now, not being able to rely on long-range visual contacts. They were flying almost blind, dependent on gyroscopes and fleeting ground sightings to establish position and airspeed. Once or twice, coming from far off in the fog, Quillon heard the booming discharges of artillery. He couldn't tell if they were being fired in exercise, or levelled against barely glimpsed enemies. Once, victim of some unspecified error in navigation, *Cinnabar* came racing out of the whiteness into the heart of Swarm, her engines all at cruise power. It was only by dint of some seriously rapid course adjustment and thrust-reversal that she avoided ramming two waiting tankers. The resulting conflagration, he imagined, would have taken out several dozen ships in the vicinity, including *Purple Emperor*. After that, the mood only turned frostier. He wondered if there would be disciplinary inquiries, courts martial, floggings, plank-walking or some entirely more arcane and ingenious forms of execution involving, perhaps, propellers, grapples or control linkages.

He was on the balcony, enjoying – or at least consuming – a cigarette (it was Swarm-made and tasted oily, but had the same soothing effect on his lungs as its Spearpoint equivalents), when he became aware of Spatha's presence beside him.

'It's a beautiful day for staring into fog, Doctor. Or do you have something else on your mind?'

Quillon pinched the butt between his fingers to extinguish it and pocketed the remains. God alone knew how much damage a stray spark would do in these conditions. 'I wondered when you'd show up, Spatha. I suppose you've come to take me back into confinement?'

'I assumed you were glad to still have your liberty.'

'I am. I'm also wondering what the catch is. I lied about Nimcha. I concealed something of vital strategic importance from Swarm. Shouldn't that be grounds for locking me up again?'

'You've argued your position quite eloquently. You had to protect the girl. In your shoes, I'd probably have done the same. When you saw that the position was untenable, you did the right thing in confessing.'

'It wasn't a confession.'

'Semantics.' Spatha took a bracing inhalation of cool air. 'The thing is, you're a sensible man, Doctor. I know you'll do the right thing to protect the girl.'

'She's in Swarm's hands now, not mine.'

'Nearly.' Spatha paused and looked at the pale outlines of the nearest ships, breaking through the fog like looming sea-cliffs before being swallowed up again. Even the engine drone was more muffled than usual, softer on Quillon's ears. 'Ricasso's taken a shine to you, you know,' Spatha added. 'He finds you interesting, both as an acquaintance and a thing of curiosity in your own right. You're the perfect dinner guest: a foil and a puzzle in the same package.'

'I'm glad to be of use.'

'He's not a bad man. He's served Swarm well in the past; there's no denying that. But these are different times. He won't take the fight to the Skullboys. Spends more time pottering down in his laboratory, trying to coax his precious serum out of his vorgs. That's not what we need now, Doctor.' The skin at the side of Spatha's mouth creased, an improbable fissure forming in the otherwise waxily smooth countenance. 'What we need is decisiveness. Listen to those ships, Doctor. Does that sound like unity to you?'

'It sounds like ships.'

'There are nearly two dozen captains standing ready to act in Swarm's best interests. Revolution's too strong a word. I wouldn't even call it a coup or a mutiny. There'll be no blood, no prop-fodder. More the natural transference of power, but sooner rather than later. The question is, which side of the fence will you end up on when that happens?'

'If all you've got are twenty-odd captains, I think I've already decided.'

'It doesn't take much to start an avalanche, Doctor. Twenty dissenters, spearheaded by *Ghost Moth*? Not many, I'll grant you. But there are many more captains out there whose loyalty to Ricasso is largely a matter of nostalgic attachment to old times. They'll shift their allegiance when they see which way the wind is blowing. More will follow. Then we'll take it to the Skulls. Finally start settling some old scores, while we have the firesap and the ammunition.'

'More killing, in other words. Whereas Ricasso at least wants to do something that might help people. I'm surprised you haven't just killed him and be done with it.' Quillon stopped talking and smiled as the realisation dawned. 'Oh, wait. I see it now. You want me to do the killing, is that it?'

'You misunderstand our methods, Doctor. Killing Ricasso would accomplish very little. He knows as much, which is why he's so lax with his personal security. One, it would have to be engineered very carefully so as not to look like a deliberate assassination or attack. Two, we'd run the very real danger of engendering sympathy for him. Kill him, wound him, and we might end up worse off than we are now. So – no – we don't want you to poison him.' Spatha allowed that remark to stand before adding, 'But there is something you can do for us.'

'What makes you think I'll do anything to help you?'

Spatha edged closer, like an old friend on the verge of sharing a confidence. 'Let me be spectacularly blunt. I know about you, and I know about the girl. At the moment, very few of us do. That could all change. A word here, a word there, and the knowledge of what she is, what she represents, will be all over Swarm faster than you can heliograph it. You may not realise this – it's not the first thing we want our guests to find out – but Swarm's history hasn't been all moonbeams and kittens. There have been convulsions. Coups. Bitter and bloody upheavals. About the only constancy is the ships. During times of crisis – which are more easily precipitated than you might imagine – mob rule can easily become the order of the day. You've seen how it is in your beloved Spearpoint. The thugs aren't slow coming out of the woodwork.'

'You weren't.'

'Weigh your predicament, Doctor. You've been treated well by Curtana and Ricasso, but you're still technically a prisoner, albeit one with generous benefits. If you doubt me, ask to be allowed to leave Swarm. See how far you get.'

'I've no interest in leaving.'

'My point is merely that you don't owe these people anything. You were rescued by Swarm, not by Curtana personally. She was just doing her job.'

'And I'd like to be able to get on with mine.'

'You will. And you'll be able to continue to do that job after the power structure has changed – if you do the right thing now. If you don't, however, we'd have to regard you as ideologically tainted ... and, of course, I wouldn't be able to guarantee your safety once your nature – and the girl's – becomes generally known.'

'And who'd engineer that, I wonder?' Quillon sighed, knowing he had no choice but to face the inevitable. 'Tell me what you want me to do.'

'Nothing too troubling. There's a document in Ricasso's possession that we'd very much like to have a look at. It's a blue leather-bound volume kept in the rack under the table where he plays that game of chequers with himself. We believe it contains a record of his experiments on the vorgs to date, in his own hand, a record that is far more truthful and accurate than any of the progress reports he has released for wider consumption.'

'You think it'll undermine him?'

'It'll show, in his own words, the continued futility of his efforts. We'll let the citizenry make their own minds up about it.'

'If you know about this book, why not just take it?'

'Because it's proven quite impossible for any of us to get near it with Ricasso in the room – and we don't have access to the stateroom when he's absent.'

'Haven't you heard of picking locks?'

'Too many safeguards, Doctor. Ricasso's a ditherer, but he's no fool. You, on the other hand, are still his new best friend. He entertains you alone in the stateroom. You have long discussions. There must be occasions when his back is turned.'

Quillon thought of the long monologues Ricasso had delivered while looking out of the window, or while preparing drinks.

'I will not compromise his research programme. If those notes are genuine, then they're invaluable.'

'He'll have a duplicate copy somewhere. And besides, we're not going to burn or tear up the very document we'll use to incriminate him. The log is and will remain Swarm property – and when the regime change is complete, there's no reason why it can't be released to you, to continue – if you so wish – his work.'

'I won't do it,' Quillon said. 'I can't do it. Even if I wanted to, even if I had the chance – I wouldn't be able to smuggle that book out of the stateroom without him noticing.'

'Ah, but that's where you're wrong. We'll find a way, between the two of us.' Spatha patted him on the back, in the soft hollow between his wing-buds. 'It's been good to talk, Doctor. Don't, of course, say a word about this to another living soul. Because I will find out if you do.'

Quillon watched him go back inside. Then he returned his own attention to the fog, and the shifting, atavistic forms that were barely discernible within it.

Ricasso leaned across the table to recharge Quillon's glass from an ornate decanter, frost-etched with airships and improbable billowing cloud-scapes. It was evening. Together with Curtana, Agraffe and Gambeson, they had just finished dining. Meroka, so far as he could tell, had either declined or not been invited. Quillon suspected that the former was more likely.

The stateroom talk had been terse and superficial, skirting around anything of substance. Matters had not been improved by the endless stream of aides filtering in and out of the room to whisper morsels of intelligence into Ricasso's ear. Nor were they assisted by the microscopic tremors and surges, detectable only by the movement they caused in the drinks, that made Ricasso halt in mid-conversation and hold his breath, no doubt anticipating some fiery conjunction of air and fuel and ponderous, combustible moving bodies. When the aides left, or the anxious moments passed, he generally struggled to regain the thread of whatever they had been talking about.

There was much to be tense about. Just before sundown one of the protector ships had returned to report a hard visual contact with another airship skulking thirty-five leagues from the fuel depot. It had only been a glimpse, a sighting of a few moments when a clearing opened in the fog, but it had been observed by several reliable spotters and there could be no doubt of its authenticity. The other ship had all the characteristics of a Skullboy raider. Beneath its baroque, intimidating embellishments its outline had even been tentatively identified as matching *Grayling*, a Swarm vessel that had been captured with all hands fifty years earlier. The Skullboys would have another name for it, of course: *Eviscerator*, perhaps, or *Gouger*. They were known for a certain single-minded literalness in the naming of their craft.

In response, Ricasso had ordered more ships to peel away from the main body to provide additional recon patrols and flanking cover. It was tactically risky, as he had explained to Quillon. There was no guarantee that the raider had even seen the protector ship, and it might now have moved on without any notion that it had come so close to Swarm. Even if there were other ships out there, they might simply be waiting for the weather to clear. But merely by committing more ships to the patrols, Ricasso risked exposing their position.

'I have to do it, though. If there are Skullboys out there and they stumble on us with half the fleet docked onto fuel towers, they'll cut us open like squealing pigs.'

'At least you can't be accused of turning your back on the Skullboy problem,' Quillon said mildly, glad that Ricasso had dispensed his metaphor after the meal's completion.

'There are plenty who'd argue that I've done just that.' Ricasso placed the stopper in the decanter. 'Fools, of course. They think that all we have to do is concentrate our main force on a handful of Skullboy nests and the problem will magically wither away. They don't grasp that the Skullboys are infinitely dilutable. While there are dirt-rats down there, and drugs that turn dirt-rats mad, there will always be Skullboys, or something so close it makes no difference.' He studied Quillon with his head cocked, like a dog that had just heard a suspicious footfall. 'Actually, I'm surprised that you'd take much of an interest in the matter.'

'Just a passing one.' Quillon smiled briefly.

'Anyone who has a problem with Ricasso's handling of the Skullboy problem,' Curtana said, 'can take it up with me first.'

'They wouldn't have the balls, my dear.'

'Has there been any more news from the semaphores?' Quillon asked.

'Not a chance, Doctor,' Ricasso said regretfully. 'We're far too far away from any of the lines, even if they are sending now. What we've got from *Brimstone* is all we're going to get, I'm afraid.'

'And you wouldn't consider sending out another scout to the same position where Brimstone intercepted the original transmission?'

Ricasso gave a short, sorrowful shake of his head. 'It really isn't practical. I'm truly sorry that the news from Spearpoint wasn't better, but you've seen how desperate things were. All you can do, Doctor – and I realise this is more easily said than done – is begin to put your old life behind you. Spearpoint's ending is a tragedy, unquestionably, but there's nothing anyone can do about it now. The onus, instead, is on the rest of us to start preparing for the future.'

'Spearpoint isn't dead,' Quillon said. 'It's dying. But a doctor doesn't abandon a dying patient. And we shouldn't abandon Spearpoint.'

'It had no compunctions about abandoning Swarm,' Agraffe said, reaching up to loosen his tunic collar, his face flushed with the evening's consumption.

'Then you have the moral high ground.' Quillon met the young captain's eyes. 'Why not think of capitalising on that, instead of digging into an even more entrenched position?'

'Noble and uplifting sentiments,' Ricasso observed, pausing to dab a napkin against his crumb-flecked lips. 'But rather irrelevant, I'm afraid. There's nothing we could do for Spearpoint, even if we had the will. We're just Swarm; a handful of airships.'

'I wouldn't call a hundred and fifty a handful,' Quillon retorted. 'Or however many it is.'

'Still a scratch against Spearpoint,' Ricasso said. 'Granted, we were once much more numerous. A force to be reckoned with. But that was before the Salient; before perfidious betrayal and the predations of time ate into our number.'

'I'm not talking about attacking it,' Quillon said. 'I'm talking about offering material assistance. We've all been privy to the news Brimstone picked up. Surely there's *something* Swarm could do.'

Ricasso looked genuinely puzzled. 'Why on Earth would you want to go back there, Doctor, of all places? They'd as soon flay you alive!'

'Some of them. But should the others suffer just because of that?'

'Again,' Ricasso said, irritation beginning to break through his normal unflappability, 'it might make a difference if there was something that could be done. Some tiny gesture. But there isn't. Nothing. And even if there was ... the storm began in the Mire, in the heart of Spearpoint.' He emphasised this point by tapping the table. 'To some, that suggests Spearpoint brought this on itself.'

'We don't all hold to that notion,' Gambeson said tartly. 'Just in case you were wondering, Doctor.'

Quillon acknowledged the other man's common sense with a nod. 'I doubt Ricasso holds to it either. Unless that spirit of sceptical enquiry he likes to present to us is a facade, draped over superstition and prejudice.'

'This is getting too intense for me,' Curtana said, glancing at Agraffe for signs of support.

He shrugged and made an agreeing noise. 'Bedtime?'

'It's very tempting.' But instead of making to leave she paused, sighed and looked around the room. 'Sure, I've got no love for the Spearpointers – I'd have thought that was fairly obvious by now – but if there was something we could do, I'd jump on it. If only to poke them in the eye and make them really bitter and twisted about what they did to us.'

'I could go along with that,' Agraffe said.

'But there *isn't* anything,' Curtana said. 'That's the point. You've seen how stretched things are here, Doctor. We're scrabbling around just to find fuel to keep our engines running. We're low on ammunition and basic supplies: it's not very noticeable yet, but we can't afford to go dispensing favours to any needy cause.'

'A gesture would still be better than nothing,' Quillon said.

'A gesture that would cost precious fuel, put ships at risk and force us to overfly the territory around Spearpoint that the Skullboys are now occupying,' Ricasso said.

'We're not afraid of a fight,' Curtana retorted, as if her personal honour was being disputed.

'No,' Ricasso said. 'We're not. Never have been. But at the same time we've never indulged in futile, risky exercises for the sake of it. Now, more than ever, we need to protect what we have. Spearpoint's managed without us since the Salient. It must manage without us now.'

'It's asked for help,' Quillon said. 'Doesn't that change things?'

'Not from us specifically,' Ricasso returned.

'As if that makes a shred of difference. If a man's drowning, do you wait until he calls your name before throwing him a rope?'

Ricasso smiled tolerantly. 'This is getting us nowhere, Doctor. I appreciate your sentiments. It's entirely right and proper that you should feel a measure of loyalty to Spearpoint. But I must remind you that you are a guest of Swarm, not part of our decision-making hierarchy. We will indulge your opinions, but you cannot expect to have influence here. You barely knew of our existence before we rescued you.' There was a stinging emphasis at the end of the sentence, Ricasso firmly reminding Quillon of the debt he still owed Swarm. 'Now can we put an end to it, please? What's done is done. We have our own problems to deal with.'

Doctor Gambeson, who had said very little that evening, cleared his throat delicately. 'Tell them,' he said in Ricasso's direction.

'What, Doctor?' Ricasso asked.

'About Serum-15.'

Quillon said, 'I thought it was Serum-16.'

'That's the one he's working on now,' Gambeson answered. 'Serum-15 was the previous batch, one of the rejected trials. Tell them, Ricasso. I think they all have a right to know now.'

'This is an unfortunate betrayal of confidence, Doctor,' Ricasso said warningly.

'And these are unfortunate times. Tell them about the batch, or I'll do it for you.'

Ricasso had their attention now, so he milked it unashamedly. He poured himself another drink, making a protracted spectacle of swilling the fluid around in the glass before taking a cautious mouthful. 'Serum-15 was a failure,' he said slowly. 'It didn't do what I wanted it to do. That's why I progressed to Serum-16.'

'But it didn't fail in the way everyone around this table undoubtedly assumes,' Gambeson said. 'Did it, Ricasso? It failed to meet your objectives. In other respects it might be deemed ... considered ... something of a success.'

Curtana narrowed her eyes. 'What's he talking about?'

'I was looking for something to free us from dependence on antizonals,' Ricasso said. 'A drug or treatment that could be administered once, and which would then give long-lasting protection against the effects of zone transitions. Not permanent immunity, perhaps, but something almost as good. A drug that you didn't have to match to every individual, one whose effects didn't depend on change-vector. A drug that could protect us where the best now fail. Serum-16 is another step in that direction.'

'And Serum-15?' Curtana pushed.

'Serum-15 offered some benefits, but it wasn't what I was looking for. I moved on—'

'Ricasso,' Gambeson said.

Ricasso lowered his glass. His eyes were deep-rimmed and slightly bloodshot. 'Serum-15 had some mild, non-fatal side effects. In all other respects it was at least as effective as clinical grade Morphax-55, or the equivalent we use on Swarm. The tests I ran showed that it provided just as much protection against zone sickness, up to and including alleviating the worst effects of massive maladaptive trauma. It was, in short, better than our best drug against zone sickness.' His pinkish eyes turned pleading. 'But it was a distraction, that's all! We don't *need* a better Morphax-55: what we have is already sufficient for our needs.'

'Ours, perhaps,' Gambeson said.

'Can you make more of this stuff?' Quillon asked.

Ricasso shook his head. 'Not easily. It's enough of a task to persuade the vorgs to achieve one result. Once you move beyond a given outcome, you may as well go back to the start.'

'But you still have some left over,' Gambeson said. 'You didn't destroy the old batches.'

'A little.'

'How much?' Quillon asked.

Ricasso gave a careless shrug. 'Fifty flasks, give or take.'

'The Boundary Commission used to distribute Morphax-55 in vats, not flasks,' Quillon said. 'Even then it had to be rationed and tracked. Every drop counted.' He felt something between sadness and relief: other than as a token gesture, Ricasso's drug wasn't going to be useful after all. Part of him wanted to return to Spearpoint. Another was terrified at the thought, anxious to cling to the flimsiest excuse for not going back.

'Tell him the rest,' Gambeson said.

Ricasso had the weary resignation of a defendant about to collapse under cross-examination. 'The flasks contain the drug in its maximum concentration,' he said. 'That's how it comes out of the vorgs. It's far too strong in that form. Needs to be diluted.'

'How much?' Quillon asked.

'A lot.'

'*How much?*'

'About ... ten thousandfold. At that point you can treat it much as you would liquid-form Morphax-55.'

'So in fact,' Quillon said, 'what you're really telling us is that this ship holds the equivalent of ... half a million flasks of clinical-grade Morphax-55?'

'Near enough.'

'And you didn't think this worth bringing to our attention earlier because ... ?'

'We have all the actual Morphax-55 we need. And I did say there were side effects.'

'Mild ones,' Curtana said.

'When the alternative is slow and painful death,' Gambeson said, 'almost anything would count as a mild side effect.'

'A flask is ... how big, exactly?' Quillon asked.

Ricasso lifted up the decanter. 'Give or take.'

'If that was Morphax-55 there'd be enough in there to provide antizonal protection to hundreds of patients for hundreds of days,' Quillon said.

Gambeson nodded. 'He's right. We're sitting on the difference between life and death for the citizens of Spearpoint.'

'It won't save the city,' Ricasso said. 'It'll just delay the death agonies. Is that really what we want to be doing?'

'You can make more of it,' Quillon said.

'I told you, it's not so easy to go back with the vorgs.'

Quillon leaned forwards to emphasise his point. 'You did it once, you can do it again. Perhaps even come up with something more effective the second time around. Forget your miracle cure, Ricasso: it's a noble objective, but even if it's feasible, it'll take too long to create to actually be of benefit to anyone. But you can do something *here and now* with what you already consider a failure. This can save lives.'

'They'll spit it back in our faces,' Ricasso said.

'After they've already asked for help? Maybe we ought to let them decide first,' Curtana said.

'You've never had any love for these people, my dear,' Ricasso said. 'What's changed now?'

'Nothing,' Curtana replied vehemently. 'They've still got to answer for what they did to us. But that doesn't mean they aren't human beings, in need of help. Even the angels, if it comes to that. I'm not proposing that we do this out of the goodness of our hearts, all right? But we're Swarm. We're better than Spearpoint, and this is our chance to prove it, instead of just basking in a warm glow of self-satisfaction.'

'What she said,' Agraffe said, grinning fiercely, as if he couldn't wait to go and start his engines.

'So we just ... return to Spearpoint?' Ricasso asked, as if there was something fundamental that he simply wasn't getting. 'Just cruise back, as if nothing's happened? Hello, it's Swarm? Remember us? We've brought the medicines you asked for?'

'If that's what it takes,' Curtana said.

'You're the one always telling us that we have to adapt to changing times,' Gambeson said. 'Now's our chance to actually do it. We don't have stop being Swarm, or repudiate our history. We just do something different, because we can. Take a leap into the unknown, and see what happens.'

'I'll do it,' Curtana said. 'Even if no one else does. As soon as *Painted Lady*'s patched together, I'll take those fifty flasks of concentrated Serum-15 all the way myself. They can dilute it when we arrive.'

Ricasso looked pop-eyed. 'Without a mandate from Swarm?'

'If it comes to it. Did my father always act on a mandate, Ricasso? For that matter, have you?' The question was evidently rhetorical, for she did not give him a chance to respond. 'No, thought not. But of course that was your generation, when things were different.'

'If one ship goes, we all go,' Agraffe said, clenching his fist. 'It'll really put the shit up them when they see Swarm arriving en masse. I'd almost want to be a Spearpointer, just to know it feels!'

'In your heart, Ricasso, you know we must act,' Gambeson said forcefully. 'And soon, too, if it's going to make a shred of difference. They're running out of Morphax supplies already. If we sit here and dither and argue for a month or three, we may as well not bother at all. There'll be hardly anyone left alive when we get there.'

'Look,' Ricasso said, 'even if I accept that this is something we should be doing, I still need a show-of-flags.'

Curtana looked distinctly unimpressed with this line of argument. 'Have you asked the other captains?'

'Of course not. It wasn't even a remote possibility until about five minutes ago. And what about the dissenters? How will they take it? They like Spearpoint even less than the rest of us, and that's saying something.'

'Never mind them,' Curtana said. 'It's the moderates you need to bring onto your side, and this is exactly the kind of thing that could galvanise them. For too long they've had to make excuses for you, how you've shirked your responsibilities to Swarm, how you spend more time with your vorgs than you do in the tactical room. I don't agree with any of that stuff, but that's only because I know you. See it from outside this stateroom and things don't look so clear-cut. It's no wonder some of the captains have started listening to Spatha and those idiots. At least the dissenters are proposing Swarm *do* something, instead of skulking around on the margins avoiding a fight.'

'Curtana's right,' Gambeson said. 'No one could accuse you of lacking vision if you put this to the captains.'

Ricasso looked stricken. 'They might accuse me of lacking sanity.'

'Not if we have a plan,' said Curtana, 'and a number of high-influence captains ready to back you. You've got two already, and I can think of at least twenty more who'll join Agraffe and me.'

'Don't put it to the flags just yet,' Agraffe said, smiling as he caught himself on the edge of insubordination. 'What I mean is, Curtana and I can put the word out to the other captains, those we think we can trust with a secret. We'll convene here and put together the basics of a plan, something watertight. Then you can put it to the flags. If you ... um ... want my recommendation, that is.'

'Noted,' Ricasso said tartly.

After he had undressed in his cabin, after he had examined his wing-buds in the mirror above the basin, after he had studied his tapering, waiflike anatomy – the bones standing out like topographic features on a map with exaggerated contours – Quillon tried to sleep. It was not easy. Later that night word had arrived of a closer sighting of a Skullboy craft, dead-reckoning its way through the fog, quartering the terrain in a search pattern. While the refuelling continued, yet more ships were dispatched to intercept and harry however many of the enemy were out there. The probing forays had more in common with blind groping in a darkened room than anything the captains were normally used to. If close action ensued, they could expect losses, damaged ships and damaged crew. Quillon volunteered to assist in *Purple Emperor's* hospital, but Gambeson told him to rest while he was able; if Swarm had need of him, it would not be slow to call on him.

But he couldn't sleep; not really. Although the station-keeping engines, and the engines of the circling escorts, served to drown out some of the noise, his ears had become keenly attuned to the monotonously shifting drone. He could begin to hear *through* it now, out into the quieter airspace beyond Swarm's inner cordon. He could hear the noises of battle, sometimes distant as thunder on the horizon, sometimes louder than fireworks going off next door. The engagement lasted for hours. It sent hectoring reports deep into his brain, penetrating the shallow, free-associating state of mind that was as close to dreaming as he was going to get. He saw gondola-sized skulls pushing their eyeless visages through the fog, suspended under flaccid grey balloons, wrinkled and convoluted as human brains, armoured, skull-headed men hanging from the lolling, laughing jawbones, edged weapons glinting with steely promise in the grey half-light. He dreamed of a vorg, escaping from its cage, sliding and crawling, dragging its limbless hindquarters through the dark bowels of *Purple Emperor*, navigating corridors unseen, leaving a slimy trail of discarded internal organs as it went, yet still finding its way to his cabin, leaning over him, its snout-mechanisms whirring and rotating, gearing up like a demented clock about to strike the hour.

Vorg/want/feed. Give/brain/vorg. Vorg/make/good/drug.

Later, Gambeson came for him. His manner was diffident, almost apologetic.

'I could use some assistance, Doctor.'

There was still blood on his wrists, where the gloves had not completely covered the skin.

Quillon reached without hesitation for his medical bag, which remained with him in his quarters whenever he was there. But when he lifted it from the dresser he knew immediately that something was wrong. The bag felt too heavy. Frowning while Gambeson looked on, he opened the bag and saw the long blue spine of a leather-bound volume jammed into the bag's middle compartment, between the pouches and pockets containing his equipment and potions.

'Reference material?' Gambeson asked.

Quillon stared at the blue book, his mind spinning. For a moment, stupidly, he wondered if he had somehow stolen the book from Ricasso's stateroom and then forgotten about it. But the dream logic collapsed. This couldn't be the book Spatha wanted him to extract from the room. Even if Spatha had somehow managed to obtain the book himself, he would have no reason to hide it in Quillon's bag. Unless the theft had been accomplished and he was expected to return it . . .

'Doctor?' Gambeson asked.

'It's nothing,' Quillon said, flustered but praying it didn't show. 'I . . . requested it from the main library, that's all.'

'You seem surprised to find it there.'

'I forgot putting it in the bag. But I remember now.' He drew the volume out slowly, almost as if it might be wired to a bomb. But in his hands it had the dull solidity that told him it was nothing more than a book.

'Might I see it?' Gambeson asked.

'It's nothing.'

'Nonetheless. Indulge my curiosity. I'm wondering what you couldn't find in my library, that you had to go to the main one.' Without invitation, Gambeson took the book and opened it. It fell open at a random page.

It was blank.

The volume was a logbook. As Gambeson leafed through its pages it became apparent that not a single entry had been made anywhere in it.

'I thought I might start a journal,' Quillon explained, improvising desperately. 'Of my time in Swarm. My experiences, and anything I felt I ought to commit to paper. To assist in my adaptation.'

'I could have supplied you with any number of blank logbooks.'

'I felt it best not to trouble you.'

Gambeson closed the book, then slid it back along the dresser towards Quillon's bag. 'Something's not right here, Doctor, but at the moment I don't have time to worry about what it might be. Not while the butcher's bill is waiting. Grab your bag and follow me. We've work to do.'

The bill, when it was accounted, could have been steeper. The first ship had returned to the fold in the small hours of the morning. It had sustained engine and steering-system damage, but only light injuries. The second came in thirty minutes later, engines still operable, but with a ragged, door-sized hole punched through the gondola's forequarters. Two officers and three airmen had been killed, and nine of the survivors had sustained serious but treatable injuries. Another two ships crawled back during the ensuing hours. They had both taken damage, but there had only been one death between them. Quillon and Gambeson worked hard, sometimes as a team, sometimes attending to different patients. All the while Quillon was aware of Gambeson's silent scrutiny, whenever the other man didn't have his hands deep inside the red mysteries of a wound. Quillon, for his part, tried to force the matter of the book from his mind, but even as he worked it kept bobbing to the surface of his thoughts. He now understood perfectly what was expected of him. The blank book was to be taken into the stateroom in his medical bag and substituted for the real one. The swap could be effected in seconds; Ricasso need never know, at least until he came to make an entry in the original log. And if Commander Spatha had his way, Ricasso might never get that chance.

He returned to his cabin after the surgery, finding the book where Gambeson had left it. He picked it up, feeling an evil, belligerent potency between his fingers, as if the book itself had become a willing conspirator in his downfall. He would have thrown it out of the window were it not sealed. Not that the book was in any way incriminating. It was a blank series of log pages.

Something fell out of it. He knelt down and retrieved it from the floor. It was a card figurine, flat enough to have been slipped between the pages. It was an angel, with the head snipped off. He did not think it could have been in the book when Gambeson had looked through it.

He crushed the angel in his fist, crumpling it until it was an unrecognisable ball of mangled card. Then he slipped the book back into his medicine bag, where he had first found it.

A little before noon he was called to Curtana's quarters. He had lied to Doctor Gambeson out of simple reflex, because it cost him nothing and gained him a little more time to evaluate Spatha's threat. But he could not keep lying indefinitely, and regarded it as entirely possible that Gambeson had already confided his suspicions to Curtana.

But she did not seem interested in his secrets.

'I allowed you to sleep in,' she said, 'because I know how hard you worked last night. I've thanked you once for your assistance on behalf of *Painted Lady*; now you have Swarm's gratitude as well.'

Her manner was brusque, as if all this was merely a preamble to some unspecified disciplinary action.

'Have there been any developments?'

'A number. Agraffe and I contacted those captains we felt could be entrusted with the outline of our intentions. They've been arriving aboard *Purple Emperor* as discreetly as possible, trying not to make it look as if anything's afoot. Preliminary discussions are already taking place. As far as I know – I've left Agraffe to report back to me – there's the beginning of a plan. We've got a possible route back to Spearpoint, avoiding Skullboys as much as possible, using prevailing wind patterns to conserve fuel. In the meantime, Gambeson's running further tests on the Serum-15 to verify that we really do have as much of it as we think. He's also looking at batches 14 and 13 as well, just in case they have some benefits Ricasso overlooked. I gather the testing's quite involved.'

'If Gambeson didn't sleep, you shouldn't have allowed me to either,' Quillon said.

'The difference is that Gambeson doesn't look like a two-day-old corpse, Doctor. I'm sorry to have to spell it out to you.' Curtana looked down at her fingers. 'After everything you told me, I was surprised that you made such a persuasive case for returning. Isn't Spearpoint the last place you'd want to be?'

'Where I want to be and where I need to be aren't necessarily the same things.'

'Ever the doctor.'

'You're no different. You can dress it up however you like, make it look as if you only want to go back to Spearpoint to spite them, but I don't believe that for a minute.'

'I admit I don't see things in quite the same simplistic terms as Agraffe.' She allowed a fond smile to touch her lips. 'Nor does Agraffe, actually, but he's smart enough to know the best way to present this to the other captains. Not as us extending the hand of friendship, but showing Spearpoint that we're better than it. And I don't necessarily think that's wrong. There would be something admirable about delivering the medicine without a word and turning our backs on them again. You know, as in, we're so morally superior to you we don't even need your gratitude.'

'Sooner or later Swarm and Spearpoint are going to have to deal with the fact that they share the same planet.'

'But not necessarily in my lifetime. Let's hand over the medicines and ... cross any other bridges at some later point, shall we?'

'That has to be your decision, not mine.'

Curtana tapped a nail onto her desk. 'As for the girl, she's not ceased to be a concern simply because of this other matter. You were right to bring her to Ricasso's attention, but his powers of protection aren't limitless. He'll want proof sooner or later, or he'll start convincing himself she isn't real.'

'He told me it wasn't a good time.'

'It wasn't. And right now I can't tell you when it might be. I'm just saying you might have to be flexible. The important thing is to keep Spatha away from her.'

'I'm aware of the risks Spatha poses.'

'Has he spoken to you privately?'

'Enough to leave me in no doubt that he's a dangerous man. You were right to warn me about him, back on *Painted Lady*. I won't let my guard down.'

'Don't. He's a snake. Prop-fodder, if I had my way.' A shrewdness appeared in her face. 'What has he said to you?'

Quillon hesitated on the brink of two momentous alternatives, anxious to confide in Curtana but equally anxious to protect Nimcha from being exposed for what she was.

'It's been made clear that I'd be better off not speaking about it to anyone.'

'About what?'

'I think that would amount to speaking about it.'

'Fear and panic, Doctor. If there's one person in Swarm you can trust, it's me.'

'I don't doubt that.'

266

'But you're still concerned. All right, Ricasso, then. Will you speak to him?' Seeing something in his face – she was better at reading him than most – she said, 'Or is it *about* Ricasso?'

'Is anything not about Ricasso?'

'Fair point. But this does concern him, doesn't it? Spatha's asked you to do something? To kill him?' She shook her head. 'No, that wouldn't make any sense. They've had ample chance to do that already. Make him ill, or issue some kind of statement regarding his ability to command? Can't see what they'd gain by doing that, either.'

Quillon knew then that he had run out of room to lie. 'I'll speak to Ricasso. Can we agree that I volunteered this information?'

'With some arm-twisting. But if Spatha's up to his usual tricks, I understand why you might have wanted to keep things to yourself.' She regarded him levelly. 'I have a lot to deal with that doesn't involve politics. Is this something I need to know about right now?'

'I don't think so.'

Curtana appraised her expensive fleet-issue watches. 'Speak to Ricasso. I promise he'll protect you and your friends. That's the one thing Spatha and his army of weasels can't allow for – you placing your trust in another human being, and that trust not being violated. Spatha thinks the world revolves on fear and betrayal.'

'He might be right.'

'Not in my Swarm. If those dissenters want to do things differently, they're welcome to break away and see how long they last. I'd give them about a year before the Skulls are picking through their bones. If it wasn't for the ships, I'd be more than glad to see the back of them right now.'

'Do you think Ricasso will get a majority vote for the medicine run?'

'Probably, if only because it means doing something, and even his enemies will go along with it if they think there's half a chance of him failing. Whatever happens, we won't be staying here. It's become much too dangerous.'

She told him something of what had happened during the engagement.

The Skullboys had been beaten back. It had been a small raiding party, five ships according to the best intelligence. Two had been destroyed by close-action spingun and cannon fire, shredded in the air. A third had been crippled, engines shot away leaving it at the mercy of the winds. Upon last sighting it had been drifting in the general direction of the zone boundary, eighty leagues to the north. Another ship had sidled away with light damage. The fifth had been taken by a party from the long-range scout *White Admiral*. None of the Skullboys had been captured alive – they preferred to don wings and jump overboard – but they had failed in their efforts to blow up the abandoned ship. *White Admiral* had fired grapples and dragged her home at half-speed. Tainted with the stench and blood of Skullboys, the ship was of no interest to Swarm. But she would be stripped of anything of material value, and her maps and logbooks subjected to the closest examination, before the hulk was set adrift for target practice.

In the meantime, efforts were made to catch up with and engage the ship that had got away. But the fog had masked her departure, and none of the pursuing ships obtained another sighting before the search encompassed a hopelessly large volume of airspace. Swarm's ships turned back home.

As to the intentions of the fleeing craft, it was guesswork at best. There might have been a larger force out there somewhere, but the ship could equally well have been operating autonomously. What was clear was that the knowledge she had acquired would eventually reach others. Skullboys, as Ricasso was fond of pointing out, were essentially self-organising. They formed like rust spots on armour plating, with multiple points of origin. They spread and coalesced. They had nothing resembling a centralised command structure. It didn't matter. They had no objectives beyond chaos and anarchy and making the world more convivial to Skullboys. They turned some of their prisoners into more of themselves and raped and killed the rest. They weren't particular.

What the Skullboys did have was something resembling an intelligence network. Sooner or later the escaped ship would make contact with another party, and then Swarm's position would be compromised. It wouldn't take long for Skullboys to find the fuel depot, now that they knew something had drawn Swarm this far north. The depot had not been tapped out, and not all of the tankers had been refuelled.

'But that's no reason to stay, waiting for them to close in on us,' Curtana said.

'The Skullboys couldn't take on all of Swarm if they tried, could they?'

'They could hurt us badly, if they caught us with half our ships still being refuelled. Not worth taking a chance on, especially now that we have a reason to move, an objective beyond just surviving. You can take some credit for that, Doctor.'

'You'd have intercepted that semaphore transmission whether I was here or not.'

'Yes, and we'd have had the medicines. But we wouldn't have had you to speak up for Spearpoint and we wouldn't have had you and Meroka to prick our collective conscience.' Curtana looked diffident. 'I'm not saying it needed pricking, but ... I'm not saying it didn't make a difference either.'

'Meroka and I aren't exactly a shining example of hope and reconciliation.'

'I'll see what I can do about that. In the meantime ... we're taking a lot on faith here, Doctor. You might just have given Ricasso a political lifeline, and if that's the case I'm more grateful than you'll ever know. I'm also hoping and praying none of us is making the worst mistake of our lives in going along with you.'

'If you are,' Quillon said, 'it's the worst mistake of my life as well.'

He was about to leave when she said: 'Doctor, what I told you earlier ... the two-day-old corpse thing?'

'Accurate, if not perhaps the terminology I might have chosen.'

'It was hurtful, and you didn't deserve it. I'm sorry. Can we ... put it behind us?'

Seeing the genuine remorse in her face, he said, 'It's already done.'

'I guess Ricasso's told you about his angel bones, the ones he likes collecting.'

'Yes,' Quillon said, not entirely sure where she was headed.

'I don't pay too much attention to his interests, except where they intersect with my duties as a captain. But I saw one of his angels once. It was when I was a girl. My father had taken me to visit Ricasso, down in his collection rooms aboard *Emperor*. It was a very old skeleton, found out near Paradise Flats. He'd taken the bones and fitted them together properly, replaced and repaired what was missing or broken. Then he'd covered them with a layer of clay. Actually it wasn't clay, but a kind of insulating caulk we use on engine lines to stop them freezing and cracking, but ... I'm digressing, aren't I? The care he'd taken with the angel, the attention to detail ... the way he'd remade the wings, using glass and metal ... the eyes and the face ... it was probably the strangest, most beautiful creature I've ever seen. And you know what?'

He saw something in her expression. 'You hated it.'

'Because of the wings,' she said, nodding. 'Because that damned ... *thing* ... made a mockery of my world and everything in it. Meroka was right, you know – Blimps. That's all we've got. And you angels own the sky like you were fucking well born to it. Excuse my language. I'm pretty handy with the rudder of an airship, all right? I know a thing or two about jet streams, about static and dynamic lift. I can turn *Painted Lady* on a sunbeam. But that's not really *flying*, not the way you do it. Is it any wonder we harbour resentment towards you?'

'If it's any consolation, I barely remember how it feels to fly. They

269

buried my memories when they sent me down to Neon Heights. It was nine years ago, anyway.'

'But you did it once.'

'More than once,' he admitted.

'You're wrong, Doctor. It's no consolation whatsoever.'

CHAPTER EIGHTEEN

He went to see Ricasso just before the show-of-flags. It was the middle of the afternoon and the fog had begun to lift, affording glimpses of powder-blue sky and arid, treeless horizons. The air was clear of Skull-boys, to the limit of vision.

'It's a good day to vote,' Ricasso said, turning from his window as Quillon entered the stateroom. 'A tiresome formality, of course – they *will* endorse me – but it must still be done. Don't you just hate tradition?'

Quillon and Ricasso were alone. Quillon placed his medicine bag next to the table where the chequer game was in progress. 'We don't have much that isn't tradition in Spearpoint. When you've been going in circles for five thousand years, it's hard not to echo the past. It's like keeping a diary, until you realise that every new entry's the same as one you've already written. So why waste your time, if nothing new ever happens? Swarm's different, I think. You haven't exhausted all the per-mutations yet. You're new enough that you still bother having history.'

'You make it sound like a youthful indulgence we'll grow out of sooner or later.'

'You will, if you get the chance.' Quillon sat down next to the table. 'May we talk? There's something I think you ought to know.'

'A medical matter?'

'Not exactly.' Quillon opened the bag and slid out the blue volume. 'Commander Spatha gave me this book. It's blank.' He riffled the empty pages. 'The idea was for me to substitute it for the one under the table, while you weren't looking. I was to sneak the original book out of the room in my medical bag and give it to Spatha.'

Ricasso blinked, but in all other respects did a good job of maintaining his composure. 'Whatever for?'

'I thought you'd know. Spatha told me the original book contains laboratory notes on the vorg serum programme. He thought that by exposing your lack of progress to date, he could undermine your authority.'

'Spatha's right,' Ricasso said. He went to the table and pulled out the original book. 'These are laboratory notes.'

The book was dense with numbers and formulae and cryptic annotation, recorded in different inks and with different degrees of neatness. Some parts were sober and methodical. Others were frantic scrawls, scratched out late at night by a man on the verge of exhaustion. There were hundreds of pages, all nearly filled with handwriting. There were even things that looked like abandoned puzzles, cross-hatched drawings with dots filling in some of the squares. Quillon couldn't help wondering if they had something to do with the chequer game, as if Ricasso was working through theoretical puzzles in the margins, as a distraction from his main work.

'But they can't damage me,' Ricasso said. 'For a start, look at the dates. This is work I finished more than two years ago. My current notes stay down in the laboratory. And even if these were current, do you honestly think anyone else would be able to make sense of them? This isn't work tidied up for public presentation. These notes are only required to mean something to me, and half the time even I can't figure them out!'

'Spatha's no fool. He must have thought he could get something out of it.'

'Maybe he can. But even if he somehow manages to understand all these notes, what use will it be to him? All he'll be able to show is that, more than two years ago, I hit a slow patch. So what? I still know more at the end than I did at the beginning.'

'He didn't go into any more detail than what I've told you,' Quillon said. 'I was told to extract the book, or he'd make life difficult for Nimcha and me.'

'And did he tell you not to mention it to anyone?'

'Of course.'

'Then I'm at a loss. Why didn't you just take the book? You've had any number of chances, and if I'd caught you, I'd have understood that you were acting under coercion. I'd have had to throw you off the ship, of course, but we'd have still parted as friends.'

'I thought about it,' Quillon said. 'But then I decided the book must be a test, so that Spatha could see how much control he had over me. What you've just told me makes me even more certain I was right. If I'd taken it, and not said a word to you, he'd only have asked me to do something else, probably something bigger and more dangerous.'

'Almost certainly.'

'So my choice was either go along with him indefinitely, or take the chance of speaking to you now. I decided to take the chance.'

'Even with the threat to Nimcha and yourself?'

'If the leader of Swarm can't protect us, who can?'

Ricasso smiled sadly. 'If only it were that simple. I can't just arrest Spatha – he'll have made sure there were no witnesses to his blackmail, and I'm afraid your word naturally carries less weight than if you were one of us. He knows this, which is why he would have felt free to be so brazen in his threats. Think about it, Doctor: if he cared about you knowing his identity, he could have easily concealed it, or contacted you some other way.'

'If you can't arrest him, can you remove his power in some way?'

'Not at such a delicate time. There are twenty captains – at least – on his side, and probably as many again ready to turn against me if they sense that my leadership is crumbling. Under such circumstances, I can't be seen to be trying to silence my critics, or marginalise my enemies. It'll make me look desperate.' Ricasso rolled his eyes in mock frustration. 'I know the bastards' names, of course – captains and ships, and whether the crews are loyal to me or the captains. But that doesn't help me when I have nothing on Spatha except your testimony.'

Quillon felt a dizzy sense of falling, as if he had misjudged the number of steps on a staircase, his foot encountering air when it expected solid ground. He had hoped to be able to confide in Ricasso and have the weight of all his problems removed. No more lies, no more evasions. But instead he felt he had gained nothing.

'If you can't protect Nimcha, then perhaps I shouldn't have said anything.'

'No, because in telling me you've lost nothing.' Ricasso passed Quillon the real logbook, taking the blank one in return. 'Spatha doesn't need to know we had this conversation, does he? You can give him my notes, exactly as if you'd gone ahead with his plan. He'll think his persuasion worked, and that'll buy Nimcha a little more time.'

'But what about you?'

'I told you, the book's useless. Best of luck to him trying to find something in it to hang me with.'

'You might not see it again.'

'Good riddance, in that case. It's old work, and I've moved on.'

Quillon slipped the real book into his medical bag. It was not quite the same as the fake – a slightly different, more turquoise shade of blue, a fussier binding, the edges more dog-eared – but it still fitted easily inside. 'If you're sure,' he said, closing the bag.

'Spatha wants to play games, he's come to the right man.'

Quillon nodded at the chequerboard. 'I noticed.'

There was, now that he paid it proper attention, something not quite right about Ricasso's chequerboard. It was actually two boards connected together in the middle, but which did not match properly. The squares on one board were larger, so that the cells did not line up neatly. And yet Ricasso's chequer pieces spanned the divide, with the black markers arrayed in winding, spidery formations across both boards, like straggling birds at the edge of a denser flock.

'It's not a game, Doctor,' Ricasso said. 'It's the very stuff of life and death.'

'The cellular grid,' Quillon said, suddenly recalling something Gambeson had told him. 'Gambeson was talking about the zones, and he said that the cellular grid didn't have enough resolution. Is this something to do with that?'

'There's a lot you and I could talk about,' Ricasso said. 'Unfortunately, by my watches I make it time for the vote.'

The show-of-flags was in progress. The winter sun did its best to sparkle on the long, fluttering banners of coloured emblems, as the fleet delivered its collective opinion on Ricasso's decision.

Quillon was with Ricasso, Curtana, Agraffe and Gambeson. They were on the balcony, watching the display. Everyone was dressed against the cold, the Swarmers wearing their best uniform coats for the occasion. Ricasso swept binoculars from ship to ship, reading the banners as they were lowered down beneath each gondola. They were strung from a stiff wire that whipped back in the wind, the flags arrowing towards the airships' tails. He held his binoculars in spotless white gloves, struggling to work the focus wheel as he switched from a close ship to a distant one. Every now and then there was a glint from the observation deck or balcony of some other ship. Conscious that binoculars might very well be trained on him, Quillon kept his goggles on and his hat jammed on tight. His hands were thrust deep into fur-lined pockets. By now word of his existence must have reached all of Swarm, and he was certain there had been a degree of informed speculation about what exactly he was. But until there was an official statement on the matter, he was determined to conceal his appearance. He wanted a cigarette very badly, but didn't think it would be good manners to light up except when he was alone.

'It's not normally this serious,' Ricasso muttered. 'I come out here and survey the flags, but I don't normally care what they're actually telling me. I just nod a lot and look interested. It's not usually been an issue.'

Quillon couldn't make head or tail of the coloured banners. No two seemed alike, but he had yet to detect any specific consternation in his hosts. There was a lot of ceremony here, many layers of impenetrable tradition. Swarm used heliographs for routine signalling between ships, but clearly all serving officers were required to maintain a working familiarity not only with the flags, but with several different systems of flags. Each ship appeared to employ entirely different protocols. No one was in the least bit fazed.

'Assent from *Clouded Yellow*,' Agraffe murmured, as if his voice stood a chance of being heard above the steady drone of station-keeping engines. 'Assent from *Silverheath* and *Gatekeeper*.'

Curtana, who was scanning a different part of the formation, said, 'Provisional assent from *Argus*. Conditional abstention from *Ruby Tiger*.'

Ricasso made a sound like man being kicked in the testicles.

'It's not a vote against you,' Curtana said. 'She's always been on your side until now. They just want more information about what we're going to do for fuel after we've delivered the medicines. Actually, I wouldn't mind some reassurance about that myself.'

'We'll cross that bridge,' Ricasso answered.

'Steal it from the Spearpointers, you mean? They're no better off than we are,' Gambeson said.

'Assent from *Ghost Moth*,' Agraffe said.

'*Ghost Moth*? You've misread the flags.'

'I don't think so. Of course, there's always that saying about giving someone enough rope to hang themselves.'

Curtana wasn't going to let it drop. 'If we burn all our fuel just getting to Spearpoint, we'll be sitting targets for Skullboys. We already know they've massed around Spearpoint's base, and they're not going anywhere.'

'We'll manage,' Ricasso said.

'I've seen the charts,' Agraffe commented. 'Even with the winds at our backs, it's looking dicey.' His attention flicked sideways. 'Assent from *The Vapourer*, by the way.'

Ricasso nodded. 'That's good. She's got influence.'

It went on like this, banner after banner, ship after ship. By the time of reckoning, about three dozen ships had voted against Ricasso's proposal, with another dozen or so abstentions. Though some of the known dissenters had cast negative votes, by and large the divisions had not fallen along predictable schisms. Some of Ricasso's staunchest allies had problems with the idea of giving assistance to Spearpoint. Some of his severest critics supported the idea because it promised the likelihood of engaging with Skullboys along the way and reinforcing Swarm's moral superiority over the despised city-dwellers. Others, like *Ghost Moth*, were cynically supportive of the plan precisely because they saw it as doomed to failure, and therefore the surest route to undermining confidence in Ricasso. Every conceivable streak of chicanery and guile was present and accounted for.

But there was also a sizeable majority who supported Ricasso for no other reason than that they thought it was the right thing to do. Many ships had articulated quibbles or reservations with the precise terms of the proposal. Yet there was a solid block of consensus – a good hundred ships – that were ready and willing to go ahead with the medicine run. From what he knew of the man, Quillon believed there had been times when Ricasso would have regarded anything less than absolute unanimity as a crushing blow against his authority. Now he appeared to take it as a welcome reassurance that he still had an effective mandate to govern. The dissenters were not numerous enough to stop the medicine run from happening.

When the others had filtered indoors, Quillon remained outside to smoke a cigarette. Already there were signs of Swarm mobilising. The banners had been retracted and engines were being pushed harder, in readiness for the long flight to Spearpoint. Rather than leave behind a protecting force to guard what were fairly limited fuel stocks, and to prevent those stocks from falling into enemy hands, the depot was to be destroyed. Guns were being trained on the towers: it was useful target practice. Incendiary bombs were being dropped on the storage tanks. Swarm would not be passing this way again.

A door opened behind him. He felt the warmth on the back of his neck and steeled in readiness for another meeting with Commander Spatha. Perhaps he had come to collect the blue book, expecting Quillon to have done his bidding by now. But when he glanced to his side it was Meroka who had joined him. She was wearing one of the Swarmers' high-altitude coats, almost lost in it with only the top half of her head protruding above the fur-lined collar.

'Heard we're moving on, Cutter.'

'So it seems.'

'Also heard you had something to do with this.'

He answered carefully. 'I ... stated my position. I don't doubt that they'd have come to the same conclusion sooner or later. Doctor Gambeson was already of the same mind as me, and I don't think Curtana needed much persuading.'

'And you know what's waiting for you in Spearpoint?'

'Nothing good.'

'What I figured as well.' She was silent for a while, her attention seemingly caught by one of the fires burning below. Towers of black smoke, folded into brainlike convolutions, rose from the flames. 'I still have problems with what you are, Cutter,' she added.

'Entirely understandable.'

'But I'll say one thing. You pushing for this ... knowing what your fate is likely to be ... that takes some balls.'

'Then I infer you approve of the decision?'

'Whole-fucking-heartedly.'

Quillon sniffed. 'I'm glad. And I'm sure you'd have exerted just as much persuasion, if you'd been in my position. I just hope it's worth it, that's all. The medicine's only a stopgap, really. Better than nothing, but it won't solve the city's problems for ever.'

'That's where you're hoping Nimcha will come in.'

'Hope's probably too strong a word. But what else have we got, if she can't put things right?'

'How much do the others know?'

'As far as I'm aware, most of the fleet doesn't even know she exists. Ricasso knows she's a tectomancer, or at least looks like one – but you knew that already. I've said nothing about how she needs to return to Spearpoint, and I don't plan on doing so.'

'They'd doubt your motives.'

'Precisely.'

'You think you can keep this a secret indefinitely?'

'I don't know. There's interest in her from an undesirable direction. I've been put in something of a bind.' He smiled quickly. 'I'm more or less on top of things, though.'

'You could tell me, Cutter.'

'It's my problem for now. I think it might be best to leave it like that for the time being.'

She gave a noncommittal shrug that was only barely visible through the thick cladding of her coat. 'Your call.'

'Thank you.'

'One other thing, Cutter. The Testament they took off me?'

He looked at her with what he hoped was only mild interest. 'Yes?'

'Curtana tells me you were the one who talked her into giving it back.'

'I—'

'Just wanted to tell you it was appreciated. That's all. Doesn't mean we're square, exactly. I don't know if we'll ever be square, you lying to me and all, and the angels doing what they did. But ... it's a step.' She paused. 'That book ... it means more to me than just a place to hide a knife, all right?'

'I never imagined otherwise.'

'You did good, Cutter. Pains me to say it, but that's the way it is. Now excuse me while I go inside, before I freeze my tits off.'

In the end there was no need to arrange a meeting with Commander Spatha. When Quillon woke the next day his medical bag appeared undisturbed, exactly as he had left it. But when he opened it the blue book was gone. In its place was another paper angel, this time with a head.

He presumed that to mean he had done well. He also presumed it to mean that Spatha had not finished with him.

PART THREE

CHAPTER NINETEEN

Swarm had been moving south for two days when Quillon was summoned urgently to the infirmary. The call had come from one of Gambeson's assistants, rather than the physician himself. Quillon could only presume that the doctor needed his help with some operation or procedure in which he was already engaged. Yet when he arrived, he found that the patient he was required to attend was Gambeson himself. He had collapsed during his work, slumping over one of the wounded airmen as the strain of recent days and weeks finally caught up with him.

'He hasn't slept in over a day,' Quillon was told, the assistant's shifty, defensive manner suggesting that he imagined Quillon might hold him personally accountable for the doctor's condition. 'What with the injured, and the extra work he's been doing for the fat man. We tried to talk him into getting some rest, but he wasn't listening.'

'Was Curtana aware of his condition?'

'Yes, she was,' came a low voice from behind him. 'Perfectly aware. I also trusted that Gambeson was the man best suited to evaluating his own fitness for duty. He assured me he was strong enough to complete the mission, and – as we have seen – he was absolutely correct in that assessment. I took him at his word, Doctor.'

'That appears to have been a mistake.'

'I had no other option. I couldn't very well afford to turn away the services of a man like Gambeson. Had I done so, we probably wouldn't have been able to complete our mission after the storm and our casualty list would have been far worse.'

'You could have asked for a second opinion.'

'I could, and the outcome would have been that Gambeson remained here while we left Swarm on our scouting mission. But do you think for one second that he'd have worked any less diligently? He had medical responsibilities in *Purple Emperor* no less burdensome than his duties aboard my ship. He'd already made a point of helping Ricasso with his work on the vorg serum production.'

Quillon had had enough insight into Gambeson's working methods to know that Curtana was right. He nodded, softening his tone. 'You're correct, of course. Short of tying him down to a bed—'

'How is he now?' Curtana asked the assistant.

'In and out of consciousness,' the man said. 'But he's very frail and needs absolute rest.'

'We won't tax him,' Quillon said.

Gambeson had been placed in a bed of his own, in a screened-off corner of the infirmary. He was awake, but barely. He hardly had the energy to move his head as his visitors pushed through the screen. His lips moved and made a sound that was almost inaudible above the engine drone. His eyes were fixed on the ceiling.

'Doctor Quillon. Curtana.'

'We came as soon as we heard,' Curtana said. She knelt and touched a hand to the form of his arm under the sheets. 'I'm sorry, Doctor. You gave everything to Swarm. I should have ordered you to take things more easily.'

'Don't blame yourself,' Gambeson said, each word taking an eternity. 'I would have . . . ignored you anyway.'

'I don't doubt it.'

'At least you're in good hands now,' Quillon said.

'What have they got me on?' Gambeson took a laboured breath, his eyelids closing momentarily. 'They wouldn't tell me, and I'm the God-damned physician around here.'

Quillon had asked the same question of Gambeson's assistant. 'Agulax-12 as a blood-thinning agent. Chronox-6 to normalise your heart rhythm.'

'Do you concur?'

'It's exactly what I'd have given you. With rest, there's every chance you'll make a good recovery.'

'Good, but not complete. You choose your words carefully, Doctor.'

'You'll have to take things more easily from now on,' Curtana said. 'If that means a reduction in your duties . . . even partial retirement . . . then that's something you'll need to face.'

'How is Merai doing?' Something in him seemed to rally at the stirring of professional interest. 'I want that stump dressing changed every three hours. No matter how much she complains.'

'Merai's doing fine,' Quillon said. 'But she isn't your concern any more. Nor are any of the other patients, or the serum tests.'

'The doctor's right,' Curtana said sternly. 'Rest means rest. No checking on your assistants to make sure they're doing the job you've already trained them for. If I can't trust you to take your own rest seriously, I'll move you to one of the sealed rooms.'

'No need to do that, Curtana.' He gave an exhausted smile. 'I like the hustle and bustle. I promise I won't interfere. I won't need to, anyway. My staff are more than competent. And in matters of medical judgement ...' he paused to gather his breath, 'you can always turn to Quillon.'

'I'll always be ready to provide any assistance I can,' Quillon said.

Curtana nodded. 'Good. Not that I'm anticipating anything, of course.' She paused and returned her attention to Gambeson. 'I want you back on your feet, Doctor. But as my friend, not my physician. If you never hold another scalpel in your life, Swarm will still owe you a debt it can't ever repay. But I'd miss our conversations even more than your skills.'

Down in Ricasso's laboratory, the vorgs stirred from whatever state of animation passed as rest for them. They had heard the door being unlocked, they had responded to the coming of light as Ricasso and Quillon entered the windowless vault. With what limbs remained to them they shifted their postures, their head-assemblies tracking the visitors, lenses clicking and whirring. They made metallic scraping sounds, as of junk shifting in a scrapyard pile. One of them said, 'Vorg/need/brain. Give/vorg/brain. Make/vorg/happy. Happy/vorg/make/good/drug.'

'The first thing I always do is check the secretion lines are still embedded and delivering,' Ricasso said. 'But you need to be careful. Don't get any closer to the cages than you have to, and hold this at all times.' He had pulled a red-handled axe from a wall mounting. 'You'll always carry a revolver – I'll have one signed out for you. And you'll always have this in one hand. It's in case one of them grabs you and tries to pull you into the cage.'

Quillon looked doubtfully at the axe. 'It'll cut through vorg metal?'

'No, but it'll cleave bone well enough. And don't think they won't try it. They're always on the lookout for muscular tissue, internal organs, neural material. They'll rip it away from you if they get half a chance, and they're strong enough to drag you between those bars.'

'The bars aren't wide enough.'

'You'd think that, until you've seen what a vorg can do, when it sets its mind on it. If one of those things does get hold of you, you'll be better off losing a hand or an arm than your life.' Ricasso said this with a kind of cheery fatalism, as if he had personal experience.

'I'll remember the revolver and the axe,' Quillon replied. 'What else?'

'If you find anything amiss, don't try to fix it yourself. Alert me, and I'll come down and look at it. I'm serious about this, Doctor. I've had some experience handling these things, and they still manage to frighten the living excrement out of me about three times a month. Your job is not to put right anything that's wrong. You'll have enough work to do just analysing the serum samples.'

The bench where Quillon would be doing the majority of his testing and preparation was safely distant from the vorgs. They'd still be in the same room, but he wouldn't need to keep an eye on them all the time. They'd just be a brooding, watchful presence.

'I don't know why you didn't just chop all their limbs off,' he said.

'I tried, but they don't secrete as efficiently. Something to do with cumulative body mass. Or spite, if vorgs are capable of spite.' Ricasso gave him a hearty pat. 'But please don't be unduly alarmed, Doctor. I merely emphasise these things so that there's absolutely no doubt in your mind how dangerous they are. Provided you don't linger near the cages, you'll have nothing to fear.'

'Aside from that, do I have free rein to test and refine the Serum-15 samples as I wish?'

'Do what you must: I trust your expertise in this matter. You'll find most of the reagents and preparations you're already familiar with, albeit at different concentrations than you might expect. Some of the names may be different, but I've written down the common variations next to Gambeson's notes. I hope that'll be enough to get you started. Remember we almost certainly can't synthesise more of the basic Serum-15 run, so preserve as much as you can for medical purposes.'

'I will. Are you sure about me taking over Gambeson's work down here?'

'Gambeson's in no fit state to carry on with it, and he only took it on when I was too busy to do it myself. That's still the case, especially with the navigational uncertainties ahead of us.' Ricasso paused at the side of a green upright cabinet with a series of dials in its upper face. He adjusted a lever and the apparatus responded with a soft click and whirr.

Quillon thought of all the work that had gone on down here, the long, unrewarded hours of patient experimentation. All the dulling setbacks and brief, heart-lifting promises of breakthrough – most of which must have turned out to be mirages. He could smell the toil in the air, ingrained in the furniture, the walls. If every citizen in Swarm could have been marched through this room, made to experience that same sense of disciplined, dutiful endeavour, there wouldn't have been one of them who didn't believe that Ricasso had Swarm's best interests at heart.

'It's still a gesture of trust,' he said softly. 'I don't take it lightly.'

'We need that Serum-15, Doctor, and you're the man for the job. Frankly I don't have the luxury of *not* trusting you.'

Quillon smiled ruefully. 'I've been in that position a few times myself. It's almost getting to be a habit.'

'Then you know how it feels.' Having inspected the cages, Ricasso sauntered back to the wall and hung up his axe. The green cabinet clicked and whirred again. 'All right, I admit that I had my doubts about you. Lingering ones. You lied to us, and I wasn't sure we'd stripped back all the layers. But when you came to me about Spatha's threat, you silenced my qualms.'

'Nothing's come of that business with the book yet. It makes me wonder what Spatha's really after.'

'Biding his time, that's all. The snake still has venom. We'd both of us best be on our guard, I think. The strike *will* come. It's just a question of when and where.' Ricasso clapped his hands. 'But for now, we both have business to attend to. Can I leave you to get on with things? I'll make sure you have a revolver next time, but there's no need to check the secretion lines now that I've done it.'

'I'll be fine,' Quillon said.

But as the door locked behind Ricasso – he never left the room without securing it – Quillon felt the vorgs studying him, tracking his movements with the watchful patience of cats.

Swarm travelled slowly, conserving fuel, edging cautiously along the western margin of the Bane. Skirting the uninhabitable zone offered the quickest path to Spearpoint, but there was no escaping the mood of nervous apprehension amongst the airmen. Though the boundary remained over the horizon, they dreaded it the way ancient mariners must have feared some ocean region fabled to host whirlpools, sirens and sea monsters. Instruments were checked with extra diligence, in case the margin of the Bane had shifted. Engines were attended to with loving care, for propulsion was the only thing holding Swarm against the whim of the winds, and the winds had no compunctions about blowing into the Bane.

Quillon kept his head down. It was easy to stay busy the whole day, and had he not needed sleep, he could have occupied himself through the night watches as well. He helped out with the sick and injured aboard *Purple Emperor*, taking on more responsibility now that Gambeson was bedridden. He worked for hours at a stretch in Ricasso's laboratory, as often as not alone, although Ricasso would drop by when he was able, scrutinising Quillon's notes, double-checking the concentrations and reagents involved in the testing and refinement of the Serum-15. Quillon now had his own key, another token of Ricasso's trust. It sat heavy in his bag and travelled with him at all times.

When he wasn't in the laboratory or the sickbay, he busied himself reading. He had spent a little time in Gambeson's private library before, going in to retrieve some reference text or other, but now he felt justified in spending hours in there. The collection – much too bulky to be taken aboard *Painted Lady* – was a palace of leather-bound enchantments. Apart from containing the compendious shipboard notes of every surgeon who had ever served on Curtana's vessel, it held numerous texts and treatises on illness, deformity and the healing arts. Many of these books and scrolls were not even written in an extant or translatable language, but their illustrations were still of lingering academic interest. One ancient volume, which almost fell apart upon examination, contained holo-graphic plates of startling beauty. As Quillon gently touched the pages, a succession of neural slices flickered past, captioned with a slanting cursive text. The book was one of those rare and precious artefacts that appeared largely immune to zone changes, suggesting that its underlying technology was organic rather than mechanical. He felt the weight of centuries in its dust, and when he turned to the frontispiece the date printed there – in recognisable, though slightly odd, numerals – was a thousand years ahead of the present. The book had not fallen from the future, Quillon knew. It had survived from an era that used another calendar entirely, before the clock was reset to zero.

More than anything – and he felt mildly guilty that Gambeson's illness had been a contributing factor – Quillon was grateful to be busy. It kept his mind off Commander Spatha, and him away from the parts of the gondola where he was likely to meet the man. He'd had no contact with him since their last encounter and Quillon was beginning to believe that Spatha had lost interest in him after the incident with the book.

Even as he thought this, however, another part of his mind recognised that he was engaged in quiet self-delusion.

On the morning of the third day he was asked to come to the state-room. When he arrived he found Meroka already there, sitting on one of the low chairs next to a coffee table. She was scratching idly at her bandaged shoulder. The only other person in the room was Ricasso, who was turning from the window as Quillon came in.

Meroka looked up. 'Man wouldn't say a word to me until you arrived, Cutter.'

'Is something the matter?' Quillon asked.

'Not necessarily,' Ricasso answered. 'I need your help with something – both of you – and I thought it best to wait until you were both present. It's about Spearpoint. We've received some new intelligence.'

'I wasn't expecting any more news until we got nearer,' Quillon said.

'Nor was I. But I reckoned without the Skullboys. That ship we captured, the night before our departure from the fuel depot?'

'I didn't think there were any prisoners,' Quillon said.

'There weren't. But we did take her with all documents still intact. Some of them have proved most ... illuminating. For ones so given to barbarism, the Skullboys are remarkably diligent log-keepers. Before she joined the pack we encountered, the *Lacerator* had been acting independently. They'd been listening to the signals on Radial Nine, the same semaphore line that *Brimstone* reported as still being operational.'

'I thought the Skullboys were trying to disrupt those lines, not listen in on them,' Meroka said.

'One ship couldn't have taken on a signal station,' Ricasso said. 'In any case, they're as interested as we are in the state of the city. They listened in on the semaphore transmissions for much longer than *Brimstone* was able to.' He nodded at the brown-covered intelligence transcripts on the coffee table. 'This is what we got. It's taken until now to decode the Skullboy logs, and there are still some passages we can't decipher, but there's enough to be going on with. If it's accurate, it gives us a much clearer picture of the condition of the city than we've had so far. Nothing in it actively contradicts anything we learned from *Brimstone*, but it does put things into a new light.' He gestured invitingly. 'Open the documents. Read the transcripts. You have unlimited clearance. All I ask is that, as Spearpointers, you be alert for anything that doesn't ring true. We've no other way of deciding if the Skullboy intelligence is reliable.'

Quillon had joined Meroka at the table. He opened one of the dossiers and examined one of the pale pink, tissue-thin transcript papers inside.

'Why wouldn't it be?'

'They're Skullboys,' Ricasso answered. 'I'd like you pay particular attention to one name in particular, if at all possible – it keeps coming up. If this man isn't responsible for these transmissions going out in the first place, he's clearly a player of some importance in post-disaster Spearpoint.'

'Tulwar,' Meroka said, frowning hard, as if she was certain she must have made a mistake. 'Here's his name. And again.' She shuffled the papers. 'Here again. He's all over this like a rash.'

'You know this man?'

'Sort of.'

'Tulwar helped us to get out of Spearpoint,' Quillon said, spotting the name for himself on another of the transcript sheets. The sentence read: *Tulwar continues to urge all citizens to use existing antizonal stocks responsibly.* A little further down: *Tulwar reports that supplies are holding and there is no need for further panic.* Further still: *Tulwar has indicated that mob law and punishment beatings will not be tolerated. While looting, the theft of rationed supplies and the breaking of curfew cannot be allowed to go unpunished, miscreants must and will be exposed to the full measure of the Emergency Law.*

'This doesn't make any sense,' Meroka said, shaking her head. 'I mean, why Tulwar?'

'You mean,' Quillon said, 'why not Fray?'

'I suppose it could be someone else with the same name,' Ricasso put in doubtfully.

'No, it's our Tulwar,' said Meroka. 'I'm pretty sure of that.'

'*Brimstone*'s intelligence did say something about criminal elements moving into the power vacuum,' Quillon said. 'I suppose Tulwar would have to be considered a criminal element by anyone's definition. But then again, so would you and I.'

'Tulwar was just a cog in Fray's machine,' Meroka said.

'A cog with ambitions, maybe. He already had a network in place: you saw how easy it was for him to arrange for us to be shipped down to Horsetown with the frozen corpses. He'd have been in a fairly advantageous position when the orthodox authority crumbled.'

'So would Fray.'

Quillon scanned the handful of papers for any mention of Fray, but the name didn't leap out at him.

'He doesn't seem to be mentioned at all.'

'This Fray was another contact?' Ricasso asked.

'More than that – he was a friend to both of us. Tulwar got me out of Spearpoint, but it was Fray who made it happen. I'd known him for years. He wasn't a paragon of virtue, but he wasn't a bad man either.' He looked at Meroka, hoping she would say it before he did.

'You don't think he made it.'

'We both saw the storm hit Spearpoint, and we know what *Brimstone* told us about the change in the zones. It hurt Neon Heights more than

288

it hurt Steamtown. From Tulwar's position that change might almost have been beneficial.'

'Enough to go from being a fairly prominent player in the Steamtown underworld to the most powerful man in Spearpoint?'

'The most powerful man in the part of Spearpoint still capable of communicating with the outside world,' Quillon said. 'For all we know, Fray's still alive; he just can't get a message out. We're only seeing a small part of the picture here.'

'But it seems to be a vaguely plausible part?' Ricasso asked.

'If you take it as a given that Tulwar's expanded his influence,' Quillon said, 'then yes, I suppose it does.'

'I agree with Cutter,' Meroka said.

Ricasso nodded, a cold gleam of satisfaction in his eyes. 'That's what I was hoping. I wasn't counting on either of you actually knowing this man, but that's a bonus. My main concern was that all this might turn out to be a Skullboy fabrication, for whatever reasons they might have had. I can't rule that out even now, but the fact that they mention this Tulwar gentleman so many times—'

'It's real,' Quillon said. 'The only doubt in my mind is about what we're *not* being told. But it doesn't change anything, does it?' He tapped a finger against one of the sheets. 'Looting. Riots. Ration shortages. Medical supplies going astray. All this tells us is that the situation is just as grave as we anticipated. Maybe worse. They really do need that Serum-15.'

'And we'll deliver it,' Ricasso said. 'As soon as we possibly can. Maybe sooner.'

Quillon found out what Ricasso meant by his remark later that day, when he was called to the stateroom again. This time there were at least a dozen captains present, as well as Curtana, Agraffe, Meroka and, of course, Ricasso himself, who stood with hands on hips and his proud belly pressing against the enormous chart table, around which the gathering had assembled. He was staring at his audience with a look of pugnacious defiance, eyes flashing from one person to the next, alert to the merest hint of dissent.

'This is our existing course,' Ricasso said, dragging a fat thumbnail along the map. 'Skirting the edge of the Bane, but spending another three days of flight actually getting further from Spearpoint by the hour, before we clear the southern extremity, pick up the prevailing winds and begin to make easterly progress.'

Curtana, who must have sensed something of what was afoot, said,

'And your point is, exactly? We talked this over at length. We're committed to it. Now is emphatically not the time to go changing our minds about the right approach.'

'And you're quite right about that, my dear. That is, you would be right if the information available to us had not altered. In the light of new intelligence, it behoves us to re-examine our original decision.'

She stood with hands on hips. 'What new intelligence?'

'We pulled recently amended charts from the *Lacerator*. The Skullboys came close enough to the Bane's limit to detect the changes. But they found nothing, no hint of a gradient along hundreds of leagues. There's only one reasonable conclusion to be drawn from that: the Bane has shifted, or contracted. We shouldn't have expected it to remain the same: every other zone has undergone a boundary change, so why not the Bane?'

'You trust these charts?' Agraffe asked. 'For all we know they're bogus, made up to lead us into disaster.'

'That's a reasonable point. But other information extracted from the same ship has been independently verified.'

Quillon glanced at Meroka, who glanced back at him at the same moment. Her expression told him that she felt exactly the same way he did. Failing to find a glaring inconsistency or implausible detail in the semaphore logs was not the same as independent verification.

'That's—' he started saying.

'Doctor?' Ricasso asked interestedly. 'Your opinion, please? I'm most anxious to hear it.'

'You know we can't ever be certain those transcripts are authentic. But even if we were, it still wouldn't give us any reason to presume the charts haven't been faked.'

'The changes the Skullboys have mapped dovetail with those measured by *Brimstone*, *Painted Lady*, *Cinnabar* and *Iron Prominent*, Doctor, so it's highly unlikely that they've been completely fabricated.'

'We don't know how far the boundary has moved,' Quillon said. 'The Bane may have shrunk, or changed its shape, but that doesn't mean we can go sailing into that territory without a care in the world. We may run into the boundary again, just a bit further in than it used to be.'

'That's why we'll be paying due attention to the clocks, every second of the way,' Ricasso said. 'We're not fools. We learned a hard lesson from the Salient. But even if the boundary has only retreated a little way, we'll still save time and fuel by cutting across the edge of what used to be the Bane. Can you deny that saving time will be beneficial to Spearpoint?'

'Of course I can't.'

'As I expected. We'll send ships ahead of the main formation, mapping the gradients across a broad swathe, establishing a safe corridor. If the clocks tell us to change our course, we will. But in the meantime, we'll shave days off our journey to Spearpoint, and avoid tangling with several known concentrations of Skullboys.' Ricasso leaned forwards, his belly billowing up onto the edge of the table. He took a pointing stick and drew it across the edge of the tract, skirting the terrifyingly blank interior. 'Given the urgency of our mission, and the saving in distance, we simply can't debate this. It must be done. We'll reach Spearpoint sooner, and since their instruments aren't as sensitive as ours, I very much doubt that any Skullboys will come after us. As a by-product, we'll end up compiling the first modern charts of this territory – something that we'd have to do eventually.'

'First charts, period,' Curtana said. 'Unless you know better.'

Ricasso said nothing, just tapped the pointing stick against the map.

'How long would we be in the Bane?' Quillon asked.

'From a standpoint of medical interest, Doctor?'

'I'm just wondering how long we'd be able to last if conditions changed, and we had to fall back on antizonals.'

'Two days at the most,' Ricasso said. 'That's assuming we never push the engines to maximum power, which of course would always be an option. Is that acceptable to you, given what you know of our drug supplies?'

'Acceptable, I suppose,' Quillon answered cautiously. 'Which, to be clear, doesn't mean the same as "embrace unquestioningly".' He felt Doctor Gambeson's phantom presence at his side. While the man himself was not well enough to voice an opinion, Quillon knew that the onus had fallen on him instead.

'I'm not saying we should rush into this,' Ricasso said. 'Equally, I see no rational alternative. The Bane's retreat offers us a short cut to our objective – what airship captain wouldn't leap at a short cut?'

'Um, me for one,' Curtana said.

'Yes, my dear. Articulate your reservations. Deep inside I know you'd be bitterly disappointed if we turned away now.' He clenched his fist. 'Just think! We could well be the first organisms to enter the Bane in more than five thousand years.'

'You're really selling it to me now,' Agraffe said, to a murmur of amused agreement from some of other captains. 'Don't get me wrong, I'm all for the medicine run. But at least that was a calculated risk.'

'The benefits outweigh the risk,' Ricasso said. 'For one thing, we can be reasonably sure we aren't going to encounter any Skullboys in the

Bane. Or anyone else, for that matter. And we won't be stopping unless we're forced to. We'll keep the main body of Swarm at cruising speed for the entire duration of the passage. The scout ships may occasionally run faster, but we'll avoid overtaxing the engines.'

'If we're really going to do this,' Curtana said, sighing, 'then *Painted Lady* should lead the way.'

'Is she ready?'

'Ready enough.'

'Excellent,' Ricasso replied. 'Six airships will proceed Swarm in arrow-head formation – *Painted Lady* first, two behind her, and three behind them. With no ship more than five leagues from another, we'll still establish accurate readings across a ten-league-wide track – more than enough to ensure Swarm's safe passage. Two further escort craft will flank Swarm, and a final one will follow behind, continuing to make readings, and also watching for anyone attempting to follow us.'

Curtana shook her head. 'They won't, take it from me.'

'Then the trailing ship will have all the more time to take meas-urements,' Ricasso said. He had, Quillon was beginning to realise, a maddening ability to twist any seeming disadvantage in his favour.

'Don't expect a majority show-of-flags on this,' Agraffe said. 'There were waverers last time. There'll be even more now.'

'There'll be no need for a show-of-flags, my boy.' Ricasso looked almost apologetic at his own cleverness. 'I covered this eventuality in my last proposal, the one for which I secured a hundred-ship mandate.'

'Ninety-eight, but who's going to quibble?' Curtana asked.

'The point is – and this is not mere constitutional hair-splitting – I expressly requested permission to vary the course en route as I saw fit, subject to improved intelligence on boundary shifts, weather patterns and the locations of enemy forces. I now have precisely that improved intelligence.'

'You won't get away with that,' Curtana said.

'No, you won't,' Agraffe agreed. 'That clause specifically forbids you from crossing any zone boundaries without a new show-of-flags.'

Ricasso looked at him, his expression one of stupefied incom-prehension. 'But I won't be crossing any zone boundaries, will I? Unless you mean the *old* boundaries on the *old* maps – but since when have we let them concern us?'

Under her breath Curtana said, 'You sly old fox.' But there was nothing remotely affectionate or approving in her voice.

'He may have a point,' one of the other captains said. 'Constitutionally speaking, that is.'

'Look,' Ricasso said, striking a conciliatory tone. 'Once people understand that the boundary has moved – that what we'll be flying over is simply barren land that has yet to be reclaimed by living things – they'll put aside their anxieties.'

'The same way I can feel all my anxieties just melting away as we speak,' said Curtana acidly.

She spoke to Quillon privately afterwards. 'You're probably surprised that I didn't put up more of a fight.'

'I think you had the intelligence to see the sense in crossing the Bane, even if you didn't like the way Ricasso forced us into it.'

'Very tactful of you.'

'I just hope I didn't cast the deciding vote.'

'I didn't see much voting going on, Doctor – or did I miss something?'

'You know what I mean. Ordinarily it would have been Gambeson Ricasso leaned on for medical advice. But in that room it was just me. He must have known I'd endorse almost anything that gets Serum-15 to Spearpoint even marginally quicker.'

'You feel manipulated.'

'I feel like there's something going on that I can't quite work out.'

Curtana's expression was rueful. 'I've had that feeling about Ricasso since I was able to count my fingers.'

'No one in their right mind would willingly go into the Bane unless there was an excellent reason, right?'

'Nobody,' Curtana said. 'But as you say, no one "in their right mind" – that's the clincher.'

'I don't think he's mad. I don't think he's even *slightly* mad.'

'I hear a but.'

'The amount of time he must have spent down with those vorgs, pursuing his magic serum – at the very least, it betokens a certain … monomania. A willingness to chase his obsessions beyond the point where any reasonable person would have turned back. I'm just wondering how that obsessiveness might relate to the Bane.'

'I guess we'll find out. I'm not planning to mutiny. Not yet, anyway.'

'At least it gets you out of Swarm again. You may not have liked the idea of crossing the Bane, but you liked the idea of someone else leading the mission even less.'

'My father would have done it. Doesn't mean I'm living in his shadow, incidentally, or trying to live up to his achievements. Any more than he was trying to live up to his father's, or his father's before that. It's the ship, Quillon. She demands it of us, makes us rise to the occasion. If

I backed out now, I'd be letting down *Painted Lady* more than anyone else.'

'I'd like to be aboard, if that isn't a problem.'

'I was planning on insisting on that anyway. You know about zone transitions, and their effects on human and animal physiology. Gambeson's staff can deal with the routine sick and injured aboard *Purple Emperor*, and you'll always be within heliograph range should your opinion be needed. Will Ricasso miss you in his laboratory?'

'Almost certainly, but I think I'll be of greater value aboard *Painted Lady*. If Gambeson is feeling a little stronger, he can return to his work in the laboratory.'

'Fine – I'll leave you to argue the fine points with Ricasso. I'm afraid you'll be the only medical man on the ship – think you can handle it?'

'I'll do my best.'

'Good. I'm running a tight ship – we'll be down to the bones, operationally speaking. There'll be no one aboard who doesn't need to be.'

'What about Commander Spatha?'

'He'll be enjoying the crossing from a different vantage point. You have my word.'

'In which case I think Kalis and Nimcha should travel with us, aboard *Painted Lady*.'

She frowned slightly. 'Wouldn't *Purple Emperor* be safer? That way they'll have advance warning if we run into a zone boundary; we'll have almost none at all.'

'It's not the zones I'm concerned about,' Quillon said.

CHAPTER TWENTY

The Bane was a scuffed margin on the horizon, pale as the foaming, breakered edge of an ocean. As the sun sank, the ebbing light stained the hulls of the airships in fiery shades of brass and copper, catching the hard edges of longitudinal ridges, navigation vanes and stabilising fins. Lights had begun to come on in some of the gondolas and along the pennanted bridges, ladders and ropeways that spanned the gaps between the ships. He watched figures move behind the lit windows, or cross from ship to ship on errands, and detected nothing out of the ordinary – no sense of crisis or disharmony. The picture was one of grand order and continuity, conveying a sense of stolid civic permanence – something that had been around for many centuries and might last even longer. And yet as he watched from the balcony Quillon grasped with renewed force how utterly transient and vulnerable this aerial squadron actually was. The darkening skies were empty of visible enemies for now, but that did not mean they would be untroubled before they reached the questionable sanctuary of Spearpoint. Each and every ship in Swarm was a perilously delicate thing, and the whole was no stronger than any of its constituents.

By now news of Ricasso's intentions had reached the entire fleet. His plan was to make the turn towards the Bane in the early hours of the morning and to cross the zone's former boundary by sunrise. That would give his navigators several hours to assess the nature of the terrain and evaluate its tectomorphic stability. If it was decided that the zone was unstable, then Swarm could still return to the other side of the former boundary without losing too much headway. There had been no show-of-flags, and as yet any disquiet about the decision was simmering rather than overt. Quillon found this lack of obvious dissent more troubling than he had expected.

Never mind; he would soon be free of the main body of Swarm.

It suited him well to be assigned to *Painted Lady*. She would be travelling with more instruments, fuel and weaponry aboard than she normally carried, and the trade-off for that was that she was, perforce, obliged to carry fewer rations and therefore fewer crew. Because of this, Curtana had been at liberty to draw up a rota that excluded anyone she didn't want aboard.

Quillon still had unfinished business in Ricasso's laboratory. He had conducted sufficient tests on the concentrated Serum-15 to know that it could be prepared for use as a general, broad-spectrum antizonal with no serious side effects. But it was not simply a question of diluting it, sucking it into hypodermics and then injecting away. The secretion had to be refined; other reagents had to be mixed into it at trace dosages, and at every stage the quantities involved had to be measured precisely. Looking weeks or months into the future – long after Swarm's presumed arrival at Spearpoint – Quillon could envisage the development of a method of batch production that would enable medical-grade serum to be produced in useful quantities. But he was not at that point yet, and until he was the preparation of the end-stage serum was intensely laborious, involving several steps where a small error would spoil that entire sample. More than once, he cursed Ricasso for tormenting the vorgs into going beyond Serum-15, when Serum-16 was all but useless except as a stepping stone. Of course Ricasso had his sights set on something better than a mere antizonal, but the social utility of Serum-15 – a cheap, potentially mass-producible substitute for Morphax-55 – was beyond calculation. Perhaps with time the vorgs could be goaded into making more of the stuff. But for now there was no hope of that, and Swarm would have to make do with what it already had.

Recognising this, Ricasso and Quillon had agreed that the unprocessed Serum-15 was too valuable to be stored in one place, even aboard an airship as well defended as *Purple Emperor*. Quillon had therefore divided the flasks up into quantities that could be crated and hidden elsewhere in the fleet, in the trusted care of captains sympathetic to Ricasso's cause. It was a matter of debate whether or not one of those ships would be *Painted Lady*. Trust was not the issue there; of course Curtana would protect the drugs as best she could. But if the Bane contained trouble, *Painted Lady* would be the first ship to encounter it, and so there was a very real risk of losing not only the dirigible but her irreplaceable cargo. Weighed against that were two other factors. Knowing Curtana, *Painted Lady* would be amongst the first ships to reach Spearpoint – she would not have it any other way – and would therefore be best placed to provide early dispensation of the drug. The medicines could be transferred between ships later, but who knew what complications might ensue once the fleet had cleared the Bane? Better to have at least some

Serum-15 aboard her now, Curtana argued, in case Swarm became dispersed or weather conditions prohibited ship-to-ship transfers. And as Quillon pointed out, it would not be too difficult to continue the processing work aboard the smaller ship, if he equipped himself with the necessary potions and glassware before they set off for the Bane.

It was finally decided that *Painted Lady* would carry both processed serum, which would need only a single-stage dilution before it was ready for human use, and a quantity of the unrefined material. Quillon would continue his processing work, and by the time they reached Spearpoint, there was every expectation that the unrefined serum would be completely processed. It was risky, certainly, but so were the alternatives.

But once he was aboard *Painted Lady* and she had pulled away from Swarm, he'd be stuck there for the duration without access to any chemical or piece of tubing he'd neglected to bring along for the trip. It was imperative, therefore, that he neglect nothing that would be required. Alone in Ricasso's laboratory, observed by the crouching steel-and-offal forms of the vorgs, he emptied his medical bag to the bottom of its black guts, spread its contents on the bench and began to refill it with the systematic care of a surgeon putting organs back into a patient. Next to the bag was also a wooden, straw-filled crate that would contain the larger glass and ceramic items and any drug-filled vessels too bulky or fragile for the bag. Curtana had provided him with a list of the crew, and because he had already tested each of them individually and had access to their medical histories, he knew their precise antizonal tolerances and therefore the drugs that would serve no purpose aboard *Painted Lady*, other than to add dead weight.

It took him an hour to fill the bag and the crate, and as much time again to reflect on his choices. The crate was too cumbersome to manage at the same time as the bag, so he left the bag locked in the laboratory while he carried the crate to the quartermaster who was supervising the loading of Curtana's airship. 'Be gentle with it,' Quillon advised, at the risk of insulting the man's competence. 'You're holding human lives, not just glass and chemicals.'

'Spearpointer lives,' the man said, as if there was a distinction.

'I've cut enough of you open to know we all bleed the same colour,' Quillon answered.

Night had fallen when he returned to *Purple Emperor's* under-levels. He didn't relish his visits to the laboratory under any circumstances, but night was his least favourite time. The vorgs never slept. They just waited and watched, and smelled of maggoty, fly-ridden meat that should have been thrown out days ago. At night the space between his bench and the cages seemed to contract, bringing the horrors closer.

He slid the key into the lock and turned it. Except the key wouldn't turn, as if he had already unlocked the door.

With a terrible sense of dread, Quillon pushed the door. For all its heaviness, for all that it was designed to keep in fire and vorgs and keep out the curious and malicious, it swung open with almost insolent ease.

He had left the laboratory unlocked. For a moment that was all he could focus on. And yet he remembered withdrawing the key on his way out with the crate. He had locked it, hadn't he? Or had he meant to, and then been distracted by the heaviness of the supplies?

The lights were still burning. He stepped inside and locked the door properly behind him. From his present vantage point, nothing appeared untoward. The vorgs were still in their cages, and at first glance the serum lines looked undisturbed. Still his heart was racing. He had not always heeded Ricasso's guidance concerning the axe, and he had neglected to sign for the revolver Ricasso had promised him, but now he walked to the wall and lifted the axe from its mounting. It felt bludgeon-heavy in his hands. It would be difficult enough to hold and carry, let alone swing. With each day his muscular strength ebbed another degree. It was not something he would have needed in the Celestial Levels.

The room was as quiet as it ever got. There was still the drone of *Purple Emperor's* engines, the steady drip from the filtration apparatus, the occasional metallic sound as one of the vorgs stirred in its confinement, the soft click and whirr of the tall cabinet, going about its hidden business. But nothing had altered since his departure. He moved along the cages, getting only as close as he dared. The caged things regarded him with the open chassis-work of their gristle-filled head-assemblies. Camera eyes clicked and whirred and hypodermic fangs telescoped in and out, glistening with ropes and threads of sticky mucus. To his intense relief all was well. He still could not understand why he had not locked the door, but the mistake had not led to anything more serious. Given the rush to prepare *Painted Lady*, the error had been – if not forgivable – then at least human.

He returned the axe to the wall and walked to the bench, ready to collect the bag.

He sensed a dark, stealthy presence at his shoulder. Heard the click of a mechanism and felt cold metal touch his neck. His first thought was absurd: that one of the vorgs had escaped and was now about to sink its fangs into him. But all the cages were still occupied. The moment passed and he realised that what he had heard was a gun's safety being clicked off, and that the hot breath on his ear was human.

A voice breathed, 'Careless, Doctor, leaving that door open.'

'I didn't, Spatha.' There was no need to turn around. He knew who he was talking to.

'The door unlocked itself?'

'It must have, if you managed to get in here.' Quillon swallowed, trying to regulate his breathing. 'But then again I suppose I shouldn't be surprised. You managed to get that book in and out of my bag, and those ridiculous paper angels. It can't have been difficult for you to make a copy of Ricasso's key, even though I thought I kept my eye on it all the time.'

'For an intelligent man, you're not very bright,' Spatha said. 'The key was the least of our worries. You think *that* would have stopped us? We could have found a way into this room any time we desired, with very little difficulty.'

'Then why didn't you?'

'I'll leave you to work that one out.' Spatha jabbed the gun into Quillon's skin. 'Here's a clue, though. If we wanted to sabotage Ricasso's work, we needed a scapegoat. For a long time there wasn't one. But then you came along and ... well, it's all falling into place now, isn't it?'

'Why would I sabotage this work? I'm the one who was pushing to get the medicines to Spearpoint.'

'You're also an exiled freak who has every reason in the world to hate that place. And a proven liar.'

'Whatever your arguments against Ricasso, this isn't the way to hurt him. We all need these drugs. He's doing useful work.'

'I can see you've been spending far too much time in his presence.' Spatha shoved Quillon towards the door. 'Unlock it. Leave it open. Then come back here.'

Quillon did as he was told. He knew there was no point in running. Perhaps if he had still been holding the axe he might have been able to do something ... but no, that was just wishful thinking. Spatha would have put a bullet through his skull before he managed to swing the axe.

He unlocked the door and pulled it open. The corridor – the clear route to the rest of the ship – beckoned.

'Very good, Doctor. Now open one of the vorg cages.'

'What?'

'Open a cage. The nearest one will do.'

It was the vorg that Ricasso had shown to Quillon on his first visit to the laboratory, the one without hindlimbs. The keys were kept on the opposite side of the room, near the axe mounting.

'Whatever you think you'll achieve here—'

'I won't say it again. Open the cage.'

Quillon went to the keys and selected the right one. The axe was close enough to grab, but useless against an adversary standing a dozen paces away with a gun aimed straight at him. He could see the weapon properly now – not a service revolver, but a heavy automatic with a long barrel and an under-slung magazine.

'If you're going to kill it, you don't need me to open the cage.'

'Killing it will come later. First it has to do a little damage, cause a little mayhem, just enough to make it plain that it was always a mistake to keep these things aboard ship.'

'The vorg will kill me as soon as I open the cage. Then it'll kill you.'

'No, it won't. Not while I'm aiming the gun at both of you, and not while it has a chance to make a break for freedom through that open door. They're not clever, but they're not stupid either. Do it, please, Doctor.'

Quillon looked at Spatha's weapon and mentally compared it with the heavy machine guns he remembered being used against the vorgs on the ground. Those guns had ripped the vorgs apart but he wasn't certain that a few bullets from an automatic would have anything like the same impact. All he could do was hope that the vorg would leave quickly, enact the chaos Spatha hoped for and then be killed.

He opened the cage, allowing the iron door to swing wide. The vorg, which had so often moved within the cage when escape was an impossibility, now appeared quite inert. It was lying down – crouching on its forelimbs, its hindlimbs gone, its segmented tail still present. The secretion line was still embedded in it, running back to the dripping apparatus on the bench.

'Remove it,' Spatha said. 'Do whatever you have to do to make it wake up.'

'It's perfectly awake,' Quillon said. 'It's just working out what to do next.' He was guessing, of course, but he thought it was a good guess.

'I won't ask again.'

Quillon took hold of the secretion line and ripped it from the vorg. The tip of the line sprang out of the metal ribcage, dragging a gobbet of meat with it. The vorg reacted to that. It twitched, a convulsive movement running from its tail to its mechanism-packed snout. At last the blue-taloned foreclaws tensed. The vorg scraped the floor of its cage, and then heaved itself forwards. It reached the horizontal bar under the open doorway of the cage and dragged itself slowly across the threshold, metal scraping against metal, until its abdomen, limbless hindquarters and tail were free of the cage. Then it halted, as if either exhausted or disorientated, or perhaps not quite believing its luck.

Quillon was still tense, still half-expecting to be shot at any moment, but he no longer considered the vorg to be the threat he had imagined. Forced to crawl on its belly, it was too slow to hurt anyone, provided they stayed out of reach of those foreclaws and snout-mechanisms. Little chance of it causing much mayhem, either. Perhaps the mere fact of its escape would be enough to undermine Ricasso, and to frame Quillon as a saboteur in whom Ricasso had foolishly placed his trust.

He was wrong about the vorg, though.

Perhaps its faculties had been dulled by the secretion process, or perhaps the sudden change in circumstances had forced it to truly *think* for the first time since its capture. Whatever the explanation, it was neither exhaustion nor the limitations of its anatomy that made the vorg move so slowly at first. The vorg did not gather speed; rather it exploded into motion as if a tightly wound spring had just been released. Perhaps the absence of its hindlimbs slowed it to a degree, but from Quillon's standpoint it was difficult to imagine anything moving faster. The forelimbs worked in a blur, the claws achieving traction against the floor, biomechanical musculature hauling the rest of the creature forwards, the tail coiling and uncoiling behind, adding its own propulsive force. Out of the corner of his eye, Quillon saw the reaction in Spatha's face: the dawning, stupefied realisation that he had set in motion something he couldn't control. The vorg rocketed towards them, crashing through benches and equipment, its tail flicking obstacles aside with ostentatious disregard. And then it was on them, or at least ready to strike – Quillon and Spatha with their backs against the wall, Spatha aiming the gun at the looming monster but frozen into inaction, unable to decide whether shooting the vorg would help or hinder their predicament. For a long moment it crouched before them, taut, ready to pounce, its snout-mechanisms clicking and whirring with the anticipation of nourishment. Red and purple things bellowed and pulsed inside the chassis of its metal ribcage. Flies had already caught up with it, buzzing in and out through gaps in its body.

And then it was gone. The tail flicked past them as it left, cutting the air with a whipcrack, but it had touched neither of them. There was just the empty cage, the open door, the two men in the chaos that had once been a laboratory.

Spatha's stasis of indecision lasted a few moments longer, and then his old self returned.

'You wanted mayhem,' Quillon said. 'Looks like you're going to get it.'

'Turn around, Doctor.'

'Are you going to kill me?'

He didn't have to wait for an answer. Spatha took his gun by the barrel and smashed the butt against Quillon's skull. Pain flowered between his eyes and he slumped to the floor.

Spatha couldn't shoot him, of course. Quillon realised this as his mind cleared and the pain shifted from agonising to merely intensely unpleasant. He had not blacked out, or if he had it had only been for an instant, not long enough to interrupt his thoughts. No, he couldn't be shot because that would place Spatha in the laboratory, and it had to look as if Quillon was the one who had released the vorg. Knocking him unconscious made it look as if he had been injured by the vorg's escape, as if he had been the only one down there.

He forced himself to his feet, fighting throbbing waves of dizziness and nausea. Touched a hand to the side of his head where the gun had struck him, winced at the contact, but came away with his fingers dry rather than bloody. The skin had not been broken. He took slow, calming breaths, trying to shuffle his thoughts into order. Spatha was gone and the vorg was still out there.

Perhaps it was the pain, but he experienced a sudden unexpected clarity of perception. He understood now why he had been asked to steal the blue book. It had nothing to do with the book's contents, which even Ricasso had considered valueless to his enemies. It had, instead, everything to do with what Quillon had done subsequently. He had informed Ricasso of the matter and by doing so had entered deeper into Ricasso's confidence. Perhaps Ricasso would have allowed Quillon access to the laboratory without that gesture, but it had undoubtedly ushered the process along. And all of that had allowed Spatha to engineer the sabotaging of Ricasso's experiments and make it look like Quillon's handiwork. For a moment, he could only marvel at Spatha's chicanery, and feel bitterly repulsed at the ease with which he had been manipulated.

The snake still has venom, Ricasso had said.

The fog was lifting from his mind. Forcing himself to act calmly, he looked around the laboratory, making sure he absorbed all the details. The other vorgs were stirring, but their cages remained secure and their nutrient lines were still delivering. He had no projectile weapon, but the axe was still on the wall. He took it, and this time adrenalin turned it paper-light in his hands. He wasn't sure what good it would do but he felt better for it.

He grabbed his bag in his other hand, left the laboratory and made doubly sure that he had locked the door on his way out. The vorg could only have gone one way, which was through the storage rooms that connected the laboratory with the rest of *Purple Emperor*'s multilevel gondola. As he passed through the first room he saw nothing out of place, suggesting that the creature had taken the path of least resistance. He entered the second room and heard a voice, raised and anxious. In the darkness he made out Spatha. He was standing – leaning, rather – against a wall, with a speaking tube raised to his lips. 'One of them's escaped. It's in the lower levels ... broken through the wall, into the service space. Get men down here now, before it reaches the rest of the gondola. Automatic weapons, everything. Repeat, a vorg is loose!'

Quillon took in the hole that the vorg had punched through the storage room wall into the compartment beyond. The panelling was thin wood of no structural utility, the kind that even a determined fist could have punched through. The hole led not into another room, but a dusty, unlit crawlspace, threaded with pipes and tensioned control cables.

'Not going to plan, is it?'

Spatha blinked, but that was as much surprise as he showed at Quillon's arrival. He returned the speaking tube to the wall.

'I should shoot you now, Doctor. It would spare both of us a great deal of trouble.'

'Then you'd have even more explaining to do.' Quillon surveyed the hole, wondering how far the vorg had already travelled. 'What were you hoping for, Spatha? That it would make a bolt for daylight, and your security men could take care of it with the minimum of inconvenience? A death or two, just to make your point? Were your people already on standby, ready to pounce?'

'Of course not. How were they to know you'd do this?'

'Oh, good. Very good. Settling into your story already.'

'Stay here,' Spatha said. 'Stay here or go back where I left you.' He aimed the gun to emphasise his point, and Quillon backed off, raising his hands – still holding the medical bag and the axe – in surrender. Again he reminded himself that the only thing stopping Spatha shooting him now was that it would be difficult to fit into his narrative afterwards. He wasn't supposed to be down here, after all, and would already have enough on his hands explaining how he knew about the vorg breakout so promptly. Quillon could only presume that there was no way to trace the origin of an utterance placed through the speaking tube system unless the speaker indicated their location.

And then Spatha was gone, leaving the way they had both entered, Quillon waiting two or three minutes before judging it was safe to follow him up into the public levels of the gondola. Generally when he left the laboratory he ascended into daylight, but not this time. The upper decks were gaslit, and as always there were fewer citizens walking around than during the hours of normal civic duty. But already there was more activity than was usual at this time. Spatha's announcement had been piped through to the whole ship and people were beginning to respond. A mechanical siren – the general alarm for a shipboard emergency – wailed through the speaker grilles. Doors were opening, citizens and administrative staff stumbling out into the corridors, security officers appearing with guns and crossbows, or sprinting to the nearest armoury to equip themselves. Quillon set off for Ricasso's quarters, but he had covered less than half the distance when he saw the man himself, along with Agraffe and Meroka.

'What the hell's happened?' Ricasso asked, barking his question at Quillon.

'Spatha,' Quillon said. 'He let it out. Got into the laboratory somehow and forced me to open the cage at gunpoint. If I hadn't done it, he'd have opened it himself.'

'The fucker,' Meroka said, scathingly, but not without an undercurrent of admiration. 'You all right, Cutter? Looks like you took a hit on the head.'

'He tried to knock me out, make it look as if I'd done all this on my own. But I'm all right. Our problem is the vorg. I think Spatha was hoping it'd come up this way, make a nuisance of itself and then get shot. But it had other ideas.'

'You saw where it went?' Agraffe said.

'Yes.' Quillon looked around distractedly. 'Where are Curtana and the others? Are they safe?'

'Curtana's aboard *Painted Lady*, getting her ready for the crossing,' said Agraffe. Kalis and Nimcha haven't been shipped over yet.'

'I don't want that thing getting anywhere near them, not after what almost happened on the ground,' Quillon said.

'Is it the same one?' Ricasso asked.

'You tell me. The left-most cage. No hindlimbs.'

'One of my older ones, then. But no less problematic. Spatha said it broke into the service space – is that correct?'

'Unfortunately. Do you think it'll stay there?'

'Where vorgs are concerned I've learned not to second-guess. They don't think or reason the way we do. It may not even realise it's in the air, aboard a ship.'

'They're going to crucify you for this,' Quillon said.

'We'll see. First things first, and then we'll worry about the repercussions. How's the laboratory?'

'A bit of a mess. I managed to get some of the supplies over to *Painted Lady* beforehand, but I'm not sure how much difference they'll make.'

'You did what you could, Doctor, which is all anyone can expect of us. You – um – did lock up, didn't you?'

Quillon marvelled at how anyone could absorb such potentially devastating news with barely a murmur of discontent. 'I did,' he said, 'but someone else should still get down there and protect the place. Spatha already has a way of getting in and out.'

Ricasso turned to the younger man. 'Agraffe – can you take care of that? Find some men we can trust, and secure the laboratory and all the rooms leading to it. Be quick about it, too. Vorgs are fast, and they won't miss a chance.'

'I'll take care of it,' Agraffe said. 'Doctor, I'll have that axe if you have no objections.

As he handed over the axe, Quillon heard gunfire from the direction of the gondola's stern, a hundred or more spans away. The shots were rapid, as if there was more than one shooter, but it was not automatic fire. Voices were raised, commands barked. The armed airmen who had been milling around waiting for specific orders began to move in the direction of the disturbance, weapons at the ready.

'It might be nothing,' Ricasso said. 'There are enough rats living on this thing to make anyone jump at shadows. Or it might be our vorg. I think I'd best go and see for myself.'

'Cutter and I'll take care of the mother and kid,' Meroka said, as if they had already discussed the matter.

'I can do it on my own,' Quillon said. 'I only have to get them aboard *Painted Lady*.'

'And if they need protecting, you aren't the best man for the job. No offence, Cutter, but that's the way it is.'

They reached Kalis and Nimcha without incident, moving against the flow of airmen and armed citizenry heading towards the front of the gondola. By the time they arrived – Quillon doubted that more than ten minutes had passed since the vorg's breakout – Kalis was already on her feet, knocking on the door, wanting to know what was happening. He could hear her through the grille. Quillon didn't know if Spatha's broadcast had been piped through to her quarters, but she could not have failed to hear the commotion as half the citizenry were roused to action.

'They're under quarantine,' the attending guard told Quillon, as he asked for the door to be opened. He was a young man with a shaving cut above his collar and a permanent curl to his lips.

'Special orders from Ricasso,' Quillon said. 'Quarantine's suspended. Kalis and Nimcha are to be relocated to *Painted Lady* before she departs.'

'I'll need to see paperwork on that.'

'There's a vorg loose,' Meroka explained. 'In case that escaped your attention. Ricasso's doing his bit for Swarm, trying to kill the thing before it sucks someone's brains out. Now, he might be able to find time in his schedule to file that paperwork you need, but I'm guessing it's going to be a stretch, what with a monster on the loose and the ship being in a state of fucking emergency and all.' She smiled sweetly. 'So what's it going to be? You going to let them out, or do I have to get, you know, truculent?'

'We were just speaking to Ricasso,' Quillon said, hoping to make their case more persuasive. 'I was down in his laboratory when the vorg escaped.'

'That was your doing, was it?'

'It's more complicated than it looks. But the thing is loose and these two people have already seen enough vorgs for one lifetime. They'd have been shipped over tomorrow; we're just moving things up a few hours.'

'You'd better not be lying, Spearpointer.'

'If I'm lying, that's the least of your problems. But there's a very simple solution. Escort us to *Painted Lady* and surrender us to Captain Curtana. She'll either accept that the quarantine's over or clap all four of us in irons.'

'Man's talking sense,' Meroka said. 'Quarantine always was horse-shit, anyway.'

'What the rumours said all along,' the guard answered. 'That it was nothing to do with them being dirt-rats. That it's about the mother, or maybe the girl, and what's under her hair.'

'If either of them are tectomancers,' Quillon said breezily, 'I think we'd know by now.'

The guard opened the door. 'Bring them out. I'll take you over to *Painted Lady*. One word, one trick, and it's over. Don't think I won't shoot the four of you. State of emergency, no one would quibble.'

'What is happening?' Kalis asked.

'Special orders,' Quillon said. 'You're being moved back to the first ship, the one we came in on.'

'Something is wrong here,' Kalis said. 'Why are they shooting? Have the Skullboys come back?'

'Not the Skulls,' the guard said. 'Got us a vorg on the loose.'

Kalis took in this news with equanimity, as if it was no more or less than she had been expecting. 'Where is it?'

'A long way from here,' Quillon answered. 'And we'll be even safer aboard *Painted Lady*.'

'Where will Meroka be?' Nimcha asked.

'I'll be right there with you, kid. And no vorg's coming anywhere near us.'

'You'd best put on cold-weather clothes,' Quillon said. 'We'll be spending some time outside.'

Nimcha asked, 'Will you read the stories, Meroka?'

Meroka looked down at the picture books, spread open on the table. 'If that's what you want.'

'I don't like them,' Nimcha explained. 'They're stupid.' She said this with the withering disdain only a child could adequately convey. 'They're about things that don't matter. But I like it when Meroka reads them, and shows me how the words match the pictures. I like Meroka.'

'Guess I have my uses,' she said.

'It makes both of you happy,' Kalis said. 'But my daughter is right. The stories are stupid.'

Watching the party being escorted through *Purple Emperor*, a casual observer would have struggled to tell whether they were being treated as prisoners or protected guests. Quillon supposed that it barely mattered now. His own liberty, if it still existed, was unlikely to last long. It would be his word against Spatha's that he had not been responsible for the vorg's release, and who would believe a foreigner, a man from Spearpoint with goggles over his eyes and secrets under his coat, a man with a demonstrable record of untruths? The best he could hope for now was to get Kalis and Nimcha to safety, while the authorities were preoccupied with the vorg.

There were two ways to reach *Painted Lady* – either by ferry craft, or by traversing the connecting walkways between airships – and both required the party to move through the gondola in the direction of the open-air loading dock where Quillon had first embarked. He willed the guard to lead them faster, but the young man seemed intent on dawdling, taking an unnecessarily circuitous route, perhaps in the hope of hearing some official confirmation of Ricasso's order. The gunfire had abated while they were talking: he had heard no discharges at all after they had started moving.

They were very near the loading dock – no more than a corridor from it – when a pair of armed airmen appeared around a bend, weapons drawn.

'Where are you taking them?' the guard was asked, none too civilly, by the older of the pair.

'Ricasso's orders. They're leaving the ship.'

'Any orders Ricasso gave today are suspended with immediate effect. He's under administrative restraint.'

'I spoke to him about ten minutes ago,' Quillon said, astonished. 'He was going back to help you find the vorg.'

'We found it. It isn't going anywhere. No thanks to Ricasso, though.'

'He had no part in its escape,' said Quillon. 'I was there when it got loose, and it wasn't my doing either.'

'You can explain all that to Commander Spatha. He wants you rounded up and brought to him.' The man smiled at his companion. 'Looks like we got here in the nick of time, doesn't it?'

Quillon knew better than to resist: these were hotheads fired up with the possibility of an overnight change in the power structure, secure in the knowledge that if blood was shed, they would not be held accountable. The young guard was relieved of his responsibility for the party, while the two airmen walked them back into the main section of the gondola, retracing their steps part of the way before veering sternwards. It was still quiet, and some of the citizens who had been roused were beginning to drift back to their quarters and duty stations, reassured that the emergency – if not the political upheaval triggered by it – was at an end.

Presently they arrived at one of the observation rooms near the stern. The room was windowed on one side, and some of the panes had been shot out or punctured by stray rounds. A panel was missing from the back wall, where the vorg appeared to have forced its way out of the service space. An airman had his rifle aimed warily at the dark aperture, though the vorg itself had been captured and incapacitated. It lay on the carpeted floor, with Spatha and his coterie of loyalists forming a semicircle around it. Ricasso was there as well, neither at gunpoint nor under any visible restraint, but forced into cowed submission by the dissident airmen who now held power in this quarter. His face was red, his eyes wide and disbelieving, and the rumpled state of his clothes suggested that he had been handled none too gently. Spatha stood a few paces to his left, kicking a shiny-toed boot against the fallen vorg. It twitched on the floor, limbless, glossy entrails spilling from its metal chassis, mechanical eyes clicking and whirring in their housings. It been shot, and impaled through its ribs with crossbow bolts. It wasn't dead yet.

Spatha, who was sweating, nodded at the arriving party. 'Very good. You weren't attempting to leave the ship, by any chance?'

'We both know what happened,' Quillon said.

'What happened,' Spatha said, 'is that a crisis very nearly overtook the ship. If it hadn't been for the quick thinking of security personnel, the consequences could have been catastrophic. But that was always your intention, wasn't it?'

'My intention was to help Ricasso produce the serum we need to save Spearpoint.' Quillon glanced around the assembled onlookers, wondering who amongst them might be sympathetic to his side of the story. 'That's what I was doing. That's all I was doing.'

Spatha pursed his lips, a pout that conveyed how deeply unimpressed he was with this line of argument. 'But is it not the case, Doctor, that you were entrusted with access to that laboratory? That Ricasso gave you the means of entering it, knowing full well the dangers posed by his vorgs?'

'I trusted Quillon,' Ricasso said. 'I still do.'

'It was a risk to bring these things into Swarm in the first place,' Spatha said. 'It was practically cavalier to hand the keys to an outsider.'

'Quillon has already saved Swarmer lives. We should be grateful to him, not suspecting him of sabotage.' Now it was Ricasso's turn to look around in the hope of finding allies. 'I know what's happening here. Quillon's been set up to reflect badly on me. But he had nothing to do with this.'

'What happened to the vorg's forelimbs?' Quillon asked.

Spatha looked at him mildly. 'Why should that be a concern, Doctor?'

'It had them when it escaped – when, let's be blunt about it, you followed me into the laboratory and forced me to release it.'

'I'd be very careful about throwing around that kind of accusation,' Spatha said, smiling at his audience as if he expected them to share the joke.

Just then a speaker grille erupted with sound. The harsh, breathless voice had been amplified by passing through a chain of resonant chambers, and in the process had lost much of what made it recognisable. But Quillon still identified it as belonging to Agraffe.

'I'm down at the laboratory. We've got trouble, I'm afraid. The bastard must have doubled back and forced its way through the door. All the cages are open. Repeat, all the cages are open. All the vorgs are loose.'

Ricasso did something then that Quillon had not expected him capable of. He moved with startling, bearlike speed, shrugging off any attempts at restraint, and before anyone could react he had the speaking tube off the wall and up to his lips.

'Agraffe, listen to me. There's a coup in progress. Signal Curtana. She'll know what to do. This must not spread beyond *Purple Emperor*!'

He had to shout the end of his statement as the tube was snatched from his hands, and he was manhandled away from the wall.

'Everyone will have heard that,' Spatha said. 'Not just Agraffe and whoever's with him.'

'That's what I'm counting on,' Ricasso said. 'And you can follow my announcement by putting the whole ship back on emergency alert. The vorgs haven't finished with you, not by a long stretch. You know why this one was so easy to kill?'

There was a twitch of unease in the corner of Spatha's mouth. 'We cornered it.'

'You cornered a cripple. Wondering where its forelimbs got to? I'll tell you. The other vorgs took it apart. They cannibalised this one for anything they could use and then threw it to you like a scrap of meat. That's what vorgs do. And somewhere aboard this ship there is almost certainly one that now has full locomotive functionality.'

Spatha's facial twitch became more insistent. He cleared his throat. 'Pass me the tube,' he told one of his men, even though he was close enough to reach for it himself. 'This is ... Commander Spatha. The vorg outbreak is not yet ... contained. All citizens and active staff to maximum vigilance.'

'You might want to rethink that takeover,' Meroka said. 'Just until this shit is cleared up.'

That earned Meroka a jab in the belly from a crossbow stock, causing her to double up in pain, compounded no doubt by the wound she had already suffered.

'You didn't have to do that,' Quillon said.

'Be careful, Doctor,' said Spatha. 'A man in your position should watch what he says.' Then he nodded at the two airmen who had brought them to him. 'Bring the girl to me.'

310

Kalis tried to hold on to Nimcha, but her daughter was wrenched away from her and dragged over to Spatha.

'They mean a lot to you, don't they?' Spatha asked Quillon.

'They're human beings.'

'One of them, certainly. This one I'm not so sure about.' He glanced at Kalis for an instant. 'Do you mind?' In a single quick movement he had one hand around Nimcha's head, cupping her gently but firmly, while he used the other to part her hair. 'It's real, isn't it? So neat and regular. Of course, we can't really see it properly now; the hair's in the way.'

'It's just a birthmark,' Quillon said.

'Of course it's a birthmark, Doctor – what else could it be? The point is that it's an eerily regular and intentional-looking birthmark.'

'Let her go,' Kalis said.

Spatha allowed Nimcha's hair to fall back over the birthmark. Still holding her with the other hand, he reached into a sheath attached to his belt and drew an elegantly lethal-looking dagger. Kalis moved to tackle him, but Spatha was quicker; he brought the blade to within a hair's breadth of Nimcha's face and held it there.

'Stay back. I'm not going to hurt her. I just want to get a better look at this . . . thing.'

He started cutting her hair away in clumps, concentrating on the back of her head. The knife whispered through the matted strands, making barely a sound as it sliced. Nimcha trembled. Her eyes were wide and frightened.

'What do you want from us?' Quillon asked.

'The truth, Doctor. No more lies. You had the chance to choose sides, but you made the wrong decision. Now **Swarm**'s turning over a new leaf. The citizenry deserve to know what **they've** been sheltering.' He flung one of the clumps to the floor. Nimcha flinched as the blade touched her scalp, drawing a tiny nick of blood.

'She's just a girl,' Quillon said. 'That's all.'

Spatha returned the knife to its sheath, his work completed. Aside from a few ragged tufts where the blade had missed it mark, he had removed most of the hair that had originally hidden the birthmark, leaving Nimcha with a bald spot like a misplaced tonsure.

He had only cut her in one or two spots, the blood already drying.

'She's a tectomancer,' he said. Then he spun her around for the benefit of his audience. 'They're real. We've always known it. But I never thought we'd stumble across one.'

'She doesn't mean us any harm,' Ricasso said.

'Then why were her mother – and you – so determined to keep her true nature from us?'

'Pricks like you might be a contributory factor,' Meroka said, and was immediately on the floor again, coughing out a tooth this time from where she had been smacked in the face.

'Return them to custody,' Spatha said. 'Proper holding cells this time – and make sure they're separated, including the dirt-rats.'

'You can't separate the mother and daughter,' Quillon said, raising his voice. 'They've done nothing!'

He was hit in the chest with a rifle stock, punching the wind out of him in a single explosive gasp. He dropped his bag, crumpling to the carpet with his head only a span from the twitching, goggling head-assembly of the vorg.

'I did warn you,' Spatha said.

Quillon was dragged to his feet. He had no strength to resist; barely enough to stand up. He caught Ricasso's eye and all Ricasso could offer him was a plaintive shake of his head, conveying the utter helplessness of their situation.

Several events then ensued in remarkably quick succession. The first was a flash of movement from the hole in the wall where the vorg had burst through. The second was a discharge from a rifle as the airman who had been guarding the hole attempted to shoot at the steel-and-sinew thing that had sprung with jack-in-the-box speed through the gap. The third was a scream as the airman realised that the vorg had him, its blue metal fore-talons digging into his right arm, piercing flesh and muscle until they snagged bone, dragging him along as it retreated into darkness. The rifle clattered to the floor. The airman disappeared through the gap like a sack of garbage being hauled away for disposal. His screams continued, echoing around the confined space.

A second had passed, possibly two – sufficient time for those present to realise what had happened, but not enough for any of the armed airmen and guards to do anything about it. By the time they had swung their weapons towards the aperture, the vorg and its prey were gone. Only a scuttling, scraping sound – receding by the second – gave any sign that the creature was still on the move.

'... the fuck,' Spatha said, and for a second his veneer of confidence was gone. When it returned there was something translucent and paper-thin about it, like a drumskin stretched too tight. 'Into the service space. I want that man brought back!'

One of the airmen worked a lever on his gun. 'Permission to use semi-automatic fire, sir.'

'No ... no. Too many firesap lines. Single-fire only. Get after it!'

Three of the men ventured cautiously through the aperture. 'It's too dark, sir!' one of them called, his voice muffled. 'We can only see a few spans either way!'

'Perhaps we should wait for daylight, sir – it'll be easier to root them out,' said another of the men.

Spatha drew his own weapon, the same one he had used to threaten Quillon, and ducked into the darkness. 'Someone find a firesap torch,' he called. 'Quickly!'

'It's all right, sir,' the first of the men shouted out excitedly. 'We've found him – it's not taken him very far!' There was a pause as the airman clambered further into the service space, and then his voice turned softer. 'Still breathing, sir – it must have decided he was too much trouble to carry.'

Spatha, who was still pausing on the threshold, said, 'Bring him out – and then the rest of you carry on after the vorg. Fear and panic, where is my damned firesap torch!'

Scuffles and grunts of exertion signalled the unconscious airman being dragged out of the shaft. At last someone brought a firesap torch to Spatha – it was a detachable wall-lantern, but served the same effect – and he directed wavering illumination into the recess beyond the panelling. Quillon saw now why it would have been unwise to use automatic fire. The service space carried a multitude of red fuel lines, as well as communications tubes and aerodynamic control wires. In any situation other than a close-action engagement, it would have been madness to use machine guns.

'Let me see him,' Quillon said, as the airmen dragged their comatose comrade into the light, feet first. Still winded, he knelt down to recover his bag. Spatha's men were being as gentle as circumstances allowed, so not very gentle at all. Aside from the pipes, there were reinforcing spars every few spans and the man's body had to be dragged over them, his head clattering against metal every time.

'His arm's pretty gouged,' one of the men said. 'But the vorg didn't take it, sir. Oh, wait. Oh no, sir ...'

'What?' Spatha said.

'His head, sir.' The man's upper torso and head were finally dragged into the light, and for a moment all seemed well, the play of light and shadow hiding the worst of his wounds. But as Spatha brought the firesap torch closer, there could be no escaping the truth. The man's skull had been punctured above the brow, a hole wide enough for a thumb to be pushed all the way into it. There was surprisingly little blood for a head wound, and despite the vorg's brutal surgery, the man was still, in a technical sense, alive.

'It's harvested frontal cortex matter,' Quillon said, staring down the tunnel of scarlet, white and grey. 'Quite a lot of it, by the look of things.'

'He's still alive,' another man said.

'Technically speaking. But don't expect him to pull his weight aboard ship any more.'

'What are you saying, Doctor?' Spatha asked.

'I'm saying that it's very unlikely that this man will ever lead anything resembling a normal life.' Quillon hesitated. It was against his instincts to make such a casual diagnosis, but he saw little margin for doubt. 'He'll need to be cared for, treated like a child.'

Spatha suddenly sounded interested. 'He'll be a vegetable, you mean?'

'I wouldn't put it quite like that, but—'

Spatha aimed his gun and shot the man through the forehead. 'We're carrying enough ballast as it is. Just did him a favour.' He looked around, irritated. 'Now what's wrong with her?'

Kalis had Nimcha back in her arms. Nimcha was convulsing, her spine arched, her neck bent back, her eyes rolled into their sockets. Her limbs were moving all the while, not so much kicking and punching as grasping and running on thin air, but her face was quite still, her mouth halfway open, a line of silvery drool spilling from her lips.

'It's got her again,' Quillon said, Kalis giving a tiny, helpless nod in return.

'What has her?' Spatha asked.

'The Eye of God. The Mire,' Kalis said.

The Mire might have her, Quillon thought, but it was the distress of what had just happened that had opened the door to let it through.

'Can she control it?' he asked.

'I do not think so,' Kalis said.

From the next room came a languid thump. It was no more eventful than the sound of a consignment of dirty bedding arriving at the bottom of a laundry chute. For a few seconds no one even responded, so preoccupied were they with the dead man and Nimcha's intensifying convulsions. But then one of the airmen looked through the door and saw what had happened. He let out a small, childlike gasp of surprise and horror. A body lay on the floor. It was another Swarmer, a woman this time, but dressed in off-duty clothes. She was on her back, her face turned their way, blood spreading out from beneath her. Quillon didn't recognise her. She'd come through a hole in the ceiling, a dark square where a panel had been dislodged. There was just time to recognise the vorg – *a* vorg, he corrected himself, since he couldn't be sure it was the same one – coiling back into the darkness, the pale tip of its segmented tail the last part of it to disappear.

Spatha ran to the spot where the woman had fallen and aimed his gun at the ceiling, tracking the sound of the vorg's slithering, scuffling motion through the panels. He fired, drilling a line of bullet holes, not stopping until he had exhausted the magazine.

Quillon knelt and examined the woman. He didn't need a pathologist's table to tell him she was dead. Nothing in her face except frozen incomprehension. The vorg had snatched her quickly, and whatever it had done to her had been equally swift.

He rolled the woman onto her front. Where her spine should have been, from her coccyx to the base of her neck, was a bloody trench. The vorg had cut it out of her, through fabric and skin and subcutaneous fat, ripped that articulated structure of bone and nerves right out of her, then dumped what it didn't need. He realised then that it hadn't been the vorg's tail he had seen vanishing into the ceiling.

He turned around, not wanting Nimcha to see any of this.

'Keep her back—' he started to say.

It came then, as he had half-anticipated. A pressure in his skull, a throb that built and built until it felt as if something was trying to lay an egg inside his brain, a burning white egg that was too large to fit, that would split the bones along their sutures. His vision tunnelled. Nausea tightened his throat. He could barely keep himself from blacking out, let alone organise his thoughts.

'What's happening?' Spatha asked, the effort of speaking written on his face.

'Zone tremor,' Quillon said.

'We're hundreds of leagues from the present boundary – a tremor can't touch us at this range,' Spatha said, his tone aiming for dismissive but betraying the frightened realisation of what he was witnessing.

'Then it's more than a shift. What you felt on the ground was just a hint of her abilities. She can change entire swathes of tectomorphic geography just by thinking about it.'

'Then she ought to stop.' He made to aim the gun at Nimcha – forgetting perhaps that it was empty, or trusting that no one else would have realised – and Kalis turned around to shield her daughter.

'She might be the only thing that can save us!' Ricasso bellowed. 'The vorgs are only just alive! Push the zone too far, they won't be able to survive at all.'

'Or us,' Spatha said. He clicked the trigger, the gun dead in his hand.

315

'Someone give me a revolver! If she pushes things in the wrong direction—'

'She will not,' Kalis said.

The effects of the zone transition continued to intensify. The floor of the gondola appeared to tilt and then return to the horizontal, signalling that *Purple Emperor* had lost propulsive power.

'Nimcha,' Quillon said, with all the forcefulness he could muster even as he felt his mind being squeezed in a vice. 'You mustn't make the change too strong, or it will break the engines for good. And we need those engines!'

Spatha had managed to snatch a service revolver from one of his men and was now holding the wavering barrel in Nimcha's direction. But he wasn't trying to fire. Either his nerve had left him, or he recognised that a zone storm might be the one thing that would hinder the vorgs, provided the shift was in the right direction.

'Put the gun down,' Ricasso said, with surprising tenderness. 'It's over, Spatha. You're not going to win this one. You think you can take Swarm in the middle of a zone shift?'

'This isn't your ship any more,' Spatha said.

Someone bent double and vomited. Forcing his mind to work, Quillon opened his bag. Knowing there was no time for anything but the most crude of calculations regarding dosage, he fumbled a dozen or so pills into his own trembling hands. 'Take these,' he said, passing them to Meroka. 'One each for everyone here. Half a pill for Nimcha. I mean it, Kalis. She may be able to bring on the zone changes, she may even have some resistance to their effects, but that resistance isn't perfect.'

Spatha lowered the revolver. 'You'll still answer for this, Ricasso. You brought this on us.'

Ricasso took a pill from Meroka. 'It's my fault now, is it? I thought you were blaming it on Quillon.'

'You gave him the opportunity to do the sabotage he always intended,' Spatha replied.

'If Quillon meant to sabotage us, there are a thousand other ways he could have gone about it.' Ricasso closed his eyes as the antizonal took effect. 'Well done, Doctor. I can feel the worst of it lifting already. Will she hold the zone where it is, or let things snap back?'

'I don't know,' Quillon said.

Spatha waved the revolver at the remaining airmen. 'Get into the service spaces. Find the vorgs, before the zone rebounds.'

Quillon looked at Nimcha. The severity of her convulsions was easing,

Kalis holding her tightly, comforting her daughter as she came through the worst of her nightmare of possession.

'I am sorry,' Kalis said. 'She could not help it.'

'Don't apologise,' Quillon answered. 'She may very well have saved Swarm.'

Footsteps – heavy, multiple footsteps – pounded in their direction. Quillon and the others looked past the dead woman, down the length of the room to the wide, balconied corridor beyond. Despite the loss of propulsion, firesap burners were still alight. At least a dozen uniformed men and women were marching towards Spatha and his gathering. They had weapons drawn, glinting orange and brassy in the firesap light, and none of the party appeared touched by the zone storm. At the front, marching with a look of iron determination on his face, was the red-bearded Agraffe.

'Did you speak to Curtana?' Ricasso asked, as Agraffe neared.

'I did. The fleet's still ours, Spatha. The rest of your supporters were too spineless to show their faces.'

'This man is under administrative restraint,' Spatha said. 'Captain Agraffe – I require you to submit to emergency rule under my authority.'

'Require all you like. I'm still answering to Ricasso.'

Spatha carried on speaking as if Agraffe had not answered him at all. 'You will submit to my rule. You will instruct your men ... whoever's with you ... to coordinate with security personnel in tracking down the remaining vorgs. We may not have much time.'

'One of us certainly doesn't.' Agraffe levelled his own service revolver towards Spatha. 'Surrender your weapon. You're under arrest for attempted mutiny.'

Spatha gave a hollow laugh. 'That's an extraordinary claim. I hope you have something suitably extraordinary to back it up.'

'Did you speak to Curtana?' Ricasso asked again.

'I did, and I retrieved what she asked me to. It's in safe hands now.' Agraffe nodded at Quillon. 'I've also been told to escort Doctor Quillon and the rest of his party to *Painted Lady*. They can be on their way within the hour.' Agraffe glanced at Nimcha, concern in his eyes. 'Will she be all right?'

'She won't be any worse off aboard *Painted Lady*,' Quillon said. 'And now that her true nature's more widely known, that may be the safest place for her. I'd like to see what we can salvage from the laboratory first, though.'

'Don't get your hopes up,' Agraffe said.

Nimcha made a mewling, nonverbal moan. Her eyelids began to

flutter. Quillon felt it then: the zone receding, returning to something like its old position, if not snapping into exactly the same shape. Consciously or otherwise, Nimcha had done what needed to be done.

From somewhere outside, an engine coughed and spluttered and then roared back into life. Then another.

'She timed it well,' Ricasso said, unable to hide his delight at the phenomenon he had just experienced. 'Brought it just long enough to sow some confusion, but not long enough to effect permanent transcriptional errors. We'll just have to hope it was enough to kill the vorgs for good.'

'They were only just clinging on to life,' Meroka said. 'Which is what made them such snake-mean sons of bitches in the first place. My guess is they're rotting away as we speak. Best find them, though, if you don't want the place stinking like a Horsetown whorehouse by sun-up.'

'There'll be due process,' Spatha said, as he surrendered his weapon. 'Criminal neglect still took place here. Align yourself with Ricasso, you're only prolonging the inevitable.'

Ricasso smiled briefly. 'We'll see.'

A little while later they were on their way to *Painted Lady*, riding one of Ricasso's personal ferries. It was still dark, with the light from the gondolas the only illumination in any direction. Swarm was on the move again, with all but a handful of engines having been successfully restarted, and with few indications that the zone storm – squall, tremor, however one wanted to term it – had caused any serious harm. As for Quillon and his fellow passengers, things could have been much worse. The physiological correlatives of the zone transition were now almost entirely past, save for the lingering influence of the antizonal medicine. Quillon had done his best, but no doctor in the world could have made an accurate allowance for the zone snapping back so quickly. Now his head buzzed like a recently struck bell, but it was not merely due to the after-effects of the pill. He was also working through the implications of what had just happened, his thoughts a ringing, throbbing dissonance of political cause and effect, like a rowdy argument going on between the two hemispheres of his brain.

'Spatha's right,' Quillon told Agraffe, as the little craft ducked and bobbed its way between the looming black envelopes. 'They can lock him up and throw away the key – kill him, for that matter – but the damage is already done. The unavoidable truth is that the vorgs escaped, killed at least two of your citizens, possibly more, and none of that would have happened if Ricasso hadn't brought them aboard.'

318

'It was a calculated risk,' Agraffe said. 'Ricasso knew that the potential rewards made it worthwhile.'

They had left Ricasso aboard *Purple Emperor*, where he was best placed to restore order, marshal his supporters and quench Spatha's stillborn rebellion. With Nimcha and Kalis also on their way to Curtana's ship, Quillon was glad to put the night's business behind him. But he could not rid himself of the feeling that Agraffe, Ricasso and the others were too confident of ultimate success.

'If he'd got anywhere with the all-purpose serum, they might see his argument,' Quillon said doubtfully. 'As it is, his existing work hasn't been successful enough to justify the risks he's taken. This incident can only damage Ricasso in the long term.'

'It was deliberate sabotage, Doctor. That's an entirely different matter.'

'Can't prove it, though,' Meroka said.

'She's right,' Quillon said. 'Spatha was brazen, but only because there were no other witnesses. Unless you include the vorgs.'

'And if there had been another witness?' Agraffe asked. 'Someone who saw what happened down there, how you were threatened and forced to open the cage?'

'That would be something. Unfortunately I was alone.' He paused, seeing something in Agraffe's eyes. 'Wasn't I?'

'Of course.'

'But there's "alone" and there's "alone". What was Ricasso asking you, when you arrived with all your men? Something about speaking to Curtana, and then you said something about something being in safe hands?'

Agraffe sighed slightly, then allowed himself a thin smile. 'Evidence,' he said. 'Evidence that – provided it was retrieved and put into safe keeping – will almost certainly give Ricasso all the backing he needs.'

Quillon closed his eyes, reviewing the time he had spent in Ricasso's laboratory. Thinking back to how something had been different the first time, when Ricasso had given him the first tour. Different in the sense of something not being there at all, when on later occasions it had been present.

He recalled the regular mechanical click of some piece of apparatus. He had taken it to be a form of clock or recording instrument, and that had made perfect sense. But he did not remember it making any sound the first time they had gone down there.

'I was being photographed, wasn't I? That's what Ricasso wanted you to safeguard. But you didn't know about it and Curtana did. She told you where to look, what to recover.'

'You shouldn't feel badly about it, Doctor.'

'I shouldn't feel badly about being spied on?'

'Ricasso trusted you enough to leave you alone in his toy room. He just didn't trust you completely. But being almost trusted is still better than not being trusted at all, wouldn't you say?'

'My experience, you take what trust you can get away with,' Meroka said. 'Ninety per cent, eighty, still a fuck of an advance on zero.'

'Thank you,' Quillon said, giving her a sarcastic smile. 'That's clarified things enormously.'

'Always ready to help, Cutter.'

'Look on it as a positive development,' Agraffe said. 'If Ricasso hadn't spied on you, you'd have no way of defending yourself. Now we can prove that Spatha was down there.'

'The plates show him, do they?'

'They'll need to be developed, which will take time. This isn't Neon Heights. But if he was in that room for more than thirty seconds, he'll have been caught.'

Quillon decided to let go of his anger, his sense of having been violated. He could either carry it with him all the way to the other side of the Bane, or discard it now.

'You think it'll be enough?'

'Spatha with a gun pointed at you, and then one of the vorgs breaks out? Yes, I think that might do the trick.'

'What will they do to him? You mentioned arrest. You didn't tell me what the sentence might be.'

'It'll be the death penalty,' Agraffe said. 'The only question is, which one.'

'And they say civilisation ends at Horsetown.'

'Don't judge us, Doctor. Just because your city doesn't have a death penalty doesn't mean it doesn't kill people. It just does it behind its back, and takes its slow, sweet time over it. The people who don't fit in, the ones it can't make work for itself, it sucks them in, grinds them down and spits them out. At least we're clean and fast out here in Swarm. Well, fast, anyway.'

'Spatha wasn't acting in self-interest. He was concerned about Swarm's survival.'

'Go back and defend him, if it matters so much to you. Where I'm sitting, self-interest and Swarm's survival add up to the same thing.'

'Fucker had it coming,' Meroka said. 'You saw how he hurt the kid.'

Nimcha was asleep in her mother's arms. Even Kalis looked on the edge of exhaustion, as if she had borne part of her daughter's torments herself.

'He is a bad man,' Kalis said. 'He should die. But quickly. I will draw the knife, if this is allowed.'

'Well, first things first,' Agraffe said with a hasty smile. 'Due process and all that. There'll still be a trial, with all the trimmings. And now that this has brought matters to a head, Ricasso will want to see a real binding show of loyalty from the dissenters. If they're not ready to – how did Spatha put it? – submit to his authority, I wouldn't be surprised if Ricasso invites them to take their ships and head for the other side of the Earth.'

'He'd do that? He'd split Swarm?'

'More like amputate the part of it that isn't healthy. Any other time, Ricasso'd rather cut his own arm off than lose one good ship. But now? We're actually going to *help* the Spearpointers.' Agraffe grinned at the very idea, a proposition so utterly at odds with the natural order of things that the only rational response was hilarity. 'If that isn't a sign that we've begun a new chapter, I don't know what is.'

'We've a way to go yet.'

'Swarm's come through harder crossings than this. Granted, we'll have Skullboys to deal with when we get near Spearpoint. But until then? I don't know what all the fuss is about. It's just dead landscape. The only thing we're likely to die of is boredom.'

They were coming up on *Painted Lady*. She loomed out of the darkness, looking astonishingly, absurdly small after the cavernous, gilded luxury of *Purple Emperor*. Quillon's heart tensed at the thought of making any prolonged crossing in that metal bucket of a gondola, for all her armour and equipment. But the Bane would be a crossing like nothing attempted in recorded history.

'I know what you're thinking,' Meroka said, as they readied to disembark. 'Piece of piss, right?'

'Yes,' Quillon said, ruminating on the words. 'A piece of piss. Exactly the sentiment I was searching for.'

CHAPTER TWENTY-ONE

Come the morning, what had been a pale line on the horizon had transformed into a broad swathe, coming nearer with each watch.

'I can't tell you how weird this feels,' Curtana said, when the other officers had left the dining table. 'We're actually steering for the damned thing, at full cruise power. I've spent most of my adult life doing everything possible to keep away from it.'

'How are the instruments?' Quillon asked, finishing the last drop of coffee. It was as black as crude firesap and preternaturally strong, as if all the coffee he'd tasted in his life before that point had been diluted.

'All readings are absolutely normal, for this zone. Ordinarily we'd be seeing strong signs of transition by now, as we get closer to the boundary. Mechanical systems would be starting to fail – engines overheating, clocks and gauges jamming up, just like when Nimcha did her trick. You'd be doling out the antizonals and even then it wouldn't be enough to stop us feeling ill.'

'Then that's a good sign. Ricasso was right to extrapolate from those earlier readings.'

The zone disturbance initiated by Nimcha's fit had been more of a tremor than a squall or storm. Back in Neon Heights it would have been a seven-day wonder, with the Boundary Commission likely needing to make only trifling alterations to their maps. So it was here. More widespread changes could not be ruled out beyond the limit of Swarm's instruments, but the conditions the fleet was moving through now were in no measurable way changed from those before Nimcha had brought the disturbance. All of Swarm had felt it, both on a physiological and mechanical level, but the tremor had been too short-lived to cause lasting damage. A few engines would need to be overhauled, and a few airmen would require additional medication to deal with the after-effects, but in all other respects Swarm was left unscathed.

They had been lucky: incredibly so. And for better or worse, Ricasso had finally got his demonstration of Nimcha's powers.

'Doing this still makes me uneasy,' Curtana said. 'It's not just me, either. Of course, none of the other officers are letting anything show.'

'Perhaps when we've crossed the former boundary, and things still haven't changed, they'll begin to adjust to it,' Quillon said.

'Let me show you something. It won't take long and I could use some fresh air anyway.'

Outside on *Painted Lady*'s balcony Quillon breathed in the cool and humid morning air, letting it flood his lungs. Coils of vapour loitered over the dark, densely vegetated landscape below. It was one of the thickest tracts of woodland they had crossed since being rescued near Spearpoint, proof not only that the city's reach was limited, but that the effects of the cooling world were not yet uniform.

The drone of the engines was steady and reassuring, like a mother's heartbeat. They were the only engines to be heard. After so long in Swarm, it was strange to have empty sky in all directions.

'Notice anything different?' Curtana asked.

Quillon surveyed the landscape, the monotonous canopy reaching away in all directions, uninterrupted by anything except the approaching margin of the Bane.

'I'm no botanist,' he said. 'If there is some change in the vegetation, you'll have to point it out to me.'

Curtana pulled a speaking tube from the gondola's wall. 'Engines. Immediate dead stop for two minutes. Resume normal cruise speed thereafter.'

Painted Lady's motors sputtered to a halt. Robbed of power, the airship began to slow down abruptly as wind resistance overcame her momentum. Quillon reached to steady himself as the gondola seemed to tip forwards. With the engines shut off, the only sound was a faint creaking from the rigging lines supporting the propulsion struts.

'Listen,' Curtana said, in little more than a whisper. 'All the birds and animals down there, you'd think they'd be at their loudest now. It's morning, after all.'

'I'm not hearing much.'

'That's because there's nothing to hear.'

'Nothing at all?'

'Only trees and plants.' Curtana was leaning over the railing with a cavalier disregard for her own safety. 'We call it the Deadening. It's marked on most of the maps, a pink margin around the red line of the Bane. This is where nature starts giving up. If we put you down in that forest right now, you'd find a mausoleum, a green crypt. You'd be the only thing down there with a nervous system. Animals – birds, insects, mammals – they just can't survive. Their cells don't work properly any more – it's like the machinery inside them becomes too complicated to function, falls apart like a broken toy. Metabolic pathways suddenly become metabolic blocks. Plants survive, more or less – they're slower and hardier, and not as complicated inside. But as you go deeper and deeper into the Deadening, even the toughest of them find it hard going. Eventually plant life stops altogether. You've got some basic life forms on the fringe of the Bane, clinging on to existence – single-celled organisms and simple bacterial colonies. Then there's nothing. Absolute sterility. This is a lush paradise compared to what's ahead.'

'We're flying over it now, and we're still alive,' Quillon said. 'But we're just animals as well. There's no reason why birds, insects and mammals couldn't follow us in.'

'They will, given time. In a few years, they'll have colonised this entire jungle, so long as the Bane doesn't snap back, and the world doesn't freeze over. But that just means there's a new Deadening somewhere else. When the shift happened, it was death for millions of creatures. They wouldn't have had time to escape, even if they had the instincts to start moving.' Curtana paused. 'The Deadening's an omen. It's the last warning, when all your instruments have lied and you've somehow remained immune to the onset of zone sickness. It's telling you to turn back now, while you still can.'

One by one the engines rattled back into life and *Painted Lady* began to move again. With her motors roaring, it should have been impossible to tell that the forest was dead. But now that Quillon knew what was below, now that he was aware of the profound absence of higher life beneath that dark canopy, he swore there was a sinister quietness lapping at the edge of his thoughts, a ravenous absence seeking to swallow everything into its own all-consuming silence.

He returned indoors and busied himself with matters medical.

The Deadening was a narrow margin, never wider than fifteen leagues. By the middle of the morning they had passed all the way across it, into what – according to the maps – was the beginning of the Bane proper. Quillon had watched as the foliage thinned out from dense dark canopy to an impoverished, bleached scrub, and soon only pockets of tenacious green persisted amidst a landscape of dead, biologically inert soil and bare, bone-coloured rocks. The green pockets were the hardiest mosses and lichens, their simple, robust biologies able to keep them alive when more complicated organisms failed. But even they could only push so far into the zone of lifelessness, and eventually even these basic organisms could not sustain themselves. They grew warped and atavistic, and then not at all. The landscape changed to rock and dust, totally bereft of living things. It was not a desert, for in the many lakes and pools there was an abundance of fresh water, gleaming back at them under the blue sky with mirrored purity. But there was nothing that could make use of that water, so even the shorelines were devoid of life. Had normal conditions prevailed, the crew would already have been dying in the most wretched way imaginable.

No one had yet come to him with any complaints, and Quillon was as certain as he could be that he was free from symptoms of zone sickness. His mind was clear, his recall and concentration excellent, his coordination acute. And yet there *was* something: the faintest twinge of nausea, a lingering tightness at the base of his throat. Unless it had something to do with the motion of the airship it could only be psychosomatic.

Quillon allowed himself to believe that – provided external conditions remained stable – there was no reason for it to worsen. On this matter, at least, there were grounds for cautious optimism. The clocks and gauges in *Painted Lady*'s chart room were obstinate in their conviction that the airship was still passing through perfectly normal airspace. No hint of a change-vector had yet been detected.

Quillon was as fond of the chart room as he was of Gambeson's library back on *Purple Emperor*. The windowless, vibration-proofed, brown-veneered room, with its caged birds, shelves of ticking instruments, whirring springs and weights, scratching pen-traces and slowly winding paper rolls was a place of lulling, hypnotic ease. As often as not one of the other crew members was present, doting on the birds, taking down readings or making some tiny adjustment to one of the glittering mechanisms, but Quillon's intrusions were tolerated, and he was grateful for the company himself. He passed many hours in technical conversation with the crew, fascinated by the subtle principles embodied in their instruments.

It was not difficult to build a device that would detect the transition to a lower-state zone, the kind that normally infested the Bane. Finely meshed gears would bind up as microscopic tolerances became unworkable. Clocks would slow and then stop. So, too, would the pistons and other precise moving parts in *Painted Lady*'s internal-combustion engines, rendering the motors inoperable. Such failures warned of biological changes that could be expected as the zone transition intensified. It was considerably more difficult to build instruments that could register

325

transitions in the other direction. *Painted Lady*'s chugging engines would keep working even if she drifted into a zone where they were technologically obsolete. But for the ship's passengers, the effects could be just as unpleasant as if the change was in the other direction. Humans were adaptive organisms, and from the earliest stages of foetal growth their nervous systems had developed under the influence of the prevailing zone. By the time they reached adulthood, their minds had become highly attuned to its characteristics. Hereditary factors played a role as well, since many individuals were descended from chains of ancestors who had only ever lived in the same conditions. Over time, each habitable zone had selected for those best able to function and reproduce within it.

The chart room contained a few instruments capable of registering higher-grade transitions, but they were staggeringly complicated and correspondingly difficult to maintain and operate. As such, they were accorded both respect and a certain degree of disdain, like attention-seeking divas in an opera company. Experienced crew preferred to put their faith in the caged zebra finches, which had been raised in Swarm and would stop singing – and eventually drop off their perches – long before human beings sensed a zone transition. The chirruping of the birds seemed to accord perfectly with the tick and whirr of the instruments.

And all was well. The birds were active, the readouts all perfectly normal. The accuracy of the clocks was constantly being cross-checked against readings taken aboard the other airships, flashed over by heliograph. So far there had been no hint of change across the entire formation, from *Painted Lady* to Swarm to the trailing airship. Had the Bane retreated by only a hundred leagues, there would have been clear evidence of that by now. It must have shifted at least one hundred and fifty leagues and perhaps further – a reshaping of the entire hemispheric geography.

By the early part of the afternoon, they had pushed far enough into the Bane that even the Deadening had retreated to a dismal grey-green strip on the horizon. The monotonous landscape of rock and water rolled underneath like a loop of film being played over and over again, or so it seemed to Quillon after spending only a few hours on the observation deck. A forest could be monotonous as well, but it was the monotony of abundance rather than absence. This was a world stripped to the bones, the skull poking through the face.

Swarm did not slow once the sun had set, even though they were travelling into unknown territory without the benefit of even the sketchiest of charts. When the sun had still been up, *Painted Lady* had climbed to nearly the limit of her operational ceiling, allowing the horizon to be scrutinised for any obstacles – weather systems or mountain ranges – that would have to be steered around. Balloons, some with automatic cameras and some with spotters aboard, were raised on long tethers to gain even more altitude.

But the clear air had revealed nothing troubling, and so the decision had been taken to push ahead at normal speed, relying solely on gyroscopic and celestial fixes to maintain a constant heading. If the atmosphere on the craft had been tense during the daylight hours, it reached a state of acute apprehension in darkness. The devices in the chart room were now under constant, nervous observation. Since the finches were asleep at night, their cages cloaked with black fabric, they were of no use in detecting a zone transition. The crew were therefore entirely reliant on the more temperamental and tricky-to-calibrate gauges. And, of course, their own physiological responses. Thus far the readings had continued to be flat, conditions unchanging, but there was a palpable sense that things had to alter at some point. Quillon registered it in the gravely resigned expressions he saw on the officers' faces when they came and went, conveying the latest readings to the bridge. They were like men waiting to sail off the edge of the world.

Quillon never allowed himself to be anything but busy. He was glad that he had packed and delivered the crate before Spatha's interruption, because many of the supplies and reagents inside it would surely have been destroyed when the vorg broke loose. He waited to hear what the final toll of the damage would turn out to be, and in the meantime occupied himself by preparing further batches of medical-grade Serum-15, ready to be delivered to the city. When he had no choice but to leave some chemical process running, he did what he could to help with the business of chart-making. There were not enough spare hands on *Painted Lady* to man all the survey cameras or make all the accompanying log entries, and Curtana's crew welcomed such assistance as he was able to offer. The stereoscopic survey equipment was easy to use once the rudimentary principles had been demonstrated to him. Thereafter he had loaded and exposed hundreds of plates, noting the airship's position and altitude by reference to the chart-room instruments, so that each dual exposure could be related to the hand-drawn maps being compiled at the same time. He concentrated on those ground features that were in some way noteworthy: the larger lakes, striking patches of mineral discoloration, or prominent outcroppings of rock that might one day form navigational landmarks, should crossing the Bane ever become commonplace.

But no measurements could be made at night, and there was a practical limit to how much work could be done in the laboratory before his own tiredness began to overcome him. When he had done all he could, and the airship was travelling in darkness, he found Curtana on the bridge. Meroka was manning the heliograph station, Agraffe at her side as she sent and received transmissions. Quillon peered into the night and made out the twinkling flicker of one of the sending ships, and it looked as distant and unreachable as the furthest star.

'There's good news and there's not-so-good news,' Curtana said, making a small course adjustment before locking the wheel.

'I'll go with the good news first.'

'Ricasso says he's salvaged more than he expected to from the laboratory. Some of the Serum-15 was destroyed, along with supplies of the other stuff we need to refine it, but it could have been worse. He's lost almost all the Serum-16, but that's moot: without the vorgs, he had no way of going beyond it.'

'And the vorgs?'

'Located and neutralised. None of them survived Nimcha's storm. But if Ricasso wants any more, he's going to have to start from scratch.'

'At least we have the Serum-15. How much did we manage to save, including the flasks I brought here?'

'About two-thirds. We won't be saving quite as many Spearpointers as we hoped, but as I said, it could have been worse.'

'I suppose so,' Quillon said. 'And if it had been an accident, I could almost accept it. But we didn't have to lose any of that medicine. Spatha and his supporters should pay.'

Curtana gave him a sly look. 'Coming round to the idea of the death penalty, are you?'

'I didn't say that. But he should be held accountable for the lives we won't save in Spearpoint, not just the people killed by the vorgs. What was the final toll, by the way?'

'Four. We found two more bodies, both harvested. And we almost lost another man in the search, simply because it's dangerous crawling around inside an airship.'

'Four people dead to make a point about Ricasso.'

'Spatha will be held accountable, I assure you. And the plates definitely prove he was in the laboratory – your innocence is not in doubt.'

'Nor my true identity, I suppose, or Nimcha's.'

'Swarm knows. And most of them are ready to accept you – or will, given time. Patience – they're only human, Quillon.'

'You mentioned not-so-good news.'

Her face tightened, as if she had allowed herself to forget about it until then. 'It was inevitable, I suppose. Under other circumstances Ricasso would have stripped the dissenting ships and crewed them with loyalists, men and women he knew he could rely on. But even if that was an option now, it wouldn't be a permanent solution. He's got Spatha, and a handful of his supporters, but how many others are lurking out there, unsuspected, waiting for another chance to rebel? The Bane was a test, I suppose. If you're with Ricasso, you'll follow him all the way to the other side, come what may. If not ...' She trailed off, something catching in her throat, before she gathered her composure. 'Ricasso's given them the option of leaving, and at least twenty captains are already lined up to steer away. If they don't want to sail with us, they can take their ships and the fuel, guns, food and medicines they have aboard and do what they will, provided they keep out of Swarm's way. And by that Ricasso means he doesn't want to see even a glimmer of one of those ships on the horizon. Because if he does, Swarm will engage.'

Quillon thought of these beautiful, dandified ships tearing into each other like so many cannibalistic vorgs.

'It's that serious?'

'Spearpoint betrayed us in our hour of need. And now Swarm is betraying itself. That's almost worse. No, no almost about it. It makes my blood boil that they'd even consider this.'

'You weren't exactly all sweetness and light about crossing the Bane,' Quillon said.

'No, I wasn't. But then I committed to it.' Curtana unlocked the wheel, ready to make another tiny adjustment to their heading. 'That's the difference. I committed. And now I'm going to see this through to the bitter fucking end.'

'Amen to that,' Meroka said.

Dawn revealed a few clouds on the horizon, but no mountains or hills, and certainly nothing to suggest that Swarm had crossed more than a hundred leagues during the hours of darkness. It was as if they had stopped, and were only now resuming progress. Quillon needed the reassurance of the chart-room staff before he was ready to accept, at least on an intellectual level, that they were still on schedule. On the main chart – the one that was being amended as they completed the crossing – an inked blue line showed their progress to date, cutting across an otherwise empty blankness. A scattering of surface features had been drawn in along the line and on either side of it, but at its widest this strip of mapped terrain was no more than fifteen leagues wide. If anything, the strip only served to emphasise how little of the Bane they would have seen by the time they crossed back over the Deadening.

Still, progress had undoubtedly been made. They had completed nearly half of the crossing without incident, and from both a technical and medical standpoint there was little immediate cause for concern. *Painted Lady* and the other ships were running well; the crews and the citizens were healthy, and those incidents of incipient zone sickness reported to Quillon could be safely ascribed to psychosomatic effects. Quillon had even found his own symptoms retreating as time passed, and the reality of crossing the Bane began to seem less outrageous. It was, after all, just territory.

Quillon came indoors from the balcony. He had been studying Swarm through binoculars, counting ships as best he could.

'The dissenters are still with us,' he said. 'Either that, or my sums are off.'

'For now,' Curtana said, 'but Ricasso's ultimatum still stands. I think they're just biding their time, weighing the pros and cons. Strike off on their own and they can do things their way. But then every decision they make has to be theirs and theirs alone – they can't rely on the technical and navigational expertise of the hundred and more other ships.'

'Out here, with no reference points, I don't blame them for being cautious.'

'Damn their caution. We're doing something new here – of course it's frightening. That's the point.'

'You've changed your tune.'

'If Spatha achieved anything, it's to make me realise that we need Ricasso more than ever. He was right all along. And we're forging a path here that others will follow. One day, if the tectomorphic shift is permanent, this crossing will be perfectly routine. There'll be way stations and signal posts. There'll be accurate maps and weather forecasts. There may even be the beginnings of a larger civilisation. Things don't have to be so fragmented from now on.'

'Be careful,' Quillon said. 'That sounds dangerously like optimism.'

He spent the morning fussing with the medicines, examining the crewmembers, exposing more stereoscopic photographs, and then joined the others for a short lunch. They were on light rations so there was nothing sumptuous about it. When he arrived, Meroka and Curtana were already sitting at the table, talking about something in raised voices that stopped as soon as he came in through the door. They hadn't been arguing.

'Did I interrupt?'

'Just telling Meroka that if she doesn't like life in post-reconstruction Spearpoint – and who could honestly blame her if she doesn't? – I'm sure we could always find her something to do in Swarm. Even if it didn't involve shooting things.'

'Spoilsport,' Meroka said, in mock woundedness. 'At least let me blow up some shit.'

'I'm sure we'd be able to find some ... shit ... for you to blow up,' Curtana said, voicing the word as if she was holding it in mental tongs, at a distance.

'Little Miss Sky-Princess is starting to thaw,' Meroka said triumphantly. 'Cursing would do her a world of good, don't you think, Cutter? Get shot of some of that tension of hers. Girl walks around like she's got a steel rod jammed up her ass. Fine, she's a captain and all – got to keep up appearances. But that can't be good for you your whole life. Bit more time with me and we'll have her profaning enough to make Fray blush.'

'It's good to have objectives in life,' Quillon said. It was, he thought, remarkable that Meroka and Curtana had found not only common ground but also the beginnings of something that looked like friendship. He supposed he should not have been too surprised; despite their wildly different backgrounds, both women were possessed of a streak of uncommon independence, albeit one that had manifested itself in wildly different forms.

The conversation took on a more formal tone as the other officers and airmen filed in. Even Agraffe, who had been posted to *Painted Lady* at Curtana's specific insistence, had to maintain appearances. He called Curtana 'captain' most of the time, only slipping out her name when his guard was down, and then looking flush-cheeked at the indiscretion, even though none of the other skeleton staffers were in any way annoyed by it. Agraffe, for his own part, appeared completely willing to submit to Curtana's command; it was, he said, doing him a world of good to get his fingers dirty again, tinkering with engines and instruments, relearning hands-on crafts he had almost forgotten since assuming command of *Iron Prominent*. Quillon liked the man and was glad he was aboard during the crossing.

Curtana had seemed awake and energetic during their earlier conversations, but now that he had time to study her discreetly, while she was engaged in discussion with one of the other officers, he noticed how strained she really looked. He wondered if she had slept at all, even if only for a couple of hours.

There was a knock at the door. One of the watch officers entered, visibly anxious about something. Quillon's heart sank. What could it be, but an indication from one of the instruments that a transition had been detected?

'What's the bad news?' Curtana asked. 'I thought everything was normal half an hour ago. Please don't tell me the finches have decided to stop singing.'

'It's not the finches, Captain, or any of the clocks. Everything's still giving the same readings we had last night, flat as can be. It's what's ahead.'

'The horizon was clear. No mountains or weather systems.'

'It's not like that, Captain. It's a thing, an object, lying more or less directly in our path, about fifteen leagues ahead of us. At our present speed we'll be over it inside the hour.'

'And this thing just popped up in front of us?'

'It was hidden from view. The terrain's very gentle, but it only took a shallow ridge to block the object until now.'

'All right. What kind of thing are we looking at?'

'You'd better see for yourself, Captain – none of us have a clue what it might be.'

Curtana stood up from the table, taking the napkin from her lap. 'Guess I'd better do what the man says.'

Quillon followed her onto the bridge, where one of the officers was peering through the forward-mounted telescope, the barrel aimed slightly downwards. Quillon could tell where the telescope was aimed since there was a twinkling point of light in the rocky landscape ahead, a few degrees below the horizon. It was too concentrated and bright to be the reflection from water; rather it resembled a mirror or a piece of highly polished metal being held up at them. The light wavered, shimmering like a mirage, but there was nothing to suggest that it was any kind of signal or attempt to communicate.

'Can they see this from Swarm yet?' Curtana asked.

'Pretty certain they can't,' the officer answered. 'We didn't notice it until a league back, and we were sweeping the horizon constantly. By the time they get to our present position, the sun angle will have changed as well, so it may not be as prominent. But unless it's small it'll be hard to miss if we keep on this heading; whatever it is, we'll be passing within a league of it.'

'That's rather a big coincidence, don't you think? All this empty vastness, and something pops up right in our path?'

'There's coincidence,' Meroka said, 'and then there's someone jerking our chain.'

'Unless it's the only one of these things we can see,' Quillon said quietly. 'Because of the sun angle, and so forth. It might not be unique, or intended specifically for us. The landscape could be dotted with them, and we just happen to see that one.'

'Whatever it is, I still don't like it. Book says there's nothing out here – not a single bacterium. Let me look through the scope.' Curtana took the eyepiece and made a tiny, finicky adjustment to the focus wheel, squinting with her other eye, her mouth open in expectation.

'Can you make out anything?' the officer asked.

'Could you?'

'Not much, Captain. Maybe a hint of elongation, but that's about all. I'd estimate the size to be no more than ten to fifteen spans across. Do you have any idea what it might be?'

'Some kind of machine, or metal structure. Doesn't seem to be doing anything, or going anywhere.'

'Concur, Captain. Nothing's changed since we sighted it. Whatever it is, of course, should easily be able to see us by now.'

'If it's looking.' She pulled away from the eyepiece and offered the view to Quillon. 'Take a gander, see if anything leaps out at you.'

Quillon peered through the telescope, but all he could make out was a kind of bright silvery smudge, dancing and flexing with thermal distortion from the warming landscape. He had no idea how large it might be, except by reference to the graduated scale on the telescope's cross hairs. But it could clearly not be any kind of city or settlement, for even at this distance a small community would still have spread across a larger apparent area than the bright object.

Curtana was right. Unless it was some kind of highly reflective geological feature, it could only be a single building, or some kind of machine.

'Has anyone else reported this?' she asked.

'No, Captain,' the officer said.

'And have we flashed anyone else about it?'

The officer shook his head. 'Thought you ought to see it first, Captain.'

'You were right. But you can alert the other escort ships now, and tell them to keep quiet about it until I say otherwise. I'd like to know if they can see anything we can't. Also signal Swarm, for Ricasso's eyes only. Tell him we've seen something ahead and are evaluating our response.'

'Aye, aye, Captain. And in the meantime, should we hold this course?'

'Did I say anything about changing it?'

'No, Captain.'

Ricasso's response came back within five minutes of the outgoing signal being flashed. Curtana read the transcription with steely impassiveness, then mumbled something under her breath that sounded to Quillon like, 'Orders are orders.'

'What's happening?' he asked.

'Ricasso's signalled all the other captains to change course. He's taking Swarm to the left of the object, while we stay on this heading.'

'Does that mean he's already gone public about it?'

'No, he's just hoping none of the captains question his orders and that the citizenry don't think there's anything unusual in a course change.'

'Will they notice?' Quillon asked.

'These people were born in the air. They feel it when the watch changes, let alone when Swarm changes direction deliberately. But they won't necessarily assume the worst. In the meantime, we'll stay on this heading, snoop whatever it is, then fall back into position at the head of the fleet.'

Quillon glanced around the bridge. 'Might we speak in confidence?'

'It's a medical matter, I presume?'

'Not unrelated.'

They retired to Curtana's quarters, she closing the door behind them then standing against one of the walls, conspicuously not inviting Quillon to take a seat. 'Better make this quick – I need to supervise our drop in altitude.'

'Then I'll get straight to the point: it's about Ricasso. I think he knows something he's not telling us.'

'About the Bane?'

'Exactly.'

Curtana looked at him guardedly then gave a small nod. 'I've had that feeling ever since he hatched this plan.'

'Then I'm not the only one. I'm not sure if that makes me pleased or worried.'

'I'd go with worried if I were you. But you're right – he's hiding something, definitely. Our maps are just big sheets of blank paper, but he knows something, or at least thinks he does.'

'About the thing lying ahead?'

'Maybe, maybe not. But he gave that order to change course pretty damn quickly, and it was very detailed in the specifics. Almost as if he was half-expecting us to run into something, and already had a scheme worked out.'

'Does that change your stance with regard to his orders?'

'No.'

'I didn't think it would,' Quillon said.

They returned to the front of the gondola. In the time since he had first seen it, the glint had come visibly nearer, beginning to take on the same extended attribute that had until then only been apparent through the telescope. It was a little less like a mirror, a little more like a large piece of silvery metal tossed onto the landscape.

Curtana strode to the command pedestal and took control of the airship, her stance – back straight, legs braced apart – communicating authority. 'We're descending,' she announced loudly. 'We'll drop altitude to two hundred spans above the surface and resume a level trajectory until I say otherwise. All engines at normal cruise power; all navigational and tectomorphic readings to continue as before.' She turned sharply to Quillon. 'There's no reason to expect any zone transition between here and there, but I'd appreciate it if you could be scrupulously vigilant for symptoms, Doctor.'

'Consider it done.'

'The slightest twitch or hiccough and we're out of here.'

'For the record, I feel absolutely normal right now, and I see no evidence of illness amongst the crew.'

'And the finches are still singing. All the same, I don't want to lose a second if we have to turn tail.'

Heliograph signalling continued unabated, despite the change in disposition of the fleet. Quillon watched Curtana scan the incoming transmissions even more alertly than usual. He learned that Swarm had completed its gentle turn, deviating from its original heading by a mere five degrees – enough that it would miss the object by a comfortable margin. The other escort ships had made the same course change, leaving *Painted Lady* alone in following the original line. So far there were no reports that the course change had led to any disagreement or consternation amongst the captains and ordinary citizens. If pressed, officers were under instructions to refer to a developing weather system that had been sighted by the forward scouts, around which Swarm needed to steer. The fact that the horizon was still as clear and unbroken by cloud as ever was obviously a detail Ricasso hoped no one would notice.

The descent to two hundred spans was uneventful. The landscape was so monotonous, so absent of obvious markers for scale, that it was only the airship's growing shadow that gave any indication that they were lowering at all. Quillon watched it ripple and flow over the rocky surface like some eager fish skimming the ocean bed. The object remained ahead, its form becoming steadily clearer in the telescope. It was a slender metal tube, lying on the ground as if it had been dropped there and then crushed, with smaller pieces surrounding it.

'It's dead wreckage now, whatever it was,' Curtana said, taking her eye from the telescope. 'Still doesn't explain what it's doing here, but I don't think there's anyone alive in it.'

'If a machine managed to make it into the Bane under its own power, our assumptions about what does and doesn't work here might need adjustment,' Quillon said.

Curtana pulled one of the speaking tubes to her lips and said, 'Nose-gunner. You see something you don't like, you have my permission to respond immediately.'

'This wasn't always the Bane,' Quillon said quietly. 'A long time ago, before the last shift, things could have survived here. We might just be seeing ancient wreckage.'

'There's still weather here,' Curtana answered, hanging the speaking tube back on its peg. 'Rain and dust storms. Lightning. Maybe I'm wrong, but I figure something that's been here for five thousand years ought to look a little less shiny.' Then she turned to one of the other officers. 'Range and status?'

'Two leagues, Captain. All clocks and gauges normal; all mechanical systems functioning well. Finches still singing.'

'Thank you. Maintain present speed and altitude.'

Quillon felt his nervousness rise by slow degrees as the two leagues of unremittingly bleak landscape crawled underneath. He had reviewed the possibilities many times since learning of the glint, and each time he had come to the conclusion that there could be nothing harmful out there. And yet his fears lingered. The mere existence of something in this long-dead place was profoundly anomalous. There was no reason to assume that logic and reason had any further say in the matter.

When they were less than a league out, Curtana surprised him by ordering the airship to descend half the remaining distance to the ground. As *Painted Lady* sank even lower, he wondered whether Curtana was making a clear-headed tactical decision, a rational response to improved data, or whether her ingrained fear of the Bane was compelling her to act in a bold or even cavalier fashion. But even when *Painted Lady* had reached its new cruising height, there was no change in the status of the object. At a range of half a league, its nature was now clear even to the naked eye. The cylinder was flared at one end and tapered at the other, and the broken things around it had the blade-like sharpness of wings, or the shattered pieces of wings.

The object must once have been a flying machine, or a missile.

'It could have come from outside, maybe,' he said. 'Like a stone lobbed into water.'

'Nothing could have flown this far into the Bane,' Curtana said. 'Even if the adjoining zones allowed someone to make a heavier-than-air flying machine with a range of more than a few leagues, it would never have got this far inside. The pilot would have died as soon as it crossed the Deadening. Everything else would have stopped working soon after.'

'Could something have glided in, even if every mechanical system was dead, and the pilot incapacitated?'

'Maybe, if that *looked* like a glider, which it doesn't.'

'You think it's a rocket, or a jet.'

'Either of which didn't get this far by gliding, or coming in ballistically.'

'I'm inclined to agree. Which really leaves only one possibility, as I see it. That it came from somewhere inside the Bane, not from outside.'

'Range to object now one-quarter league,' called the officer.

'All engines to dead slow and reduce altitude to fifty spans. We're going to get this close anyway, may as well make it count.'

The next six minutes dragged excruciatingly. Even when they were almost on top of the fallen machine, he still could not entirely shake the feeling that it was about to lash out at *Painted Lady*, spearing her out of the sky in some fierce demonstration of concealed potency.

When they were directly overhead, there was still no response. Cameras clicked. Machine guns tracked from their bubble-turrets, aimed straight down. Seen from above, the object had clearly been an aircraft of some kind. The wings had sheared off and shattered, but their elegant, swept-back form was still evident. And there was a dark porthole in the visible side of the hull which seemed to imply the presence of a pilot or crew when the machine had flown.

'Flash Ricasso,' Curtana called to her signals officer. 'Tell him it's just a wreck. The position's logged, so someone can come back and have a better look after we've reached Spearpoint.'

In a low voice Quillon said, 'There could be things inside that wreck that Swarm can use.'

'We're not stopping. The objective was to short-cut our way back to your city, not stop off at every point of interest along the way. Unless Ricasso's got other ideas.'

But when Ricasso's reply came back he had no such requests. He thanked Curtana for diverting her ship, and requested that the undeveloped photographic plates be conveyed to *Purple Emperor* at the earliest opportunity, for his inspection.

An hour later, *Painted Lady* had resumed her position at the head of the fleet, which was now moving parallel to its earlier heading. So far as Quillon could tell, no significance had been attached to the course change, the citizens neither more nor less alarmed and agitated than they had been before noon. As the sun went down, and normal conditions continued, Quillon even sensed an easing in the onboard tension. The birds had fallen silent, but that was only because they were sleeping. The instruments in the chart room recorded nothing of concern. The engines droned a steady, melodic song, like a well-schooled choir. Quillon read through the medical summaries flashed through from Swarm – terse to the point of cryptograms, given that they needed to be laboriously encoded and decoded – and concluded that there were no more than the expected number of citizens reporting symptoms of zone sickness, all of which could be safely assumed to be phantom cases. Aboard *Painted Lady*, the crew were still healthy, their collective morale restored by the uneventful passage over the mysterious wreck. As he dined with the others (Kalis joined them, having left Nimcha asleep) he felt some of that ease rub off on him as well, glad to have his rational instincts confirmed. The question of who had launched that ill-fated machine was one for another expedition, in which Quillon would be happy to decline participation.

He slept well, and woke refreshed. He felt no ill effects: quite the contrary, in fact, since he was alert and curious as to what the day would bring. He washed and groomed himself, dressed and made his way to the front of the gondola. The crew and their polished instruments were bathed in the golden light of the early sun.

'Good morning,' he said.

No one answered, not even Curtana, who had her back to him. She was leaning against one of the windows, while another of her officers sighted through the telescope. Another was busy with the heliograph, sending a long and evidently complicated transmission. It was only then that Quillon noticed that the usual drone of the engines had been replaced by a quiet purr. The crew were intense and focused, as if engaged in a silent battle, one that required absolute concentration and the readiness to act with deadly speed. Even Meroka was there, looking through binoculars, seemingly fixated on a steep-sided mountain looming on the horizon, its base sliced through with a line of atmospheric haze.

Quillon coughed lightly. 'Is there a problem?'

'Twenty-two ships have just pulled away from Swarm and started making their way back west. Do you want to know why?'

He moved to the window next to her and peered through the glass. There was an instant when the landscape did not look any different from the day before, when he feared that Curtana and her crew were seeing mirages. Then his eyes began to pick out what the Swarmers had already seen.

Wrecked machines everywhere.

Little silver and white blemishes on the ground, like the discarded tinsel-foil litter of the Gods. He took in dozens, and then hundreds, of the smashed things. There was hardly a square league that did not contain some piece of broken machinery.

'I see,' he said, the closest he could come to a useful observation.

'They weren't there when we lost sight of the ground last night,' Curtana said. 'But since sunup, we've flown over thousands of the things, and they're everywhere, in all directions as far as we can see.'

'Are we running slow because of a fault?'

'No, there's nothing wrong with the ship. We're just trying to assess what it means and confer with Swarm – what's left of Swarm – about how we respond. According to the flanking airships, the wrecks go all the way to the horizon. This isn't something we can steer around.'

'I suppose it isn't something you can hide from Swarm either.'

'No,' she said on a falling note. 'Everyone knows now. That's why the dissidents have decided to cut their losses. They don't like the omens.' Curtana grimaced. 'For once, I can't blame them – it's not an encouraging sight, is it?'

'Whatever happened to these machines, there's no reason to think it's going to happen to us.'

'No, and just because you find a skull nailed to a tree, it doesn't mean you're entering a really bad part of the woods. But still.'

Quillon took in more of the slowly passing scene, awed by the scale of the destruction. 'So many of them,' he said. 'It's hard to credit. Do you think they're all from the same civilisation?'

'Fair bet. They look basically similar to the one we found yesterday. Maybe a few details changed here and there, but clearly made by the same culture. And now that we've surveyed a large number of the wrecks, for the most part they're pointing in roughly the same direction.'

Quillon had already noticed as much. 'Back the way we've come – implying that they flew here from somewhere ahead of us.' As he spoke he found himself glancing at the mountain, the one that Meroka was peering at through the binoculars.

'Right, and there seem to be more of them the further we go. I guess only a few made it as far as the one we saw yesterday.' Curtana hesitated. 'Here's the hard part. We've seen bodies as well. Pilots who survived the crash, crawled out of the wreckage and died soon after. I was expecting skeletons, but they look like they only just died.'

'Nothing decays out here,' Quillon said. 'If a body fell in the right position, sheltered from winds, a corpse could last a long time.'

'I think that's what really pushed those twenty-two captains to leave, not the wrecks.'

'Is that the end of it? Has everyone left who isn't absolutely behind Ricasso?'

'He hopes do. But morale's somewhat fragile.'

'Perhaps the citizens would feel a little more reassured if they knew that those pilots could have been here for thousands of years. I could make a statement—'

'We've already circulated one. Problem is, there's a limit to how much rational argument people will swallow when they're flying over a desert littered with incorrupted corpses.'

'Understandable.'

After a while she said, 'Do you think they were suicide pilots?'

'I sincerely hope not.'

'So do I. But I keep wondering, how much chance of success did these bastards really think they had? And what kind of desperation made them strap themselves into those machines? Do you think they even knew where the Bane ended?'

'We may never know.'

'I guess they didn't all die at the same time. Some of them outlasted their machines by a little while, and some of them were probably already dead by the time the aircraft stopped working. I suppose they were the lucky ones. At least they didn't have to crawl outside and die, knowing there was no chance of rescue.'

'Perhaps they had suicide pills, to ease the suffering in the event of a crash. Perhaps some of them even made it out of the Bane, into habitable territory.'

'And were then captured and tortured by the nearest bunch of pre-technological dirt-rats. Sorry. I am trying to look on the bright side here, honestly.'

'If it happened thousands of years ago, our history books won't have recorded it. But we can't always assume the worst.'

'There you go with that optimism thing again.'

After a few moments Quillon asked, 'What does Ricasso make of all this?'

'Whatever he knew in advance, I don't think he was expecting anything on this scale. But it's either turn around and follow the others, or keep going. And I know what my father would have done.'

By noon, the density of crashed machines had doubled compared to his first sighting. Aside from the occasional wreck that must have been a more advanced craft that had fallen short, these vessels were visibly less sophisticated than the ones they had overflown earlier. Bright, stainless metal was now replaced by tarnished and rusting panelling, with the occasional dab of faded and flaking paint. The craft were clumsier looking, insofar as it was possible to judge from their smashed ruins.

'While you were asleep,' Curtana said when she joined Quillon on the observation balcony, 'a boat caught up with us and ferried the unexposed plates back to *Purple Emperor*. Ricasso's been looking at the images all morning. According to the latest flash, he's pretty confident that the first machine we saw was a rocket, rather than an air-breathing machine. Probably liquid-fuelled, semi-ballistic, like a missile with a pilot strapped in. Once his motor burned out, he'd have been hoping to glide all the way to safety.'

'And now?'

'Ricasso doesn't need us to send photographs back to him – he can just look out of the window. He reckons these were mostly powered by jet turbines – you can sometimes see the intakes where the air gets sucked in for combustion. Making jets work obviously wasn't a problem for these people. And after they'd developed jets, they moved on to rockets, which are even tougher to build. You need high-speed pumps, sophisticated metallurgy, cryogenic cooling systems, automated control systems ... all way beyond anything *we* can get to work.'

'And you're confident all these machines originated from the same people?'

'I'd say so. Whenever we've seen any markings, it's always the same basic symbol – a red rectangle with some stars in it – and the same kind of lettering. The symbol varies in design – as if we're seeing different iterations of it – but it's always the same basic form.'

'And the language – is it something you're familiar with?'

'No, it's like nothing in the books. Which makes sense, if these people have been cut off for as long as we think. There's no reason why we should expect to understand them.'

'I wonder how long they kept trying to break out,' Quillon said.

'Hold that thought. I suspect we're going to find out whether we like it or not.'

Hour by hour, the picture underneath underwent subtle changes. The density of fallen machines rose and fell in slow waves, implying periods of intense, industrialised escape activity, followed by fallow times when the effort was less concentrated. The jet aircraft became increasingly basic, until they gave way to propeller-driven machines of a design and sophistication that would not have been out of place in Swarm. By turns, even these sleek monoplanes, with their enclosed cockpits and retractable undercarriages, gave way to ungainly biplanes and triplanes, fashioned (insofar as it could be judged) as much from wood and fabric as from metal. Eventually even these carcasses gave way to the huge, proud-boned remains of ancient airships, lying on the ground where they had fallen.

That was when Meroka said, 'There's something you all need to know.'

'What is it?' Curtana asked.

'That mountain ahead of us . . . well, it ain't no mountain.' She paused and swallowed hard. 'It looks a fuck of a lot like Spearpoint to me.'

CHAPTER TWENTY-TWO

Between Swarm and the mountain lay a tremendous wall. Quillon realised that it was the thing he had mistaken for atmospheric haze when looking at the mountain earlier. It cut across the landscape like a knife slash. As the telescopes were trained on it, the line revealed itself to be an obviously man-made structure, punctuated at regular intervals by towers and fortified gates, its heights gleaming like polished ivory, its lower flanks lost under wind-blown mounds of dirt and dust. Here and there the structure was riven by vast cracks, or punctured by the scorched craters of what must have been ferocious lightning bolts. But it had endured.

It was tall: two or three hundred spans, at the very least, and taller again where the towers and battlements rose. It spanned the horizon to the limits of visibility, blocking their way – symbolically, at least – for hundreds of leagues in either direction, perhaps further.

But the wall was not the most awesome thing, nor even the second. The second most awesome thing was a wreck. It had crashed down onto the wall five or six leagues to port, sagging broken-spined with one half on the nearside and the other half on the far side, like a colossal maggot trying to wriggle over an obstacle. It was not an airship. It had never been an airship. The wreck's shape echoed an airship's envelope, but there the similarity ended. It was much too large, to begin with: easily a league from one end to the other, and perhaps a tenth of a league in height. It had no gondola or engines or empennage. It had ruptured as it crashed onto the wall, its upper surface zipping open like an overcooked sausage. The skin was weathered white, offset by the faded remnants of orange or red markings: oblique slashes and hyphens, chains of angular hieroglyphics, tiny pinprick dots of windows laid out in lines at all angles, rather than merely parallel to the ground. There were bulges and protuberances at various points along the bent hull, antenna-like spines or probes thrusting forwards (or back – it was impossible to tell which way the ship had been flying before it crashed). Unlike an airship, this vessel's interior was definitely not hollow. It was full of tight-packed machinery, broken and bent but still otherwise much as it would have been when the ship crashed. It glinted with absurd, festering detail, like a cliff seen through binoculars. The ship managed to convey both overwhelming scale and immense, cunning miniaturisation, almost as if, somehow, it should have been even huger.

'No one made that,' Curtana said, breaking the awed silence. 'No one could *ever* have made that. It's just too ... just too ...' She trailed off, shaking her head in frustration.

'I imagine Ricasso has a theory or two,' Quillon said. 'He thinks we used to be able to travel through the void above the atmosphere, from world to world. I suspect that may be one of his void-crossers. A ship of space.'

'Ordinarily I'd laugh at something like that,' Curtana said.

'But not today.'

'We couldn't even *fake* something like that. And that's not a fake. That's something that used to be in the air, flying around.'

'The technology is way beyond anything we've seen so far – the rockets, the aircraft. Do you think it came later, or before?' Agraffe asked.

'That's one for Ricasso to figure out, not me,' Curtana replied.

The void-crosser had crushed part of the wall beneath it, but not demolished it completely. *Painted Lady* hovered now, her guns pointed with timid ineffectualness at the forbidding structure. Curtana flashed Ricasso and waited for his answer. This time his response did not arrive immediately. There was time for Swarm to move close enough to view the wall for itself; time for Ricasso to digest the significance of the wreck, the wall, the looming, paradoxical thing beyond the wall, and consider the combined ramifications.

Then an answer flashed back from *Purple Emperor*.

'We continue,' Curtana muttered, reading the transmission when it was handed to her by the signals officer. 'As if there was ever any doubt.' She grabbed the speaking tube. 'Engines to cruise power – trim for five hundred spans. I want a close look as we go over the top. Machine-gunners are authorised to fire at will if necessary, using short controlled bursts.'

The intervening terrain was as littered with machines as the desolate leagues that had preceded it. Few winged aircraft now, save for a handful that must have come down short, but numberless smashed and skeletal airships, many balloons, their ruined envelopes lying across the ground like the flattened bodies of beached jellyfish. Closer in – within the last few leagues – there were wheeled machines that had clearly never been meant to fly: huge, ponderous contraptions like moving statuary or siege engines, some of the larger ones with metal smokestacks jutting from their backs like the defensive spines of ancient lizards. Some of them appeared to be made entirely of wood, right down to their huge spokeless wheels. One even had the remains of sails and rigging rising from its back, with tiny pale corpses lying amongst the collapsed ropes and shattered timbers. Had they seriously meant to *sail* their way beyond the wall? Quillon wondered. Perhaps from the vantage point of the wall, there appeared to be a navigable path, a ready-made road that would take them over the horizon when the winds were in their favour. But that would have been a treacherous lie. Those men had effectively been dead the moment they passed beyond the wall, or whatever earlier structure existed at the time they had begun their doomed journey. The wall as it now stood – damage and all – was surely the work of a mature society, the kind that could build flying machines. The wind-powered land-yachts belonged to a more rustic culture, one that crafted objects from wood and canvas and crudely fashioned iron. It was easy to imagine that a thousand years separated the balloons from the rockets. Maybe more than that.

And always, always, that red rectangle of which Curtana had spoken. Five stars in the corner – one large, four smaller. All the smashed machines carried some form of it, if they carried any symbology at all. The sole exception was the void-crosser.

Quillon didn't want to think about how much time separated that cloud-sized argosy from everything else. Perhaps it – and the wall – were the oldest things of all. Save, of course, for Spearpoint.

It wasn't, as they had quickly realised, *their* Spearpoint – but in all other respects it was clearly the same type of structure. It rammed out of the ground, a slowly narrowing helical spike, tapering to perhaps half a league across at the point where it ended, its soaring rise abruptly terminated six leagues from the ground. Their Spearpoint went on upwards, narrowing to the merest sliver as it daggered out of the atmosphere above the Celestial Levels. This one just stopped. It was a flinty black in colour, and nowhere on it, save for the very lowest part, was there any indication that people had ever called it home. No city-districts winding their way up the spiral ledge, no empty buildings, disused roads, commuter lines, elevators and funicular tracks. It was Spearpoint lopped off at the top and scoured back to its skin.

'Ricasso knew about this,' Curtana said in a barely audible mutter. 'It's too much of a coincidence otherwise. He knew there was something here, something he was interested in. Must have been a clue on one of those old charts of his.' In an even softer hiss she added, 'The lying bastard.'

'He was still right to push for crossing the Bane,' Quillon said.

'He's still got some explaining to do. Now I know why he got over the smashing of his laboratory so easily. He knew *this* was coming up as a consolation prize.'

Painted Lady climbed to five hundred spans. Curtana aimed her over the flat-topped section of wall between two of the towers, while the other ships hung astern to watch what happened.

As the airship neared the great structure, so the wall's immense size and age impressed themselves upon Quillon with renewed and demoralising force. Had this not been deep inside the Bane, he was certain that vegetation would have smothered the edifice from its ramparts to the tops of its towers, reducing it to little more than a peculiarly regular green ridge, thrusting up from jungle canopy. But here nothing, not even the lowliest weed, had been able to endure. Yet the wall was still subject to the weather, and countless storms must have dashed against those white cliffs over the centuries and millennia. They'd had almost no measurable effect.

At last the top of the wall was directly under them. It was twenty spans across, room enough for garrisons and weaponry, but the fortifications he had noted earlier were clearly ornamental. The walls curved away in a gentle arc to either horizon. If the ends joined up, Curtana said, it could easily be a hundred leagues from side to side.

The inner face of the wall fell in steps rather than a single smooth descent. Connecting the ledges was a complex arrangement of ramps and stairways, some clearly grafted on to the worn remnants of older constructions. Plain white buildings crowded the lower ledges, tall houses and tenements piled in leaning, haphazard ranks like books in an untidy library. Again, it was clear that many phases of building and renewal had occurred. There were structures on the ground, but they were grouped into distinct communities with tracts of open space between them, rather than a single vast city pressing against the wall. Quillon made out the pale scratches of arrow-straight roads threading from one village or hamlet to the next. Many of them radiated out from the base of the broken Spearpoint, echoing the semaphore lines of Quillon's home. Perhaps these roads and towns had once been set amongst trees and grassland, rather than the dusty rock and dirt that now surrounded them.

'Flash Ricasso that we're over the wall and there's no sign of life,'

Curtana called out to the signals officer. 'Inform him that I'm taking *Painted Lady* down to fifty spans to get a closer look. We'll be out of line-of-sight until I bring her back up.' Then she grabbed the speaking tube. 'Machine-gunners. Keep on your toes.'

Without waiting for Ricasso's acknowledgement, Curtana took the airship down to just above the roof level of the tallest buildings. They were overflying a village of perhaps thirty or forty distinct structures, laid out in a grid pattern with an open square near the middle. The white buildings were obviously designed for warm, dry weather. Their windows had shutters rather than glass, and there were open courtyards at their hearts, enclosed by galleried floors on all sides. If there had ever been ornamentation or colouration applied to the walls and floors, it had long since been scoured away by the wind, bleached by centuries of relentless sun. Nothing moved below except *Painted Lady*'s ominous shadow, her propellers a blur of whirling motion and her gun turrets swivelling nervously from target to target.

It was, Quillon knew, futile to speculate about the kinds of people who had lived here, at least on the basis of the evidence gathered so far. They could have formed the most civilised and enlightened society imaginable, a community of infinite wisdom and kindness. Or they could have been bloodthirsty cultists with a lingering death fixation. It was impossible to tell from their ruins. Everyone needed a roof over their head, even the barbarous and depraved.

'There's something,' Curtana said, pointing to the next community along, another thousand spans or so out from the wall. 'Let's check it out.'

Quillon wasn't sure what she'd seen, and for a moment he wondered if curiosity wasn't overcoming her natural instinct to protect the airship. Yet how could there be anything down there that could harm them, even unintentionally? No animals, no people, no possibility of hidden weapons, for nothing of any sophistication could have survived the Bane. It was just ancient brick and clay: inert matter. Nothing, not even a scorpion or a rat, not even a bacterium, had lived in these streets for hundreds of years.

'Take us lower: thirty spans,' Curtana ordered. 'All engines to dead slow.'

Painted Lady's motors quietened to a drumming chatter, barely ticking over.

'What have you seen?' Quillon asked.

'That,' she said, pointing to the thing that was now hoving into clear view, in the open centre of the village.

It was something half-made, surrounded by the sun-bleached, wind-scoured remains of wooden scaffolding. A wooden machine as tall as any of the houses, rising proud on solid wooden wheels several times higher than a man, with the remains of a rickety wooden track leading away from the unfinished machine. The track, such as it was, pointed back towards the wall, although it ended abruptly just beyond the village limits.

'They were building another one of those things we saw out there,' Curtana said. 'One of those sailing engines. Look: you can even see the big tree-trunk they were going to use for the main mast, laid out on those trestles.'

'Does that mean we got it wrong?' Quillon wondered. 'They were building these *after* they built the aircraft and the rockets?'

'That's a depressing thought,' Agraffe said.

'I guess it depends on when this area became uninhabitable,' Curtana said. 'Could be everything we're seeing here was abandoned ages before they developed the flying machines. But the people who built these wooden machines – I'm not sure they'd have been capable of building the wall, and the wall had to come first.'

Quillon nodded. 'And even from the top of the wall they wouldn't have been able to see where the rockets fell down. They'd have had a hard time seeing the biplanes and airships, in fact. No wonder they still thought that sailing out might just be worth a shot.'

'The poor bastards,' Agraffe said.

'Let's reserve judgement on that,' Curtana replied. 'For all we know they were abject xenophobes intent on raping and pillaging the next society they had the misfortune to bump into.'

'You want to go down and take a closer look at the machine?' Quillon asked.

'It can wait.' She turned to one of her officers. 'Take us back up to five hundred, resume our previous heading and flash *Purple Emperor*. Inform Ricasso we've found the remains of several communities but no signs of life. There's no reason for Swarm not to follow us. Tell him that we'll pass the structure ... the other Spearpoint ... on our starboard side, at our revised altitude.'

Quillon sensed the mood around him. No one was in a hurry to debate the implications of the other Spearpoint. It was too unexpected to fit into anyone's preconceived notions about the world. There was one Godscraper, and one only. Why was there a second such structure, not only abandoned and uninhabited but broken and forgotten in the middle of nowhere?

Too much to deal with, too much to think about. He understood perfectly. He felt it as well.

'Return flash from *Purple Emperor*,' said the signals officer. 'It's Ricasso, Captain. Says he wants to come aboard.'

'Flash him back. Tell him it's not ... expedient.'

A flurry of heliograph transmissions ensued. Ricasso was coming aboard anyway. Curtana took it with stoic forbearance.

Swarm and its entourage of support airships passed over the wall without incident. Shortly afterwards a boat detached from the main formation and sped out to meet *Painted Lady*. As it drew alongside, Quillon recognised the black and gold livery of one of Ricasso's personal taxis. The man himself disembarked with enough luggage to fill a small room.

'You're going to have to return some of that ballast,' Curtana said.

'I presumed, my dear, that since you had burned fuel, there would now be a surplus in your weight allowance.'

'We lose sungas through the cells,' Curtana said. 'They're not completely pressure-tight, even with the new coatings. Plus we'll be clear of the Bane in less than a day. You didn't even need to bring an overnight bag.'

'I may as well see out the rest of the journey here, now that I've made the crossing.'

'From a security perspective, wouldn't it be better if you stayed aboard *Purple Emperor*?'

He made a theatrical show of looking around the room. 'What, you think someone's likely to assassinate me here? Someone from your hand-picked and hugely loyal crew?'

'I was thinking more of the risk that we might run into something, or have an accident,' Curtana said.

'That risk applies equally to the entire fleet.' He raised a pudgy finger before she could frame an objection. 'Oh, I'm perfectly aware that *Painted Lady* would be the first vessel exposed to any danger. But knowing this ship, you can run a damn sight faster than that slow, bloated beast called *Purple Emperor*.'

'We don't run,' Curtana said testily. 'We engage.'

He waved aside the distinction. 'Whatever you say, my dear. What matters now is altitude more than speed.' He clapped his hands together briskly. 'Now, I realise it's an imposition, but might I trouble you to pass over the other Spearpoint, rather than around it?'

'We can't. Its tip is far above our operational ceiling, as you well know.'

'Then as high as we can manage, and we'll launch a pressurised spotter balloon when we're at the limit. That's feasible, isn't it? You still have a balloon aboard?'

'Yes,' Curtana said, with obvious effort. 'And I take it this isn't the kind of request I'm able to turn down?'

Ricasso grimaced awkwardly. 'Not really, if I'm going to be brutally honest. Consider it part of your risk-assessment duties.'

'That makes things so much easier.'

'Splendid. I can't tell you how excited I am about this, you know. I mean, of all the things to find.'

'Yes, who'd have thought it? Who could possibly have anticipated this, when crossing the Bane was first mooted?' Curtana turned away before he could answer – a direct insolence only she could have got away with – and snapped her fingers at the two *Emperor* men lingering by the connecting bridge. 'Get his junk stowed back aboard your boat. I need to start making speed again.'

A few minutes later the bridge was reeled in and the taxi was on its way back to Swarm, carrying newly drawn maps and photographic plates that had been exposed since the last exchange. Curtana's men showed Ricasso to his improvised quarters – little more than a large storage cupboard with a small grubby window, adjacent to the chart room. Rolls of emergency repair fabric, crates of unexposed plates and boxes full of dressings, potions and unguents had to find other homes aboard the already tightly organised airship. Quillon, who was never far from Ricasso, surmised that the man was not displeased with the arrangements, however improvisatory their nature. There was even room to unfold a bunk in his new quarters, provided some of the other items were moved around temporarily.

While he was helping Ricasso settle in – it had fallen to him, since almost everyone else seemed to be preoccupied with rigging for high-altitude flight – Quillon said, 'So this really was a surprise?'

'Of course, my dear fellow!'

'But you had – let's say – suspicions we'd find something out here.'

Ricasso ruminated before answering. Quillon imagined him weighing the benefits of concealment versus candour. 'Not suspicions, precisely. That would be too strong a term. But did my investigations turn up something that intrigued me, something that led me to think crossing the Bane would offer us more than just a short cut? I won't deny it. But we're not even talking about a rumour here, Quillon. We're talking about less than a scrap of one, a figment most educated men wouldn't hesitate to dismiss.'

'Something you'd like to share?'

'There was a map, a fragment of a map, with something on it. Something deeply puzzling and strange. It looked like another Spearpoint – but that would be impossible, surely?'

'Now we know better. You've got a theory, haven't you?'

'I had one,' Ricasso said forlornly. 'Spearpoint – our Spearpoint – happens to be located quite close to the equator. For a long time, I've had a notion that Spearpoint was a kind of bridge between the Earth and the heavens. There have been treatises ... scholarly speculations ... on the possibility of constructing a kind of cosmic funicular, one that would ferry people and goods far above our atmosphere. I've made a point of collecting these articles, sifting the good from the bad, the sane from the demented. I do not pretend to understand every nuance of the mathematical underpinnings, but one thing has remained constant. You do not build such a structure up from the face of the Earth. You hang it down from a point in the void, so that its weight is exactly counterbalanced by the outward force it feels due to its orbit around the world. It must, of course, hover above the same spot on the ground to be of use. And it must be located close to the equator, if not exactly on it.'

'I've seen the charts,' Quillon said. 'We're still thirty or forty degrees from the equator.'

'And yet here is something very like Spearpoint, except that it's snapped.'

'Meaning that Spearpoint cannot be the thing you imagined,' Quillon said, wary of making his point too forcefully, for he knew how much of Ricasso's self-worth was invested in his scholarship.

But Ricasso didn't seem to take it too badly. 'No, you're right. It can't be. Whatever Spearpoint is – whatever Spearpoint *was* – it was almost certainly never a cosmic funicular. Unless our whole world has tipped on its axis. Which means that if I was wrong about that, there's a chance I was wrong about everything else as well.'

They were gaining height. Of all the ships in Swarm, *Painted Lady* was the one best equipped for high-altitude work, but even at her operational limit she would still be two leagues below the broken summit of what was now being called Spearpoint 2. Ricasso had known that, of course, just as he'd known that she still carried a spotter balloon that could be released and recovered in the thinning air. The balloons were used only rarely, since they were unpowered and therefore could not be employed as survey aides from fast-moving ships. But all the larger escort craft carried them, for the balloons had occasionally proved the decisive factor in aerial engagements where long-range observation was crucial. That didn't make them popular, for Swarmers – as Quillon had quickly recognised – were universally contemptuous of any airborne contraption lacking an engine, steering system or stiffening structure. Even blimps were beneath their dignity.

The deflated balloon and its airtight passenger pod travelled in a recess just behind the main turret on the upper surface of *Painted Lady*'s envelope, ready to be launched directly into the air with the minimum of fuss. The airship had to slow to a virtual standstill for the balloon to be inflated, filled with hot air from a firesap burner, but the procedure had obviously been well drilled and despite having to be handled by a reduced number of airmen, it proceeded without incident. Quillon, who had agreed to travel with Ricasso in the pod, watched matters with only mild apprehension. Set against all the dangers he had faced since leaving Spearpoint, a spot of high-altitude ballooning seemed in no way extraordinary. No one had made any concerted efforts to talk Ricasso out of the enterprise, and as ship's physician, Quillon was at a loss to find medical grounds against it. Ricasso was – despite appearances – fairly healthy, and conditions inside the pressurised compartment would differ very little from those in the gondola.

The passenger pod was a brass-coloured thing with angular, down-sloping riveted sides, hemispherical portholes set into three of the four faces and a pressure-tight door in the other. A small selection of instruments poked down through the floor, worked from inside. There were two seats and some rudimentary controls, enabling the occupants to work the firesap heater on the roof of the balloon, to drop ballast when it was required and to adjust the flow of air from the bottled supply within the cabin. That was it. No wireless to communicate with *Painted Lady*, since wireless didn't work in the zones. No means of steering or choosing a landing spot, beyond such control as was achievable through varying altitude and thereby intercepting different windstreams. None of that really mattered, though. Ricasso, who claimed no particular proficiency with balloons, only wanted to go up and down. If they landed on *Painted Lady* again, so be it. If they missed and had to be picked up from the ground, it would entail only a small delay, inconsequential against the tremendous saving already achieved by passing through the Bane.

'You sure you're cool with this, Cutter?' Meroka, clad in cold-weather gear, was with them as they prepared to board the cabin.

'Done much ballooning?' Quillon asked with a smile.

'About as much as you've done horse burying.'

'Then I'll be fine.' He slipped on his goggles. He had not been wearing them routinely since leaving *Purple Emperor* – his nature was no secret to *Painted Lady*'s crew – but now the wind made his eyes sting. 'Besides, if anything goes wrong with the air tanks, the fact that one of us is already adapted for high-altitude breathing may help matters.'

'Half-adapted, Cutter. Don't get ideas above your station.'

'I won't.'

Curtana stamped her feet against the cold. It had been pleasant enough at their normal cruising altitude, but the air was chillier up here. 'With the wind direction as it is right now, you should drift clean over the summit. Suggest you start losing height almost as soon as you're over it. You don't have long before those bottles run dry.'

'We'll be the very epitome of haste,' Ricasso said.

They got into the compartment, knees touching as they took up opposing seats. Curtana pushed the airtight door shut, allowing Ricasso to lock it from inside. He increased the firesap burner, fully inflating the balloon. The pod clanged against its fasteners as it tried to rise into the air. Curtana peered through one of the portholes and gave a hand gesture indicating that they were ready to depart.

'This is it, Doctor,' Ricasso said theatrically. 'No going back now!'

'Then let's get this diversion over with, so we can return to the serious business of the medicine run.'

'Intellectual spoilsport.' But Ricasso was smiling.

Ricasso worked a release mechanism and suddenly – dreamily – they were aloft and rising. It wasn't silent – there was the steady hiss of the air supply, and the on/off rumble of the firesap burner – but it was immediately obvious that they were not in a powered craft, and the motion, smooth as it was, had a sense of not being under their direct control. *Painted Lady* diminished with considerable speed, falling away and below as winds snagged the balloon. Quillon had just enough of a view of her to see her engines rev up again as the airship resumed powered flight. Very soon they had the sky to themselves, save for the looming tower of Spearpoint 2. The air currents were conveying them towards that edifice at considerable speed, but they were also rising steadily. Already the angle of view had changed, and Quillon was able to make out the upper surface of a ledge that had not been visible from the airship. Unlike Spearpoint's ledges, it showed no sign of ever having been lived on.

'If it's not a . . . what did you call it? Cosmic funicular?'

'A working hypothesis, now gratefully discarded.'

'Then what is it?'

'I don't know. That's rather the point of this little exercise.' But Ricasso leaned forwards, rising to the theme. 'I was wrong, and so was everyone who ever speculated that Spearpoint might have been a cosmic funicular, at least in the conventional sense. But all those fables about it being a bridge to the stars? They can't *all* be wrong.'

'Unless, that is, they're all wrong.'

'That wreck we saw – the fallen void-crosser?'

'Yes?'

'Something that big, we'd have noticed it if it came down anywhere else in the world. The Bane preserved it to some degree, but even with five thousand years of weather and war, if one of those had crashed somewhere else, there'd still be something left. Don't you think, Doctor?'

'I suppose.'

'So why aren't there any?'

'I don't know.'

'I think the answer, quite literally, is staring us in the face. The void-crosser's here because it had something to do with Spearpoint Two. The one is intimately related to the other.'

'So why aren't there any fallen void-crossers lying near our – my – Spearpoint?' Quillon asked.

'Because, Doctor, your Spearpoint isn't broken.'

The balloon's course was straight and true, the winds clement. Quillon's ears popped slightly on the ascent – cabin pressure was obviously lower than aboard *Painted Lady* – but in all other respects he felt clear-headed and alert, and he saw nothing in Ricasso's boyish demeanour to indicate that the other man was suffering any ill effects.

'Look,' Ricasso said at one point, gesturing excitedly through one of the windows. 'There's Swarm! I've never seen it from so high up before.'

Quillon turned to follow Ricasso's down-pointing finger. It took him a few moments to identify Swarm against the confusion of background scenery. Far from the city-sized agglomeration of ships he had grown accustomed to, Swarm now appeared to be little more than a hectic concentration of slightly elongated dots, darkening near the middle where the larger ships were gathered. He could cover all of it with one hand. Even the sharp curvature of the Earth failed to diminish the sense of the landscape being vast and permanent compared to Swarm's fragility.

'Not much, is it?' Ricasso said, reading Quillon's thoughts as if they were written on his face. 'But it's all we've got, most of us.'

Quillon recalled looking back at Spearpoint, the night the storm turned out the lights.

'Home is where the heart lies,' he said quietly.

They kept rising. The cabin creaked and clanged with the rising pressure differential. The sky overhead was a deeper blue than even the view from the Celestial Levels, shading almost to black at the zenith. Quillon wondered whether a healthy, fully formed angel could have endured at this altitude. He didn't know for sure, but he was certain that his own chances for survival were not much better than Ricasso's. He stood between two worlds, without a confident foothold in either.

Before very long they were level with the summit and still rising. Ricasso adjusted the firesap burner to level their flight. If Spearpoint 2 resembled a wine glass with the cup snapped off, they were now at approximately the point in the narrowing stem where the break had occurred. It was close to half a league across, Quillon estimated. The edges were jagged, like the serrated wall of a circular crater. He had felt nothing resembling vertigo until this point, but as the balloon sped towards the summit, the feeling began to reassert itself. He was able to look all the way down the rising structure, to the point where it emerged from the ground. He was tiny and it was huge, and the balloon wouldn't leave so much as a scratch if the winds changed and dashed them against that imperturbable black wall.

And then, suddenly, they were above the summit. Quillon wasn't quite sure what he had been expecting until that moment. It had never occurred to him that Spearpoint might be hollow, but if this broken twin was any indication it was, and the thickness of the walls was no more than a twentieth of the diameter of the broken stem. The sun could not have reached more than a league or so down the shaft, but from what they could see, it was both perfectly smooth and of perfectly constant diameter. He had the ominous sense of looking down a rifle-barrel.

'That void-crosser we saw,' Ricasso said, 'would easily have fitted inside that shaft, don't you think?'

'I suppose.'

Ricasso was busy working the cable-release for the underbelly camera.

'Spearpoint's diameter decreases from the base, but – and you'll have to take my word on this – it's never less than one-eighth of a league across. From the Celestial Levels upwards, it doesn't get much narrower. A ship could travel all the way up, until it reached vacuum. Actually, it wouldn't necessarily be a question of *reaching* vacuum; if the shaft pushed sufficiently far above the atmosphere, it could hold vacuum all the way down to the surface of the Earth. That ship was probably never meant to travel in air at all. It was a ship of space, a creature of the true void.'

'Why?' Quillon asked.

'Why what?'

'If it's so much trouble, why bring a ship like that down to the ground at all? It seems a lot of effort, building something like Spearpoint – or Spearpoint Two, for that matter – just to bring a ship the last few leagues.'

'Perhaps that's the way they wanted to do things.' But even as Ricasso spoke, Quillon heard the dissatisfaction with the glibness of his own explanation. 'No, perhaps not. Wait a moment, Doctor. There's still something else we can do.' He leaned over to grab one of the instrument controls. 'Flare drop. It's meant for illuminating the ground in darkness, if you're looking for somewhere to put down.'

They were still over the open mouth of Spearpoint, albeit much nearer to the far edge now.

'Do it,' Quillon said.

Ricasso tugged at the lever and a mechanism made a reassuring solid *clunk* somewhere under their feet. The flare, presumably, had just detached itself from the base of the pod. Quillon couldn't see it at first, but as they travelled on, and the flare fell further below, it came into view. It was an incandescent blob under a tiny parachute.

They watched it fall into shadow, whereupon it began to illuminate the hitherto unseen part of the shaft. Alas, the wind was pushing the balloon too quickly for them to watch the flare as it travelled all the way down. It had barely reached halfway to the ground when the balloon's motion took it over the edge, and the shaft was no longer visible.

'We'll have to come back,' Ricasso said. 'Do it properly. Maybe even send someone down there.'

'How far down do you think it goes?'

'Below the surface of the Earth, I'm pretty sure. If the ships were only meant to travel down to the base, wouldn't we have seen somewhere for the passengers to disembark?'

'It's been a long time. Maybe the ground's covered up the entrances and exits.'

'That's possible. And of course, Spearpoint's riddled with tunnels through the walls, so we can presume this one is as well. I wonder, though ... You said it yourself, Doctor – there wouldn't be much point building all this just to come the last few leagues. So what if the ships were meant to go further than that? Deeper, I mean?'

'Into the Earth?'

'That's what I'm getting at. How far below, I wouldn't care to speculate.

356

But – presumably – many leagues at the very least. Otherwise – why bother with all this?'

'Why bother going into the Earth, is another question,' Quillon observed.

'Yes,' Ricasso said. 'That it is. And of course, none of this gets us anywhere near the really big one.'

'Which is?'

'What is the Mire? Or, more generally speaking, what are the zones? And why do they originate in Spearpoint?'

Quillon was about to answer when he glimpsed the plunging, spiral-ledged wall on the other side of Spearpoint, and felt his heart skip a beat.

'Look,' he said.

Ricasso did, and for an instant Quillon saw the same reaction he had just experienced. Recognition, followed by a wrenching sense of wrongness.

Cut into the black face of Spearpoint 2, between two rising turns of the spiral ledge, was a baubled star. It was mirror-bright even now, the reflected horizon-line cutting through it, tawny brown below, pastel blue above.

The sign of the tectomancer.

'Now that,' Ricasso said, 'does put rather an interesting complexion on things.'

They came down in a series of giddy, bucking descents as Ricasso worked the firesap burner and the balloon tangled with the twisting winds around Spearpoint 2's base. Any hope of landing back on *Painted Lady* was utterly forlorn, Quillon now saw. Perhaps with the balloon in more expert hands, and with more predictable winds, it could have been accomplished. But not today, with Ricasso at the controls.

Ancient structures, similar in style to those that lapped against the encircling wall, pressed around Spearpoint 2's base and crawled partway up the ledge. It was the start of something like Horsetown, but for one reason or another, it had risen no higher. Whatever the function of the ledge, it now seemed probable to Quillon that it had never been intended as a place for people to build on. Perhaps it had something to do with the winds, deflecting them up, rather than around, the soaring structure. Or perhaps the ledge had been installed to allow gargantuan machines to toil up and down the outside, repairing and modifying where necessary.

'There she is,' Ricasso said.

'What?'

'*Painted Lady*. She's shadowing us. That's good. I was a little worried she might lose us in all this sky.'

'You didn't mention that before,' Quillon said.

'I didn't think it would be helpful.'

'Probably not. And this may be premature, but do you have the vaguest idea how that thing we just saw – that symbol – relates to Nimcha, and all the other tectomancers?'

'Honestly? No. But here's a thought – that mark on her head ... those powers she has ... they didn't just arise by magic. Will you indulge me?'

'I'm not going anywhere.'

'Let us suppose – and I stress that this is merely a supposition – that the tectomancers once served some specific and useful purpose in society. You have guilds in Spearpoint, do you not? And we have traditions of generational ownership in Swarm, parents passing airships to their children, and so on. It's not that unusual for humans to keep it in the family, so to speak.'

'You think the tectomancers were a guild of some kind?'

'The term will suffice, for now. But a more complex guild than anything we have experience of. Let us again suppose that those marks and powers arose through the direct manipulation of inherited factors, in much the same way that angels were shaped from orthodox humans. Whatever work they did, whatever purpose their guild served, it required of them an inordinate degree of alteration. And it would have been hereditary, so that each generation passed the powers down to the next. That mark on Nimcha's head is merely the external signifier of far more profound differences inside her skull.'

'Then there would have been many of them, once.'

'Hundreds, thousands, who knows? Enough to do whatever great work this society required of them. And they would only ever have bred with other tectomancers, of course. The guild would have been insular and self-perpetuating. Perhaps they would have introduced outsiders occasionally, to maintain the diversity of the population. But it would have been strictly controlled.'

'I understand. But I don't see how we get from there to here, with tectomancers so rare as to be almost mythical.'

'Something happened, clearly. Might it be too outrageous a leap of speculation to suggest that it was the intrusion of the Mire, the breaking through of the Eye of God, the coming of the zones? Perhaps I've gone too far; it's a weakness of mine. But consider this: if civilisation fell, then what became of the guild? Did its members hide themselves away, or were they forced out into the wider world, to survive amongst ordinary humans as best they could? Did they marry into the wider population, diluting their inheritance factors?'

'Diluted,' Quillon said, picking up on Ricasso's line of reasoning, 'but still present, still capable of producing a tectomancer if the right combination of factors came together again. But after five thousand years, or however long it's been, that would be very unlikely indeed.'

'Agreed – it must be unlikely or we'd be swimming in tectomancers. As it is, they only arise very rarely indeed – a statistical fluke. And for every genuine, functioning tectomancer – for every Nimcha – there must be another that has almost the right set of inheritance factors, but not all of them. A child with the powers, but not the mark. A child with the mark, but no ability to move zones. They exist, Doctor. There may not be very many of them, but given Nimcha's existence, we can be sure that she's not alone.'

'You truly believe there are others out there?'

'Not in huge numbers, certainly. And some will be older than Nimcha, some younger. Some may not even realise what they are. But I doubt very much that she's alone.'

'But something's different now, isn't it? The storm that hit Spearpoint had been building for years – such things don't happen more than once every century, and maybe not as often as that.'

'Nimcha may be special, even amongst tectomancers. Or it may be that something in the Mire has changed, something that makes it more responsive, more willing to obey them.'

Quillon thought about that for a moment. 'If Nimcha is exceptional, then it's even more of a coincidence that we ran into her when we did.'

'You'd prefer to think you weren't the victim of cosmic happenstance?'

'If Nimcha is a tectomancer, but merely one of many ... however "many" might be ... then it's easier for me to accept that we might have crossed paths. It also makes me wonder if Kalis was entirely right about her daughter.'

'In what sense?'

'Kalis believes Nimcha brought the big storm. It's clear that Nimcha's powers are genuine, so I don't blame her mother for making that assumption. But what if she's wrong about the rest of it? If there are other tectomancers out there, all of them feeling the pull of the Mire, all of them capable of reacting to it and shifting the zones, would Kalis be able to single out the influence of her daughter?'

'You don't think Nimcha is as strong as Kalis believes.'

'Alone, no. But collectively – acting in concert with the others – she might very well be. Or else we've got it all wrong, and there's just one of them, and Nimcha is exactly as powerful as Kalis imagines.'

'We don't have enough evidence to decide either way,' Ricasso said, 'so for now we may as well keep open minds. But let's be clear about one thing. It's Spearpoint calling Nimcha home, not the Mire. The Mire may be the very thing it needs the tectomancers to put right. To heal the wound in the face of the world where the Eye of God burned through.'

'What would happen then?'

'Something we haven't had a lot of in the last five thousand years,' Ricasso said. 'History.'

The balloon had continued to shed altitude as they spoke. Ahead, at an intersection of several pale, weather-scoured roads, lay a cluster of white buildings around a dome-shaped central structure. The off-white dome was marbled by black fractures. Judging by the scale of the windows in the surrounding buildings, it must have been fifteen or twenty storeys in height at its apex. Under other circumstances, it would have been impressive, but today it just looked like an act of pathetic underachievement.

'Try to avoid landing on that,' Quillon said.

With dreadful inevitability, the winds made every effort to ensure that was exactly what happened. Ricasso tried to lose height more rapidly, but thermals keep buoying them up. The pod had already sunk below the top of the dome and was now scooting along at about the same height as the tallest buildings. When a collision looked inevitable, Ricasso abandoned his efforts to lose more height and instead dropped ballast, firing up the burner again. Ponderously, the balloon and its cargo began to rise upwards. They cleared the roofs of the outermost buildings, clanged against a wall, and bobbed higher. The buildings climbed up in steps, getting taller the closer they were to the rim of the dome.

'When I said *avoid* landing on that—'

'I know,' Ricasso said. 'You meant "avoid" in the more commonly accepted usage.'

They weren't going to clear the dome, that much was apparent. What was the worst that could happen, though? Quillon wondered. They were still aloft, still airworthy. Even if they crashed into the side of the dome, the winds could do no more than drag them to the zenith, and then they would be free again.

'I think we'll be all right,' Quillon said. 'If we can just avoid hitting one of those—'

'Cracks,' Ricasso finished for him. 'Like the one we appear to be headed directly towards?'

The crack in question ran down from near the apex of the dome to the point where it met the tallest of the surrounding buildings. It was wider at the base than the top. Just about wide enough, Quillon reckoned, for the pod to pass right through. But not, he felt fairly confident, for the balloon the pod was hanging from.

They passed between the dome's ripped sides, the pod still moving as quickly as ever. Then it slowed, far more violently than was generally appropriate for balloons, and came to a halt. The pod creaked and swayed in the gloomy half-light of the dome's interior. The angled windows prevented Quillon from looking up, but he didn't need his eyes to tell him that the balloon had snagged itself in the gap.

The pod jerked down and stopped. Both men caught their breath. They were still far above the floor of the dome, which they were presuming lay at the same level as the surrounding land. The pod might conceivably survive such a drop; it was questionable whether Ricasso and Quillon would.

'Curtana'll get here quickly,' Ricasso said, undermining the reassuring thrust of his statement with a desperate, confirmation-seeking grin. 'One imagines.'

The pod jerked down again. The balloon, which was open at the bottom, would have completely deflated by now. They were just hanging by snagged fabric, a dozen or so storeys up.

'At least we solved the mystery of Spearpoint,' Quillon said.

Something ripped. The pod dropped. Quillon gripped his chair in reflex and closed his eyes.

The pod landed. It crunched down onto something reassuringly solid, then tipped slightly to one side. The entire drop must have taken no more than half a second.

'As I was saying ...' Quillon let go of his seat arms, coming to the surprised conclusion that he was not only alive, but not necessarily facing imminent death. 'Where do you think we are?'

'Let's get out and see,' Ricasso said.

He equalised pressure before working the door mechanism. The door swung open and banged into rubble. Quillon and Ricasso climbed out, blinking against dust. It hovered in the air, pinned there by slanting sunbeams ramming through the dome's many cracks. The pod had come to rest on a rubble slope, perhaps the crumbled remains of the part of the dome that had collapsed to form the crack where the balloon had jammed. It formed a steep but traversable ramp all the way down to the floor, covering about a third of it.

'Will Curtana see us?'

'She'll have seen where we were headed,' Ricasso said, 'and part of the balloon's still sticking out of the crack. She'll find us, don't you worry about that.'

They set off down the ramp, picking their way with great care, stumbling occasionally, helping each other down the steepest and loosest parts. All the while Quillon's attention kept drifting to the thing down on the floor. It was a dome in its own right, a glass hemisphere partly covered on one side by the rubble. Dust had coated it almost to the point of opacity, but – like Ricasso, who was no less fixated – he could see things inside the glass.

'There's something I meant to ask you,' Quillon said, 'before I was distracted by the star symbol, and all that talk of tectomancers and guilds and history.'

Ricasso lost his footing, recovered it by windmilling his arms. 'Ask away, Doctor.'

'I was thinking back to what Gambeson said to me, about the cellular grid – which seemed to have something to do with the zones – and how we were going to talk about that game board of yours, the one with the black pieces. When you mentioned the Mire, and how we didn't understand it—'

'Mm.' Ricasso carried on for a few paces. 'That's tricky stuff to explain.'

'Could you at least give it a try, before one of us breaks our neck?'

'It's about the zones, Doctor – you're right in that regard. About their very nature. It's been something of a conundrum to me, you see. I've been trying to puzzle out exactly what they are, rather than just accepting them as a feature of a world, like the length of the year or the distance to the horizon. It's one thing trying to develop medicine to help us better tolerate them, but that doesn't really get to the essential nub of things, does it?'

'I wasn't aware there was a nub. The zones are the zones. They exist. We have to live with them. What more is there to it than that?'

'On a practical level, very little. Still, wouldn't it be better to understand them, if there was the slightest chance of that? At least then we'd know what our options were.'

Quillon still wasn't convinced, but he decided to humour Ricasso anyway. 'So tell me about this theory.'

'We've already spoken of something going wrong, something that sent the tectomancers out into the world. I think the zones are the visible manifestation of a quite profound wrongness, a wrongness that happens to afflict the very warp and weft of reality.' Ricasso paused meaningfully. 'I use the term "warp and weft" advisedly, Doctor.

Consider, if you will, a piece of woven fabric, composed of threads going up and down and left to right. That's your basic cellular grid: a pattern of repeating elements. Squares, in that case, although they don't have to be. The point is that there's a uniform pattern, a repeating structure.'

'As in your game board.'

'Precisely, Doctor. Now suppose that there are pieces covering some of the squares and leaving others uncovered. The reality that you and I experience – I contend – depends in its absolute totality on the precise arrangement of those pieces. Everything we do – everything that happens to us, from the flow of blood in our bodies to the tiniest flicker of electricity in our heads – relates to a specific, changing pattern on that game board.'

'We're made of atoms,' Quillon said. 'This much I know.'

'True enough, Doctor. The game board also encodes a complete description of matter on the atomic scale. In point of fact it goes deeper than that, down to the clockwork inside atoms. But here's the singular thing.' Ricasso kicked a rock from under his feet. 'It isn't an infinitely fine mesh. Sooner or later you hit the finite resolution of the grid: the limiting size of the squares. You can't have two pieces in one cell, and a piece mustn't lie between two cells. Which is of no particular concern to us, since it's what we've evolved with. There's implicit structure that seems to go down further than the squares, but that's really just an illusion, like a tiny image in a convex mirror. What we're dealing with here is truly the base layer of reality.'

'Intriguing. Please continue.'

'I think something's gone wrong with the game board. The cellular grid used to be the same wherever you looked: it was just the game pieces that moved around. Not now, though. Not since the zones broke out.' Ricasso paused to steady himself as a lozenge-shaped chunk of rubble tilted under his feet. 'The grid has become discontinuous, for a start. There are tears, rifts, between different parts of it. Those are the zone boundaries. We'd scarcely notice them if the zones were all the same inside, but they're not. They don't match up any more, because the grids aren't the same size on both sides of the boundary.'

Quillon thought back to the game board, and the mismatch he had noticed between its two halves.

'What could make the grids end up like that?'

'One can only speculate. It seems probable to me – probable, but not certain – that there's some hidden parameter, a variable that governs the coarseness of the grid inside each zonal division. Once, it must have been set to the same value everywhere, like a great collection of gyroscope needles all pointing in the same direction. Then the incursion happened – the Mire erupted out into our world, the Eye of God shone through, if you will, and everything went to pot. The gyroscope needles spun around randomly before jamming at certain settings, each of which resulted in a particular zone being fixed at a certain limiting resolution. And that's what we're stuck with now: a world made up of different game boards glued together at the edges. The boards can shrink and ooze around each other, but they can't vanish entirely.'

The rubble was loose under Quillon's boots. The pod had disturbed a tremendous quantity of dust into the air upon its arrival and now each footfall was adding to the grey choke. He coughed and cleared his throat. 'It's a theory. But I still don't see how it relates to our world.'

'Consider the passage across a zone boundary. We get mapped from one board to another. If the difference in the cell sizes isn't severe, our bodies are able to adjust to the change. We're squishy and adaptable, you see – I don't need to tell a medical man that. Our atoms fall into slightly different configurations as the grid shifts under them, but on a physiological level, we barely feel it. It's a small effect, and the neurological symptoms of having your brain very slightly rewired are easily handled by simple drugs.'

'Antizonals.'

'You're ahead of me already, Doctor.'

'All right. What happens when we cross back over?'

'You're remapped to a finer resolution again. Transcription, I call it. You adjust. The key thing, though, is that there must always be a degree of information loss. You can't travel through a low-state zone – a zone with low cellular resolution – without losing something. It's just that people – animals, organisms – are rather adept at absorbing the transcription losses. Machines, less so. The change hits them hard at the atomic level because they're rigid, inflexible. They depend on things fitting together very accurately. Errors propagate all the way up to the macroscopic level. Anything built with very fine tolerances simply can't survive the passage from a high-state to a low-state zone. It's like passing a complicated message through a room full of sloppy translators. Stuff drops out. Stuff gets misinterpreted and doesn't come out the other side the right way. If you're not careful you end up with gibberish. Machines break, Doctor. And the damage doesn't get undone when they pass back into a high-state zone.'

'Again, it's a nice theory.'

'But no more than that, you're thinking. And you know what? You're absolutely right. It's not verifiable. It's not testable. It's not even something you can mention in polite company.'

Quillon felt the urge to be charitable. 'Let's assume you're right. It's not as if anyone has any better ideas, is it?'

'You're far too kind, Doctor.'

'How did this happen, though? How did the Eye of God break through? And what does it have to do with Spearpoint? What does it have to do with the tectomancers and their guild?'

'Pertinent questions, one and all. Questions that, at least at the present juncture, I am singularly ill-equipped to answer.'

At length they reached the floor, rubble- and dust-strewn in its own right, but not quite as treacherous as the ramp. The glass dome was perhaps fifty spans across. Remarkably, it showed no evidence of damage, even though huge chunks of rubble must have fallen on it. Quillon scuffed a hand over the glass, which was strangely cold and gelid to the touch, and the patch he exposed was as clear and unscratched as diamond.

'There's something inside,' Ricasso said, holding a hand over his brow to screen out the glare from the sky. 'Looks like some kind of tableau or shrine.' He said this on a falling note, as if he had been expecting something more spectacular. 'Little statues, that's all.'

Quillon widened the clear patch until he had a better view. Inside the dome was a patch of sandy ground, dotted here and there with rocks and boulders. In the middle of the patch, more or less directly under the apex, was a kind of house raised up on splayed stilts. The house was angular and mechanical, with something of the machine about it, but it didn't look like any kind of vehicle or aircraft Quillon had ever heard of.

The statues were even more puzzling. There were six of them, arranged in poses around the central feature. They were small enough to be children, none of the figures coming higher than Quillon's abdomen. But if they were meant to be children – rather than pygmies or little people – then there was no way to tell from their faces. They were clad in white armour, with curved black visors covering their faces. They were humpbacked and they had what looked like accordions fixed to their chests. Their gloved hands appeared out of scale with the rest of them. Some of the 'children' had tools with which they were poking or raking the ground, while others were posed as if looking into the far distance, shielding their faceless visages from the sun in eerie mimicry of Ricasso's posture.

'What a strange tableau,' Quillon said.

'Look, Doctor,' Ricasso said. 'On that one's shoulder.' He was indicating the nearest figure. 'Do you recognise it? It's the same symbol we saw on those crashed machines, on the far side of the walls. The rectangle, with the five stars?'

'It still doesn't mean anything to me.'

'Nor to me, but one must presume it meant something to the people who made this dome.' He craned his neck upwards. 'The main one, I mean. The glass one, and these statues, must be even older. If they stumbled on the tableau, the way we've done, there's no telling what significance they might have placed on it.' Then he paused, made a small laughing sound and said, in an overly emphatic tone, '"*And in that time, before the gates of paradise were closed to them, men and women were as children."*'

Quillon remembered enough of the quote to complete it for Ricasso. '"*And so plentiful were the fruits and bounties of paradise that they lived for four-score years, and some lived longer than that. And in that time the Earth was warm and blue and green and many were its provinces."*' He waited a few moments, conscious of a spell that he did not wish to break, before adding: 'Do you think it means anything?'

'Probably not,' Ricasso said, wiping his dust-smeared hands on his knees. 'I'm all for looking for meaning in ancient texts. But now and then you have to just accept the fact that you're dealing with so much religious gibberish.' Then he looked back up the rubble slope, to the darkening crack of sky. 'We'd better not keep them waiting, had we? Not when we've got a city to save.'

Quillon and Ricasso paused on their way out to unload the exposed plates from the balloon cabin's underbelly camera, then completed their descent via the abandoned buildings fringing the dome. Curtana had set *Painted Lady* down on the nearest patch of open ground, taking the opportunity to carry out certain inspections that would otherwise have been impractical away from Swarm. Quillon and Ricasso were ushered back aboard without comment, Ricasso clutching the plates to his chest protectively.

Then they were airborne, speeding to the east, racing the lengthening shadow of Spearpoint 2. By the next day they had cleared the Bane and the Deadening, and were back over charted territory. Ricasso's crossing had succeeded, and it had undoubtedly saved them valuable time and fuel. But the mood was not one of jubilation. Swarm had sundered, losing part of itself not to war or accident but to political dissension.

And while they had completed the longest part of the journey, they had not necessarily completed the hardest part. They still had to reach Spearpoint, and that meant crossing ground that was now occupied by Skullboys.

With the Bane behind it, Swarm regrouped, pulling in *Painted Lady* and the other scouts. Taxis and cargo ferries fussed between ships. Quillon and Ricasso returned to *Purple Emperor*, the two men wishing to assess the status of the serum stocks aboard the larger ship. Meroka accompanied Quillon, but Agraffe and Curtana had elected to remain aboard *Painted Lady*, to make sure she was readied for the final leg of the journey to Spearpoint. Quillon was reluctant to leave Kalis and Nimcha, but he had been assured that his absence need only be a brief one.

He did not realise he had been tricked – or at least hoodwinked – until the ferry docked and Ricasso announced that his presence was required at Spatha's tribunal.

Quillon was taken aback. He had assumed that the matter of Spatha's punishment lay safely in the future, where it need not trouble him.

'I don't have to be part of this.'

'On the contrary, you're central to it. If Spatha had got his way, we'd both have been hung out to dry. Or did you think the new administration would let bygones be bygones, welcome you into the fold? No, Doctor, I think not. There'd have been another trial – a farce, with only one possible outcome – and you'd have been executed as an example to the waverers.' Ricasso took firm hold of Quillon's arm as he steered him into *Purple Emperor*. 'Those plates didn't just convict Spatha. They saved both of us from the propeller.'

'Is that still how you do it nowadays?'

'We've made some advances, but there can always be exceptions.'

When they were safely inside, Quillon said, 'About those plates. We still haven't really talked about them.'

'What's to talk about?'

'You spied on me. All the time I was down in the laboratory, you were taking photographs.'

Ricasso shrugged off the criticism. 'It was my life's work. Do you honestly think I wasn't going to take some precautions?'

'I thought I'd earned your trust.'

'You had. But that doesn't mean I could be certain that you were *competent*. Suppose I saw you mixing up the reagents by mistake?'

'From a single photograph?'

'It was a precaution, that's all. Let's not allow it to spoil a perfectly amicable relationship.'

'I was ready to forget about it, until you dragged me back into Spatha's trial.'

'You're one of us now, Doctor. Consider it your civic duty. It won't take long, anyway. It's about as open-and-shut as they come.'

Ricasso was right about that, at least. The tribunal was over in little more than an hour, and much of that had been taken up with formalities. There were no more than twenty people in the sealed, windowless room, including Spatha and his diffident, half-hearted defence counsel, who entered proceedings with the mildly distracted air of a woman who knew nothing she did or said would make the slightest difference to the outcome. The prosecution, such as it was, consisted of Ricasso and five senior captains: they were, Quillon was given to understand, the nearest thing to a standing military court Swarm had to offer. Another ten captains, from a range of ships – including both hard-line Ricasso loyalists and moderate waverers – constituted the jury. Quillon was the only witness called to testify, and his contribution was mercifully brief. He was cross-examined over the matter of his coming to Swarm, then regarding the blue book, and finally about his involvement in the escape of the vorgs. He answered truthfully, since he no longer had a thing to hide. Had he been asked about Nimcha, he would have told them all he knew.

But they weren't interested in Nimcha, and they weren't overly interested in him. It was all about Spatha, who stood proudly despite being cuffed and under armed guard. Throughout the tribunal he maintained a look of stoic composure, the unashamed facade of a man who believed he had acted in Swarm's best interests, or at least wanted his questioners to believe as much.

Quillon certainly did. And when by an act of mental contortion he managed to put himself in Spatha's place, he could see nothing in the man's actions that had not been utterly consistent with his stated aims. Swarm was a democracy only insofar as it suited Ricasso. And if one truly did believe that Ricasso's leadership was bad for Swarm, and that the fight had to be taken to the Skullboys, what else could one do but gather supporters and plot a takeover? In that sense Spatha had acted reasonably, even fairly. The personal animosity that Quillon had felt emanating from the man in no way undermined that thesis. Spatha's hate, both for him and Nimcha, had been incidental.

The verdict of the jury was not unanimous, but nor was it required to be. All agreed that Spatha was guilty of releasing the vorg and precipitating the deaths that had followed. All agreed that his actions had cost both lives and the loss of precious medicines. Where they differed was on the question of whether those actions constituted mutiny, or merely an overzealous regard for the security of Swarm, in the sense that Spatha had not necessarily been acting in his own self-interest.

It made little difference to the outcome. Seven captains were not only convinced of Spatha's guilt, but that his crimes merited execution. Two recommended administrative restraint pending further investigation. One abstained on the grounds that it could not be proven beyond all doubt that the incriminating photographs were genuine. The minority voices clearly pained Ricasso, who had been hoping for unanimity.

But seven were sufficient. Under Swarm law, Spatha was deemed guilty of material sabotage, the murder of four citizens, perversion of the course of justice by attempting to shift blame onto both Quillon and Ricasso, and, almost as an afterthought, attempted mutiny. The weight of the other crimes would have been sufficient, but mutiny carried an automatic death penalty.

Sentence was carried out promptly, with surprisingly little ceremony. The court moved to one of *Purple Emperor*'s boarding platforms, where Spatha was strapped into a leather harness of obvious antiquity. The harness in turn was fixed to a line, and the line to a winch. Spatha was swung out over empty sky and then lowered to a distance of about one hundred and fifty spans under the airship. Armed airmen took up station and directed pedestal-mounted machine guns at the barely recognisable form on the end of the line. With his arms and legs trussed, Spatha was incapable of visible movement.

But the gunners didn't open fire immediately. Instead they waited for the winch line to be swung gently back and forth. What was a relatively small motion at the platform level soon became a wide, pendulous arc at the other end of the line. Spatha's motion gradually took on the form of an ellipse, moving back and forth as well as sideways. It took Quillon a moment to realise that all this was deliberate, to make the target harder to hit. At a signal, the machine-gunners let their weapons roar, aiming not at the gyring figure but at the point in the sky where the figure was likely to be a fraction of a second later. It turned out to be much more difficult than it looked, and the winch operator only complicated things by adjusting the length of the line and the amplitude of the swing. It was probably only seconds, but it felt to Quillon as if minutes passed before any of the bullets found their mark. Even then, the shots did not look to have been decisive. The gunners seemed to be wilfully prolonging Spatha's execution, chipping away at him rather than going for the lethal shot.

'Don't judge us too harshly,' Ricasso said, straining to make himself heard over the chug of the guns. 'It would have been far easier just to have shot him at point-blank range. But then we'd be denying him the right to contribute something useful to Swarm.'

'Wouldn't a sack of dirt serve much the same purpose?'

'Dirt's useful,' Ricasso said. 'You never know when you'll need it for ballast.'

Quillon was glad when it was all over, when at last the hanging form had been deemed to have served its purpose. It was winched back up, the ragged, bloodstained form extracted from the harness – itself peppered with bullet holes, but essentially repairable – and tossed overboard.

'You don't approve,' Ricasso said. 'I can see that. But then, you don't really have the option of not dealing with us, do you? We've got the medicines.' He smiled and nodded, as if in his presence Quillon had crossed some threshold of moral complexity, leaving the naive world behind. 'Welcome to politics, Doctor. We don't get to pick our allies. The best we can hope for is that we don't despise them quite as much as our enemies.'

After the execution Quillon and Ricasso returned to *Painted Lady*. Curtana's ship was provisioned and ready to resume its position at the head of Swarm, equipped and armed for the final approach to Spearpoint. A day after Spatha's execution, they picked up Radial Nine again and received the first news from the city since before the crossing.

A day later, they could see it.

'From Tulwar, sir,' the airman said, handing Quillon the thin sheet of transcript paper.

'You're already in contact?'

'Yes, sir. Via the semaphore line so far, although we're close enough now that we should be able to establish a continuous heliograph exchange, provided the visibility keeps up. Which is good, because no one expects Radial Nine to hold out much longer. The Skulls are chipping away at it station by station.'

Quillon read the transcript. Rather than the general report that had been picked up by the Skullboy airship *Lacerator*, this was a direct communication to Swarm, in response to an earlier announcement sent to Spearpoint along the faltering semaphore network. Swarm had informed the city – taking particular pains not to mention Tulwar by name – that it was responding to the earlier call for help, with the intention of bringing sufficient antizonal supplies – albeit in concentrated form – to treat millions of citizens. Swarm requested guidance for offloading the cargo and ensuring it reached the right hands. It also mentioned that any direct medical queries should be addressed to the physician aboard *Painted Lady*, without mentioning Quillon's name. The response had come back six hours later, suggesting that lines of communication, both in and out of Spearpoint, remained fragile. This time it appeared to be directly authored by Tulwar. Digesting the transcript, Quillon was left in no doubt that it was the same man they had dealt with before his escape.

Meroka agreed. 'The place where he's suggesting we offload isn't too far from his part of Steamville. Too much of a coincidence, Cutter.'

'You think so?'

'Yeah. Looks like our wheezing friend really is running the show now, probably out of the same bathhouse.' Meroka gave a noncommittal shrug. 'But if the man can get the job done, ain't no skin off my nose.'

'Although you'd rather it was Fray.' He nodded. 'I feel the same. But we can't go asking what happened to him. If we do that, anyone who reads our signal will know we had some prior connection with Fray. And if that's someone who happens to be looking for me—'

'You don't have to say it, Cutter. I know what you mean.'

'It also means we can't let Tulwar know that we know who he is either. At least not until we're face to face, and we know there's no one listening in. The other thing we can't mention is Nimcha. Not until we're sure she's going to be safe.'

'Maybe we should cross that bridge after we've delivered the drugs, don't you think? Ain't gonna be no walk in the park, just getting to Spearpoint. Just so you're clear on that, Cutter.'

'Under no illusions,' he said, forcing a stoic smile.

Meroka fell silent, and for a moment he thought she had said all that she meant to. Then she started speaking again. 'Gave you a pretty hard time, didn't I?'

'No more or less than I deserved.'

'Because of you being an angel?'

'There's no escaping it.'

'No, I guess there isn't. But I was wrong all the same. Not wrong to hate them for what they did, but wrong to take all that out on you. So you lied. I guess you did it with Fray's blessing, though.'

'I lied to almost everyone I ever met in Neon Heights. Fray was the only one who got anywhere near the truth. And there were still things I didn't even tell Fray.'

'Guess we all have our little secrets.'

'All of us,' he affirmed. 'Doesn't make it right or wrong, of course – it's just the way we are. For what it's worth, I'm glad Fray put us together. I know it meant dragging you out of Spearpoint, I know it meant you getting shot ... but, as selfish as it sounds, I wouldn't have had it any other way.'

'Can't say I was sorry not to be back in Spearpoint when it all turned to shit.'

'You'd have done well, I suspect.'

'Maybe. Maybe not. Sometimes it's just how the dice fall. Look at Fray. Look at Tulwar.'

'I see what you mean.'

'I'm glad I met Curtana. Glad I met the kid, as well. Gotta say, mother still creeps me out a bit. But the kid's all right.'

'Thank you for reading to her. I think she liked the stories.'

'The stories?' Meroka laughed. 'I hate those fucking airship stories. But she seems to like me reading them, so I guess we're stuck with each other.'

'All of us,' Quillon said.

CHAPTER TWENTY-THREE

Less than twenty leagues separated Swarm from its destination. The fleet had been on a survival footing as it crossed the Bane. Now it was at war-readiness, and with impeccable justification. Long-range observers had peered through leagues of trembling, smoke-wreathed air, mapping Skullboy positions all the way to the dusty margins of Horsetown, where Spearpoint commenced its soaring climb from the plains. Swarm had no option but to cross that occupied terrain.

'There are no airships in the air or on the ground,' Agraffe said, looking from face to face as he delivered his news, 'but that doesn't mean the Skullboys haven't been busy, or that we're not going to encounter moderate resistance on the way in. We're too far out to detect artillery or gun emplacements, although you can be sure they're there. At our usual cruising altitude, they won't pose us any great difficulties, and in any case we should be able to take out most of them with our long-range guns before we're anywhere near them. But our observers have seen balloons. They're tethered to the ground, laid out in concentric lines all the way back to Spearpoint, most of them already inflated – big, obvious targets.'

'We'll cut them to ribbons,' Curtana said.

'Perhaps.'

'You're not convinced?' Ricasso asked, glancing up with heavy-lidded eyes from the heliograph report that had been handed to him a few minutes earlier.

'Skullboys may be insane, but they're certainly not stupid. They know our capabilities, what they can and can't get away with. If they want to stop us, why aren't they putting airships in the air?'

'Maybe they're all out of airships,' Meroka said.

'Skullboys are a self-organising rabble,' Agraffe said patiently. 'We may have shredded one part of the organism, but that doesn't preclude it from growing another limb. Weaker, perhaps – but still capable of hurting or slowing us. Perhaps they just couldn't get any other ships here in time – that's a possibility, I admit.'

'But not one you're inclined to go with,' Ricasso said.

'They have the means to organise those balloon lines, but not to get a single ship into the air? I don't buy it.'

'Nor do I.' Ricasso put the heliograph report down on the chart table, setting it under a skull-shaped paperweight, some captured, shrivel-headed trophy from an earlier glory. 'I don't have to, either. We've just heard from Tulwar again. He was brief and to the point, as needs must. It isn't good news.'

'What's the problem?' Quillon asked. 'We've come this far; Spear-point's practically within spitting distance. We know Tulwar's still in some kind of control, or he wouldn't have flashed you. All we need to know is where exactly to land and who to give the medicines to.'

'Tulwar isn't the problem,' Ricasso said. 'It's the zones around Spearpoint.'

Curtana groaned. 'What's the matter now?'

'It used to be possible, at least in theory, for us to fly Swarm right up to one of those ledges. In the old days there were even docking towers. It was probably still possible before the zone storm, although I suspect the towers were long gone. But now there isn't a navigable path through the air: not one we can use, anyway. The Skullboys know that, of course. That's why they haven't put any ships into the air. They wouldn't work.'

'It took Tulwar until now to tell us this?' Meroka asked.

'Tulwar didn't know,' Ricasso replied. 'Surveying the airspace around Spearpoint hasn't exactly been the highest priority – not when people have been dying in droves, and Spearpoint's been under attack on two fronts. They've only just been able to make some measurements out there. Unfortunately, they're bad news for us.'

He pressed his belly to the chart table and ran a finger over the map of Spearpoint. It was an old one that Quillon and Meroka had done their best to bring up to date, their annotations a scribble of bright-red ink over faded black and sepia.

'At our preferred altitude,' he continued, 'we'll hit a boundary ten leagues out. Beyond the boundary, wrapping Spearpoint from all dir-ections, is a low-state zone, roughly equivalent to the old Horsetown.' He met Quillon's eye. 'You've been through it, so you'll know exactly how much works in Horsetown.'

'Almost nothing that isn't made of meat.'

'Simple machines, that's all. Iron clocks, waterwheels, flintlock pistols. Internal-combustion engines, air-cooled or gas-powered machine guns, sensitive navigation devices – not so much.'

'Could we race through and hope it doesn't affect our engines before we get out the other side?' Quillon asked.

'Doesn't work like that, I'm afraid. There are some latency effects, so we wouldn't lose all power immediately after crossing the boundary. But even if we hit the boundary at maximum speed, we still wouldn't get more than a few leagues into it before we lost engines. Guns would follow shortly afterwards.'

'Does it reach all the way to the ground?' Curtana asked.

'No,' Ricasso said. 'At least not according to Tulwar's information, which even he admits isn't necessarily accurate. We could come in very low, and still retain engines. But then we'd be at the mercy of those ground emplacements. They'd rip us to pieces.'

'Even if we got through, there'd still be the main formation behind us,' Curtana said.

Ricasso shook his head. 'Not a hope. We just don't have enough escort strength to protect them, or even enough airspace to guard the unarmed ships from below. We have civilians to think of, not to mention the reason we're doing this in the first place.'

'The reasons,' Quillon corrected under his breath.

'Quite.' Ricasso nodded.

'All right,' Curtana said. 'If not down, then what about up? Can we come in over the top?'

'Just as impractical, I'm afraid. The low-state zone extends well above our normal ceiling.' Before she could raise an objection he said, 'Yes, I know *Painted Lady*'s flown higher than almost every other ship in Swarm, and I don't doubt she could do so again. But one ship's simply not enough, and I won't risk all the medicine in one hold. Besides, high altitude brings its own risks. You'd be exposed to angels and anything else capable of flying around up there.'

'So in other words,' Meroka said, 'we're screwed whichever way we come in. May as well turn tail now and head back to the Bane. Is that what you're saying?'

Ricasso stood back from the table. 'No, I'm saying that the only option open to us may strike you as rather unpalatable.'

'Which would be?'

'We push on. Three ships go first, with the processed serum stocks divided between them. The unprocessed stocks remain aboard *Purple Emperor* for now, until it's safe to bring her in.'

'Cross the boundary and eventually lose all power and weapons,' Curtana said.

'But we'll still be *airborne*,' Ricasso answered. 'Hydrostatic lift doesn't depend on any clever gadgetry; the ships will still fly.'

'Drift, you mean. The whole point of a dirigible is that it's *dirigible*. You get to choose which way it goes, and how fast.'

'That will be decided for us,' Ricasso said. 'The prevailing wind happens to be on our side. Even if we lose all power, the ships will keep moving in the right direction.'

Curtana looked offended. 'We're pilots, not balloonists. Leave that to the Skullboys.'

'I've done some ballooning recently. It has its attractions.'

'And look how well that ended.'

He smiled at Curtana. 'Thank you, my dear, for that frank assessment. I'll remind you that we're airmen above all else. And all we have to do is get the laden ships down on that ledge.'

'You mean crash.'

'That will depend on the skill of those involved, wouldn't you agree? There are twisty thermals near Spearpoint, which would be a problem even if we had engines. We can also expect to encounter resistance from the occupying elements, not to mention the hostiles around Spearpoint's base.' He flashed a challenging smile. 'But I have the utmost confidence in my captains. The question is, do they have confidence in themselves?'

Curtana rolled her eyes. 'Oh, don't start that again. You got me to fly into the Bane. That was bad enough, but at least I stood a slender chance of having a ship at the end of it.'

'Land her gently enough and you'll still have a ship.'

'I'll have a gutless skeleton, if I'm lucky. No engines, no guns. Just a heap of metal and skin and gas. That's not the way *Painted Lady* was meant to go. Down in flames, maybe. But ending up like some paralysed cripple?' Curtana looked away disgustedly, as if they were discussing the betrayal of a close friend.

'If we do this one thing,' Ricasso said, looking around the room for support, 'then everything changes. Everything. Not just Spearpoint, not just Swarm, but the entire landscape of our world. Who knows if we'll even want ships when the dust has settled? Maybe we'll have found something else to care about.'

'You'd have thrown someone overboard if they'd spoken like that a year ago,' Curtana said.

'I'd have been right to. But that was then and this is now. They've lost their city. What do a few ships matter, set against that?'

She looked amazed. 'Fear and panic, you're actually serious. What did you and Doctor Quillon actually see on that ballooning trip? The face of God?'

'Very nearly,' Ricasso said.

'How long until we hit the boundary, at our present speed?' Quillon asked.

Ricasso looked at his paperweight. 'Tulwar doesn't know exactly where the limit is; his information wasn't that detailed. We might hit it in an hour, maybe two. The lead ships will need to climb, since they're going to lose dynamic lift as soon as the engines conk out. The wind will carry them on, but the ships will be sinking all the while. Apart from venting gas and dropping ballast – neither of which they can carry on doing for ever – they'll have no control over that descent rate, so they'll have to make sure they're high enough at the start not to miss Spearpoint completely.'

'I'm liking this more and more,' Curtana said. But in her face Quillon could already see a hardening resolve; calculations of static and dynamic lift whirring behind her eyes, sums she had been doing all her adult life, as effortlessly as breathing.

'And then?' Quillon asked. 'How long will it take the ships to pass through?'

'Again, I can't say with any certainty. The total passage shouldn't last longer than two hours. Why?'

'There's not enough time for antizonals. It's hard enough calculating the right dosage when you don't know the conditions in advance. But even if I got the dosage right, the drugs would still be in our systems when we come out on the other side.'

'There are corrective drugs,' Ricasso said.

'Only suitable for a small adjustment, to refine a dosage or to negate the residual effects of an earlier treatment. It'd be madness to use them at the necessary concentrations. And Serum-15 won't be any more use to us right now.'

'So this thing that's already going to be incredibly difficult,' Curtana said, 'we'll be doing while under the effects of zone sickness?'

'I can order the dispensing of a low-strength, broad-spectrum antizonal as soon as we hit the boundary,' Quillon said. 'It won't offset all the effects, and the benefits will begin to fade within about half an hour, but it'll still be better than nothing.'

'It'll have to do,' Ricasso said. 'The transition shouldn't be too severe, anyway. We're only talking about a small change, aren't we?'

'We'll know when we hit it,' Quillon said.

After a mildly combative three-way argument between himself, Curtana and Agraffe, Ricasso reluctantly agreed to return by boat to *Purple Emperor*. It was safer there – marginally, at least – and there was much for him to do in connection with the unprocessed Serum-15 reserves that the larger ship still carried, those that had been salvaged from Spatha's sabotage.

Swarm's assault on Spearpoint would be led by *Painted Lady*, *Cinnabar* and *Iron Prominent*, while the other ships held back on the safe side of the zone boundary. But as the lead ships climbed into the cold air of the low stratosphere, edging perilously close to their operational ceiling, all of Swarm followed their ascent. *Painted Lady* and some of the other escort ships were used to climbing to these altitudes, but for many of the larger ships it was the first time in years that anything like this had been asked of them. It was as much of a challenge for the crews and citizens as it was for the labouring engines. Few of the gondolas were pressurised, so it was necessary to break out oxygen bottles and masks to alleviate the effects of the thinning air. Children, the elderly and the sick were permitted to breathe continuously, but the adults had to ration their intake, using the masks just enough to stave off hypoxia. Anything else would have been entirely impractical in any case. Orders still needed to be shouted; intense conversations still needed to take place. More so than at any other time, in fact, for the higher Swarm went the more there was to go wrong; the more that needed immediate repair. The thinning air began to affect engine power, requiring the manual adjustment of fuel-to-air mixtures. Airmen had to climb out onto icebound engine struts, working gloved and goggled to alter carburettor settings. Fuel lines and seals turned brittle, requiring immediate repair. One man was lost overboard as he slipped on ice; another suffered severe burns to his hand when he removed his glove and touched freezing metal. Other men came back inside hypothermic or frostbitten, and yet there were always volunteers ready to go back outside and continue the work. Most of the ships had some power in reserve, so they could keep climbing even when an engine or two was lost to the cold, but this was not always the case. With painful inevitability, elements of Swarm began to drop back, unable to maintain the climb. They would have to look after themselves from now on; the other ships had enough worries of their own.

Quillon spent the climb making sure all the other ships were informed of his orders regarding the antizonals, regardless of whether they would be making the crossing now or later. His instructions were simple enough – the dosage per person was small, and could easily be met with the normal supplies carried aboard each ship – but as the orders were relayed from ship to ship, there was still surprising scope for confusion. Queries were flashed back, doubting that the original order had been received correctly. Even after Quillon had reissued his instructions, he still had a handful of outstanding requests for confirmation to deal with. It was only when he had dealt with these that it occurred to him he still had to dole out the drugs for the crew of *Painted Lady*. All the while he was engaged in examining his own faculties for evidence of sudden-onset zone sickness.

Curtana found him in the chart room. She had been breathing oxygen and a black mark encircled her mouth where the mask had dented her skin.

'Thought I'd let you know that we've levelled off. We're at four leagues now. This is as high as we go without popping rivets.'

'How many ships made it up this far?'

'Sixty-five, last count. A few stragglers may still catch up, but I'm not counting on it. It's still going to be hard. I've got men outside nursing every engine. We've been firing the guns just to keep the barrels from icing up.'

'They won't be much use to us once we cross over, will they?'

'Nothing will happen instantly. It's all going to come down to percentages and training.'

'The zebra finches seem to have gone very quiet.'

'They're dead,' she said bluntly. 'Or unconscious, anyway. It's probably the altitude rather than zone sickness. Trouble is, our instruments are freezing up just as quickly as everything else. We're not going to have much advance warning.'

'We'll just have to do our best.'

Curtana noticed the wooden box set on the chart table before Quillon, with his mask and oxygen bottle still inside it. 'If you're trying to prove something, it isn't necessary. We need you to be sharper than any of us.'

'I'm not trying to prove anything.' Quillon smiled awkwardly, aware that they were having a conversation that would have been impossible only a few weeks earlier. 'I just don't feel the altitude or cold the same way you do. And no, I'm not deceiving myself. I've been scrupulous in testing myself for zone sickness, so I know I'm not missing anything. My faculties are undiminished.'

'It must feel like coming home.'

'I don't think it could ever feel like that.' He paused and touched the unopened box. 'If I sense I need it, I promise I'll take the oxygen.'

'Won't be long now. Soon after we hit the boundary we'll start to sink back down into thicker air.'

He passed her a glass vial. 'Here are the pills, enough for the entire crew, including Meroka. Make sure no one takes anything until I give the order, and make doubly sure no one takes more than one pill. Can I entrust you with that?'

'Of course. I've already stationed Meroka in the underbelly turret, but I'll make sure she gets her dosage. And Nimcha and Kalis?'

'I'll attend to them myself. They have somewhat different requirements.' He was silent for a moment. 'This isn't going to be easy, is it? Even with the three best ships in Swarm, and the best crews in the world running them, there's no guarantee that we'll get through.'

'We have to try.'

'How would you rate our odds?'

'Of all three ships still being intact by midnight? About the same as your chances of growing a full set of wings by teatime.'

'Give me time, and I might surprise you.'

Curtana reached out and squeezed his shoulder. 'I'd best be getting back to the bridge. When we hit the boundary, it's going to get interesting. Think I'll feel happier with my hands on the controls.'

'Ditto.'

Then she was gone, leaving Quillon to gather his things and walk to Kalis's quarters. On his way he listened to the engines' ululating drone, alert to the slightest shift in tone, anything that would herald the transition to the low-state zone. He heard nothing untoward, but the certainty that it was going to happen sooner or later kept him on edge. He would probably sense the transition before it affected any of *Painted Lady*'s mechanical systems, but where zones were concerned nothing could be guaranteed.

'It's going to happen soon,' he told Kalis. 'You'll feel it, even if it doesn't affect you as much as it will the rest of the crew. Hopefully it won't last too long, and then we'll be down on Spearpoint, safe and sound.'

'Where all our troubles end,' Kalis said. She and her daughter were both wrapped in layers of clothing, with fur-lined hoods drawn over their heads. They had been breathing oxygen, but placed the masks aside when he arrived.

'One step at a time,' he said, taking a seat. 'At least we have allies in Spearpoint who want to make sure we'll be all right.'

'Is it us they care about, or what we carry?'

'Both, in all likelihood. It doesn't make them monsters. They've suffered a lot and they want the drugs very badly. We can't blame them for that.'

'They don't know about me,' Nimcha said. 'Do they?'

'It's best that they don't. That doesn't mean you're in any more danger than any other little girl in Swarm.' It was a lie, and he knew she could hear it in his voice even as he spoke. If she was a normal little girl, she would be with all the other families, in the safe belly of *Purple Emperor* or one of the other capital ships.

'I can feel it,' Nimcha said quietly.

'Spearpoint?'

'The Mire,' she corrected darkly, as if it was a mistake no sane adult should ever have made. 'The Eye of God. Stronger than before.'

'It's calling to her,' Kalis said. 'Urging her on. Reaching out to her, as she reaches out to it. It knows that she is near now. It will not let her go.'

'It's what she was born to do,' Quillon said soothingly. 'We shouldn't fight it. It's stronger than any of us, and above all else it doesn't mean her any harm. Far from it: she's the one thing in this world it wants to protect above all else.'

'It sings to me at night,' Nimcha said. 'It used to whisper. Now it sings. I can't really hear the songs properly, it's like they're too far away. But I know what it's trying to tell me. It's broken, too broken to make itself better. It's tried, and it's not as broken as it used to be, but it still needs me to help it mend itself completely.'

'That's what you can do, that none of the rest of us can. One day people will see that that mark on your head is the most beautiful thing in the world.'

Nimcha took a gulp from her oxygen mask. 'I'm still scared.'

'It would be strange if you weren't.'

'I don't know what's going to happen.'

'None of us does.' He looked at Kalis, wishing he could find a way to reassure both mother and daughter that all was going to work out for the best. But he would have to reassure himself first, and he wasn't sure that was possible. He swallowed to wet his mouth. 'Things can't get much worse, that's all I know. If Ricasso's right, then everything we've endured for five thousand years has come to pass because there's something wrong with the Eye of God. This isn't the way the world is meant to be, not the way it was before. Now, I'm not saying you can put all of that right. But if the Eye has started trying to make itself better, and if you can lend a helping hand – which seems to be what it wants of you – then perhaps things can be improved even by a tiny amount. A little would make a lot of difference right now. None of those people down in Spearpoint are waiting on a miracle. They just want their existence to be a little easier than it is now. They'll take what they can get, Nimcha. Even if all you can do is move the zones around so that not so many people are going to die, that'll still be something to be thankful for.'

'But what if everything changes?' she asked. 'What if I change the world, and they don't like it?'

'You're brave and strong and wise beyond your years. The Eye wants you for a reason. It needs the wisdom you have that it lacks. I think it can repair itself now, but it's worried that it'll do more harm than good when it does. That's why you have to guide it. It wants you to help make the world better, not worse.'

'You believe this,' Kalis said.

'I'm trying to,' Quillon answered.

'You have been kind to us. You have made my daughter well. But she is not yours to give away.'

'I never imagined she was.'

'When the moment comes, it will always be her decision. And mine.'

'I understand.'

'If she turns from the Eye, if she does not have the will to enter it, you must respect her choice.'

'I shall.'

'Because for all the kind things you have done, for all that I know you to be a good man, I will still kill you if you make my daughter act against her wishes.'

'I'd expect nothing less,' Quillon said. But the truth of her words had cut him to the marrow. She meant everything – about his kindness, and most especially about killing him.

He had no doubt that she'd find a way, too.

'It's—' he began, feeling a cold claw of subepidermal tension close around his brain.

The captain's voice came over the speaker. 'Transition to boundary detected. Antizonal medicines to be ingested immediately.' Her voice was shaky, as if she was trying to speak while someone dug a bullet out of her. 'Battle condition now at indigo. All crew to failure-readiness stations. All long-range gun batteries to target Skullboy ground positions and balloon emplacements with HE shells, discretionary fire. Other gunners hold targeted fire until my order. Weapons will be cascaded in sequential order. Only senior officers may authorise the dropping of failed pieces.'

The tension was still there, the icy fist caressing delicate limbic structures, but as the moments passed he knew he could still function. There was no crippling disorientation, no stomach-voiding nausea. Yet.

'We've crossed the boundary,' he said. 'It was always going to be a fast transition at airspeed. Hopefully, we'll be out of it just as quickly. How do you feel?'

'I'm all right,' Nimcha said.

'We will manage without your medicine,' Kalis added, as if there had been any doubt in his mind.

'Don't suffer unnecessarily – we'll need both of you fit and well when we reach Spearpoint. If you need me I'll be on the bridge.'

'We will come with you now,' Kalis said.

'It's probably safer here. It's likely that we'll encounter some resistance as we approach for landing.'

'Safer, but still not safe,' Kalis said. 'Besides, she wants to see it.'

He led them forward, reeling a little as he stood too quickly, the effects of the zone sickness hitting like a kind of mild intoxication. Under normal circumstances the effects would increase in severity over the ensuing hours, but he hoped that they would be out the other side before it had a chance to worsen dramatically.

They made their way to the bridge, Quillon aware that the engines were still droning and the guns still being fired occasionally to keep them from icing over. He heard rather than felt the machine guns, but when the long-range cannon were fired, once every few minutes – they were using practice shells, rather than the normal high-explosive rounds – the whole ship lurched with recoil. Beyond the relative sanctuary of the gondola, goggled and masked crewmen still attended to the engines and aerodynamic machines of the ship. They hardly moved, the frost painting their stiff overcoats so that they looked like statues under a light dusting of snow. Behind, flying at nearly the same altitude, came *Cinnabar* and *Iron Prominent*, the two other escort ships that had fallen into formation with *Painted Lady*. Though they were there to provide mutual cover, to Quillon's eyes they looked pitifully distant and frail, like hanging ornaments made out of wire and rice paper. A thought formed with unsparing clarity: *if we count on them, we're finished. If they count on us, they're finished.* The best any of them could do was fight like devil-dogs.

He wondered if he was starting to think like Curtana.

She was on the bridge, standing at the main control pedestal, an oxygen mask dangling from her neck, both hands on the wheel, but ready to adjust any of the brass-handled power and elevation control levers at a moment's notice. Her feet were spaced wide apart and her back held ramrod straight. She looked as if she was about to face down a rampaging animal, with only her wit and will to save her.

'Number one engine: holding,' reported Agraffe, reading off a series of gauges. 'Number two: holding. Number three: holding. Number four: holding. All engines at three thousand r.p.m. and operating within normal temperature and fuel-consumption ranges.'

Targe, the heliograph operator, called out, 'Incoming flashes from *Cinnabar* and *Iron Prominent*. Both ships report safe transition and continued functioning of all mechanical systems.'

'We're not going to be this lucky,' Curtana said, dropping one hand to make a precise, expert adjustment to one of the levers. 'That's not the way it works. Down lookout: anything going on under us?'

The periscope operator answered her without taking his eyes from his instrument. 'Continued movement of Skullboy forces, but no offensive reaction to our presence so far. Balloons are still tethered, and I've yet to see any cannon fire.'

'It won't be long. Agraffe: keep those engine updates coming.' As Agraffe spoke – and without glancing around – she added, 'Doctor – good of you to join us.'

She must have seen his reflection in the window, for he had not announced his arrival.

'I trust everyone's taken their medicine?'

'Like good little children.' She lifted the oxygen mask to her face and took a few nourishing breaths. 'When can we expect the pills to kick in?'

'This is as good as you're going to feel, I'm afraid. On the plus side, you shouldn't feel much worse than you do now.'

'I feel like someone's tightening a vice on my head, while spinning me round and round in a barrel.'

'If you can't function, I can administer a higher dose. But you'll pay for it when we cross back over.'

'Pass, in that case. I'm going to need to be sharp all the way into Spearpoint.' For the first time she looked over her shoulder, only for an instant, before snapping her attention back to the controls and the view in front of her. 'Kalis and Nimcha – I wasn't expecting you on the bridge. Wouldn't you rather be back in your quarters? It's going to get a little ... tense in here.'

'You mean that I should protect the child from things she might find upsetting?' Kalis asked.

'You want to put it like that, then yes.'

'You have no idea of the things she has already lived through. This is nothing to her.'

'Fine; stay if you want to, I won't argue. But keep away from the instruments and windows.'

The big guns roared, the gondola jolting from the recoil.

'Balloons are loose and rising,' the periscope operator called at almost the same time. 'Three, no four, ascending quickly. Skullboys are aboard ... I make it five or six per balloon. Fully armoured air-raiders, strapped to the outside of the basket.'

'Belly turret, concentrate fire on those balloons,' Curtana said.

'Over-temperature condition on engine three,' Agraffe said excitedly. 'All other engines running normally.'

'She's beginning to cook,' Curtana said. 'Feather three to fine pitch. I'm cutting her down to two thousand revs, see if we can make her last a little longer. Deep breaths, everybody. This is where it gets interesting.'

Agraffe raised a speaking tube to his lips to give the order to alter the propeller pitch, a rarely made adjustment that could only be performed by someone stationed at the end of the outrigger. His voice would be relayed in chains out to the shivering airman.

'Pitch adjusted,' he reported, ten or twenty seconds later.

'Adjusting trim vanes,' Curtana said, tugging at stiff, wire-linked levers, the exertion showing in the tendons of her neck. 'Damn things are so heavy ... here she comes. Nose straight again. Losing some airspeed, but I don't want to start shedding height just yet.' She reached for her own speaking tube. 'Ballast drop, five bags, immediate.'

Quillon felt the floor lurch up as *Painted Lady* shed weight, regaining the equilibrium she had lost when her forward speed decreased. Curtana made another precise trim adjustment. For now the craft was flying straight and level again, but everyone on the bridge knew that this was only a temporary state of affairs.

Quillon sensed the tension as a quivering, gelid presence in the air.

At least it was daylight, he thought. Visibility was excellent, as good as it had ever been even on the clearest days in the Bane, and every detail of Spearpoint sparkled with hallucinatory clarity, the city breathing like a living thing in the corkscrewing mirage of spiralling thermals. Because it was day – rather than night, when the absence of lights would have been telling – there was very little to suggest that anything catastrophic had happened to Spearpoint. Even though they still had leagues to cross, he felt as if he could reach out and seize their destination, hauling them in across the gap with only his strength.

'Two balloons down with all raiders,' the periscope man reported.

'Belly gun maintaining fire. Looks like they're preparing to release the next line of balloons as soon as we pass over.' He drew breath, his face still pressed to the hooded eyepiece of his instrument. 'One more balloon down. Fourth is still rising.'

'Over-temperature condition on one,' Agraffe said, his voice hollow with dread inevitability. He had the earpiece of his speaking tube pressed to the side of his head.

'Feather her,' Curtana said. 'I'll cut revs again.'

'No use. Fire control engaged. We've lost one for good.'

Quillon looked out of the starboard window and saw the propeller blades winding down, curds of black smoke coiling from the engine slats, almost enveloping the airman who had been tending it. The airman began to negotiate the strut, returning from his vigil. There seemed to be something almost cowardly in the haste with which he had abandoned it, but Quillon reminded himself that the engine had not simply failed, it had ceased, in every sense of the word, to be an engine. Parts that had once fitted with precision tightness would now be welded seamlessly together, as if that was the way they had come out of the forge. The engine could perhaps be made to work again, but only by melting it down and starting from scratch.

'Two and four holding,' Agraffe reported. 'Three still running hot.'

'Feather all remaining engines to fine pitch,' Curtana said. 'I'll nurse what I can from them before they turn to scrap on me.'

'Fourth balloon is down,' said the periscope operator. 'We'll be above the second wave in just over a minute.'

'Flash from *Cinnabar*,' said Targe. 'She's lost an engine. *Iron Prominent* also reports loss of hydraulic turret control on forward spingun battery. Presently able to effect manual steering, but it's stiffening up quickly.'

'Tell them to lock at forty-five degrees below horizontal before it seizes on them completely. At least they'll be able to shoot at something.' Curtana grabbed her speaking tube again. 'Ballast drop, ten bags, immediate.'

The floor lurched up again. Curtana worked levers, still standing rigid, taut with concentration, at the control pedestal. 'No good. Can't get enough nose-up trim. We're descending.'

'Too fast?' Quillon asked.

Curtana lowered her head to squint at cross hairs. 'No, we're still good for landing, provided we can hold this vector. Wind's still on our side, even if nothing else is.'

'Is your ship dying?' Nimcha asked, in exactly the tone a child might have used to enquire about the colour of the sky.

'No,' Curtana said. 'She's just becoming a different kind of ship. No better, no worse. Just different.'

'Then why do you sound like you're crying?' Nimcha asked.

'Engine three is dead,' Agraffe reported.

'Trimming,' Curtana said, and Quillon heard it in her voice as well, the crack as she tried to hold herself together.

'Second wave is loose and rising,' the periscope operator said. 'Ascending just behind us. Wind's carrying them forwards, but we still have faster ground-speed.'

'That's good news, isn't it?' Quillon asked. 'If they've misjudged their ascent, they can't possibly get ahead of us.'

'Not what they have in mind,' Curtana said.

'It isn't?'

'Standard Skull attack pattern, Doctor. Rising behind, then swooping down on us with the wind against their backs.' She grabbed the speaking tube. 'Belly guns: maintain fire on those balloons. Aim for the bags rather than the baskets, no matter how tempted you are to splatter a few Skullboys.'

'Balloons still can't touch us, though, can they?' Quillon asked. 'I mean, not with everything we have on this ship, the guns, the armour?'

'Pretty soon, Doctor, we're all going to be ballooning.' She slammed a lever hard over, biting her lip with the effort of concentration. 'And pretty soon those guns won't be worth anything more than their value as ballast.' She grinned without turning around. 'But never mind. I like an even fight best of all. Makes the winning all the sweeter.'

'Over-temperature condition on two,' Agraffe called out.

'Oh, thank you very fucking much.' She twisted around to inspect the ailing engine. 'No point even thinking of trying to save that one. Ballast drop! Ten bags, immediate. And tell the crew to start preparing to ditch those dead engines.'

'Two balloons from the second wave down,' the periscope operator said. 'Two still rising, but with damage to one of the baskets.'

'*Cinnabar* and *Iron Prominent* report further engine failures,' interjected Targe, compounding Curtana's anguish.

'I should be over there with them,' Agraffe said.

'Nothing you could do about it if you were,' Curtana replied. 'Tell them to lay down a deflection pattern over those balloons, but to watch their own backs as well.'

The periscope operator called out, 'Third balloon wave now lifting under us. Four units, six raiders per basket.'

'How many more lines before we're clear?' Curtana asked.

'After this one, three, maybe four, depending on how many decoy positions they have.'

The spinguns, which had only been fired in short, snarling bursts to keep their barrels warm, were now firing almost continuously. Quillon could hear them, feel them through his bones, but he could only trust that they were firing in a useful direction. The wind was carrying the remnants of the second wave of balloons astern of *Painted Lady*, so they were all but invisible from the gondola's bridge. Punctuating the spinguns came the heavy *chug* of the long-range guns, aimed low to smash the Skullboy emplacements. The shells scooped monstrous craters in the terrain ahead of the airship, but it was clear from their random spread that it was all but impossible to achieve precision hits. The best Curtana could hope for were a few lucky strikes, in the expectation that they might be sufficient to demoralise and scatter the other Skullboys. Quillon wasn't even sure that Skullboys were capable of being demoralised.

It was only in the intervals when the spinguns were being reloaded, and the big guns were silent, that he realised how much quieter the airship had become. She was running on one engine now, an engine that had been throttled back from its usual power. The ground was still racing under them, but most of that forward progress was now due to the wind pushing against *Painted Lady*'s hull. Had Curtana wanted to turn around, she would not have had the power to do so; she would still have been driven towards Spearpoint.

'Second wave is now finished,' Agraffe reported, relaying observations from the rear of the gondola, since the rising balloons were now out of the periscope operator's line of sight. 'Clear hits – they're both going down with all raiders.'

'And the third wave?'

'Possible strike on one basket; all four units still rising.'

'How the hell can they hit the basket and not the bag?' Curtana asked, her exasperation breaking through.

'Could have been stray fire from the ground,' Agraffe replied.

'Fourth wave is rising,' the periscope operator said. 'Four units, usual lading.'

Because it was the only engine he had to listen to, Quillon heard the dying cough of engine four quite distinctly. Agraffe didn't even bother reporting it this time: he just exchanged a loaded glance with Curtana, both of them knowing that the ship had given them all she could. And then in the intervals between the guns being fired it wasn't just quiet; it was eerily, beautifully silent. There wasn't even the nail-scrape of wind against the gondola, the martial drumming of it against the envelope. *Painted Lady* had been fighting the elements of the sky since the moment she first took to the air; she had now become their willing slave.

'Maintaining descent slope,' Curtana said, finally relinquishing control of the wheel. It was all but pointless now; she could no more steer *Painted Lady* than a leaf could navigate its own path down a river. 'Ballast drop: one bag, every twenty seconds, unless I say otherwise. Gas crews: prepare to vent on my order.'

The long-range guns roared, but on the second discharge something went audibly, catastrophically wrong. The recoil felt more savage than usual, the sound more ragged and clanging.

'HE shell jammed in barrel!' Agraffe shouted.

Curtana inhaled to say something, to swear or exclaim, but on the point of speaking she halted, her mouth open. The moment stretched, second upon second. Quillon looked around, but all he saw were frozen faces slowly melting into anger and frustration rather than the absolute, staring-into-the-void terror that had been there for an instant.

'We're all right,' she said, barely raising her voice above a whisper. 'If it was going to blow—'

'We can't risk a breech burst from the other gun,' Agraffe said.

'You're right – stand it down.' She hammered the heel of her hand against the control pedestal. 'Damn; we needed those guns. What I wouldn't give for a muzzle-loading cannon right now.'

'What just happened?' Quillon asked.

'Shell jammed,' Agraffe said. 'It's a very tight fit down the barrel. Has to be, or else the combustion gases won't work efficiently and the rifling won't give the projectile enough spin. Problem is it just became fractionally *too* tight. Tolerance shifted, locking the shell in place. Welding it, most probably.'

'Will it go off?'

'Would have, if it was going to. But we can't chance another; some-times they *do* detonate.'

'It was always a risk,' Curtana said. 'Just hoped I'd know when to stop using the guns before it happened.'

'Two balloons down from the third wave,' Agraffe said. 'Two still rising. One unit from the fourth wave down; three still rising.'

'Fifth wave loose and rising,' the periscope operator said.

'Four balloons,' Curtana said. 'Right, I get it now.' She snatched up the speaking tube. 'How are those severance crews coming along? I want those engines ditched and falling inside thirty seconds!'

'You're cutting the engines away?' Quillon asked.

'Damn-all use to us now, Doctor. They're only deadweight, steepening our descent slope. Bit of luck, they'll squash some Skulls on the way down.'

'Always good to maintain a positive attitude,' Quillon said.

The airmen were at work on the ends of the struts, still labouring in their enormous coats, masked and goggled forms all but indistinguishable from each other as they battled with mammoth shears and spanners to unharness the engines. Doubtless the disconnection had been anticipated in their design and installation, the severance made as easy as it could possibly be given the complexities of control and fuel linkages, but it still struck Quillon as desperate work to be doing in the middle of a battle. One blessing was they didn't have the wind to contend with now. Nonetheless the bravery of the men impressed him with renewed force. They loved Curtana and would do anything for her.

At least the spinguns were still working. They sounded much louder now, and in the intervals of silence he heard, distantly, the booming of Skullboy artillery and what he guessed to be the remaining weapons of *Cinnabar* and *Iron Prominent*. The Skullboys had the advantage that they could still fire heavy guns from the ground, but *Painted Lady* was still much too high for their shells to touch, and if Curtana held her course she would never fall within range of them. He supposed that they were only firing the guns now to intimidate; to leave Swarm's citizens in no doubt that the Skullboys owned the ground and the airspace immediately above it.

'Balloon down,' Agraffe called. 'Only one left from the third wave now.'

'One more than I'd like,' Curtana said.

'She's passing level with us about now. Dorsal and flanking guns should be able to start picking her up,' Agraffe said.

'All spingun units to continuous fire,' Curtana shouted into the speaking tube. 'If you can't see anything to shoot at, aim at the ground. I want you to run out of ammunition before your guns seize on you. It's no use afterwards.'

Quillon turned to the front windows, peering through the narrow armoured slits at Spearpoint. Not only was it larger than when he had last looked, it was clear that they had shed at least one shelf turn's worth of altitude. They were still far above what had once been Circuit City, the air still treacherously thin and cold, but there was no doubt that they were sinking. He had no option but to trust that Curtana had done her calculations correctly, and that their present rate of descent would not slam *Painted Lady* into the ground short of the city. If that happened, crashing would be the least of their problems.

'Spingun hit on the fourth wave,' Agraffe said. 'One down, Captain. Fifth wave still intact.'

'Sixth wave loose and rising,' the periscope operator said. 'Reckon that's it, Captain. Only two balloons in the sixth wave. Cannon must have got the rest.'

Curtana asked, 'How many balloons still in the air?'

'Nine in all: six from the fifth and sixth waves, three from the fourth and third waves.'

'So a mere fifty-four Skullboy raiders, assuming none of them took a bullet on the way up.' A sudden lurch signalled the jettisoning of one of the useless engines. Curtana was still adjusting trim when two more engines dropped off their struts. Freed of tons of dead metal, the airship rebounded upwards. 'That'll buy us some time,' she said, just as the fourth engine was cut free. 'I don't mind coming in too shallowly. We can always vent at the last minute and drop hard. But I won't give those bastards the luxury of picking us off with their howitzers. How are we doing with that last balloon of the third wave?'

'Dorsal gun's giving it all she's got,' Agraffe said.

Just then there was a terrible, aching silence. Neither the dorsal nor flanking spinguns were firing.

'Please tell me they're just changing a belt,' Curtana said.

One of the guns – Quillon couldn't tell which – sputtered back into venomous, fire-spitting life. But it was only one gun he was hearing. The gunners had missed their chance, he thought. If they couldn't hit the rising balloon when it was level with *Painted Lady*, the task would only get harder as it climbed above them.

'The Skullboys,' he said. 'Can they even survive up here, without pressurisation?'

'Not for long,' Curtana said. 'But they don't need long, either. They climb fast and get down just as quickly. High-altitude exposure doesn't last more than a few minutes. Maybe they lose a few digits, get a few new frostbite scars. You think that's going to be a deterrent when you're already ugly as fucking sin?'

'I still can't see what possible good it does them.'

Agraffe called over from his speaking tube. 'Dorsal spotter reports raiders are loose from third-wave balloon,' he said. 'Six units, standard attack formation.'

Curtana snatched up the speaking tube again. 'All stations! Raiders incoming. Repeat, raiders incoming! Secure for close action! I don't want those bastards getting their nails into my ship!'

'Is this going to get bloody?' Quillon asked.

Curtana nodded gravely. 'I sincerely hope so. Feel like lending a hand?'

'Certainly, if there are injuries to be treated.'

'Not quite what I had in mind. We could use extra help topside, now that we're down to one spingun. You've a head for heights, haven't you?' She turned to one of the other officers. 'Poitrel: show the doctor to the armoury and issue him with something useful. If you want to kill a few Skullboys while you're up there, be my guest.'

'Come with me,' Poitrel said.

CHAPTER TWENTY-FOUR

They went to the armoury. Poitrel took out four rifle-like weapons, slinging one over Quillon's shoulder and handing him another. Then they started up the narrow spiral staircase that climbed all the way from the gondola up through the echoing vault of the airship's interior, the buoyancy cells looming huge and vulnerable as dragon's eggs.

They came out topside next to the dorsal spingun turret, still manned and operational. The air was breezeless, precisely as if *Painted Lady* lay becalmed in the sky. Halfway to the front, two airmen were manning a small machine-gun position – two pedestal-mounted weapons set on a railinged platform – but as yet they weren't firing. Presumably they didn't have the range of the spinguns, and so wouldn't be used until the raiders were closer.

The turret was drilling death into the sky. Without the bulk of the airship to muffle them, the noise from the twin spinguns was nearly unbearable. Quillon watched the hot barrels dervish round at a fearsome cyclic fire rate. Through a slit in the back of the turret he could just see the two masked and goggled gunners, with a third man peering through fixed binoculars and working hard on the crank wheels of the manual steering gear. The guns could be elevated and lowered with relative ease, but turning the turret had now become a laborious, muscular business. For the moment it scarcely mattered: the raiders were still far enough away that the guns could be concentrated on a fixed spot in the sky. Quillon saw them with his own eyes: a tight cluster of sickle-thin wings, a flock of cadaverous birds passing at great height. Behind the shapes, the balloon that the raiders had jumped out of, before unfurling their wings, was still hauling its empty basket. Closer still – almost level with *Painted Lady* – the remaining two balloons of the fourth wave were still rising with their cargoes. The balloons of the fifth and sixth waves – however many were left – were still beneath the ship.

It seemed quite impossible that the raiders could withstand the continued assault from the turret, but that was exactly what they were doing.

Quillon reminded himself that the bullets were subject to parabolic deflection as well as momentum loss, and that while the wind velocity was steady around the airship, it would take very little variation to bend the bullets off-target once they had travelled half a league or so. In reality, the raiders were probably spread much further apart than they appeared at this distance, with a lot of sky between them.

'Follow me,' Poitrel said, leading Quillon around the turret, along the narrow, railinged walkway running the length of the airship's spine, until they were halfway to the rear of the envelope, with the bulbous fin of the empennage blocking the view to the immediate rear. Here, the walkway widened to accommodate another pair of pedestal-mounted machine guns equipped with double-handed grips. 'It's simple,' Poitrel said, shouting to be heard above the spinguns. 'Point and shoot. They come in fast, so you'll need to fire deflection shots. Aim the gun to where they're going to be, not where they are, keep the trigger down and let them fly into your bullet stream.'

'What are they hoping to do?'

'Land on us.' Poitrel released a safety catch on the starboard gun. 'And then take the ship and slaughter every one of her crew, you included. They're fully capable of it, believe me.'

'No doubt.'

'They'll be within range in about twenty seconds. Wait for me to start firing, then join in.'

Quillon placed his hands on the grips and swung the starboard gun around until the aiming cross hairs lay centred on the six approaching raiders. They were visibly larger than even a few moments ago, streaking towards *Painted Lady* at a surprisingly shallow angle. He began to make out details of their bat-black wings, the hard, paperlike angles of fold-points and stiffening spines. The human fliers were knots of armoured darkness where the wings met.

Poitrel had not yet opened fire with the port gun when the spingun turret found its mark, ripping apart one of the flanking raiders. The attacker's wings disintegrated into dark flapping shreds, losing integrity as the bullets tore through stiffening veins and control ligatures. In the same instant the raider erupted into a cloud of shattered armour, splintered bones and crimson gore. It was as if a drab firework had just gone off at midday.

As their dead comrade spilled towards the ground, the five remaining raiders closed up formation. For a few moments it looked as if the spinguns would be able to maintain their simultaneous fire, but then the noise from the turret changed, and Quillon realised that only one of the guns was now operational. The zone was intensifying its hold on them, slowly robbing *Painted Lady* of anything that might have given her a significant edge over the enemy.

Poitrel opened fire, Quillon a moment later. Even though it was mounted on a pillar, he could still feel the machine gun's recoil, trying to wrench itself from its mount. Flames belched from the gun's exhaust vents, bright enough to obscure his view of the raiders unless he released his hold on the trigger from time to time. Poitrel, more practised, maintained continuous fire. Again the remaining spingun found its mark, and another of the flanking raiders yawed away from its companions in a lazy arc, wings collapsing behind it as it arrowed to the ground. Then that spingun ceased firing, leaving only the dorsal machine-gun positions. The four surviving raiders split into two groups, veering apart to present fast-moving targets breaking to port and starboard. They were very close now, almost alongside *Painted Lady*, and Quillon could make out details of their armour and weaponry. They needed both arms to control their wings, so there was no possibility of them aiming pistols or rifles. But the raiders all had small strafing cannon strapped to their bellies, aimed to shoot slightly downwards if the raiders were flying horizontally.

Poitrel took one of them down. It was a textbook deflection shot – laying a razoring line of bullets ahead of the flier, letting him fly into it as if it were invisible cheese wire. A pink horror of entrails bannered the sky. In the instants of consciousness left to him the grinning raider still had enough wing control to flex around and bring his belly-cannon onto *Painted Lady*. The gun fired once, a muffled bark. The projectile howled into the airship's side, punching a surgical line straight through, sucking tattered fabric in its wake.

'We're holed!' Quillon called, swinging his gun around to chase the two raiders on the starboard side, trying to anticipate their line.

'We'll manage,' Poitrel shouted back. 'Don't think it took out a gas cell.'

Quillon's gun sliced the last half from one of the raider's wings, severing his arm at the wrist and sending him spinning out of control. Two more succumbed to the other machine-gun position, dying before they could bring their belly-cannons to bear.

'Well done,' Poitrel said, easing back on his trigger. 'But we're not home and dry yet. The next twelve are incoming, and this time we don't have the spinguns. Think you're ready for them?'

'I'll do my best.'

It seemed to Quillon that the raiders came in faster this time: two groups of six from the two remaining balloons of the fourth wave. He was acutely aware that the four balloons of the fifth wave were beginning to climb above *Painted Lady*, ready to disgorge their own raiders. Twelve this time; twenty-four the next.

It can't be done, he told himself. *We're going to lose.*

Poitrel started firing. Quillon joined in, the gun quivering with demonic rage. In the confusion of battle, with the machine-gun fire criss-crossing around the ship, it was soon all but impossible to tell who had killed who. It was equally impossible to keep tally of the surviving raiders. He couldn't survey the whole sky at once, and *Painted Lady* obscured a huge percentage of it. It was almost like standing on the ground, except that the enemy were able to dart beneath the horizon and under his feet. The raiders came in hard and then cranked their wings forwards at the last instant, matching the airship's speed and circling around, above and below her, flexing to bring their belly-cannons into use. They grinned and howled and screamed, tearing through the air like banshees. The cannon fired and he felt *Painted Lady* shudder every time something went through her. Once he felt the sickening lurch that surely meant a gas cell had been punctured, robbing her of vital lift. A short while later came the counter-lurch that meant Curtana had dropped more ballast (whatever now counted as ballast), and thereby regained the slope that would eventually bring them to Spearpoint. With all the spinguns now out of commission, it was down to machine-gunners and riflemen to defend the ship. The air crackled with an unending fusillade.

None of the twelve raiders from the fourth wave managed to land on the ship, but they had inflicted damage on her and the machine guns were beginning to overheat and jam. One gunner had been killed by cannon fire, decapitated at his position, so that for a few moments some dire reflex kept his headless body working the gun, appearing to track the raider who had killed him. Then his body slumped and the gun was silent and smoking.

But by then assistance was beginning to arrive from below. Spingun and long-range gunners had abandoned their useless weapons and grabbed rifles and small arms. They were emerging from the hatch next to the turret, goggled and masked, scanning the sky with the expressionless glass circles of their eyeholes. When at last Quillon's machine gun jammed into scrap, he remembered the rifle slung over his left shoulder and swung it into position. There was no possibility of laying down deflection shots now, but in compensation it was much easier to track the incoming raiders as they swooped by. Two appeared to die when Quillon was shooting at them, but by then it was all but impossible to know who was responsible for the kills. He was content just to be playing his part in *Painted Lady*'s defence.

For all that there were now more airmen on the narrow spine of the envelope, there were also more raiders to deal with. Soon none of the machine guns were operable and the men had turned to rifles. When the rifles failed, or exhausted their magazines, the men switched to muskets or clumsy single-shot pistols, making each shot count. The fusillade had become more attenuated; now every shot was audible and distinct, and there was enough silence between the shots for shouts and screams to ring through. Though the muskets and pistols continued to function in the zone, they were cumbersome to reload and some of the airmen had switched to crossbows. Aimed skilfully, they proved surprisingly effective against the raiders' armour. But the raiders were arriving in such numbers that they could absorb more losses than before, and with each swooping approach they came closer to landing on *Painted Lady*. When at last a raider did touch down, landing just beyond the turret, he shrugged out of the complicated harness of his wings and pulled twin pistols from hip-holsters, hitting two of the airmen before they had a chance to return fire. Someone shot him through the throat with a crossbow, the arrow ramming out from the back of his neck. The raider slid from the walkway, slipping between the railings and down the ever-steepening slope of the envelope, long-nailed fingers scratching at the rushing surface for a handhold, until the curvature of the hull took him out of sight.

Quillon's rifle was dead and he was reaching for his musket, trusting that it was loaded and ready to be used, when he heard his name.

'Doctor Quillon,' Agraffe called, emerging from the turret, bereft of either mask or goggles. 'We need you down below!'

Poitrel took the musket from him. 'Go. You've done your bit out here. Now put your hands to better use.'

'There are injured?' Quillon asked. He had seen casualties on the deck, but in the heat of the battle it did not seem likely that anyone could have been taken below.

'Enough to keep you busy,' Agraffe said, cupping a hand around his mouth to shout. 'Captain's hoping you can stitch at least some of them back together before we hit Spearpoint.'

Quillon started along the walkway, crouching to avoid being shot by either side. At the other end of the envelope a raider touched down and was immediately set upon by scimitar-wielding defenders. Another joined his comrade, shrugging out of his wings just in time to join in

397

the vicious engagement. Quillon understood now precisely what Curtana had meant by close action. It was metal on metal, blade against blade. Victory would lie not with those who could shoot with the most skill, but with those who could hack and stab with the most vigour.

Then he was inside the envelope, descending the metal staircase, his hands shaking so hard he could barely grasp the rail. Something was different, and it took him a moment to realise what it was. The once gloomy vault was now a cathedral of wintery light, the envelope punctured in so many places that it was almost like being outdoors again. One of the gas cells was gone, the deflated bag lying in folds, and a handful of airmen were struggling to effect some emergency repair on a second cell. One man lay dead on the floor; from his broken-limbed posture Quillon judged that he must have fallen from one of the overarching scaffolds of the airship's rigid frame. Of the battle going on above him he could hear almost nothing save the drumming of booted feet on the walkway, and the occasional muffled boom of a raider's bellycannon. He was nearly down when a shot tore through the envelope, missing the gas cells but wrenching part of the staircase away right under him. He had to squeeze past the gap, trusting that lightning would not strike twice. By the time he reached the gondola, he was shaking more than ever.

He didn't need to be told where to go. The most severely injured airmen had been brought to the infirmary room, while those who were merely wounded were stationed in the chart room. There were no dead in the gondola, which surprised him until he realised that Curtana would have no compunctions about disposing of useless weight if it meant the continued survival of the airship.

The preliminaries of surgery steadied his nerve. He assessed his patients, moved one man from the infirmary to the chart room and another back in his place, and set to work. The injuries were many and various, but almost all had been occasioned by belly-cannon shots ripping through the envelope or the less well protected parts of the gondola. Only one airman had survived a direct strike, but he would lose the remains of one leg below the thigh: even with the best medicine in Neon Heights it couldn't be saved now. Others had been hit by splinters of wood, metal and glass, resulting in deep cuts, lacerations, simple and compound fractures and profuse bleeding. Few of the injuries would have been troubling under normal circumstances. But these airmen were all suffering from the combined ailments of altitude, residual zone sickness and the side effects of the antizonal medicine they were supposed to have taken. Some of the most effective drugs in

Quillon's arsenal would have killed them instantly, so he was forced to make do with less potent medicines, falling back on the wisdom he had gleaned from Gambeson's notebooks.

As always when he was working, the outside world shrank to a tiny, buzzing distraction, a fly trapped between windowpanes. He was intermittently aware of the ongoing battle; he processed the shudders and lurches of the airship's continuous descent; he was conscious of other wounded being brought down from above; but at no point did these matters impinge on his ability to heal, or where healing was not an option, to provide comfort to the dying. Not all of the injured could be saved, even with an angel at their bedside.

It was only during a lull, when one patient was being moved off the table and another prepared, that he found the time to ask, 'What about Kalis and Nimcha? Are they all right?'

'They're safe,' Agraffe said.

'And Meroka?'

'Fine. We pulled her out of the turret screaming and kicking, but there was nothing else she could do down there once the guns seized. We've got her on signals now.'

'And Curtana?'

'She'll die at the wheel rather than let someone relieve her. I feel I should force her to take a rest: it would, technically, be within my rights as another captain. Then again, I'm not sure who else I'd trust to bring us in.'

'You?'

'I know my limitations, Doctor.'

Quillon nodded: there was no point flattering the man when they both knew Curtana was the better pilot. 'We're still on target for Spearpoint?'

'We've just seen off the last of the fifth wave – we should break through the zone before much longer. The Skullboys are still taking pot-shots at us from the ground, but they don't have any more balloons left now. We haven't lost too much altitude, as far as I understand.' Agraffe hesitated, the strain written on his face. 'You did well up there, Doctor. It wasn't expected of you, but we're all grateful.'

'You didn't think I could kill as well as heal.'

'Now we know. And so do you. Sometimes we surprise ourselves with what we're capable of when push comes to shove.'

'Perhaps,' Quillon said, turning away before Agraffe could press him on the matter.

He delved into the work again, cleaning and cutting, sewing and sawing, doing his best with the limited tools at his disposal. The sounds of battle had faded some time ago; he could not say exactly when he had heard the last shot or the last scream or had the last injured man delivered to his care. Occasionally there was a rumble from below, as of distant thunder, but *Painted Lady* sailed on oblivious. The zone had cost her much – stripped her of the very essence of what she had once been – and the battle had cost her even more in terms of her living crew. But she had endured, and the winds were still guiding her to her destination.

When he had done all he could, he disposed of his bloodied apron, washed his hands and returned to the bridge. He supposed that it had been no more than an hour and a half since he had last stood here, but such a span of time now seemed ludicrously short for the events it was required to contain.

Before he had said a word, or had his presence acknowledged, he saw Spearpoint. Curtana had the armoured shutters flung wide for maximum forward view. The sun had shifted, and now the light falling on his city had the lambent, beaten-gold quality of late afternoon. It was so huge, so stupefyingly tall, so hypnotically dense with teeming human poten-tial that it stole his breath away. He had never seen it like this. Even when he was an angel he had never strayed far from the friendly thermals of the Celestial Levels, and when he had fled the city with Meroka he had not allowed himself to look back until they had set up camp, by which point Spearpoint had been much more distant. But now it filled half the sky, and it was drawing nearer by the second, and he knew he would never be able to leave it again.

'I think that's the ledge where Tulwar wants us,' Curtana said. 'Right, Meroka?'

Meroka nodded. 'Dead ahead, almost level? That's your landing spot.' She was grubby-faced from the turret's fumes, except around her eyes, where she had been wearing goggles. 'Hey, Cutter. Heard they've been keeping you busy in the operating theatre.'

'I did what I could.'

'Did anyone else die on you back there?' Curtana asked.

He grimaced at her tone. 'I'm afraid you might have to wait a little longer for more ballast to shed.'

'Thermals should start picking us up as soon as we reach the base.' Into the speaking tube she said, 'I want everything that isn't breathing overboard now. Even if it's still working. Guns, instruments, clocks, maps and almanacs, they all go. No matter how ancient and valuable.'

'Will that do?' Quillon asked, as she hung the tube back on its hook.

'It's all we've got left. If I could get everyone up in the envelope and cut the gondola loose, I'd do it. Hell, if I thought I was surplus mass I'd throw myself off first.'

'I believe you.'

He felt the change from one breath to the next, the first hint of the slow unclenching of the fist that had been locked around his skull since they had entered the zone. Curtana looked at him, waiting for his acknowledgement that he had felt the same thing she had, and that it was not merely wishful thinking. He nodded once.

'It lasted longer than I expected.'

'Tulwar did the best he could,' Curtana said. 'If we hadn't been fore-warned, the Skullboys would be picking through our bones about now. Is there anything you need to do?'

'There's no point making any medical decisions until we know we're completely through the boundary. But if the conditions on the other side are similar to those we were experiencing before, the crew should be able to carry on without any additional medication from me.'

'That's good. You'll have your hands full with the injured.' She hesi-tated, and something of her usual humanity – the Curtana who existed when she was not fighting wars – broke through the facade of military callousness. 'What I said earlier, about any of them dying—'

'You didn't mean it. I know.'

'Actually, I *did* mean it, more or less. But it was the wrong thing to say to you, and I'm sorry for that.' She angled her head to sight through the window, judging their approach vector and gradient. 'Gas crews – five-second vent from aft cell,' she said into the speaking tube, then to Quillon, 'One second we're too high, the next we're too low. If we don't hit that ledge square on, we've had it.'

'You've done well to get us this far.'

Curtana sneered. 'As if that counts.'

'How are the other ships?'

'*Cinnabar*'s down with all hands. *Iron Prominent* is with us, but they're still mopping up Skullboys. The rest of Swarm's hanging back on the other side of the zone. They won't cross until we've taken the sting out of the enemy.' She let out a small, astonished laugh. 'Fear and panic, I never thought I'd see this day. Spearpoint looming out of the ground like God's own hard-on and I'm actually *hoping we get there*. Not long ago I'd have thrown myself into a propeller for thinking this way.'

'You had your reasons. But whatever that thing is, it's not the Spearpoint you used to hate. It's something else, something different.'

'Nimcha couldn't have known what she was starting.'

'I think she knew a lot more than she's ever likely to admit – to us, at least,' Quillon said.

'You'd better go back and see how they're doing.'

'Is there anything more I can do for the ship?'

'Keep some of those wounded men alive and you'll have more than earned your keep. We're not out of the woods yet, though, just so you know.'

'I appreciate the dangers.'

'Tulwar's been in touch. They're ready and waiting for us, and doing what they can to keep the Skulls occupied on the lower ledges. But we can still expect some resistance.'

'We'll get through it.'

Without warning the gondola nosed up. 'Thermals starting to kick in,' Curtana said. 'We're over ... what's that squalid-looking place below?'

'Horsetown. And it's not nearly as bad as it looks from up here.'

'Actually,' Meroka said, 'it's worse.'

'It's going to get bumpy from now on – prevailing winds hit the updraught and you get some interesting turbulence. A big ship like this, you wouldn't think the air could toss it around like a ball, but it will.'

'Is there anything you can do?'

'Pray really hard.'

He left her to her work, certain that Curtana still had some control over their destiny and that no one was better equipped to make use of that control. Nimcha and Kalis were waiting where he had left them, both of them unhurt, although visibly rattled by what they had been through. He told them that they were very close to Spearpoint now, and – without wishing to cause them further distress – that all would hinge on what happened in the next hour. The thermals continued to buffet the ship, lurching her up and down, the nausea of motion sickness beginning to push aside the last, drowsy remnants of zone sickness. The mother and child had adjusted well to the transition, and despite their apprehension and discomfort it was at least a blessing that they were no longer required to breathe bottled air.

'You must feel glad,' Kalis said. 'To be returning to your city, when you must have thought that would never happen.'

'I left the city because certain people were planning to murder me,' Quillon explained gently. 'The same people who did murder – or at least sanctioned the killing of – someone very close to me. None of that's changed. My enemies are still there. I may or may not still be of the same interest to them, but you can be sure they haven't suddenly decided to let bygones be bygones.'

'Will they kill you?' Nimcha asked guilelessly.

'Hopefully they'll accept me for what I am, not what I was. That's all we can ever hope for, isn't it?' He tried to raise a smile from Nimcha, but the effort was wasted. 'Anyway, I don't feel the same way I did when I left. I had very few friends then. Now I feel like I have an army at my side.'

Something pinged against the bottom of the gondola, making them all start. It sounded as if the shot had struck immediately under their feet, but Quillon knew how easily noises could carry from one part of the metal frame to another. 'It's to be expected,' he said. 'The Skullboys have control of the lower parts of the city and they don't want us to land. But they won't stop us.'

It was easy to sound that confident; less easy to believe it in his heart. That they had got this far did not give them an automatic guarantee of success. The world did not work like that. It took pleasure in punishing the cocksure.

'I'd best see to the wounded,' Quillon said, standing unsteadily as another thermal pitched the floor.

'Did many die?' Kalis asked.

He nodded. 'We're lucky to be alive. *Cinnabar* didn't make it, and *Iron Prominent* took even heavier losses than we did.'

'She brings luck and death,' Kalis said. 'That is what they always said of the tectomancer.'

'They were foolish and ignorant,' Quillon replied. 'She's just a girl with some unusual inheritance factors, that's all.'

He visited the patients, made a cursory inspection, adjusted a dressing here or a splint there, but their status was the same as before. The men were all on stretchers, ready to be lifted down to safety. He already had his suspicions about who would live and who would die, but even his most optimistic forecasts were contingent on conveying the wounded to Neon Heights. Here there were too many sick men in too small a place, the air itself beginning to thicken with disease and corruption.

By the time he returned to the bridge shots were ringing against the gondola every few seconds. They were coming up from the ledge below them, where the Skullboys had control. The target ledge was very close now: he could even see tiny figures near the edge, with wave upon wave of dark-windowed buildings rising behind them, jostling for space and height until they met the soaring edifice supporting the next ledge above. He saw roads and bridges, and more people moving on them, but no slot-cars, slot-buses, trains, funiculars or elevators. Tulwar had mentioned electricity, but there was obviously so little of it to go around that most of Neon Heights was still without power, pushed back to the level of Horsetown, only without the benefit of horses.

'Less than half a league now,' Curtana said. 'We're slowing, though. The wind's losing its effectiveness, meeting the city. I just hope we've got enough drift to carry us all the way in.'

'And if we don't?' Quillon asked, shocked that it had all come down to something so utterly arbitrary.

'We only have to get close, that's all. Then we can grapple in.'

'How close?'

'Best that you don't know, Doctor, otherwise you'll be a nervous wreck.'

'And we wouldn't want that to happen,' Quillon said.

He willed the city closer, striving to blot the sound of gunfire from his mind. The shots were intensifying the closer they got to the landing point. The Skullboys must have occupied the tallest buildings on the underlying ledge, meaning that they had less distance to shoot across as *Painted Lady* drew nearer to her destination. With her own guns now all but derelict, *Painted Lady*'s crew had few options for retaliation. Airmen were firing muskets and crossbows down from the walkways and engine struts, but achieved little. The incoming bullets could be withstood: most of them ricocheted off the gondola's heavy under-plating, or punched harmlessly through the envelope, never touching a gas cell. But then came the rockets, streaking up from rooftops on pillars of zigzagging flame. They were little more than fireworks converted into crude incendiary devices, most of them missing the airship even if they struggled to her altitude. But again the distance they had to span was lessening, and the proportion of misses was decreasing. 'The fuckers,' he heard Curtana say – he knew there was nothing an airman feared more than fire.

By then the wind had pushed *Painted Lady* almost side-on to the ledge, all vestiges of aerodynamic control surrendered. In the dense and darkling sprawl of buildings it was difficult to see where Curtana intended to put her down, assuming she had ever allowed herself the luxury of thinking that far ahead. On the roads, promenades and squares between the structures people were massing in bewildering numbers, drawn by the spectacle. Some of them held torches against the gathering gloom of dusk, creating feeble pools of moving light. Quillon wondered why Tulwar wasn't keeping them free of possible landing sites, then reminded himself that no one, not even Tulwar, had that authority now.

There was a bell-like clang, quite distinct from the impact of a bullet, as a rocket glanced against the underside of the gondola. It might have been a lucky shot, but there was no doubt that *Painted Lady* had fallen within range of the Skullboys. Quillon tensed, realising that it now required an effort of will to keep breathing normally. In his estimation less than a quarter of a league now separated them from the ledge. As if in recognition of this, the massed citizenry were beginning to fan back from the square that now lay directly ahead. Buildings hemmed it from either side, surely squeezed too tightly together for the airship ever to fit between them. Not that fitting really mattered now, Quillon decided. It would be enough if *Painted Lady* rammed herself home, even if the impact mangled her once-proud frame.

Another rocket struck home, this one with more ferocity.

'Don't you have any defence against these?' Quillon asked.

'We do, actually. It's called not ever getting in range of Skullboy rockets. Normally it works pretty well for us.'

'What will happen if they hit the envelope?'

'It'll burn,' Curtana said. She turned to Poitrel. 'Grappling teams ready?'

'All at station,' he answered.

'They'd better not mess this up. We'll get maybe one chance before the thermals push us up and out again, and I don't fancy our hopes of ever finding our way back to Spearpoint without engines.' She reached for the speaking tube, wiping dried spit from her mouth before bringing it to her lips. 'Curtana here. This might be my final announcement as captain of *Painted Lady*, so I'll keep it brief. We're coming in fast, so I can't promise you an easy stroll to the ground or a smooth docking. A crowd of good people down there want our medicines very badly, but we can't just hand them out like candies. The supplies have to go through Tulwar's distribution network so that they reach everyone who needs them, not just those within grabbing distance. We have sick and injured to offload and hospitalise. It's going to take discipline and organisation and the best damned crew in Swarm working like a well-oiled machine. The ship's done us proud to get us this far. Let's show her what she meant to us.'

She hung up the speaking tube.

'If that doesn't do it, nothing will,' Quillon said.

A rocket slammed past the gondola, its tail still spitting fire. He could hear the crowd now, the massed roar of all those people waiting on the ledge, the crackle of guns as men directed fire down onto the Skullboys.

'The ship won't be the safest or most secure place once we're grappled in,' Curtana said.

'Meaning what?'

405

'You've done your bit for us. You shouldn't feel obliged to put yourself at further risk.'

'Am I still the surgeon on this mission?'

'You haven't been formally discharged from duty.'

'Then I will continue to perform those duties, if you have no objection.'

She gave him a smile, cracked at the edges with fatigue. 'None whatsoever, Doctor Quillon.'

'It's not as if I'm going to be massively popular down there when they find out what I am.'

'They'll adapt. We did, in the end.' She looked through the gondola's side window, the ledge – which had looked so far away for so long – now rushing closer like a black tidal wave, a froth of tiny figures massing at its crest. At the last minute, a side-gust began to rotate the airship again, bringing the ledge back into the forward windows. Curtana must have been out of options, but still she could not relinquish her grip on the controls. 'One hundred spans,' she said, in not much more than a whisper, estimating their distance by eye. 'Fifty.'

Quillon felt a soft fist grab the ship and begin arresting its forward drift. He had to grab a handhold to remain standing.

'Grapples ... *now*,' Curtana said, but she was not issuing an order, merely voicing a prayer. The task of firing the grappling lines, Quillon surmised, required such expert timing and aim from the individual teams that it could never be directed from the bridge. Perhaps for the last time, Curtana had placed her utmost faith in the ability of her crew.

The grappling lines sang out, whipping through the air as their spring-loaded launchers were released. The first fell short, its iron fingers scratching down the black wall of the shelf. There would not be time to reel it in, re-arm the launcher and try again. But the second found its mark, the grapple tangling with railings, the line tautening as the grappling crews worked the manual windlasses. The third whipped out and overshot the railings, crashing down in what looked like the middle of the crowd.

'I told them to clear us a landing zone,' Curtana said dolefully, as if it was no more or less than she had expected. 'I told them that if there were too many people, it was going to get messy.'

'They'd be dead in a month anyway, if we hadn't come,' Quillon said.

'That's very pragmatic, Doctor. I think you've spent too much time with us.'

Now *Painted Lady* had lost all forward motion, and for a moment she hung in space, serenely becalmed, separated from the ledge by little more than her own length. A brave man could have crossed the gap hand-over-hand. Then winds began to tug her away from Spearpoint, and the lines, which were already taut, instantly became as rigid as iron cables. The railing began to buckle outwards under the load. Even in the gondola, Quillon heard the creak and groan as the windlasses resisted the tension. Then the grapple ripped itself free of the railing, dragging its horrible cargo with it, and *Painted Lady* jerked viciously as the second grapple took her entire burden. He watched the claw slide down the railing, the railing bowing out in a sinuous curve as it struggled to hold the airship. For a moment he was struck by the sure and certain knowledge that they were going to fail. Then two more grappling lines whipped out and found their mark, and the airship was once again secured. The lines were tightened and then began to haul in *Painted Lady*. The pace was excruciatingly slow, for the only motive power now available was human muscle. But though the winds continued to buffet her, Quillon finally dared to believe that she was safe.

'You did it,' he told Curtana, when he had seen another two grappling lines be deployed. 'You got us here. You got us to Spearpoint.'

'We're not touching dirt yet,' she said, as irked as if he had broken some sacred taboo of airmanship.

'You can't take any pleasure in this, can you? I suppose if you still had the ship in one piece it might be different.'

'I'll worry about *Painted Lady*. You worry about the sick men and the Serum-15. I want the crates ready to be lowered in sixty seconds. The mission's not over until we've delivered our cargo. Understood?'

'Of course.'

Those able-bodied airmen who were not already manning the windlasses were beginning to gather in the gondola, some of them bearing stretchers, others hefting the cupboard-sized medicine crates, ready to lower them down through the belly hatch as soon as they were over solid ground. The medicine crates, Quillon realised, were one of the few commodities that hadn't already been thrown overboard to lighten the load. He took a crate himself and stood back from the belly hatch as an airman let it hinge down, revealing a rectangle of distant rooftops. The Skullboys were still down there, still firing guns and rockets, but it would take extraordinary luck for one of them to find that tiny open door in the gondola's underside. Nonetheless Quillon kept well back from the edge, willing time to pass more quickly. The rooftops were sliding by, but the rate at which the airship was being hauled in was agonisingly slow.

Then, suddenly, the black wall of the ledge began to hove into view, and as suddenly again they were over the buckled railing, the gondola's lowered hatch almost scraping the top of it as they came in. Whatever altitude she had been at when the grapples were fired, the tautening lines had brought the gondola almost level with the square. They were passing over a seething mob of people now, hands reaching up to grab at anything that came within reach. The roar from the crowd was overwhelming, but there was more to it than simple jubilation. There was something frayed and desperate about it, something that could turn the crowd into a frenzied, indiscriminate mob at the tiniest provocation.

Now ropes were being dropped down from the gondola and engine struts to augment the grapples. The airship came to a sudden halt, almost knocking Quillon off his feet and through the open hatch. Either the windlasses were tight or the envelope had jammed against the surrounding buildings. He supposed that it didn't matter much now. With the anchor lines tight and the gas cells still providing some lift, the gondola was safe for the time being.

The crowd was clearing around a party of red-hatted militia approaching the belly-hatch. They had guns, aimed at the sky, but ready to be brought to bear on anyone hindering their progress. Behind them, clearing a wider swathe, came a steam-powered truck with another group of armed men riding on its running boards. The militia cleared a circle under the gondola, forcing back the crowd with threatening jabs of their guns. The crowd capitulated without much fuss, even clearing a path of their own volition to allow the truck to halt just beneath the open hatch.

Curtana emerged from the bridge, grabbed a loaded double-barrelled pistol from the armoury rack, tugged back its paired flint-tipped hammers and swung down onto the ladder, holding on with one hand and grasping the pistol in the other. She tried to say something to the red-hatted men, but she couldn't make herself heard over the crowd. Gritting her teeth, she aimed the pistol at the sky, angling her shot so that it would skim past the envelope. She fired.

The crowd subsided into an uneasy, belligerent silence.

'I'm Captain Curtana. Where's Tulwar?'

One of the red-hatted men spoke up. 'Tulwar can't make it.'

'He was meant to be here.'

'He's having medical issues. He said to bring you to the Red Dragon Bathhouse.'

'Just like that? On trust? Us not knowing who the hell any of you are?'

'My name is Kargas,' said the red-hatted man. 'You'll have to be satisfied with that for now. Do you have the medicines?'

'Got the advance supply here,' Curtana said. 'It'll have to tide you over for now. I take it you've got a distribution plan in place?'

'Tulwar's got it all worked out,' Kargas said. 'There are local bosses for every district, every quarter. They've all been allocated consignments, depending on how many people are under them. No one goes without.'

'So there'll be no skimming, and none of the medicines will ever turn up on the black market?' Curtana said.

'I won't make promises I can't keep. This is a city without a government. Things get porous. All I can tell you is that if you hand over those medicines, Tulwar and the rest of us will do our damndest to make sure most of them get to the people who need them.'

'You think I came halfway around the world for that half-assed plan?'

'We're doing the best we can.'

'I think we should take the man at his word,' Quillon said in a low voice. 'There'll never be absolute guarantees, so he's just being honest with us. At some point we just have to decide to trust someone.'

Curtana still looked dubious. 'I'll need some assurances on my side.'

'Go ahead,' Kargas said.

'Got a lot of injured people here. I want them taken somewhere to rest and be looked after. Any hospitals still open for business?'

'Hospitals are ... not doing too well. Most of them don't have lights, power, hot running water or anything much resembling trained medical staff. Frankly, your people would be just as well off at the bathhouse. They can be treated there, and it's safe and clean.'

'I've been there,' Quillon confided in a near-whisper. 'I can't vouch for the safe part, but it looked clean enough.'

'You got any more of those trucks?' Curtana called down.

'Two more waiting to move in as soon as this one's loaded,' Kargas said.

'I'll send down four crates as a goodwill gesture, but that's your lot until all my injured are on that first truck, along with my doctor.'

'We need those medicines.'

'And you'll get them, as soon as I'm convinced that my people are safe. I'm sorry some Spearpointers got hurt when we grappled in, but if anyone even lays a finger on one of my crew I'll smash the rest of the crates before you can blink.'

'Your people will be safe. But just give us the medicines as quickly as you can.'

Curtana nodded at Quillon. 'Lower down the injured. And get someone to bring Kalis and Nimcha. Are you all right about going with them, Doctor?'

'I have to deal with Tulwar sooner or later.'

'Make that two of us,' Meroka said, pushing alongside him.

'Send word back as soon as you get to the bathhouse,' Curtana said. 'I'll join you as soon as the ship's secured.'

'Ever the captain,' Quillon said with a ghost of a smile, hoping she'd take it for the compliment he intended.

Even with the best of preparations, it was not an easy matter to lower the injured airmen onto the back of the truck. The militia did their best, as did Quillon and the rest of the able-bodied crew, but there was no way to avoid causing some discomfort. If anything, though, their grunts and groans at least served to demonstrate that *Painted Lady* had paid a heavy price to deliver her cargo. Quillon hoped it would convince the Spearpointers that they had not been alone in their suffering, even if Swarm's time of hardship had come late in the day.

Before leaving the airship he shrugged on a heavy coat, disguising – as best he could – his wing-buds. He put on airmen's goggles and his hat. Then he shimmied down the ladder and helped with the arranging and securing of the stretchers, satisfying himself that none of the broken limbs had suffered any grave displacement during the unloading process. Meroka came next. Then came Kalis, wearing an airman's coat and a hat to hide her tattoo, little about her to mark her as being anything other than an ordinary member of the crew. Meroka helped her down, and then both women assisted Nimcha. Then came the four crates Curtana had promised. Kargas levered the lid off one and inspected the straw-packed vials of Serum-15.

He lifted one of the vials up for inspection. 'I'm no doctor—'

'But I am, and the medicine's real,' Quillon said. 'It needs five-to-one dilution, but once that's done you can use it the same way you'd use Morphax-55.'

'That's a Spearpoint accent.'

'Neon Heights,' Quillon said. 'Isn't that reason enough to trust me?'

'That would depend on how you ended up with Swarm.'

'The same way you got mixed up with Tulwar, I suspect – something that worked for me at the time.'

'Who're the women with the kid?'

'Friends of mine,' Quillon said, as Kalis turned to look at Kargas with fierce interest. 'Who also happen to be patients under my care. Now can we get on to this place you mentioned? The bathhouse?'

Kargas gestured at the driver, who eased the hissing machine into motion and began to carve a path through the crowds. Quillon looked back at the gondola, meeting Curtana's eyes for an instant, a world of understanding passing between them. It was entirely possible that they would never meet again, given what had happened to Spearpoint. Things had become porous. But neither owed anything to the other. Quillon had served the ship, and Curtana had fulfilled her part of the bargain by getting them this far. If they parted now it was as equals and friends, bound by comradeship and shared experience rather than duty and obligation. He hoped they would meet again, and soon. But he knew they could not count on it.

As the truck worked through the crowds, Tulwar's militia had to keep fighting off people who were trying to climb aboard for the medicine, jabbing at them with the butts of their rifles, or firing warning shots just above their heads. Once, a claw of a hand closed around Quillon's sleeve and threatened to pull him into the mass. Kargas seized him, his quick reflexes probably saving Quillon's life.

'They're not bad people,' Kargas said, as he pulled Quillon back from the brink, 'but they've been through hell.'

'If I'd been in Spearpoint when the storm hit, I'd be down there with them now.'

'If you'd lasted this long,' Kargas said. 'It's been difficult. We've all lost good friends, people whose zone tolerance wasn't great to begin with. It hit them worst of all.'

'Things will get better now,' Quillon replied.

'For the time being. Don't get me wrong: we're grateful for any assistance. But medicines will only last so long, and then we'll be back where we started. For a while we held out hope that the zones were going to revert, snap back the way they used to be. It's becoming increasingly difficult to believe that'll ever happen now. This is starting to feel like something we have to get used to.'

Quillon tried not to glance at Nimcha as he spoke. 'We'll do what we can.'

As they pushed towards the edge of the square, away from the shelf's edge, the other two trucks were moving to receive the rest of the medicine. Quillon looked back to see one of them park under the gondola, the crates being handed down via an efficient chain of arms from man to man. It was only now that he saw exactly what had become of *Painted Lady*, how precariously, with what devastating finality, she had come to rest. The envelope was jammed between buildings, the armoured fabric tearing back along the sides to reveal grotesque anatomical mysteries: the circular stiffening rings, the riblike scaffolding of lateral spars, the soft and vulnerable interior of lifting cells, strung out along her gashed length like a chain of dark lungs, some of them still inflated, others sagging and useless. The engine struts, long since unburdened of engines, were buckled back from the gondola at almost ninety degrees. The empennage, the great bulbous flaring of her tailpiece, was still jutting into space. The empennage was on fire.

The empennage was on fire.

Quillon must have realised it in the same instant as the crowd. He had not thought it possible that the roaring mass could make any more noise than it was already producing, until he heard the screams. The people began to surge away from the airship, bright tatters of burning fabric already beginning to rain down on them, the flames consuming more and more of *Painted Lady*'s tail. At first there was room for the people to move, but then some began to fall, and in the confusion others trampled and tripped over them, and then there was only a swarming, squirming chaos. By that point the airmen in the gondola must have known what was happening. Quillon saw them exiting the side doors onto the railed balcony. They were moving quickly but without obvious panic, lowering ladders and ropes, some of them climbing down, others taking their chances and jumping. The flames had all but skinned the empennage now, leaving only a burning skeleton outlined against the darkening sky, the spars and struts picked out in a flickering blue-orange nimbus. The flames were steadily working their way forwards, already beginning to lick at the envelope immediately over the rear part of the gondola. The medicines were still being lowered down from the belly-hatch: more hastily now, almost being thrown from man to man, but still with order and discipline. The first truck was almost loaded, the second waiting to move into position. The rear quarter of *Painted Lady* was beginning to sag as the heated metal lost integrity. Curtana kept appearing at the top of the hatch, lowering crates to the man below her. 'Get out,' Quillon mouthed to himself. 'This isn't worth dying for.' Each crate was precious, but a few more wouldn't make any practical difference to the welfare of the Spearpointers.

Not that Curtana appeared to see it that way. They were lobbing the crates down now, one after the other, but she wasn't going to leave the job unfinished. For all that he had his injured to look after, for all that he felt protective of Kalis and Nimcha, the only place he wanted to be was back in the gondola, either helping her or throwing her out through the hatch with the crates.

Above the roaring and screaming of the crowd came a new and entirely inhuman sound of distress, an agonised metallic groaning. The rear quarter of the ship was breaking off completely. He watched the spars buckle and snap one by one. Then it was falling, slow as a dream, dropping away into the void beyond the edge of the shelf. He wondered

412

if it might fall onto the Skullboys and for a moment hoped that it would. Then he thought of them writhing in fire and knew there were things he would not wish even on his enemies.

The rest of the airship, suddenly unbalanced, tipped forwards, bringing the gondola closer to the ground. But the buildings were still pinning the envelope in place, at least until the fires took the rest of her. He couldn't see the hatch now that the angle of the gondola had changed – the crowd was in his way. But the fires were already wreathing much of the envelope and beginning to lick down onto the metal plating and armour of the gondola.

'Get out,' he said again.

And then the truck swerved between buildings and the city snatched the burning airship from view.

CHAPTER TWENTY-FIVE

Now that night was falling the city turned dark, with only the occasional fire or feebly burning light to suggest that anything resembling civilisation still had a hold on Spearpoint. They were driving through what had once been Steamville, before the storm rendered the old boundaries moot. Meroka had borrowed or wrestled a rifle from one of the militiamen and was jabbing it at every shape or shadow they passed. The majority of citizens had retreated indoors with the setting sun, leaving the streets to gangs of nocturnal scavengers and vastly outnumbered militia. Every other house or building appeared to have been gutted by fire, and there were wrecked steam-cars and -carriages on every street. The corpses of dead horses lay rotting under foul blankets, abandoned where they had fallen. There was a vile sewer smell in the air, enough to make Quillon want to gag. Part of him hoped he would never get used to it, because he did not ever want to feel that this was a normal condition to live in.

As far as he could judge, most of Spearpoint was like this. There were a handful of enclaves where electricity could still be made to work, and fewer still where anything like the technology of the Celestial Levels was still theoretically workable. But electricity was power, and power needed to be generated, and that required an able workforce. In the near-anarchy now prevailing throughout much of Spearpoint – the parts that weren't already anarchic no-go zones or urban battlegrounds on the edge of the Skullboy incursion – it was almost impossible to organise and motivate people to do their old jobs. That might change when the medicines became more widely available, and people no longer had to contend with the debilitating, mind-fogging effects of zone sickness. Until then the best that Steamville could manage was a few isolated blocks where basic power and amenities had been re-established. The Red Dragon Bathhouse was one such place, helped no doubt by the fact that it possessed its own steam supply. Apart from now being the only illuminated building on the street, it hadn't changed in any visible way when the truck delivered them to the main entrance. There were still people hanging around in front of it, drawn like flies to light. The paper lanterns were still burning, casting pastel ovals across the pale-green frontage. With all the dead horses lying around, Quillon didn't suppose that tallow was in short supply.

Kargas and the other militia established a cordon around the entrance, allowing the injured men to be stretchered inside, Kalis and Nimcha to enter unmolested, and for the crates to be safely unloaded. Quillon adjusted his coat before he stepped off the truck. There had been enough gloom under the gondola that he had not felt conspicuous, but he was certain now that the bulges of his wing-buds were showing through the fabric. Someone even pawed at his back as he walked up to the bath-house's portico, but whoever it was got a rifle butt in their face – possibly administered by Meroka – for their troubles. Quillon hoped they had just been after the coat, rather than curious as to what lay underneath it.

Then they were inside the steamy, perfumed haven of the bathhouse. He had found it oppressive before, but now he welcomed anything that might dispel the city's rank odours. There were fewer lights on inside than he remembered, but the bathhouse was clearly still functioning, and it still had clientele. Kargas led them to Madame Bistoury's office, at the end of the long corridor that also led to the cellar door. One of the waxlike girls came out of the office as they approached, ignoring them – because they were here on business, not pleasure – with expert insouciance. Madame Bistoury looked up from her double-entry accounting as they entered the office. 'Good of you to return to us, Doctor,' she said, masking any surprise she might have felt, as if Quillon had merely stepped out for a short stroll. She had recognised him instantly. 'And you too, Meroka ... how unexpected.'

'We liked it so much, we came back,' Meroka said.

'Quite,' Madame Bistoury said delicately. 'As you can see, the bath-house abides. We've endured more changes than almost any other institution in Spearpoint, and I don't doubt that we'll endure many more. Not to downplay the recent unpleasantness, you understand – this has certainly been one of the more troubling episodes in the bathhouse's history. But we've come through it, and thanks to your arrival there is a measure of hope for all of us.'

'What would you have done if we hadn't made it?' Quillon asked.

She gave a bored shrug, before making some tiny correction to her accounts. 'What we always do. Adapt.'

'We may have lost some of the medicines when the ship caught fire. And we still don't know how many of the other ships will get past the Skullboys.'

If Madame Bistoury had not already been informed of the fire, the news appeared to hold no great interest for her. She dipped her pen back into the inkstand. 'You'll be here to see Mister Tulwar, of course. That's to be expected. He's been very useful to us, there's no point in denying it.'

'Someone has to stoke the boiler,' Quillon said.

'Not in that sense. Mister Tulwar's business connections ...' She glanced at Kargas, perhaps thinking of the most politic way of phrasing her thoughts. 'Let's just say they've proven advantageous, in terms of guaranteeing the bathhouse's security during a ... challenging period. I always knew he was an influential man. I never quite grasped the *extent* of that influence. Perhaps he was a flower that needed darkness to bloom.'

'I take it he's still where I met him last time?'

'No. Mister Tulwar has gone up in the world, as befits his rising influence. Kargas will show you the way. And you mustn't be alarmed by what has happened to him.'

'We already know what happened to him,' Meroka said.

'I mean since. There've been changes. Some of us find them ... disquieting.' Again she glanced at Kargas. 'But Mister Tulwar doesn't like it when people stare or comment. And it's better for him now, not being confined to the boiler room.'

'I assure you that there is nothing in this world now capable of shocking me,' Quillon said.

'Something in your face tells me you aren't exaggerating. It was hard out there, wasn't it?'

'Challenging.'

Madame Bistoury withdrew her pen from the inkstand and looked at Kalis and then Nimcha, appearing to notice them for the first time. 'I don't believe we've met.'

'Kalis and her daughter Nimcha are friends of ours,' Quillon said.

'From beyond Spearpoint?'

He nodded, certain there was nothing to be gained from lying. 'We travelled together, and then found ourselves guests of Swarm. We've all been well looked after.'

'Your first visit to Spearpoint?' Madame Bistoury asked, directing her question not to Kalis but to Nimcha.

'Yes,' the girl answered.

416

'You must find it very strange.'

Nimcha seemed to give the question due consideration before answering. 'No.'

'But you've never seen anything like this, have you?'

'In my dreams,' the girl said. 'But in my dreams it was better. In my dreams it worked.'

'The city still works, after a fashion.'

'No, it doesn't. It's broken. It's been broken for ever and ever. But now it wants to make itself better.'

'These recent days must seem like for ever to a child,' Madame Bistoury observed, with an uncertain smile.

'I mean thousands of years,' Nimcha said.

'What an uncommon little girl.' She looked to Quillon for confirmation. 'She has a peculiar intensity about her, Doctor. She seems to look through me as if I'm made of smoke. I've never felt so utterly tenuous in all my life.'

'She's been through a lot,' Quillon said. 'It does that to you.'

'You've been through a lot as well. You look much thinner. More drawn and pale than I recall. Almost like a ghost of yourself.'

'There are sick and injured men in our care. I was told they'd be looked after here,' Quillon said.

'Naturally. Anything for our noble benefactors. I'll have the girls clear one of the floors; we can spare it presently. Do they have any particular medical needs?'

'I'll check on them later, but they should be well enough for now. Those that are able to sit up would undoubtedly appreciate food and drink, and perhaps some soap and water.'

'I'll see that it's arranged. In the meantime, you'll doubtless be wanting to speak to Tulwar?'

'Will you let us?' Quillon asked.

Madame Bistoury looked momentarily abashed. 'You don't need my permission, not if Mister Kargas is with you.'

'I'll show them through,' Kargas said. 'My men will bring the medicines and the injured airmen upstairs.'

'Very good.' Madame Bistoury leaned across the table to take Quillon's hand. 'I'm glad you returned to us, Doctor. Surprised, but glad. I knew you wouldn't forsake the city. We're all equally its children, aren't we? No matter where we come from.'

'No matter where,' Quillon said, waiting until she had released her grip on his hand.

'The mother and child may remain with me, if they have no business with Mister Tulwar.'

'We have business,' Kalis said resolutely.

They were led to another part of the bathhouse, on the same floor as Madame Bistoury's office but several twisting, windowless corridors away. The wood-panelled walls all looked alike to Quillon, and by the time they had arrived at the end of one of the corridors, facing a large pair of heavily framed double doors, he had lost all sense of direction. Music came from behind the doors, the repetitive notes of a simple tune played on brassy, piping instrumentation. Kargas knocked on one of the doors and a moment later it was opened slightly. Kargas spoke to the man on the other side, the music becoming louder through the gap between the doors. Steam was hardly in short supply in the bathhouse, but Quillon was still surprised by the quantity that came curling between the doors.

'He'll see us now,' Kargas said.

The doors were pulled wide. The room beyond must have been one of the largest in the bathhouse, even though its true dimensions were obscured by billowing steam, reaching all the way to the vague limit of the ceiling. Not just steam, Quillon corrected himself, for there was also the unmistakable smell of woodsmoke, even though the air had been heavily perfumed to disguise it.

'Come in,' a voice boomed over the music. 'Don't be shy.'

They stepped inside. Tulwar was waiting for them, standing like a fog-enshrouded statue somewhere near the middle of the room. Quillon wiped sweat from his brow with the end of his coat sleeve. From what he could make out, Tulwar hadn't changed in any obvious way. He was still a steam-driven cyborg, bulky around the lower body where his life-support system enclosed much of his torso, like a man wearing a kettle. His right eye was still missing, covered by a patch of iron, leather and wood. There were still plates in his skull. His left arm was still mechanical, and there was still a segmented cable trailing behind him. Quillon had the impression that he was standing more upright, with more strength in him, but that was the only outward change he was sure of.

'Doctor Quillon. I can't say you were the first person I was expecting to walk through that door. Or that Meroka would be the second. Ah, the endless capacity life has to surprise us.'

'It's good to see you,' Quillon said.

'You're lying, of course,' Tulwar answered, raising his voice over the music. 'No one ever thinks it's good to see me. What you mean is that it's useful and expedient that I survived; even more so that I appear to have retained some lingering influence in this godforsaken ruin of a city, because it will make the distribution of our medicines all the easier.'

'Doesn't that amount to the same thing?'

'Perhaps,' Tulwar conceded. 'And I shouldn't give the impression that I'm ungrateful for what you've done. None of us ever expected it of Swarm, let alone that you'd be involved. We'll talk about that later; I'm sure you've much to tell us. For now, let's say you must have exerted considerable persuasion.'

'They would have come to Spearpoint's assistance sooner or later,' Quillon said. 'They're not bad people, any more than we are. They just needed to let go of the past.'

'You speak of Swarm as if no one from it was present.'

'No one is, properly speaking.' Quillon indicated his companions. 'You know Meroka. Kalis and Nimcha became guests of Swarm, as did I. We've been treated well – practically given the rights of citizenship. But like me they were born outside it.'

'And they have something to do with the distribution of the medicine?'

'Not exactly,' Quillon said. 'But we'll get to them in a moment.' He peered beyond Tulwar, in the direction from which the music was coming. There was a bulky shape there, intermittently hidden and revealed by the steam. He kept having to wipe condensation from his goggles. 'I see you've made some alterations to your medical arrangements.'

'You noticed.'

'Hard not to,' Meroka said.

Tulwar took a difficult step towards them, the umbilical line stiffening behind him. With a creak of heavy iron wheels the calliope inched forwards.

'The old boiler developed a fault not long after the storm and I had to be unplugged at short notice. Rather than wait for it to be repaired – a procedure that, frankly, I wouldn't have survived – I had that infernal steam organ brought around to the back of the bathhouse. Negotiations of a somewhat one-sided nature ensued with the owner. I was plumbed in, thereby acquiring my own mobile steam supply. It's a far superior state of affairs in that I'm no longer confined to the basement. On the negative side of the ledger, there wasn't time to disconnect the music-making apparatus. I'm assured that it can be made silent at some later stage, but – to my considerable chagrin – that hasn't yet proven possible. The calliope must be kept stoked, and while there is steam pressure the music must of necessity play. Fortunately the repertoire may be varied now and then, meaning that I can listen to as many as twelve different tunes during the course of a day. One must be grateful for such mercies. I just wish that the gentleman who punched those twelve tracks into the cards had thought to make one of them cause the machine to play silently.'

'But in time, something can be done?' Quillon asked.

'Doubtless, provided I am willing to let someone tamper with the innards of the very mechanism keeping me alive. Which, presently, I am not. Nor am I willing to chance disconnection and re-attachment to the old boiler while they tinker around with this thing. I almost didn't survive it the first time, nearly died the second and don't rate my chances very highly for a third. For now I tolerate the calliope. Truth to tell, I do more than tolerate it. My enemies know about it now. It's begun to gain a certain notoriety. I'm told that grown men have been reduced to sobbing wrecks because they've heard music from the room next door, and think they're going to be sent to see me.'

'Take more than a rumour to do that,' Meroka said.

'I've had to exercise a firmness of hand, I won't deny it. The city was going to the dogs. If the angels didn't take us, the Skullboys would have. Someone had to step into that void and provide structure. I never expected that someone would be me. I would have been happy just to lie low and wait for someone else to save the day. But when no one stepped up, I realised I had a moral obligation to play my part. Cometh the hour, as they say.'

'What happened to Fray?' Meroka asked.

'Fray's dead. I'm sorry to break it to you like this, but you'd have found out sooner or later. He didn't make it through the first day of the storm. It was bad up there, all right? You know what kind of condition he was in before it happened. Not exactly built for endurance.'

Meroka sounded surprisingly matter of fact. 'How'd it happen?'

'He just died. It was very sudden, by all accounts. MMT. Ask the doctor – he'll tell you how it plays out.'

'Massive maladaptive trauma,' Quillon said. 'It makes sense, Meroka. His nervous system was in a bad way before any of this. In a sense, it would have been a blessing. Better than dying slowly of starvation, or because you've drunk infected water.'

'From what I've heard, MMT isn't exactly a nice, painless way to go.'

'It's quick,' Quillon said. 'Compared to the alternatives.'

'Fray was the kind of man we needed most,' Tulwar continued. 'I won't deny it. The best I can do is try to think the way he would have thought, do the things he would have done. I know I'm not doing anything like as good a job, but it's still better than nothing.'

'At least you've provided a framework for getting the drugs out to those who need them,' Quillon said.

'A framework, yes. And you've done your part by bringing the medicines here.' Concern flashed over his face. 'They're safe, aren't they?'

'What we managed to get aboard *Painted Lady* and then unload before she caught fire. I don't know about the other crates, or how the rest of Swarm's doing,' Quillon said.

'In a seller's market, anything is better than nothing. You've done very well. I'll see that you're rewarded for your efforts.'

'Believe me, reward's the last thing on my mind.' Quillon paused. 'Aren't you curious about the fire?'

'I was already informed. It's an unfortunate business. But then, what isn't?' Tulwar flashed a lop-sided smile before continuing. 'Now: your friends. You mentioned their names, but I confess they've slipped my mind.'

'I am Kalis,' the woman said. 'Nimcha is my daughter.'

'I was beginning to wonder if you were mute,' Tulwar said. 'Welcome, in any case. You'll both be taken care of. I can't promise you the luxuries that our city was once capable of furnishing, but you'll be kept safe and warm and well fed.'

'We do not seek your charity,' Kalis answered. She stood behind Nimcha, with one hand on her daughter's shoulder.

'They survived outside Spearpoint, under conditions at least as lawless as anything here,' Quillon explained. 'That's not to say that I don't want them properly cared for. But that isn't why I've brought them to see you.'

'It isn't?'

Quillon glanced at Tulwar's lieutenant. 'There's something delicate that we need to discuss.'

'Mister Kargas, would you be so kind as to leave us momentarily?'

Kargas was understandably indignant. 'They haven't been searched.'

'I trust them, just as I trust the doctor and Meroka. Dismiss the organmaster as well. Pressure will hold for a few minutes.'

'Very well,' Kargas said, making no effort to hide his displeasure.

When the doors had been closed and they were alone again – save for the still-piping calliope, churning through the same banal melody – Tulwar nodded once. 'Continue, Doctor. What is it that can only be entrusted to my ears alone?'

'I came here to save your city,' Nimcha said.

Tulwar seemed at least as unsettled by her answer as he was amused by it. 'Did you?'

'She's a tectomancer,' Quillon said.

Tulwar smiled again, but there was a quality of fading expectation in his smile, as if he had anticipated better of Quillon. 'Some would say they don't even exist.'

'They exist,' Quillon affirmed. 'But tectomancers are ... not what we imagined. There's much that we still don't understand about them – much that we may never understand. But I know this: there's something in her mother's blood, some cluster of inheritance factors, that has expressed itself in Nimcha. She has the mark. Show him, Nimcha: he won't harm you.'

Nimcha's hair had still not grown back where Spatha had cut it away. She presented her scalp to Tulwar. He took a step forwards, the calliope creaking behind him.

'It's just a red blemish on her skin,' he said.

Quillon nodded. 'Yes, but it's a perfectly formed blemish intended to mark her as one with a special, world-altering power. It's a symbol, not a disfigurement.'

'And this world-altering power is ...?'

'She can shift the zones. They bend to her will.' Quillon hesitated, mindful that it would be unwise to mention Nimcha's part in the storm that had brought Spearpoint to the edge of ruin. 'I've seen her do it,' he went on. 'She doesn't yet have full control of that power, but her ability's growing by the day. This isn't magic, Tulwar. It's just a kind of technology we don't understand any more.'

'Technology,' Tulwar said, as if the word itself had sordid implications.

'I don't know how or why it works. But I do know that Spearpoint isn't what we thought. It's not unique. We found another one in the middle of the Bane – smashed and lifeless, not at all like the city we know. But the underlying structure was unmistakable. Someone made these things for a purpose, and it wasn't just about giving us somewhere to live. And the tectomancers, the people like Nimcha, were in some way vital to that purpose.'

'Sounds a lot like guesswork to me.'

'Ricasso – Swarm's leader – and I saw the same symbol, the same baubled star, marked on the side of the structure. It must have been there for thousands of years, unseen by human eyes. Had anyone been able to live there, they would have covered it or worn it away almost as long ago. That's why we have no record of it here, except via the myth. *Had* we remembered, things might have been different.

Perhaps if we hadn't been persecuting people like Nimcha for so long – treating them like witches and mad women – we might have got somewhere.'

'Some would say the world works fine as it is, Doctor.'

'For some. But I've seen what it's like beyond Spearpoint, and now Spearpoint's had a taste of that as well. It can be better, though. Nimcha can put things back the way they were.'

'Before the storm?' Tulwar asked.

'I'm optimistic. So is Nimcha. The city's been calling to her, speaking to her on an almost telepathic level. She's linked to it by some bond, some communicational channel, something that can reach right through zone boundaries as if they don't exist.' He shrugged helplessly. 'I don't pretend to understand it, only to accept that it functions.'

'And the city wants what, exactly?'

'Spearpoint – or whatever Spearpoint really is – needs her to take control. Her powers work at a distance, but to be truly effective she needs to be here, as close to the Mire, even the Eye of God, as she can reasonably get.'

'She's pretty close already,' Tulwar said.

'It's not close enough for the city. It needs her to be nearer. I don't think it's trying to hurt her, but while she's not where she needs to be there's a deep-rooted conflict that's making her ill. For Nimcha's own good, I must see that this conflict is resolved. If that also works for the good of Spearpoint, all the better.'

'That's a lot to take on board, Doctor.'

'If there was another explanation, I'd embrace it willingly. But as I said, I've seen what she can do. I haven't suddenly started believing in witchcraft.'

'Meroka . . . is this on the level?'

'As apeshit as it sounds, yes. Cutter's telling the truth.'

Tulwar raised a finger, provisionally. 'Let's – for the moment – take what you've said as gospel. What exactly do you envisage happening next?'

'We get into the tunnels. Meroka knows the way.' He looked at her, inviting her to take over.

'They go plenty deep enough,' she said. 'Be a long walk, but we can manage that. There's a sub-shaft not far from the launderette entrance – that'll take us most of the way down.'

'To the Mire?' Tulwar asked.

'Near as anyone's going to get,' Meroka said.

'It's the only option,' Quillon said. 'We need to take Nimcha into those tunnels, Tulwar. But with the city the way it is now, only you can make that happen.'

'You've no idea what will transpire when you take her there.'

Quillon glanced at Kalis and Nimcha in turn, knowing that neither of them deserved easy consolation. 'I don't, no. But if she's precious to Spearpoint, it stands to reason it won't want to harm her.'

'And when it's finished with her?'

'She'll still be a tectomancer.' Quillon thought back to the conversation he had had with Ricasso, in the spotter balloon. 'Once, I think they were the masters. Spearpoint – whatever Spearpoint was – was just the instrument they controlled. The city remembers that. It wants – needs – a guiding hand. It needs a human mind to help it help itself. She'll still be valuable when the zones are put back the way they should be.'

'This must be done,' Kalis said.

'You're willing to see this happen to your daughter?' Tulwar asked.

'It is her desire as much as it is the city's,' Kalis answered. 'And I have seen how sick the city made her, when she could not answer its call. My mind is clear of doubt.'

'None of this has been taken lightly,' Quillon said. 'We've had the voyage back to Spearpoint to think it over. Our decision is already made. Now all we need is access to those tunnels.'

'Won't be a walk in the park,' Tulwar said.

'Don't like parks much anyway,' Meroka said.

'The angels have Circuit City now and they're making inroads into what used to be Neon Heights. My men are holding them back as well as they can, but Fray's entrance is slap bang in the middle of the battle.'

'The launderette entrance would make more sense,' Meroka said.

'No better, I'm afraid. Look, I'm not saying it's impossible. Just that you're not going to be able to stroll up to the Pink Peacock without a fight.'

'We're not afraid of that,' Quillon said.

'I don't doubt it. But logistical arrangements will need to be made. When are you thinking of going in?'

Quillon glanced at Meroka. 'How does right now sound?'

'Take a look in the mirror some time,' Tulwar told him. 'You're a walking shadow. Matter of fact, you all look like you could use a wash, some food and a decent night's sleep. Nothing's happening tonight, understood? I'll need to clear a safe route to one of the entrances and that means reinforcing my troops. At the moment

424

they're operating close to one of the new zone boundaries, which means I'm having to cycle them in and out before the sickness gets too bad. But now you've shown up with new medicines, I can put more men into the area.'

'The idea was to prioritise distribution to the citizens, not the militia,' Quillon said.

'Your call. You want access to that tunnel system badly enough, you're going to have to make some tough choices about resource allocation. Sleep on it.'

'If you issue the medicines, we can go in tomorrow?' Quillon asked.

'That'll depend on reports from the front line. If Nimcha – it is Nimcha, right? – is as precious to the city as you claim, I'm not going to commit her to the danger zone until I've got a cast-iron guarantee that it's secure for civilian passage.' Tulwar paused. 'I'll do what I can, all right? But tonight you rest here. Now someone go and bring Kargas and the stoker back in again.'

'What we've spoken of,' Quillon said. 'It stays a secret, understood? You know about the superstition surrounding tectomancers. We can't risk anyone finding out about Nimcha.'

'Nothing goes beyond this room. Kargas will have to know about the plans for entering the tunnel, but he doesn't need to know why. How many of Swarm know about this?'

'By the time we got to Spearpoint? Only a few people. Their leader, Ricasso; *Painted Lady*'s captain, Curtana; Curtana's second-in-command, Agraffe. They're all people I'd trust with my life.'

'Must have been hard work, keeping a lid on that. But then I suppose you've had lots of practice, Doctor Quillon, you being what you are. I'm assuming your companions know all about you.'

'They've accepted me for what I am.'

'Better hope the rest of the city follows their lead, because you're starting to stand out from the crowd.'

'I'm fortunate to be alive. I'll take whatever else is dished out to me.'

There was a knock at the doors. After a moment they opened, admitting Kargas. 'I'm sorry to interrupt,' he said, 'but they've brought Captain Curtana to the bathhouse. She survived the fire.'

Quillon smiled, momentarily relieved, but there was an edge in Kargas's voice that he couldn't ignore. 'But she's not unhurt.'

'You'd best see for yourself, Doctor. I've had her taken to the same floor as the other injured airmen. The good news is that she managed to get almost all of the medicine out in time.'

'Good, Kargas,' Tulwar said. 'You were right to bring this to our attention. I'm sure the doctor will want to be with Captain Curtana. We'd concluded our discussion in any case. It was very illuminating. Now would you be so kind as to order the organmaster to return? I need more steam. And while he's at it, have him change the God-damned tune; it's starting to piss me off even more than usual.'

CHAPTER TWENTY-SIX

Quillon, Meroka, Kalis and Nimcha ascended to the makeshift infirmary on the next floor, passing demure girls and sweating, sheepish clients on their way upstairs. It was dark outside now, with barely any sign that the city extended beyond the black panes of the windows. No lights, no fires, not even the subliminal urban hum of distant traffic and commerce, blocks or districts away. It felt exactly as if the bathhouse was afloat on a still, black sea, countless leagues from land and civilisation.

'Do you trust this man?' Kalis asked when they were safely out of earshot.

'I see no option but to trust him,' Quillon said. 'If Tulwar meant to betray us, he could have done so the last time we met. We can't always choose our allies, I'm afraid.'

'Cutter's got a point. Man helped us get out of Spearpoint.'

'What happened to him, to make him the way he is?'

'He got on the wrong side of the angels. And that, at least, gives us something in common.'

'Amen to that,' Meroka said.

'We may not like it, but it makes perfect sense for his militia to get the drugs ahead of everyone else. If it's that or see the city slide even further into chaos, the militia must take priority.' Quillon gave an awkward, self-justifying shrug. 'In any case, it's not as if we brought enough Serum-15 on *Painted Lady* to make more than a token difference to the citizens anyway. Mass treatment will have to wait until the other ships arrive. It's best that the limited supply we have now is given to those who can make the best use of it.'

'You say this, but you do not believe it in your heart.'

Quillon paused on the staircase, bile rising in his throat. 'What do you want me to say? That I don't think we should do everything we can to get Nimcha where she needs to be? I'm not superhuman, Kalis. No one handed me written instructions on how to do the right thing by you,

Nimcha, the city and her millions of citizens. I'm just trying to do my best, without a script, without any real idea who I can and can't trust, and in the sure and certain knowledge that I'll be torn limb from limb by just about anyone who discovers my true nature.'

Kalis looked down. 'I did not mean to criticise.'

He made an effort to soften his tone. 'This hasn't been easy for any of us, not least you and Nimcha. But if you don't think I can get you the rest of the way, you only have to tell me to stop trying to help and I'll gladly step aside. I'm sure there are thousands of sick people out there I could be treating this very moment, instead of trying to heal Spearpoint itself.'

'You are doing the right thing,' Kalis said.

'Yes,' Nimcha added. 'Please don't leave us, Doctor. I don't want to go into the tunnels without you.'

'We'll be all right,' Meroka said, giving her an affectionate squeeze on the arm.

'I do not know how far you will be able to come with us,' Kalis said. 'Even if you want to.'

'As far as the city lets me,' Meroka said. 'That's my promise to you.'

'The same goes for me,' Quillon added.

'As our doctor?' Nimcha asked.

'As your friend.' He paused and added, 'And doctor, of course. You don't get away from my medical services *that* easily. Speaking of which, we really should be on our way to see Curtana and the others.'

'Do you think she'll be all right?' Nimcha asked.

'I expect so,' he said.

But there was a tightening knot of trepidation in his chest as he answered.

An entire floor had been given over to the sick and wounded, with the patients spread throughout several rooms. Quillon collected his medical bag at the door to the largest, where it had been placed on a table waiting for him. The news was both better and worse than he had been expecting. Worse, because there were many more men and women who had received injuries of varying severity when the fires took *Painted Lady*. Better, because Agraffe's wounds were superficial, and better still because Curtana was not as badly burned as he had feared. They had placed her in a small room adjoining one of the larger rooms, a windowless chamber with a paper lantern hanging from the ceiling and elegant lacquerwork designs on the walls. Agraffe was there already, his hands bandaged, his cheekbones sooty, his eyebrows and downy effort at a beard singed, but otherwise unhurt.

'How are you?' Quillon asked, casting a critical eye over Agraffe's dressings.

'Burned my hands climbing down one of the ladders, but other than that I got off pretty lightly.' He looked down at the white-bandaged balls at the ends of his wrists. 'There are people here who know basic medicine – I think they've been looking after Tulwar's militia. They think I'll keep the use of my hands, although I have a feeling I'll probably need grafts.' Agraffe managed a philosophical smile. 'Whether anyone can perform grafts now is something I'd rather not think about.'

'I'm sure we'll find a way.'

Curtana had not been quite so fortunate. Quillon imagined her staying on the gondola until the bitter end, until there wasn't a medical crate left to unload.

'She wouldn't leave,' Agraffe said. 'Not until the last of the supplies were unloaded. By then half the gondola was on fire and the flame-retardant on the envelope was dripping off like hot wax. There were dead airmen on the floor, citizens and airmen screaming from their injuries. One of the connecting bulkheads jammed shut when the airship re-settled. In the confusion we lost contact with each other. I got out thinking I was the last one alive. I didn't realise she was still aboard.' He shook his head in regret and frustration. 'If I'd known—'

'There's no sense in thinking like that. You both stayed aboard long after I did. As far as I'm concerned, neither of you has anything to prove about your courage, least of all to me.'

'Do you think she'll be all right? They haven't told me much.'

Quillon appraised the unconscious form of the airship captain. 'Has she woken?'

'She was awake when they brought her here but they gave her something to put her under. She said she didn't need anything, but I knew she was in pain.'

Her right arm was bandaged from hand to elbow, her left to the shoulder. Another bandage encircled her head, covering her ears and forehead. Her hair spilled messily over the dressing. She breathed shallowly, lying on her side with her face turned away from her visitors. 'Is that the extent of her wounds?' Quillon asked quietly.

'I think so.'

Quillon set his medical bag by the side of the bed, opened it and sifted through the compartments for a pair of tweezers. Without waking Curtana – whatever they had given her had put her into deep unconsciousness – he began to undo the dressing on her left arm, peeling back the bandage to inspect the skin underneath. It was raw, but he did not think the burn had reached deeper than the surface tissue layers. Suspending judgement until he had examined the rest of her, he removed the dressing and applied a sterile salve from his bag. Then he called for a fresh bandage and wrapped the arm again. He repeated the procedure for the other arm. There were patches where the burn was more serious, but nothing that he considered life-threatening. There would be scarring, certainly, but he did not think grafts were warranted. He applied the salve, redid the dressing and began cautiously to examine her head wounds, breathing a private sigh of relief as he saw that the burns were not serious.

'She'll be all right,' he said in a near-whisper. 'I don't doubt that she was in pain, but she was also exhausted to the point of collapse from commanding the ship. If they gave her something to keep her asleep, they did well.'

Curtana stirred and murmured something. For a moment he thought she was returning to consciousness; but the moment passed and she subsided into restful silence.

'Thank you,' Agraffe said, attempting to clasp his bandaged hands together in his lap.

'You say most of the medicine was saved?'

'All but a couple of crates that caught fire or smashed. The rest, as far as I know, made it here intact. We'll need to run a proper inventory, of course, and make sure we've got enough clean water for the dilution. Have you spoken to Tulwar about the distribution programme?'

'That and the, um, other matter.'

'He speaks of Nimcha,' Kalis said, still standing by the door with her daughter in front of her.

'How did Tulwar take it?'

'Surprisingly well, all things considered,' said Quillon. 'He needed less persuasion than I'd expected. The medicines will be distributed fairly, with the advance supplies going to militia. It leaves a bad taste in my mouth, but I see no alternative. If the militia can hold back the angels in what used to be Neon Heights, we can get Nimcha into the tunnels.'

'And Tulwar understands what'll happen then?'

'I've told him what she can do,' Quillon answered. 'I'll leave it to him to work through the consequences. If all goes well, we may leave as early as tomorrow. I pushed for it to happen sooner, but Tulwar wasn't having it.'

'I'm sure you did your best. Any news on *Iron Prominent*, or the rest of Swarm?'

'Not since we landed.'

430

'Most of the ships don't have medicine, so there's no sense throwing them against the Skullboys, or risking a high-altitude approach. The others won't come in until the ground resistance has been at least partially neutralised – and that's not going to happen tonight.'

'Wouldn't night give them a practical advantage?' Quillon asked.

'In some respects,' Agraffe said, 'but not in others. You've seen how much trouble we had hitting those ground targets even when the sun was up. At night, it'll be harder still. The Skullboys won't be able to go ballooning so easily, but they'll still have their artillery positions and rockets. And as the ground cools, we'll lose even more lift. There's only so much ballast you can throw out. Anyway, it's not as if Ricasso's going to bring all the ships in anyway, not while there's a dead zone around Spearpoint. That would be the end of Swarm, and I don't think even he's prepared to go that far.'

'Perhaps it's time for Swarm and Spearpoint to reunite.'

'Reunion doesn't have to involve throwing away perfectly good ships, Doctor.'

'Perhaps it won't come to that. If Nimcha can put the zones back the way they were ...' Quillon trailed off, weariness washing over him. He clapped his hands and made an effort to sound energised. 'Now: to more immediate matters. I'd like to look at your dressings, if you'll let me. Afterwards I'll do what I can for the other men. And then, I think, I shall take Tulwar up on his invitation to be fed. You could probably use something to eat yourself, Agraffe. My recollection is that you were on duty for just as long as Curtana, and I didn't see you taking any rest either.'

Agraffe held up the useless white mittens of his bandaged hands. 'Eating's going to pose some difficulties, I'm afraid.'

'Not while you're amongst friends,' Quillon said.

It was close to midnight when Quillon decided that he had done all he could for the injured airmen; that while the survival of some might still be in jeopardy, nothing he could do now would make any tangible difference to the outcome. He packed his tools and medicines back into his bag, hands numb from overwork, eyes blurring with tiredness, and – although he lacked any great appetite – forced himself to join Meroka, Kalis, Agraffe and the others in the room that had been set aside for dining. It must have been over Tulwar's quarters, for repetitious, steam-driven music could occasionally be heard rising through the floor. The candlelit meal was a banquet compared to anything he had lately experienced aboard *Painted Lady*, the food – despite the prevailing hardships – prepared to a surprisingly high standard. It was perhaps best that the diners did not enquire too deeply into the nature and origin of the various heavily salted meats, or quiz the bathhouse cooks on how long those meats had been left to cure. The main thing was it all tasted good. Quillon nibbled for appearance's sake, washing down what little he consumed with pungent, purple-tinged wine. Nimcha, he learned, was already asleep, doubtless dreaming of things no one around the table could easily imagine. Meroka had washed, but he could still make out the dark margin around her eyes where she had been wearing goggles in the gun turret. Kalis was helping Agraffe with his food, cutting it for him and lifting it to his lips with a pearl-handled fork. The other airmen – there were no militia or civilians present – were caught between the euphoria of having made it to Spearpoint, and doleful reflection on the terrible price that had been paid by so many of their comrades. Everyone around the table knew they were fortunate to have made it this far; that, irrespective of whatever happened now, they had done something good and lasting for the city. Nothing could take that deed from them. But they were also fully aware that the main bulk of Swarm had yet to complete the crossing, and that there would be a similarly heavy toll on them.

At last the tired comrades began making excuses and left for the rooms that had been allocated to them. Meroka said she was going to check on Curtana before retiring. Quillon remained seated, until he was alone with Kalis.

'You wonder what I really think about my daughter,' she said, as Quillon sipped at the acrid remnants of the purple wine. 'Whether I can really love her, when I know what must be done.'

He shifted in his seat, finding a more comfortable position now that he did not need to worry about people seeing the bulges of his wing-buds.

'I've never doubted your love for her. Not once. Not for a moment.'

'I do not know what will happen to her.'

'No, but you've always known what would happen if she wasn't allowed to come here. Those bad dreams and convulsions wouldn't have gone away with time. They'd have become worse and worse, and eventually my medicines wouldn't have been able to stop them. She'd have died, Kalis – but not before enduring a great deal of suffering. You've done the only possible thing a mother can, which is to care for your daughter. Bringing her to Spearpoint was the only choice open to you. And now you have no choice but to finish the journey, come what may.'

'What if the city does something to her?'

He reached across the table to lay his hand on hers. 'It already has. But I meant what I said to Tulwar. The city needs her badly, which is why it's been calling her closer. But for that very same reason, the last thing it's going to do is hurt her now that she's arrived.'

'You want to make me feel better, but at the same time you do not wish to lie. Yet the truth is you have no idea what will happen.'

'I don't,' Quillon said, sighing. 'But I can always hope for the best. I think that's all any of us can do.'

'You will come with us, if we leave tomorrow?'

'As far as I'm able. Until the city won't let me go any further. You have my word.'

'Thank you.' She raised her head to look hard into his eyes. 'You are a good man, Doctor. You must never forget this.'

'Other men would have done just as much as me.'

'But there were no other men. There was only you, and your bag of medicines. You saved us, when you could have walked on. Then you made Swarm save this city.'

'Not yet,' he cautioned. 'There's still work to be done. No matter what happens tomorrow.'

'But the work has begun,' Kalis said. 'That is all that matters now.'

Quillon rose at dawn, feeling better for having slept, but still with a burden of tiredness that the rest had not alleviated. His wing-buds itched, as if there was some vigorous new phase of growth going on inside them. When he had washed and dressed he went out onto one of the bathhouse's balconies and stood with his hands resting on the flaking paint of the wooden railing. He had scrounged a cigarette from one of Tulwar's men and now smoked it gratefully.

At some point overnight it had rained, washing away the worst of the city smells that had dogged the district the night before. The air was cool and invigorating on his skin, perfumed with the faintest hint of woodsmoke. It was a bright, clear day, ideal for ballooning. The balcony faced outwards from Spearpoint, and by some stroke of fortune it also afforded him a view of the fleet. Swarm lay massing on the horizon. Even with the improved acuity of his eyes he could not identify the individual ships, or tell if their engines were still running. The best he could do was make out a dense knot of craft that he felt sure contained *Purple Emperor* somewhere near its heart. He thought of Ricasso somewhere in that congregation of airships and wished him luck. They would all need it.

'You frosty, Cutter?' Meroka asked, by way of greeting.

'Frosty as in ...?'

'Alert. Awake. Ready and able to deal with whatever shit the day's got in store in for us.'

'In that case, I'm frosty.'

'Too bad about *Iron Prominent*.'

'I didn't hear.'

'You will. Came in bad. Spilled her guts. Now it's an unholy free-for-all to see what they can save, before the Skulls get their shit-stinking hands on the meds.'

The news hit him like a punch to the abdomen.

'We need every drop.'

'Ain't nobody'd argue with you on that one, Cutter, least of all me. Matter of fact, I'm wondering whether I wouldn't be better off going down and seeing what I can do to help. But then another part of me says, fuck it, go with Cutter.'

'I suppose I ought to be flattered.'

'Don't be. I just don't want to see you screw this one up. Not with Nimcha and Kalis depending on you.'

'Then let's see what our host's managed to arrange for us.'

They re-entered the bathhouse and followed the throb of organ music until it brought them to Tulwar. He was standing – leaning – over a broken crate, his life-support umbilical straining behind him as he assumed an unnatural angle, sifting through straw and glassware, picking out the occasional broken flask and discarding it in an empty crate next to the straw-filled one.

'When all this is over,' Quillon said, 'I promise that I'll do what I can for you. There has to be a better way than this. Even if the best I can do is turn off the music.'

Tulwar dug an intact flask from the straw and held it up for inspection, entranced by the clear, valueless-looking fluid within it. 'Turn off the music and you'd start undermining my reputation.'

'No one would have to know.'

'No, you have a point there. They wouldn't.' He fell silent for a moment, sagging forwards on his feet as if his steam pressure had fallen catastrophically. Then he straightened and said, 'Guess Meroka filled you in on the bad news?'

'About *Iron Prominent*?'

'Not exactly what you'd call a textbook landing, that's for sure. Broke her back, ripped her gondola in half and dropped her cargo onto the roof of a building on the ledge below.' He shook his head, as if vivid

434

images were still playing behind his eyes. 'Skullboy rocket strike. She lost a lot of hands. When it was obvious that she was going down they managed to get the spotter balloon launched with some medicines aboard, but it's come down a few blocks up from here and my men haven't managed to get to it yet. Other than that . . .'

Quillon was willing to grieve for the crew, but only when he knew what had happened to her cargo of Serum-15.

'Aside from whatever's in the balloon, how much have we saved?'

'You're looking at the first crate out of there,' Tulwar said. 'Been a mad scramble to reach them before the Skullboys do. Fortunately they didn't have anyone on the roof of that building, or we'd have lost everything—'

'And?'

'We managed to lower men down on lines to secure the roof. Lost good men in the process, too: the Skulls don't give up without a fight. Judging by this crate, I'm afraid at least a third of the flasks didn't make it. You'll excuse me for taking a personal interest, but if these drugs have been contaminated, or sabotaged by the Skulls, I don't want them leaving this room.'

Quillon's mood see-sawed between crushing disappointment and blessed relief that they had been able to save anything. After the loss of *Cinnabar*, the drugs had become even more precious.

'Does Agraffe know what happened to his old ship?'

'I've informed him. Word is Curtana's a little more responsive this morning. I understand she took it stoically.'

'She always knew there'd be losses. She nearly didn't make it herself.'

Tulwar replaced the lid on the broken crate as best as he could. 'I suppose we should celebrate our successes rather than dwell on failure. The medicines you brought are already doing good, you'll be pleased to hear. They're in short supply, of course, but I've made sure they reached the men who needed them most.'

'I'll be glad to offer such help as I can when I return,' Quillon said.

'It will be received gratefully. And I have good news, I think. My men have secured the entrance to the tunnel complex at the Pink Peacock.'

'Is Malkin still running the joint?' Meroka asked.

'Not much of a "joint" to run, I'm afraid. There's no power, no running water, no clients. Kind of takes the edge off the happy-go-lucky party atmosphere. You knew Malkin well?'

She caught the past tense. 'He's dead as well?'

'He made it out, got all the way down to Second District before he was caught up in a food riot, or instigated it, for all I know. He'd been trampled to death. It wasn't pretty, the first few days – just dealing with the bodies was a major headache. We couldn't leave them lying around, and throwing them over the ledge was just passing the problem down to someone else. They take a lot longer to burn than you'd imagine.'

'You'd be surprised what I can imagine,' Meroka said.

'I'm sorry about Malkin. I didn't know him that well – that was Fray's turf, not mine – but by all accounts he had his uses. Still ... let's not dwell on what can't be put right. The important thing is that we have access to the Pink Peacock.' He corrected himself with a grimace. 'Or at least we do right now. The angels are responding with a renewed push of their own, so it's not clear how long we'll be able to hold that area, or provide a safe path through Neon Heights. If you want access to the tunnels, I'd say don't delay.'

'There's no reason why we should,' Quillon said. 'We don't need anything, except your help in getting to the entrance.'

'You sure about the launderette not being accessible?' Meroka asked. 'It's just that it'll make things a fuck of a lot easier for us once we're inside.'

'No, I'm afraid that area's quite unreachable now.'

'Then we'll take what we're given,' Meroka said.

At least Tulwar sounded pleased. 'That much I can arrange. After all you've done for us, it's the least I can offer in return. Do you really think this is going to work, Doctor Quillon? Do you really think she's going to make things better?'

'If she can't, no one else can.'

CHAPTER TWENTY-SEVEN

Meroka was on the truck before Quillon, working the mechanism of a rifle vigorously back and forth to free it up. She had one booted foot planted on a crate, the other on the bed of the truck, a hard, determined look on her face. Only a slight stiffness in her posture betrayed the fact that she had been recently wounded. *Let's get this done*, her expression seemed to say. No matter what the day might bring.

She used a free hand to help him up onto the back of the vehicle. His medical bag was slung over his shoulder: he had borrowed a belt from the Red Dragon Bathhouse and looped it through the bag's handle, so that he could keep both hands free. Four militiamen were already aboard the truck, in addition to those stationed around the perimeter of the bathhouse. 'Help yourself,' Meroka said, indicating an assortment of gleaming, oiled weapons laid out on top of a crate. 'They're all loaded and good to go.' Quillon picked up the smallest pistol he could see and dropped it into his coat pocket, trusting that with all the firepower around him, he would be very unlikely to have to make use of it. The morning air was cold, and black shadows lingered between the buildings. He still wore the goggles, trusting that if anyone wondered about them they would take them for an affectation, rather than a necessary element of disguise.

'Fine day to save the city,' Quillon said. 'I just wish Fray was here to help us.'

'Yeah,' Meroka said. 'It's a real pisser about Fray.' Then she clicked the rifle's mechanism again, grunted with something like satisfaction and slung it over her shoulder. 'Here they come.'

Kalis and Nimcha emerged, blinking in the half-light, led by two of Tulwar's men. They both wore heavy coats and airmen's hats. They were helped aboard without ceremony. Quillon wanted to say something reassuring to the mother and daughter, but when he searched for the right words all he could come up with was easy platitudes. None of them needed that now. They all knew what they were getting into, including Nimcha.

Signals were given and the truck hissed into motion. It picked up speed quickly, the militia cordon letting it through into the streets beyond the bathhouse. They only passed one vehicle going the other way, and that was also one of Tulwar's. The two crews slowed and exchanged brief words. Quillon saw two dented, battered crates on the rear platform, and guessed they'd been rescued from *Iron Prominent's* spilled cargo.

In daylight, even the brittle daylight of early morning, the city was even more of a wreck than Quillon had realised the night before. Night had hidden many things, not all of them welcome. Only a few blocks from the bathhouse, they passed a long line of hanged bodies, strung from makeshift gibbets. A little further on, a head had been spiked onto the top of a railing. Kalis moved to shield her daughter, but Nimcha was much too quick. She stared at the scene, expressionless.

'It's worse than we thought,' Quillon said.

'I know what you're thinking,' Meroka said. 'Is this fucked-up place really worth saving? But the answer's yes. Always and always. Because where else are we going to go?'

The truck bounced over cracks and bumps in the road. At one point the wheels rolled across a bulging tarpaulin, crunching whatever dead, decaying thing lay under it; at another intersection the truck had to ram its way past a steam-coach that had toppled over, forming what was either an innocent obstacle or an attempt at an ambush. The militiamen loosed a few shots into the shadowed doorways of buildings, but Quillon never saw anyone moving inside. In fact the only signs of life were the rats and cats scrabbling to escape the rolling wheels.

A long, laboured climb lay ahead of the truck even after it had crossed the old boundary into Neon Heights. Now the hinterland was just a strip of unusually pronounced desolation between equally squalid margins. The truck navigated backstreets until it passed the railway station where Quillon and Meroka had been forced to flee by taxi. Now the station was a burned-out ruin, its roof supports open to the sky like ribs. The few slot-cabs still outside were either blackened wrecks or had been tipped over on their sides, or both. There was garbage everywhere. Quillon spotted a hunched, dark-hooded figure picking through the detritus, but there were no other indications of inhabitation. The advertising billboards around the frontage had been torn or defaced where they were within easy reach, but their colours and slogans were still vivid, promoting products and services of questionable relevance, such as an improved brand of shaving cream, shoe polish and slot-car insurance. But Meroka was right, Quillon thought. They didn't have a choice about which city to save, so they might as well make the best of the one they had.

The truck had little option but to make most of its ascent the long way around, climbing the rising ledge. The steeper connecting ramps were either blocked, collapsed or not yet secured for safe passage, and none of the funicular vehicle-lifts was operating. The truck kept under the elevated legs of the railway line for most of its journey. By the time they reached Third District, more people were about, although most of them appeared unwilling to stray too far outside the buildings. A couple of shots clanged against the elevated structure, Meroka and the other riders returning fire, but not in any obvious expectation of hitting anyone. Once, they sloshed through the run-off of a waterfall cascading down from the next ledge. Quillon spotted a dismal huddle of men, women and children trying to collect what they could, with pots and pans and any other receptacles they could manage. No matter that the water had come from somewhere else in the city, somewhere that was probably just as filthy and disease-ridden as Neon Heights. In their shoes, Quillon supposed, he would have been forced to take the same chances. It was then that he realised that getting medicine to these people wasn't even going to be half the battle. It was going to be a tenth, or a hundredth part of it. But it was the one part that had to be in place before any other reconstruction could begin.

At last the truck arrived in what Quillon knew to be the old Fourth District. On the face of it, the streets didn't look any different from those they had already passed through. But the militiamen grew noticeably edgier and the driver picked his way with increased care, as if wary of booby traps and snares. Quillon, Kalis and Nimcha were encouraged to crouch as low down as they could. Quillon found his hand returning to the pocket where he had secreted the pistol. They no longer had the cover of the elevated railway line and were now easy prey for anyone taking potshots from the tall buildings on either side of the street.

Then he saw one of his own, flitting effortlessly across the gap between two tenements. He knew immediately that the creature was an angel. Like him, it lacked fully developed wings. Like him, it had been adapted to some degree for life in the lower levels. But the manner in which it moved spoke nothing of normal human physiology. This was a creature shaped not for infiltration but for occupation, probably very similar to the ghouls that had chased them out of Neon Heights.

Then he saw a second, ghosting across the same gap. They were pale and fast and seemed to disdain the usual constraints of gravity and momentum. They moved fluidly, like organised smoke. He caught a flash of metal and heard a shot drum against the front of the truck. The militiamen fired back, blasting away at the roofline of the nearest building. He caught another grey blur and the sputter of automatic fire. At least the angels didn't have energy weapons, Quillon thought. Now that the prevailing zone was equivalent to Steamville, angel-level technology would be even less workable than it had been in the old Neon Heights. The infiltrators had to use rifles and machine guns, just like the defending forces. It was a level killing field, with the exception that the angels were fast and numerous.

The driver kicked the truck into high gear, apparently deciding that any risk from snares was to be preferred above being ambushed by angels. They sped around a bend and passed along a backstreet faced on either side by drab brick tenements and zigzagging iron fire escapes. Machine-gun fire receded into the distance. The truck careered through a row of garbage cans, then twisted around onto the next street. Quillon recognised the district again – they were very near the rising wall of the next ledge, soaring up on the left like a frozen black fogbank. There, ahead, was the alley that housed the Pink Peacock. Abandoned cars had been dragged out of their slots to form a crude barricade around the entrance to the side street. The truck barely slowed as it made the turn, yawing to the right so that the crates started sliding and the passengers had to grab for anchors. There was a narrow gap between two of the cars, not quite wide enough for the truck to fit, and the heavy wheels gouged their way through, ripping away fenders and door-panels. Militiamen, unseen until now, were stationed behind the barricade. Beyond was what passed for a secure area, leading up to the Pink Peacock's undemonstrative entrance. Quillon allowed himself a partial sigh of relief. Tulwar had kept his word.

The truck came to a seething, simmering halt. Quillon and Meroka sprang off and helped Kalis and Nimcha down. The Pink Peacock's front door was already open, with two of Tulwar's men guarding it. They had the chipper look of local ne'er-do-wells who couldn't believe their luck that the city had turned upside down and they'd come out floating on top.

'Better not plan on staying in those tunnels too long,' one of them said to Quillon. 'We might not be here when you come out.'

Quillon and the others went inside. The Pink Peacock had never been the brightest of places but now it was a dimensionless cavern of barely relieved gloom. There was no electricity. Illumination was offered by a number of portable gas lanterns placed on tables and shelves, turned down to little more than a flicker. Quillon sensed Kalis's lingering consternation.

'What is this place?'

'Nowhere we'll be spending any time,' he said. 'It's just the easiest route into the tunnels.'

Meroka made her way to the bar. She peered over the back of it as if looking for a drink. 'It's a real shame what happened to Malkin,' she called. 'Him abandoning the place and all.'

'Shit happens,' a militiaman said.

'Yeah, that it does. Which is good, or else people like me'd be out of business.'

'What are you looking for?'

Meroka was scratching behind the bar. 'His cash box. Where he kept his fluid assets. Figured if he didn't want it, I'd help myself. Seeing as I was a long-term business associate. Figure some of that money belongs to me or Fray, whichever way you cut it.'

The militiaman laughed at her patent naivety. 'Forget it. Even if he somehow forgot to take the box – and Malkin wasn't *that* stupid – that money isn't worth dick any more. 'Cept as something to light a fire with, or wipe your arse on. Haven't you ever heard of hyperinflation?'

'Thanks for the succinct economic analysis, dickhead.' She gave up searching behind the bar. 'Money's gone anyway. Guess he wasn't that stupid, like you say.'

'No, I guess not.'

'Something up?' Quillon asked, annoyed with Meroka for delaying matters when all he wanted to do was get into the tunnels and confront whatever lay ahead.

'Just thought it was worth a look, that's all.'

'If you can bear to put your mercenary instincts aside for just a few moments, we actually came here to help Nimcha, not make ourselves richer.'

'I didn't forget about them, Cutter.' She sounded less irritated than he expected. 'C'mon. Let's get on with it.' Then she bellowed, 'Tulwar's people – I take it none of you is coming with us?'

'Do we need to?' the militiaman asked.

'Not really. I know my way through these tunnels about as well as anyone.'

'Then we'll leave you to it.'

Meroka grabbed one of the handheld lanterns, told Quillon to grab another and led them into the windowless nook where Quillon had met

Fray on the evening of his escape. Nothing much had changed. There was even a half-finished drink on the table. Meroka fished a set of keys from her pocket, opened the door in the back wall and ushered Quillon, Kalis and Nimcha into the claustrophobic space beyond, and then worked the lock on the interior door.

'Close that one behind us,' she told the militiaman. He kicked shut the outer door, leaving them in darkness save for the wavering, tentative glow of the gas lanterns. 'Go forwards,' she told the others, before shutting and locking the main door behind them.

'It doesn't smell good in here,' Nimcha said.

'You get used to it,' Meroka said, pushing past them with her lantern held high. 'Trust me on this. Now let's walk on a bit. We need to let them think we're going deeper into the tunnels, as per the plan.'

'We aren't?' Quillon asked.

'Just walk on.'

He kept walking, bringing up the rear with Kalis and Nimcha just ahead of them.

'I don't understand,' he said, when they had gone on for another minute or so.

'Haven't you figured it out yet, Cutter? This is a set-up. Tulwar's lured us into these tunnels so he can kill us and pretend we never happened.'

'Tulwar?'

'Yeah, Tulwar. The guy with the steam-powered heart.'

'I thought you – we – trusted him.'

'We did.'

Kalis spoke for the first time since entering the tunnel. 'I did not like that man. But why would he want to kill us, if we are here to make the city better?'

'You've answered your own question,' Meroka said. 'Tulwar likes being at the top of the food chain. It's working out for him. Only problem is, he needs things to stay nicely fucked-up for that to continue. We come along, threaten to sprinkle fairy-dust on everything and put it back the way it used to be, that's not exactly – pardon the expression – music to his ears.'

'Tulwar could have killed us in the bathhouse, couldn't he?' Quillon asked.

'Sure. But then he'd have risked being found out by Curtana and the others. Same thing if he'd tried killing us on the way here. Too many questions: more medicine coming in any time now, and he's going to want to keep on Ricasso's good side. Man needs that Serum-15. Wants to be the linchpin of the distribution operation. Got a taste for

442

controlling the supply and demand, wouldn't you say? Take away the disaster, you take away his living.'

'That's only a hunch, though,' Quillon said.

'Yeah. Until about five minutes ago.'

'I don't understand.'

'Tulwar lied about Malkin. He's not dead. Or if he is, he didn't go the way Tulwar said.'

'Maybe Tulwar got it wrong.'

'Don't think so. That stuff about the cash box? I made it up. In case you didn't figure that out already. I was just checking for the keys behind Malkin's bar.'

'Which keys?'

'The spare set. Fray gave me a bunch of keys to open the door back there, and all the others in the tunnels. I held on to it all this time. Fray had his own, which he always kept on him. But Malkin had the spare set. He knew about the tunnels, how to use them if the heat came down.'

'And Malkin's set?'

'Wasn't there.'

'Aren't you reading a lot into some missing keys?'

'I know Malkin, Cutter. If those keys are missing it's because he took them. And if he did, it's because he wanted to get into these tunnels. Which means Tulwar was either lying, or very mistaken, and I know which one I'm putting my money on.'

'All right,' Quillon said, sighing. 'Let's assume you're right about this – where does it leave us?'

'In, not to put too fine a point on it, a world of shit.'

'You know these tunnels well.'

'Yeah. Problem is, so do a lot of people connected to Fray. Tulwar might not be able to fit into them, but that doesn't mean he can't draw a map for someone else.'

'But we've locked the door behind us. Aren't we safe now?'

'Not really. Someone could have come in ahead of us, and in any case there's another entrance: the one I took you out of, in the launderette.'

'Tulwar said it wasn't secure,' Quillon said.

'Tulwar said a lot of things. I'm starting to wonder about several of them.' She took a deep breath. 'I think we've been set up for execution, Cutter. They could change the locks and let us die in here slowly, but I don't think that's Tulwar's style. He'll want to know the job's been done. That means he'll have sent someone into the tunnels ahead of us.'

'We must leave,' Kalis said.

'We can't,' Meroka said. 'Go back the way we came in, they'll just shoot us anyway.'

'Can they get into the tunnels, if they don't have the same keys?' Quillon asked.

'I don't know how many sets were floating around, or what happened to Fray's. Even without the keys, Tulwar had all night to come up with a workaround. You think the man doesn't know a good locksmith? Someone could easily have got through those doors by now, and locked them again from the other side.'

'Then you're right,' Quillon said. 'We're in trouble.'

'Or we would be,' Meroka said, 'if I wasn't the one leading us. I told Tulwar we were headed for the sub-shaft near the launderette entrance, so that's where they'll be expecting us to show up. But that's not the only option open to us. There's another way down to the Mire, and it doesn't involve us going anywhere near the other sub-shaft.'

'I'm hearing a "but",' Quillon said.

'It's not the option I'd have preferred, but when the alternative is walking into a trap, it begins to have its attractions.' Her tone turned urgent. 'But we need to move now, all right? We need to move and you need to trust me when I tell you I know what I'm doing. If they get impatient, Tulwar's men may decide to meet us halfway, and that wouldn't be good.' She paused. 'Oh, and there's a catch. We'll almost certainly be crossing into a different zone.'

'We expected that,' Quillon said.

'With machines in it,' Meroka said. 'Mad ones.'

'As in . . . the Mad Machines? The ones you told me didn't exist, except in bedtime stories?' Quillon asked.

'Yeah.' She raised her lantern and gave her companions a grin of demonic wickedness. 'So I guess I lied about some stuff as well.'

CHAPTER TWENTY-EIGHT

Meroka forced a hard pace, driving the party on through the twisting black warren, passing open shafts and branching junctions without comment. If they led anywhere, Quillon supposed, they were not to places Meroka deemed presently useful. The warm, wet air carried decay on its breath. Perhaps Quillon's nose had become more sensitive since leaving Spearpoint, but it seemed to him that the smell was more pronounced this time. More intense and more obviously redolent of death.

He had seen Spearpoint 2 and that had changed everything about the way he visualised this tunnel system. He had known of the tunnels before his escape, but only in the vague sense that he was aware of other hidden structures, such as sewerage pipes and telecom ducts, which, rather than being cut through Spearpoint's underlying fabric, channelled through the compacted, granite-like substrate that was all that remained of earlier building phases. If he had pictured the tunnels at all, he had imagined them branching and threading their way through Spearpoint's solid trunk like worm tracks. But Spearpoint wasn't solid, he now appreciated. Most of it – if it was anything at all like its broken twin – was hollow, all the way up and all the way down. There might not even be atmosphere inside it, if Ricasso was right and the vacuum integrity had withstood the centuries. The tunnels, as bewildering and labyrinthine as they were, lay solely within the walls.

Meroka had told the party to make as little noise as possible, and while they couldn't do anything about their breathing, Quillon and the others resisted the urge to speak. Even when they had travelled for what felt like far longer than his original journey (though that was probably his mind playing tricks) he knew better than to question Meroka about her plan. They were in her hands, totally dependent on her knowledge, and now was not the time to start having second thoughts about her abilities.

At last, Meroka stopped and held the lantern at eye level. There was a gap in the wall with an armoured door set into it, fixed to a crudely welded frame that was itself caulked into place, rather than being drilled or screwed. Quillon couldn't remember if he had noticed it on his first trip. He didn't think it was the junction where Meroka had shot the rat, since that had been much closer to the launderette exit. At least, that was what his jumbled recollection told him. But that had been a night of flight and fear, and fear was not conducive to the laying down of accurate memories.

'This is the place,' Meroka said in a hiss-whisper. She jangled her way through the bunch of keys, nerves beginning to tell. Quillon watched as she tried various keys in the lock, none of them working the mechanism. She tried one final key and there was a reassuring – but ominously loud – clunk from the lock mechanism that seemed to echo away for infinities. It was the loudest sound they had made since locking the door back at the Pink Peacock.

The door huffed open and Quillon felt a cool, dry gust. His lantern roared brighter, then returned to its normal glow: there was a pressure differential.

'It's a steep slope,' Meroka said, removing the key and slipping it into the lock from the other side. 'I'll go first. Kalis and Nimcha – follow me, but watch your footing all the way down. Don't want to start sliding. Cutter – lock up behind us, quietly as you can.'

He held his lantern high and nodded.

Meroka disappeared from view. Kalis went next, followed by Nimcha, their faces underlit by Meroka's bobbing light as she descended ahead of them. Quillon moved to the door and surveyed the shaft. The slope was steeper than he had expected, but the floor wasn't completely smooth. There were steps cut into it, or rather the rounded, smoothed-off traces where steps might once have been, before time softened their forms. The others were just about able to use these ghost-steps to keep themselves from sliding, but it was still treacherous. It was especially difficult for Nimcha, who had to step further than the others, relative to her size.

Quillon eased through the door and was about to swing it gingerly shut when there was a flash and a rattle of automatic gunfire, unbearably loud in the tunnel's confines. Bullets clanged into the door from the other side, punching thumb-sized dents all the way through the metal.

'Cutter! Shut the door!' Meroka shouted back at him.

He heaved at it and the door hinged towards closure, but not before more bullets had rained into it. He heard shouting and hurried footsteps. Through the narrowing gap he saw bright-yellow lights and heard more gunfire, closer this time.

446

'Guess you were right about that ambush!' he called down to Meroka. 'Remind me never to doubt another thing you say!'

'Yeah. Now shut the fucking door!'

He tried turning the key. The lock moved partway then jammed, as if the door had not closed completely. He tried again but with no luck.

'It's stuck!' he called. 'I can't turn the lock!'

'I don't need a sermon on it, Cutter!'

He tried one last time, but the key still would not rotate all the way. The door seemed tight in its frame; he could only guess that the gunfire had damaged the lock on the other side. There was nothing to be done about it now. He withdrew the key, then started down the slope, Nimcha only ten or so steps further on. The gunfire had stopped for now, but even though the door was closed he heard the voices growing nearer. He quickened his pace, using his free hand to steady himself against the wall.

'How far down?' he called.

'Not far!' Meroka shouted back.

He heard a scrabbling sound behind him, a hand on the door. A grunt and the sound of safety catches or magazines being clicked into place. The door hinged open, the yellow light spilling down the slope. He risked a glance over his shoulder and saw men with lanterns, bigger and brighter than their own. One of the men shouldering a gun and aiming it down at him—

Quillon crouched. On an impulse he lobbed the lantern in the direction of the yellow glow, putting all his strength into the swing. The lantern smashed into something. He heard a cry and then a series of barking yelps, and he imagined burning oil spilling over one of the ambushers. Someone loosed a short burst of automatic fire down the sloping shaft, but without the lantern to guide them, Quillon was all but invisible. He took another few steps after his companions. With both arms now free he reached his right hand into his pocket and pulled out the pistol, released the safety and aimed the gun at the widening yellow glow. He fired. Someone screamed and there was another sharp burst of return fire. He felt something tap his left arm, like a gentle blow from a small hammer. Another tap followed, this time striking him below his left collarbone. Both blows packed an unfeasible amount of momentum. He lost his balance and crashed into the tunnel wall. The door opened fully and a squall of gunfire lashed his way. He crouched, fired off two more shots and resumed his descent. The men at the top were beginning to come down the shaft, but they appeared unwilling to follow him too closely. He had been using his left arm to steady

447

himself as he descended the shaft, but the strength that he'd had a moment before wasn't there now.

'Cutter!' Meroka yelled. 'You still breathing?'

'On my way,' he said, and to his surprise the words came out in a pained grunt. He sounded like a wounded man. It was only then that he began to suspect he might have been shot. There was, now that he gave some attention to the matter, quite a bit of pain in both his arm and chest.

Miraculously, the shaft began to level out. He picked up his pace, conscious that the others were now some way ahead. He was moving in darkness now, the bobbing glow of Meroka's lantern before him – she and the others were clearly almost running – and the brightening glow of his pursuers behind. Shots continued to ring out, but as the tunnel became horizontal, so the curve took him out of reach of the bullets. He broke into a hobbling, off-kilter run. Slowly he began to catch up with the others.

The tunnel widened. His footfalls grew more echoey, the walls around him receding beyond the range of Meroka's lantern. He had the impression that they had entered an enormous vault, a cathedral-sized void in the black fabric of Spearpoint.

'Where are we?' he gasped, between ragged breaths.

'Give me the keys,' Meroka snapped. 'You *did* take the keys out, didn't you?'

'Of course.'

He passed her the set, conscious that Tulwar's men would not be long in arriving. Meroka handed her rifle to Kalis.

'Anything comes through that door, you shoot it. It's set for single-fire mode. You've got twenty rounds. When I shout, you follow me.'

'Why don't we follow you now?' Quillon asked.

'Because I need the lantern to find the door out of here, and the lantern's the thing they're going to be shooting at. Any other dickhead questions, while we're at it?'

'I'm good for the moment.'

Meroka sped off, her footsteps diminishing into the distance. Wherever they were, it was immense. His arm and chest were still hurting. He touched the arm wound with the back of his pistol hand and the hand came away sticky and warm. He aimed the pistol at the yellowing maw of the tunnel and waited, knowing there was nothing else to be done.

'Go into the darkness,' Kalis told her daughter. 'We will find you.'

Nimcha hesitated, then scampered away.

'I'm sorry,' Quillon said. 'This isn't the way it was meant to happen.'

'Was any of this your fault, Quillon?'

'I don't think so.' He reconsidered. 'Some of it, possibly. Not all of it.'

'Did you try to do what you could for my daughter?'

'Yes,' he answered.

'Then you need not apologise.'

He heard the jangle of keys, a lock being tested. The sound came from right next to him and a thousand leagues away. 'It won't open!' Meroka called, and for the first time since leaving the Red Dragon Bathhouse he heard real fear in her voice. She had been in control until now, even when she knew that they were walking into an ambush. It was an ambush on her territory and that changed everything. It had been manageable.

This wasn't.

'Here they come,' Quillon said.

They shot into the brightening yellow glow. The men spilled out into the vault, shadows and silhouettes impossible to distinguish. Kalis started firing and Quillon did likewise, until the pistol clicked and became just another useless chunk of metal. There were three men, then four, then five. He had hurt one of them with the lantern, possibly wounded another, but there were still too many of them. Shots began to come in their direction, drawn by the muzzle flash from Kalis's rifle. Quillon flinched, and then the rifle was silent. Twenty shots. It wasn't much.

'You can stop now,' a voice said. A man stepped forwards from the tunnel mouth. He carried one of the bright lanterns, a small pistol held loosely in his other hand, as if he had no expectation of using it. 'It's over. Just the formalities to attend to now.'

It was Kargas. Quillon said nothing, letting the man find him in the darkness. For a moment they faced each other, Kargas inspecting him, looking up and down his body as if what he saw was a piece of dead meat rather than a living thing. 'You took a hit, Doctor Quillon. Looks nasty. Where's the girl and Meroka?'

Quillon said nothing. He tried to hold Kargas's gaze.

'I guess Tulwar couldn't make it, right?' Meroka said, sauntering over with the other lantern. She had avoided being shot, but must have realised there was no point in making any further escape efforts. The useless keys were still in her hand. 'Sent his spineless fucking sidekick instead.'

Kargas let out a brief, sarcastic laugh. He looked over his shoulder. 'Bring the ghouls. It's time they were reacquainted.'

There was an exchange of words, a quick patter of footsteps, and

Tulwar's men moved aside. Two angels came into the vault, moving with their not-quite-normal gait, not so much walking as gliding, the way mist might drift across a midnight lagoon. They wore hats and long brown coats, cinched loosely at the front. Even as they approached they were undoing the cinches, shrugging the human garments onto the ground. They wore nothing underneath. In the yellow light they were pale as bone, as thin as sticks. They appeared too frail to stand upright, let alone to animate themselves. One was female and the other male, although Quillon doubted that any of the humans would have been able to make the distinction. The creatures were essentially sexless in appearance, reproductive and mammary organs sleeked away for maximum aerodynamic efficiency. It was only by the subtlest of cues that he was able to determine their gender with any confidence. Even as his body became more like theirs, it felt quite impossible that they had ever had anything in common.

With a flourish, a whoop of disturbed air, the angels unfurled their wings. They flicked out with the swiftness of spring-loaded blades, sharp-edged and faintly luminous, patterned with a pastel delicacy of water-colours. The wings flexed to provide lift, only needing to move gently for the angels to rise and fall, their feet leaving the ground with each downbeat. The show served no purpose other than to emphasise what they were, and what he was not.

'We've come back for you,' they said, in exact, trilling unison. 'To return you to the Celestial Levels.'

'If you can come down here as you are,' Quillon said, 'then there's nothing you need from me. I don't even remember any of the details of the old infiltration programme.'

'You don't need to remember them,' the female angel said. 'They're in your head all the same. They just have to be extracted. Dug out.'

'And we do need those memories,' the male angel said. 'We can visit, but we cannot remain. Even the best of our current infiltration units lack what you possessed: the ability to stay in a different zone – a very different zone – for months, years on end.'

'Other people besides me were aware of the protocols.'

'Dead, or vanished,' the female said dismissively. 'You, on the other hand, have endured. You are very precious to us. More so now than ever. We would, of course, like to take you alive. That will make the data-extraction work more straightforward. But the main thing is that you not fall into the hands of our enemies. They would find your knowledge equally useful.'

'Except they'd want it for a different purpose,' Quillon said. 'To do good, to benefit all of Spearpoint. Not just to make a better army of occupying angels.'

'Goodness is a question of perspectives,' the male said. 'We have ours. You have yours.' The angel's beautiful, porcelain head, with its lustrous blue eyes, swivelled towards Kargas. 'We have what we came for. The girl is yours, when you find her. We ask only that her frozen corpse be presented to us for examination. It will be of interest to compare her with the others.'

'Take him,' Kargas said, jabbing a finger at his men. 'The rest of you, fan out and find the girl. She has to be in here somewhere: if there was a way out, Meroka would already have found it. Tulwar doesn't need her alive, but try not to make too much of a mess.'

A voice rang out from the darkness. 'You mind if I chip in at this point?'

There was a ringing silence. No one spoke. The voice was not one any of them had been expecting to hear. Quillon thought he recognised it. He didn't dare believe he was right.

Then Meroka said, 'Fray?'

'Aw, you spoiled the surprise. Ah well, guess the secret's out now – may as well come clean.' Without a sound, a lantern brightened. It was far off to one side of the vault, not too distant from the door Meroka had been trying to open. 'Heard the commotion, thought it was worth investigating,' the voice went on. 'After all, it's been a mite quiet down here lately.'

'Hasn't it just,' said another voice: not so easy to pin down, but which Quillon thought he also recognised. Another lantern brightened, a few paces to the right of the first. The lanterns must already have been lit, light-tight shades now pulled off them, allowing the illumination to spill out.

The two men – Fray and Malkin – were standing near each other. They were not unarmed. They were quite seriously not unarmed. Both men were carrying – or at least aiming – what could only be categorised as small artillery pieces: two bulky gas-powered spinguns, so heavy that they had to be strapped to their bodies via thick leather girdles. Malkin was aiming at the angels, more or less; Fray at Kargas and the other ambushers.

'So,' Fray said, 'anyone want to take a scholarly guess as to what's going to happen next?'

'I think, whatever it is, it's going to need cleaning up afterwards,' Malkin said.

Fray thought about this for a second, then nodded. 'Yep. Me too.'

There was a momentary hiatus, as if the world had stopped breathing.

The angels were the first to react, predictably enough. Their wings twitched. *Fight-or-flight reflex*, Quillon thought: it manifested in angels as surely as it did in unmodified humans, just in a different form.

Malkin opened fire. He had a clear line of fire onto the angels. He didn't so much shoot them as dismantle them. They came apart in mid-air, as if they were being held there by fine wires, like dummies in a shooting gallery. The spingun burst probably didn't last more than three seconds, and the direction of fire hardly shifted.

It didn't matter. It was enough.

Malkin cut off his spingun, yanking the lever that interrupted the gas supply to the rotating barrel assembly, but by then Fray had started up his weapon and was enacting his own brand of wrath on Kargas and the other Tulwar traitors. He started and stopped, started and stopped, the spingun hosing a line of fire across the vault, the stuttering light limning details that had been invisible until now: soaring black pillars, a ceiling spanned by ebony arches.

At last Fray cut the gas supply and the gun spun down, sighing like a tired dog.

He raised his lantern higher and peered into the gloom. The look on his face was that of a man who'd lifted the seat on an unflushed lavatory.

'Like you said,' he affirmed to Malkin. 'Some cleaning up.'

CHAPTER TWENTY-NINE

It was only when Fray unbuckled the still-smoking spingun and placed the heavy piece on the ground that Quillon saw how badly he was trembling, how gravely the storm must have hit his already damaged nervous system. Malkin didn't look much better, but then Malkin never had. Both men looked as if they had been living down in this black vault for years, as if daylight was no more than a distant memory.

Meroka put down her lantern and walked over to Fray. In the last few paces she broke into a loping run. She wrapped her arms around his tree-like girth, Fray looking down at her as if this was some arcane anthropological behaviour he had never counted on witnessing. He looked pleased and surprised and not quite sure how to react.

'Guess you missed me.'

'Tulwar told us you were dead, you big fucking oaf.'

'And you believed him?'

'He made it sound plausible,' Quillon said, glad to walk away from the splattered remains of the two angels. He slipped the empty pistol back into his pocket and cupped his right hand over the wound in his left arm. 'Told us you'd died of zone sickness. Said Malkin was dead too.'

The snake-thin barkeeper ran a hand through his oiled-back hair. 'Do I get a hug as well?'

'Some other time,' Meroka said. Her attention was all on Fray. She released her hold, letting him breathe. 'Did you really not know we were coming?'

'You might find it difficult to believe, but we're a bit thin on current affairs down here,' Fray said.

'We felt the pressure changes when the doors opened. Then we heard the shooting,' Malkin explained. 'Decided to see what all the fuss was about.'

'Of course I guess I was hoping that if you *did* make it back to Spearpoint, you'd have the sense to work out where I'd gone,' Fray said.

'I don't think Tulwar worked it out,' Meroka said. 'Fucker knew about the tunnels, but didn't figure you'd made a bolt for them. And obviously didn't know about this place, or what's down here.'

'It's always good to keep a few secrets, even from your most trusted associates,' Fray said.

'Did you have your suspicions about him?' Quillon asked.

'No more than I have my suspicions about most people, Cutter. It's good to have you back, by the way. I wasn't expecting to see you for months, after we said goodbye. How was life outside? You did make it outside, didn't you?'

'For a little while.'

'Guess we've got some catching up to do. You look like shit, by the way. Just between friends.'

'You should see me in daylight.' Quillon drew his hand away from his wounded arm.

'How bad is it?' Meroka asked.

'I'll mend.' He realised that she hadn't noticed the other wound, the one in his upper chest, and for now he saw no point in mentioning something that couldn't be treated until they were back in daylight. 'I don't think it went deep; I can take care of it with what's in my bag.'

'We've got clean water and light,' Fray said, looking past Quillon as he spoke. 'Who are the other two, by the way? We haven't been introduced.'

'You will be,' Meroka said.

Fray touched a hand to his forehead. 'My hospitality's slipping. Come with me. It's not the height of luxury, but it's kept Malkin and me alive down here. We'll get Cutter fixed up in no time.'

He collected the spingun and started walking, limping with each stride, his shoes squeaking on the floor.

'Tulwar's going to send more people down here sooner or later,' Meroka said. 'He's got a whole army up there. Guy's practically operating Spearpoint, the parts that haven't been overrun by Skullboys and angels.'

Fray nodded. 'That's the way it was going before I decided to lie low. But we'll deal with Tulwar in due course. He's just an appliance that needs unplugging.'

They followed him to a black door in the black wall. He worked a key and unlocked it.

'I couldn't open it,' Meroka said.

'That was the idea, I'm afraid – I changed the locks. Not to stop you getting any further, but to stop Tulwar or anyone else I didn't want down here. I figured if anyone did make it this far, I'd know about it.' He shot her a grin. 'Worked, didn't it?'

'Don't go changing no locks on me again, all right? Nearly pissed in my shoes when I couldn't get that door open.'

'Meroka,' Fray chided. 'There's a child present.'

On the other side of the door was a short tunnel, and at the far end of the tunnel was a room, much smaller than the main vault, which Fray had turned into his bolt-hole. It had metal doors leading out from it, the same kind they had already passed through. There were a couple of beds laid out on the floor, several crates stacked up around the beds, a couple of folding chairs, a card table. Quillon looked into one of the open crates and saw ammunition, packets of clinical-grade Morphax-55, candies, bottled water, cigarettes and alcohol. The place smelt inhumanly stale, but he supposed that was to be expected. Fray hadn't promised them the heights of luxury.

Quillon sipped at bottled water – it had the gritty taste of collected run-off – and helped himself to one of the cigarettes. He had removed his coat and hacked away at his sleeve to expose the wound, but although he was unconcerned now about anyone seeing his wing-buds or the increasingly skeletal condition of his anatomy, he preferred not to draw attention to the chest wound. There was enough blood on his shirt from the arm wound to hide the evidence of it anyway. It could have been worse: the bullet had gouged a bloody trench through what little muscle bulk he retained, but it had left no trace of itself behind. With Kalis's help he had staunched the bleeding, sterilised the wound, stitched the skin and applied a pressure pad and dressing. When it was done he shrugged the coat back on again, forcing his arm into the sleeve with difficulty. A knot of pain, hardening with each breath, told him that the chest wound would not be so easily treated.

'You good, Cutter?' Meroka asked.

'I'm good.'

She shared a slug of Firebird with Fray, while Kalis and Nimcha declined the offer of anything to drink.

'Meroka's right – we can't stay here now,' Fray said, sorting through one of the other crates, his drink in the other hand. 'Tulwar's men will find their way down here eventually, if only to figure out what happened to the last bunch. There'll be more of them, and they'll have bigger guns. But that's fine – Malkin and I were about ready to check out anyway.'

Malkin blinked. 'We were?'

'Oh, yeah.' Fray finished his drink and slammed the glass to the ground. 'Place stinks like a shit-tip anyway. Pardon my language.'

'It's about time we told you about Nimcha,' Quillon said, beckoning the girl away from her mother. 'She's the reason we came here, Fray. She's the reason Tulwar tried to have us killed.'

'I thought he set you up with the angels.'

'That was just incidental. I don't doubt they made it worth his while, a trade-off of some kind. You give us Quillon, we'll let you keep Neon Heights. For the time being.'

'So what does Tulwar have against Nimcha?'

'Show him,' Quillon said.

Nimcha reached up and removed her hat. She stared at Fray for a few moments then turned around slowly, presenting the back of her head to him, exposing the baubled star where her hair had been hacked away by Spatha.

'Right . . .' Fray said, on a falling note.

Quillon asked, 'You know what this means?'

'Kind of.'

'And your opinion on the matter?'

'You wouldn't have brought her here if you didn't think there was something in it. Right, Cutter?'

'She can do it,' Meroka said. 'Make the zones change. I've seen – felt – it happen.'

'There's something in her head,' Quillon said. 'Machinery, I suppose. Machinery made of living matter, shaped from the moment she was conceived. But not like any machinery in our experience. I met a man called Ricasso while I was outside – he's studied the zones and contemplated tectomancers and what they mean. I don't think I understood all of it, but from what I can gather, the things we make – even the things angels make – aren't very good at adapting to zone changes. They're too clunky, too rigid. Living things make a better job of it – we're squishier, as Ricasso put it, more able to adjust to changes in the cellular grid. I think the stuff in Nimcha's head must be like that as well.'

Fray looked sceptical but interested. 'What stuff?'

'She can feel Spearpoint. Or more specifically the Mire, or the Eye of God. She's like a radio, and the Eye is the transmitting station.' Quillon winced, as much over his inability to communicate his thoughts as from the throbbing pain in his arm. 'But it's not radio, or anything we can even begin to understand. Whatever it is, it's able to reach through hundreds, thousands of leagues, into the mind of a girl.'

Malkin asked, 'Why?'

'That's the hard part, the bit I don't think even Ricasso understands. But we have to stop thinking of tectomancers the way we do. They're not witches, that's for sure. If that symbol on the back of her head means anything, then it was people like Nimcha – people with whatever gift she has – who made Spearpoint. They built it, for whatever purpose it was meant to serve. They were the architects, and perhaps the caretakers as well.'

Fray squinted. 'Caretakers?'

'Whatever Spearpoint is – and after the things we saw in the Bane, I'm starting to have an idea – it isn't working now. The Mire, the Eye of God, is part of what's gone wrong with it. The incursion, Ricasso called it: the intrusion into our world of something wrong. The world isn't meant to be divided up into zones. They're a mistake, a symptom, a sign that something isn't right. But whatever's wrong, it's *been* wrong for so long that we've got used to it. We've been building our world around that wrongness for five thousand years. But it can't go on.'

'I kind of liked things the way they were,' Fray said.

'So did a lot of us, but that's irrelevant. The world is dying. It's getting colder and soon there won't be enough trees to give us the wood and the firesap we need to keep things running. We have to leave, if only so that we can look back and see what's gone wrong, and start thinking of ways to mend it. But the zones won't allow us to escape. We can be as clever and ingenious as we like, but we can't beat them.'

'So we're fucked, is what you're saying. Not to put too fine a point on it.'

'No, Fray. We're not. Because we don't need to fight the zones for ever. Whatever happened to Spearpoint all those years ago, I think it's starting to put itself right. Perhaps it needed five thousand years to even begin to heal itself. All I know is that the process has begun, and that Nimcha is part of it.'

'A kid?'

'It's what she can do that matters. What's in her head, the talent. She's probably not the only one it's been calling out to. It's been going on for generations: inheritance factors shuffling around in the population until they combine in the right way and give rise to a tectomancer. Someone who feels the zones, someone who can make them move. But for centuries – thousands of years even – they were wasted. Spearpoint couldn't respond to them, couldn't sense them, and they couldn't sense Spearpoint. If they did discover their abilities, it was only enough to get them branded as witches and lunatics. But that's not what they were at all. They were caretakers. Healers.'

'Gatekeepers,' Meroka said.

'Yes,' Quillon said emphatically, remembering the passage in the

Testament. '"*And the mark of the keepers of the gates of paradise shall be upon her, and she shall be feared.*" But we don't have to fear her! Revere her, possibly. Respect? Definitely. But fear? I don't think so. She's come to save us, not annihilate us. The Mire's been calling her, seeking her guidance. It's come all this way on its own, but now it needs a human mind to shape the process of recovery. That's what she has to provide.' He paused for breath. 'That's why we brought her here.'

Fray widened his eyes, nodded, then rubbed his palms together. For now, at least, his shaking had abated. 'In which case, Cutter, I guess she'll want to meet the Mad Machines. Because nothing happens in here without their say-so.'

'Are they near?' Kalis asked.

'Just the other side of the zone.' Fray flashed a devil-may-care smile. 'Hope you're all feeling up to the crossing.'

As Meroka had told him during their escape from Spearpoint, the zones became progressively more compacted within the structure. A boundary might span many leagues in the open lands beyond the city, several blocks inside Neon Heights or Horsetown, but now the transition between zones might easily be measured in hundreds of spans or less. Fray opened one of the doors leading out of the bolt-hole and led them down another shaft, one that became progressively steeper and more difficult to traverse. At length they came to another opening, and it was here that Quillon felt the first physiological tingles of an imminent transition, over and above the steady pressure that had been present since the last leg of the airship crossing.

'We're close now,' he said.

'You got that right.' Fray set down his lantern. 'Change vector's pretty steep, just so you all know what to expect. Gonna feel like you've stepped from Steamville to Circuit City without taking a breath. Maybe worse than that. Think you can work out the Morphax dose for that, Cutter?'

'I'll do my best.' By lantern light he dug inside his medical bag, sorting through the by now rather depleted supplies until he found the vials he wanted. He doled out pills to Meroka and Malkin, then turned to Kalis and her daughter. 'I admire your strength,' he told them, 'but now isn't the time to prove your self-reliance. I've seen it, and I don't need any further convincing. But if Fray's right, this is going to hit us hard unless we're medicated.' He demonstrated his own conviction on the subject by popping two of the pills. 'I'm committed now,' he said, swallowing them down. 'I have to cross the zone now.'

Kalis's expression was one of steely resolve, but at last she nodded and extended her hand. 'If you think this is necessary.'

'I do.'

He gave her two pills to swallow, and a third for Nimcha. He watched to make certain they complied. Then he went back to Fray, who was beginning to shake again, his ragged nervous system anticipating the stress of the crossing. Whatever benefits the alcohol had given him were beginning to wear off.

'You don't have to come with us,' Quillon said. 'You've already done enough.'

'And miss this, Cutter? You've got to be kidding me.'

'You're not well.'

'And I'll be even less well if I attempt that crossing without Morphax inside me. Your choice, of course.'

'Like I have any,' Quillon said, unstoppering the vial and palming two pills. 'You're the man with the spingun, after all.'

'There is that,' Fray said.

They set off again. The boundary came on them more quickly than Quillon had been expecting, and at first the sharpness of the transition was enough to make him worry that he had misjudged the dose. But as they carried on walking, the Morphax-55 began to kick in and take the edge off the worst of the effects, even going some way to dulling the pain from his bullet wounds. He still felt wrong, as if there was a pressure in his head that was only being masked, not alleviated, but it was enough to enable him to function and retain some clarity of mind. He surveyed his companions and saw nothing immediately untoward in any of them. Even Fray appeared to be coping. Perhaps his body still had a few transitions left in it after all.

They passed through more tunnels. By now Quillon had given up trying to guess where they were in relation to Spearpoint's hollow walls, whether they were nearer the inside or the outside. All he could be certain of was that they had not descended far from the level of the Pink Peacock. The Mire, whatever it was, must still be a great distance under their feet.

'We're getting near now,' Fray said. 'Not to cause any offence or anything, but when we meet the Mad Machines, it'll be best if Meroka and I do the talking. Just to break the ice, so to speak.'

'I'm all for ice-breaking,' Quillon said. His apprehension was rising like mercury in a thermometer, creeping steadily up the shaft. 'These machines ... the mad ones – have you been acquainted long?'

Fray seemed to take it as a straight question. 'Long enough. We only get to deal with two or three of them – there's some sort of hierarchy. The shallow tunnels are all fine and dandy if you just want to take a few short cuts or get away from the local heat for a few hours. But to go deep – which is what we're doing now – you have to deal with the things that live down here.'

'Why isn't their existence more widely known?'

'It used to be, but the city authorities were glad to turn a blind eye, provided the machines kept to their side of the zone. Storm shook things up a bit, but not enough to let them break out onto the ledges. Mostly, the authorities just didn't want to deal with anything they couldn't exploit or understand. All the cops I worked with knew about them, but they were the thing you never talked about. You'd use them to scare confessions out of people, say you were going to leave them in the tunnels and let the Mad Machines find them.'

'That's what parents tell their children will happen, if they're naughty.'

'Well, one thing's for certain: some of us have been very naughty indeed.'

They emerged into what was evidently another large vault, judging by the way the acoustics changed and the lantern light fell away without being reflected from adjoining walls or ceiling. The party walked on for some distance until Fray raised his lantern and brought them to a halt. The lantern trembled in his hand, the little flame quivering. When he spoke, it was with atypical reverence. 'This is where they come. They'll be here sooner or later, one or more of them.'

'How can you be sure?' Quillon asked.

'Because this is how it always happens, Cutter. You come here. You wait. The machines show up. Now remember what I said about letting Meroka and me do the talking? The one thing you don't want to do is piss these things off.'

'What are these machines?' Kalis asked.

'Take a guess. I don't think even they know for sure. Maybe they were put into Spearpoint to keep it running, like janitors.'

'They're not doing much of a job,' Quillon said.

'Well, you don't know how fucked it would be if they weren't around, do you? Maybe they're the only things that have been stopping this place from crumbling to dust all these years.'

Quillon thought about the broken stump of Spearpoint 2. 'Perhaps.'

Then he felt a breeze that had not been there a moment before. Fray met his eyes and nodded once. Kalis wrapped her arms around Nimcha, drawing her daughter closer to her. Without a word being said, the little party formed a cordon around mother and daughter: Fray and Quillon on one side, Meroka and Malkin on the other. The breeze ebbed, but in its place was a distant but approaching sound: a continuous metallic clattering. It sounded like garbage being bulldozed down an alley, a building avalanche of junk and debris. Insofar as Quillon had given the Mad Machines any thought, nothing had prepared him for this.

'Juggernaut,' Fray said, speaking just loud enough to be heard over the growing clatter. 'I think it's Juggernaut.'

'Sounds like it to me,' Meroka said.

'Is that good or bad?' Quillon asked.

'Depends what kind of mood she's in. Juggernaut has off-days,' Fray replied, then ran a finger across his lips, telling Quillon to zip it.

The machine stopped somewhere in the darkness. There was an oily smell on the air, accompanied by a low, barely perceptible humming. The clattering had all but ceased. Quillon could see nothing, even with the lantern light, but he still sensed Juggernaut's looming presence. The sense of powerlessness, even with Nimcha at his side, was more intense than he had ever felt in his life.

Lights came on. Quillon squinted against the blue-tinged brightness, striving to see details beyond the glare. They were looking up at Juggernaut, the lights coming from the machine itself, stabbing down at them. Juggernaut was not what he had expected.

The Mad Machine was a towering, teetering pile of animate junk, tall and wide as a four-storey tenement and about as long as a city block. It was just barely symmetrical, like a heap of scrap that had been compacted into a roughly rectangular shape, but with enough gaps and lopsided protrusions to upset any hint of regularity or orderedness. He could see that it was a single entity, of sorts, in that all the visible parts were either articulated or fixed together by some means or other. But there was no sense of Juggernaut having been designed, or even that Juggernaut had evolved in steps from some earlier, more ordered state. It just looked like a heap of trash that had been flung together and which had, astonishingly, spontaneously, aggregated into a kind of building-sized robot.

It did not have wheels or legs or any other obvious means of locomotion, but many parts of it appeared capable of independent movement. It had nothing resembling a head. The lights – which to Quillon had the bug-eyed look of car headlamps, although all of different makes and sizes – had been arranged across its front in an entirely random pattern. He could see no means by which the machine was able to view its visitors, but that it was aware of them was beyond question. He had seldom had the impression of being more intently studied.

Fray was the first to speak. He raised his voice and said, 'Thank you for letting us come here, Juggernaut. It's good of you to allow us to come this far. I'm afraid we don't have much to give you, but you're welcome to what we have.'

Meroka took Malkin's weapon in her hands, but not as if she intended to use it. Silently, as if the act had been rehearsed, she and Fray stepped forwards several paces and placed their spinguns on the floor. Then they walked back to the group, all without turning their backs on the machine.

Juggernaut did nothing for several seconds. The humming continued, perhaps a little louder than before. The clattering was also more emphatic. It was almost as if the machine was drumming fingers, thinking things over.

Part of its frontage moved. Pieces of articulated machinery hinged away from the lamp-dotted edifice, unfolding and elongating into a kind of mechanical trunk. The trunk swung through the air, lashing over their heads. Quillon couldn't help but flinch. It was easily powerful enough to crush them all with a single flick.

But Juggernaut was more interested in Fray's offering. The trunk curled around the spinguns. It lifted them into the air as if they were twigs, then folded back into the main mass. Just before the arm vanished back into the robot, Quillon saw pieces of the frontage maw widen, opening an impromptu mouth into glowing, red-lit mechanical innards. It was like the inside of a furnace or foundry. The spinguns had been consumed.

Clattering sounds ensued. Then Juggernaut quietened again.

'Welcome, Fray,' it said. 'Welcome, Meroka. Welcome, companions of Fray and Meroka.'

Inasmuch as Quillon had been expecting the Mad Machine to speak at all, it was not with this voice. This was polite, dignified, almost ceremonial. It was just barely louder than if there had been someone standing there addressing them. It was the voice of a slightly disciplinarian but basically kind-hearted schoolmistress, not a machine as large as a building.

'I'll bring more next time,' Fray said. 'This is all we had on us. I'm afraid we weren't planning on this visit right now.'

The machine cogitated. It clattered and hummed. 'This will suffice, Fray. You have been generous in the past. You will be generous in the future.' It said this with flat assurance, as if it either had a complete grasp of human nature, of Fray, of future events, or all three.

'We need your help,' Meroka said, electing to speak for the first time. Quillon heard a quiver in her voice that was entirely new to him.

The lamps swivelled en masse to focus on Meroka. 'What is the nature of the difficulty?' Juggernaut asked.

'It's not so much a difficulty, as . . .' Meroka faltered. 'We brought this girl with us. She needs to get somewhere. We thought maybe you could help us with that.'

'Where does she need to go?'

'We don't know. Near the Mire, maybe. Or not. Just somewhere she can act, or do whatever it is Spearpoint wants her to do.'

'I do not understand you.'

'Show them your head,' Meroka said. 'Maybe it'll help.'

Nimcha hesitated at first, then took a brave step away from Kalis. She walked into the glare of the machine, the lamps angling onto her, turning her into a silhouette with multiple shadows. She stood resolute, with her arms at her sides. Then she turned slowly around and presented the back of her head for Juggernaut's inspection.

'She's the genuine article,' Fray said, glancing back at Quillon as if to say he sincerely hoped this was the case.

'I have been instructed to act on this symbol. She will come with me, to the other machines. They will know what to do.'

And even as it spoke, Juggernaut folded out its arm again, the configuration not quite the same this time, as if the jumbled components had locked together in a different permutation. The arm ended in a flattened, paddle-shaped platform, which it placed on the ground just in front of Nimcha. 'Step on,' the machine commanded, not without kindness.

'No,' Kalis said, taking a step towards her daughter.

Quillon reached out and took her arm. 'We brought her this far because she was dying, Kalis. If she doesn't complete this journey, she'll only get worse.'

'This is what must be done,' Juggernaut said. 'She must be taken.'

'Taken where?' Kalis cut in, her own voice higher and louder than Juggernaut's.

'To the others,' the machine replied.

Nimcha looked back, torn between the opposing poles of Juggernaut and Kalis. On some level, Quillon was certain, she felt compelled to go where the machine wanted her to. The thing in her head – the thing that had expressed itself via the birthmark, and which had given her the link to Spearpoint – was urging her to take that final step. On another, she was just a girl on the point of being wrenched away from the mother who had nurtured and protected her all her life. He could almost feel the psychic strain of that conflict, threatening to snap her in two.

'We have to go with her,' he said, his own voice coming from some-where inside him that he barely knew existed. 'Is that possible, Jug-gernaut? Can you take us with her?'

'You don't know what you're getting into,' Fray said warningly.

'I know,' Quillon replied. 'Trust me on this.'

'I will not leave her,' Kalis said. 'I will do all that I can to see her healed, but I will not leave her.'

Juggernaut clanked and clattered and hummed. 'You may come,' it said finally, as if the matter had been given due process. 'Those who wish to.'

'I will not leave my daughter,' Kalis said.

Quillon nodded. 'And I won't leave my patients. I can't say I've been much use to either of you, but I am still your doctor. Will you let me come with you, Kalis?'

'Why do you ask me, and not the machine?' she asked, taken aback.

'Because you also have a say in this.'

She looked at him for lingering moments, then nodded slightly. 'If you will, Quillon.'

'Sign me up as well,' Meroka said.

'No,' Quillon said sharply. 'You've done enough for all of us, Meroka. You don't have to come any further. There's nothing left to prove.'

'It was never about proving anything, Cutter.'

'My point still stands. I don't know where we're being taken, or what's in store for us when we get there. If we're being taken anywhere near the Mire, then the zone transitions are going to be rapid, severe and essentially unpredictable. Nimcha and Kalis have natural tolerance. I have the tolerance the angels gave me, before they sent me down to Neon Heights. It's still going to be difficult for us, and you don't have either of these advantages.'

'Cutter's right,' Fray said, putting a hand on her shoulder. 'Anyway, your talents would be better put to use elsewhere. You can be sure Tulwar's in the tunnels by now, and he'll have the usual entrances and exits covered. But of course, those aren't the only ways in and out. You, um, didn't tell him about the other routes, did you?'

Meroka glared at him.

'No, of course you didn't,' Fray said hastily. 'Point is, they don't know about the other bolt-hole. Take Malkin there and tool up. There are more spinguns and ammunition and enough supplies to hold out there for a few days if you need to.'

'*Purple Emperor* and the rest of the fleet still think Tulwar's the man to deal with,' Quillon said. 'Someone needs to get word to them, without Tulwar finding out.'

'We could always burn down the bathhouse,' Malkin said.

'Curtana and Agraffe are friends of ours from Swarm, and they're currently recuperating in the bathhouse. We don't want them or any other innocent people caught up in this. But the head needs decapitating. Ricasso and the others must be warned that this isn't a man they can trust. If they can get enough airmen down to take control of the bathhouse ...' Quillon trailed off, trusting he could leave the details to someone better equipped to furnish them. 'We need to get someone to the bathhouse if we can. Or at the very least flash a heliograph message to the other ships.'

'Shaving mirror in the other bolt-hole,' Fray said, rubbing his stubble-free chin. 'Good job I care about appearances. They're coming in from the west, right?'

Quillon nodded. 'If the wind holds.'

'Use the exit by the old Second District Gas and Electric substation. That'll put you within range of the bathhouse, and you should have no problem getting a line of sight from anywhere in that district.'

'Tulwar never mentioned that entrance,' Quillon said.

'Because Tulwar doesn't know about it. You think I wanted my lieutenants to know *everything*, Cutter?'

'Hope one of you knows how to signal those ships,' Malkin said, 'because I figure I must have skipped school the day they taught about heliographs.'

'Yeah, well I didn't,' Meroka said. 'Not saying I'll be as fast as a Swarmer, or that I won't make a few screw-ups, but I should be able to get something through.'

Fray looked impressed and proud at the same time. 'Really?'

'That time on the blimps wasn't completely wasted, you know.'

'You never fail to surprise me,' Fray said.

Juggernaut clattered and hummed. There was an edge of brooding impatience in the sounds it made.

'I think we'd better be on our way,' Quillon said. He turned to the machine. 'How do we ... travel with you, Juggernaut? If that isn't a stupid question?'

'I shall provide for your comfort and safety. The journey will not be long, but we will be passing through a number of change-boundaries.'

'The vectors must all be towards higher-state zones, or you wouldn't be able to function there,' Quillon surmised. 'This zone is probably the lowest state you can endure.'

'Correct.'

'I think we'll be back,' Quillon said slowly, 'but I'm not sure. We shouldn't take anything as a given. Meroka . . . I know we haven't always seen eye to eye. We've both kept things from each other, me particularly.'

'There were reasons for that, Cutter,' Fray said.

'It's all right,' said Meroka. 'Cutter and me . . . we're good. He got Swarm to come back here and . . . that wasn't nothing. Can't say I'm ever going to be the angels' number-one fan but they're not all bad. Some of them have even got the balls to do the right thing, when it needs doing.'

'High praise,' Fray told Quillon. 'I'd quit while you were ahead, if I were you.'

'Are you going, Meroka?' asked Nimcha.

'Can't come any further, girl. Someone needs to get that message to Swarm, and I don't think we want to trust it to Malkin.' Meroka reached out and took Nimcha's hands. Meroka was a small woman but her hands were still much larger and more grown-up than Nimcha's. She squeezed them gently. 'You're going to start being well again, kid. This is what this has all been about.'

'Thank you for reading to me.'

'Did you like the stories?'

Nimcha did something which, until then, Quillon would not have said she was capable of. She smiled. It was a hesitant, gap-toothed smile, but it was a smile nonetheless. 'Not really.'

'Me neither.' Meroka gave a big grin in return, the two of them sharing a joke. 'They sucked, didn't they? All that airship stuff?'

'They sucked,' Nimcha agreed, sounding, for a moment, like nothing so much as a smaller, feistier version of Meroka.

'Thank you,' Kalis told her. 'You have been kind to us. You did not have to be.'

'Thank Cutter. He was the one overruled me when it came to rescuing you.'

'I thank you both.'

'And now,' Quillon said, 'I really do think we need to be on our way. We don't want to test Juggernaut's patience indefinitely.'

CHAPTER THIRTY

The machine took them. It folded out parts of itself to make platforms they could stand on, like the running boards of limousines. Quillon and Fray, Nimcha and Kalis climbed aboard, the four of them holding on to the ragged metal side of Juggernaut and each other as the machine rumbled and cranked itself into something approximating uniform motion. It felt as if they were riding an accelerating avalanche. Beneath their feet, huge chunks of Juggernaut detached from the main mass and moved up, down, backwards and forwards, no part of it appearing to be in any way coordinated with the next, but the whole somehow conspiring to make the machine move along, as if it was on wheels or tracks.

They moved along tunnels wide enough to take not just trains, but perhaps an airship or two. The slope steepened, climbing and diving, until at times they were travelling down shafts that were practically vertical. Juggernaut protected its human cargo, constantly rearranging its tumbling, shifting, chaotic form so that they were always kept upright and out of harm's way.

The boundaries came hard, like a series of waves breaking one after the other. Quillon compensated as best as he could, dispensing Morphax-55 from his medical bag even as the effects intensified and impaired his own ability to think clearly. This was testing the limits of his own tolerance, just as surely as it was testing the limits of Nimcha and Kalis's. As for Fray, he didn't want to think what this was doing to the already damaged, decaying infrastructure of his nervous system. Fray, though, was surely aware of that as well. Quillon just hoped that the massive dose of antizonal medicine Fray was now receiving would be sufficient to keep him going for a little while, even at the expense of his longer-term health.

But for all that, the journey was still astonishing. They were moving through regions of Spearpoint that had hardly been witnessed by human eyes in thousands of years. Certainly, he suspected, by very few people who had ever had the chance to report back on what they had seen. At one point the wide shaft down which Juggernaut was passing became transparent on one convexly curved side, and he realised – or guessed – that they were looking into Spearpoint's central shaft, akin to the one that he and Ricasso had looked down into from *Painted Lady*'s spotter balloon. Then that passed and the tunnel was windowless again, and the zone changes continued, each more abrupt than the last.

But then there came a point when he felt the change-vector shift in the opposite direction, and suddenly they were passing back into lower-state zones, the symptoms easing, though never quite fading completely. When Juggernaut eventually brought them to a halt, he judged that they had returned to conditions not radically different from those in the vault where Juggernaut had first appeared. The effects of all the boundaries they had passed through could not be shrugged off, nor was it possible to ignore the levels of Morphax-55 they had all been forced to consume. But for now this was a kind of respite, and he sensed all of them welcoming it.

It was another vault, at least as big, if not bigger, than the first. But this one was illuminated from the start, so he had no difficulty in surveying their surroundings. Juggernaut lowered them almost to the ground and they stepped off, all save Nimcha, who was helped down by her mother. Juggernaut's clattering and humming was but one component in a louder chorus now, for there were other machines present, about a dozen of them.

They were all similar to Juggernaut, in that they appeared to be composed largely of junk and mechanical detritus, scavenged and refashioned into enormous, jumbled components. Six or seven were roughly Juggernaut's size and shape, but the others were larger, and one was larger still, twice as tall and wide and long as any of the others. By the manner in which the other machines were situated around this one, Quillon couldn't help but think of it as their leader, or at the very least the one that was owed the most respect. Juggernaut, indeed, shuffled and clattered to one side as soon as the humans had disembarked. And then the large one spoke.

'Bring her.'

The voice was louder, more commanding than Juggernaut's. It was female, but with a markedly different timbre and inflection. And as the machine spoke, the jumbled elements of its front moved in such a way as to suggest, between moments of shifting chaos, a woman's face.

'Do you know this one?' Quillon whispered.

'New to me, Cutter,' Fray said. 'Never been this deep before.' He was trembling badly, a line of sweat on his forehead, having to lean with one hand on his knee to support himself.

'Bring her!' the machine commanded again, this time with more emphasis.

Nimcha and Kalis stood hand in hand. Fray shuffled in front of them, still stooping, until he stood before the great, shifting face of the largest machine.

'We'll bring her if we feel like it. First it might help if we knew who – what – we're dealing with.'

A volcanic rumble emanated from the machine, as of terrible potent fury welling up from within. It sounded angry enough to smite them all to bloody pulp in an instant. But – Quillon tried to tell himself – the sound might have been no more than the audible correlate of powerful mentation going on inside.

'I am ... the final one,' the machine announced.

'The final what?' Fray persisted. 'Help us out here, please.'

The face broke apart. It quelled its shifting and cracked open along fracture lines, peeling wide like a flower, exposing part of the machine's glowing red core. Quillon was reminded of Juggernaut's mouth, the furnace into which Fray's offering had been placed. This was not quite the same, however. There was something in there. It resembled, at first glance, an elaborate wheel-shaped sculpture, tipped up to face them. At the hub of the sculpture was a glass sarcophagus, and inside the sarcophagus, though barely discernible behind a layer of frost, lay an adult human figure, a bald, white-gowned woman, orientated with her head uppermost. The woman's eyes were closed, her arms folded in front of her so that they crossed at the wrists, the posture conveying a saintlike dignity. Grouped around the woman, each at the end of one of the wheel's spokes, were other sarcophagi, ten in all, and of those, five were presently occupied.

Fray glanced back at Quillon, then returned his attention to the machine. 'That's you, I figure, in the middle. You were a human woman, and now you're ... this. Asleep, I guess. Plumbed into whatever it is the others are plumbed into.'

'I think they're the same as Nimcha,' Quillon said. 'Tectomancers.'

'Tell us what happened,' Fray called.

The woman did not move or respond in any observable sense. But Quillon, like Fray, was in no doubt that on some level they were communicating with her.

'There was a mistake,' she said. 'We opened the wrong door. We let it through.'

'Let what through?'

'The Mire,' Quillon said. 'The Eye of God.'

'The network collapsed under the influx, branch by branch, all the way back to here, back to Earthgate, back to the control nexus, from which we had given the command to open the door.'

'The door into what?' Fray persisted. 'What door?'

'It had been thousands of years. Our measurements told us it had restabilised, the annealing complete, that the tract could once again be opened for passage. But the measurements were flawed. Our data was incomplete, our interpretation incorrect. Our decision was . . . disastrous. It brought calamity to Earthgate, this ancient, once-dead world. If Earth itself was spared, then that is a blessing we did not deserve. Our hubris knew no bounds. Our misjudgement brought death to this planet and shame to our birth-guild.'

Fray, shaking with the effort of holding himself together, glanced back at Quillon. 'This making any sense to you, Cutter?'

'I think she's telling us that they made a mistake, and it let the Eye of God break through.'

'Some fucking mistake.'

'I think she's also telling us that the people who were in charge of running this thing were born into it. Like a family business, I suppose.' Quillon smiled. 'I wish Ricasso was here. He'd have known what to ask.'

'Ten thousand years . . . ten thousand Earth years . . . have passed since the intrusion,' the woman said. 'For much of that time, all we could do was maintain the merest thread of functionality, in readiness for the time when the repair could begin. Now it has begun. The tract has undergone changes, utterly beyond our control. It has begun to recover integrity, exactly as our flawed measurements led us to believe all those thousands of years ago. We take no credit for this: how could we? But these changes have had repercussions all the way back through the network. At last, damping and containment devices have begun to reactivate and provide a measure of control. The possibility of repair is now within our grasp. The incursion may be undone, and the network made passable once more. Earthgate may be reopened for passage. But this work requires subtle guidance.'

'It requires, in other words, tectomancers,' Quillon said.

'You're ahead of me, Cutter,' Fray said. 'What the hell is Earthgate, anyway? Why doesn't she just say "Earth" and be done with it?'

'I don't know. And I don't know what she means when she says Earth was spared, either. I don't suppose it matters much right now: we've come here once; we can always return, with more questions. For now this is about Nimcha, and what she's meant to do.'

'Which is?' Fray asked.

'Be like this woman. She's another tectomancer – or at least she was, once upon a time. Like Nimcha, she was born for this work, given the right machinery in her head to enable her to talk to ... whatever it is she – they – were meant to control. The network, whatever that was. But something went wrong, and they either died out or were scattered to the four winds.'

'Until another one showed up. Right?'

'Right. And now Nimcha must take her place, or the strain of resisting it's going to kill her.' He looked at the girl apologetically, but there was no escaping the truth of it, and he was sure she was no less aware of that now than he was. 'It's what she was born to do, Fray. To put this mess right.'

'You mean ... get into that thing?'

'This must happen,' the woman in the machine said. 'She has come, as the others came. She is not the first. She will not be the last. More will come, now that the calling grows stronger. More will come and then the healing will be guided, and the mistake will be undone.'

'I am her mother,' Kalis said. 'I want only to see my daughter made well again.'

'There's only one way that's going to happen,' Quillon said, anxious to comfort her however he could, but knowing that nothing he said or did would make this any easier. 'She has to take her place. Until she does, the conflict will continue to eat her up inside.'

Kalis looked at her daughter, then at the vacant sarcophagi, one of which was surely waiting for her.

'Can I sleep with her?'

'No,' the woman in the machine said. 'Only those who carry the mark may enter the composite.'

'Why?'

'It would be harmful to you. You are not equipped. And the space you would occupy must eventually be taken by another.'

'How long?' Quillon asked. 'If she joins you, if Nimcha assumes her place in the composite, how long will it take before the work ... the healing ... is done?'

'I cannot say. But the work will be difficult until the composite is complete.'

He looked at Kalis, then Nimcha. 'The choice has to be yours. You can't be forced into this. But I've stated my medical opinion: it's this or death, Nimcha. Nothing in my medical bag can stop what's happening to you.' He gestured at the wheel of waiting sarcophagi. '*That* can. And perhaps it doesn't have to be for as long as we fear.'

'You do not know this,' Kalis said.

'No, I don't. And I can't make any promises. But things have been happening quicker lately and that has to be a sign. You've already made a difference, Nimcha, just by existing. Spearpoint felt and responded to you long before you got here, so imagine what you're going to be able to do once you're part of it. You've moved zones already, Nimcha. I shudder to think what else you're capable of.'

'But the others must come,' Kalis said. 'It told us.'

Quillon nodded again. 'So we'll make it easier. We'll go looking for them. Swarm – what's left of Swarm – needs a new purpose now. What could be better than scouring the Earth looking for other tectomancers? Chasing after them not because they're witches, something to be feared, but because they're the most precious, vital people alive?'

'Cutter's right,' Fray said. 'It's the way it has to be. And you have to go back out there and help Cutter do this. You know what it's like to bring up a tectomancer – such knowledge will be invaluable.'

'I will not leave my daughter alone.'

'She won't be alone.' Fray made an effort to stand up straight, without leaning on his knee for support. 'I'll stay down here. Not much chance of me surviving that return trip, anyway, so I'm not making much of a sacrifice. But I'll be here, for as long as I'm able.'

Until you die, Quillon thought. But even Fray wasn't able to state his prospects that bluntly.

'You don't have anything,' Quillon said. 'I can give you my medicine bag, what's in it, but even then—'

'I'll make do. I've dealt with Juggernaut before, remember? Juggernaut can find me food and water, and probably just about anything else I care to name. Main thing is, I can stay alive down here, and I'll be with Nimcha. That's my promise to you, Kalis. I know it won't make this much easier for you, but at least you won't be leaving Nimcha on her own down here. I'll be watching over her.'

'You would do this?'

'Part of me would like nothing better than to rip Tulwar's steam supply out of his backside and watch him keel over. But that's not really an option, I'm afraid. Best leave that kind of thing to Meroka and Malkin. They won't let me down, I'm sure of that.'

'They won't,' Quillon said.

Fray's tone turned cautionary. 'Same goes for you, Cutter. Know it won't be easy for you, back on the outside. But you've survived until now, so I figure you must have learned a thing or two from me. What we just talked about, finding the other ones like Nimcha? Don't let me down on this, all right? Scour the planet for them, as if they're precious jewels, and bring them back to Spearpoint. You know the drill now.' He raised a finger. 'And remember, you're doing this as much for Kalis as you are for me. Sooner they fix this mess, whatever it is, sooner she gets her daughter back.'

'We'll find them. You have my word on it.'

'We never did break our word to each other, did we? Guess now wouldn't be the time to start.'

'Definitely not,' Quillon said.

'Nimcha,' Fray said, beckoning her to come over to him. 'Say goodbye to your mother now. You and I have work to do.' And he wrapped his powerful arm around her shoulders, and for a moment, only a moment, the shaking was gone and he looked to Quillon like the strongest friend he could ever have known.

They left the Hall of the Mad Machines, Juggernaut taking Quillon and Kalis back to the vault where they had first encountered it. Kalis was numb and silent during the return journey, still reeling from having to part with her daughter. The more he reflected on events, the more certain Quillon became that there had been no other option, and that Kalis also knew this to be true. It was a course she had been on since they had arrived in Swarm, perhaps for even longer than that, and she must always have known that the end would be harrowing. Yet he kept telling himself that it could have been worse. It had been a separation, not death, and in that there was always hope. If they had not yet saved Spearpoint, they had started a process that might lead to something close to salvation, and perhaps the opening of great doors that had been closed longer than history remembered.

'We will return,' he told her. 'We'll find the others, and we'll bring them here. You'll see Nimcha again.'

'Do not make promises you cannot keep, Quillon.'

'I don't,' he said. 'Not now, not ever.'

She nodded, not so much because she believed him, he sensed, but because she wanted to, and that was better than nothing.

Fray had given him his set of keys when they parted, so that Quillon would be able to pass through the tunnel system's doors on his way out, but he had been able to give Quillon only the sketchiest of indications as to how he might find his way to the other exit, the one that Meroka and Malkin had been headed towards. He was gloomily resigned to getting lost, even with Kalis to share the burden of interpreting Fray's instructions. But he need not have worried.

'Figured I'd wait a while,' Meroka said. 'Just in case you decided you hadn't had enough of me for one lifetime.'

Quillon laughed. He was delighted to see her. It felt like centuries since Juggernaut had carried him away. 'Where's Malkin?'

'Sent him on ahead. It won't make much difference, and it'll give him time to load up the guns. Probably going to need them.' She paused. 'Um ... can't help noticing there's only two of you.'

'Fray and Nimcha decided to stay a while,' Quillon said.

He didn't need to say anything else. Meroka looked at him, and she understood.

'Did it work out?'

'I think so, but we won't know for sure for some time.' He was holding Kalis's hand, he realised. 'Which is good. We still need to get that Serum-15 delivered and distributed. If the Mire closed now, it would be worse than the storm. But I don't think it's going to happen for a little while. We have time to prepare, time to get stronger.'

'We have work to do,' Kalis said, speaking clearly, strongly, echoing Fray's words to Nimcha. 'All of us.'

As they emerged from the concealed tunnel entrance, near the silent, tomblike mass of the Second District Gas and Electric substation, the air snapped against Quillon's skin like a flap of airship canvas and he knew that the wind direction had not changed since the day before. It was, astonishingly, not long after noon. The streets were empty, but from only a few blocks away, and perhaps a little further down the gentle slope of the ledge, came a brief exchange of gunfire. The fighting was still going on. Quillon didn't know if this was a part of the city controlled by the angels, or by Tulwar's militia. In a little while, he fervently hoped, it would make very little difference.

'I can get us to the bathhouse,' Meroka said. 'I know enough rat runs and back alleys to avoid most of the heat. Not saying it'll be easy, but I think I can get us there.'

'Think you should send that signal first?' Quillon asked.

'Let's be optimistic and assume we'll do it later. Nice view from the roof of the bathhouse, so I gather.'

'Hope you weren't planning to shoot your way inside when you arrive, because I don't think you'll get much further than the hatstand.'

'Even Fray wouldn't be that rash,' Meroka said. 'Besides, plenty of

474

people in there we don't want to hit if we can help it.'

'So we just . . . stroll up, and ask to be let in? Pretty please? With Tulwar crossing his fingers we're already dead?'

'No,' Quillon said. 'We don't need to do that. If we're lucky, and they haven't finished with *Iron Prominent*, there's still a way we can get right inside.'

Malkin narrowed his eyes. 'Run that by me one more time, Cutter.'

So he did, and when he was done they had a plan. What pleased him most of all was that Meroka said it was a good one.

'Put them down there,' Tulwar told his men, as they sweated and grunted under the burden of the crates. There were three in all: the last of the supplies to be recovered from the spilled cargo of the airship, whatever it was called. Until the other ships arrived – *if* the other ships arrived, he corrected himself – this would be the last batch of good medicine to reach Spearpoint. Looking through the steam-filled room at the buckled and crushed crates, he wondered how much could have reasonably survived. The medicine had its uses – you couldn't control the city without it, on some level – but it was very much a case of less is more, as far as Tulwar was concerned. He was surprised at how easily Quillon and the others had believed his story about wanting to inspect the crates personally, to make sure none of the flasks had been contaminated or tampered with by the Skullboys down on the lower level. Fact was, the purity of the medicine was not exactly central in his concerns. He was much more anxious to make sure that not too much of it got out there in one go. Yes, his militia needed it to help them in their push against the Skulls. But there was no reason why the rest of it had to be recklessly squandered on the sick and needy. They'd get it in good time, when it suited his requirements, not theirs. For the moment he was intent on stockpiling good flasks here in the bathhouse, until such time as he felt it expedient to dispense them. The airship spilling its guts – making it hard for the Swarmers to track the crates and their cargo – had been the kind of fateful intervention he could never have planned for. Sometimes life just played out like that. For all that had happened to him – for all that half of what made him human had been ripped away – he still considered himself an unusually lucky man. But then you made your own luck. That was the part that Fray had never got, the hopeless fool.

'You can leave now,' he told the men. 'And tell the stoker to come back in twenty minutes.'

'You can last until then?' one of them asked.

'Pressure's fine. I can last.'

When the heavy doors were closed he moved to the first crate. The umbilical tightened and he felt the calliope creep along behind him. He glanced at the quivering needles in his belly gauges. The music had been playing so repetitively that he was scarcely aware of it now. If he ever got silence again it would be silence filled with the cavernous holes where the music used to fit.

He levered the lid off the first crate, leaned in to dig through the padding of straw until his wooden hand touched glass. He pulled out a flask, observed the clear fluid filling it nearly to the stopper. Lives in the palm of his hand, quite literally. He moved to place the flask to one side – he would decide later whether to send it out or stockpile it – but some impulse gripped him and he opted instead to smash the flask against the side of the crate. The medicine treacled through the hinge-points of his wooden fingers. He couldn't say that it had felt good to destroy the Serum-15, but it had certainly felt significant.

Something came out of the straw.

He didn't have time to react, only to register the fact that it was happening. He had not even begun to take a step back when the figure uncurled to its full height, still covered head to toe in straw, but recognisable, very recognisable.

'Figured there was some unfinished business,' Meroka said.

She already had a gun aimed at him. She fired it point blank into one of his steam-pressure dials. Then she fired again, and again, directing each shot into a different part of him. Tulwar staggered back, the umbilical sagging behind him. A jet of hot white vapour speared out of his belly, only adding more steam to the room.

'Those first three were for Fray,' Meroka said, stepping out of the crate, flinging open her coat, discarding one gun and drawing another. 'The rest're on me.' She aimed something heavy and black and semi-automatic and opened up on him. Now he was geysering steam in six or seven directions, squealing like a kettle on the boil. He raised his wooden arm against her and she turned it into a splintered, fingerless stump. Tulwar collapsed back onto the thick tail of his umbilical.

The double doors opened. From his vantage point he made out two or three of his men coming back into the room, drawn by the ruction. His eyes were watering and he couldn't make them out clearly. One of them was trying to bat the steam away from his face. Another pointed a gun barrel vaguely in his direction, and then swung it onto Meroka.

'Shoot!' Tulwar cried.

The man – he didn't even know his name, couldn't recognise his face either – only had time to fire off one shot before Meroka took care of him and whoever else had come through the door. The bodies – there were three, he was sure of it now – slumped to the ground, their guns clattering as they hit the hard wooden flooring.

'Fray's dead,' he said, the words coming out wet and bloody, something bubbling down in his windpipe.

'No,' Meroka answered, pausing to change a magazine. 'Fray's just doing some babysitting. The last time I saw him he was just fine. Ain't that a bummer? Exactly the news you don't want to hear on your deathbed.'

She strolled to the doors, kicked them shut again and made a point of securing the internal lock. Then she started shooting him again, concentrating on his legs this time.

There was a splinter in one eye and spitting steam in the other, each as painful as the other, but he still had enough vision to see the other crates opening up, the figures coming out. Two thin men, both of whom he knew, neither of whom he'd expected to see alive again. Malkin was one; Quillon the other.

'No!' he said, scratching at the air with his good hand, like a man beset by night-terrors.

Malkin reached down into the straw and pulled out a massive-barrelled rifle. Still standing up in the crate, he aimed the rifle at the calliope and punched booming holes through the steam. Took his sweet time cocking, aiming and firing each time, as if there was no reason to hurry any of this. The steam was rocketing out of Tulwar now. It was doing something funny to the music, making it speed up. Deep in the calliope, the pressure loss – or maybe the shots Malkin had drilled into it – was having some detrimental effect on its regulator.

Quillon emerged from his crate, long legs articulating fluidly as he cleared the rim and stepped onto the floor. The angel was the only one who didn't seem to have a weapon on him.

'That's enough,' he called, over the accelerating music.

'Spoil our fun, Cutter,' Meroka said. 'That's you all the way.' But she made a show of holstering the semi-automatic weapon, letting her coat flap closed again. Malkin stood behind her, the rifle barrel tipped up towards the ceiling.

Quillon walked slowly over to Tulwar and then knelt down, picking his spot carefully so that the steam jets missed him.

'It didn't have to happen like this,' he said, speaking so quietly, so slowly and calmly that it was as if he didn't hear the music at all. 'We came back to the city ready to trust you. All you had to do was help the people when they most needed it. No one was asking for the world. No one was asking for anything you couldn't deliver.'

Tulwar spat blood and something horrible that he wasn't sure was ever meant to come up through his throat. 'Like you ever cared, angel. Like this was ever about anything but your own survival.'

'Maybe that was true once,' Quillon said. 'But I moved on. Realised I wasn't the centre of my own universe. Wasn't even anywhere near the centre. Pity you didn't have it in you to make the same adjustment.' He tilted his head left and tight, taking in what was left of Tulwar, not looking too encouraged by what he saw. 'Still, water under the bridge now. You want us to change the reel?'

The music was now a skirling, screaming cacophony.

'You're the doctor,' Tulwar said. 'Put me out of my misery.'

Quillon began to stand up. 'Sorry,' he said, and for a moment there was regret on the otherwise stiff mask of his face. 'I appear to have forgotten my bag.'

But even as he was rising to his feet, something seemed to give way inside him. He collapsed to his knees and retched a spray of blood into Tulwar's face. Quillon reached up to shield his mouth, coughing again but this time catching most of it in his hand. He looked down at the red mess on his palm with a kind of apologetic bemusement, as if this was exactly the wrong thing to have done in polite company.

'Cutter,' Meroka said. 'You don't sound too good there.'

'Looks like we might both be doing well to make it to sundown,' Tulwar said.

'I might,' Quillon said, and wiped a sleeve across the bloodied gash of his mouth. 'You'll be doing well to make it through the next five minutes.'

'Why settle for minutes?' Meroka said, drawing and aiming the gun.

A great deal happened afterwards, but for much of it he was at best semi-conscious, cognisant of movement and noise and – beyond a sense that events of significance were taking place – completely unable to process the information in a coherent manner. He was lying on the ground for much of the time, with someone's coat forming a pillow under his head, his own coat parted so that his friends might assess the damage he had worked so assiduously to conceal from them. He heard gunfire, too loud and echoing to be outside the bathhouse, but not coming from within the room itself, and raised voices, shouts and arguments and low, conspiratorial murmurs. He fell in and out of black dreamlessness, each time renewing his determination not to fall into unconsciousness, each time failing. He was injured, possibly fatally, but he did not want to die. He had been present at the start of something he wished to see to its conclusion. He had made promises, and the thought of breaking them was worse than the fear of death.

But he had been shot, and he was already weak. In the narrowing moments of clear, rational thought he grasped that these were not happy bedfellows. He was also someone for whom even the best human medicine was essentially useless.

He slipped between moments, and then a figure assumed solidity before him.

'Quillon, you dumb son of a bitch. Why didn't you tell us?'

His own laughter surprised him. 'Because we might have turned around.'

'Just because you were hit?'

'I thought so.'

'Not while I was on watch. We'd come that far, I'd have shot you there and then.'

'Just as well I didn't tell you, then, isn't it?'

Meroka glanced aside. She was swimming in and out of focus, for all that the room was now free of steam. 'You found that bag of his yet?'

'It's here.'

The bandaged apparition that came into view was, impossibly, Curtana. He knew then that he must be hallucinating, for there was no way at all that she could have found the strength to leave her bed, not with the injuries she had sustained. But the realisation that he was delirious only strengthened the apparition's hold on reality. It leaned in closer and spoke softly.

'Quillon. Listen carefully. There must be something in here, something in these medicines, that can help you. I want you to tell me what it is, and how we use it.'

'No use,' he said, smiling at the illusion's persistence. 'Internal bleeding. Nothing you can do.'

'Have I formally relieved you of duties caring for the crew of *Painted Lady*?'

So the phantom wasn't perfect. It didn't realise what had happened the night before. Almost sorry to shatter the delusion, he said, 'The ship's gone. It burned. No more *Painted Lady*.'

'Yes. Very good. None of which matters a damn to me when I still have my crew, one of whom needs you to keep him alive. The bag, Doctor. The drugs. Tell me what I need to do.'

'There's nothing you can do.'

Her voice turned to a snarl. 'I am Captain Curtana of the rapid scout *Painted Lady*. You are my physician, and I am ordering you to treat yourself.'

Again he laughed, but this time at his own supine willingness to go along with the charade. 'Open the bag. The second pouch ...' He watched her dig through the contents. 'Yes, that one. Take out the vials.'

She held them up for inspection. 'Which one?'

'On the right. My right. Now find the clean syringe and uncap the needle.'

He faded; eternities passed and Curtana was there again, with the syringe plunged into the vial. 'How much, Doctor?'

'To the first graduation. Find a vein in my arm and ...' He slipped out of consciousness again.

He came around sharper, everything back in focus, including the pain of having been shot. Remarkably, Curtana was still there talking to him. 'I've done it,' she said. 'I hope it's enough for now. If it isn't, you'd better tell me what else I need to do. I'm afraid it might be a few hours before we can find someone I'd trust to operate on you.'

For the first time since Tulwar's death he felt as if his thoughts were moving in rational patterns. 'How are you?'

'Better than my ship.'

'They shouldn't have let you out of the infirmary.'

'They didn't want to. But with all the noise you were making down here, it's not as if the infirmary felt like the safest place in the city any more.' She looked over her shoulder. 'I see you settled your grievance with Tulwar.'

'Yes. But he owes Spearpoint much more than he could ever repay just by dying. He stole the drugs it cost us lives and ships to bring here. What's happening now?'

'A period of transition, I think you'd best call it. My people are impressing on Tulwar's people the wisdom of surrender and a rapid shift of allegiance. I'm counting on most of them being opportunist thugs who'll recognise a good thing when it's offered to them.'

'A bitter pill to swallow, though. Suddenly being told they're working for Swarm.'

'At least I'm giving them the choice.'

'Yes. And the alternative is ... what, exactly? Fight you?'

She gave a spirited grin. 'They can try.'

'You have almost no guns, after crossing the zone. Nor will any ship that makes it into Spearpoint by that approach.'

'Whisper it, Doctor. At the moment we're hanging on to the illusion of superiority by our fingernails. They think we're stronger than we really are.'

'Tulwar knew what the zone would do to Swarm's equipment.'

'Tulwar's dead. Most of his men are fools who barely know there's a world beyond Spearpoint.' Her face hardened with resolve. 'Anyway, we're not powerless. We still have trained men, the crews of two ships, and they're very good with crossbows and edged weapons. I invite anyone doubting this to put it to the test. Besides, there's another factor. We still have the rest of Swarm, and the rest of Swarm is still very much armed.'

'But on the wrong side of the zone.'

'For now. But the landscape's changing. Tulwar's militia – our militia, now – have at least some access to Serum-15. It means they can push into the lower levels of the city, places denied to them before. The Skulls are in retreat – a surge of resistance is the last thing they were expecting. There's still a long way to go, and it may be days or weeks before we see any change in the control of the surrounding lands. But it will happen, and when it does there will be no military impediment to a low-level approach, skirting beneath the zone boundary. It'll still be difficult, and there may be pockets of resistance. Maybe more than pockets. But we'll be able to keep our engines running the whole way in, and we'll still have working guns when we dock.'

'Days or weeks. You think we can hold out that long?'

'There's another factor that means we may not even have to. While you were gone there've been ... negotiations, I suppose you'd call them. We've been in contact with a faction of angels. They saw what happened to the first two ships and sent an envoy out to meet with the rest of Swarm. The angel was nearly dead by the time it reached *Purple Emperor*: it had been forced to fly much higher than they usually do, to skirt the top of the zone, and its propulsion pack had failed not long after it left Spearpoint. Frozen half to death and almost too weak to fly. But it got to us, and opened a channel of communications with the Celestial Levels.'

'It's angels from the Celestial Levels who are trying to occupy Spearpoint from above.'

'Not all of them, Quillon – you told us as much yourself. There must still be some angels up there you and I can trust, or they wouldn't have sent someone down to warn you to get out of the city.'

'That was a while ago.'

'I know, and it's anyone's guess as to how much influence the pacifists still have over the warmongers. But they wouldn't have sent that angel on a near-suicidal flight for nothing. The warmongers have overstretched themselves, trying to occupy the lower levels.' Doubt crossed her face for a second. 'That's what the angels are telling us, anyway.'

'And they'd have no reason to lie, not when there's so little at stake.'

'I don't know. Maybe they are lying, saying they can guarantee the fleet's security if it comes in high, rather than low. But here's the thing. Sooner or later everything boils down to trust. You just have to make that leap of faith. In fact it's sort of the point. If there were cast-iron guarantees, you wouldn't need trust in the first place.'

'So Ricasso will risk all of Swarm on a promise, from angels he's never dealt with before today?'

'Not all of Swarm. But a portion of it – enough ships to make a difference, by bringing in more Serum-15? I think so. And he'll make sure he's on one of those ships when it crosses.'

'The one thing I've never doubted is his courage.'

'But you don't think this is wise.'

'It's a gamble.' Quillon sighed, the fight – the energy for argument – draining out of him. 'But then I understand your position. If you want to keep a lid on Tulwar's rabble, then you need to assert your strength. Bringing in more ships will do just that, especially if you can demonstrate that you have the collusion of at least some of the angels.'

'No one said it would be pretty. But if that's what it takes to keep this city from slipping back into chaos, Ricasso won't hesitate.' She paused. 'There's so much I'd rather be talking to you about. What happened down there, inside Spearpoint? Meroka and Malkin told me some of it, but I'm still only getting part of the story. Is Kalis going to be all right?'

'She wouldn't have made it this far if she wasn't strong.'

'And Nimcha?'

'I don't believe in destiny. But if I had to, she'd be living proof of it. She was born to serve Spearpoint, Curtana. Born to heal it and make it work again.'

'By doing what?'

'It's not a city. It's a gateway, a terminal. A road to the stars. But to reach them, you don't go up.' He smiled. 'You go down. Deep beneath our feet, in the bowels of the Earth, is ... something. Something I don't think you or I are quite capable of understanding. An aperture into ... something even stranger, I suppose. That's the road.'

'Can we travel it again?'

'I think we may have to.'

'That'll take some doing.'

'It will. And I suppose we'll need ships and good pilots to fly them.

They won't be like your ships, and I'm guessing the piloting skills will be somewhat different. But I don't doubt that the necessary adjustments can be made.'

'I think that might be a problem for my grandchildren.'

'Perhaps. But the world isn't going to wait for us. It's getting colder, and the forests are dying. We either do something about that, or find somewhere else to live.'

'I'm glad you're thinking about the future.'

'Yours. Not necessarily mine.' And he coughed again, the blood welling in his mouth, and the next breath felt as if there were knives in his lungs, jumbled this way and that like the contents of an untidy cutlery drawer.

'Quillon, what I said about getting someone to operate on you. There's another possibility.'

'If you think I can operate on—'

'Not you, no. But another angel. If we have friends up there, and we can get you to them—'

'It's hopeless, Curtana. The city's a war zone. We ran into enough trouble just getting to the Pink Peacock.'

'And if there was another way? One that didn't involve cutting through the city?'

'There isn't.'

'There is now. I think I can get you to the Celestial Levels. We'll have to be quick, though, and I can't guarantee that any of this is going to work, or that it'll be easy on you. But I think there is a way we can make this happen.' She tucked her good hand, the one that wasn't bandaged, under the crude pillow formed from Meroka's coat. 'I'm going to move you now, Quillon. It may hurt. But you're my physician, and I'm not giving up on you that easily.'

He was unconscious by the time they got him onto the roof of the Red Dragon Bathhouse. Unconscious but still breathing, albeit shallowly and with each breath shifting something horrible and loose in his chest. Still alive, though. That, Curtana thought, was all they could hope for now. And if he could manage not to die before he reached the angels, that would be even better. But she had never felt less optimistic in her life.

They were all there now, Meroka, Malkin, Kalis and Agraffe, crowding around the waiting capsule of the spotter balloon as the gasbag was inflated. Her crew had not dared begin the process before now; the balloon would be far too tempting a target for potshots, even before it began its ascent. As it was the gasbag had needed emergency repairs and the inflation – aided by hot air supplied by the bathhouse's furnace – was taking longer than she would have liked. Would it even work at all? she wondered. The spiralling thermals would drive the balloon higher, but if it fell out of their grip the prevailing winds would soon carry it beyond Spearpoint, far beyond the possibility of rescue or help for Quillon. Having failed to land *Painted Lady* in one piece, she had a ready appreciation for just how malicious those thermals and winds could be when they collided with each other. She felt it in the tingling of burned skin under her bandages. Still: what else could they do, but this one daring thing?

Two of Madame Bistoury's girls had brought Quillon's stretchered form up from the lower floors. They shivered on the roof, drawing their flower-patterned nightgowns around themselves, but unwilling to return indoors until they had witnessed the departure. Curtana helped to manoeuvre Quillon into the observation cabin, making sure he was adequately protected from whatever jolts lay ahead. Once he came close to stirring, but his eyes were drowsy and unfocused and she did not think he retained any real sense of what was going on.

'This isn't the way it was meant to happen,' Agraffe said. 'We were supposed to save the city, not lose Quillon.'

Curtana adjusted the blankets she had used to cushion Quillon. He looked like a little baby wrapped up in them: an ugly, strange, birdlike baby. 'We haven't lost him, not yet. And we haven't saved the city. We've begun to save it, that's all.'

'Good. Now leave the rest of it to us. You can get back down to the infirmary, where you belong.'

'While there's some ballooning to be done?'

'No. Absolutely not. You're not riding in that thing. Look at you: you've got one good hand, and you can barely work the arm it's attached to!'

Trust Agraffe to fall back on a purely technical objection, she thought, rather than an appeal to emotion. He knew her far too well. 'It's a balloon. It's not exactly over-endowed with controls. You go up or down. And we don't need to go down.'

He held up his own bandage mittens. 'You know I'd be doing this, if I could still pull a lever.'

'You can't, and I can.'

'Sky Princess has made her point,' Meroka said, buttoning the coat she had donated for use as Quillon's pillow. 'And it's a good one. No damn doubt about it. But I've got two hands, which kind of settles the argument.'

'You've never flown a balloon before,' Curtana said.

'No. But like you said, it goes up or down. Reckon I can get my head around that, if I try really hard. And there's another point, one that won't mean much to you but means a hell of a lot to me.'

'Which is?' Agraffe asked.

'Quillon's still my package. I do the delivering around here.' She finished putting on the coat, pausing only to draw the collar higher around her neck. 'Now show me how to work those God-damned levers, before I have to get argumentative about it.'

Agraffe looked at Curtana. 'If it's a choice between sending Meroka and sending you, you know which side I'm going to come down on. No offence, Meroka.'

'None fucking taken. You carry on.'

'She only needs to know how to slow her ascent, when she reaches the Levels. If the angels are there to meet her, they'll find a way to bring her in. And if they're not, she can turn off the burner and drop down again.'

'And hope she hits the civilised part of Spearpoint, not the part still occupied by Skulls,' Curtana said.

'Same risk would apply to you,' Agraffe pointed out.

'Yeah, and at least I'm prepared for it,' Meroka said, patting her coat, metal chinking through the leather. 'But, you know, it's not coming to that. If the good angels aren't yanking our chains, I'll bring Cutter to them. Just make sure they know we're on our way.'

Kalis nodded at Curtana. 'Let her do this. It is her wish. She has travelled far with Cutter. Let her continue the journey.'

Malkin walked over to Meroka and drew a revolver out of his pocket. He passed it butt-first to Meroka and reached out his own hand to close hers around the grip. 'Take this. Used to belong to Fray, when he was in the force. Then it became mine. Never let me down when push came to shove. If it comes to it, take out a few of them flutter-winged bastards for me.'

'If it comes to it,' Meroka said, 'I'll be aiming to take out more than just a few.' But she took the gun and slipped it into one of her own coat pockets, where it would be ready for immediate use.

'Pulls a little to the left,' Malkin said.

'I'll keep that in mind.' She gave a heavy shrug under the coat. 'You ready to show me how to fly this thing, Curtana? 'Cause if you don't, I'm taking it anyway. We don't want to keep Quillon waiting much longer.'

Curtana helped Meroka into the cabin, jabbing a finger at the very few salient points of interest, while Meroka buckled herself in for the ascent. 'Altimeter. Firesap burner. Ballast drop. Gas release – go easy on that, because you'll sink faster than you can get hot air back into the envelope.'

'I'll figure it out.'

'The cabin's pressurised, but you'll only have two hours of breathable air. Admission valve is here, but don't even think of opening it unless you're below at least Circuit City.'

'I guess what we're saying here is, the angels better be on our side up there. Or Quillon and I are both screwed.'

'If we don't have friends up there,' Curtana said, 'I think that goes for most of us. You'll just be the first to find out.'

'Seal me in. Got me a sudden hankering to do some ballooning.'

'Good luck, Meroka.'

'Same to you, Sky Princess. Hope they give you another blimp. You've earned it.'

Curtana's eyes met Meroka's; there was an unspoken exchange between them, and then she closed the door and motioned for Meroka to work the internal latch.

Curtana stepped back. While they had been talking, the team had achieved inflation of the balloon. It was straining to lift the cabin off the roof, into the wild heights above. She realised she had forgotten to demonstrate the release catch to Meroka. She pointed through the glass at the heavy lever to Meroka's right. Meroka nodded and reached down to work the control. And then, with a swiftness that always startled Curtana, for all the balloon deployments she had witnessed, the cabin was rising. Perhaps it was her imagination, but it seemed to her that Quillon stirred from unconsciousness at precisely the moment of release, coming to wakefulness long enough to take in his surroundings and find Curtana beyond the glass, watching as he ascended. And then he was gone, as the balloon rose and took its occupants out of view.

'Come back,' she whispered. 'We could use you.'

She was still craning to follow the balloon's progress when Agraffe joined her and wrapped his arm around her side, taking care not to apply pressure to any of her bandages. 'She's in the thermals,' he said, cupping a hand over his eyes. 'Non-stop all the way to the Celestial Levels.'

Someone fired a single desultory shot; it clanged uselessly off the underside of the cabin.

'I wonder if we'll ever see either of them again,' Curtana wondered.

'We couldn't have left Quillon in safer hands. You know that. And at least he has a chance now.'

'It could have been me up there, not Meroka.'

'Like she said, Quillon was her responsibility, not yours. Anyway, you and I have more than enough to be getting on with here. We have to signal Ricasso, so he can let the angels know what's coming up to them. And find out what his plans are.'

'He'll be sorry he didn't get a chance to talk to Quillon again.'

'Maybe he will,' Agraffe said. 'That's the thing. Nothing's certain now. The only thing I'm sure of – if that isn't a contradiction – is that nothing is going to be the same. I mean, look at us – we grew up in Swarm, educated from birth to spit on the memory of this place. And now we've risked our lives to get here and damn it all if I don't want to see it survive.' He was, despite everything, quite unable not to grin. 'Maybe Swarm's finished, at least the one we knew. But if that's the case then Spearpoint isn't going to be the same either. I want it to make it through this – somehow I know it will – but I also know it's going to come out the other end different.'

'Why stop at Spearpoint?' Curtana said. 'If Nimcha and the rest do their work, the world itself won't be the same. And if the world changes, so does that.'

'What?' Agraffe asked.

She was pointing at the sky, but not at the balloon, which had climbed so rapidly that it was now little more than a tiny brassy speck against the sheer, ever-climbing face of Spearpoint. She wasn't even pointing at the Celestial Levels, where the balloon was headed.

She was pointing into the empty, angel-less heavens beyond.

Everything else. The universe.